W9-CHV-724

"ONE OF THE MOST HONEST AND IMPORTANT WORKS OF OUR TIME"

Alfred Kazin

"Nowhere in fiction has the sensuality of boys and girls, innocence smeared with desire, lasciviousness mixed with brutality, been done with more skill and ruthless pen. . . . No history, no report, no photographs or paintings will be needed for this Chicago street of the first third of the twentieth century. It is all there in STUDS LONIGAN."

Saturday Review

"A GREAT PIECE OF AMERICAN REALISM."

The New Republic

Studs Lonigan
James T. Farrell

Young Lonigan

The Young Manhood of Studs Lonigan

Judgment Day

AVON
PUBLISHERS OF BARD, CAMELOT, DISCUS AND FLARE BOOKS

AVON BOOKS
A division of
The Hearst Corporation
959 Eighth Avenue
New York, New York 10019

First Avon Printing, in a single volume, February, 1977

AVON TRADEMARK REG. U.S. PAT. OFF. AND IN
OTHER COUNTRIES, MARCA REGISTRADA,
HECHO EN U.S.A.

Printed in the U.S.A.

WFH   10   9   8   7   6   5   4

To Marjorie and James Henle
Whose encouragement was so helpful
in completing this trilogy

Contents

Young Lonigan

East Side, West Side,
All around the town,
The tots sing ring-a-rosie,
London Bridge is falling down.
Boys and girls together,
Me and Mamie O'Rourke,
We tripped the light fantastic
On the sidewalks of New York.

POPULAR SONG.

A literature that cannot be vulgarized is no literature at all and will perish.

FRANK NORRIS.

except in the case of some rarely gifted nature there never will be a good man who has not from his childhood been used to play amid things of beauty and make of them a joy and a study.

PLATO, "REPUBLIC," Jowett translation.

The poignancy of situations that evoke reflection lies in the fact that we really do not know the meaning of the tendencies that are pressing for action.

JOHN DEWEY, "Human Nature and Conduct."

SECTION ONE

CHAPTER ONE

I

Studs Lonigan, on the verge of fifteen, and wearing his first suit of long trousers, stood in the bathroom with a Sweet Caporal pasted in his mug. His hands were jammed in his trouser pockets, and he sneered. He puffed, drew the fag out of his mouth, inhaled and said to himself:

Well, I'm kissin' the old dump goodbye tonight.

Studs was a small, broad-shouldered lad. His face was wide and planed; his hair was a light brown. His long nose was too large for his other features; almost a sheeny's nose. His lips were thick and wide, and they did not seem at home on his otherwise frank and boyish face. He was always twisting them into his familiar tough-guy sneers. He had blue eyes; his mother rightly called them baby-blue eyes.

He took another drag and repeated to himself:

Well, I'm kissin' the old dump goodbye.

The old dump was St. Patrick's grammar school; and St. Patrick's meant a number of things to Studs. It meant school, and school was a jailhouse that might just as well have had barred windows. It meant the long, wide, chalk-smelling room of the seventh- and eighth-grade boys, with its forty or fifty squirming kids. It meant the second floor of the tan brick, undistinguished parish building on Sixty-first Street that had swallowed so much of Studs' life for the past eight years. It meant the black-garbed Sisters of Providence, with their rattling beads, their swishing strides, and the funny-looking wooden clappers they used, which made a dry snapping sound and which hurt like anything when a guy got hit over the head with one. It meant Sister Carmel, who used to teach fourth grade, but was dead now; and who used to hit everybody with the edge of a ruler because she knew they all called her the bearded lady. It meant Studs, twisting in his seat, watching the sun come in the windows to show up the dust on the floor, twisting and squirming, and letting his mind fly to all kinds of places that were not like school. It meant Battleaxe Bertha talking and hearing lessons, her thin, sunken-jawed face white as a ghost, and sometimes looking like a corpse. It meant Bertha yelling in that creaky old woman's voice of hers. It meant Bertha trying to pound lessons down your throat, when you

11

weren't interested in them; church history and all about the
Jews and Moses, and Joseph, and Daniel in the lion's den,
and Solomon who was wiser than any man that ever lived, except
Christ, and maybe the Popes, who had the Holy Ghost to back
up what they said; arithmetic, and square and cube roots,
and percentage that Studs had never been able to get straight
in his bean; catechism lessons . . . the ten commandments
of God, the six commandments of the church, the seven capital
sins, and the seven cardinal virtues and that lesson about the
sixth commandment, which didn't tell a guy anything at
all about it and only had words that he'd found in the dictionary
like adultery which made him all the more curious; grammar
with all its dry rules, and its sentences that had to be diagrammed
and were never diagrammed right; spelling, and words like
apothecary that Studs still couldn't spell; Palmer method writing, that was supposed to make you less tired and made you
more tired, and the exercises of shaking your arm before each
lesson, and the round and round ▨▨▨▨ and straight and
straight, ▨▨▨▨▨ and the copy book, all smeared with ink,
that he had gone through, doing exercise after exercise on
neat sheets of Palmer paper, so that he could get a Palmer
method certificate that his old man kicked about paying for
because he thought it was graft; history lessons from the dull
red history book, but they wouldn't have been so bad if America had had more wars and if a guy could talk and think about
the battles without having to memorize their dates, and the
dates of when presidents were elected, and when Fulton invented the steamboat, and Eli Whitney invented the cotton gin
or whatever in hell he did invent. School meant Bertha, and
Bertha should have been put away long ago, where she could
kneel down and pray herself to death, because she was old and
crabby and always hauling off on somebody; it was a miracle
that a person as old as Bertha could sock as hard or holler as
loud as she could; even Sister Bernadette Marie, who was the
superior and taught the seventh- and eighth-grade girls in the
next room, sometimes had to come in and ask Bertha to make
less noise, because she couldn't teach with all that racket going
on; but telling Bertha not to shout was like telling a bull that it
had no right to see red. And smart guys, like Jim Clayburn, who
did his homework every night, couldn't learn much from her.
And school meant Dan and Bill Donoghue and Tubby and all
the guys in his bunch, and you couldn't find a better gang of
guys to pal with this side of Hell. And it meant going to mass
in the barn-like church on the first floor, every morning in
Lent, and to stations of the cross on Friday afternoons; sta-

tions of the cross were always too long unless Father Doneggan said them; and marching on Holy Thursday morning in church with a lily in your hand, and going to communion the third Sunday of every month at the eight o'clock mass with the boys' sodality. It meant goofy young Danny O'Neill, the dippy punk who couldn't be hurt or made cry, no matter how hard he was socked, because his head was made of hard stuff like iron and ivory and marble. It meant Vinc Curley, who had water on the brain, and the doctors must have taken his brains out, drowned and dead like a dead fish, that time they were supposed to have taken a quart of water from his oversized bean. The kids in Vinc's class said that Sister Cyrilla used to pound him on the bean with her clapper, and he'd sit there yelling he was going to tell his mother; and it was funny, and all the kids in the room laughed their guts out. They didn't have 'em as crazy as Vinc in Studs' class; but there was TB McCarthy, who was always getting his ears beat off, and being made to kneel up in front of the room, or to go in Sister Bernadette's room and sit with all the girls and let them laugh at him. And there was Reardon with horses' hoofs for feet. One day in geography in the fifth grade, Cyrilla called on Reardon and asked him what the British Isles consisted of. Reardon didn't know so Studs whispered to him to say iron, and Reardon said iron. Sister Cyrilla thought it was so funny she marked him right for the day's lesson. And St. Patrick's meant Weary Reilley, and Studs hated Weary. He didn't know whether or not he could lick Weary, and Weary was one tough customer, and the guys had been waiting for Studs and Weary to scrap ever since Weary had come to St. Patrick's in the third grade. Studs was a little leery about mixing it with Reilley . . . no, he wasn't . . . it was just . . . well, there was no use starting fights unless you had to . . . and he'd never backed out of a scrap with Weary Reilley or any other guy. And that time he had pasted Weary in the mush with an icy snowball, well, he hadn't backed out of a fight when Weary started getting sore. He had just not meant to hit Weary with it, and in saying so he had only told the truth.

St. Patrick's meant a lot of things. St. Patrick's meant . . . Lucy.

Lucy Scanlan would stand on the same stage with him in a few hours, and she would receive her diploma. She would wear a white dress, just like his sister Frances, and Weary's sister Fran, and she would receive her diploma. Everybody said that Fran Lonigan and Fran Reilley were the two prettiest girls in the class. Well, if you asked him, the prettiest girl in the class was black-bobbed-haired Lucy.

He got soft, and felt like he was all mud and mush inside; he held his hand over his heart, and told himself:

My Lucy!

He flicked some ashes in the sink, and said to himself:

Lucy, I love you!

Once when he had been in the sixth grade, he had walked home with Lucy. Now, he puffed his cigarette, and the sneer went off his face. He thought of the March day when he had walked home with her. He had walked home with her. All along Indiana Avenue, he had been liking her, wanting to kiss her. Now, he remembered that day as clearly as if it had just happened. He remembered it better than the day when he was just a punk and he had bashed the living moses out of that smoke who pulled a razor on him over in Carter Playground, and a gang of guys had carried him around on their shoulders, telling him what a great guy he was, and how, when he grew up, he would become the white hope of the world, and lick Jack Johnson for the heavyweight championship. He remembered the day with Lucy, and his memory of it was like having an awful thirst for a cold drink of clear cold water or a chocolate soda on a hot day. It had been a windy day in March, without any sun. The air had seemed black, and the sky blacker, and all the sun that day had been in his thoughts of her. He had had all kinds of goofy, dizzy feelings that he liked. They had walked home from school along Indiana Avenue, he and Lucy. They hadn't spoken much, and they had stopped every little while to look at things. They had stopped at the corner of Sixtieth, and he had shown her the basement windows they had broken, just to get even with old Boushwah, the Hunkie janitor, because he always ran them off the grass when they goofed on their way home from school. And she had pretended that it was awful for guys to break windows, when he could see by the look in her eyes that she didn't at all think it so terrible. And they had walked on slow, pigeon-toed slow, slower, so that it would take them a long time to get home. He had carried her books, too, and they had talked about this and that, about the skating season that was just finished, and about the spelling match between the fifth- and sixth-grade boys and girls, where both of them had been spelled down at the first crack of the bat, and they had talked about just talk. When they came to the elevated structure near Fifty-ninth, he had shown her where they played shinny with tin cans, and she said it was a dangerous game, and you were liable to get your shins hurt. Then he had shown her where he had climbed up the girder to the top, just below the elevated tracks, and she had shivered because it was such a dangerous brave thing to do, and he had felt all proud, like a hero, or like Bronco Billy or Eddie Polo in the movies. They had walked home lazy, and he had carried her books, and wished he had the price to buy her candy or a soda, even if it was Lent, and they had stood before the gray brick two-story building where she lived, and he had wanted, as the devil wants souls, to kiss her, and he hadn't wanted to leave her because when he did he knew the day would get blacker, and he would feel like he did when he had been just out of his diapers and he used to be afraid of the night. There had been something about that day. He had gone on in school, wishing and wishing for another one like it to come along. And now he felt it all over again, the goofy, dizzy, flowing feelings it had given him.

He puffed, and told himself:

Well, it's so long to the old dump tonight!

He wanted to stand there, and think about Lucy, wondering if he would ever have days with her like that one, wondering how much he'd see of her after she went to high school. And he goddamned himself, because he was getting soft. He was Studs Lonigan, a guy who didn't have mushy feelings! He was a hard-boiled egg that they had left in the pot a couple of hours too long.

He took another drag of his cigarette.

He wanted that day back again.

He faced the mirror, and stuck the fag in the right-hand corner of his mouth. He looked tough and sneered. Then he let the cigarette hang from the left side. He studied himself with satisfaction. He placed the cigarette in the center of his puss, and put on a weak-kneed expression. He took the cigarette out of his mouth, daintily, barely holding it between his thumb and first finger, and he pretended that he was a grownup mama's boy, smoking for the first time. He said to himself:

Jesus Christ!

He didn't know that he bowed his head when he muttered the Lord's name, just as Sister Cyrilla had always taught them to do. He took a vicious poke at the air, as if he were letting one fly at a mama's boy.

He stuck the fag back in his mouth and looked like Studs Lonigan was supposed to look. He lowered the lid on the toilet seat, and sat down to think. He puffed at his cigarette, and flicked the ashes in the sink.

He heard Frances talking:

"Get out of my way, Fritzie . . . Get out of my way . . . Please . . . And Mother . . . Mother! MOTHER! . . . Will you come here, please . . . I told you the hem was not right on this dress . . . Now, Mother, come here and look at the way my skirt hangs . . . If I ever appear on the stage with my skirt like this, I'll be disgraced . . . disgraced . . . Mother!"

He heard the old lady hurrying to Frances's room, saying:

"Yes, Frances darling; only you know I asked you not to call Loretta Fritzie . . . I'm coming, but I tell you, your dress is perfectly even all around. I told you so this afternoon when you tried it on with Mrs. Sankey here."

He could hear their voices as they jabbered away about her dress, but he didn't know what they were saying, and anyway, he didn't give two hoots in hell. Girls had loose screws in their beans. Well, girls like his sister anyway. Girls like Lucy, or Helen Shires, who was just like a guy, were exceptions. But there he was getting soft again. He said to himself:

I'm so tough that you know what happens? Well, bo, when I spit . . . rivers overflow . . . I'm so hard I chew nails . . . See, bo!

He took a last drag at his cigarette, tossed the butt down the toilet, and let the water run in the sink to wash the ashes down. He went to the door, and had his hand on the knob to open it when he noticed that the bathroom was filled with smoke. He opened the small window, and commenced waving his arms around, to drive the smoke out. But why in hell shouldn't they know? What did his graduating and his long jeans mean, then? He was older now, and he could do what he wanted. Now he was growing up. He didn't have to take orders any more, as he used to. He wasn't going to hide it any more, and he was going to tell the old man that he wasn't going to high school.

The bathroom was slow in clearing. He beat the air with his hands.

Frances rapped sharply on the door and asked him to get a move on.

He waved his arms around.

Frances was back in a moment.

"William, will you please . . . will you please . . . will you please hurry!"

She rapped impatiently.

"All right. I'll be right out."

"Well, why don't you, then? I have to hurry, I tell you. And I'm in the play tonight, and you're not. When you had your play last May, I didn't delay you like this, and I helped you learn your lines and everything, and now when I have to be there . . . William, *will you please hurry* . . . PLEASE!

. . . oh, Mother . . . Mother! Won't you come here and tell Studs to hurry up out of the bathroom?"

She furiously pounded on the door.

Studs was winded. He stopped trying to beat the smoke out. The smoke was still thick.

"All right, don't get . . . a . . . don't get so excited!"

He whewed, and wiped his forehead, as if there had been perspiration on it. That was a narrow escape. He'd almost told his sister not to get one on, and then there'd have been sixteen kinds of hell to pay around the house.

Whew!

You'd a thought he wanted to stay in there, the way she was acting. Well, he was going to walk out and let 'em see the smoke, and when they blew their gobs off, he would tell them from now on he was his own boss, and he would smoke where and when he damn well pleased; and furthermore, he wasn't going to high school.

"William, will you please . . . please . . . *please* let me in . . . Mother, won't you please . . . please . . . OH, PLEASE, come here and make him get out. He's been in there a half-hour. He's reading. He's always mean and selfish like that . . . Mother, please . . . PLEASE!"

She banged on the door.

"Aw, I heard you," Studs said.

"Well, if you did, come on out!" she snapped.

He heard his mother coming up to the door, while Frances banged and shouted away. He took a towel . . . why didn't he think of it sooner? . . . and started flapping it around.

His mother said:

"William, won't you hurry now, like a good son? Frances has to go in there, and she has to finish dressing and be up there early because she's going to be in the play. Now, son, hurry!"

"All right. I can't help it. I'll be right out."

"Well, *please* do!" Frances said.

The mother commenced to tell Frances that William was going to let her right in; but Frances interrupted:

"But, Mother, he's been in there almost an hour . . . He has no consideration for other people's rights . . . He's selfish and mean . . . and oh, Mother, I got to go in there . . . and what will I do if I spoil my graduation dress on his account . . . make him, Mother . . . and now I'm getting unnerved, and I'll never be able to act in the play!"

The old lady persuaded. And she told Studs that she and his father couldn't go until they had all the children off, and they would be disgraced if they came late for the entertainment on the night their son and daughter graduated.

Frances banged on the door and yelled.

"Aw, don't get so darn crabby," Studs said to her while he fanned the air with his towel.

"See, Mother! See! He says I'm insane just because I ask him to hurry after he's been in there all day. He's reading or smoking cigarettes . . . Please, make him hurry!"

"Why, Frances, how dare you accuse him like that!" Mrs. Lonigan commenced to say.

Studs heard his sister dashing away, hollering to the old man to come and do something. He fanned vigorously, and his mother stood at the door urging.

II

Old man Lonigan, his feet planted on the back porch railing, sat tilted back in his chair enjoying his stogy. His red, well-fed-looking face was wrapped in a dreamy expression; and his innards made slight noises as they diligently furthered the process of digesting a juicy beefsteak. He puffed away, exuding burgher comfort, while from inside the kitchen came the rattle of dishes being washed. Now and then he heard Frances preparing for the evening.

He gazed, with reverie-lost eyes, over the gravel spread of Carter Playground, which was a few doors south of his own building. A six-o'clock sun was imperceptibly burning down over the scene. On the walk, in the shadow of and circling the low, rambling public school building, some noisy little girls, the size and age of his own Loretta, were playing hop-scotch. Lonigan puffed at his cigar, ran his thick paw through his brown-gray hair, and watched the kids. He laughed when he heard one of the little girls shout that the others could go to hell. It was funny and they were tough little ones all right. It sounded damn funny. They must be poor little girls with fathers and mothers who didn't look after them or bring them up in the right home atmosphere; and if they were Catholic girls, they probably weren't sent to the sisters' school; parents ought to send their children to the sisters' school even if it did take some sacrifice; after all, it only cost a dollar a month, and even poor people could afford that when their children's education was at stake. He wouldn't have his Loretta using such rowdy language, and, of course, she wouldn't, because her mother had always taught her to be a little lady. His attention wandered to a boy, no older than his own Martin, but dirty and less well-cared-for, who, with the intent and dreamy seriousness of childhood, played on the ladders and slides which paralleled his own back fence. He watched the young-

ster scramble up, slide down, scramble up, slide down. It
stirred in him a vague series of impulses, wishes and nostalgias.
He puffed his stogy and watched. He said to himself:

Golly, it would be great to be a kid again!

He said to himself:

Yes, sir, it would be great to be a kid!

He tried to remember those ragged days when he was only
a shaver and his old man was a pauperized greenhorn. Golly,
them were the days! Often there had not been enough to
eat in the house. Many's the winter day he and his brother
had to stay home from school because they had no shoes. The
old house, it was more like a barn or a shack than a home, was
so cold they had to sleep in their clothes; sometimes in those
zero Chicago winters his old man had slept in his overcoat.
Golly, even with all that privation, them was the days. And
now that they were over, there was something missing, something gone from a fellow's life. He'd give anything to live
back a day of those times around Blue Island, and Archer
Avenue. Old man Dooley always called it Archey Avenue,
and Dooley was one comical turkey, funnier than anything
you'd find in real life. And then those days when he was a
young buck in Canaryville. And things were cheaper in them
days. The boys that hung out at Kieley's saloon, and later
around the saloon that Padney Flaherty ran, and Luke O'Toole's
place on Halsted. Old Luke was some boy. Well, the Lord
have mercy on his soul, and on the soul of old Padney Flaherty.
Padney was a comical duck, good-hearted as they make them,
but crabby. Was he a first-rate crab! And the jokes the boys
played on him. They were always calling him names, pigpen
Irish, shanty Irish, Padney, ain't you the kind of an Irishman
that slept with the pigs back in the old country. Once they
told him his house was on fire, and he'd dashed out of the
saloon and down the street with a bucket of water in his
hand. It was funny watching him go, a skinny little Irishman.
And while he was gone, they had all helped themselves to
free beers. He came back blazing mad, picked up a hatchet,
called them all the choice swear words he could think of,
and ran the whole gang out into the street. Then they'd all
stood on the other corner, laughing. Yeh, them was the days!
And when he was a kid, they would all get sacks, wagons,
any old thing, and go over to the tracks. Spike Kennedy, Lord
have mercy on his soul, he was bit by a mad dog and died,
would get up on one of the cars and throw coal down like
sixty, and they'd scramble for it. And many's the fight they'd
have with the gangs from other streets. And many's the plunk
in the cocoanut that Paddy Lonigan got. It's a wonder some

of them weren't killed throwing lumps of coal and ragged
rocks at each other like a band of wild Indians. To live some
of those old days over again! Golly!

He took a meditative puff on his stogy, and informed himself
that time was a funny thing. Old Man Time just walked along,
and he didn't even blow a How-do-you-do through his whiskers.
He just walked on past you. Things just change. Chicago was
nothing like it used to be, when over around St. Ignatius Church
and back of the yards were white men's neighborhoods, and
Prairie Avenue was a tony street where all the swells lived,
like Fields, who had a mansion at Nineteenth and Prairie,
and Pullman at Eighteenth and Calumet, and Fairbanks and
Potter Palmer and the niggers and whores had not roosted
around Twenty-second Street, and Fifty-eighth Street was
nothing but a wilderness, and on Sunday afternoons the
boulevards were lined with carriages, and there were no automobiles, and living was dirt cheap, and people were friendlier
and more neighborly than they now were, and there were
high sidewalks, *and he and Mary were young.* Mary had been
a pretty girl, too, and at picnics she had always won the prizes
because she could run like a deer; and he remembered that
first picnic he took her to, and she had won a loving cup and
gave it to him, and then they went off sparking, and he had
gotten his first kiss, and they sat under a tree when it was hushed,
like the earth was preparing for darkness, and he and Mary
had looked at each other, and then he knew he had fallen,
and he didn't give a damn. And the bicycle parties.

> *Daisy, Daisy, give me your answer true,*
> *We won't have a stylish marriage,*
> *We can't afford a carriage,*
> *But you'll look sweet,*
> *Upon the seat, of a bicycle built for two.*

And that Sunday he had rented a buggy, even though it
cut a terrible hole in his kick, and they had driven way out
south. Who would have ever thought he and she would now
be living in the same neighborhood they had driven into that
Sunday, and that they would have their own home, and graduate
their kids from it? Now, who would have thought it? And
the time he had taken her to a dance at Hull House, and
coming home he had almost gotten into a mixup with some
soused mick because the fellow had started to get smartalecky,
like he was a kike. Yessir, them was the days. He hummed,
trying first to strike the right tune to *Little Annie Rooney*,
then the tune of *My Irish Molly 'O.* He sang to himself:

Dear old girl, the robin sings above you!
Dear old girl, it speaks of how I love you,
Dear old girl, it speaks of how I love you . . .

He couldn't remember the rest of the song, but it was a fine song. It described his Mary to a T. His . . . Dear Old Girl.

And the old gang. They were scattered now, to the very ends of the earth. Many of them were dead, like poor Paddy McCoy, Lord have mercy on his soul, whose ashes rested in a drunkard's grave at Potter's Field. Well, they were a fine gang, and many's the good man they drank under the table, but . . . well, most of them didn't turn out so well. There was Heinie Schmaltz, the boy with glue on his fingers, the original sticky-fingered kid. And poor Mrs. Schmaltz, Lord have mercy on her poor soul. God was merciful to take her away before she could know how her boy went up the road to Joliet on a ten-year jolt for burglary. The poor little woman, how she used to come around and tell of the things her Heinie found. She'd say, in her German dialect, My Heinie, he finds the grandest things. Vy, ony yesterday, I tell you, I tell you, he found a diamond ring, vy, can you himagine hit! And that time she and Mrs. McGoorty got to talking about which of their boys were the luckiest, and about the fine things my Heinie found, and the foine things my Mike is always pickin' up. Good souls they were. And there was Dinny Gorman, the fake silk-hat. When Dinny would tote himself by, they'd all haw-haw because he was like an old woman. He was too bright, if you please, to associate with ordinary fellows. Once a guy from New York came around, and he was damned if High-hat Dinny, who'd never been to the big burg, didn't sit down and try to tell this guy about New York. Dinny had made a little dough, but he was, after all, only a shyster lawyer and a cheap politician. He had been made ward committeeman because he had licked everybody's boots. And there were his own brothers. Bill had run away to sea at seventeen and nobody had ever heard from him again. Jack, Lord have mercy on his soul, had always been a wild and foolish fellow, and man or devil couldn't persuade him not to join the colors for the war with Spain, and he'd been killed in Cuba, and it had nearly broken their mother's heart in two. Lord have mercy on his and her and the old man's souls. He'd been a fool, all right! Poor Jack! And Mike had run off and married a woman older than himself, and he was now in the east, and not doing so well, and his wife was an old crow, slobbering in a wheel chair. And Joe was a motorman. And Catherine, well, he hadn't even better think of her. Letting a traveling salesman get her like that, and expecting to come home with her fatherless baby; and then going out and becoming . . . a scarlet woman. His own sister, too! God! Nope, his family had not turned out so well. They hadn't had, none of them, the persistence that he had. He had stuck to his job and nearly killed himself working. But now he was reaping his rewards. It had been no soft job when he had started as a painter's apprentice, and there weren't strong unions then like there were now, and there was no eight-hour day, neither, and the pay was nothing. In them days, many's the good man that fell off a scaffold to die or become permanently injured. Well, Pat Lonigan had gone through the mill, and he had pulled himself up by his own bootstraps, and while he was not exactly sitting in the plush on Easy Street, he was a boss painter, and had his own business, and pretty soon maybe he'd even be worth a cool hundred thousand berries. But life was a funny thing, all right. It was like Mr. Dooley said, and he had never forgotten that remark, because Dooley, that is Finley Peter Dunne, was a real philosopher. Who'll tell what makes wan man a thief, and another man a saint?

He took a long puff. He gazed out, and watched a group of kids, thirteen, fourteen, fifteen, boys like Bill, who sat in the gravel near the backstop close to the Michigan Avenue fence. What do kids talk about? He wondered, because a person's own childhood got so far away from him he forgot most of it, and sometimes it seemed as if he'd never been a kid himself, he forgot the way a kid felt, the thoughts of a kid. He sometimes wondered about Bill. Bill was a fine boy. You couldn't find a better one up on the graduating stage at St. Patrick's tonight, no more than you would see a finer girl than Frances. But sometimes he wondered just what Bill thought about.

He puffed. It was nice sitting there. He would like to sit there, and watch it slowly get dark, because when it was just getting dark things were quiet and soft-like, and a fellow liked to sit in all the quiet and well, just sit, and let any old thoughts go through his mind; just sit and dream, and realize that life was a funny thing, but that he'd fought his way up to a station where there weren't no real serious problems like poverty, and he sits there, and is comfortable and content and patient, because he knows that he has put his shoulder to the wheel, and he has been a good Catholic, and a good American, a good father, and a good husband. He just sits there with Mary, and smokes his cigar, and has his thoughts, and then, after it gets dark, he can send one of the kids for ice cream, or maybe sneak down to the saloon at Fifty-eighth and State and have a glass of beer. But there was many another evening for that, and tonight he'd have to go and see the kids get a good sendoff; otherwise he wouldn't be much of a father. When you're a father you got duties, and Patrick J. Lonigan well knew that.

While Lonigan's attention had been sunk inwards, the kids had all left the playground. Now he looked about, and the scene was swallowed in a hush, broken only by occasional automobiles and by the noise from the State Street cars that seemed to be more than a block away. Suddenly, he experienced, like an unexpected blow, a sharp fear of growing old and dying, and he knew a moment of terror. Then it slipped away, greased by the thickness of his content. Where in hell should he get the idea that he was getting so old? Sure, he was a little gray in the top story, and a little fat around the belly, but, well, the fat was a healthy fat, and there was lots of stuff left in the old boy. And he was not any fatter then old man O'Brien who owned the coal yards at Sixty-second and Wabash.

He puffed at his stogy and flicked the ashes over the railing. He thought about his own family. Bill would get himself some more education, and then learn the business, starting as a painter's apprentice, and when he got the hang of things and had worked on the job long enough, he would step in and run the works; and then the old man and Mary would take a trip to the old sod and see where John McCormack was born, take a squint at the Lakes of Killarney, kiss the blarney stone, and look up all his relatives. He sang to himself, so that no one would hear him:

> *Where the dear old Shannon's flowing,*
> *Where the three-leaved shamrock grows,*
> *Where my heart is I am going,*
> *To my little Irish Rose.*
> *And the moment that I meet her,*
> *With a hug and kiss I'll greet her,*
> *For there's not a colleen sweeter,*
> *Where the River Shannon flows.*

He glowed over the fact that his kids were springing up. Martin and Loretta were coming along faster than he could imagine. Frances was going to be a beautiful girl who'd attract some rich and sensible young fellow. He beat up a number of imaginary villains who would try to ruin her. He returned to the thought that his kids were growing up; and he rested in the assurance that they had all gotten the right start; they would turn out A No. 1.

Martin would be a lawyer or professional man of some kind;

he might go into politics and become a senator or a . . . you never could tell what a lad with the blood of Paddy Lonigan in him might not become. And Loretta, he just didn't know what she'd be, but there was plenty of time for that. Anyway, there was going to be no hitches in the future of his kids. And the family would have to be moving soon. When he'd bought this building, Wabash Avenue had been a nice, decent, respectable street for a self-respecting man to live with his family. But now, well, the niggers and kikes were getting in, and they were dirty, and you didn't know but what, even in broad daylight, some nigger moron might be attacking his girls. He'd have to get away from the eight balls and tinhorn kikes. And when they got into a neighborhood property values went blooey. He'd sell and get out . . . and when he did, he was going to get a pretty penny on the sale.

He puffed away. A copy of the *Chicago Evening Journal* was lying at his side. It was the only decent paper in town; the rest were Republican. And he hated the *Questioner,* because it hadn't supported Joe O'Reilley, past grand master of Lonigan's Order of Christopher lodge, that time in 1912 when Joe had run for the Democratic nomination for State's Attorney. Lonigan believed it was the *Questioner* that had beaten Joe; he wouldn't have it in his house. He thought about the Christys, and decided he would have to be taking his fourth degree, and then at functions he could be all dolled up with a plume in his hat and a sword at his side that would be attached to a red band strung across his front. And then he'd get a soup-and-fish outfit and go to the dinners all rigged out so that his own family wouldn't know him. He wasn't a bad-looking guy, and he'd bet he could cut a swath all togged up in soup and fish. And when his two lads grew up, he was going to make good Christys out of them too. And he'd have to be attending meetings regularly. It might even help his business along, and it was only right that one Christy should help another one along. That was what fraternalism meant. He looked down at the paper and noticed the headlines announcing Wilson's nomination at St. Louis. There was a full-length photograph of long-faced Wilson; he was snapped in summery clothes, light shoes and trousers, a dark coat and a straw hat. He held an American flag on a pole about four feet long. Next to him in the photograph was the script of a declaration he had had drafted into the party platform forecasting the glorious future of the American people and declaring inimical to their progress any movement that was favorable to a foreign government at the expense of the American Nation. The cut was worded, THE PRESIDENT AND THE FLAG.

Now, that was a coincidence. On the day that Bill and Frances were graduated, Woodrow Wilson was renominated for the presidency. It was a historic day, because Wilson was a great president, and he had kept us out of war. There might be something to coincidences after all. And then the paper carried an account of the day's doings at the Will Orpet trial; Orpet was the bastard who ruined a girl, and when she was in the family way, went and killed her rather than marry her like any decent man would have done. And the baseball scores. The White Sox had lost to Boston, two to one. They were only in fifth place with an average of five hundred, but things looked good and they might win the pennant anyway. Look at what the Boston Braves had done in 1914. The Sox would spend the last month home. He'd have to be going out and seeing the Sox again. He hadn't been to a game since 1911 when he'd seen Ping Bodie break up a seventeen-inning game with the Tigers. Good old Ping. He was back in the minors, but that was Comiskey's mistake. Cicotte and Faber were in form now, and that strengthened the team, and they had Zeb Terry at shortstop playing a whale of a game, with Joe Jackson on the club, and Weaver at third, playing bang-up ball and not making an error a game like he had playing shortstop, and Collins and Schalk, and a better pitching staff, they would get going like a house on fire, and he'd have to be stepping out and seeing them play regular. Well, he could read all about it, and about the food riots in Rotterdam, and the bloody battle in which the Germans had captured Vaux, afterwards. Now, he'd have to be going inside, putting on his tie, and going up with Mary and the kids for the doings. He sat there, comfortable, puffing away. Life was a good thing if you were Patrick J. Lonigan and had worked hard to win out in the grim battle, and God had been good to you. But then, he had earned the good things he had. Yes, sir, let God call him to the Heavenly throne this very minute, and he could look God square in the eye and say he had done his duty, and he had been, and was, a good father. They had given the kids a good home, fed and clothed them, set the right example for them, sent them to Catholic schools to be educated, seen that they performed their religious duties, hustled them off to confession regularly, given them money for the collection, never allowed them to miss mass, even in winter, let them play properly so they'd be healthy, given them money for good clean amusements like the movies because they were also educational, done everything a parent can do for a child.

He puffed his stogy and sat there. The sun was imperceptibly burning low. Old man Lonigan looked about. He puffed on his stogy, and his innards made their customary noises as they diligently furthered the digestive process.

III

Frances rushed upon him, and with excited little-girl madness she asked him to make William get out of the bathroom.

The old man rapped on the bathroom door and told Bill to hurry up.

"Father, he's just a mean old brute. He's been in there an hour. He's reading or smoking cigarettes."

"Why, Frances!" the mother said.

"No, I ain't."

"Bill, tell me . . . are you smoking?"

"Aw, she's all vacant upstairs."

"Why, that is no language for an educated Catholic boy to use," the mother said.

"Father, he's mean and selfish. He's a brute, a beast. He isn't fair, and he doesn't give anyone else the least bit of consideration. I'll be late. I can't go. You'll have to get my diplomas, and they'll have to let someone else act. I can't go. I can't go. He's made me all nervous and unstrung. I'm unstrung, and I can't act now. I can't. And I'm worried because I'm not sure if my dress is even or not and I have to *go* in there. Father, *please* make the brute come out," Frances said melodramatically.

"All right. I'll be right out. I can't help it," Studs said.

"Make him, Father!"

"Goddamn it, Bill, hurry!"

"I will."

"He's always like this," Frances said.

"I ain't."

"Every time I'm in a hurry, he's getting in the way. He's selfish, and don't think of anyone but his dirty old self, and he always monopolizes the bathroom . . . he's an ole . . . goat," said Frances.

"Aw, shut up and go to hell," said Studs as he fanned the air.

"Why, William Lonigan! Father, did you hear him insult me, swear at me, like I was one of those roughnecks from Fifty-eighth Street I sometimes see him with?"

"Bill, come right out. I'll not have you cursing in this house. I'm boss here, and so long as I am, you will use gentlemanly language when you address your sister. Where do you learn to speak like that, you, with the education I've given you? You don't hear anyone around here speaking like that," said the old man.

"Aw, heck, she's always blowing off her bazoo," said Studs.

"William, I wish that you wouldn't use such language. After receiving such a fine education . . . I'm shocked," said the mother.

"He doesn't know any better. He couldn't be a gentleman if he tried to," Frances said.

"Now, Frances, don't add fuel to the fire," the mother said.

"All right. I'm coming right out. I couldn't help it. Only it gets me sore to hear her yelling her ears off like that, over nothin'."

"Well, it's a good thing I do. Someone ought to expose him, and tell him how mean and selfish and inconsiderate he is, and how he only thinks of himself."

"Now, children, this is your graduation night, and you know your graduation night ought to be one of the happiest of your lives," the mother said.

The smoke had cleared now, so Studs could take a chance. He marched out, leaving the bathroom in perfect order. Frances indignantly brushed by him, her head held proud.

Frances was a very pretty girl of thirteen. Her body had commenced to lose its awkwardness, and she had a trim little girlish figure. Her plain white graduation dress set her off well, with her dark hair and her blackish eyes. She looked older than Studs.

"William, you should be more considerate," the mother said, unheard.

"Bill, you're gettin' at the age where you should be more . . . more chivalrous toward the ladies," the old man said as he chewed away at the remains of his stogy.

"Yeah, but heck, the way she yells over nothing, and starts raisin' all kinds of Cain when there ain't no reason," he said.

Father and mother cautioned him on the use of the word ain't. It was not polite, or good diction.

"Bill, you have to put up with the ladies, and make allowances fer their . . . defugalties," the old man said pompously.

He nudged Studs, intimately, and slipped him a buck as a graduation present. Studs felt good over getting the buck, and went to his bedroom to put on the white tie he hated to wear, but had to. He looked at the tie, feeling uncomfortable. He looked out the window, and Goddamned the tie.

He heard his old man and his old lady speaking.

"Well, Mary, we got our children started now. We got Bill and Frances pretty near raised."

"Yes, Patrick, and I'm so happy, because it's been such a hard job, you know."

"Yeah, we done well by 'em, and paid their way, and now

it won't be so hard as it was, and when we get 'em all raised, and brought up, and educated, we'll take a trip to Ireland. It will be our second honeymoon . . . And, Mary, you and I'll have to give more time to ourselves and spark about a little. This summer sure, we'll go out to Riverview Park and have a day of our own, like we planned for so long," he said.

"Yes, Patrick . . . And, Patrick, these little spats the children have, they're nothin' at all," she said.

"Nope. They happen in the best regulated families," the old man said; he laughed, as if he had cracked a good joke.

"And nobody can say we ain't done right by our children," he said.

"They certainly can't."

"And we paid their way," he said.

"Yes . . . and Sister Bernadette Marie told me how fine a boy William was, and how grand a girl Frances is," Mrs. Lonigan said.

"Yeah!" the old man said.

Then the old lady started to talk about the high school they would send Studs to. Studs knew what was coming. She was going to suggest that he be sent to study for the priesthood. He got sore, and wanted to yell at her. But the old man dismissed the whole subject. He said they could decide later, adding:

"I got the money, and we can send the lad any place we want to."

"But here, you get your tie on and comb your hair. We have to go, Patrick . . . And, Martin, come here and let me see your fingernails and behind your ears. Did you wash your neck? That's a good boy. And your teeth? Open your mouth . . . Well, for once you are presentable . . . and Loretta, is your dress on? Come here. Yes, you look like a little lady . . ."

She entered Studs' room, retied his tie, and recombed his hair, much to his discomfort, and made him go over his fingernails again; he felt as if they were trying to make a molly-coddle out of him. She pinned on the long class ribbons of golden yellow and silvery blue. He sat on the bed, waiting for them, thinking about all kinds of things.

Looking like Sunday, or as if they had just walked out of a dusty family album, the Lonigan family promenaded down Michigan Avenue. Studs and Frances marched first. Studs felt stiff; he told himself he must look like some queer egg or other. Frances marched along, proud and lady-like. She did not deign to glance at Studs, but she teased him in a voice so loud that all heard her. He walked along, looking straight ahead, his eyes vacant; he thought up all the curse words he could and silently flung them at her. Loretta and Martin followed. Loretta was carrying the beautiful bouquet of white roses and carnations that were for Frances, and she walked along imitating her sister. She even teased Martin with the same words that Frances was using. Martin had to be cautioned by his parents, because he did not suffer in sulky silence, as Studs did. Father and mother formed the rear guard; parental pride oozed from them like healthy perspiration; the lean mother looked frugal, even in the plain but expensive blue dress she had bought for the occasion. Passersby glanced at them a second time, and they smiled with satisfaction. The old man kept repeating that he hoped Father Gilhooley would give the kids a big send-off.

"Studs got long pants on," Martin said, to escape the teasing of Fritzie.

Fritzie giggled.

"Close your beak," Studs turned and said.

"Martin, how many times have I forbade you to call him that awful name . . . and William, don't talk like that to my baby . . . The two of you cutting up like that in public . . . I'm ashamed of you," the mother said.

"Now, cut it out," the old man said authoritatively.

"I ain't a baby," Martin said.

"I'm walking with the baby," Frances said.

The Lonigans promenaded along Michigan Avenue, looking like Sunday.

CHAPTER TWO

I

Father Gilhooley floridly faced his audience. He pursed his fat lips, rubbed his fat paws together and suavely caressed his bay front. A fly buzzed momentarily above him, and almost settled on his gray-fringed dome. He stood forward on the crowded little stage, pausing to create a dramatic effect. To his left, and a trifle out of line with him, Father Doneggan and Father Roney, the two parish assistants, stood, their faces expressionless. Back of him the graduating class was phalanxed; the blue-suited boys fidgeted on the left; the white girls stood, like wax models, on the right. All clutched their diplomas, while many also held green-bowed Irish history diplomas and Palmer method certificates.

Every atom of the June heat seemed to be compressed in

little cubes that dripped wet discomfort over the heads of
the packed audience. Heads constantly turned and switched
to gaze at the cool patches of blue sky that were framed in
the windows lining the two side walls. The audience had enjoyed
the entertainment; at least, it had heartily applauded each
number from the very cute little group piece the first-grade
girls had spoken to the group dancing of Fritzie's fourth-grade
class, the elocution recitation of the sixth-grade girls, the
special numbers by prodigies like little Roslyn Hayes and
Dorothy Gorman, and the adaptation of a play from *Little
Women* that the seventh- and eighth-grade girls had presented.
And now the good priest was going to conclude the entertainment with a brief talk . . . at least many hoped that
it would be brief.

The good priest blandly commenced:

"This is a *joyous* evening for all of us here at St. Patrick's.
We have all enjoyed the skillful and well-acted entertainment
to the utmost, just as we enjoyed the similarly well-presented
entertainment of the boys of this parish school last May. We
could ask nothing more of our children, or of the good sisters
who trained them. It has been, and I utter these words without
the least iota of doubt in my own mind, an entertainment as
amusing and as entertaining as many a professional show. It
has also been, my dear friends, an evening which we will
carry with us through the years as a golden treasure. And
it will be an especially sacred and hallowed memory to you
who are the fathers and mothers of the boys and girls in St.
Patrick's banner class of 1916. It is you parents who have
made this grand evening possible, who have suffered and worried
and fretted, sacrificed, stinted yourselves luxuries, in order
to send your children off daily to the good sisters where they
might receive Catholic training. You have had your fears and
your worries sending these sturdy, well-behaved, beloved, and,
yes, handsome children to school. But now these fears and
worries must be scattering like the fog dissipating before the
warming rays of Gawd's golden morning sunlight. Your little
ones have been safely steered beyond all the early rocks and
shoals and sands in their voyage on the sea of life. The dis-
tribution of diplomas, which you have just witnessed on this
small stage, symbolizes the arrival of your little ones in the
first safe haven on their journey across the stormy and wave-
tossed sea of life. It symbolizes the victory and achievement
which is the result of eight hard years of patience and care;
a triumph whose ultimate crown of success will be forged at
the very throne of Gawd Almighty."

He talked on, his language fat with superlatives. Then, becoming as skittish as a portly and dignified pastor from the old sod can be, he said that while he was opposed to gambling, he was still willing to *bet* that there was not a parish in the great city of Chicago that could have put on a finer display or have turned out a more stalwart graduating class than St. Patrick's had on this June evening. He was interrupted by loud clapping, and he smiled . . . magnificently.

He continued his talk, reminding his dear friends that in this, their hour of joy, they must not forget the good sisters who had trained the children, not only in reading and writing and arithmetic, not only for the splendid performance they had made that evening, but also for the more serious and important task of . . . saving their immortal souls.

"After all, we are made to love, to serve, and to obey Gawd in this world, and to be happy with Him in the next, just as the catechism teaches us," he said profoundly.

And it was the religious training, the daily example and inspiration provided by the modest, self-sacrificing, holy virgins who had pointed out the path of salvation for the children of St. Patrick's parish. The graduates of St. Patrick's parish all walked in the ways of Gawd, grew up into sterling-silver specimens of Catholic manhood and womanhood, because of the teaching, the kind nurturing in goodness that they met with in the classrooms of St. Patrick's school. The entire parish owed a heartfelt tribute to these white-souled women.

In the rear of the hall, left-hand side, were three ex-little ones of St. Patrick's who had worn out the patience of the holy women, three naughty little boys who had been canned from school and who might even end on the gallows. They were kids of Studs' age, Paulie Haggerty and Tommy Doyle, who were famous not only because they were hard guys but also because they had such fat butts, and tough Red Kelly, whose old man was a police sergeant. Hook-nosed, bow-legged Davey Cohen and Three-Star Hennessey, fourteen, small and considered nothing but a tricky punk, were also with them. They had all snuck in and were having a good time, making trouble. Davey suddenly whisted to Red, Tommy and Paulie. They whispered, and laughed quietly, and Red told Davey to go ahead. Davey goosed Hennessey. Hennessey was goosey anyway, and he jumped; his writhings disturbed a surrounding semi-circle of dignity. But Three-Star suddenly saved himself; he pointed out Vinc Curley. Vinc was better goose meat.

The priest spoke on, and the boys on the stage grew more restless. Weary Reilley told Jim Clayburn that he wished old Gilly would pipe down, but Jim didn't answer, because Jim knew how to act in public, and anyway he was almost like

a boy scout. TB McCarthy told Gunboats Reardon that it
was all a lot of hot air, and Reardon nodded as he shifted his
weight from the right to the left gunboat. Father Doneggan
heard TB, and gave him a couple of dirty looks. Studs wiped
the sweat from his face and fidgeted less than the others. He
told himself that he wished Gilly would choke his bull and
let it die. Gilly spoke of Catholic education, praising the
parents who had possessed the courage, the conscience and
the faith to give their children a Catholic schooling. He
contrasted them with those careless, miserly and irreligious
fathers and mothers who dealt so lightly with the souls of
the little ones Gawd had entrusted in their care that they
sent them to public schools, where the word of Gawd is not
uttered from the beginning to the end of the livelong day.
Such parents, he warned, were running grave risks, not only
of losing the souls of their children but also their own immortal
souls. Of such parents, the good priest said:

"Woe! Woe! Woe!"

And many of the boys and girls on the stage were going on
in their schooling. To the parents of these boys and girls he
felt it his duty to give warning. The shoals would become more
dangerous, the rocks larger. If their souls were to navigate
successfully on the stormier seas of life, he commended them
to the Catholic high schools of Chicago, where the boys would
be trained by holy brothers and consecrated priests and the
girls by holy nuns. No sacrifice would be too great to see
these fine boys and girls continue in Catholic hands. Let
not the parents, after such a fine beginning, fall into the class
of those about whom he must monotone:

"Woe! Woe! Woe!"

And his verbal thickets grew thicker and thicker with fat
polysyllables. They wallowed off his tongue like luxurious
jungle growths as he repeated everything he had said.

II

The Lonigans sat in the rear of the hall. Mrs. Lonigan strained
forward in a visible effort to devour every syllable that dropped
from the tongue of the noble priest. Patrick Lonigan sat back
listening, as comfortable as he could possibly be seated on
a camp chair in a hot and crowded hall. Once or twice he
yawned, and his wife nudged him. He mopped the perspiration
from his brow. At Mama's side the two youngest darlings
laughed, squirmed and childishly muttered, much to her annoyance. She nudged Papa, who was just falling into a drowse,
and said that William and Frances took the show away from
the others; why there wasn't a girl who looked as pretty,

or who had acted as well as Frances; and William was a pretty handsome boy, too.

"Uh huh!" the old man said.

"And we don't owe a penny on their education," she said.

"Uh huh!" he grunted.

They listened, and their pastor's words made them feel that they had participated in a great work, that they had done the Will of the Great Man Who sat on the Heavenly throne.

She strained forward again to listen attentively while the priest explained that it would be a shame if St. Patrick's could not dedicate, from among this class on the stage, a few lives to the service of God. Now was the time for the graduates to consider whether or not they had the call, for the mothers and fathers to encourage their children who might have the call, to resolve that they would put all aside and prepare for the consecrated work of the priest and the holy work of the nun. As Mrs. Lonigan listened, a dream of hope lit an ecstasy on her thin face. At this moment Loretta said something to Martin and the two children giggled. Mrs. Lonigan, severely angry, pinched Fritzie and warned her to be quiet. She told Loretta that she acted as if she had not been brought up in a good home and taught politeness and manners. She told Loretta to have respect for the priest and the people listening to him, and she made more disturbance than her daughter.

III

Facing the graduates, the priest gravely said:

"And now comes the painful duty, my dear young friends, of bidding you . . . farewell. It is a duty which I would gladly shirk, if shirk it I could. But . . . *Tempus fugit!* Time flies! Time is sometimes like a thief in the night, or like some lonely bird that comes to the banquet hall of this earth where man is feasting; it comes from a black unknown, flies through while man eats, and is gone out in the black night; and I may add, my dear young friends, the black night is black indeed, unless one has abided by the will of Gawd. Friends, it would be my fondest wish to keep you here with us at St. Patrick's, studying, serving the Lord, playing your happy innocent games of childhood out there in our large playground; but . . .

"Tempus fugit! For alas! . . . . Time flies!

"Tonight you put aside the joys of childhood to become young men and young women. And just as we, who are older, now recollect the joys and happiness of childhood, so will you one day remember your golden days with us here at St. Patrick's. They will be memories of gold and silver, memories richer than all the treasures of this world. And, my dear young friends, I want you to remember that, no matter what you may become, no matter if you are rich or poor, famous, as I sincerely trust some of you will be, or just one of the poor, honest workers in the Master's Vineyard, we at St. Patrick's will always remember you as friends, we will always remember the banner class of 1916."

IV

"Vinc, listen to this!" said Three-Star Hennessey.

Vinc listened.

Three-Star made lip-noises.

The others almost strangled themselves checking guffaws. Davey held his nose and whispered to the guys that it was Vinc.

"Ugh!" he muttered.

People near them looked askance.

The guys all told Vinc that he should be ashamed of himself.

"It was him! It was Three-Star, Dave. I didn't do it. I didn't. Hones'! Hones'! Hones'! I didn't. I tell you I didn't. I'll take an oath. Cross my die and hope to heart, I mean, I'll cross my heart and hope to die if I did it. I'm tellin' you that I didn't. Hones'!" pleaded Vinc with pained sincerity.

Three-Star told Vinc to tie his bull to another ash can.

"Why, Three-Star!" Vinc said, shocked.

Someone in the audience told them to shut up.

"Didn't your old lady teach you any better manners?" said Paulie.

"She's better'n your old lady," said Vinc aloud, but his remark didn't carry up to the stage. People turned, annoyed.

"Yeah!" whispered Paulie to Vinc.

Vinc was open-mouthed and hurt; hurt that he should be treated so unjustly.

V

"Alas, my dear young friends, you must move down the hard and stony paths of life. And at times, it will be a difficult road. It might be a long and lonely journey, unless you take, Gawd forbid, that false path which the great and Catholic-minded William Shakespeare described as the primrose path to the everlasting bonfire; *the primrose path to the everlasting bonfire* sown with the flowers and fruits of the Devil, bounded by beautiful rose bushes behind which hide old Nick and his fallen angels; the foxy, the sly and foxy hordes of hell. You must beware of old Nick, and you must not allow him to snare your souls. Old Nick, the Devil, is tricky, full of the blarney, as they say in the old country. He is like the fox, tricky, cunning, clever. He will always make false promises to you; he will seek to deceive you with all the pomp and gold and glory of this world. He is a master of artifice, and he will pay your price in this . . . if you will pay his price in the next world; *if you pay his price in the next world,* where hell hisses and yawns, and the damned suffer as no earthly being can or has suffered. False friendships, fame, riches, power, success, all will be strewn at your feet by old Nick, if only you sell your soul, like Mephistopheles . . . *if only you deny our Lord, Jesus Christ."*

From the second row, center, Mr. and Mrs. Reilley listened to the priest. She was a reddish woman, generously supplied with flesh and bust. He looked like a conventional cartoon of a henpecked husband.

"Sure, isn't he the walkin' saint of God? And isn't he the saint?" she said.

Reilley nodded his head from a long-standing habit of acquiescence.

"And isn't he the grand scholar?"

Reilley nodded.

"And maybe the lad will take all of what he says to heart."

Reilley nodded.

"And maybe he'll not run around like he does."

"I hope so," Reilley muttered.

"And sure, doesn't the lad and the lass take the cake up there on the stage?"

"Uh huh!" from Reilley.

VI

The priest described the glee of the Devil when he, Lucifer, snares a young and innocent soul; and the boy Studs Lonigan on the stage had an imaginative picture of Satan in a tight-fitting red-horned outfit, like the creature on a Pluto water bottle, hopping out from behind a bush, clutching the soul of a young guy or a girl from the stony road of life and dragging it away as he smiled, showing all his teeth just like Deadwood Dick in the newspaper cartoons. Father Gilhooley told how cunning Satan took the Master up to the mountain tops of the world and offered him all the pleasures and riches of this life, if He deny His Father, and Jesus resisted, saying, Get thee behind me, Satan, for He must be about His Father's work. The priest said that Satan must have, symbolically, taken the German Kaiser to the mountain tops and offered him the world and Kaiser Bill must have accepted, and that was probably why we had the terrible war devastating Europe. Yes, they must beware of old Nick, and they must persevere in the

ways of the Master, who died that agonizing death on that
terrible cross to redeem mankind. They must always remember
that Christ died for them, and they must never put a thorn
in His side by sinning. And they must not forget the advice
and example, the teachings of the good sisters. They must
say their prayers morning and evening and whenever they
were heavily beset with temptations, they must keep the
commandments of God and of Holy Mother Church, receive
the sacraments regularly, never willfully miss mass, avoid
bad companions and all occasions of sin, publicly defend
the Church from all enemies and contribute to the support
of their pastor. If they did these things, and if they dedicated
their lives to God's Holy Mother, and to the good and great
patron saint of their parish who had driven the snakes out
of Ireland, converting it to the true faith so that it had become
the Isle of Saints and Scholars, they would all be among the
sheep and not the goats on that grand and final day of judgment, when the God of Love would become the God of Justice.
Wishing that they would all go forth to lead holy and happy
lives, he gave them one final word of warning. On this very
night of their graduation, when they and their parents were
so proud, so happy, so righteously gratified, there was many
a work-worn father and many a gray-haired mother sitting
by the lamplit parlor window, waiting and praying for the
return of that prodigal son, that erring daughter, who would,
alas . . . never return. He prayed Gawd forbid any graduates
of St. Patrick's to cause gray hairs to a father or a mother.
Gawd wished that the fourth, above almost all other commandments, be kept . . . *Honor thy father and thy mother; that
thy days may be long upon the land which the Lord thy Gawd
giveth thee.*
     He blessed them, and the ceremonies were closed.

VII

     The graduating class shuffled off the stage into the side
room on the left. The boys gathered around wrinkled Sister
Bertha; the girls giggled about smiling, youngish Sister Bernadette Marie.
     Studs stood off by himself, wanting to join the guys and
say goodbye to Battleaxe Bertha. He found himself suddenly
sad because he wanted to stay in the eighth grade another year
and have more fun. He told himself that Bertha was a pretty
good sport, all things considered; and anyway, she hadn't treated
him so rotten like she had TB McCarthy, or Reardon, whose
old man was only a working man and couldn't afford to pay
any tuition. Yes, she was a good sport at that. He wanted to

go up to her and say goodbye, and say that he felt her to be a pretty good sport at that, but he couldn't, because there was some goofy part of himself telling himself that he couldn't. He couldn't let himself get soft about anything, because, well, just because he wasn't the kind of a bird that got soft. He never let anyone know how he felt. He told himself that anyway he'd join the guys and say goodbye to her. He made several starts to approach the guys, but didn't go up. He stood watching, hoping that someone would recognize him and call him up. But he felt that he didn't belong there. There was Frances, near Bernadette, and there was Lucy Scanlan; but they didn't see him. His old not-belonging feeling had gotten hold of him. He eased out of the door. It was just as well, because he wanted to slip around to the can and have a smoke before he joined the folks out in front to be told he looked so swell and all that boushwah. Inside the damp boys' lavatory on the Indiana Avenue side of the building, he leaned against a sink and puffed away, absorbed in the ascending strands of smoke. He wondered if it was really a sin to smoke, and told himself that was all bunk.

He puffed and looked about the dark and lonely place. He could hear himself breathing, and his heart beating away, and the queerness of the place seemed to put strange figures in him, and the strange figures just walked right out of his head and moved about the place, leering at him like red-dressed Satan. He felt like he used to feel when he was a young kid, and he would have nightmares, and strange boys, like demons, and as big as his father, would come and lean over his bed, and he would get up and run screaming into the dining room, where he would tear around and around the table until his old man came and shagged them away. Hell, he wasn't afraid of spooks any more, and all this talk of spirits was a lot of hokum. It was just that he felt a little queer about something. He puffed nervously, and watched the way the rays of moonlight fell into the room and dropped over the damp floor like they were sick things.

Whenever Studs had queer thoughts he had a good trick of getting rid of them. He imagined that his head was a compartment with many shutters in it, like a locker room. He just watched the shutters close on the queer, fruity thoughts, and they were gone, and he'd have a hell of a time bringing them back, even if he wanted to. He saw the shutter close in his mind now, and he puffed away and felt better. He coughed, because he tried to inhale and got too much smoke in his throat and nose. He thought about Gilly's speech, and told himself that, whew, Gilly had talked a leg off of everybody;

he talked as much as High-Collars Gorman, the lawyer. He thought of some of the things Gilly had said, and told himself that he didn't care so much about making any long, hard journey, like Gilly had described. He had always wanted to grow up and become a big guy, because a big guy could be more independent than a punk; a big guy could be his own boss. But he felt a little leery about leaving it all behind and going out into the battle of life.

He had long pants, and he wasn't just a grammar school punk any more, and he could walk down the street feeling he wasn't, but well . . . sometimes he wasn't so glad of it. And now he'd have to go to high school, when he didn't want to, and meet new kids and get in fights all over again to become somebody in a new gang.

He told himself that he'd have to go out now in the battle of life and start socking away. It was fun thinking about it, but that was different from the real thing. And when you had to fight, you got socked in the mush, and a good sock was never any fun. Anyway, he had the summer ahead of him, and he could have fun with the guys around Indiana.

Weary Reilley came in. Weary was carrying his diploma, but he didn't have any Irish history or Palmer method certificates. They were boushwah anyway, and just a lot of extra work.

Studs gave Weary a cigarette, and they stood facing each other. They were a contrast, Weary taller, and with a better build, and looking like a much badder guy. Weary had a mean, hard face, square and dirty-looking.

"I'm glad it's over," Studs said.

"Me, too. This for the works," Weary said, making noises by compressing his lips outward and blowing.

"I'm glad I'm through with Battling Bertha," Studs said.

They laughed in mutual agreement and understanding.

"Wouldn't she get one if she saw us in here smokin'!" said Weary.

"Yeah," said Studs.

They laughed and lit new fags.

"She's too old to teach anyway," said Studs.

"She's a crab," Weary said.

"I never liked the old battleaxe," Studs said.

"Remember when she kept me after school and started to sock me, and I wouldn't let her?" Weary said.

"Yeah. You had to fight with her, didn'cha?" said Studs.

"Well, the old cow went to swing on me, and I told her hands off. No, sir! I'm not lettin' no one take a poke at me and get away with it. Not even Archbishop Mundelein himself," Weary boasted out of the side of his mouth.

"Neither am I!" said Studs.

"Neither am I!" said Weary.

They looked each other in the eye, and kept staring for several long seconds to prove that they were unafraid of each other.

"No one can get away with takin' a poke at me," Studs said.

"Well, I never let anyone get away with takin' a poke at me neither, and I didn't intend to start by lettin' blind Bertha smack me," Weary said.

"After that she never bawled you out, did she?" Studs said.

"She was afraid of me," bragged Weary.

"She used to treat me all right. You see, my old man always gave the nuns a turkey on Thanksgivin' and Christmas," Studs said.

"Say, by the way, did you see Doneggan take a wham at TB?"

"No. Why?"

"Well, Muggsy McCarthy made some crack when Gilly was speakin', said Doneggan didn't like it, so he cracked his puss," Weary said.

"Yeh! Say! You know TB gets it in the neck every shot. I kinda feel sorry for the guy," Studs said.

"He's nuts anyway. I know I wouldn't take what that loogin takes. I don't give a good goddamn who it is, nobody is gettin' away with anything on this gee," said Weary.

"You know, they got a hell of a lotta nerve haulin' off on a guy just because they're priests or nuns," said Studs.

Studs casually shot his butt, just like all tough guys did.

"Well, if a guy stands for it, that's his tough luck," Weary said.

"Yeah, but goofy McCarthy is helpless. Christ, the poor guy's got one foot in the grave. His brother Red ain't so bad, but he's a sap. I tell you he's fruity," said Studs.

"The loogin's rotting away with TB anyway," said Weary.

"But lemme tell you . . . he's damn smart. Jesus! You know, if he'd a wanted tuh work, he could of had the scholarship to St. Cyril or any of those schools that hold scholarship exams and give scholarships," Studs said.

"But what the hell does that mean?" said Weary.

"Nothin'," said Studs.

"Anyway, I'm glad I'm through with old Bertha, . . . say, gimme another fag?" Weary said.

They lit cigarettes.

"Remember her, how she'd rush down the aisle to hit a guy, and she'd never hit the right one because she's as blind

as a bat and she couldn't see enough to take the right aim?"
said Studs.

They laughed because Bertha was funny, blind as a bat like
she was.

"But she is one lousy crab," said Studs.

"Anyway, I'm damn glad to be out of the dump," said Weary.

"Me, too," affirmed Studs.

"But we had a pretty good time at that," Weary added.

"Yeh, even if we did have Bertha in seventh and eighth grade,
and even if we did have guys like Clayburn in the class making
it hard for us by always studying," said Studs.

"Clayburn ought to be in the boy scouts," Weary said
derisively.

They laughed.

"Say, remember the time we shoved bonehead Vinc Curley
through the convent window, and there was a big stink, and
Bernadette lammed blazes out of him when he bawled that
he didn't do it and she said he did and she would break his
head before she let him call her a liar?" said Studs.

"That was funny," Weary said.

"And the time Muggsy hit Bertha with an eraser, and she
went sky high, and looked like she'd bust a blood vessel, and
she blamed Reardon and nearly put lumps on his head by
beaning him with her clapper?" said Studs.

"And the fights we used to have with the Greek kids from
the school across the way, and their priest would come over
to Gilly, because he and Gilly are friends even if he is a Greek
Catholic priest, and Gilly would send Doneggan up to read
the riot act to us?" said Weary.

They laughed.

"And remember the time when Bertha fell on the ice?"
said Studs.

"That was good because we were off three days," said Weary.

"You know, about the only decent thing about Bertha was
that she was always falling on the ice or getting sick so she
couldn't teach and we were getting holidays," said Studs.

"Well, Bertha always gave me a pain right here," Weary
said, pointing to the proper part of his anatomy.

A pause.

"Are you going to high school?" asked Weary.

"I don't know. I don' wanna," said Studs.

"I'm not goin'," said Weary.

"I don't think I'll go," said Studs.

"Schools are all so much horse apple," said Weary.

"I don't want to go, but the gaffer wants me to, I guess,"
said Studs.

"Well, I ain't goin', and my old man can lump it if he don't like it," said Weary.

"Gonna work?"

"Maybe," said Weary.

"Maybe I'll get myself a jobber," said Studs.

"Say, by the way, Gilly didn't ask for any dough in his speech, did he? I wonder if the old boy is sick or startin' to get feeble," said Weary.

"Well, he told us all to remember and not forget to contribute to the support of our pastor," said Studs.

"Yeah, that's right. He's never yet made a sermon without askin' for somethin', a coal collection, or a collection for the starvin' chinks, or for Indian missions, or some damn thing," said Weary.

"He's always asking for the shekels. He's as bad as a kike," said Studs.

"And did you hear his crack about the playground?" said Weary.

"Yeah," said Studs.

"Well, I couldn't keep a straight face when he made that crack about our large playground. Boy! a yard full of cinder where you can't play football, or even pompompullaway without tearin' hell out of your clothes and yourself, and they won't let you play ball in it because they're afraid you'll break a window, and he's too damn cheap to put up baskets for basketball. Like the gag he worked on us in winter. We were the snow brigade, and got a lot of praise for shoveling snow off of his sidewalks, and he saved the money he'd of had to pay to have it done . . . and he patted us on the head, said we were good boys, and gave us each a dime," said Weary.

"Well, I gotta go," said Studs.

"Me, too," said Weary.

"Here's some gum to take the fag off your breath," said Studs, sticking some Spearmint in his mouth.

"S . . t, the old man knows I smoke anyway," said Weary.

They walked out to the front to meet their proud, waiting parents.

VIII

Small crowds gathered in front of the parish building, to converse, laugh and reflect the glory of the children and elders of St. Patrick's parish. The Lonigans stood in one such small group. Lonigan spied Dennis P. Gorman. Mr. Dennis P. Gorman was a thin, effeminate man with a dandified mustache, and his nose was sharp. He was exceedingly well tailored in a freshly pressed gray suit; he wore a clean white shirt, a

high stiff collar and a black tie. His meek, satellite wife was
at his side; she was moron-faced, and looked younger than
her thirty-six years. These well-known parishioners were standing under the arc light, bowing profusely and elegantly to
the passers-by. Lonigan moved from the group he was in,
without excusing himself; his wife followed. He hastened up
to Gorman, held out his hand and said:

"Hello, Dinny!"

Dennis P. Gorman proffered a limp hand. Mrs. Dennis
P. Gorman bowed and offered saccharine compliments for
the Lonigan children.

"Well, Dinny, what did you think of it?" Lonigan asked.

While Dennis P. Gorman paused and cleared his throat
for oratorical delivery, Mrs. Lonigan approached, and she
and Dennis's wife engaged in mothers' talk.

Dennis's effeminate voice was now prepared for action,
and he said in tones of mingled melodrama and sing-song:

"Well, I believe, in fact, I am firmly convinced, that Mr.
Wilson's nomination today was an excellent choice . . . yes,
an excellent choice. I am profoundly gratified that he has been
renominated. I shall be proud to give him my own humble
vote, and believe that it is the positive duty of every public-
spirited citizen to do likewise. I shall endeavor, within my
own limited power, to assist in his campaign for reelection.
There is not one iota, no, not one slightest crepuscular
adumbration of doubt but that Mr. Wilson is more qualified
to wield and sway such power as resides in the chief executive
position of the United States than his opponent, Mr. Hughes.
He has brains, administrative capacity, diplomatic skill, integrity, ability, courage and a brilliant record. It was due to his
efforts that we have, today, the Federal Reserve System, which
shall, in our own lifetime, render panics impossible. It was
his diplomacy that has kept America minding its own business
and out of the dreadful militaristic war that now bleeds and
devastates Europe, and leads some to believe that we have
come to Armageddon. I say, with rich and full conviction,
that there is not the slightest doubt, no question whatever, as
to the relative merits of the two men. There is absolutely
no comparison; it is all contrast, that makes Mr. Wilson's star
scintillate with added brilliancy. Were he a Republican, I
believe that I would bolt my party to give him my vote. However,
I know that a man of Woodrow Wilson's stature, character
and all-round ability and integrity could never remain a Republican, because, as every unbiased observer well knows,
the G. O. P. is helplessly, hopelessly and irredeemably corrupt.
Have I made my opinion clear, sir?"

The keen grayish eyes of Mr. Dennis P. Gorman roamed the spaces of the starry June evening.

"Oh, yeh! I'm for Wilson, too. A brilliant scholar! Wilson's a scholar, the brainiest President we had since Lincoln. And he kept us out of war. I think I'll make a contribution, of course it will be small, a drop in the bucket, but then I'll make my little contribution to the campaign," said Lonigan.

Dennis P. Gorman told Lonigan quickly, but with his customary aloofness and dignity, that every contribution, no matter how small, would be appreciated, and that Wilson was not the President of Wall Street, but of the common people, and the common people were the ones he needed. And the Democratic party, Gorman called it our party, is the voice of the common people, the average, good, honest Americans like those of St. Patrick's parish.

"Yeah, I'll see you later, Dinny, and make a small contribution. But what I meant is how did you like the works tonight, Dinny?"

Lonigan saw Dennis P. Gorman frown at his use of the word Dinny. It was unintentional, a habit carried on from earlier days.

Mr. Dennis P. Gorman paused, and then expostulated:

"Oh! It was excellent. Excellent. Did you hear my daughter rendering a selection from Mozart and a nocturne from *Sho-pan?*"

"She was swell. I liked her," said Lonigan.

"Well, I wouldn't say that she was precisely swell; but I do believe, I do believe, that she interpreted the masters with grace, charm, talent, verve and fire," said Mr. Dennis P. Gorman.

"Yes, Dennis," said Lonigan.

"And your daughter did an excellent piece of acting," said Dennis.

"Yeh, she did pretty well," said Lonigan, his assumed modesty breaking across his face.

The two mothers also talked. They had finished on the superbness of their respective daughters, it was Mrs. Dennis P. Gorman's word, and were now commenting on what a grand speech the pastor had made. Mrs. Gorman used the word new, and she redescribed the entertainment as nice. Mr. Dennis P. Gorman paused from his conversation with Lonigan to inform his wife that nice was not the correct word, and that she had mispronounced *new;* it was not *noo.*

Dorothy Gorman came out with Frances Lonigan; they both received their flowers. Dorothy Gorman was a plain-featured, almost homely girl, and standing beside Fran she

looked pathetic. The appearance of the daughters led to gush-
iness and many cross compliments. When these were duly
finished, Mrs. Lonigan invited Mr. and Mrs. Dennis P. Gorman home for a chat and a bit of ice cream. Mrs. Gorman
accepted the invitation, but turned to her husband for his
consent.

"Well, I'd like to, Mary, but you know that Dorothy here
has had a trying time, and I believe that she had better come
home, and we had better see that she gets the proper rest
. . . But thank you, exceedingly, Mrs. Lonigan. And sometime I should enjoy the company of you and Patrick at our
home."

"Yes, do come for tea, but be sure and telephone before-
hand to be certain that I'm in, because Dennis and I have a
number of social engagements these days," said Mrs. Dennis
P. Gorman.

"Yes, May, and thanks," said Mrs. Lonigan.

"Well, so long, Dinny," said Lonigan, again an unintentional slip.

Mr. and Mrs. Dennis P. Gorman and their well-guarded
daughter strode magnificently home.

The Lonigans moved over to chat with the Reilleys, who
accepted their invitation. Fran Lonigan and Fran Reilley,
a very pretty dark-haired girl, rounded up some of the kids.
Just then Studs and Weary appeared, and the group trooped
down to the Lonigans'.

IX

An extravagance of electricity, with almost every light in
the house on, swelled the significance of the evening in the
Lonigan household.

"I feel relieved that it's all over," said Mrs. Lonigan as
she sat in one of the imitation-walnut dining-room chairs,
sipping ice cream.

"It was grand," responded Mrs. Reilley, who sat next to
her hostess.

"Well, we did the right thing. I'm glad Father Gilhooley
gave it to the people who send their children to the public
schools, because the public schools ain't no place for Catholic
children, and I say it's the bounden duty of parents to see
that their children get the right upbringin' by sending them
to Catholic schools. It's only right, and I say, I say, that when
you do the right thing, you're happier. You know, when you're
not happy, you're worried and nervous, and you worry, and
worry causes poisons in your system, and poisons in your system
ruin your digestion and harm your liver. Yes, sir, I say that

from a hygienic standpoint it pays to do the right thing, like we all done with our children," said Lonigan as he expanded in comfort in the dining-room Morris chair.

He sat there and sucked enjoyment from his stogy.

"And ain't it the truth?" said Mrs. Reilley.

"Yeh," muttered Reilley, who was slumped back in his chair seriously engaged in the effort to enjoy the stogy Lonigan had handed him.

"The Catholic religion is a grand thing," Mrs. Reilley said.

Lonigan told how he had heard two little Catholic girls, no bigger than his own youngest daughter, swearing like troopers. It was because their parents didn't send them to the sisters' school. They all agreed, with many conversational flourishes; and Mrs. Reilley said the girls would sure be chippies.

Mrs. Reilley stated, with swelling maternal pride, that her son, Frank, would attend a Jesuit school and then prepare for the law so that he could some day be a grand Catholic lawyer, like Joe O'Reilley, who had almost been state's attorney.

"The Jesuits are grand men and fine scholars," said Mrs. Lonigan.

"They got these here A. P. A. university professors skinned by a hull city block," Reilley said.

Mrs. Lonigan said that yes the Jesuits were grand men, and she would like to make a Jesuit out of her son William.

"But has he the call?" jealously asked Mrs. Reilley.

"I think so. I say a rosary every night, and I offer up a monthly holy communion, and I make novenas that God will give him the call," Mrs. Lonigan said.

"And wouldn't I give me right arm if me son Frank had the call?" Mrs. Reilley said.

"But, Mary, you know I'm gonna need Bill to help me in my business. Why do you want to start putting things like that in the boy's head?" protested Lonigan.

"Patrick, you know that if God wants a boy or a girl for His work, and that boy or girl turns his back on the Will of Almighty God, he or she won't never be happy and they'll stand in grave danger of losing their immortal souls," said she.

"Isn't it the truth?" said Mrs. Reilley.

"But Mary . . . "

"Patrick, the Will of God is the Will of God, and no mortal can tamper with it or try to thwart it," his wife replied.

Lonigan protested vainly, saying how hard he had worked, and how a father had some right to expect something in return when he did so much for his children.

Mrs. Lonigan opened her mouth to speak, but Mrs. Reilley beat her to the floor and said that when a body gets old, all that a body has is a body's children to be a help and a comfort, and that a body could expect and demand some respect from a body's children. She and her old man had worn their fingers down to the bone working for their children. Reilley had been a poor teamster, and he had gotten up before dawn on mornings when the cold would almost make icicles on your fingers in no time, and she had gotten up and got his breakfast, and fed the horses, and both of them had worked like niggers in those days back of the yards before their children were born. And a mother doesn't have her back near broken with labor pains for nothing. She held up her red, beefy, calloused hands. Then she boasted that she was proud that her children would not have such a hard time. Frank would be educated for the law; Frances would teach school; and maybe she would make a Sister of Mercy out of little June.

Reilley yawned. Lonigan detailed how hard he had worked.

They could hear the young people laughing, having a *harmless* good time in the parlor. Lonigan said it was great to be a kid, and then spoke of the Orpet murder trial. Everybody felt that hanging was too good and too easy a punishment for such a cur. Mrs. Reilley, in a blaze of passion, said that if a boy of hers ever did such a vile thing to an innocent girl she would fasten the rope around his neck; but her Frank would never be that kind of a cur; her flesh and blood, he couldn't be. Lonigan made a long speech averring that it was a beastly violation of the natural law. June Reilley and Loretta appeared, and Mrs. Lonigan signaled her husband to pause until she shooed the innocent ones off to Loretta's room. They scampered out of the room, and enjoyed their own discussion of forbidden topics. Then the parents joined in a general denunciation of Orpet, adding that no Catholic would ever commit such a foul deed.

"Sure, that's so," Lonigan orated profoundly as if he were shedding the fruit of long and consistent thought.

"And isn't the Catholic Church the grand thing?" Mrs. Reilley said lyrically.

"And just think how awful the world would be without the Church," said Mrs. Lonigan.

"There's nothin' like the Church to keep one straight," said Lonigan.

"It keeps you toeing the mark. That's one thing to say for it," Mrs. Reilley said.

Reilley agreed with a feeble nod of his sleepy head.

"That is the reason we gave our children a Catholic education," Mrs. Lonigan said.

"And isn't it the truth that a mother never need worry when she sends her byes and girls to the good sisters, the holy virgins!" Mrs. Reilley said.

There was a nodding of heads.

"Isn't the Church the grand thing," insisted Mrs. Reilley.

The conversation drifted and dribbled on amidst increasing barrages of yawns.

X

It was the first evening of the official maturity of the young people in the parlor, and after getting seated they wondered what to do; the boys sat stiffly on one side of the room, and gazed furtively at their long trousers; the girls faced them, acting prim and reserved. Growing up had always meant more freedom, and here they were after their graduation, afraid to do anything lest it seem kiddish; afraid, particularly, to play the kids' kissing games they used to play at parties.

"Well, what'll we do?" grumbled Weary, who sat between Studs and sallow-faced TB on the unscratched piano stool.

"Yeah, let's do something," Studs suggested.

Soft-skinned and fattish Bill Donoghue was seated under the floor lamp near them. He said:

"Now that's a bright idea!"

Studs made a face at Bill, as if to say: Go soak yer head!

"Bill's a loogin who always tries to wisecrack," Studs said.

"Studs is a little fruity!" Bill said, and they laughed.

"Such awful slang you boys use," Helen Borax said.

Studs scowled at Helen and said:

"Bill, I'm going to slap your pretty wrist!"

Helen colored slightly, and elevated her nose.

Bill got limp like a sissy, and tapped his own wrist daintily, and everybody laughed at his comics, because Bill was really very funny.

"Well, anyway, I'm glad I'm through school," said Tubby Connell, a kinky-haired, darkish boy who had plunked, uncomfortably, in the corner easy chair that Mrs. Lonigan always said must be beautiful, because it had cost over a hundred dollars.

"Ope! Look what the wind blew in!" Bill said, looking at Tubby.

"Another lost country heard from," muttered Studs.

Tubby blushed bashfully.

"Anyway, I'm darn glad to get out of that joint," Weary said.

"Frank, it isn't a joint . . . And you jus' wait. You'll be sorry and wish you were back at St. Patrick's just like Father Gilhooley said we'd all remember our days there," his sister said.

"Weary didn't hear him say that. When Gilly was talking of that, I heard him snoring," Bill said, and they laughed.

Peggy Nugent said you shouldn't speak of a priest like that, or something awful might happen to you. You should always say Father Gilhooley. She smiled, and everybody could see she thought it was thrilling to call him Gilly.

"Well, he has gills like a fish," Bill said.

"How disrespectful," Lucy Scanlan said, twinkling her blue eyes.

Weary made faces at his sister. Tubby reiterated that he was glad to get out of jail because he felt that he had to say something. He was blushing.

They laughed, and TB said he, too, was darn glad to get out of the pen, and they laughed again.

"I'll be glad to get to high school," said well-behaved Dan Donoghue, and just as he did, Bill aimed a peanut at Tubby. Connell told him to cut it out, and Bill asked what in a very innocent voice.

He and Tubby carried on a side-dialogue.

"You will, Dan? Why?" asked Fran Lonigan.

"Oh, I just will," said Dan.

"Well, I don't know if I'm glad or not," said Fran.

"What school do you think you'll go to, Studs?" asked Lucy, smiling with her sweet baby-face.

"None."

"William, you know you're going to high school," his sister said sternly, as if she were an adult scolding him.

"Yeah, I suppose I don't know what I'm gonna do," said Studs.

"You most certainly do not," said she.

"We'll see," said he, trying to save his scattering dignity.

"Father will see!" said she with finality.

He scowled, felt unmanned, felt that Weary was sneering at him as if he was a weak sister. He looked at his meaningless long trousers.

Weary said with great braggadocio he wasn't going to high school and his sister protested. Tall Jim Clayburn said he thought going to school was sensible and necessary if you wanted to get ahead. He said he thought that Sister Bertha had once told them the truth when she said you needed education and stick-to-it-iveness to get ahead in life. Lucy said Jim was so sensible, and she had a devilish look in her eyes. Dan commenced to agree with Jim, but his brother interrupted him:

"Say, did you see High Collars?"

"Yeah, I saw him walkin' with Dorothy and his wife," Tubby said, glad to get back in the conversation.

"He wouldn't let her come to the party. He told Mother that Dorothy needed her proper rest," said Fran Lonigan.

"He's an old mean thing," said Lucy.

"The poor kid! She's all right, and awfully sweet, but she can't ever do anything on account of her father. Sometimes she tells me about it, and cries," exclaimed Fran Reilley.

"I wouldn't want an old man like him," TB said.

They looked at TB, because his old man was nothing to brag about.

"Anyway, he didn't wear his silk hat tonight," Dan said.

"I wonder if he uses perfume?" TB said.

"I'll bet he wears ladies' underwear," contributed Bill Donoghue.

The guys haw-hawed, and the girls giggled modestly after stating that Bill's language was not exactly nice.

They talked on, and wondered what they would do. Bill goofed Tubby, because Connell looked like a smoke, and Bill said that now Tubby was graduated, he shouldn't find no trouble becoming a Pullman porter. TB said that every time he saw Tubby he thought it would rain because of dark clouds all around. Tubby hock-hocked in imitation of Muggsy, and the girls said Tubby was too frightful for words.

Jim Clayburn went to the baby grand, and Bill said that they would now listen to Good Old Stick-To-It-Iveness. Jim played, and they crowded around, singing, but they couldn't get any harmony because Bill bellowed and Tubby and Muggsy tried to be funny. They sang *Alexander's Rag Time Band, The River Shannon Flowing, It's a Long Way to Tipperary, Dear Old Girl, Dance and Grow Thin,* and *Bell Brandon.* Then Jim started *In My Harem.* Bill got in the center of the floor and did a shocking hula-hula that was so funny they nearly split laughing; he sang:

> And the dance they do . . .
> Is enough to kill a Jew . . .
> Da-Da-Dadadada-Da . . .
> In my harem with Pat Malone.

Jim played *When It's Apple Blossom Time in Normandy,* and just as they started the chorus Bill goosed Tubby, and Studs did the same with TB. The two victims jumped, yelling ouch. It broke up the singing and everybody laughed. Bill

asked Rastus where the ghosts were, and Tubby replied by
calling Bill snake Irish, so low that he crawled in the mud.
Studs said that trying to decide which was the worst, an Irishman
or a jigg, was like shooting craps for stage money with loaded
dice; and he was proud of his crack even if they didn't laugh.

"Let's dance!" Helen said, interrupting all the tomfoolery.

The fellows who knew how foxtrotted with the girls while
Lucy played. Studs, TB and Weary stood in a corner whispering dirty jokes. When the others tired of dancing, they sat
down; this time the fellows weren't all on one side of the room
and the girls on the other. They talked some more, and wondered what they would do, and Bill kept the party going by
his clowning. Martin wandered in, looking oh-so-darling, and
the girls made a fuss trying to pet him. Tubby finally grabbed
him and said:

"Let's fight, you little rascal!"

Martin biffed Tubby, and Bill said:

"The kid takes after his big brother, only he's got it on him
with the dukes."

Tubby then grabbed Martin again, and the child said:

"Lemme go, you boob!"

The guys clapped, and the girls were taken by his cuteness.
Fran said it was the wrong way for Martin to take after his
brother.

Lucy pulled Martin toward her, tied him with her arms,
said he was just too darling for words; she kissed him.

"Yeah, he's got it on his brother all around. As a Romeo,
he's got Studs backed off the boards," Bill said.

Studs blushed and got exceedingly interested in the stale
joke with which Tubby was laboring.

Martin fought free, and as he rushed out of the room he
yelled back:

"I wish to hell you'd lemme 'lone!"

They laughed; Fran Lonigan frowned.

The conversation went on; everybody wondered what they
would do. Lucy set them at ease by boldly suggesting wink.
The girls blushed and giggled while they were getting into
their places. But the game went off stiffly because there were
too many boys. They changed to kiss-the-pillow. Everyone
got into the spirit of the game, even Weary. He found it wasn't
so goofy kissing girls. And Helen Borax acted like she might
have a crush on him. He'd never thought much of her, except
that she was the kind of a chicken who never tried to act
her age and who seemed to think she was a queen. But it
wasn't hard to kiss her. And Studs got gay because he was
getting his chance to kiss Lucy, and he didn't have to keep

his liking for her under cover. He told himself he liked her, and repeated this; he liked her around him, liked to look at her, liked her laugh, liked her near him, liked to think of doing things for her, suffering, fighting, playing football, defending her against demons and villains, and anybody.

As they played, Fran Lonigan said: "Gee, what would Sister Bernadette Marie, what would she say if she saw us now?"

"I wonder," smiled Helen Borax.

"Particularly you girls. She'd expect it of me, because she always said I was only a chicken, anyway, and not serious like Helen and you girls," Lucy said.

Helen colored.

Bill smiled broadly, and said that if Bertha knew about it she'd get jealous and wish that she'd been around to play. He said she joined the convent because she'd been disappointed in love, and maybe if she got the chance she'd get a crush on TB or Tubby.

"What do you mean she's been disappointed in love?" asked TB.

"Sure. She acts just like an old maid," Bill said.

"But what I want to know is who'd love her?" asked TB.

They laughed, and the girls thought it was horrid.

Bill kept the floor and said he knew the old battleaxe would like to play. He said he'd show just how she would play. He put on a sour pan, hunched himself a trifle, the way she was hunched, talked shrilly and goofily, and dropped the pillow in front of Muggsy. He kissed Tubby, who blushed with embarrassment, and they nearly all split their sides laughing.

The game went on. Studs dropped the pillow, by accident, in front of Helen. They looked meanly at each other, and neither moved until everybody yelled at them to play the game square, so they knelt down, each at an edge of the pillow, peck-kissed each other, and deepened their mutual hatred.

They changed to post-office. Tubby was suggested as postmaster, but Bill demanded the job, saying he was the logical person to examine all transactions. Fran Lonigan, as hostess, started the ball rolling. As she walked into the bedroom right off the parlor entrance, Bill grabbed her, and kissed her; it was his tax. She laughed and didn't get angry. Fran called Dan. Dan kissed Bill on the way of entry. It was funny.

Dan called Fran Reilley, and kissed her. She called her brother. She stamped his toe, and ran out saying it was for a special delivery letter. He got sore, but she had gotten away too quickly. He told Bill to call Borax.

Weary kissed her flush on the mouth. He held her there, and when he finally released her, she sighed deeply.

He kissed her again, and she powerlessly tightened against him. He forced her to the bed.

"Stop touching me there. Stop!" she whispered.

When he paused, breathless, she demanded an apology.

"Shut up!" he muttered.

He bent down and kissed her.

"Unhand me, you cur. Take your hands off!" she whispered. "Take your hands off there, or I'll scream!"

He pulled her to him and kissed her. She became limp in his arms. He kissed her again, and she pressed to him. He loosed her. She called him a cur and demanded an apology.

"Shut up!"

She bit her lips, fought back tears, and said in a low, strained voice:

"Apologize!"

"Kiss me!"

She was a girl suddenly baffled by a woman's impulses.

She flung herself around him. Then he walked out.

Regaining her composure and rearranging herself, she called in Jim. In the parlor they looked at Weary, surprised and over-curious. There was a tight silence, which Bill broke by saying that Weary had received a delayed letter. They laughed, and Weary's frown broke into a smile.

Jim, in the meantime, had called in Lucy; and she called Studs. She pursed her lips before she kissed him. It was so sudden, and her lips had such a sweet, candy taste that he was pleasantly surprised and stood there, not knowing what to do or say. He had never kissed sweet lips like that before. He faced her, and she was something beautiful and fair, with her white dress vivid in the dark room. She looked beautiful, like a flame. She pursed her lips, moved closer to him, flung her arms around him, kissed him, and said:

"I like you!"

She kissed away his surprise, looked dreamily into his eyes, kissed him again, long, and then dashed out.

Jesus Christ! he said to himself.

The game went on. Studs and Lucy, Helen and Weary kept calling each other into the post office. All the guys except TB and Tubby got their share of kisses. Tubby was called a few times for charity's sake, but TB was left out in the cold. He sat in a corner, wisecracking as if he didn't mind. He knew he didn't belong there anyway. Probably he did have the con, as everybody said and believed.

XI

After all the guests had departed, the Lonigans sat in the parlor talking.

"Well, I'm tired," Lonigan said, yawning.

"I'm dead tired," said the mother.

"It was hard work," said Lonigan.

"Isn't Mrs. Reilley common, though?" yawned Mrs. Lonigan.

"But she's a nice, good, wholesome, sincere woman," said Lonigan.

"She's green," the wife said.

"She's ignorant; she's a greenhorn," said Frances.

"Frances!" the mother said.

"Well, she is!"

"But you needn't say so . . . so . . . crudely."

"Anyway, she and her old man are pretty old-fashioned, but they are nice people. They are too nice for that boy of theirs. If he were my son, I'd lambast the stuffings out of him; he's a real bad actor," Lonigan said.

"I'm afraid no good will ever come out of him, and I'm so glad William here is not like he is. Did you hear the way he talked to his mother and father, so disrespectful, saying he'd do what he wanted to, and he wouldn't go right home with them. William, I don't want you to have anything to do with him. He's a bad one. He'll probably end up in the penitentiary," she said.

Studs admired Weary, his enemy. Weary's parents had told him to come home with them, and Weary had wanted to walk home with Helen Borax; there had been a row and he had walked off. Studs was almost impelled to defend Weary, but didn't, because then his old man might have talked all night.

"Well, it's a good thing he isn't my son, or he'd get the stuffings lambasted out of him. I'd knock some good sense in his head," Lonigan said with finality.

"Mrs. Reilley uses awfully bad grammar, too," Mrs. Lonigan said.

"Well, I'd rather have people use bad grammar than have 'em be smart alecks like Dinny Gorman. Why, I knew him when he didn't have a sole on his shoe; and then him stickin' up his nose and actin' like he was highbrow, lace-curtain Irish, born to the purple. And all just because he's got a little book-learnin' and he bootlicked around until he became a ward committeeman. Why, he was nothin' but a starvin' lawyer hangin' around police courts until Joe O'Reilley started sendin' some business his way. What is he now . . . nothin' but a shyster. Maybe he might have a little more booklearnin' than I, but what does that mean? Look here, now: Is he a better and more conscientious father? Does he pay his bills more regularly? Has he got a bigger bank account than I got?" said Lonigan in heated indignation while no one listened to him.

When the old man had finished orating, Studs said:

"All the kids call him High Collars!" The old man laughed.

"And the crust of May! Won't you come to tea, but do call first, as we have so many, oh, so many, social engagements these days!" Mrs. Lonigan said.

"She can't hold a spoon up to you with all her damn society airs," Lonigan said.

"I know her kind. She's just like a cat, all soft and furry, and with claws that would scratch your eyes out," the old lady said.

There was a pause in the conversation; Martin looked mischievously at Studs and said:

"Studs got long pants; Studs got long pants."

"Shut up!"

The old lady reprimanded Martin for using the nickname, and the old man admonished Studs that he shouldn't talk like that to his brother.

"But I do think William looks darling," teased Fran.

"You look pretty slick, Bill. Don't let 'em get your goat," the old man said.

"Yes . . . so cute. Even Lucy Scanlan thought that he looked so . . . cute," said Frances.

Studs gave his sister a dirty look; the old man tried to kid Studs about having a girl; Studs shut up tight as a clam.

"Now, children," the mother conciliated.

"They're not just children any more," the old man said.

"Yes, they are. They are, too. They're my children, my baby blue-eyed boy and girl. They can't be taken from me, either," the mother said, tenaciously.

The old man looked at Studs as much as to say: What can you do with a woman?

"Now, Mary, you know that people have to grow up," the old man said.

"Dad!" Studs said hesitantly.

"Yes," responded the old man.

"How about my workin' with you now, instead of goin' to school? You'll want me to sooner or later, and I might as well start now," said Studs.

"Well . . . I'll have to think it over."

"Why, William!" protested the mother.

They had a discussion. Mrs. Lonigan kept wondering out loud what the neighbors would think, because it would look like they were too cheap, or else couldn't afford to send their boy to high school. She repeated, several times, that she would be ashamed to put her head in St. Patrick's Church again or to look Father Gilhooley or any of the sisters in the face if their boy were sent out into the cold world to work, with only a grammar school education, when all his classmates went on to high school. Lonigan kept nodding his head in thought, and soliloquizing that he didn't know what to say, because she was right, and yet a lot of this education was nothing but booklearning, nothing but bunk. He had some new thoughts, and these fed further soliloquizing. It was pretty true that in a way knowledge was power and a person could never know too much, as long as he was right-thinking. And then he didn't want nobody to think that he wasn't doing the right thing by his children; and maybe people would misinterpret it if the boy didn't try high school, at least for a while. And anyway, an education could never hurt you as long as you were right-thinking.

Studs tried to dissent, but he was inarticulate.

His incoherent protests were cut short by his mother suggesting that he ought to study for the priesthood. She said one could always change one's mind, up to the taking of the vows, and a priest got a wonderful education, and even if he didn't go on with it, he would be more educated than most people. She said it was, just as Father Gilhooley said, the duty of all parents to see if their children had the call. How would God and his poor Mother, and great St. Patrick, guardian saint of the parish, feel if Studs turned a deaf ear on the sacred call? Lonigan opened his mouth to say something, but Studs said decisively he didn't have the call. The mother said he should pray more, so he would know, and God would reveal to him if he had. Frances interrupted to say that Studs should go to Loyola, because everybody of any consequence was going there and it was the school to go to. They talked on, and it was decided, against Studs' wishes, that he go to Loyola.

Then the parents rose to retire, yawning.

Mrs. Lonigan put Martin to bed. She hugged the boy close to her meager bosom and said:

"Martin, don't you think you'd like to be a priest when you grow up, and serve God!"

"I want to be a grave digger," Martin answered sleepily.

She left the room, her cheeks slightly wet with tears. She prayed to God that he would give one of her boys the call.

After they had left the parlor, Studs sat by the window. He

looked out, watching the night strangeness, listening. The darkness was over everything like a warm bed-cover, and all the little sounds of night seemed to him as if they belonged to some great mystery. He listened to the wind in the tree by the window. The street was queer, and didn't seem at all like Wabash Avenue. He watched a man pass, his heels beating a monotonous echo. Studs imagined him to be some criminal being pursued by a detective like Maurice Costello, who used to act detective parts for Vitagraph. He watched. He thought of Lucy on the street and himself bravely rescuing her from horrors more terrible than he could imagine. He thought about the fall, and of the arguments for working that he should have sprung on the old man. He thought of himself on a scaffold, wearing a painter's overalls, chewing tobacco, and talking man-talk with the other painters; and of pay days and the independence they would bring him. He thought of Studs Lonigan, a free and independent working man, on his first pay night, plunking down some dough to the old lady, for board, putting on his new straw katy, calling for Lucy, and taking her out stepping to White City, having a swell time.

Frances came in. She wore a thin nightgown. He could almost see right through it. He tried to keep looking away, but he had to turn his head back to look at her. She stood before him, and didn't seem to know that he was looking at her. She seemed kind of queer; he thought maybe she was sick.

"Do you like Lucy?"

"Oh, a little," he said.

He was excited, and couldn't talk much, because he didn't want her to notice it.

"Do you like to kiss girls?"

"Not so much," he said.

"You did tonight."

"It was all in the game."

"Helen must like Weary."

"I hate her."

"I don't like her either, but . . . do you think they did anything in the post office?"

"What do you mean?" he asked.

She wasn't going to pump him and get anything out of him.

She seemed to be looking at him, awful queer, all right.

"You know. Do you think they did anything that was fun . . . or that the sisters wouldn't want them to do . . . or that's bad?"

"I don't know."

Dirty thoughts rushed to his head like hot blood. He told himself he was a bastard because . . . she was his sister.

"I don't know," he said, confused.

"You think maybe they did something bad, and it was fun?"

He shrugged his shoulders and looked out the window so she couldn't see his face.

"I feel funny," she said.

He hadn't better say anything to her, because she'd snitch and give him away.

"I want to do something . . . They're all in bed. Let's us play leap frog, you know that game that boys play where one bends down, and the others jump over him?" she said.

"We'll make too much noise."

"Do you really think that Weary and Helen did anything that might be fun?" she asked.

She got up, and walked nervously around the room. She plunked down on the piano stool, and part of her leg showed.

He looked out the window. He looked back. They sat. She fidgeted and couldn't sit still. She got up and ran out of the room. He sat there. He must be a bastard . . . she was his sister.

He looked out the window. He wondered what it was like; he was getting old enough to find out.

He got up. He looked at himself in the mirror. He shadow-boxed, and thought of Lucy. He thought of Fran. He squinted at himself in the mirror.

He turned the light out and started down the hallway. Fran called him. She was lying in bed without the sheets over her.

"It's hot here. Awful hot. Please put the window up higher."

"It's as high as it'll go."

"I thought it wasn't."

He looked at Fran. He couldn't help it.

"And please get me some real cold water."

He got the water. It wasn't cold enough. She asked him to let the water run more. He did. He handed the water to her. As she rose to drink, she bumped her small breast against him.

She drank the water. He started out of the room. She called him to get her handkerchief.

"I'm not at all tired," she said.

He left, thinking what a bastard he must be.

He went to the bathroom.

Kneeling down at his bedside, he tried to make a perfect act of contrition to wash his soul from sin.

He heard the wind, and was afraid that God might punish him, make him die in the night. He had found out he was old enough, but . . . his soul was black with sin. He lay in bed, worried, suffering, and he tossed into a slow, troubled sleep.

SECTION TWO

CHAPTER THREE

I

Studs awoke to stare sleepily at a June morning that crashed through his bedroom window. The world outside the window was all shine and shimmer. Just looking at it made Studs glad that he was alive. And it was only the end of June. He still had July and August. And this was one of those days when he would feel swell; one of his days. He drowsed in bed, and glanced out to watch the sun scatter over the yard. He watched a tomcat slink along the fence ledge; he stared at the spot he had newly boarded so that his old man wouldn't yelp about loose boards; he looked about at the patches in the grass that Martin and his gang had worn down playing their cowboy and Indian games. There was something about the things he watched that seemed to enter Studs as sun entered a field of grass; and as he watched, he felt that the things he saw were part of himself, and he felt as good as if he were warm sunlight; he was all glad to be living, and to be Studs Lonigan. Because when he came to think of it, living had been pretty good since he had graduated. Every morning he could lie in bed if he wanted to, or else he could hop up and go over and goof around Indiana Avenue and see the guys and . . . Lucy.

He reclined in bed and thought about looking for a job; he did this almost every morning, and usually he had good intentions. Then he would start pretending, as if his good intentions had been carried out and he was working, earning his own living, and independent, so that his old man couldn't boss him. But every morning he would forget his good intentions before he got out of bed. And a morning like this was too nice a one to be wasted going downtown and trying to find a job, and maybe not finding it; and anyway, it was a little late, and most of the jobs for guys like him had been probably grabbed up by other kids.

Studs got up. He thought about saying his morning prayers,

but he decided to wait and say them while he was washing; a wise guy could always kill two birds with one stone. He knelt down by the open window and took ten inhales; on colder mornings, when the temperature of the room was not the same as the temperature outside, it was swell and invigorating taking inhales, and Studs liked to do it because it made him feel good, but in summer like now, it was only a physical culture measure that he took, because some day Studs Lonigan was going to become big and strong and . . . tough. He turned and went over to the dresser, thinking about how tough a guy he might become. He studied Studs Lonigan in the mirror, and discovered that he wasn't such a bad-looking guy, and that maybe he even looked older than he was. He took a close-up squint at his mug and decided that it was, after all, a pretty good mug, even if he almost had a sheeny's nose. He twisted his lips in sneers, screwed up his puss, and imagined himself telling some big guy where to get off at. He said, half aloud:

See, bo, I don't take nobody's sass. And get this, bo, the bigger they are, de harder dey fall. See, bo!

He took his pajama top off and gave his chest the double-o. It was broad and solid, all right. He practiced expanding his chest, flexing and unflexing his muscles to feel their hardness, tautening his abdomen to see if he had a cast-iron gut. He told himself that Studs Lonigan was one pretty Goddamn good physical specimen. Scowling like a real bruiser ought to scowl, he shadow-boxed with tip-toed clumsiness, cleaving the air with haymakers, telling himself that he was not only tough and rough, but that he was also a scientific boxer. He swung and swished himself into a good perspiration, knocking out imaginary roughnecks as if they were bowling pins, and then he sat down, saying to himself that he was Young Studs Lonigan, or maybe only Young Lonigan, the Chicago sensation, now in training for the bout when he would kayo Jess Willard for the title.

He snapped out of it, and went to the bathroom. He washed in clear, cold water, snorting with his face lowered in the filled bowl. It felt good, and it also felt good to douse water on his chest. After drying himself with a rough bath towel, he stood up close to the mirror and looked to see if there were any hairs on his upper lip. If he wasn't so light, maybe he'd have to shave now. He imagined himself with the guys, walking, and him saying well, he wouldn't be able to get around so early that night because he had to shave, and shaving was one lousy pain. And maybe girls would be there, and he'd say the same thing, only he wouldn't curse. Himself letting

Lucy know he shaved by complaining of it, or by talking about how he cut himself with the razor, or about how it had been hard because the razor was dull. Well, anyway, he could trim a lot of guys who did shave. He was nobody's slouch. And some day he'd be shaving, and have hair on the chest, too. It was like that Uncle Josh piece on the Victrola, I'm old but I'm awfully tough. Well, for him it was: I'm small but I'm awfully tough.

Studs left home immediately after breakfast so he could get away from the old lady. She was always pestering him, telling him to pray and ask God if he had a vocation. And maybe she'd have wanted him to go to the store, beat rugs, or clean the basement out. He didn't feel like being a janitor. He would work, but he wouldn't be a janitor. Janitor's jobs were for jiggs, and Hunkies, and Polacks, anyway. He'd asked the old man again to take him to work, but the old man was the world's champion putter-off. Every year since Studs could remember, he'd been promising that he was going to take the old lady to Riverview Park, and he was still promising. That was just like the old boy. Studs walked along, glancing about him, feeling what a good morning it was, walking in the sun that was spinning all over the street like a crazy top. He could feel the warmness of the sun; it entered him, became part of himself, part of his walk, part of his arms swinging along at his side, part of his smile, his good feelings, his thoughts. It was good. He walked along, and he thought about the family; families were goddamn funny things; everybody's old man and old woman were the same; they didn't want a guy or a girl to grow up. His mother was always blowing off her bazoo about him being her blue-eyed baby, and his old man was always giving advice, bossing, instructing him as if he was a ten-year-old. Well, he was growing up in spite of them; and it wouldn't be long now before he had long britches on every day. Let 'em do their damnedest; Studs Lonigan would tell the world that he was growing up.

He goofed around for a while in the vacant lot just off the corner of Fifty-eighth and Indiana. He batted stones. He walked around kicking a tin can, imagining it was something very important, some sort of thing like an election or a sporting contest that got on the front page. Then he thought about Indiana Avenue. It was a better street than Wabash. It was a good block, too, between Fifty-seventh and Fifty-eighth. Maybe when his old man sold the building, he'd buy one in this block. It was nearer the stores, and there were more Catholics on the street, and in the evening the old man could sit on the front porch talking with Old Man O'Brien, and his old lady could gossip with Mrs. O'Brien and Dan's mother, and Mrs. Scanlan. The house next to Scanlan's would be a nice one to live in. Some people named Welsh owned it, but they were pretty old and they'd be kicking the bucket soon. There were more trees on Indiana, too, and no shines, and only a few kikes. The building on the right of the lot was the one where yellow-belly Red O'Connell lived, the big redhead. Studs wondered if he could fight him. He'd love to paste O'Connell's mush, but Red was big. Maybe the old man would buy the building and kick the O'Connell's out. Down two doors was the wooden frame house where the O'Callaghans lived. Old Man O'Callaghan had been one of the first guys to live in the neighborhood, and he was supposed to be lousy with dough. And then the apartment buildings where the Donoghues lived. And then the series of two-story bricks, where Lucy, Helen Shires and the O'Briens lived. And then the home where those Jews, the Glasses, lived, and then the apartment buildings on the corner, where punk Danny O'Neill, and Helen Borax, and goofy Andy lived, and they had that bastard of a janitor, George, who was always shagging kids. Some Hallowe'en they were going to get him, good. If Studs lived on Indiana, he'd see more of Lucy. He walked down Indiana, thinking he might call for some of the bunch; but then, he was an independent guy, the best scrapper of the gang; let 'em call for him. He stopped at Johnny O'Brien's gangway and checked himself when he was on the verge of shouting up for Johnny. He came out on the sidewalk, and looked back toward Fifty-eighth. He walked backward.

"Hello, there," sighed Leon.

"Hello!" said Studs, turning sharply, a little surprised.

Studs looked at Leon; he almost looked a hole through him.

Leon was middle-aged and fat. He had a meaty rump that always made the guys laugh, and a pair of breastworks like a woman. His skin was smooth and oily, his eyes dark and cowy, his lips thick and sensuous, his nose Jewish. Leon was a music teacher, and Studs always felt that he was goofy enough to be . . . just a music teacher.

"I say! Why do boys look backward? I always wanted to know," he said in a half-lisp.

"I was just lookin' to see if any of the guys were down the street."

"Well, you know, it's the funniest thing. It really is. Because I see so many boys looking backward, and I'm always asking myself why they do it. Never for the life of me have I been able to understand," said Leon.

Studs shrugged his shoulders.

Leon placed his hand on Studs' shoulder, and patted his head with the other hand. It made Studs feel a little queer, he felt as if Leon's hands were dirty, or his stomach was going to turn, or something like that. Sometimes his mother tried to hold him and kiss him, and that made him feel goofy. This was a hundred times worse. Once over in the park, an old man sat down by him and asked if he liked the girls, or ever took them over on the wooded island at night, and he tried to feel Studs. The guy had been goofy, and Studs had had an awful feeling that he couldn't describe. He hadn't gone to the park for over a week, and every time he thought of the old guy, and wondered what the bastard had wanted, his thoughts turned sour. He felt the same way with Leon, only Leon was funny and he could laugh at him.

"When are you going to come and see me and let me teach you how to play the piano; you know, you little rascal, that I offered to give you lessons free."

"Oh, some time," Studs said.

"You're missing a wonderful opportunity, my boy. You don't understand now, but you will some day, how fine music can make a life beautiful," persuaded Leon.

What the hell is the damn fool talking about? Where in hell did he get that way? Studs said to himself.

Leon had taken his hands off Studs. Now he patted his head.

Studs stepped back a little.

"You're young now, but I'll bet you're an artist. If you let me teach you, I'll make a musician out of you."

Studs thought he might as well string the guy along a little.

"Then I can play in movie houses?"

"No, not that. I only do that to make a living. I mean a real musician. An artist."

Studs wondered what he meant by artist. He thought an artist was a guy who painted pictures, and always raved like a maniac because nobody liked his pictures.

Holy Jumpin' Jimminy! Studs almost laughed right in the guy's face.

"You must come over now and start those lessons."

"Some time I will," said Studs.

"Don't hesitate. He who hesitates is lost. You have your opportunity now, my boy, and opportunity strikes but once. Now tomorrow morning I'll be free. My mother will be out at eleven, and suppose you come then, and we'll be all alone and there won't be no one to bother us, and we'll be free . . . for our first lesson."

Leon placed his arm around Studs' shoulder.

"Well, tomorrow, I gotta beat rugs for my mother."

"But mother might let you off if you say it's to take music lessons."

"You don't know my mother."

"But mothers can be convinced. Now, I know. I have a mother who still tries to boss me."

Studs didn't have any answer for Leon. Leon tried to convince Studs. Then he had to rush to get to a lesson. He gave Studs a final pat, and told him to think it over. As he started to wriggle his rump along, he turned and said:

"Well, ta, ta! Now, don't forget the lessons . . . and don't do anything naughty-nasty . . . like tickling the girlies. Ta! Ta!"

He waved his arm womanishly, and went on. Studs watched him. He laughed. He felt a little queer. He wondered why Leon was always placing his hands on a guy.

II

Studs kept futzing around until Helen Shires came out with her soccer ball. Then they dribbled back and forth on the paving in front of her place. She lived next door to the Scanlans. It was a drearily lazy June morning now, and they played. Helen was a lean, muscular girl, tall and rangy, with angular Swedish features, blue eyes and yellowish white hair. She was tanned, and wore a blue wash dress, which was constantly ruffling up, so that her purplish-blue wash bloomers showed. She looked very healthy.

They played. Helen took the ball to dribble. She strode down about six yards, turned around, and dribbled forward, straight and fast, with the form and force of a star basketball player. All the guys used to say she was a natural athlete. Studs stood squat, his hands spread fan-wise, his body awkwardly tensed for sudden effort. As she approached him, she feinted toward her right, changed her stroke from left to right hand, and passed him on his right, making him look quite sick.

Studs side-glanced up at the Scanlan parlor window. He'd never before been jealous of Helen's athletic skill, but now he was. Maybe Lucy had been peeping behind the curtain. He had hoped she was. Now he changed his wish.

"I don't like basketball so well," he said, grinning weakly.

"You will after you learn the game," she answered, dribbling back.

She dribbled again, and Studs, with a chance swing of the right arm, batted the ball out into the street. He changed his wish, and covertly side-glanced at the Scanlan window. Helen complimented him on his good guarding.

It was his turn. He came forward, awkward, clumsier than usual because he tried to show form. He bounced the ball too hard and too high, and he was slowed down. He lost control of the ball before he reached her, and it bounded onto the grass.

It was good he was only pretending that Lucy watched him. They kept dribbling, and she kept making him look sick. She was having a better time than he, because she could do the thing, and she could get the satisfaction one gets out of doing a thing right. But he stuck on.

Once when they paused, she said:

"You ought to make the football team at Loyola."

"I'd like to," he said.

"You will," she said.

They talked for a while, and resumed dribbling. She dribbled and he guarded. He took a turn, and she snatched the ball from him, pivoted gracefully, and dribbled down the other way. They alternated, and he kept side-glancing at the Scanlan window.

After a half-hour, they were both a little fagged, and they sat on Helen's front steps.

"Say, Studs, there's a can house around on Fifty-seventh Street," she said.

"There is?"

"Yeh."

"You sure?"

"Sure! Paulie Haggerty was around the other day, and he told me about it, and I went and looked the other night, and saw a lot of cars parked there and a lot of men enterin' and leavin'. One guy even wore a silk hat."

"Whereabouts was it?"

"The flat building on the other side of the alley on Fifty-seventh. It's on the first floor," said she.

"The red one where we climbed on the front porch that afternoon when it was rainin' and shot craps?" he asked.

"No. Next door to it," she said.

"We'll all go round there some night and look in," said Studs.

"All right," said Helen.

"Say, Weary hasn't been around. I wonder if he's workin'?" said Studs.

"I don't like him," she said.

"I don't care so much for him," Studs said.

"He's too fresh," she said.

"Yeh?"

"Yeh, he's too darn fresh."

"Why?"

"Well, he tries to take liberties with girls. You know what he tried to do to me, don't you?"

"No?"

"Well, one day he asked me to let him see my kid sister's playhouse in the back, and I did. Then he went and tried . . . well, you know what he wanted to do to me, and I wouldn't let him. I don't care to do that sort of thing. I like to play with fellahs because, generally, they're fellahs like you an' Dan and Tubby, and they're square and decent, and not rats like those guys from Fifty-eighth Street, or like Weary Reilley, and they're not fussy and babyish, like girls. Girls are always tattling, and squealing, and snitching, and I can't stand them. With decent guys, you can be . . . well, you can be yourself. Anyway, he tried to do that to me, and I wouldn't let him. He kept arguin' with me, and grabbin' me, and I wouldn't let him fool around and have a feel-day, so he lost his temper like he always does, and he got sore as blazes, and I was afraid, so I rushed out. He tried to get me to come back, and said he was only foolin' and he didn't mean anything, and all that sort of bull. But I didn't fall for it, so he left me, sore as blazes, and sayin' he'd get me some time."

"I never knew that," Studs said.

"Well, he did. I don't like him; I hate him, the skunk; he's a bastard," she said.

"I don't care so much for him, either. But you got to give him credit for being a damn good scrapper. He ain't yellow."

"You can fight him, can't you?"

"I'm not afraid of him," Studs said.

"Sure, you can lick him," she said.

"Well, I never backed out of a fight with him," Studs said.

"Say, let's get a soda," Helen suggested.

"I'm broke," Studs said.

"I'll treat," she said.

They walked down to Levin's drug store at the corner of Fifty-eighth and Indiana and they had double chocolate sodas; they sipped with their spoons, so that the sodas would last longer. Studs told himself that there was something very fine about Helen. She was a square shooter, and she understood things. If he tried to sip a soda with a spoon before anybody else, they would laugh at him. When he and Lucy got to be sweethearts, she'd understand things, like Helen did. A guy couldn't find a pal like Helen every day. They sat, and Studs mentioned Lucy, saying that she was a nice-looking kid. Helen smiled like a person who knew too much. She said she liked Lucy, because she was a sweet kid, and full of fun, and not an old ash can like Helen Borax, who was too stuck up to live on a street like Indiana. She said it served Helen right that she had gotten a crush on a guy like Weary, because Weary would take some of the snootiness out of her and, well, Weary would probably make her do you-know with him, and it would be a good thing for her to be ruined, because she might come down off her high horse, and it would be a swell chance to talk about her, instead of having her talk about everybody else. But Lucy was a good kid for a guy to like, she said; and Studs said he wasn't so sure how much he liked her. She said, well, a guy like Studs was better off liking a girl like Lucy, and going with the bunch around Indiana Avenue, than he was, say, hanging out with the gang around Fifty-eighth Street. Red Kelly, Tommy Doyle, Davey Cohen and those guys were all louses; the only decent one among them was Paulie Haggerty; and Paulie had been better off when he used to come around Indiana and he was sweet on Cabby Devlin. Studs said he didn't give two whoops in hell for them; but he wasn't afraid of any of 'em.

Finishing their sodas, they returned toward Helen's. They paused before the clapboard frame house of the O'Callaghans. It was set about twenty yards back from the sidewalk, with a well-kept lawn and a large oak in front. Studs and Helen wondered why people lived in such an old-fashioned house, especially when they were rich like the O'Callaghans were. They were stumped by this. Studs tried to think what the neighborhood had been like when Old Man O'Callaghan first settled there and built his house, cutting down trees and living alone just like a pioneer. It must have been like a forest. That must have been good except for the wind at night. Even now, when you lived in a brick house that was all burglar-locked, and there weren't any trees for the wind to blow through, the wind at night was something you almost couldn't stand to hear. What must it have been then? It must have sounded like a horde of ghosts rising from a rainy cemetery, or an army of devils and demons; and he didn't know how Old Man O'Callaghan and his wife stood it. And what about the pioneers? The wind in the trees all around their houses must have sounded like Indians, and they must have jumped out of bed every five minutes and grabbed their guns. He would have liked to be a pioneer and go out to fight Indians and build log cabins. He would have had a swell time, pot-shotting Indians, rescuing girls like Lucy from them, and from smugglers and hold-ups. Or maybe he'd have been an outlaw like Jesse James. That would have been the real stuff, and no outlaw as tough as he would have been would have feared the wind. No, sir!

They played kicking goals between two lampposts. A punt passing over the goal line untouched was a point, and a drop kick was three. They were about even as kickers, and gave each other a good match, and they trusted each other and knew there was no cheating, so they could go ahead and play, not having any squabbles or having to talk and chew the rag a lot. It was swell for Studs to play, kicking, watching the ball soar up and away, and maybe fall in back of the goal line, knowing he had made the good kick and scored that point, or to make a drop kick, or to run back and pick one of Helen's southpaw kicks out of the air. And just to go ahead playing, not bothering to talk or think of anything, except now and then to imagine that Lucy was in the window watching. They played a long time, and winded themselves; when they quit, Studs was leading thirty to twenty-five.

They sat on Helen's front steps.

"You know, I always used to think I'd feel a little different when I graduated from grammar school, but here it's a couple of weeks ago, and I don't see any difference yet. Everything seems pretty much the same, and well, I don't know. Here I am graduated, and I'm wearin' short pants again, and got to listen to my old man the same as I did before I was graduated, and I come around, and everything and everybody's the same, kidding the punks, playing chase-one-chase-all, and blue-my-blackberry, and baby-in-the-hole, and all that sort of thing, just like before, and, well, in the fall I'll have to go to high school, and, well, things are just not like I imagined they would be after I graduated."

"I feel the same way," Helen said.

"I feel the same; and it's no different when you get confirmed. You are supposed to change, and something that's a mystery called a character is stamped on your soul, that is, if you're a Catholic; but you don't really seem to change any. Anyway, I didn't seem to," Studs pondered.

"Well, I never got confirmation, but I think I know what you mean. But my father and mother, they don't think so much of confirmation," said Helen.

"Of course we're taught different than you. We're taught that you shouldn't feel that way about the thing. You should believe in God and in the Church, and do all the duties that God and the Church say you should, or else you won't be doin' right and you'll go to Hell. Of course, if a person's not Catholic, but if they're sincere in bein' whatever they are, well, they'll stand a good chance of gettin' into Heaven. That's the way we're taught," said Studs.

"My father and mother say that it's all right what you believe, so long as you live up to that belief and don't do nothin' that's really wrong, or really hurt your neighbor, and if you do that, you ain't got nothin' to worry about from God," Helen said.

"Well, you know, it seems funny. Last night I was thinkin'. I remembered how I thought all the time that I'd feel so different after graduation. But now! Well, I'm just . . . I don't know. When I was a punk in the first grade, I used to look up to the guys ahead of me and feel that eighth-grade kids were so big, and now when I'm graduated I still wish I was bigger, and I don't feel satisfied, like I used to think I would when I was only a punk," Studs said.

"That's just the way I sort of feel."

"Yeh . . . but, oh, well," said Studs.

He felt that there was something else to be said, but he didn't know how to say it; he wondered if he was blowing his gab off too much. Sometimes, with Helen, he could talk more, and say more of what he really meant, than he could with any other person.

"Yeh," said Helen, meaningfully.

He glanced at her; he told himself that she was nice-looking. He felt soft inside, as if his feelings were all fluid, all melting up and running through him like a warm stream of water. He didn't know what he ought to say. He hurriedly glanced across the street. He saw Dennis P. Gorman tote his cane and his dignity down Indiana Avenue on his way to the police court. He laughed at High-Collars; and Helen said her father always called Gorman a mollycoddle who ought to be wearing corsets.

"You know, we'll have to take a look at that can house sometimes," Studs said, because he felt that he had better say something.

"Yeh!"

"I'd like to know what's inside of a can house," said Studs.

He was calmed down again, and he could look at her without feeling strange, and he wasn't in danger of giving his feelings away. He noticed that she, too, had been looking away.

"Well, I suppose one of those places has got a lot of expensive furniture, and the whores all sit around in their underclothes and maybe they drink a lot, and you know," she said.

"I'd sure like to see one some time," he said.

"Me, too," she said.

"Maybe we can sneak up on the porch sometimes," he said.

"Yeah," said Helen.

"We might see someone doin' it, too," he said.

"Yeah," said Helen.

"Sometimes I wonder what it's like," he said.

"So do I," she said.

"I don't think it's so much," said he.

"All the kids act as if they knew, but I'll bet that none of them really do," she said.

"I guess you're right."

She told him of the time that her dog, Billie, had cut its nose, and had accidentally rubbed a little blood on her night-gown. Her mother had seen the blood spot, and had gotten excited, and had tried to explain to Helen what things were all about, but Helen had known what her mother told her; and her mother hadn't told about the thing that was the real bother; her mother hadn't said a word of what it really felt like. As Helen told this to Studs, he got all excited, and seemed to see her before him, melting and fading. He felt like he'd have to do something, and he was afraid to try.

"Say, wouldn't it be nicer back in the playhouse?" he said, keeping his voice under control as much as he could.

"We can't go back and sit there now. My sister Marion and her girl chums are in it," she said.

"Oh!" he said.

Nothing had seemed wrong in his asking, he guessed. So they sat there and talked. Helen asked him if he knew this Iris who took all kinds of guys up to her house when her mother wasn't home, and let them all have a gang-shag. Studs said he didn't know Iris, but he'd heard of her. Helen said that was going too far; it was like being a whore. Studs said yes.

But he wished he could horn in on one of those gang-shags.

Weary Reilley ambled around, and Helen grumbled a greeting to him. He asked if they'd seen Helen Borax, and they said no. Weary fooled around with the soccer ball, and they barbered about nothing in particular. Then they dribbled, one taking the ball, and the other two standing in a line to block the dribble. Weary had never played basketball, so he was awkward and clumsy and couldn't do the trick right. He went at it rough-and-tumble. He got sore because Helen could make such a monkey out of him. He finally lost his bean and dribbled head on into her, bucking her breasts with his football shoulders. It hurt her. She cried; she knew he had done it meanly and on purpose. She told him so, and he called her a liar. She slammed him in the mush with the ball, and his eyes watered.

"Listen," he said, preparing to rush her and let her have one.

Studs gripped Weary from the rear and held him in a firm clasp.

"Let me go, you sonofabitch," Weary yelled.

Studs flung Weary around and then faced him.

"Who's one?" asked Studs.

"Both of you, and she's a whore," said Weary.

"Why, Goddamn you," said Helen.

"Take that back," said Studs.

"From . . . *you!*" sneered Weary.

Weary socked Studs in the jaw; Studs' jaw flushed, Studs was confused; his breath came fast; maybe he was afraid; he had to fight; he forgot about everything but Weary in front of him. He hauled off and caught Weary on the knob with a wild right haymaker. They rushed into each other and swung. They broke their clinch and circled around. Weary rushed, and a wild uppercut that Studs had started from the ground a trifle before Weary had come in, caught Reilley on the button, Reilley was jogged back; he shook his head, and then walloped Studs with a left and right. But neither of them felt a lot. They fought, absorbed in punching each other. Every time they landed, a feeling of pleasure ran through them, pleasure at having done something physically successful. They fought, slugging, socking away, rushing, swinging with haymakers and wild swishing roundhouses.

Johnny O'Brien, thirteen and fattish, came around and watched. He didn't yell who he was for, and asked Helen how the scrap had started.

"Oh, Weary got snotty and called me an' Studs dirty names. If Studs can't bust hell out of him, I'M GONNA . . . Come on, Studs! Bam him! . . . Attaboy, Studs!"

Helen attaboyed Studs because he had just given Weary a good bust in the nose. Weary rushed back and made Studs' left ear red from a wallop. Studs missed Weary with a wild haymaker, and almost fell over. Weary jolted him when he was off balance. Studs came back with a rush and caught Weary in the mouth. Weary busted Studs. Studs busted Weary.

A crowd had formed a circle around them, watching, blocking the sidewalks. Women, mothers, yelled unheeded from nearby windows for them to stop. Screwy McGlynn, the fat guy who drove a laundry wagon, and who bragged that he had put the blocks to nearly every K. M. in the neighborhood, climbed down from his wagon and watched the fight with a professional eye. He stood next to Johnny O'Brien, similarly professional, and said the little guy had guts. He rooted for the little guy. Danny O'Neill, twelve, small, curly-haired, four-eyed, joined the mob and yelled for Studs to bust hell out of the bully. Dick Buckford, from Danny's gang, came around and rooted for both of them to win. The mob around had a swell time, shifting, shouting, yelling; it was the fight they had been waiting for. Mrs. Dennis P. Gorman tripped along. She paused and made a vain attempt to tell someone that it was a nasty spectacle which should be stopped. She heard Helen yelling for Studs to slam the cur; she picked up her skirts, crossed the street and tripped on.

Screwy McGlynn chewed on his cigar, grew more professional, and said: "That little guy is sure game . . . Well, he's one of them guys that believes in the old adage . . . the bigger they are, the harder they fall . . . And I always say that a good game little man can lick a good big man."

"Yeah, they're both good boys," said Johnny O'Brien.

Studs fought a boring-in fight. He waved his left arm up and down horizontally, for purposes of defense, so he couldn't do much punching with it, but he kept his right swinging. Weary met Studs and lammed away with both fists. It was anybody's fight.

Studs cracked Weary with a dirty right. They clinched. Weary socked in the clinch.

"HEY! FIGHT FAIR!" young Danny O'Neill yelled.

"DON'T LET 'IM GET AWAY WITH IT, STUDS," yelled Helen.

Lucy Scanlan deserted the carpet sweeper and stood on her front steps watching, rooting for Studs. Helen Borax, on her way to the store, stopped to watch from Lucy's porch. Helen said it was disgusting, and hinted that it would be a roughneck like Studs Lonigan to start such a fight. Lucy was too busy rooting for Studs to hear. She kept yelling:

"BUST HIM, STUDS!"

Helen watched with an aloof expression on her precociously disdainful face.

Weary again socked in a clinch.

"Fight fair," said Studs, a little breathlessly.

"Up your brown!" sneered Weary.

They clinched. Studs swung low, and experienced animal pleasure when the foul punch connected. Weary tried to knee Studs, but it was only a glancing blow off Lonigan's thigh. They clinched again, tumbled onto the grass, rough and tumbled, with first one and then the other on top, socking away. Dan Donoghue and lanky Red O'Connell dragged them apart, and they squared off. O'Connell yelled for Weary. Everybody else cheered Studs. They rushed each other, swinging, fighting dirty, cursing, scratching. Studs connected with Weary's beak, and Reilley got a bloody nose. He asked Weary if he was licked yet; and Weary thumbed his nose at Studs. Weary socked Studs, giving him a shiner. Studs smashed Weary with rights on three successive rushes. Studs seemed to be winning, although he lumbered tiredly. Weary was bleeding, breathing almost in pants, and his shirt was torn; his shoulder was scratched; and there were scratches on Studs' arm. They fought, and Studs kept connecting with Weary's mush, hitting twice for every one he took.

Diamond-Tooth, tough, red-faced, big-mouthed, hairy-handed, looking as much ape as man, came around; he separated them with his crane-like paws.

"Now, you fools, shake hands," he commanded.

Weary refused. He told Diamond-Tooth to mind his own Goddamn business and go to hell.

"Oh, you're tough! I see! Thanks for the tip! You're a tough punk, not afraid of nothin'. Huh! You want your snotty puss bashed in a little more. Huh? Didn't this little squirt here give you enough?"

Most of the kids laughed.

Weary retreated a few paces and picked up a boulder.

"PUT THAT BRICK DOWN!"

Weary didn't reply.

"I see! I GOTTA SLAP YOUR PUSS, and run the gang of you in, give you a nice little ride in the wagon and let your old ladies come down to the station bawlin' to get you out."

The kids drew back nervously. Screwy McGlynn, who had moved forward to remonstrate with the stranger, retreated, hopped onto his wagon, and was gone. Diamond-Tooth cowed the gang with his detective's star.

"Gee, he's a real bull," Danny O'Neill whispered too loudly.

Profound silence!

"Yeh, he's a real bull, punk; and you better clamp that trap of yours tight!"

"Come on, you guys. Maybe you'll change your minds."

He dragged them along. Studs was meek and afraid; Weary was sullen, glowering. The others started to follow them toward Fifty-seventh, and he turned and snottily told them to blow, before they were hauled in.

He asked, after the three of them had turned the corner:

"What were you punks scrappin' over? Huh?"

"He called my mother a name," Studs said.

"He called me one, too," Weary said.

"Maybe you were both right," Diamond-Tooth said.

They stood there.

"Now, shut up and shake hands; if you don't, I'll fight the two of you," said the dick.

They shook hands, insincerely. Weary walked east along Fifty-seventh, toward Prairie Avenue. His pride was even more bruised than his face. He walked determining revenge, entertaining extravagant schemes of cold-blooded murder, of framing Studs on some stunt or other, of getting him from the back sometimes with a rock or a beebe gun or a knife, or maybe a twenty-two, of some day walking up to him and renewing the fight, taking an advantage by busting him right square between the eyes before he knew what was coming, or maybe cracking him in the neck and choking his windpipe, or in the solar plexus. He was angry. He sensed his own weakness. He could get little satisfaction out of planning revenge. He hated Studs, hated him with the face Studs had punched, with the body he'd battered; and that face and body told Weary he was licked when his mind refused to believe it. He was interrupted by Helen Borax, who called him from behind. She said that she was sorry, and that Studs was a beast, and she knew that Studs must have hurt him, and she was awfully sorry. Her pity made him see white. He drained off his hatred by glaring at her, calling her a bitch, and telling her he had gotten all he wanted from her under her back porch on the night they had graduated.

Studs, the conquering hero, returned to the gang. As he walked back, he thought up a brave story, about how he had told the gum-shoe to lump it, which he would tell the gang. But when he was sitting in the center of the adulatory group, he couldn't tell it. Damn it, he couldn't spread the bull on thick; he didn't know how to string people along and tell lies like some people did. He told them what had happened, and they had fun talking it over. They talked about the battle, showering Studs with praise, telling him how great he was and how he was the champ of the neighborhood. Johnny O'Brien had been going around telling everybody how thick he was with Red Kelly, and every time he got in dutch with anybody bigger than he was he would always threaten to get Red Kelly after him. Now he told Studs that he could clean up Kelly. Studs was tired, sick in his stomach, aching all over. And he kept feeling his swollen eye. Johnny O'Brien ran home and copped a piece of beefsteak from his old lady. Helen and Lucy applied it. Studs was happy, even though he felt rotten. He was now the cock of the walk, and the battering he had gotten from Weary was worth this; but he'd hate to have to fight him again; his jaw was all cut on the inside; well, Weary was probably worse off. Weary Reilley had been licked; he, Studs Lonigan, had pounded the stuffings out of him. Now, that was something to be proud of.

He listened to the sycophantic comments: they poured sweetly on his ears. Helen gave a vigorous redescription of how the fight started. Red O'Connell, who hated Studs, and was kowtowing to him only because he had cleaned up Reilley, kept saying, it had been a bear of a fight. Dan Donoghue said there hadn't been a fight like it in the whole history of the neighborhood. Dick Buckford told Studs he could fight like blazes until they all told the punk to keep quiet. And Lucy said it showed Studs was brave.

Studs told himself he had been waiting for things like this to happen a long time; now they were happening, and life was going to be a whole lot more . . . more fun, and it was going to make everything just jake; and he was going to be an important guy, and all the punks would look up to him and brag to other punks that they knew him; and he would be . . . well, in the limelight. Maybe it would set things happening as he always knew they would; and he would keep on getting more and more important.

It was all swell; and it made him feel good, even if he was tired and aching. After they had all talked themselves almost blue in the face, they decided that it would be cooler in the Shires' playhouse. They went back there, and Helen chased away her kid sister's gang. The guys all chipped in to buy lunch, with Johnny O'Brien putting up most of the money. Red, Dan and Johnny went to the delicatessen store for grub; coming back, they copped a couple of bottles of milk from iceboxes. It was a fine lunch, and afterward they played post office, and Lucy gave her hero plenty of kisses. Life was fine and dandy for Studs, all right, and the only thing bothering him, besides his headache, was that he would have a heck of a time explaining his shiner to the old lady.

CHAPTER FOUR

I

Studs couldn't stay in one place, and he kept walking up and down Indiana Avenue, wishing that the guys would come around. As he passed Young Horn Buckford and some punk he didn't know, Young Horn said hello to him. He gruffed a reply. He heard Young Horn say, as he walked on:

"You know who that is? That's STUDS LONIGAN. He's the champ fighter of the block."

Studs laughed to himself, proud.

He came back to Fifty-seventh, and sat on the curb, watching two kids race each other up and down the street with barrel hoops. They pretended they were auto-racers. A little kid in a blue shirt? kept saying he was Dario Resta; and the other called himself Ralph De Palma. Resta and De Palma raced back and forth, and at the conclusion of every race there was an argument between the two winners. He would have liked to play in such a game, but it was too young for him. He smoked a butt.

"H'lo, Studs!"

"Hello, Half-Wit," said Studs to snotty-nosed, Jew-faced, thick-bodied, thirteen-year-old Andy Le Gare.

"Studs, can I feel your muscle?"

"I will if you will show me how you can bat your head against a brick wall."

"G'wan," said Andy.

"Say, Wilson's gonna get skunked," Studs said.

"He won't. My father said so; and he knows," said Andy.

"Listen! Wilson's a morphidite," Studs said.

"What's that?"

"A guy that's both a man and a woman at the same time, like fat Leon," said Studs.

Andy looked at Studs, hurt, puzzled, betrayed.

"I don't believe it. I'll bet you ten bucks," said Andy.

"Where'd you get the ten bucks?" sneered Studs.

"Never mind, I'll get ten bucks," said Andy.

"Boushwah!"

A pause. Andy again asked Studs if he could feel his muscle. Studs consented if Andy would show his stuff. Andy said it was a bargain. Andy felt Studs' muscle, and said: Gee! He again gripped Studs' hard-fibered right arm, and repeated his exclamation of admiration. Studs then made Andy carry out his part of the bargain; so Andy went over to the corner building, and, laughing idiotically, he snapped his head against the brick wall six times. Studs watched him open-mouthed, and said:

"Your bean must be made of iron. Watch out they don't take it some day to use on the elevated structures."

Andy went off. Studs watched him, laughing and muttering exclamations of surprise.

Studs hung around until the gang dribbled along. They sat on the grass in front of the apartment building on Indiana, where Danny lived. They whiled away the time with kid trivialities.

Danny O'Neill said that he had a good one on Three-Star Hennessey.

"Spill it," said Dan Donoghue.

"Well, it's funny; it's a good one," said Danny. Danny laughed like the goofy punk that he was.

"Well, for Christ sake, out with it before we take your pants down," said Johnny O'Brien, who acted as if he were a big guy like Studs and Dan.

"Well, Hennessey was under the Fifty-eighth Street elevated station . . . and gee, it's funny . . . !"

"Well, then, shoot it while you're all together," said Studs.

"Well, he was under the Fifty-eighth Street elevated station . . ."

"Yeh, we heard that," said Johnny O'Brien.

". . . lookin' up through the cracks to see if he could get an eyeful when the women walked up and down stairs . . ."

"Yeh, and we know what he was doing. That's nothing new," said Johnny.

"He once had a race with Paulie, and they both claimed the other had fouled," said Studs, and they laughed.

"But this time it's funny . . . You see, a dick caught him and shagged him down the alley. Three-Star got away, because nobody could catch him anyway, but the guys told me it was funny, him legging it, with his stockings hanging . . . and he didn't even have time to button up," said Danny.

They gabbed and laughed. Bill Donoghue interrupted the discussion on this latest of Hennessey's exploits to say:

"That's a warnin' for you, TB."

"Say . . . I don't do that," said TB.

"No!" said Studs ironically.

"What you got them pimples on your forehead from?" asked Johnny O'Brien.

"Why, you're gettin' so weak that young O'Neill here can toss you," Studs said.

TB and Danny were made to wrestle. O'Neill dumped Mc-Carthy with a crotch hold. TB squirmed, and O'Neill tried to turn and pin him with another crotch and a half-nelson, but Muggsy slid free. He was just getting behind O'Neill, when he was shoved by Bill and Studs. He squawked about dirty work being done him, and called Danny names, threatening to get him alone sometime. The guys told Muggsy that just for that he would get the clouts. They held him from behind, and encouraged Danny to sock him in the puss. Then they made Danny jerk open his buttons. It was fun.

"Jiggers!" yelled Johnny O'Brien.

Across the street, where Johnny pointed, they saw TB's old man, a tough, red-mustached, Irish police sergeant. They legged it to O'Brien's basement by a circuitous route and peered up from the basement window in time to see the old man finish slapping TB around. He bawled out Monk, kicked him in the slats, and told him to go on home.

When the coast was clear, they came out and sprawled on the grass, laughing over Muggsy's punishment. He was a goop, anyway.

They gassed. Studs suddenly reflected:

"You know, Hennessey must have some screws loose."

"Just some? That loogin is all loose, his bean is all screwy," said Johnny O'Brien.

"He's a sap. The squirrels call him brother," said Bill.

"He's got bats in the belfry," said Dan.

A banana man lazily shoved his cart across Fifty-seventh Street, shouting, droning, sing-songing: Bannano-oe!

The guys had great fun listening to Bill mimic the dago.

They sat around and chewed the fat. Studs said:

"You know, even my old lady warns me to keep away from Three-Star."

"Hell, so does mine," O'Brien said.

"Is Hennessey the bull artist?" said Danny O'Neill.

"But you know, sometimes he's good-hearted," said Tubby.

"Say, he'd steal your stockings without touching your shoes if he had half a chance. He'd even steal 'em if they were stiff and full of holes," Johnny O'Brien said.

"He's cookoo," said O'Neill.

"Well, Tubby, you're older and he thought you'd make a good friend and maybe stick up for him some time, that's why he treated you. He needs someone to protect him because there's gangs of guys always out to get him, and nearly every guy his size in the neighborhood has cleaned on him," said O'Brien.

"Sometimes he will get the livin' hell pounded out of him," Dan Donoghue said.

"Yeh," said Studs.

"He deserves all he gets, though, the little degenerate," said Dan.

"He should have been a nigger or a hebe instead of Irish," said O'Brien. Johnny added that Hennessey had even been caught in a basement with his half-wit sister.

"Yeah!"

"Speak of the devil and he's sure to appear," said Tubby.

"Yeh, Rastus!" said Bill.

They spied Hennessey and Haggerty dragging themselves along Indiana toward them. They came closer. Both were chewing tobacco, expectorating the juice like dyed-in-the-wool hard guys. Three-Star's face was smeary, framing his innocent blue eyes; he had a cherubic dimpled chin. He wore an old, dirty blue shirt and filthy khaki pants that were falling down. He had holes in his stockings, and no garters.

"Hello, Falling Socks!" said Studs.

"Hey, Hennessey, don't you believe in baths?" asked Johnny O'Brien.

"Hello, Nuts and Bolts!" said Bill.

Three-Star thumbed his nose at them.

"Hey, Punk!" said Bill.

Hennessey won forgiveness by passing out wads of Tip-Top for the older guys to chew.

They goofed Three-Star about the elevated incident, but he only laughed and gave them the low-down on it; he was quite proud of the way he had given Johnny Law the slip. He told some dirty jokes he had just collected. Then he looked at Danny O'Neill, who was his own size, and said he'd like to start mooning punks. He said he was fed up on the dago chickens around State Street anyway. The guys all thought that was a new word. Studs tried to talk Hennessey into going down in O'Brien's basement and doing his stuff, but Hennessey wouldn't. They hung around and gassed. They got to shouting and talking loud. Studs tried to promote a fight between Danny and Hennessey, and got them to tip-tapping with open hands. George, the cranky janitor, came out and told them to make less noise. After he turned his back, Hennessey made faces at him and the guys laughed. George turned around and caught Three-Star. He came back, and told Hennessey that if he caught him on the premises again, he'd break his dirty neck. When George had gone, they all talked of what a crab he was. Then the older guys got Hennessey and O'Neill tipper-tapping again. Studs got in back of Danny, and Bill stood behind Hennessey. They shoved simultaneously. The two punks batted their domes together and got sore. They started fighting. Hennessey lowered his head, and rushed, swinging wildly. Danny stood off and met each rush with a stiff left uppercut. He was cleaning on Three-Star for fair, much to the delight of the gang. They all yelled too loudly. George appeared on the roof and doused a pail of water on them; everybody but Studs and Johnny O'Brien got wet. They stood there, cursing up at George. He stood on the roof and laughed down at them. Then he got sore again and yelled for them to beat it while the beating was good. They knew George, so they straggled away. They went back in the alley, and the fight was resumed. Danny cut Hennessey up some more. Three-Star quit. He went off bawling that he'd get O'Neill alone some day. When he was a good distance away, he swore at them. They didn't shag him, because he was too hard to catch.

The next day, when they came around Indiana, they found

themselves all roundly cursed in chalked markings that extended the whole length of the block. And they met George with a policeman. They were shown the mail boxes in George's two buildings on the corner. Every one of them had been smashed with a hammer or a hatchet. They all got leery, but they had alibis, and the cop only took their names and went around to their homes to find out what time they had come in.

They knew who did it, but they didn't want to be snitchers. They went back to Johnny's yard and noticed that two side windows of the basement had been broken. They armed themselves with clubs and sticks and marched forth like an army going to war. But Hennessey was nowhere to be found.

II

When the guys were out looking for Hennessey, Johnny O'Brien told Studs to come along with him, so they ditched the gang. They returned to Indiana, and met old man O'Brien. He took them with him in his Chalmers. He was a husky, grayish man, starting to get a goodly paunch. They went first to the O'Brien coal yards at Sixty-second and Wabash, and then they toured the south side while O'Brien checked up on coal deliveries.

As they were driving east on Sixty-third, old man O'Brien said, his voice exaggeratedly rough:

"Who's the hardest guy in the gang?"

"Studs," said Johnny.

Studs blushed a little, and wanted to say something to make it appear like he wasn't so awful tough after all, but he was secretly pleased. He sat there, trying to think of something to say, and he couldn't get hold of a word.

"Well, some day, Studs, let's you and I mix. I'm not so young as I used to be, and maybe I'll be a little slow and will get winded, but just let's you and I mix. I'll tell you what I'll do. I'll tie my knees together, have one arm tied behind my back, and throw a gunny sack over my head. Now is that square?" Old Man O'Brien said.

They laughed. Studs thought that Old Man O'Brien was a pretty tough one when he got going. He remembered that night when they had all been standing at the corner of Fifty-eighth and Indiana. They had just been talking there, not doing a thing out of the way. And MacNamara, the lousy cop, came around. He blew his bazoo off, and told them to get a move on, and not be hanging around corners molesting the peace. They said they weren't doing anything. He blew his bazoo off again, and told them not to talk back to him or he'd run the whole damn bunch of them in. He said they weren't no good anyhow, and wanted to know what kind of fathers they had that would let them be out on the streets at night, molesting decent people and disturbing the peace. He told them to get a move on, and he grabbed Johnny's arm and started to shove him. Old Man O'Brien had been in the drug store, and he'd taken the whole show in. He got sore as a boil and stepped up to the lousy flatfoot. He told him where to get off at in regular he-man's language. He said he was the kind of a father these boys had, and what was there to say about it? And he told MacNamara that those boys would stand on the corner as long as they pleased, and as long as they were behaving, as they had been then, no one would try and bully them . . . not while he was around. And no cop could think that he was going to get away with pushing his son. And he told the damn bluecoat that if he would take off his star, he'd punch him all over the corner, and when he got through, wipe the street with him. MacNamara had walked away like a whipped dog, mumbling apologies. If he had cracked a wise one, Old Man O'Brien would have socked him. And if he had run Old Man O'Brien in, with Mr. O'Brien being in the right like he was, well, he would have been in a jam, because Old Man O'Brien had money and a pull. Studs and all the guys had wished they had an old man like Johnny had. Now, riding in the car, Studs thought what a swell old man he was. He remembered Johnny saying his dad never once hit him. And he gave Johnny plenty of spending money. He was a real old man, all right.

They drove down South Park Avenue. Old Man O'Brien said he'd take Studs and Johnny to White City some time. He and his wife had been there only last week, and had had a dandy time. Studs felt that Mr. O'Brien was different from his own gaffer. He wasn't a putter-off, but when he said he'd do something, he did it. Old Man O'Brien turned, and said:

"Hell, you kids ain't as tough as kids used to be in my days. When we fought then, we fought. And we all had to use brass knuckles."

"You wouldn't fool us, Gov'nor, would you?" kidded Johnny.

Studs thought it wasn't every guy who could kid with his old man, like Johnny could. Most old men were, like his own, always serious, and always demanding that you show them respect and listen to everything they said, and never contradict them or think they were in the wrong. And they never understood a kid.

Johnny had some old man, all right.

"Yeh, and when I was a kid, we used to fight Indians, and if we made a slip then, well, we'd have been tommy-hawked."

"No!" Studs exclaimed with surprise. He knew what old man O'Brien said couldn't be true, and yet he half-believed it was. He had an imaginary picture of Mr. O'Brien wading through a field of Indians, throwing a whole tribe of them up for grabs.

"Yeah, I was once near tommy-hawked at the place where White City now stands."

"He's always trying to bunk a guy," Johnny said.

"That's the trouble with this kid of mine. He never believes anything I say," Mr. O'Brien said.

He turned and smiled good-naturedly at them. In the moment that he turned, the car swerved, and he had a narrow escape from hitting a rattling Ford.

He got sore, and cursed after the other driver, telling him to take his junk in the alley where it belonged, and to try riding a bicycle until he learned how to drive.

"They ought to prohibit those goddamn Fords from being driven in the streets. They are nothing but a pile of junk."

"They are automobile fleas," Johnny said.

Studs told a joke he had read in a Ford joke book. A rag man was going down the alley one day, and he was called in a back yard. The man who called him said how much will you give me for this, and he pointed to a Ford. The rag man looked, and he looked some more. Then he said vel if you give me five dollair, I'll take it avay for you. They laughed at the joke. Old Man O'Brien said it was a pretty good one.

Old Man O'Brien spoke of the good old days, gone by, of the Washington Park racetrack, with its Derby day in the middle of June and the huge crowds it attracted, its eighty acres, its race course with a gentle slope from east and north that made it a faster track than a dead level one, its artificial lakes and garden works on the inner sides of the main track, its triple deck stands, its bandstand at one end of the stand, why, it was a dream. And all the color and noise and foment, and the crowds shouting, the betting and the excitement, when Burns, or Turner, or Burnett would lead a horse into the home stretch. And some of them horses, too, they were beauts, Hurley Burley, Enchanter, Imp, and them two horses that were goddamn good nags, Ben Hadad and Saint Cataline. Johnny's mother knew how good them horses were, because she had had a good time more than once on their winnings, right after she got married, and yes, sir, them horses had bought Johnny's sister Mary something when she was learning to walk. Yes, sir. And he told them of Garrison. Garrison, he said, was the jockey who was such a good man in the home stretch that they took the word, Garrison-finish, from the way he rode a horse. He'd seen Garrison ride, and Sloan too. And he spoke of the trolley parties and picnics of yore, and the dances and prize fights at Tattersalls. All the kids used to sneak in, the way kids always sneak in. They had a million ways of crashing the gate. One of their tricks was to bribe a stable man to let them in through the stables. Well, one night during a big fight, all the lights in the place went out and the management had to give tickets for the next night. Well, you should have seen the crowd that came. Every newsboy and teamster in town must have had a five-dollar ringside seat. And of all the old fighters he'd seen in action, Bob Fitzsimmons, Jimmy Britt, Jim Jeffries, Gentleman Jim Corbett, who could wiggle a mean tongue, and don't think old Gentleman Jim didn't know how to curse. Terrible Terry McGovern, ah, there was a sweet fighting harp for you, a real fighting turkey with dynamite in each mitt and a fighting heart that only an Irishman could own. Young Corbett, who was born with a horseshoe in his hands and a four leaf clover in his hair, and who put a jinx on Terrible Terry; Benny Yanger; the Tipton Slasher whom Old Man O'Brien knew personally; Stanley Ketchell who didn't know when to quit fighting even when he had a gun jammed against him; Joe Wolcott, Dixon, Joe Gans, Young Griffo, the most scientific fighter of all times with maybe the exception of Nonpareil Jack Dempsey, who came before Mr. O'Brien's time; Tom Sharkey—all of them old boys. They didn't have fighters like that nowadays. None of 'em were no-fight champions like Jess Willard, and most of them were real Irish, lads who'd bless themselves before they fought; they weren't fake Irish like most of the present-day dagoes and wops and sheenies who took Hibernian names. None of them were no-fight champions like Jess Willard, the big elephant. Why, an old timer like Philadelphia Jack O'Brien or Kid McCoy could have spotted the big elephant all his blubber and laid him low in a round. Now, McCoy was the trickiest fighter that ever lived. He had a brain and a corkscrew punch that made the big boys see stars once it landed. Once he was fighting some big bloke, and he suddenly pointed down and told the big ham his shoe laces were untied. The ham looked down, and the old corkscrew snapped across, and the big bum was rolling in the resin; and another time, McCoy pointed to the gallery, and the big dummy he was fighting looked up, and the old corkscrew right went over and the dummy started trilling to the daisies. And the baseball games in the old days of Spike Shannon, Mike Donlin, Fred Tenney, Jimmy Collins, Cy Young, Pat Dougherty, Fielder Jones of the Hitless Wonders, and even earlier when he was a kid, and

they had the Baltimore Orioles, and he used to see Kid
Gleason pitch, and there was Hit-Em-Where-They-Ain't
Willie Keeler, Eh Yah Hughie Jennings, Muggsy McGraw,
old Robby, Pop Anson, Brothers and the Delehantys. Hell,
even Ty Cobb wasn't as good as Willie Keeler.

"And you know who was the greatest of them all?" asked
Old Man O'Brien.

"Who?" asked Studs.

Studs usually didn't give a damn about baseball. Danny
O'Neill was the one who knew all about it. But when Old
Man O'Brien talked of baseball, it was as exciting as going to
see a movie serial, like that one a long time ago, *The Adven-
tures of Kathleen*. And the ball players he named were like
heroes, as great as generals.

"Well, old Rube Waddell. Rube was a guy. He was a left-
hander, and all left-handers are cracked."

Old Man O'Brien paused. Then he said:

"Studs, you ain't left-handed, are you?"

"No, sir!"

"Don't call me sir . . . Well, my kid there ain't either
. . . but he ought to be."

"YEAH!" kidded Johnny.

He told them all the familiar Rube Waddell stories. Then
he said that poor Rube ruined his health, and practically
killed himself because he was left-handed. It was Rube's left-
handedness that made him always want to run after a fire like
a kid. Well, Rube was always leaving Connie Mack and joining
up with some hick fire department, and Connie'd have to
send his scouts out to find the southpaw. Once Rube got himself
in with the hook and ladder crew in St. Louis or somewhere,
and went to a fire. When Rube was in fighting the fire, a floor
caved in on him and he got lost with some others under the
wreckage, and they turned the hose on him. It was funny,
but that was what put the kibosh on poor Rube's lungs. Studs
sat listening, enchanted, imagining himself a great guy like
Rube Waddell.

Old Man O'Brien talked on:

"But I ain't so much interested in sports as I used to be.
Baseball's the only clean game we got left. The Jews killed
all the other games. The kikes dirty up everything. I say the
kikes ain't square. There never was a white Jew, or a Jew
that wasn't yellow. And there'll never be one. Why, they even
killed their own God. . . . And now I'll be damned if they
ain't comin' in spoiling our neighborhood. It used to be a
good Irish neighborhood, but pretty soon a man will be afraid
to wear a shamrock on St. Patrick's day, because there are

so many noodle-soup drinkers around. We got them on our
block. I even got one next door to me. I'd never have bought
my property if I knew I'd have to live next door to that Jew,
Glass's his name. But I don't speak to him anyway. And he's
tryin' to make a gentleman of that four-eyed kid of his . . .
as if a Jew could be a gentleman."

Johnny and Studs laughed, and told him that the Glass
kid was nothing but a sissy. They had nothing to do with him.

"Well, don't . . . unless it's maybe to paste him one."

A pause.

"And say, Studs, you got 'em over your way, too. What
does your old man think of 'em?"

"Well, he's always talking of selling. My father thinks they
are ruining the neighborhood."

"They are . . . only, say . . . listen . . . can that my
father stuff. Both of you kids know damn well that when you're
alone you say . . . my old man . . . come on, act natural
. . ."

Studs told himself that Johnny's old man was like a regular
pal to a kid.

They stopped in an alley at Fifty-second and Prairie. Old
Man O'Brien bawled hell out of a sweating Negro who was
putting in a load of coal. The Negro was grimed with coal
dust, and perspiration came out of him in rivers. He worked
slowly but steadily, shoveling the coal into a wheelbarrow,
pushing it down a board and emptying it down a chute through
a basement window.

They drove on, and Mr. O'Brien said:

"You got to put pepper on the tails of these eight-balls.
They're lazy as you make 'em. A Jew and a nigger. Never trust
'em farther than you can see 'em. But some niggers are all
right. These southern ones that know their place are only
lazy. But these northern bucks are dangerous. They are getting too spry here in Chicago, and one of these days we're
gonna have a race riot, and then all the Irish from back of
the yards will go into the black belt, and there'll be a lot
of niggers strung up on lampposts with their gizzards cut
out . . . My kid here wanted to wrestle in that tournament
over at Carter Playground last winter, and I'da let him, but
he'd of had to wrestle with niggers. So I made him stay out.
You got to keep these smokes in their place and not let 'em
get gay."

They stopped for sodas, and Mr. O'Brien bought them each
two. Studs could have caught his old man buying a kid two
sodas like that. While they were sitting with their sodas, Old
Man O'Brien told them of the things of yesteryear, and of

plays he'd taken Johnny's mother to. One was called *Soudan*, given way back in about 1903, and it was a humdinger! They killed forty-five men in the first act. Was it a play! They had shipwrecks at sea, and what not, and when the shooting started half of the audience held their heads under the seats until it ended, and when the villain came on the stage everyone kept going ss! ss! And the dime novels, and Nick Carter! But times had changed. Times had changed. Even kids weren't like they used to be, they had none of the old feeling of other times, they didn't have that old barefoot-boy attitude, and they weren't as tough, either, and they didn't hang around knotholes at the ball park to see the great players, not the ones around Indiana anyway. Times had changed.

They drove around. At one place, Mr. O'Brien had to see a sheeny and explain why the coal delivery had been late. The fellow talked like a regular Oi Yoi Yoi, waving his arms in front of him like he was in the signal corps of the U. S. Army. He protested, but Old Man O'Brien gave him a long spiel, and as they were leaving, the guy all but kissed Johnny's father. When they drove on, O'Brien said to the kids:

"You got to soft soap some of these Abie Kabbibles."

He winked at them and they laughed. Studs kept thinking of his old man and Johnny's, and dreaming of being a kid like Mr. O'Brien had been and wishing that his gaffer was more like Mr. O'Brien. . . . Well, anyway, he wasn't as bad as High Collars.

It had been a great afternoon, though.

III

That night when Studs was ready to go out, he walked into the parlor. The old man and the old lady were sitting there, and the old boy was in his slippers sucking on a stogy; and the two of them were enjoying a conversation about the latest rape case in the newspapers in which the rapist was named Gogarty. Studs noticed that when he entered they shut up. He wondered what the hell did they think he was. Did they think he was born yesterday, and still believed in Santa Claus, the Easter Rabbit and storks? He wanted to tell them so, tell them in words that would show how much of a pain they gave him when they treated him as if he was only a baby. But the words wouldn't come; they almost never came to him when he wanted them to. He stood swallowing his resentment.

The old man said:

"You know, Bill, a fellow ought to come home some time. Now when I was your age, when I was your age, I know I liked to get out with the fellows, and that's why I can understand how you feel about bein' a regular guy, and bein' with the bunch, and I don't want you to think I'm always pickin' on you, or preachin' to you, or tryin' to make you into a molly-coddle, because I ain't. I know a kid wants a little liberty, because I was your age once . . . BUT . . ."

Studs got Goddamn sore. He knew what was coming. The old man always worked the same damn gag.

"You see, Bill, you're stayin' out pretty late, and you know, well, it's as your mother says, the neighbors will be thinkin' things, wonderin' if we, the landlords here, set a good example for our children, and live decently, an' if we are takin' the right sort of care of our children. I'm the owner of this here building, you see, and I got to have a family that sets the right kind of an example. Now what do you think they'll think if they see you comin' in so late every evenin', comin' in night after night after most respectable people have gone to bed?"

"But what is it their business?" asked Studs.

"And, William, you know you have to look out for your health. Now what will you do if you go on getting little sleep like you do? You know you should get to bed early. Why, this very day in the newspapers, there was an article saying that sleep gotten before twelve o'clock was better and healthier sleep than sleep gotten after midnight. You're wearing your-self out, and you're wearin' out me, your mother, because I worry over you, because I can't let my baby get tuberculosis," the mother said.

"I'm all right; I'm healthy," Studs said.

"Well, I think, Bill, I think a fellow could get enough play all day and until ten o'clock at night. You always want to remember that there'll be another day," the old man said oracularly.

Studs said that all kids stayed out, sitting on someone's porch, or in the grass in front of someone's house, talking and there wasn't anything wrong with it, because it was so nice in the evening. And the other kids' fathers didn't care. Mr. O'Brien never kicked about Johnny being out, and Johnny O'Brien was younger than he was.

"If Johnny O'Brien jumps in the river, do you have to?"

That was the way his old man always was!

Studs just stood there. The old man told him to save some-thing for another day. Studs sulked, and told himself there wasn't any use arguing with his old man and old lady. They just didn't understand.

The old man brought out a Lefty Locke baseball book, which he had bought for Studs and forgotten to give him.

He said it would be a good thing if Studs stayed in and read it. Studs ought to do more reading anyway, because reading always improved a person's mind. Studs sat down, pouted and read the book for about ten minutes. But Lefty Locke wasn't anything at all like Rube Waddell; it was a goofy book. He fidgeted. Then he said hesitantly that he'd like to take a little walk, and the old man, disappointed, said all right.

When Studs met the guys, he told them that he'd won a scrap with the old man. That evening they played tin-tin with the girls, and Studs kissed Lucy. It made him forget that his old man and his old lady and home weren't what sisters and priests made them out to be at school and at Mass on Sundays.

IV

It was a hot early July afternoon, and life, along Indiana Avenue, was crawlingly lazy. A brilliant sun scorched the impoverished trees and sucked energy from the frail breezes that simpered off a distant Lake Michigan.

The gang had all gone swimming, and Studs had not felt like going home for his suit. Danny O'Neill was at the corner of Fifty-eighth, playing a baseball game by himself with a golf ball. He threw the ball at the ledge on the side of Levin's tiled wall. Every time it struck the ledge, and the rebound was caught, a run was counted. Every throw was a time at bat. Danny played away, happy and contented by himself. Studs stood across the street, hands on hips, watching, shaking his head because he couldn't make out goofy O'Neill. He could have such a swell time by himself, playing some goofy baseball game or other or just sitting down playing knife. Danny was such a crack knife player that no one would play pull the peg with him. He was goofy, though. Studs crossed the street and said:

"Hello, Goof!"

They played the baseball game, and Danny beat Studs four times. Studs didn't like to get beat at anything, so he quit playing. He pulled Danny's cap over his eyes, almost bending the punk's glasses, and said:

"You're dizzy!"

He started tip-tapping with the kid, telling him that he was a good young battler but needed training. Studs said he was going to train Danny so he could lick any punk in the neighborhood. They tip-tapped. Studs let loose a rough slap, telling Danny he had to learn to take it. The slap hurt, but Danny bit his lip and didn't cry. They sparred, tapping easily. Danny stepped around Studs and slapped him with lefts. Studs hauled off, and let Danny have a pretty stiff one. Danny bit his lip.

He was the kid who could take punishment, so he didn't cry. Studs put his hands on his hips, and looked surprised at the shrimp, as if to say, Christ, but you're goofy. They sparred on, and Studs kept hauling off on Danny, training him to take punishment. Then Studs told O'Neill he'd show him some tricks in scientific fighting. Studs got on tip-toe, danced and lumbered around, and almost fell over his own feet. So he gave the punk a vicious slap in the puss. Breathless, they paused.

"You're good! you kin clean up any of the punks around here, even ivory-domed Andy Le Gare. None of them can hurt you," Studs said.

"It's because I know how to breathe. You see, when the kids fight, they breathe out of their mouths, and they lose their wind, quick; while I breathe out of my nose and save my wind, and we fight until they are winded, and I win. That's the way I beat Andy," Danny said.

Studs said Danny was a goof. The reason he could fight was that he was so goofy that he couldn't be hurt. They sparred a little more, but Studs had lost interest in training Danny. They talked.

"Say, did you ever hear of Rube Waddell?"

"Sure, I got an autographed ball from him."

"Don't goof me. You're too young to have got it."

"Well, he gave it to my uncle for me when he was playing in the American Association, and I got it at home. He was the greatest left-hander in the game, and I know Stuffy McInnis, the greatest first baseman in the game. He gives me balls when the Athletics are here," said Danny.

Studs said the Rube was no good. Danny didn't have any right to have a ball from Rube Waddell. Studs walked away, sore. He walked down Fifty-seventh Street, furtively looked around to see if anyone saw him, and when the coast was clear he sniped a butt from the street. He walked back, smoking it. Then he met Lucy, returning from the store with an armful of groceries. He carted them for her. As they walked slowly back towards her house, Studs had some of the old feeling he had had on that March day. She asked him what he was going to do, and he said he didn't know, but he thought he might take a walk over to the Washington Park playground, and fool around if that old crab Mr. Hall didn't kick him out. She told him it was a good idea, because she thought she'd go to the park, and they could walk over together. She said Mr. Hall was a mean old frog. Studs told himself that it was swell, and he was in luck. He told Lucy that he guessed they could walk together at that. He became suddenly leery and uncertain, because a guy could never be sure when he was, and when he wasn't, saying the right thing to a girl; he felt that he should have said something different to her; he hoped that he hadn't said anything that would make her sore and change her mind so she wouldn't go to the park with him. He waited and worried while she went into the house, and it took a long time, so that he got nervous and was afraid she wasn't coming, but he waited anyway. He heard some young kids in the Shires' gangway, Helen's kid sister, a couple of her girl friends, and a ten-year-old punk named Norman something or other. They were talking about having a show party in one of the basements across the street. They enthusiastically agreed to, and they ran across the street, looking quite cute and innocent. Studs watched them skip, and said to himself with a quizzical look on his face:

Jesus Christ!

He scowled, scratched his head and asked himself if he should tell Helen Shires. He decided not to, because he hated any kind of a snitcher. He laughed to himself, thinking how funny it was, and what a knockout of a story it would be for Dan and the guys if they would promise not to pass it on. He thought of his kid sister, Fritzie, telling himself that she wouldn't never do a thing like that. If he ever found her doing it, he'd certainly boot her tail around the block until she couldn't walk straight. But then, he guessed there was something in Catholic girls that made them different from the other girls. Now, there was Helen Shires; she was fine, just like a pal or a guy's best friend; but then, there was something different and purer in a girl like Lucy which stopped her from talking about the things he and Helen talked about. Yes, sir, he was pretty certain about that something purer in Catholic girls. He laughed, because the little kids had been so funny. He thought about going over and peeking in on their party, but just then he saw Lucy.

She came out wearing a reddish-orange wash dress which looked nice on her, because she was dark, curly-haired, with red-fair skin, and the dress set her off just right. And she had on a little powder and lipstick, but it didn't make her look like a sinful woman or anything of that sort. Studs didn't usually pay attention to how girls looked, except to notice the shape of their legs, because if they had good legs they were supposed to be good for you-know, and if they didn't they weren't; and to notice their boobs, if they were big enough to bounce. He looked at Lucy. She was cute, all right. He told himself that she was cute. He told himself that he liked her, and she was cute. His heart beat faster, and he scarcely knew what he was doing.

They strolled east on Fifty-seventh Street. A Negro nurse-maid came along with a bow-legged baby, and Lucy made a fuss over it; Studs thought it was a pain, but he decided that girls were girls, and if they were like Lucy, they must be higher creatures that a guy just couldn't understand, no matter how much he tried. He pretended that he was interested in the darling tot, but it gave him a pain. They strolled on, and Studs kept side-glancing at angelic Lucy, straining his mind to think of something to say. He said that it was a nice day, all right. She agreed. He said that it was the kind of a day that made a fellow want to do nothing, and she said yes. She said she liked doing nothing. Studs said that usually he didn't like doing nothing, but now he felt different from the way he felt on most days. He said that there was too much for a guy to do to want to do just nothing; he told her some of the things a kid could do, instead of doing nothing; he told her now he, Red O'Connell, and the gang had gotten Red's beebe gun, and had stood on Red's porch, shooting pigeons, and he had killed the most, three; and how Red had shot Muggsy McCarthy in the pa . . . the back and Muggsy didn't know who shot him, and it was funny, and then Red had gotten his old man's Chalmers, and they had gone riding, and Red had stepped on it, and they had gone down South Park Avenue fifty miles an hour, and they had kept shooting away, trying to break windows, and they had broken five or six of them. She said it was just horrid, and that boys just wanted to make mischief; as Sister Bernadette Marie always said, boys had the germ of destruction in them, and they did perfectly awful, horrid things; but she said it just like a girl, meaning the exact opposite.

They came to the park, where it was cooler. She walked more slowly, and they gazed idly about them. Everything was sun-colored, and people walked around as if they had nothing to do. It was nice out, all right, with the sky all so blue and the clouds all puffed and white, and floating as if they were icebergs in a sea that didn't have any waves. And he thought it would be fine if he and Lucy could have wings and fly away past the sky; he thought about their flying away, flying right through clouds, and way past the other side of the sky, where there was nothing, and they flew through nothing until they came to some kind of a place with a palace, and servants, and everything they wanted to make them happy, and all Studs had to do to get the place, for himself and Lucy, was to clean up on a couple of big boloneys, that owned it. But he called a stop to these thoughts, and told himself that Studs Lonigan was not the kind of a gee to have goofy thoughts like that. She said that it was awfully nice. Studs said that it was cooler in the park than it was outside. They glanced off at their left, and saw the playground, surrounded by shrubbery and an iron picket fence. From inside they could hear the shouts of playing children. They saw the swings, with the colored shirts and dresses of kids flashing, disappearing, flashing above the shrubbery, a momentary rhythm in the sunlight. It all sounded and seemed as if it belonged to the park. Lucy said that she thought it would be nicer to walk around than to go into the playground, because anyway, it was for little kids, and if they went in they'd get all hot and dirty, playing. Studs thought too, that if old skin-and-bones crabby Hall kicked him out for being too old right in front of Lucy, he would be so ashamed he could never look her in the face again. Studs deeply pondered the idea of not going to the playground, and said that it was a good idea; yes, he repeated, it was a good idea. As they crossed, their feet sank in the asphalt drive that was gooey on account of the heat, and they moved onto grass that was like velvet and bright with many colors from the sun. She took his hand; they walked, swinging hands, heads lowered, not saying anything to each other.

As they walked over to the wooded island, Studs felt, knew, that it was going to be a great afternoon, different from every other afternoon in his whole life. They walked on, not talking, but the way she held his hand made him feel good, and he repeated to himself that it was one of his days. They crossed the log bridge over onto the island . . . a spread of irregularly wooded and slightly hilly ground with the sheep pen at one end of it. They walked on until they came to a full-leaved large oak that stood near the bank. It looked nice and they decided to climb it, and sit on one of the large branches. Studs helped her, and saw her clean wash bloomers. He was tempted, and wondered if he ought to try feeling her up. He remembered Marion Shires, and the other little kids, and wondered if he ought to, and how he might ask Lucy to have a show party with him. He got excited. But when they were up in the tree, and Lucy was laughing about her dirtied dress and the little scratch on her hands, he forgot all about these temptations. They sat, not having much to say, and he held her hand.

Below them, a man and wife moved, watching their baby stumble and giggle ahead of them. Lucy watched the kid, a piggish-faced child, and told Studs that it was awfully cute. She suddenly lowered her head, muttered shyly that she would probably never get married and have children. Studs was

a little surprised, because girls like Lucy weren't supposed to
think about such things. He told himself that if she was like
that Iris from Carter School it would be different, and he
could understand it. But Lucy! He wondered if he ought to
try feeling her up, and he tried to think up an answer for
her; but his mouth was dry, and all he could think of was the
lump in his throat. Three times he asked himself what he
ought to say. He watched the group below disappear. He
finally said that it had been a cute kid. Lucy said yes. Lucy
said that she was never going to marry and become a mother,
because she was going to join a convent and be a nun. She
talked as if she was mad about something. Studs wondered
what was the matter. He looked at her, and her face seemed
to melt in a misty sort of asking expression. He asked her if
she thought she had the call to be a nun, and she said yes,
she was going to become a nun. Studs said that she ought to
think it over first; he told himself that he loved her, and wanted
her not to become a nun, and knew that she wouldn't if he
could only tell her the way he loved her, but he didn't know
what he wanted to say, because it wasn't words but a feeling
he had for her, a feeling that seemed to flow through him
like nice, warm water. She told him yes, she had definitely
made up her mind. Her voice sounded angry, and he wondered
what was the matter.

The breeze playing upon them through the tree-leaves was
fine. Studs just sat there and let it play upon him, let it sift
through his hair. He said that it was nice and cool; he said
that it was cooler in the trees than it was on the ground. Lucy
said yes it was, and she didn't seem interested, and it made him
still wonder what was the matter. The wind seemed to Studs
like the fingers of a girl, of Lucy, and when it moved through
the leaves it was like a girl, like Lucy, running her hand over
very expensive silk, like the silk movie actresses wore in the
pictures. The wind was Lucy's hand caressing his hair. It
was a funny thought to have, and Studs felt goofy and fruity
about having it, and felt that he hadn't better let anyone know
he had thoughts like that; he wouldn't tell her. But he did;
he told her the wind was like the hand of a pretty girl, and
when it touched the leaves, it was like that pretty girl stroking
very fine silk. She laughed, and said that it was a very funny
and a very silly thought for a person like Studs Lonigan to
have. It made him ashamed of himself, and very silent, and
he wished that he was somewhere else and Lucy was not
with him, probably laughing at him like she was in her mind.

They sat. There seemed to be a silence on the park. Nothing
but the wind. Studs could hear his heart beating like it was

a noisy clock. He felt as if he was not in Washington Park, but that he and Lucy were in some place else, a some place else that was just not Washington Park, but was better and prettier, and no one else knew of it. He glanced about him. He looked at the grass which slid down to the bank, and at the shrubbery along parts of the lagoon edge. He gazed out at the silver-blue lagoon that was so alive, like it was dancing with the sun. He watched the rowboats, the passing people. He took squints at everything from different angles, and watched how their appearances would change, and they would look entirely different. He listened to the sounds of the park, and it seemed as if they were all, somehow, part of himself, and he was part of them, and them and himself were free from the drag of his body that had aches and dirty thoughts, and got sick, and could only be in one place at a time. He listened. He heard the wind. Far away, kids were playing, and it was nice to hear the echoes of their shouts, like music was sometimes nice to hear; and birds whistled, and caroled, and chirped, and hummed. It was all new-strange, and he liked it. He told Lucy it was swell, sitting in the park, way up in a tree. Lucy said yes, it was perfectly grand. Studs said: YEAH!

"It's so lovely here," she said, leaning toward him, puckering her lips.

Studs looked at her. Without knowing what he was doing, he kissed her. It was all-swell to kiss Lucy, and it was different from a game where she had to kiss him, and everybody was kissing everybody else. And she kissed him with her red lips in a queer sweet way; and he kept telling himself that it was fine to kiss her. In the movies, and in the magazines, which he sometimes read, the fellow always kissed the girl at the end of the story or the picture, and the kiss always seemed to mean so much, and to be so much nicer, and to have so much more to it than ordinary kisses. Kissing Lucy was getting a kiss like that. And it made him feel . . . all-swell.

And everything just kept on being perfectly jake, not spoiling it there with him and Lucy. They sat. There he was, and there was Lucy, swinging her legs, singing *The Blue Ridge Mountains of Virginia*, and it was nice, and he told himself that no afternoon in his whole life had been like this one, not even the afternoon after he had licked the stuffings out of Weary Reilley. He had felt sick from the fight then, and the gang had all been around and made things a lot different from now, with himself and Lucy sharing and owning all the niceness themselves. And he had a feeling that this was a turning point in his life, and from now on everything was

going to be jake. He had always felt that some time something
would happen to him, and it was the thing that was going to
make his whole life different; and this afternoon was just
what was going to turn the trick; it was Lucy. Living was
going to be swell now, and different from and nicer than it
had ever been before. The only thing the matter with it all
was that it couldn't last forever. That was the way things were;
they ended, just when they began to be most jake.

A bird cooed above them. He usually thought it was sissified
to listen or pay attention to such things as birds singing; it
was crazy, like being a guy who studied music, or read too
many books, or wrote poems and painted pictures. But now
he listened; it was nice; he told himself how nice it was.

If some of the kids knew what he was doing and thinking,
they'd laugh their ears off at him. Well, if they did, let 'em;
he could kick a lot of mustard out of the whole bunch of
'em. He gazed up at the bird. Some white stuff dropped on
him, and somehow, seeing the bird that sang like this one
doing that, well, it kind of hurt him, and told him how all
living things were, well, they weren't perfect; just like the
sisters had said they weren't in catechism. He was glad Lucy
hadn't noticed it. They sat. Lucy touched his sleeve, and told
him to listen to the bird music. He listened. But Lucy was suddenly distracted by an oh-so-cute-and-so-darling baby, being
led below them by a nursemaid.

They sat. Studs swinging his legs, and Lucy swinging hers,
she chattering, himself not listening to it, only knowing that
it was nice, and that she laughed and talked and was like
an angel, and she was an angel playing in the sun. Suddenly,
he thought of feeling her up, and he told himself that he was
a bastard for having such thoughts. He wasn't worthy of her,
even of her fingernail, and he side-glanced at her, and he
loved her, he loved her with his hands, and his lips, and his
eyes, and his heart, and he loved everything about her, her
dress, and voice, and the way she smiled, and her eyes, and
her hair, and Lucy, all of her. He sat, swinging his legs, restless,
happy, and yet not so happy, because he was afraid that he
might be acting like a droop, or he might be saying or doing
something to make her mad. He wanted the afternoon never
to end, so that he and Lucy could sit there forever; her hands
stole timidly into his, and he forgot everything in the world
but Lucy.

"Isn't it awfully nice here?" she said.

"Yeah!" gruffed he.

He wanted to say more, and he couldn't. He wanted to
let her know about all the dissolving, tingling feelings he was

having, and how he felt like he might be the lagoon, and the feelings she made inside of him were like the dancing feelings and the little waves the sun and wind made on it; but those were things he didn't know how to tell her, and he was afraid to, because maybe he would spoil them if he did. He couldn't even say a damn thing about how it all made him want to feel strong and good, and made him want to do things and be big and brave for her.

His tongue stuck in his mouth.

They sat swinging their legs.

And Time passed through their afternoon like a gentle, tender wind, and like death that was silent and cruel. They knew they ought to go, and they sat. Accumulating shadows raked the scene which commenced to blur beneath them. They sat, and about them their beautiful afternoon evaporated, split up and died like the sun that was dying a red death in the calm sky. Lucy said that it was getting late, and she had better be going. Studs told her to wait just a little while longer. She insisted that she had to go. They sat, and Lucy puckered her lips. Studs kissed her. She stroked his hair, and it was even nicer than the wind, and she said that she liked him bushels and bushels. She said that she had to go, and she sat swinging her legs so that he could notice them; and they had a nice shape, too. She pointed to another baby. Studs thought of how babies were born, and he blushed. She asked him what he was doing, and offered a penny for his thoughts. He said he wasn't doing nothing, only looking, not thinking. He again thought of feeling her up, and again it made him feel like he was a dirty bastard.

They sat, and more precious minutes were squeezed, drained dry. Whey they finally climbed down, the sun was dead in the sky. They hurried home, half-running, not speaking. Leaving the park at Fifty-seventh, they saw Sunny Green and Shorty Leach playing tennis, lamming the ball at each other in the half darkness, playing and volleying better than most men could. Lucy asked him if he could play tennis better than the two kids, and he said yes. He was sorry he told her such a lie, almost before the words were out of his mouth, just like he felt pretty lousy because he had exaggerated the story about how he and the guys had gone riding in Red O'Connell's car, shooting beebes. He promised to teach her how to play tennis. They parted in front of her house at a quarter to eight. She stood a moment on the porch, smiling at him through the summer dusk; and the spray from the sprinkler on her lawn tapped his cheeks; the boy, Studs, saw and felt something beautiful and vague, something like a prayer sprung into flesh. She threw him a kiss and fled inside. He walked home, pretending that he was carrying her blown kiss in his handkerchief. As soon as he arrived home, he rushed to his bedroom and kissed his handkerchief. He brought out his tennis racket and gestured before the mirror like a star tennis player, and resolved to practice his game, and some day for Lucy he might make himself as good as McLaughlin. He was proud of his form, too. Then he shadow-boxed, and imagined that he was beating up some hard guy to protect Lucy's character. Soon he was beating up a whole gang of them. He imagined her rewarding his heroism with a kiss, and folding his arms around the bed-pillow, tenderly, he kissed it. He sat on his bed, and contemplated the fact of Lucy. He told himself that he was one hell of a Goddamn goof; he sat on the bed, thinking of her and becoming more and more of a hell of a Goddamn goof.

V

STUDS LOVES LUCY . . . LUCY IS CRAZY ABOUT STUDS . . . I LIKE TO KISS LUCY—STUDS . . . STUDS KISSED LUCY A MILLION TIMES . . .

Studs saw chalked writings like these all over Indiana Avenue, on sidewalks, fences, buildings. It was two mornings after he and Lucy had been in the park. On the previous day, he had cleaned out the basement for his old man, and he had been too tired at night to wash up and come around. When he read the scrawlings all over, his face got red as a tomato, and he got so sore he cursed everybody and everything. He promised himself that a lot of guys were going to get smacked. He was so sore that he didn't take the trouble to examine the childish writings, a scrawl quite like that of his sister Loretta and her girl-chum, June Reilley.

Danny O'Neill came along, and stopped at Studs' side. He read the words aloud, and laughed. Studs socked him. Danny, in a temper, stuck his tongue out at Studs, called him a bully, and said, mimicking:

"I'm gonna tell Lucy!"

Studs cracked Danny in the jaw with all his might, and the punk, holding his mush in his hands, bawled.

Most of the guys saw Danny's swollen jaw, so they didn't try to kid Studs. The older guys sat on the grass, talking, blaming the punks, planning how they would swoop down on them and get even by taking their pants off and hanging them on trees, making them eat dirt, giving them a dose of it that they wouldn't forget until kingdom come. But the punks had all smelled trouble, and they were gone. The bunch sat around

and talked about revenges. Studs didn't say much; he didn't
even look anybody in the eye. Suddenly, he got up and left,
and the guys said that when Studs walked away from his
friends like that, without saying a word, he was pretty Goddamn
sore, and when he was pretty Goddamn sore, he wasn't the
kind of a guy you'd want to meet in a dark alley. He walked
for blocks, not recognizing where he was going, feeling disgraced, feeling that everybody was against him, blaming everybody, blaming that little runt, Danny O'Neill. He felt that
he was a Goddamn clown. He blamed himself for getting soft
and goofy about a skirt. He planned how he would get even,
and kept telling himself that no matter what happened, it
couldn't really affect him, because STUDS LONIGAN was
an iron man, and when anybody laughed at the iron man, well,
the iron man would knock the laugh off the face of Mr. Anybody with the sweetest paste in the mush that Mr. Anybody
ever got. He vowed this, and felt his iron muscle for assurance.
But he didn't really feel like an iron man. He felt like a clown
that the world was laughing at. He walked, getting sorer and
sorer and filling his mind with the determination to get back
at . . . Indiana Avenue, the whole damn street. As far as he
was concerned, it could go plumb to hell. He was through hanging around with the Indiana Avenue mopes, and as for
O'Neill, well, Studs Lonigan hadn't even begun to pay that
little droopy-drawers back yet.

When Studs got home, Martin, speaking like he had been
coached, said:

"How's Lucy?"

"I seen Lucy today; she looked nice, like she was looking
for someone . . . and she had paint on her lips," Fritzie said.

Frances asked him if he was going over to see Lucy after
supper, if he was, she'd walk over with him . . . and she
said if he was he had better wash himself clean and shine his
shoes.

The old man sang monotonously:

> *Goodbye, boys . . .*
> *For I . . . get . . . married . . . tomorrow . . .*

Mrs. Lonigan seriously warned him that he was still a
little young and he would have plenty of time later on for
girls, and girls would make a fool of him, and he should not
be thinking of them, but he should be praying and meditating
to see if he had a vocation or not.

Studs walked out of the room, saying that they could all
go to hell.

He heard them laughing after him. Even the walls and

the furniture seemed to laugh, to jibe and jeer. He went out
for a walk without eating, and he met Helen Borax on Fifty-
eighth Street. She asked him how Lucy's gentleman was, and
said that she heard he was a specialist in osculation; she said
she would never have believed it, but she couldn't doubt all
the proof she had seen around the neighborhood in the last
few days. And she would never be able to understand how Lucy
mistook him for Francis X. Bushman; but then everyone had
his or her right to like people. She said she knew Lucy needed
a sort of roughneck to carry her books when she went to
high school, because Lucy was going to St. Elizabeth's, and
it was in a nigger neighborhood, and he could protect her,
and walk home with her through the nigger neighborhood.
Helen spoke so swiftly and cattishly that Studs couldn't get
in a word edgewise. She didn't stop for over five minutes,
and then she only paused for breath. After she had talked
a blue streak, they stood making faces at each other.

He said, sore as a boil:

"Kiss my . . ."

She blushed, gulped, swallowed, looked shocked and horror-
stricken. He turned his back on her, and walked away.

"Lucy's gentleman!" Helen called after him.

He turned and thumbed his nose.

VI

The next day he wandered forlorn streets, wishing that
he would meet Dan, or Helen Shires, or someone, and not
having the nerve to go around Indiana, where he might find
them. At Fifty-eighth and Prairie, he met Lucy. She was with
some girl he didn't know, and she said hello booby to him,
winking at her friend. He got sore, and stuttered goofy things
to her, like she needn't think she was so much. She said she
was a lady, and only cared to associate with gentlemen. He
said that girls were a pain. She said that girls wouldn't think
much of him after the awful thing he had said to Helen Borax;
she said her mother would certainly forbid her to associate
with such a person. He stood looking at her. She asked him
if he saw anything green. He didn't have any comeback.

They walked away, their heads stuck up, laughing at him.
He stood there, trying to figure out why girls were so un-under-
standable, and why they changed and were flighty like the
weather. He walked on in a trance, thinking about this and
about things in general. He told himself again and again that
the world was lousy and he was going to give it one Goddamn
run for its lousy money, all right. It was rotten, all right. Just
when things were jake, they blew up like they had a stick of

dynamite under them. Well, Goddamn everybody, let them lump it. He walked, thinking, dream-planning heroic revenge, telling himself how he would become something daring and famous like an aviator, a lone wolf bandit, an Asiatic pirate, a German submarine commander.

He walked. The day was fine. The wind was cool. It would have been so nice to walk with Lucy. He went over to the park, and found their tree and sat up there, imagining that Lucy was by his side swinging her legs and kissing him. He forgot where he was, and everything else. He only thought of Lucy. Then he thought he was some place else, and this time, some place else was sad, and he didn't want to be in it, and there was no place else for him to go. The wind again waved through his hair, but now it was only the wind.

He cursed.

He finally grew lonely and needed to find someone, anyone, to be with. He climbed down and walked snappily, so people seeing him would think he had some place to go and that he wasn't drooping around like a damn mope. He found himself over near the playground. He went in. Johnny O'Brien, Danny O'Neill and a number of other younger kids were playing indoors, and Miss Tyson, the pretty director, was umpiring. Miss Tyson was a pretty chicken, all right, and a good sport, and whenever she played with the guys, and had to run bases, she slid, and they could all see her legs. Studs stood and watched them for a minute, and he was just going to ask them to let him in the game, when Old Man Hall, in his tan uniform and looking like he was on his last legs, came up. He looked at Studs, sour and crabby, as if it was Studs' fault that he was an old man ready to go west.

"Come on, now. Get out of here, and don't be plaguin' them that are smaller'n you are. This is no hangout for fellows like you. You ought to be ashamed of yourself, hanging around here, a big fellow like you that ought to be working and earning a living. Come on, get out!" he said in a creaky voice, starting to shove Studs.

"Don't go shoving me!" Studs said.

"I told you to get out, and if you don't, I'll call the police," Hall said.

"Well, just watch who you're shovin'."

The indoor game stopped, and everybody collected around Studs and Old Man Hall. It made Studs feel like an even bigger clown.

Miss Tyson tried to intercede and explain to Hall that Studs was all right, but the old codger made a long speech, telling everybody that he ran the playground, and as long as he did toughs would stay out even if he had to have the police to put them out.

Miss Tyson smiled sweetly at Studs, and apologized. But she couldn't do anything. To save his pride, he said he didn't want to come in anyway, and they could all go to the devil before he'd play on their indoor team in the playground tournament, like he'd said he would when he'd been asked to. He left, Hall hobbling along beside him, and almost every kid in the playground witnessing his humiliation. At the gate Hall said:

"Now if you come back, I'll have you run in. Good riddance to bad rubbish!"

An old guy, who was so feeble he couldn't probably hold a spoon of soup without spilling it all over himself, doing a thing like that to Studs! It made him Goddamn sore. He told himself: I'm riled sure, now.

He sat outside the playground, brooding, wondering how he'd get even with Hall. Then he walked on and sat near the sun-blue lagoon, down past the boathouse. He sat. He watched the people flood over the park. He wished he was somebody else. He watched the sky roll down back of the apartment buildings that stood above the trees lining the South Park edge of the park. He watched a familiar-looking Airedale dog shag about, snapping at the heels of the park sheep, until Coady, the flat-footed, red-faced park cop, hoofed it after the dog, probably sweating and cursing his ears off. The dog scampered away from the cop, ran down to the lagoon, and took a swim. The cop sought the shadow of the boathouse. The dog came out, shook the water from its back, and ran. Studs noticed it more closely. It was goofy Danny O'Neill's dog, Lib, and it ran away every day to come over to the park and take a swim. The dog was a damn sight smarter than Danny. He told himself that Airedales were peachy dogs, they were fighters, they could swim and liked the water, and they were smart; an Airedale was too smart a dog for O'Neill to have. Studs thought of getting even with Danny by doing something to the dog, but when he watched it run, its movements so graceful, its body so alert, its ears cocked the way he liked to see a dog's ears cocked, he couldn't think of hurting it. He called: "Here, Lib!" The dog came up. Studs patted its head, softly stroked its forehead the way dogs liked to be stroked, rubbed his cheek against the dog, liked it even if it did smell like a livery stable.

"Good dog!" he said.

He stood up, grabbed a piece of branch and threw it. The dog chased the branch, grabbed it, returned, dropped the branch at Studs' feet, and spread out on all fours, waiting to be patted. Studs kept throwing the branch until it was ugly wet with saliva. He rubbed his hand in the grass and patted the dog. He told the dog to stand up, and it obeyed. Then to play dead dog. Then to roll on its back in the grass and speak. He ran, and the dog legged it with him, and rapidly left him behind.

Lib spied the park sheep and was after them. The sheep milled and bleated, and Lib tore circles around them, running like an efficient sheep dog. The cop again appeared, waddling on his defective feet. The dog ran at the sound of the cop's voice. It was too wise for the cop, Studs thought, and laughed. Coady yelled at Studs, complaining, in his Irish brogue, that he wished he'd keep that dog of his away. It was a disturbance of the peace, with it always scaring the sheep, jumping up and getting ladies' dresses muddy, and running around without a leash and muzzle, all against the law. Suppose the dog went mad and bit a baby. The next time he saw the dog, he would shoot it. It was too damn troublesome, and too damn wise.

"Sure it knows I'm after it, and runs when I come," Coady said in an Irish brogue.

Studs said it wasn't his dog.

"Well, then, bejesus, whose dog is it?"

"I don't know."

"Well, keep it away from here, or sure it'll be a dead dog."

The sun was too much for Coady. He flatfooted it back to the shade. Studs laughed. It was always fun to see a copper stumped. The dog was gone now, on its way home. Studs walked, wishing he had a dog of his own, because you could have fun with a dog, particularly when you were lonesome. A dog was almost human, and a guy was always wishing he could get closer to it, speak to it, understand what it meant when it barked. It was pretty the way the dog looked at you, the way it ran and cocked its ears. It got a guy. A dog was a real friend, all right. But his old man wouldn't have a dog, because he said dogs were dirty, and his mother said they brought bad luck into the house, because sometimes dogs were the souls of people, who had put a curse on you, come back to life.

He walked around the park, and didn't meet anyone he knew.

CHAPTER FIVE

In summer, the days went too fast. They raced. In June, right after his graduation, Studs had had no sense of the passing days. And now July was almost gone, and the days were racing toward September and school. He remembered the Fourth; he had spent it with the Indiana gang, lighting firecrackers under tin cans to watch them pop.

It had promised to be a great summer for him and it was turning out pretty punk. And now it was one of those days, like the ones that came so often in mid-August. It was hot, but there was no sun; and the wind sounded like there were devils in it; and the leaves were all a solid, deep green. It was just that kind of a day. It made him feel different, glum; and his thoughts were queer and foggy, and he didn't have the right words for them. There was the feeling that he wanted something, and he didn't know what it was. He couldn't stay put in one place, and he kept shifting about, doing all sorts of awkward things, looking far away, and not being satisfied with anything he did.

He didn't go around Indiana any more, so he had walked up and down other streets and had ended up in the Carter Playground. He fooled around. He batted out stones. He climbed up the ladders and slid down, and didn't mind doing that, but canned it, because the ladders were for young squirts. He sat on the edge of the slide and thought of Lucy, and of how he had scarcely seen her since that day. He liked Lucy. He liked her. He loved her, but after what had happened he was even ashamed to admit it to himself. He was a hard-boiled guy, and he had learned his lesson. He'd keep himself roped in tight after this when it came to girls. He wasn't going to show his cards to nobody again. He sat on the slide. He got up and climbed the ladder. He slid down. He picked up pebbles and shot them as a guy shot marbles. He went to the fountain for a drink. He wished he could think of something he'd like to do.

He thought about how he had licked Weary Reilley and become such a big cheese around Indiana, and well, he had turned out to be a different kind of a big cheese now. He walked down to Cannon's confectionery store near State and bought an ice cream cone. He licked the ice cream with his tongue so that it would last longer. When he returned to the playground, Red Kelly, Davey Cohen and Paulie were there. Guys had always wondered what sort of a showing Studs would make in a scrap with the lads from Fifty-eighth and Prairie, but none of them had ever bothered Studs. As he walked across the playground toward them, he suddenly wondered if any of them, if Red, would start something now. He saw Davey Cohen talking to Red, and pointing to him. When he got up to them, Red asked him if he thought he was tough. He asked Red why. Red said he just wanted to know if Studs thought he was tough, because if he was, well, he, Red Kelly, would knock a little of it out of him. He and Red looked at each other. Red spat. Studs spat. Davey said put a stick on Studs' shoulder. Davey picked up a stick, and handed it to Paulie. After hesitating, Paulie placed it on Studs' shoulder. Red glowered at Studs. Studs made faces back. Red spat from the corner of his mouth. Red knocked the stick off and said that he didn't even bury his dead; he let them lie. They fought. Studs gave Red a bloody nose, and Red showed a yellow streak and quit; he walked off and said he'd square matters later. Davey and Paulie sidled around Studs. They asked him why he never hung out with their gang.

"We have a swell time all the time, better than the St. Patrick's guys from Indiana," Paulie said.

"Hell, they're all mopes," Studs said.

"Yeh, well, then come on around with us," Davey said.

Studs said that he would.

Some young punks, Joe Coady and Denny Dennis, came around. Joe got the ball and bat from the instructor's office, and they played move-up piggy.

Studs batted. Paulie pitched. He served one up to Studs. Studs leaned on it, and it went out to center field on the fly. Davey caught it.

Paulie batted, and Coady pitched. Studs went out to right field.

Coady twirled the ball.

Paulie didn't hit it.

"Come on and pitch 'em right," said Paulie.

"I'm pitchin' right. What's a matter?" asked Coady.

"Pitch 'em and cut it out," Paulie said.

Studs told them to play and quit dynamitin'.

"Hey! Hey! Can the goofin'," he added.

Coady twirled the ball, and Paulie sizzled one along the ground.

"Goddamn you! Pitch right!" Paulie snarled.

"I'm pitchin' it all right. Can't you hit it?" answered Coady.

"You ain't. Come on, you Goddamn punk, or I'll fling the bat at you!" Paulie said.

"You better not. He's Tommy Doyle's cousin," young Dennis said.

"All right, punk. No one asked you tuh put your two cents in," Paulie said to Dennis.

"Hey, can it!" Studs said.

Coady made an elaborate pitching gesture, and underhanded a floater straight over the pan. Paulie let it go by.

"Damn you, pitch right," Paulie said.

Studs walked in and out. He picked up stones, and threw them aimlessly.

"I'm pitchin' all right. Why don't you hit it?" asked Coady.

"You lousy punk, pitch right!" Paulie said.

Coady twirled the next pitch, and Paulie lashed, hitting a mean, twisting foul by first base. Coady ran after it, and got his hands on the ball but muffed it.

"Come on, Joe! Let 'im hit it," Davey yelled.

"Pitch it right, you little bitch," said Paulie.

Coady did, an easy floater, and Paulie popped a fly to Denny. He threw the bat at Coady, but Joe dodged and laughed. He moved toward him. Coady ran, Paulie wriggling his tomato after Joe. Joe was too swift for Haggerty.

"If I catch you, I'll bust your neck," yelled Paulie.

"Hey, cut it out," Studs yelled.

"Aw, come on, you guys," pleaded Denny.

Paulie kept shagging Coady. Joe would slow down until Paulie got near him, then he would dodge, twist and dart off, laughing at Paulie. Joe had won medals in grammar school track meets, and he was fast. He had Paulie puffing like a balloon, and Haggerty had to give it up. Joe laughed at him.

Studs got sore and threw pebbles at both of them. Paulie lined rocks at Joe.

Studs asked Paulie if he wanted to keep on playing.

"Yeh, but I'd like to kill the lousy punk and bust his freckled neck," said Paulie.

He shook his fist at Joe.

"Can't you hit? . . . You couldn't hit the flat side of a barn . . . you couldn't hit one if it had crutches on it," Joe yelled.

"Lemme get my hands on you, and I'll hit all right," Paulie said.

"Come on, Paulie, can it! You'll get another bat," said Davey.

Paulie took his place out in center field. Denny pitched. Coady batted. He hit the first one on a line past third. No one was near it. Davey shagged after the ball.

Denny pitched again.

Coady did not swing.

"Come on! Hit it!" yelled Paulie.

"I will," said Joe.

Denny pitched.

Joe smacked another one over third.

He hit another one over third.

They all got sore and yelled at him.

Studs went over and leaned against the ladders in foul territory.

Coady lined one to right field. Studs would have had it, if he had been in position. He got sore and cursed, running after the ball.

Coady kept on placing his hits, chopping them, hitting down and lining out grounders, cutting them over third, drawing them in back of first base.

"What the hell you think you're doin'?" raged Paulie.

"I'm batting, ain't I?"

"What you think you are?" asked Studs.

Joe accidentally hit one on first bounce to Denny, and his turn would have been up, but Denny fumbled.

"Christ sake! You're all thumbs," said Paulie.

"Come on, you punks," said Studs.

Coady placed one over Davey's head in deep short. The ball rolled way out in left field. Davey watched it roll. So did Paulie. They looked at each other.

"You're the outfield," said Davey.

"I'm centerfield," Paulie said.

"I'm playin' infield," Davey said.

"I'm not gonna get it. It wasn't my field," Paulie said.

"Well, I'm not neither," Davey said.

Paulie sat down.

Davey sat down.

Studs went over and leaned against the slide bars.

"You get it, Denny," Davey said.

"I don't have to get it. It ain't my ball. I was pitchin'," Denny said defensively.

"One of you guys gotta get it," Studs said.

"It ain't mine," Paulie said.

"It ain't mine," Davey said.

"Come on and quit dynamitin'," Studs said.

"I ain't dynamitin'," said Davey.

"Commere, Denny," Studs said.

"No, I won't. I'm pitchin'. I don't have to get it," yelped Denny.

"Come on, you guys. I want my bats," Coady said.

"Hell, you got 'em," Paulie said.

"I want mine, too," Denny said.

"Well, you get the pill then," Paulie said.

"Come on and give me my bats," Coady said.

Paulie threw some stones around.

"Commere, Denny," Studs said.

Denny reluctantly went over to Studs.

"Go and get the ball, and we'll get you your bats," said Studs.

"No, I don't have to," said Denny.

"Go ahead! I'll do you a favor some time," said Studs.

"Heck! Why should I? I didn't hit it or miss it. I was pitchin'. If it was my position, I would, but it wasn't," said Denny.

"Go on, get it," persuaded Studs.

"I won't."

Studs grabbed Denny, and twisted his arm back in a hammer lock.

"Ouch! UUUUU! Damn you! You big bully! Let me go! I'll get my brother after you, and he'll kill you for this. Let me go! Ouch! UUUUUU!"

"Well, will you get the ball?"

"Owwww! Let me go, you bully! Let me alone!"

"Now will you get it?"

"Make 'im get it," said Davey.

Studs twisted again. Denny yelled. He promised he would get the ball. Studs relaxed his hold. Denny started walking away. He bawled. He called Studs a big bully. Suddenly, he turned and thumbed his nose at Studs.

"You bastard," he yelled.

Studs shagged him, and Davey and Paulie took up the chase. Denny was caught. Studs twisted his arm again. He called Studs a big bully. Davey suggested taking his pants off. Paulie ripped his buttons open.

"Let me go, you bullies. Let me alone! I didn't do nothin' to you. I didn't bother you. Pick on someone your own size. I'll tell my brother. He'll kick the crap out of you," yelled Denny, frantically.

Studs twisted his arm again.

Denny shrieked that they were sbs.

Studs twisted. Paulie slapped Denny's face. Denny bawled, large tears rolling down his dirty face. Paulie goosed him. Denny squirmed, and yelled.

"Take it all back," demanded Studs.

"No."

Studs twisted.

An agonized yes.

Studs loosed his hold.

Paulie snatched Denny's cap.

Denny begged for it.

They laughed at him. They threatened to hang his pants on the picket fence. Denny cried for his cap.

Paulie handed the cap to Studs. Denny ran toward Studs. Studs tossed it to Davey. Denny ran toward Davey. Davey passed it to Paulie. Denny picked up some boulders and moved toward Paulie. Paulie told the punk to drop the rocks while he knew he was well off. He passed the hat to Studs.

Studs wrapped some stones in it. He said to Denny: "Here it is!"

When Denny came to Studs, Studs threw the cap on the roof of Carter school.

Denny bawled, and yelled that his brother would get the whole bunch of them, and he got a kick in the slats for his mouthiness.

Studs, Paulie and Davey left the playground.

"You'll get it like that," Paulie yelled to Joe.

"Got to catch me first."

"Let's get him," said Davey.

"Hell, we'd never catch him," said Studs.

"We hadn't better. He's Tommy Doyle's cousin," said Davey.

"Listen, Studs, you ought to hang around with us guys at Fifty-eighth and Prairie. You'll have more fun," said Paulie.

Studs said he might. They told him how swell a scrapper he was.

"You're as good as anyone on Fifty-eighth. You're as good as Tommy Doyle," said Davey.

Studs felt pretty good again. He felt powerful. Life was still opening up for him, as he'd expected it to, and it was still going to be a great summer. And it was a better day than he imagined. A sun was busting the sky open, like Studs Lonigan busted guys in the puss. It was a good day.

They walked on down toward the Fifty-eighth Street corner. Davey sniped a butt and lit it. Paulie jawed a hunk off his plug of tobacco. He offered some to Studs but Studs didn't take it; chewing tobacco made him sick. Paulie's pan was stuffed with tobacco. They walked along, all feeling pretty good.

Studs heard his mother calling him, and they hurried around the corner as if he didn't hear her.

"What'll we do?" asked Davey.

"What'll we do?" asked Paulie.

"Let's do something," said Studs.

"Let's," said Davey.

They walked along. Studs took drag on Davey's butt. Paulie

got between them, putting an arm around each of their shoulders. They were a picture, walking along, Paulie with his fat hips, Davey with his bow legs, and small, broad Studs.

"We'll find something to do," said Davey.

"Sure," said Paulie.

They walked along, looking for something to do.

SECTION THREE

CHAPTER SIX

I

Studs Lonigan, looking tough, sat on the fireplug before the drug store on the northeast corner of Fifty-eighth and Prairie. Since cleaning up Red Kelly, he, along with Tommy Doyle, had become a leading member of the Fifty-eighth Street bunch. Studs and Tommy were figured a good draw. Studs sat. His jaw was swollen with tobacco. The tobacco tasted bitter, and he didn't like it, but he sat, squirting juice from the corner of his mouth, rolling the chewed wad from jaw to jaw. His cap was pulled over his right eye in hard-boiled fashion. He had a piece of cardboard in the back of his cap to make it square, just like all the tough Irish from Wentworth Avenue, and he had a bushy Regan haircut. He sat. He had a competition with himself in tobacco juice spitting to determine whether he could do better plopping it from the right or the left side of his mouth. The right-hand side was Studs; the left-hand side was a series of rivals, challenging him for the championship. The contests were important ones, like heavyweight championship fights, and they put Studs Lonigan in the public eye, like Jess Willard and Freddy Welsh. Seriously, cautiously, concernedly, he let the brown juice fly, first from the left, then from the right side of his mouth. Now and then the juice slobbered down his chin, and that made Studs feel as goofy as if he was a young punk with falling socks.

People paraded to and fro along Fifty-eighth, and many turned on and off of Prairie Avenue. It was a typically warm summer day. Studs vaguely saw the people pass, and he was, in a distant way, aware of them as his audience. They saw him, looked at him, envied and admired him, noticed him, and thought that he must be a pretty tough young guy. The ugliest guy in the world passed. He was all out of joint. His face was colorless, and the jaws were sunken. He had the most

Jewish nose in the world, and his lips were like a baboon's.
He was round-shouldered, bow-legged and knock-kneed. His
hands were too long, and as he walked he looked like a pa-
rabola from the side, and from the front like an approaching
series of cubistic planes. And he wore colored glasses. Studs
looked at him, laughed, even half-admired a guy who could
be so twisted, and wondered who old plug-ugly was, and what
he did. Then Leon ta-taed along, pausing to ask Studs' about
taking music lessons. He put his hands on Studs' shoulders,
and Studs felt uncomfortable, as if maybe Leon had horse
apples in his hands. Leon wanted Studs to take a walk, but
Studs said he couldn't because he was waiting for some guys
to come along. Leon shook himself along, and Studs felt
as if he needed a bath. Old Fox-in-the-Bush, the priest or
minister or whatever he was of the Greek Catholic Church
across from St. Patrick's, walked by, carrying a cane. Studs
told himself the guy was funny all right; he was Gilly's bosom
friend. Studs laughed, because it must be funny, even to
Gilly, listening to a guy talk through whiskers like that. Mrs.
O'Brien came down the street, loaded with groceries, and Studs
snapped his head around, like he was dodging something,
and became interested in the sky, so that she wouldn't see
him, not only because he was chewing, but also because if
he saw her, he'd have to ask her if he could carry her groceries
home for her. Hell, he was no errand boy, or a do-a-good-
deed-a-day boy scout. And there was old Abraham Isidorivitch,
or whatever his name was, the batty old half-blind Jew who
was eighty, or ninety or maybe one hundred and thirty years
old, and who was always talking loud on the corners. Abraham,
or whatever his name was, did repair work for Davey Cohen's
old man sometimes, and the two of them must be a circus when
they're together. Mothers passed with their babies, some of
them brats that squawled all over the place. Helen Borax, with
her nose in the air, like she was trying to avoid an ugly smell.
Mrs. Dennis P. Gorman, with a young kid carrying a package
of her groceries that was too heavy for him. Studs got the
gob of tobacco out just in the nick of time. She stopped and
asked him how his dear mother was. She said he should be
sure and tell her and his father to telephone them sometimes,
and to come over for tea. And she asked him how he was
enjoying the summer. Dorothy was just doing fine. She was
very busy with her music, and she was going to summer school
at Englewood, because she wanted to do the four years high
school in three. And she said that Mr. Robinson, head master
of the troop of boy scouts in the neighborhood, had been over
to her house the other evening, and he talked about getting

more boys in his organization, because that kept them out of mischief. The boy scouts, she explained, were an excellent organization, which made gentlemen out of boys, gave them opportunities for clean, organized fun and sport, and they taught boys to do all sorts of kind deeds like helping blind ladies across the street. The little boy helping her with groceries was a boy scout, and his good deed every day was to carry her groceries home; and he wouldn't take a penny for it. And her husband said that the boy scouts gave boys preliminary military training and discipline so that it would be easier for them later on in the army, if they were called to defend their country, as they might have to do with that old Kaiser trying to conquer the world. She expected to see Studs and all the other boys on Indiana Avenue join the boy scouts. She started to move on, and said in parting:

"Now, do tell your dear mother and your father to come and see us, and now don't you forget to, like little boys often do."

The boy scout struggled after her with the bundle that was too heavy for him. Studs watched them, and thought unprintable things about old lady Gorman.

He stacked some more tobacco in his mug. He sat there. He put on a show to please himself, and imagined that everybody noticed him. He tired of his tobacco juice spitting contest, and quit. He watched snot-nosed Phil Rolfe, the twelve-year-old little pest, tear after a motor truck heading north. The runt got his hitch, even though Studs yelled after him to confuse him, and wished that he'd break his kike neck. Old Man Cohen, dirty, bearded, paused and accusingly asked Studs if he had seen Davey. Studs said no. Studs felt sorry for Davey, with an old man like that. He sat there.

Nate shuffled by, and, seeing Studs, came over. Nate was a toothless, graying little man, with an insane stare in his smallish black eyes. He wore a faded and unpressed green suit that had cobwebs on it and a thick, winter cap of the kind that teamsters wore.

"What's on your mind, Nate?" Studs asked, using the same tone and manner that the older guys around Bathcellar's pool room used with him.

Nate said he was getting some new French post cards, and told Studs that he'd sell them for a dime apiece. They were *some* pictures. Oh, boy! They showed everything. Studs said that he'd take a dozen or two when Nate brought them around. Nate tried to collect in advance, but Studs was no soap for that. Nate started to shuffle away and Studs asked him where the fire was.

"Work, my boy! I was jus' tellin' myself about the chicken I made lay eggs today. I was deliverin' some groceries over on South Park Avenoo, and this chicken was the maid. See! Well! Well, I delivers my groceries, and she says the missus ain't in, and she looks at me, you know the way a chicken looks at a guy!"

Nate winked, leered and poked Studs in the ribs expressively. He continued:

"She says I should leave the groceries, and you know that ain't good business, so I calls Ole Man Hirschfield, but he says it's O.K. So I leaves the groceries. She tanks me, and she says she has jus' made a cup of tea, an' I should siddown and have one wid her. She was a looker, so I takes the tea wid her, and we gets to barbering about one ting an' anoder, about one ting and anoder . . ."

Nate paused to wipe the slobber off his whiskery chin.

"We gasses about one ting an' anoder, and soon she ups and walks by me to go to the sink, so I pinches her, and it was de nicest I ever pinched, an', my boy, I pinched many in my day, because I'm old enough to be yer grandaddy. Well, first ting you know . . ."

Nate leered.

"The first ting you know . . . why . . . I schlipt her a little luck."

"Yeh?"

Nate poked Studs confidentially, leered, and said:

"Yeh, I schlipt her a little luck."

"Yeh?"

"Yeh!"

Nate turned to gape at a passing chicken, and Studs goosed him. Nate jumped.

He shuffled away, furious, telling himself about the damn brats who got too wise before their diapers were changed.

Studs laughed.

He took out another chew, and resumed his competition. The right-hand side of his mouth won easily. He thought of Lucy, who was probably still sore at him. The old feeling for Lucy flowed through him, warm. She seemed to him like a . . . like a saint or a beautiful queen, or a goddess. But the tough outside part of Studs told the tender inside part of him that nobody really knew, that he had better forget all that bull. He tried to, and it wasn't very easy. He let fly a juicy gob that landed square on a line, three cracks from him. Perfect! He saw Lucy, and acted very busy with his tobacco juice squirting. He let fly another gob that was a perfect hit. She laughed aloud at him, and said:

"Think you're funny, Mr. Smarty!"

Studs let fly another gob. She laughed again, and walked on. Studs sat, not looking nor feeling so much like a tough guy. He didn't turn and see Lucy twist around to glance at him. He threw his wad away. He sat, heedless of the noisy street. A dago peddler parked his fruit wagon in back of Studs and he was there calling his wares for some time before Studs laughed, like he laughed at all batty foreigners. He thought of Lucy. Lucy . . . she could go plum to . . . LUCY! He shoved another thumb of tobacco in his puss, but didn't chew it with the same concentration. He almost swallowed the damn stuff. Mr. Dennis P. Gorman passed, after his trying day at the police court. Studs coughed from the bad taste in his mouth.

Kenny Kilarney appeared, and Studs smiled to see him. Kenny was thin, taller than Studs, Irish, blue-eyed, dizzy-faced, untidy, darkish, quick, and he had a nervous, original walk.

"Hi!" said Studs.

"Hi!" said Kenny, raising his palms, hands outward.

"Hi!" said Studs.

"Hi!" said Kenny; he salaamed in oriental fashion.

"Hi!" laughed Studs.

"Hi!" said Kenny.

"Hi!" said Studs. "Jesus Christ!" said Studs.

"Hi, Low, Jack, and the Game," said goofy Kenny.

They laughed and stuffed chews in their faces. Studs marveled at Kenny's skill in chewing. Juice rolled down his own chin, and he had to spit the tobacco out again.

Kenny gave a rambling talk. Studs didn't listen, and only heard the end, when Kenny said:

"And I said I'm from Tirty-turd and de tracks, see, an' I lives on de top floor ob de las' house on de left-hand side of de street, and deres a skull an' crossbones on de chimney, and blood on de door, and my back yard's de graveyard for my dead."

Studs laughed, because you had to laugh when Kenny pulled his gags. Kenny was a funny guy. He ought to be in vaudeville, even if he was still young.

"Well, Lonigan, you old so-and-so, what's happening?"

"It's dead as a doornail, you old sonofabitch," Studs said.

Kenny looked at Studs; he told him not to say that; he cried:

"Take that back!"

"What's eatin' you?"

"Nothin'. But I don't care if you're kiddin' or not. I love my mother, and she's the only friend I got, and if I was hung tomorrow, she'd still be my mother, and be at my side forgivin' me, and I can't stand and let anybody call her names, even if it's kiddin'; and I don't care if you are Studs Lonigan and can fight, you can't say anything about my mother," Kenny said. He drew back a step, wiped the tears from his face with his shirt sleeve, and picked up a wooden slab that lay on the sidewalk.

Studs looked questioningly at Kenny, who stood there nervously clenching and unclenching his free fist, determined, his face ready to break into tears at any moment.

"Hell, Kenny! I was only kiddin'. I take it all back," said Studs.

They faced each other, and in a minute or two the incident was forgotten. Kenny became his old self.

"It's too hot, or we could go raidin' ice boxes. But I don't feel like much effort today," Kenny said.

"Let's go swimmin'," suggested Studs.

"O.K.," said Kenny.

"All right. I'll get my suit and meet you here in twenty minutes," said Studs.

"But I'll have to get a suit. I ain't got none," said Kenny.

"Whose will you borrow?" asked Studs.

Kenny winked.

"What beach'll we go to?" asked Studs.

"Fifty-first Street," said Kenny.

"Ain't there a lot of Jews there?" asked Studs.

"Where ain't there kikes? They're all over. You watch. First it's the hebes, and then it's the niggers that's gonna overrun the south side," Kenny said.

"And then where ull a white man go to?" asked Studs.

"He'll have to go to Africa or . . . Jew-rusalem," said Kenny.

Kenny sang Solomon Levi with all the sheeny motions, and it was funny, because Kenny was funny, all right, and could always make a guy laugh.

Afterwards Studs said:

"If we go to Jackson Park, it might be better."

"There's Polacks there," said Kilarney.

"Well, how about Seventy-fifth Street beach?" asked Studs.

"It's O.K. But listen, sometimes Iris is at Fifty-first."

"That's a different story. I got to meet this here Iris," said Studs.

"Yeh," said Kenny.

"I hope she's there."

"She's sweet. Boy, she's just UMMMMMMMMMMMMM-MMMMM," said Kenny.

"Is she really good?" asked Studs.

"Best I ever had," said Kenny like he was an older guy with much experience.

"Well, I'm going to be a disappointed guy if she ain't," said Studs.

"But listen! Don't work so fast. Suppose she don't give you a tumble. Sometimes she gets temperment, and then she's no soap until some guy she gets a grudge against beats it . . . She's like a primadonna," said Kenny.

"I thought she was like a sweetheart of the navy," Studs said.

"Well, sometimes she is and sometimes she isn't."

"Yeah. But anyway, you just lead me to her," boasted Studs.

"Well, at that, you're talkin' horse sense," said Kenny.

"Horsey sense," said Studs.

"Well, anyway, I got to get my suit," said Kenny.

Kenny told Studs to walk down Fifty-eighth toward Indiana.

"And when I come tearin' along, you run, too, and cut through the lot on Indiana, and down the alley, and through that trick gangway to Michigan," he added.

Studs did. In a moment, Kenny came running along, and they carried out their plan of escaping, though no one was chasing them. On Michigan, Kenny pulled out the two-piece bathing suit he had copped; the trunks were blue, the top white.

"If it only fits now," he said.

They laughed together, and Studs said that Kenny had real style. Kenny laughed, and said it was nothing to cop things from drug stores. Studs told himself that Kilarney was a guy, all right.

They put their suits on under their clothes at Studs'. The suit fitted Kenny. They went over to South Park and bummed rides to Fifty-first, and did the same thing along Fifty-first and Hyde Park Boulevard. They had fun on Hyde Park Boulevard. It was a ritzy neighborhood where everybody had the kale and all the men wore knickers and played tennis and golf, and all the guys were sissies. Kenny had chalked his K.K. initials all over the Fifty-eighth Street neighborhood, so he started putting mysterious K.K. signs on the Boulevard. And he kept walking on the grass, making fun of the footmen and wriggling his ears at the well-dressed women. They saw one hot dame, in clothes that must have cost a million bucks, and Kenny commented on the large breastworks she had. He spoke too loud, and she heard him. She went up in the air like a kite, and talked very indignantly about ragamuffins from the slums. When they got out of her hearing, they laughed.

The lake was very calm, and way out it was as blue as

the sky on a swell summer evening. And the sun came down over it like a blessing. And they were tanned, so they didn't have to worry about getting sunburned and blistered. They ran out from the lockers with feelings of animal glee. The first touch of the water was cold, and they experienced sharp sensations. But they dove under water, and then it was warm. The lake was just right. They went out, splashing, diving under water, trying to duck each other, laughing and shouting. The diving board was crowded but they climbed up and took some dives. Kenny did all kinds of dippy dives, back flaps and rolls. The people about the diving board watched them and thought Kenny was pretty good. He started a stump-the-leader game on the board but he was too good for them, so they all lost interest.

Kenny and Studs swam out where it was cold and deep, and there was no one around them. They dove, splashed, floated, splashed, swam, snorted. They were like happy seals. Studs got off by himself and wheeled and turned over in the water like a rolling barrel. He called over to Kenny that it was the nuts. Kenny yelled back that boy it was jake. They swam breast-stroke, and it was nice and easy; then they did the crawl. They went out further. Only the lake was ahead of them, vast and blue-gray and nice with the sun on it; and it gave them feelings they couldn't describe. Studs floated, and looked up at the round sky, his head resting easy on the water line, himself just drifting, the sun firing away at his legs. It was too nice for anything. He just floated and didn't have anything to think about. He looked up at the drifting clouds. He felt just like a cloud that didn't have any bothers and just sailed across the sky. He told himself: Gee, it was a big sky. He asked himself: I wonder why God made the sky? He floated. He floated, and suddenly he liked himself a lot. Sometimes he was ashamed of his body, like when the old man came in to use the bathroom when he was taking a bath and didn't have anything on, or like on the night he graduated, when he was in bed and had a time trying to sleep. Now he liked his body, and wasn't at all ashamed of it. It moved through the water like a slow ship that just went along and didn't have any place in particular to go and just sailed. About ten yards away he heard Kenny wahooing and singing about Captain Decker who sailed on the bounding main, and lost his . . . and Kenny seemed almost as far away as if he was on the other side of the lake. He splashed with his hands. Then he held his toes up and tried to wiggle them, but he got a mouthful. He turned and swam a little way, taking in a mouthful of water and holding it. He turned over and

floated, spouting the water, pretending he was the most powerful whale in the seas and oceans, floating along, minding its
business, because all the sharks were leery of attacking it.
He had a sudden fear that he might get cramps and drown, and
he was afraid of drowning and dying, so he turned over and
swam. But he wasn't afraid for long. Then he and Kenny
tried to see who could stay under water the longest, and they
waved in to attract attention, so people on the diving board
might think they were drowning and get all excited. He
dove down, imagining he was a submarine, and the water
kept getting cooler, and he kept his eyes open but could only
see the water, clear, all around him. He felt far away from
all the world now, and he didn't care. He came up, choking
for air, and it was like coming to out of a goofy dream where
you are falling or dying or something. Kenny was up before
him, and Studs, after he had gotten a good breath, told Kenny
he wasn't so good.

"Drowning ain't my specialty. That's not my trick!" Kenny
yelled back.

They swam slowly in.

When they got on the beach, they gazed about and ran all
around, looking for Iris and eyeing all the women to get some
good squints. Kenny said it would be swell, like heaven, if
all women wore the same kinds of swimming suits that An-
nette Kellerman did. Studs said it would be better if they
didn't wear anything. Kenny said women sometimes did go
swimming without anything on. Studs said he'd give his ear
to see them.

Finally, they sprawled face downward in the sand, the sun
fine and warm on their backs, evaporating all the wet. They
didn't talk. They just sprawled there. It was too good to talk.
Studs forgot everything, and felt almost as good as when he
had been by himself way out in the deep water. He just lay
there and pretended that he wasn't Studs or anybody at all
and he let his thoughts take care of themselves. He was far
away from himself, and the slap of the waves on the shore,
the splash of people in the water, all the noise and shouts of
the beach were not in the same world with him. They were
like echoes in the night coming from a long way off. He
was snapped out of it by Kenny cursing the goddamn flies
and the kids who ran scuffing sand all over everybody. Studs
looked up. Then he looked out over the lake where the water
and sky seemed to meet and become just nothing. He thought
of swimming far, far out, farther than he and Kenny had,
swimming out into the nothingness, and just floating, floating
with nothing there, and no noises, no fights, no old men, no

girls, no thinking of Lucy, no nothing but floating, floating.
Kenny broke off his thoughts. He talked about swimming
across the lake, arguing that a good life guard could swim
all the way to Michigan City or Benton Harbor. Studs said
that Kenny was nuts, but then he couldn't talk as fast
as Kilarney, so he lost the argument. Kenny just talked
anyway, and it didn't matter what he talked about or make
him less funny.

At six they went home, and moving along Hyde Park
Boulevard, trying to bum rides and cursing everybody who
passed them by, Kenny said:

"It was swell today."

"Yeh! It was swell," Studs said.

"Only I wish Iris had been there," said Kenny.

"Yeh," said Studs.

"I'm so hungry, I could eat a horse," said Kenny.

"Wouldn't it have been nice to have had her there and have
had let us lay our heads in her lap, and have a feel-day, or
go out with her way out, or swim around to the breakwater,
where nobody was, and out there get our ashes hauled,"
said Studs.

"Almost as nice as eating a steak would be this very minute,"
said Kenny.

"Sure," said Studs.

They walked on. When Studs had been lying in the sand,
he had been at peace, almost like some happy guy in a story,
and he hadn't thought that way about girls, and it hadn't bothered him like it did other times, or made him do things he
was ashamed of way deep down inside himself. Now his peace
was all gone like a scrap of burned-up paper. He was nervous
again, and girls kept coming into his mind, bothering all
hell out of him. And that made him feel queer, and he got
ashamed of the thoughts he had . . . because of Lucy. And
he couldn't think of anything else.

At home they had steak, and Studs, like a healthy boy,
forgot everything but the steak put before him.

II

The July night leaked heat all over Fifty-eighth Street,
and the fitful death of the sun shed softening colors that
spread gauze-like and glamorous over the street, stilling those
harshnesses and commercial uglinesses that were emphasized
by the brighter revelations of day. About the street there seemed
to be a supervening beauty of reflected life. The dust, the scraps
of paper, the piled-up store windows, the first electric lights
sizzling into brightness, Sammie Schmaltz, the paper man,

yelling his final box-score editions, a boy's broken hoop left forgotten against the elevated girder, the people hurrying out of the elevated station and others walking lazily about, all bespoke the life of a community, the tang and sorrow and joy of a people that lived, worked, suffered, procreated, aspired, filled out their little days, and died.

And the flower of this community, its young men, were grouped about the pool room, choking the few squares of sidewalk outside it. The pool room was two doors east of the elevated station, which was midway between Calumet and Prairie Avenues. It had barber poles in front, and its windows bore the scratched legend, Bathcellar's Billiard Parlor and Barber Shop. The entrance was a narrow slit, filled with the forms of young men, while from inside came the click of billiard balls and the talk of other young men.

Old toothless Nate shuffled along home from his day's work.

"Hello, Nate!" said Swan, the slicker, who wore a tout's gray checked suit with narrow-cuffed trousers, a pink silk shirt with soft collar, and a loud purplish tie; his bright-banded straw hat was rakishly angled on his blond head.

"Hello, Moneybags!" said Jew Percentage, a middle-aged, vaguely corpulent, brown-suited, purple-shirted guy with a cigar stuck in his tan, prosperous-looking mug.

"Hello, Nate! How's the answer to a K. M.'s prayer on this fine evenin'?" asked Pat Coady, a young guy dressed like a race-track follower.

"How're the house maids?" asked young Studs Lonigan, who stood with the big guys, proud of knowing them, ashamed of his size, age and short breeches.

The older guys all laughed at Young Lonigan's wisecrack. Slew Weber, the blond guy with the size-eleven shoes, looked up from his newspaper and asked Nate if he was still on the trail of the house maids.

Nate had been holding a dialogue with himself. He interrupted it to tell them that he was getting his.

Slew Weber went back to his newspaper. He said:

"Say, I see there's six suicides in the paper tonight."

"Jesus, I knew it," said Swan.

"This guy Weber is a guy, all right. All he needs to do is smell a paper, and he can tell you how many birds has croaked themselves. He's got an eagle eye fur suicides," said Pat Coady.

Nate started to talk; he said:

"Say, goddamnit, I'm tired. I'm gonna quit this goddamn wurk. Jesus Christ! the things people wancha tuh do. Now, today I was hikin' an order, and some old bitch without a stitch on . . . "

"Naughty! Naughty! Naughty Nate!" interrupted Percentage, crossing his fingers in a child's gesture of shame.

"She was without a stitch on, and she wants me to go an get her a pack of cigarettes, an I looks at her, and I said, I said . . . but Jesus, it was funny, because I coulda killed her with the look I gave her; but I said, I said, Lady I'm workin' since seven this mornin', and I still gotta store full of orders to deliver. Now Lady how do you expect me ever to get finished, and Lady if I go runnin' for Turkish Trophies for everyone that wants 'em . . . Well, sir! Ha! Ha! She shuts up like a clam. And then I always gotta deal with these nigger maids dat keep yellin' for you tuh wipe your feet. I say, give uh nigger an inch, and dey wants a hull mile. And my rheumatism is botherin' me again. But say you oughta see the chicken I got today . . ."

Saliva and browned tobacco juice trickled down Nate's chin.

"Well, Nate, the first hundred years is the hardest," said Percentage.

"Yeh, Nate, it's a tough life if you don't weaken," said Swan.

"Say, Nate, did you ever buy a tin lizzie?" said Studs, trying to be funny like the older guys.

"Think yuh'll ever amount to much, Nate?" asked Pat Coady.

"Say, listen, when you guys is as old as me you'll be in the ground," said Nate.

"Say, I'll bet Nate's got the first dollar he ever earned," said Slew.

"And a lot more," said Pat.

Nate told them never to mind; then he started to talk of the Swedish maid he had on the string. He poked Slew confidentially, and said that every Thursday afternoon, you know. Then he said he was getting in a new stock of French picture cards, and tried to collect in advance, but they told him to bring them around first.

A girl passed, and they told Nate there was something for him. Nate turned and gaped at her with a moron's excited eyes.

Percentage told Nate he had a swell new tobacco which he was going to let him try. Nate asked the name and price. Percentage said it was a secret he couldn't reveal, because it was not on the market yet, but he was going to give him a pipeful. He asked Nate for his pipe, and Nate handed him the corncob. Percentage held the pipe and started to thumb through his pockets. He winked to Swan, who poked the other guys. They crowded around Nate so he couldn't see, and got him interested in telling about all the chickens he made while he delivered groceries. Percentage slipped the pipe to Studs, and pointed to the street. Studs caught on, and quickly filled the pipe with dry manure. Percentage made a long funny spiel, and gave the pipe to Nate. The guys had a hell of a time not laughing, and nearly all of them pulled out handkerchiefs. Studs felt good, because he'd been let in on a practical joke they played on someone else; it sort of stamped him as an equal. Nate fumbled about, wasting six matches trying to light the pipe. He cursed. Percentage said it was swell tobacco, but a little difficult to light, and again their faces went a-chewing into their handkerchiefs. Nate said they must all have colds. Nate said that whenever he had a cold he took lemon and honey. Percentage said that once you got this tobacco going, it was a swell smoke, and all the colds got suddenly worse.

Nate shuffled on, trying to light his pipe and talking to himself.

Percentage took Studs through the barber shop and back into the pool room to wash his hands. Studs said hello, casually, to Frank, who always cut his hair; Frank was cutting the hair of some new guy in the neighborhood, who was reading the *Police Gazette* while Frank worked. The pool room was long and narrow; it was like a furnace, and its air was weighted with smoke. Three of the six tables were in use, and in the rear a group of lads sat around a card table, playing poker. The scene thrilled Studs, and he thought of the time he could come in and play pool and call Charley Bathcellar by his first name. He was elated as he washed his hands in the filthy lavatory.

He came out and saw that Barney was around. Barney was a bubble-bellied, dark-haired, middle-aged guy. He looked like a politician, or something similarly important.

"Say, Barney, you think you'll ever amount to much?" asked Barlowe.

"Sure, he's something already," said Swan.

"What?"

"He's a hoisting engineer," said Swan, who accompanied his statement with the appropriate drinking gesture.

"Yeh, he's a first-class hoistin' engineer," said Emmet Kelly, one of Red's brothers.

"He hoists down a barrel of beer a week, don't you, Barney?" said Mickey O'Callaghan.

They laughed. Studs told himself that, goddamn it, they were funny all right.

"You two-bit wiseacres can mind your own business," said Barney.

They all laughed.

"But, Barney, no foolin' . . . I want to ask you a question in all sincerity," said Percentage.

"Save the effort and don't get a brainstorm, hebe," said Barney.

"Why don't you go to work?" asked Percentage.

"Times are hard, jobs are scarce and good men is plentiful," said Barney.

They all laughed.

"Well, anyway, Barney, did you get yer beers last Sunday?" asked Weber.

"Listen, brother! Them Sunday blue laws don't mean nothin' to me," said Barney.

"Nope, I guess you'd get your beer even if the Suffragettes put Prohibition down our necks," said Pat Coady.

"Why, hell! I seen him over in Duffy's saloon last Sunday, soppin' up the beers like there was no law against buyin' drinks on Sunday. He was drinkin' so much, I thought he was gonna get his false teeth drowned in beer," Barlowe said, and they all laughed.

Studs noticed the people passing. Some of them were fat guys and they had the same sleepy look his old man always had when he went for a walk. . . . Those old dopey-looking guys must envy the gang here, young and free like they were. Old Izzy Hersch, the consumptive, went by. He looked yellow and almost like a ghost; he ran the delicatessen-bakery down next to Morty Ascher's tailor shop near the corner of Calumet, but nobody bought anything from him because he had the con, and anyway you were liable to get cockroaches or mice in anything you bought. Izzy looked like he was going to have a funeral in his honor any one of these days. Studs felt that Izzy must envy these guys. They were young and strong, and they were the real stuff; and it wouldn't be long before he'd be one of them and then he'd be the real stuff.

Suddenly he thought of death. He didn't know why. Death just came into his thoughts, dripping black night-gloom. Death put you in a black coffin, like it was going to put Izzy Hersch. It gave you to the grave-diggers, and they dumped you in the ground. They shoveled dirt on you, and it thudded, plunked, plump-plumped over you. It would be swell if people didn't have to die; if he, anyway, didn't have to; if he could grow up and be big and strong and tough and the real stuff, like

Barlowe was there, and never change. Well, anyway, he had
a long time to go.

People kept dribbling by and the guys stood there, barbering
in the funny way of theirs.

Lee came along, and the guys asked him why he was
getting around so late.

"Oh, my wife invited me to stay home for supper, just
for a change, and I thought I'd surprise her and accept the
invitation," Lee said.

"Hey, you guys! did you get that? Did you? Lee here said
his old woman asked him to come to supper, just to vary the
monotony a little, and he did. He actually . . . dined with
his old woman," Percentage said.

"Next thing you know he'll be going to work and supportin'
her," said Pat Coady.

"Jesus, that's a good one. Hey, Lee, tell me some more
. . . I got lots of Irish . . . credulity," said Barney.

They laughed.

"That's a better one," said Lee, pointing to a girl whom
everybody marveled at because they said she was built like
a brick out-house.

"She has legs, boy," said Studs, trying to horn back into
the conversation.

They didn't pay any attention to him.

"Well, I object!" said Percentage.

"Why?"

"I OBJECT!"

"Why?"

"Goddamnit, it ain't right! I tell you it ain't right that
stuff like that moll be wasted, with such good men and true
around here . . . I say that it is damn wanton extravagance," said Percentage.

"Hey, Percentage, you shoulda been a Philadelphia lawyer,
with them there words you use," said Barlowe.

The guys laughed, and Percentage said he saw the objection
was sustained.

Swan, Percentage and Coady had a kidding match about
who was the best man. It was interrupted by Barney. An
ugly-looking, old-maidish female passed, and Barney said to
the three kidders:

"That's your speed!"

They trained their guns on Barney, and told him how dried
up he was.

Another dame ambled by, and Percentage repeated his
objection, and they kidded each other.

A third dame went by, and Percentage again objected.

"Them's my sentiments," said Fitz, the corner pest.

A good-looking Negress passed.

"Barney, how'd you like that?" Studs asked.

"Never mind, punk! . . . And listen, the niggers ain't as bad as the Irish," said Barney.

"Where's there a difference?" asked Percentage.

"Well, if you ask me, Barney is a combination of eight ball, mick, and shonicker," said McArdle, one of the corner topers.

"And the Irish part is pig-Irish," said Studs.

"The kid's got your number," said Percentage as they all gave Barney some more merry ha-ha's.

Studs felt grown up, all right.

Barney called Studs a goofy young punk. But they all laughed at him. Studs laughed weakly, and hated bloated-belly Barney. He told himself he'd been a damn fool for not having put on his long pants before he came out.

They hung around and talked about the heat and the passing gals. It grew dark, and more lights flashed on. Andy Le Gare came along. He spoke to Studs, but Studs didn't answer him; Studs turned to Barlowe, and said the punk had wheels in his head. Barlowe said yeh; he remembered him in his diaper days down around Forty-seventh; but his brother George was a nice guy, and a scrapper. Studs again felt good, because Barlowe had talked to him like one equal to another. Andy stopped before Hirschfield's grocery store, and started erasing the chalked announcement. He rubbed out the lower part of the B on the brick butter announcement, and stood off to laugh in that idiotic way of his. The guys encouraged the punk. They talked about baseball. Swan spilled some gab about the races. Then he told of what he had seen at the Johnson-Willard and Willard-Moran fights. He said that Willard was a ham, and that Fred Fulton would mow him down if they ever got yellow Willard in the same ring with the Minnesotan. Studs said the Irishman Jim Coffey was pretty good. Swan said he was a cheese. He said the best of them all, better than Fulton even, was Gunboat Smith, who had the frog, Carpentier, licked that time in London or Paris or wherever they fought. They wondered what they would do, and talked about the heat. Barney suggested seeing the girlies, and they said O. K. Barlowe said he couldn't go. They asked why.

"I still got my dose," he said.

They told him it was tough, and he wanted to take care of it. Coady asked him if it was bad.

"It's started again," he said casually.

"Well, be careful," Coady said.

The other lads piled into a hack, and were off. Studs watched them go, wide-eyed with admiration and envy, and yet quite disappointed. Then he watched Barlowe limp down the street, a big husky guy. He thought of the time when he'd be able to pile into a hack and go with the lads. He thought of Barlowe. He was afraid of things like that, and yet he wished he could stand on the corner and say he had it. Well, it wouldn't be long now before he'd be the big-time stuff.

Davey Cohen, Tommy Doyle, Haggerty, Red Kelly and Kilarney happened along. Kilarney had a pepper cellar, and they went over to the park to look for Jews and throw pepper in their eyes. Over in the park, Studs saw a pretty nurse, and he started objecting that molls like that should walk around and not have guys taking care of them; it was a lot of good stuff gone to waste, he repeated, and the kids all laughed, because it was a good wisecrack.

III

Studs and Paulie walked south along Prairie Avenue, eating the last of the candy. The candy came from the famous raid on Schreiber's ice cream parlor. Schreiber's place was between Prairie and Indiana on Fifty-eighth. Schreiber was a good guy, but you know he liked his nooky, and he was always mixed up with some woman or other. They caught up with him. One day when Studs was walking down Fifty-eighth Street, he saw two dicks taking the guy away. The bunch found out, through Red Kelly, whose old man was a police sergeant, that Schreiber was in on a white slavery rap. Three-Star Hennessey discovered that the back door of the candy store wasn't locked, and all the kids in the neighborhood raided the place. For five days they were filling up on sodas, having fights with ice cream and whipped cream, carting away candy. They stole wagons from little kids, and bikes, and carted the stuff to George Kahler's basement. It was a swell feed they had. Most of them couldn't eat supper for a week. But with so many hogging it, the loot didn't last as long as it should have. Anyway, it was a time to remember for your grandchildren. They talked about it, and laughed.

"Well, it's August already," Paulie said.

"Yeh, Goddamn it!"

"I wonder what school I'll go to next year?" Paulie said.

"Can't you go back to St. Patrick's?" asked Studs.

"Jesus, I don't think so. And if I did get back, they probably wouldn't pass me anyway . . . Say, why in hell is school?" asked Paulie.

Studs shrugged his shoulders and cursed school.

"Say, why don't you bring your old lady up to see Bernadette," said Studs.

"Maybe I will. Hell, St. Patrick's gets more holidays and is out sooner in June than the public schools. Only I got bounced out of there three times already," said Paulie.

"Well, maybe you can break the record," said Studs.

"That's something," said Paulie.

They walked along. Paulie sniped a butt and lit it.

"Doesn't Iris live here?" said Studs, pointing at a red brick, three-story building.

"Yeh, and I'd like to bump into her," Paulie said.

"Me, too," said Studs.

Studs suddenly resented Paulie. Paulie couldn't fight as well as he but got more girls, and knew what it was all about.

Iris, fourteen, bobbed-haired, blue-eyed, innocent with a sunny smile, walked out of the building. She had a body too old for her years; the legs were nice and her breasts were already well-formed.

Iris was glad to see them. Paulie asked her how was tricks. She said what tricks. Paulie said just tricks. She said he was naughty-naughty. She flung lascivious looks at them, and Studs was thrilled as he had never been thrilled by Lucy. He shifted his weight from foot to foot, and studied the sky. Then he became absorbed in his shoes. They were high ones, scuffed and dirty, very much like army shoes. Paulie asked how about it. She said her mother was home. Paulie said they could go over to the park. She said no, because she had to help her old woman clean house. She cursed her mother, glibly. Hearing a girl call her mother names was different from hearing a guy, and it shocked Studs. Paulie asked how about it. She said some other afternoon. She told Studs she especially wanted him to come and see her some time, because she had never met him before and everybody said nice things about him. She looked at him in that way of hers, and said she'd be nice to him. Then she tripped toward Fifty-fifth Street, and they watched her wriggle along. They had a discussion about the way girls wriggled along. Studs said the one who had them all beat at wriggling was Helen Borax. Paulie said Iris was no slouch though. Studs wondered if girls wriggled on purpose, and how about decent ones. He told this to Paulie, and added that he hadn't ever noticed if his sister did or not. Paulie said all girls had to wriggle when they walked, and he guessed there was nothing wrong with it. He said that anything a girl did was o.k. with him, as long as she was good-looking.

They met Weary at Fifty-eighth Street. Weary had his long jeans on. He looked at Studs; Studs sort of glowered back. Paulie suggested that it was foolish not to shake hands and settle old scores. They shook.

Studs tried to be a little friendly. He asked:

"What you been doing?"

"Workin' in an office downtown," said Weary.

"Off today?" asked Paulie.

"I took the day off, and my old lady got sore and yelled at me. I had a big scrap with the family. The gaffer was home and he tried to pitch in, too, and my sister Fran, she got wise. They noticed that my hip pocket was bulgin' a little. And when I leaned down to pick somethin' up, they saw my twenty-two. They shot their gabs off till I got sick of listenin' to them, and I got sore and cursed them out. I told them just what they could do without mincing my words, and they all gaped at me like I was a circus. The ole lady jerked on the tears, and started blessing herself, and Fran got snotty, like she never heard the words before, and she bawled, and the old man said he'd bust my snoot, but he knew better than try it. So I tells them they could all take a fast and furious, flyin', leapin' jump at Sandy Claus, and I walks out, and I'll be damned if I go home. Maybe I might try stickin' somebody up," he said.

They were shocked, but they admired Weary tremendously. They acted casual and gave him some advice. He showed them his rusty twenty-two, and said he needed bullets. Paulie said it might be a little dangerous carrying a loaded gat around, but Weary didn't care. Studs wished that he could walk dramatically out of the house like Weary did; he told himself that he might some day. Paulie asked Weary what he'd been doing, and Weary said he had been hangin' out at White City; he'd picked up a couple of nice janes there. One of them was eighteen and didn't live at home, and wanted him to live with her. They looked at Weary. Weary was a real adventurous kid, after all was said and done, even if he was something of a bastard. Suddenly Weary left, walking toward Fifty-seventh. They watched him. He met a girl . . . it was Iris . . . and the two of them disappeared in her entrance way.

"Well, I say she's no good," Studs said.

"Well, I'll be damned," said Paulie, scratching his head.

They looked at each other, knowingly, expressing with their faces what even the lousiest words they could think of to call Iris couldn't express.

"Some day I'm gonna up and bust that jane right in her snoot," said Paulie.

"And a guy I licked . . . I ought to hang a couple more on him," Studs said.

"Yeh," said Paulie.

Studs wished to hell there were more swear words in the list so he could use them to curse the world.

IV

Studs had stayed in the bathroom too long, as he was staying most of these days. The old man bellowed that dinner was ready. Studs came out, feeling relieved. He muttered a hasty act of contrition, promising God and the Blessed Virgin that he would try his hardest not to break the sixth commandment by thought, word or deed.

Sunday dinner of roast beef and mashed potatoes was already on the table; the family was seated.

As Studs sat down, the old lady said that they ought to say grace once in a while, thanking God that they were well off and happy and so much better off than most families. The old man agreed, and he said patriarchally:

"Well, Martin, you say grace!"

"Grace!" said Martin.

They laughed. Then Loretta said grace. The two parents insisted that hereafter grace would be said before and after each meal.

"I say this: if you keep God in the home, active and real, you'll have a happier home and can get along better in all you do," the old man said oracularly.

"You say the truth," echoed Mrs. Lonigan.

The old man carved the meat. He spoke to Studs as he sliced. He asked Studs why he was late for dinner. He said Studs was always late for dinner. Everybody else got to the bathroom early enough, so that they could be at the table when dinner was announced. He said that he spent good money for food, and that Studs' mother slaved over a hot stove so that they could have a decent meal. He and the mother both had some right to demand gratitude and respect for this. Studs said that he didn't see nothing wrong in having stopped to wash his hands; and his father, starting into rag-chewing, put Studs in a mood of opposition, made him feel that he was in the right, made him believe that he had delayed only to wash his hands, and that his father was being inconsiderate and un-understanding. The old man said that there had been plenty of time before to wash his hands. Studs said that he didn't see why there was any kicking. He was at the table now, and nothing had happened by his stopping to wash his hands. The old man told him to suppose that the meat had gotten cold. But it didn't get cold, Studs said. Lonigan told him that it might have gotten cold. Frances said that she wished the Sunday quarreling could be stopped. She was tired of sitting down to a Sunday dinner and being forced to listen to this interminable ragging. Old Man Lonigan said that there wouldn't be no quarreling if everybody did what was right. He said that he was boss of the household, and that as long as he remained boss of the household there were certain rules that would be observed, and one was that everybody must be at the table on time. It got Studs sore. The old man was always pulling that stuff. Studs said that so far as he was concerned, he wouldn't eat Sunday dinner if there was going to be the same fighting all the time. Frances said that she agreed with Studs. Mrs. Lonigan said that the name was William. The old man said that they could take or leave the rules of the household. Martin asked for meat. Loretta said that the dinner would be cold if it wasn't served soon. She said that there was awful much talking. The old man told her to be more respectful because little children should honor their parents and be seen and not heard. Passing Martin's filled plate down, he assured them that he was a good father. He said he asked very little from them. Frances and Studs looked tiredly at each other, and didn't say anything. They awaited their plates, and then they concentrated on eating.

"This is fine, Mama," the old man said, jamming roast beef into his mouth.

"I like it," said Martin.

"Any more for anyone?" said the old man.

"Me," said Martin.

"You got hookworm," the old man said, taking Martin's plate.

Finally, the old boy said, smiling expansively:

"Well, I'm filled. I ate my share."

The others said they had had their fill.

Coffee and ice cream were served, and they talked lazily.

The mother changed the stream of conversation, and said:

"William, I wish that you wouldn't be staying out so late."

"Yeh, Bill, we told you about that once before," the old man said.

Bill told himself that he was almost fifteen, and that he ought to have some rights. But what the hell could a guy say to an old man like his? He wished he had an old man like Johnny O'Brien did.

"And, William, I know you don't like me to mention this, but you're still young yet, and can't decide. I do wish you would pray to ask God if you have a vocation or not, and next month start in and make the nine first Fridays. Now that is the least you can do for Almighty God who sacrificed His only begotten Son for you on the cross of Calvary."

"All right," Studs said, knowing the best thing to do with his parents was to agree with them and let it go at that. His mother harped so much on it that he thought maybe he did have a vocation. But he tried not to think of it, when he could do so, without putting the thought out of his head deliberately, because, well, there was . . . Lucy.

"Now, Mary, you know the boy hasn't a vocation. You're putting things in his head, and maybe you'll go and make a priest out of him when I'll be needing him, and then he is not meant for the priesthood, and you know, Mary, it is as bad to send one in that hasn't a vocation as it is to keep away one who really has the call. You know, Mary, there's many the unhappy priest who don't belong in the ranks and is there because his good mother unthinkingly made a priest out of him."

"Patrick, you know I'm not doing anything of the sort. I'm only trying to put the boy in the right spirit, so he can decide whether or not he has the call."

"But, Mary . . ."

It started them off again. This time Loretta interrupted the argument to say that she had seen Studs, she meant *William*, hitching on a motor truck. The old lady shuddered, blessed herself and called on Jesus, Mary and Joseph. The old man said it was dangerous, and that Bill ought to be careful and try and have his fun doing less dangerous things. It might seem brave to hitch on trucks, but it wouldn't if Bill came home with a broken leg. Studs glowered at Loretta, and told her she would do well by minding her own business. He was reprimanded for this. Then Loretta said that she had also seen him taking a puff of that terrible Tommy Doyle's cigarette over in Carter Playground the other day. The old lady cried, and spoke of the proverb: tell me your friends, and I'll tell you who you are. She said William was too well educated to associate with such toughs. She said that smoking was a sin against God. Studs asked why; he said that men smoked. The old man said that smoking stunted a boy's growth, ruined his health, disrupted his moral sense, and was against . . . nature. He lit a long stogy. Frances said smoking was nasty, and Studs said nobody asked her for her two cents. Mrs. Lonigan said that it might give him TB. Studs kept wishing they would can the sermon. He asked them to cut it out, and he was reminded of the commandment to honor thy father

and thy mother. He said he had some rights. The blah went
back and forth.

When they arose from the table, grace was forgotten.

The old man went into the parlor, and put Cal Stewart's
account of how Uncle Josh joined the Grangers on the Victrola.
He listened to it and laughed heartily. Then he made a decision,
and called Studs into the parlor alone.

"Bill, don't you think you ought to keep going to confession
regularly?" he said.

"Yeh."

"When's the last time you were there?"

"May," said Studs.

It was April, but he could get away with telling the old
man it was May.

"At St. Patrick's you had your sodality to remind you and
keep you going regular. Now, it's up to you, and you got
to make the effort yourself . . . Now, Bill, I want you to
promise me you'll go next Saturday," the old man said.

Studs promised.

A pause.

The old man's face reddened. He started to speak, paused,
blushed and said:

"Bill, you're gettin' older now, an' . . . well, there's somethin' I want to tell you. You see, well, it's this way, after a
manner of speaking, you see, now the thing is quite delicate
after a manner of speaking but you see, I'm your father and
it's a father's duty to instruct the son, and you see now if
you get a little itch . . . well you don't want to start . . .
rubbin' yourself . . . you know what I mean . . . because
such things are against nature, and they make a person weak
and his mind weak and are liable even to make him crazy,
and they are a sin against God; and then too, Bill . . . I
wish you'd sort of wait a little while before you started in
smokin' . . ."

Silence. The boy and the father looking out at the lazy day,
which was suddenly robbed of sunlight by a float of clouds.
Studs felt self-conscious; he was ashamed of his body; he
needed air and sunlight. Maybe if he ran he'd forget his
body, or like it again, because running was good.

Studs promised not to smoke. Why the hell not? The old
man would maybe give him a little extra spending money.
The old man was glad, shook hands with him, as man to man,
and gave Studs six bits. Studs pocketed the dough and got
his cap. The old man read the Sunday paper. Studs went out.
He felt better in the open air, and walked along, snappy; he
wasn't so ashamed of his body. He felt the seventy-five cents

in his jeans. After a short debate with his conscience he lit a fag, and let it hang from the corner of his mouth. He told himself that he was tough, all right. He arranged his cap at an angle. He thought about Iris, and he wished her old lady was out, and he could go up there this afternoon. He remembered what the old man said about that thing making you crazy, and it bothered him. He tried his shutter trick to get rid of the thoughts, but it was hard. He walked fast and kept thinking his mind was a shutter, closing on these thoughts, until finally he got rid of them. He went over in front of the pool room, and spent the afternoon smoking cigarettes and listening to the lads talking.

V

One afternoon, when Studs missed the guys from Fifty-eighth Street, he wandered back around Indiana Avenue and met Helen Shires. She said hello to him, but he felt self-conscious, and said hello back, looking away and watching the clouds. He noticed some iodine on her left hand. He could ask what was the matter, and that would keep the talk off of himself not being around there any more. He asked her what had happened.

"Oh, I got a sprained thumb. It was that damn Andy Le Gare. He got fresh, and one day came up and tickled the palm of my hand. Well, I'm not letting anybody try and get dirty around me, so I hauled off on him," she said.

"You hung one on 'im, huh? Good!"

"Yeah, he started to hit me back, but I hit him again, and he changed his mind. But I sprained my thumb, and it's pretty sore," she said.

"Gee, that's good, not the thumb, but your hanging a couple on goofy Andy," said Studs, because he couldn't think of anything else to say.

She asked him where he had been keeping himself and how he was getting along. He did not seem as confused now, and he started bragging about the swell time he had been having. She invited him to her sister's playhouse, where it would be cooler and they could sit there and chew the fat.

"It's been dead around here," she said.

"Yeh!" said Studs, glad that the street was dead, because it showed that he had been a wise guy in shaking his tail from Indiana.

"I have been having a swell time," he said.

"Well, I been swimming nearly every day. But my mother keeps naggin'. You know how a kid's old lady is. They want to do what's right, but they never understand a kid," she said.

"My old lady wants me to be a priest. Can you imagine a guy like me bein' a priest?" said Studs as he lit a cigarette, just as Swan lit his cigarettes in front of the pool room.

Helen said that she wasn't getting on so well with the family, because they always kicked that she wasn't like other girls; they said she was too old to go on being a tomboy. Her old lady wanted her to do like other girls and give up playing ball, so that she could pay more attention to other things like study-ing music, dancing and dramatics. She said for her part, if she would be allowed to play basketball on the Englewood high school team, music, dramatics and dancing could all go hang. She said she was fed up on her old lady's nagging.

"But can you imagine a guy like me bein' a priest?" repeated Studs.

"The girls around here are too soft and primpy; they're cry babies. And they are always talking, talking about boys and kisses. And some of 'em like Helen Borax are too damn catty for me," Helen said.

"Well, it seems to me that the whole neighborhood around here has gone dead. Now aroun' Fifty-eighth and Prairie we got a real gang," said Studs.

"Well, I don't like them," she said.

Studs shot the butt he'd been smoking. He stocked his mush with tobacco. She smiled and asked him now long he'd been chewing. Trying to be matter of fact, he said that he'd been chewing for a long time. He rose, and walking to the window he let the brown juice fly. It was a pretty good per-formance; he was learning, all right.

He came back and asked her if she could imagine a guy like him bein' a priest. She said he wasn't such a bad guy at that.

"But can you imagine a guy like me bein' a priest?" he said.

They sat. They didn't have much more to say. Studs had feelings he would have liked to talk about, but he didn't have words, just those melting feelings that went through him and made him want Lucy more than he wanted a drink of water when he was thirsty. Helen would have liked to talk to him as they used to talk when he hung around Indiana. The words just weren't in either of them any more. After a while she tried to speak, telling him that he was being a fool hanging around Fifty-eighth Street where the bunch made a bum out of everybody. She said a guy didn't have to be a sissy or yellow not to be a bum like those louses were. She didn't like them, or like the way they picked on Jews, and beat kids up, and always got in trouble. The thing the matter with them, she said, was that they thought every night was Hallowe'en.

Studs said that she just didn't understand them, because they were great guys, and they had a lot of pep, and weren't a bunch of mopes. And they always stuck together and none of them were yellow. They were awake and lively; they weren't deadnecks.

"If I was you, Studs, I'd can 'em. First thing you know they'll have you in a jam, and you'll be ridin' in the paddy wagon."

"Naw," said Studs, letting tobacco juice fly through the opened window.

He thought about riding in a paddy wagon. It was like thinking of fighting, a lot of fun; but the real stuff wasn't always so swell.

"Well, Studs, you'll maybe find out for yourself. I like you, Studs, and you're a nice kid, but for your own good, I'd say that you ought to shake them bastards. Red Kelly's nothin' but a rat, and Tommy Doyle, he's no good. Why, he used to get drunk when he was only in sixth grade, and last summer he used to run for beer for the workmen who were over at the Prairie Theatre, and he'd drink with them; and he always goes around with older guys like Jimmy Devlin, getting girls in basements, and not caring at all if they say yes or not, but just going ahead. No wonder he got thrown out of St. Patrick's and Carter School. The only nice kid in the bunch is Paulie, but he won't be long, hanging around with those rats."

"They're all right," insisted Studs.

"And I hear Weary's around again," said she.

"Yeh, him and me made up," said Studs.

"Well, watch him; he's dangerous, and I wouldn't trust him. He's a dirty . . ."

"I don't know. I don't like him particularly, and if he ever gets noisy with me, well, I'll hang a couple more on him, but you gotta admit that he's one guy that don't let nobody run him. He don't even let his old man run him . . . Why, he beat it from home," Studs said.

"Yeh, I heard about it. He lives in basements and generally has peanuts for supper," said she.

"But he's his own boss."

"But that's all baloney. He's going straight for the pen. You mark my word. Then a hell of a lot of bossing himself he'll do," she said.

Studs said he didn't know.

They sat. Silence, and a feeling of artificiality for both of them.

Helen asked him if he had met that Iris that was around.

"I met her on the street with Paulie. That's all," he said.

Studs wanted to say he was going up there, but he didn't know how she'd take it. He remembered the time Iris had given him and Paulie a lot of hot air because she wanted Weary alone. Reilley! He hissed to himself. But maybe Iris didn't know he'd cleaned on Weary. Well, when she did, and she got to know him, she wouldn't have nothing to do with Weary. When she got to know him, well, you just watch his dust. If he had to, he'd take a few more pokes at Reilley . . . only, well, he wasn't afraid of another fight, but then, well, he'd licked the guy once, even if he did get the insides of his face all cut, and a shiner. Iris would . . . understand him. Now that was a discovery. The trouble that always bothered him was that nobody understood him. Well, maybe she would. Maybe that thing was so that fellows and girls could get to understand each other. Maybe there was more to it than just getting girls and doing it because you were curious, and because then you could brag before other guys about it. He wanted to tell Helen about his thought, but he guessed he hadn't better.

"Say, did you find anything more out about that house on Fifty-seventh Street?" asked Studs.

"Lucy's heard something about Iris, and asked me. Lucy still likes you," Helen said.

"Yeh," said Studs, getting quite misty.

A pause.

"Say, do you think there'd be anything doing at that place now? Maybe if we could climb on the porch," said Studs.

Helen shrugged her shoulders.

A pause.

"Is your mother or anybody home?" he asked.

"Why?" Helen asked.

She looked at him; she guessed what was in his mind.

"No," she said. She added, "Lucy really likes you."

Lucy! She seemed quite far away from him now. At times he liked her, and at times he tried to pretend to himself that he didn't. He wanted to tell it all to Helen, and the words choked in his throat. *The time they sat in the tree!* Helen said she could fix things up for him with Lucy. He wanted to say go ahead, but something stopped him, and he told her never mind. He could have kicked himself in the tail all the way around the block for it, but that was what he said and he didn't know why. And it was all on account of that punk, Danny O'Neill. Well, things would turn out all right in the end. Lucy liked him, and it might do her good if she did a little worrying because he acted like he didn't like her. She would come around to him. After all he was STUDS LONIGAN. He tried to keep

Helen talking about Lucy, and he sat there, as if he wasn't interested, spitting tobacco juice like sixty. He told Helen that Lucy was all right, but he didn't think he was interested in girls any more. Helen said "YEAH!" Silence. Studs tried to explain that he really wasn't, and he got himself all mixed up. Helen didn't answer him. They sat in silence.

"But say, didn't any of the guys find out about that place?" he said.

He looked at her.

She glanced away.

"I don't like to always be talking about those things. Guys always start to talk about them with me, and then, well, they get fresh and start asking me, or scratching the palm of my hand," she said.

She talked to him as if she was talking to Andy Le Gare or somebody else.

Silence. Then she asked him was he going to school. He lied that he wasn't. He guessed he couldn't talk to Helen as he used to. They looked at each other, realizing that they were changed. They looked at each other.

She said he ought to go to high school, because he would be a football star. He said he didn't know.

They sat. He got up, and she said she had to go in and take a bath. He said he'd come in and wait, as long as nobody was home. She gave him a dirty look and said he hadn't better.

She walked out to the front with him. He limped, just like he had seen Barlowe limping. She asked him what was wrong. He said he'd sprained a muscle or something, sliding in an indoor game.

He left her, and walked down toward Fifty-eighth. He thought of Lucy, and Iris, and Helen, and . . . then Lucy. He pretended that he was with Lucy over in the park in their tree, with the wind in his hair, and her sitting, swinging her legs, himself watching her, kissing her, her telling him he was a great guy, and she liked him, and was sorry for what had happened, themselves sitting there all afternoon with no one near them, and the air so cool in their hair. And maybe she'd see it was all right for them to . . . well, it might make them understand each other better.

He thought he heard her calling him, and he started his limping again. He turned sharply. There was no one behind him. He dropped his head and walked along. He tried to make himself feel good by telling himself how tough he was.

Lucy, I love you.

VI

"What'll we do?" asked Tommy Doyle.

"I don't know," answered Benny Taite.

"Uh!" muttered Davey Cohen.

"I'm pretty tired of sockin' Jew babies, or we might scout a few," said Red Kelly.

"Me, too," said Davey.

"Well, what I'd like is a glass of beer," said Tommy.

"You always do," said Davey, as he sniped a butt from the curb-edge.

The gang of them were in front of the Fifty-eighth Street elevated station.

"Ope!" laughed Studs Lonigan, pointing to Vinc Curley and Phil Rolfe, who came along Fifty-eighth Street from Calumet.

As they approached, Weary Reilley commanded:

"Commere!"

"Say, goofy, you got any dough?" Studs asked.

"Yeh," said Vinc Curley like an absent-minded dunce.

"Let me see it," said Kenny Kilarney.

Vinc said he had made a mistake. He didn't have any money. They ragged him. Weary sneered, grabbed Vinc's arm, and told the guys to frisk him. Studs grabbed Phil, and the gang got six bits out of the two of them. They ran, the victims ran after them, bawling, but they were ditched in an alley.

The group ganged into Joseph's Ice Cream Parlor at Fifty-fifth and Prairie and had sodas. The bill was more than their six bits, and they didn't see why they should pay anyway. They figured out how they would make a dash for the door, and Kenny told them to leave and say he had the bill. He told Weary to hold the door for him. To stall time, Kenny fooled around the candy case, took a couple of Hershey bars, and ordered some mixed chocolates. While Joseph was weighing the chocolates Kenny dashed. He and Weary caught up with the guys, who were crossing the north drive of Garfield Boulevard. They all tore down Prairie, and got away easily. They returned toward Fifty-eighth Street, laughing over it. After a lot of squabbling, they divided the dough evenly. They wondered what to do. Kenny and Davey goofed over a cigarette butt. Studs and Benny Taite sparred. Weary told some new dirty jokes. Paulie Haggerty then asked Weary about school, but Weary said the hell with it. He pointed to the objects in the street that symbolized school for him. He said the family had taken him back home, and wouldn't make him do what he didn't want to, because they were scared to hell that he'd bust out and become a holdup man. Studs thought it would be a good thing to run away from home, but he felt that he never would. They wondered what they would do. Two kids came along, and they were stopped and asked where they came from. The kids said Fifty-ninth and Wentworth. Red Kelly said it was an Irish neighborhood and all right, so they let the kids go. They wondered what to do, and Kenny thought he'd like to play his cat trick. The last time he had played it, he had caught a couple of cats and dropped them from a roof, and one cat had almost landed square on a cop. The cat trick was best, though, when he could get a dog, and cart the cats to a third floor or a roof and then sick the dog on them so they'd have to jump. There were no cats to be found, so Kenny said he'd like to rob ice boxes. They trailed over to a building at Fifty-eighth and Michigan, and on the way picked up Johnny O'Brien. Three buildings stood in a row facing Fifty-eighth and extending to the Michigan Avenue corner. There was a narrow walk, and a few feet of dirt in the back, and the porches extended all the way along, with no banisters dividing one from another. It was easy for the guys to split up, and for each group to take a floor, while Davey stood downstairs and Johnny O'Brien hung outside in the alley to give jiggs. They got milk, tomatoes, eggs, catsup, and butter. Kenny got most of the loot, because Kenny had a style of his own. Studs got one bottle of milk; he had been a little leery about getting caught, and in a hurry, or he could have hooked some tomatoes. He whewed with relief when they all got safely over to the vacant lot at Fifty-eighth and Indiana. No one was hungry, so they wondered what they would do with their haul. Kenny lammed a bottle of milk against the wall of the three-story gray brick house where O'Connell lived. Red Kelly said it was a shot for the lanky bastard. They flung the other bottles of milk against the wall, and watched the milk trickling into the sandy prairie. Johnny O'Brien saw goofy Andy Le Gare. Johnny flung a tomato, and it smacked Andy square in the mush. Wiping his face with a dirty handkerchief, and stuttering curses, Andy came over. He socked Johnny, who was a year older and bigger than him. They fought and Johnny gave Andy three dirty socks. He was too big for Le Gare, but the fool kept on fighting, getting himself smacked. Benny Taite suddenly gave jiggers. The janitor from the O'Connell building and the one from the building they had looted were coming across the prairie after them.

"The Germans are comin'!" Paulie yelled.

"Boushwah!" Kenny yelled at the janitors.

He flung his last tomato and it caught one of the janitors in the neck. The other guys flung their eggs and tomatoes, and then rocks. They legged it, yelling like a band of movie Indians. They ditched the janitors around Fifty-fifth, and marched on toward Fifty-third. They laughed, and Weary said they could have licked the lousy foreigners anyway, only it was more fun getting shagged. They decided to get the two of them on Hallowe'en. Kenny said every day was Hallowe'en. They laughed. Kenny said they were in little Jewrusalem now, and they could probably catch a couple of Jew babies.

Two hooknoses, about Studs' size, did come along. Andy and Johnny O'Brien, the two youngest in the gang, stopped the shonickers.

"Sock one of 'em, Andy," Studs said.

"Sa-ay, Christ Killer!" Johnny said to his man.

"We ain't done nothin'," the guy pleaded.

"Where you from?" asked Red Kelly.

"Fifty-first and Prairie."

"That's a Jew neighborhood," said Red.

"No!"

Red called him a liar, and said that all Jew neighborhoods were a disgrace, and that was enough.

Andy and Johnny each shoved one of the Jews.

They started to mosey on.

"No you don't, big-nose!" said Red, catching Johnny's man.

Weary grabbed the other.

"You're the guy that got tough with me, ain't you?" said Andy.

"I ain't never seen you before."

"Don't let 'im get out of it, Andy. Take 'im back in the alley," said Davey.

The two Jews were dragged back in the alley.

"Now, if you two sons of Abraham ain't yellow like the rest of your race, fight," said Red Kelly.

They said they didn't want to fight.

Red said they had to.

"Go ahead. These kids are smaller than you and you'll get a fair fight as long as you don't do no dirty work."

They begged to be let off.

"Oh, you don't want to fight. You're yellow. Well, you dirty yellow . . . There, take that," said Andy.

They heard the smack. It was a beaut.

"And this for you, Jewboy," said Johnny.

Johnny's man fell to his knees.

Benny Taite was behind him.

"Take that for killin' Christ," said Benny.

Johnny dragged him to his feet.

"That a boy. One eye's closed, Johnny kid," Davey said, encouraging Johnny.

Johnny's victim was down and wouldn't get up. Kenny got a few yards off, made noises, whistled, and sang:

> Fire, fire, false alarm
> Baby da-dumped
> In papa's arm . . .
> Fire, fire, false alarm.

He came up whizzing, snorting, yelling that he was the hose cart.

"House on fire! House on fire! House on fire!"

They laughed.

"Now it's out!" he said.

They laughed.

Johnny's victim tried to wipe his face with his handkerchief. Davey booted him. He rolled back, got up, and ran. Red tore after him, and aimed a good swift kick, but missed and fell on his ear. He cursed the Jew.

Andy's victim had been fighting back all the while. It was a good fight, even, with them trading sock for sock. Then the fellow's weight began to tell. Andy was breathing heavy, and his punches were lumbering ones. Studs laughed, and gave the guy a kick in the pants. The fellow turned, and as he did, Andy got him smack in the eye.

"Jesus, Andy, you got his eye swellin' like a balloon," Benny Taite yelled.

"Hit 'im again, he's only a shonicker," said Davey.

They gave the guy the clouts, and left him moaning in the alley. Kenny ran back, frisked the guy, and took a pearl-handled pocket knife.

They walked on over to the park, and Andy and Johnny gloried in congratulations. Red said they would make Andy their mascot and let him start fights with hebes, because he was small, and then they all could pitch in and finish the job.

"Now it will be a perfect day, if we can only catch a couple of shines," said Weary.

They all wished that.

They passed the duck-pond at Fifty-third, but didn't try any rough stuff there because two cops watched them. Over in the ball field they parked under a massive oak. They played pull-the-peg, and told dirty jokes while the knife passed from left to right.

The park spread away from them in a wide field of grass, shrunken and slowly withering through August, with many

spots where the grass was worn down and dirt showed. The
baseball diamonds started cater-corner from them and rimmed
the park, around to the field house that was off toward their
left. A scabby line of bushes extended almost completely
around the park, and behind the shrubbery the dazzling,
shimmering sky fell. Fellows and kids were scattered about
playing, some so far away that they seemed like white-shirted
dots, and their voices like muffled echoes. About a block to
their left, and near the field house, a gang of older fellows lazed
under a tree, watching a guy in a sweat shirt lam out flies
to four or five guys and a kid. The kid was young Danny O'Neill.
For a kid he was a sweet ball player, and it was swell to
watch him making cupped catches, spearing drives over his
shoulder as if it didn't take any effort, making one-handed running catches, snapping up line drives at his shoestrings. He
was a perfect judge of fly balls, and he never overran the pill.
They talked, deciding that Danny was cracked, but he was
a damn good player. Andy said he wasn't so good. They ragged
Andy, because O'Neill was one of the few punks in the neighborhood who had beaten Andy up. Kenny halted the knife
game while he mimicked Danny walking along Fifty-eighth
Street, unconscious, with his goggles stuck in the box scores.
They laughed, because Kenny was a scream when he took
someone off like that. The knife game ended, with Andy the
loser. He squawked when they hammered the burnt match
deeply into the ground, and refused to pull the peg. They told
him he had to, or get his pants taken off and then dropped
in the lagoon at the other end of the park. Andy bent down
and dug his teeth in the ground. He gnawed around, paused
to squawk, and finally came up with the match and his face
smeared with dirt. They kidded Andy because he was of French
extraction, and Kenny punned the word French. Andy missed
the pun and defended the French, and that was funny. Red
Kelly said that Andy wasn't a frog; he was a kike, and his
old man ate kosher, gefilte fish and noodles. Kenny said Andy
was playing a joke on them, because his old man was that
sheeny fox-in-the-bush they always saw on Fifty-eighth Street.
Studs asked Andy when his old man was going to wash his
whiskers. Andy said his old man was the best old man in
the world. Red said he couldn't be, because he belonged to
a labor union. Red said his old man was a police sergeant,
and he was always saying labor unions were a disturbance of
the peace, because they destroyed property. "That's what
my old man, and what High Collars always says," Studs interrupted. Andy repeated that he had the best old man in the
world. Davey said Andy meant the best noodle-soup drinker.

Andy said he'd get his big brother after them, and his big brother was tough because he had been in the ring, and fought a draw with Charlie White.

Shadows slowly spread and softened over the park, and the scene was like a grass idyll. They sat there talking. Studs watched Danny turn, run with his back to the ball, face around, and catch a fly simply and easily; it was pretty. Studs said Danny was good and that every Sunday he played with men. O'Brien said yeh, but he had a lot of splinters in his roof.

They sat. Kenny said that if Andy was to be their mascot, he'd have to be initiated.

"No! No, I won't have no initiation," Andy protested.

They persuaded him, saying it was an easy initiation. All he had to do was to play letter fly. He said he didn't know nothing about no letter fly, and didn't want to play it. They called him yellow, so he said he'd play.

They all stood around in a circle. The object was for everyone to say some word with fly at the end of it. When you couldn't think of another word, without hesitating, you had to say letter fly. Andy asked what happened then, and Kenny said nothing. The one who said letter fly lost, that was all. But if you didn't play letter fly, you couldn't belong to the Fifty-eighth Street bunch.

"Spanish fly!" Kenny started off.

They laughed because Kenny would always think of something like that to say.

"Shoo fly," said Studs.

"Horse fly," said Johnny.

"Foul fly," said Red.

Andy was slow. They said hurry up.

"You gotta be honest. If you're not and you cheat you can't come around with us," Red said.

"Big fly," said Andy.

The game went around again. By the time it was Andy's turn, the flies were pretty well exhausted. He stood there, his efforts to think plain on his face. They ragged him, and told him to play fair. They gave him thirty to think of some fly. He couldn't. He said:

"Letter fly."

"Come on, guys. Let ur fly!" said Kenny.

The others said let ur fly.

They all let ur fly, and Andy got so many pastes in the mush he was dizzy.

He started to protest.

"You told us to do it, didn'cha?" said Red.

"I didn't neither."

"Didn'cha say let ur fly?"

They had him there. He walked away bawling, and turned to say:

"I'll get my brother after you."

"Go on home, punk, while you're all together," said Weary.

After Andy had gone, Studs pondered and said:

"He's the biggest dumbsock I ever saw."

Red explained why he was so dumb, and Studs glanced aside to blush, because he remembered what his old man had said about going crazy.

They sat. Paulie talked of Iris, and it made Studs restless. They all got that way. Finally they couldn't stand it any longer, so they told Paulie to talk about something else. They said all he ever did was talk that way.

"Some day you'll be ruined right by the molls," Red said to Paulie.

Studs sat, wishing, hoping.

It was almost twilight when they started home, and goofy Danny O'Neill was still shagging flies. They spread out, arms on each other's shoulders, and moved along singing:

> *Hail, hail, the gang's all here!*
> *What the hell do we care,*
> *What the hell do we care*
>
> *now.*

They walked on along the tennis courts on South Park Avenue, talking away. Studs didn't listen to them. He thought of Iris. He prayed that he would get her soon. He had to, because he couldn't think of anything else these days; and even that shutter trick wouldn't work to get the thought out of his mind.

CHAPTER SEVEN

I

After leaving Iris', Davey Cohen walked around the neighborhood, brooding, justifying himself. It hurt, and made a guy pretty goddamn sore, being cut cold by Iris when she didn't bar none of the punks or the dumb Irish in the neighborhood. And she had told him no soap. Jew! All the guys were there now, and punks like Andy with them. She had let him stay there while she showed herself off to the guys. She had let him get all anxious, like the rest. Then, Jew! She wouldn't let a kike touch her. If he didn't leave she had threatened to get Studs and Weary to sock him, and they would have, because she had something to give them. Well, he was glad he hadn't touched her. She'd make him sick. He didn't want the left-overs of the Irish and of degenerates like Three-Star Hennessey. Not him. He didn't want the sweetheart of the pig-Irish.

He walked around and pretended. He pretended that he was Studs Lonigan. Then he pretended that he had long pants on, that he wasn't so bowlegged and that his nose wasn't bent like a fishhook. He pretended that he had cleaned up all the tough guys on Fifty-eighth Street. He saw himself in an imaginary fight with Studs Lonigan, Studs rushing him the way he had rushed Red Kelly, waving his left fist up and down, swinging his right one, him sidestepping and sinking snappy rights to Studs' guts and his jaw, and then hooking lefts around and catching Studs in back of the neck. Himself making a monkey out of Studs.

He had been at Iris' and they had shot craps for turns. Studs had been first; then it was his turn. When Studs came out, MMMM MMMMMMMM, he had jumped up, anxious, and gone in, and she had covered herself and called him a dirty Jew.

He walked around and didn't notice where he was going. He enjoyed hating the micks, the lousy Irish. The Irish were dumb. That was why they always had to fight with their fists. They couldn't use their noodle; they didn't have any to use. All they had up there was bone, hambones and cabbage. He thought of himself, so much cleverer than the Irish. The micks were lousy, all right. A race of beer guzzlers, flat-feets, red mugs and boneheads. Why, they even had to take a Jew Christ, and then what did they do but make a dumb Irishman out of him.

He saw all the Irish race personified in the face of Studs Lonigan, and he imagined himself punching that face, cutting it, bloodying the nose, blackening the eyes, mashing it. He had walked out of Iris', and Studs had yelled ope; he's gotta go and peddle clothes for the old man. And the others had said things: Here's your hat. What's your hurry? Where's the fire? Don't be gone long. He had walked out and hadn't said anything. But the Irish! They were all like Lonigan and that lousy Weary Reilley.

He wanted to outwit the whole goddamn gang. Well, he could do that, but he wanted to bust them one and all. First Lonigan. Bam! Then Reilley. Bam again. Then Doyle, Kelly, all of them one right after the other. He wanted to bust them and he was . . . Yellow.

But it was more than being yellow. It wasn't his yellowness,

it was his feeling. The Irish didn't have any feeling. They had
thick hides and fists like hams. Fighting made him sick. When
he went with the guys smacking Jews, he sometimes got so
sick he felt as if he'd puke. He didn't like it. He put himself
off as a battler, and talked big and hard only because he had
to. If you went around with the Irish and didn't make yourself
out a scrapper, you had one hell of a time. He had to use his
noodle even there, so he could get along with them. They didn't
know how to do a damn thing but put up their dukes . . . and
look for Iris, the dirty . . .

He knew he was . . . yellow. He had gotten himself a
rep as a tough guy by using his mouth and getting in with
Doyle and Kelly, then with Studs after Studs had taken on
the redhead over at Carter Playground, and now that Reilley
was coming around he was nosing in with him, too. Well,
he could lick some of the guys like Bob Stole, who was heavier
than he was, or Benny Taite, or goofy Kenny Kilarney. But
if anybody ever leaned on Kenny the whole gang would pile
on him and send him to the hospital. He was supposed to
be as tough as they were; but, well, it was just because a Jew
had more gray matter in one little corner of his nut than an
Irishman, or a whole gang of them, had in their whole damn
heads. Yes, sir, if Studs ever let him have one, it would be
curtains. But he had the rep for being as hard as Studs or
any of them. And Iris had threatened to put her dress on and
call the party off if he didn't get out; and he had walked out
like a whipped dog with its tail between its legs.

He walked around and sniped a butt. He smoked and brooded.
He felt that he was different from the guys. All they ever
wanted to do was to roughhouse around, make noise, give
guys the clouts, raid ice boxes and have gang-shags with
girls like Iris, the dirty . . .

He was different. He liked to read books. He thought of
the books he read when he got a chance, late at night, after
his goddamned old man was in bed, snoring. He thought of
the characters, the goddesses of his own pretendings, who
were like all the nice and fine things in the world. The Lady
of the Lake, who had a *breast of snow;* Guinevere, who
was *the fairest of all flesh on earth;* Elaine, *the lily maid of
Astolat.* He was their champion, their knight; and he roamed
through a wild world of his own imaginings . . . all for them.
They were his, and none of the Irish bastards could know them,
touch them, think of them, see them all white and fine and
beautiful and understanding, and like a fine day. They were
his. What did he care for fourteen-year-old Iris, the dirty
. . . Her age limit was eight to eighty, and maybe she even

got kids five and six. He walked and wondered which of the three goddesses he dream-loved the best—or maybe it was Rebecca from *Ivanhoe?* He tried to think of them all as one, and his thoughts got soft and beautiful like music. He wished that he could go home and read about them, imagining himself as their knight, fighting on a white charger to protect their innocence. Then Studs Lonigan and the other dirty micks could have their Iris. But if he went home, his old man would blow his snoot off, calling him a nogoodfornothing loafer, who wouldn't never deliver clothes, but always wanted to be out fighting with the Irish, or else reading books that would never do him no good. It was the sort of crap Davey could remember hearing ever since he could remember hearing anything. He hated like hell delivering clothes for the old man, but he never got any money any other way, unless he stole it. But he got sick of hanging around the tailor shop, listening to his old man nag as bad as if he was an Irish hag.

He wondered. He sniped another butt. He got chilly with fear, thinking of what might have happened if he hadn't cleared out of Iris', and she had got Studs, maybe Studs and Weary, to bust him. He kept feeling more and more sorry for himself, and making dream resolves that he would get even with them all some day. Maybe he would get rid of all yellowness and become a great fighter like Benny Leonard, who was one smart hebe that could beat the Irish at their own game; and when Benny got in the ring with Freddy Welsh, the champ, well, he'd kill Welsh. He would be a champ as scientific as Benny. They would see then. Or he would write a great poem about someone like Elaine or Ellen or Rebecca, with himself the knight, and Iris, the dirty . . . as the woman who cleaned out the chamber pots. Dirty Iris made him sore as hell. He hoped to hell she'd have a baby that looked like Studs Lonigan, only uglier, or that her old lady would come home and catch the bunch and call the police, and get them all a jolt in reform school. Then it would be his turn to laugh. She was so low that she wouldn't even bar a cockroach, a nigger, or a flea. She was nearer the ground than a snake.

He wished that he had a nickel for an ice cream cone. Studs and the other guys generally had spending money, and he always had to cadge off them. Himself with a chocolate ice cream cone, licking it with his tongue, slow. He thought of this until he passed a pretty girl, and that brought the scene at Iris' back to him. It made him sick and sore with wanting, and it cut him again, when he thought of her calling him a kike, and a Jew, and ordering him out after she had let him hang around, see her, shoot craps for his turn, and all that.

And the ice cream cone. Himself and an ice cream cone, and a jane, like the one that passed, over on the wooded island at night, when the sky was choked with stars, like diamonds on the head of Elaine, and the moon was cool and blue, and the air nice, with the smell of the trees hitting you, and . . . the jane there . . . and . . . The goddamn Irish! Goddamn 'em! Goddamn Studs Lonigan and the whole race of 'em! They got everything and deserved nothing. They were thickheaded. The dumbest Jew was smarter than the smartest Irishman. Well, some day!

He met Vinc Curley.

"Hello, Vinc," said Davey.

"Hello! Say!"

"Yeh?"

"Say!"

"What?"

"Say, Davey! Say!"

"What in hell do you want?"

"Say, did you see Andy?"

"Yeh. Why?"

"Oh, I just wondered where he was, 'cause he said he'd see me aroun' this afternoon."

Davey said that Andy was with the older guys at Iris', where they were all having a gang-shag.

"What's that?"

"You're too young to know."

Vinc slowly realized what it was, and his feelings seemed hurt.

"What did he do a thing like that for?" Vinc asked, speaking in that slow sort of drawl he had.

"He wanted to. What do you suppose?"

Davey was impatient with the idiot.

"I didn't think Andy was like that," said Vinc sadly.

"You'll be the same some day, only don't pick 'em like Iris."

Vinc asked if Davey had seen Danny O'Neill, Paulie, Studs, Red and others. And he sadly said he didn't think that Paulie would do a thing like that. Davey started to walk away. Vinc rushed up to him, tapped his shoulder, and said:

"Say! say!"

"Yeh!"

"Did you see Johnny O'Brien?"

"No, nuts!" said Davey.

"I was supposed to see him, too . . . Gee, I wonder why none of the guys came around this afternoon?"

"Say, Vinc, let me take a nickel, will you?" asked Davey.

"You say you ain't seen any of the guys? Gee, that's funny. All of them said they were gonna be around," said Vinc.

"They shoulda been, if they said they would; it was a dirty trick, them tellin' you they'd be around when they knew they wouldn't be," said Davey.

"Well, I just wondered," said Vinc.

"Well, what do you say, Vinc? You'll let me take a jit, won't you? I'll give it back to you tonight. My old man is gonna give me a couple of bucks for deliverin' clothes for him. I'll give you the jit back with a nickel interest," coaxed Davey.

There was an oblivious look in Vinc's eye. He still wondered why none of the guys were around.

"But how about leavin' me take that jit?" said Davey.

Vinc watched a kid pass on a bike. He exclaimed:

"Oh!"

Davey asked again. Vinc said that he couldn't. He didn't have any money. He wondered why no one was around.

Davey walked down the street, deciding that Vinc was another Irish bastard. Davey suddenly turned around and saw Vinc coming out of the drug store with an ice cream cone. He said he thought Vinc was broke. Vinc said he'd found a nickel in his pocket after Davey had gone. Davey said Vinc was a liar. He said that whenever Vinc got in trouble, he needn't come around for Davey Cohen to stick up for him. He'd never stick up for a liar like Vinc Curley. Vinc said he was sorry. He said: Hones' Dave! He got his tongue twisted in explanations.

Davey said the guys were coming. Vinc asked where. Davey pointed in back of Vinc. Vinc turned, Davey grabbed the cone, and blew, Vinc after him, yelling help, murder, robber, stop thief. Davey ditched Vinc in the alley under the elevated tracks.

He walked down Fifty-seventh to South Park, and down back to Fifty-eighth. At Fifty-eighth and South Park, he met Stein, an eleven- or twelve-year-old mamma's boy. Davey said hello. So did Stein. Davey got hard-boiled. Stein nervously moved away. Davey called him back.

"Where's your wrist watch and tennis racket?" Davey asked.

"I haven't a racket, and I'm going to the store."

"Well, listen!"

"I am."

"Listen!"

Davey made lip-noises.

Stein turned.

"Commere!"

"I have to go to the store for my mother."

Davey dragged Stein back, and was going to sock him. He felt powerful. Then he let him go on, and felt even more powerful.

He walked around, and thought how he was going to be a great guy, when things got different, and he got away from the Irish. He would then be understood . . . He was sad . . . He came out of his sadness by imagining himself going back to Iris', socking Studs and then hanging one on Iris.

He met Danny O'Neill. Danny asked Davey if he'd seen anybody. He talked like he wasn't a punk, but was an older guy. That got Davey a little sore. But even so, he guessed Danny wasn't such a bad kid. Davey said most of the guys were having a gang-shag at Iris'.

"Yeah!" said Danny, curious.

"She likes gang-shags," said Davey.

"Yeah!" said Danny, more curious.

"Sure," said Davey.

"How they doin' it?" asked Danny.

"They shot craps for turns, and each guy takes his turn."

"In front of everybody?"

"Be yourself!"

"Gee, you think I could go there some time?"

Davey scorned the punk.

"You're too young. You ain't got the stuff of a man."

"Well, I don't know."

"Well, I do."

"Were you there?" asked Danny.

"Oh, yeh," said Davey casually.

"Why didn't you stay?"

"I didn't want to. I don't like bitches," said Davey.

"Who stayed?"

"Oh, Studs, Weary, Tommy, Paulie, Red, Hennessey, a lot of guys."

"Yeh?"

Davey sniped a butt, and stuck it in the corner of his mouth.

They talked of fighting, and Davey told of all the scraps the Fifty-eighth Street gang had, and what a great bunch it was. Danny asked if Davey could lick Studs, and Davey said he wasn't afraid of anybody . . . but then the guys from Fifty-eighth Street stuck together and fought other guys.

After he left Danny, Davey sniped another butt. He thought of Elaine and Ellen. He became proud that he was a Jew. He recalled Chedar, not the beatings, the ugly smells and the dirty rabbi, but the beautiful sing-songed Hebrew, the beautiful-sad history of the Jews. He was proud. The Irish, goddamn them, didn't have anything like that. He hated the Irish. He vowed he'd blow the place, and go on the bum, see the world, make his own way, come back somebody, and leave them all lump it. He thought of Iris. He remembered how white she had been. The dirty . . .

He went home to supper, and the old man started chewing the rag.

After supper, he slunk in a corner and read *The Lady of the Lake*. He read and reread the line:

And Snowdoun's Knight is Scotland's King

It set his imagination ablaze, and Davey Cohen, huddled in a corner of a dirty room in back of the disordered tailor-shop, became Snowdoun's Knight and Scotland's King.

II

After being at Iris', the guys hung around the corner. They started getting hungry, so they split up and went home for supper. Studs, Weary and Paulie walked together.

"Jesus, it woulda been funny if the old lady'd found us," said Studs.

"It would have been a big joke, all right," said Weary.

"It would have been funny, all right," Studs said. "And our old men and old ladies would have found out. It would have been a big joke, all right."

"Well, my old man and old lady can't do nothin' to me. I left home on 'em once, and they're scared I'll do it again. But my old lady would sure get one on. Whew! She'd pray, and sprinkle holy water all over the house, and I'd get drenched with it, and she'd pray and have masses said for my soul, and she might even try to have me exorcised," Weary said.

"Well, there'd have been a stink that I wouldn't have wanted to get mixed in," Studs said.

"But, hell, what's a guy gonna do? If he doesn't get a girl now and then, well, he's liable to put himself in the nut house," said Paulie.

"Yes, I guess a guy does. I guess it's a sin, but . . ." said Studs, shrugging his shoulders.

"But, gee, I don't see why it's a sin if a fellow has to do it. I think the priests and sisters tell us this because they think we're a little too young. Maybe they don't mean it is a sin if you're a little older," said Paulie.

"Maybe," said Studs, who was having a time with his conscience.

"Well, anyway, they don't make machines any better than Iris," said Paulie.

Lucy Scanlan passed them. She smiled sweetly, and they tipped their hats.

"You know, Lucy's nice-looking and she's got pretty good legs," said Weary.

"You know, guys like us are too rotten to go around with girls like her, or your sister, Studs, or Frank's sister, Fran," said Paulie.

"They're goddamn different from Iris, the dirty . . ." said Weary.

They talked about the thing that made some girls, generally Catholic ones, different. Weary and Studs bragged what they'd do if they ever caught guys monkeying around their sisters. That was only half of what Studs told himself he'd do if he caught a fellow getting fresh with Lucy.

"Bet you when Lucy grows up and marries, she's going to be one swell order of pork chops," Paulie said.

Studs felt like socking both of them.

They stood gabbing at the corner of Fifty-eighth and Michigan. Paulie and Studs said it would be hell if Iris ever snitched. Weary said if she did, she knew that he'd smack her teeth down her throat. Then Paulie talked about how Iris had looked, and they compared her with other girls. Weary said Helen Borax had a better figure, but he'd never seen it. Nobody except Weary could touch Helen with a ten-foot pole; and he had gotten what he wanted from her.

"But it would be hell. Mothers get pretty wild about their daughters. I know the punks once had a party at young O'Neill's, and they played kiss-the-pillow, and that young O'Rorty girl told her old lady, and there was hell to pay. The old lady made her wash her mouth out, and then went up to the sisters and raised hell, and Sister Cyrilla gave O'Neill a report card full of zeroes," said Studs.

"I know. I was there. That's when I made a play for Cabby Devlin, and she got so sore at me she hasn't spoken to me since. She's decent, too," Paulie said.

"Well, here's one gee that's not worried," said Weary.

Studs and Paulie both admired Weary.

At home, Studs' conscience bothered him, and he still worried lest Iris would snitch. But there was nothing to do, unless he wanted to be a damn fool and spill the beans. He tried to pray, promising the Blessed Virgin that he wouldn't never fall into sin like that again, and he'd go to confession, and after this he'd go once a month and make the nine first Fridays. But he couldn't concentrate on his prayers. He had had to do it. All summer he'd been bothered by it, and then, when the guys said they were going to Iris', he couldn't have run out. He'd had to do it. At school, he'd been taught it was the terriblest sin you could commit. In Easter week of his eighth-grade year, he remembered Sister Bertha saying that God tested you with temptations of sins of the flesh, and if you were able to withstand them you needn't worry about not getting into Heaven. Ninety-nine per cent of all the souls in Hell were there because of sins of the flesh.

Hell suddenly hissed in Studs' mind like a Chicago fire. It was a sea of dirty, mean, purple flames; a sea so big you couldn't see nothing but it; and the moans from the sea were terrible, more awful and terrible than anything on earth, than the moans of those people who drowned on the Eastland, or than the wind at night when it's zero out and there's snow on the ground. And all the heads of the damned kept bobbing up, bobbing up. And everybody there was damned for eternity, damned to moan and burn, with only their heads now and then bobbing up out of the flames. And if Studs died now, with his soul black from mortal sin, like it was, well, that was where he would go, and he would never see God, and he would never see Lucy, because she was good and would go to heaven, and he would never see Lucy . . . forever.

And Studs was afraid of Old Man Death.

It was a tough break, all right, because you couldn't seem to resist temptations. It was supposed to be your weakness that made you do it. But everybody's father and mother did it. If they didn't nobody but Christ would have ever been born. The newspapers were full of stories about people who did it. Millionaires did it with chorus girls, and got sued. The older guys did it every Saturday night at a can house. Fellows who weren't Catholics said that priests and nuns did it, but that was a lousy lie. Father Shannon, the missionary, had said that he'd seen hospitals full of people who were rotting away in blindness and insanity because of it. It made Barlowe limp. Everybody was always doing it. There were movies about it, and guys in short pants couldn't go, unless they snuck in. ADULTS ONLY. Everybody doing it, doing what . . . not the turkey trot. But you weren't supposed to. It made God sorry, and put a thorn in the side of Jesus. But God was in Heaven where it oughtn't to really bother Him. If maybe Adam and Eve hadn't sinned! Studs had once heard his mother say that they were put out of the Garden of Eden because of it, and that the apple story was only a fairy tale told to kids too young to know any better. But it was supposed to be wrong for a guy to do it. It was right for the sisters to warn you, because temptation always got you. But when you didn't do it, well, you couldn't think of anything else, and it made you hot all over, and you couldn't sleep at night. All you did then was to think you were doing it, and to pretend that every woman you saw didn't have nothing on . . . and it wasn't so much, either. It didn't help guys to understand girls any better, and after it Iris didn't understand him any better, and it didn't scarcely last a minute, and it wasn't as much fun as making a clean, hard-flying tackle in a football game, or going swimming like that day he and Kenny had gone; a double chocolate soda had it skinned all hollow.

He was agitated. If Iris should snitch! If he should die now in a state of mortal sin! If God should get angry with him for sinning, and do something to him! He wasn't even worthy of Lucy now. He remembered that day in the park.

But what could a guy do? It wasn't so much, but it got you. It wasn't so much, and it made you feel dirty, and . . . He was called to supper. He walked into the dining room, acting and feeling like a man.

SECTION FOUR

CHAPTER EIGHT

It was a November afternoon. It made Studs happy-sad. He bummed from school and met Weary and Paulie. They went over to Washington Park. The park was bare. The wind rattled through the leaves that were colored with golden decay. The three kids strolled around, crunching leaves as they walked. Almost nobody was in the park, and their echoes traveled far. Just walking around and talking made them feel different.

They moved, lazily, over toward the wooded island with its trees gaunt and ugly. They talked a little.

As they walked along, Studs started to laugh to himself. They asked him what he was laughing about. He said:

"I was just thinking about the guy in the drug store out near school. Every time a gang of us guys come in, he laughs, and says to his clerk: 'Ope lookat! Hey, Charlie, here comes the higher Catholic education! Lock up the candy cases.' "

"That's a good one. Here comes the higher Catholic education. Lock up the candy cases," said Paulie.

They stood gazing at the chilled-looking lagoon that was tremulous with low waves. Leaves drifted, feebly and willy-nilly, on its wrinkled surface, and there was no sun. They wandered on along the shore line, and Weary broke off a branch from the shrubbery. He whittled a point on it and stopped to poke some ooze out of a dead fish.

"Ugh!" muttered Paulie.

"Dead as a door nail," said Studs.

"Death's a funny thing," said Paulie.

"I ain't afraid of it," said Weary.

"Well, it's a funny thing," said Paulie.

"It's different with a fish. A fish don't count anyway. It ain't got any soul," Studs said.

"Nothing counts enough to make me afraid of it," Weary said.

"How about you, Studs?" asked Paulie.

"Well, I ain't gonna die for a while," Studs said, his voice a little strained.

"None of us know when we're gonna kick the bucket," said Paulie.

"Come on, crepe hanger," said Weary.

"Yeah, Paulie, you sound like your old man was in the undertaking business," Studs said.

Nothing in particular happened, and the day seemed so different from other days. Nothing happened, and it wasn't dull. The three kids felt something in common, a communion of spirit, given to them by the swooning, cloudy, Indian summer day that was rich and good and belonged only to them.

They stopped at the squat stone bridge and looked down into the water, watching the movement of the current, noticing the leaves and branches swimming on its surface.

"How's it going today, Paulie?" asked Studs.

"Oh, the athlete is still running," Paulie said.

"Still running?" said Studs.

"Yeh, he's a good track man," said Paulie.

"If I was you, I'd get the jane that did it to you, and paste the living hell out of her," said Weary.

"So would I, if I could find her. She was a pickup," said Paulie.

"What did she look like?" asked Weary.

"I don't know much. It was at night. I know she was young; she couldn't have been more than sixteen. I guess she had dark hair. She had a voice that was kinda shrill and sharp. I might remember it, but it would be hard to pick her out of a crowd in full daylight," said Paulie.

"Janes like that are no good, and they ought to be smacked," said Weary.

"You better go to a doctor," said Studs.

"I ain't got the jack," said Paulie.

"How about telling your old man?" asked Studs.

"Hell, I can't. He'd get too sore. He's sore enough about school, and keeps yelping about me only being in seventh grade now when I shoulda been graduated," said Paulie.

"Ain't you doin' nothin' for it?" said Studs.

"I got some stuff at the drug store, but they ain't done no good," said Paulie.

"I'd look for that jane and bust her," said Weary.

"Well, you ought to do something for it," said Studs.

Studs wanted to ask Paulie questions about it, but he could see that Paulie didn't want to talk further.

They walked on and stopped at the denuded oak tree where Studs and Lucy had sat. It stirred memories in him that were sharp with poignancy and a sense of loss. Seeing the tree, all stripped like it was dying, made him doubly sad. And Lucy didn't even speak to him any more when she saw him on the street, and she had sat in the tree with him, swinging her legs. . . . He leaned against the trunk and said:

"Well, tomorrow is Saturday!"

"Yeh, and you guys won't have to take the trouble to bum from school," laughed Weary.

"That's a tough break for us," said Studs.

"Yeh, we ought to kick. Studs'll write a letter of complaint to old Father Mahin, ain't that his name, at Loyola and I'll up and see Battling Bertha, and ask her why is Saturday?" said Paulie.

"How is Bertha?" asked Studs.

"Oh, she's as big a crab as ever," said Paulie.

"You ain't seen her, have you?" asked Weary, ironically.

"Yeh, I was to school two weeks ago," said Paulie.

They talked. Paulie wondered out loud about when he would return to school, and if he would get back in class. The sisters said they were giving him his last chance when his mother went up in September and begged that he be let in. Studs said that he ought to have George Kahler write him an excuse, because George was a bearcat at forging handwriting. If Paulie got a sample of his old lady's handwriting, the trick could be turned. Then he wouldn't get canned. Studs and Paulie talked of how they hated school. Weary stood there, whittling.

Suddenly, Studs said:

"Gee, I wonder where Davey Cohen is by now."

"He hasn't written anybody, has he?" said Paulie.

"No, he blew out right after that first time we were at Iris', went on the bum like a damn fool. You wouldn't catch me doing that. I know where I get my pork chops," said Studs.

"He was a kike, and kikes are no good," said Weary.

"Well, with an old man like his, I don't blame the guy for taking to the road," said Paulie.

"He was a kike, and kikes are yellow. If a gee is yellow, I ain't got no use for him, and I ain't never seen a hebe that didn't have yellow all over his back," said Weary.

"Well, Davey's gone," said Paulie.

They wished they had cigarettes.

"And Iris. They didn't make machines better than she was," said Paulie.

"And she never snitched on you, did she, Weary?" said Studs.

"She knew better," said Weary.

"The old lady caught you with her, didn't she," said Paulie.

"And she acted like all old ladies. She went up in the air, threw a faint, cried and hollered. She went to sock me, and I told her hands off, and walked out," said Weary.

"Well, she's in a boarding school, where she can't see any guys now," said Studs.

"And she was good stuff, too, even if she was a little young," said Paulie.

Studs sat down in the leaves by his tree.

Weary said his old man still wanted him to go to school, but he wouldn't go because it was all the bunk.

They hung around Studs' tree a while. Then they walked on in silence. Finally, Paulie said:

"Gee, it's nice here!"

They said yeh, and they walked around. Studs thought of Lucy and how far away last summer was. He wanted to talk about her to the guys, but felt he hadn't better, and anyway, he couldn't hit upon words that would say what he wanted to say. He wished he could go back to that afternoon.

Paulie asked Studs about football.

Studs didn't hear him, but after Paulie repeated the question, Studs said:

"Oh, I was out for the freshman team, and the coach liked my stuff, but he finally canned me. Said it was discipline, because I didn't show up every day. Hell, if I showed up every day, that meant I'd have to go to school. And they raise hell with you for not having homework and that stuff. You can't fake knowing Latin and algebra, and, Jesus, you have to write compositions for English. None of that for me," said Studs.

"Well, you'd make good if you went out regularly," said Paulie.

"It ain't worth it," said Studs.

They walked on. Paulie got soft, and told about how he liked Cabby Devlin, but he couldn't get to first base with her since he'd been such a damn fool at young O'Neill's party. Weary said love was the bunk.

They sat down in leaves by the stepping stones. They talked a while. Then they were silent. Finally Weary said:

"It's swell here."

"Yeh," they answered.

Darkness came, feather-soft. The park grew lonely, and the wind beat more steadily, until its wail sounded upon Studs' ears like that of many souls forever damned. It ripped through the empty branches. It curved through the dead leaves on the ground, whipped bunches of them, rolled them across bare stretches of earth, until they resembled droves of frightened, scurrying animals. Studs wanted to get out of the park now.

They said so long, and each trooped moodily home. As he was leaving the park, Studs saw a tin can. He commenced kicking it, and stopped. He was wearing his long pants every day now, and only kids, punks, kicked tin cans along. He started walking on. He turned. He looked at the tin can. He came back and kicked it. He walked on. No one saw him. He thought about the day. He wondered about other days, and wished he had a lot of them back. He wished that he was back at St. Patrick's, instead of being in high school and in dutch for bumming. He wished that he and Lucy were together, instead of being like strangers. He guessed she knew about Iris.

At supper they had a quarrel, as usual. His mother asked him to pray so he could decide about his vocation. And the old man told him he ought to go to confession, because he hadn't been there since June. Then they kicked at Martin not having his finger nails cleaned and Loretta and Frances squabbled. After supper, he went to sit by the parlor window. Frances sat down to do her homework. The old man asked him didn't he have homework. Studs said he had done it in a study period at school. The old man said it would be good to get ahead. Studs said he didn't know what homework they'd have ahead. Frances called in to ask him if he knew what declension "socius" belonged to. He said he didn't. The mother said she guessed the girls learned more rapidly than boys did, and they went ahead faster in their lessons. The old man put on his house slippers. He listened to *Uncle Josh Joins the Grangers* on the Vic. Then he opened his *Chicago Evening Journal.* Looking over his paper once, he said:

"Well, Mary, now that the kids are coming along, we'll have to take more time to ourselves, and next summer we'll have to do a little gallivantin' of our own, and go out and make a night of it at Riverview Park."

Studs sat looking out of the parlor window, listening to night sounds, to the wind in the empty tree outside. He told himself that he felt like he was a sad song. He sat there, and hummed over and over to himself . . . *The Blue Ridge Mountains of Virginia.*

1929-1931

The Young Manhood
of
Studs Lonigan

"*Your woraciousness, fellow critters, I don't blame ye so much for; dat is natur, and can't be helped. . . . No use goin' on; de willians will keep a scrougin' and slappin' each oder, Massa Stubb; dey don't hear one word; no use a-preaching to such dam g'uttons as you call 'em, till dere bellies is full, and dere bellies is bottomless; and when dey do get 'em full, dey won't hear you den; for den dey sink in de sea, go fast to sleep on de coral, and can't hear not'ing at all, no more, for eber and eber.*"

MOBY DICK BY HERMAN MELVILLE

SECTION ONE

1917-1918-1919

I

The baby bawled. Lee heard a final sob from his wife. He slammed the door. Cursing in disgust, he walked along Calumet Avenue. He joined the lads in the barber shop, front of Charlie Bathcellar's poolroom, and smiled with a lightened mood.

"Congratulate me, boys!"

"What, did you get a divorce?" asked fat, middle-aged, dour-faced Barney Keefe.

"You sound like you lost your job, Lee," Jew Percentage smiled.

"Nope! I got a one-way ticket to Berlin. Leaving tomorrow," Lee said.

"Say, I see where some guy in Kansas City put a Colt in his mouth, and fired, committing suicide. That's four suicides in the paper tonight," Slew Weber said, looking up from his newspaper; he was slouched in one of the barber chairs.

"Hey, Swede, drop that morbidity!" said Barney.

"Lee, what did the missus say?" asked Percentage.

"What she says ain't nothin' out of my poke. Her old man has enough to take care of her and her goddamn brat. And I don't care if I never see her again," Lee answered spiritedly.

"She must have thrown the rolling pin at you," said Fitz, the poolroom pest.

"She acted like a goddamn bitch. She jerked on the tears. Then, she came petting around. Just like a goddamn bitch, trying to get me hot. She pulled every trick that a bitch pulls on a guy," Lee said in disgust.

"She loves you. She just doesn't want to see her man shot into sixteen pieces," Pat Coady said.

"I ain't afraid of death, and before they get me, I'll chop down a few goddamn sausage-eatin' Dutchmen. I'm glad to go and take my chances. I've been a shipping clerk for a whole goddamn year, and I'm fed up with it and that goddamn bitch of a wife I got and that squalling brat. I'm fed up, and want to see the fun. . . . And listen, lads, don't think that Lee Cole ain't going to sample some nice French chicken," he said, winking.

161

"Well, Lee, give our regards to Kaiser Bill," said Pat.

"And tell him the boys from Fifty-eighth Street want to throw a party in his honor, if he'll drop around," Slew said.

"Sure thing! And say, boys, since it's my last night, how about having a blowout?"

"You said it. We'll send you off to Berlin in the right way," said Barlowe.

CHAPTER ONE

I

Studs Lonigan walked north along Indiana Avenue. His cap was on crooked, a cigarette hung from the corner of his mouth, and his hands were jammed into the pockets of his long jeans.

Warm sun sifted dozily through an April wind, making him feel good. He liked spring and summer. There were things in winter that were all right—ice skating, plopping derbies, with snowballs—but spring and summer, that was his ticket. Soon now, there would be long afternoons ahead, at the beach and over in Washington Park, where they would all drowse in the shade, gassing, telling jokes, goofing the punks, flirting with the chickens and nursemaids, fooling around and having swell times. Like last summer, only this one was going to be even better. He was a year older now, bigger, and he knew what it was all about. After June, he wouldn't have that worry about school. It sure was a black cloud over his head. Gee, he didn't know what night he would go home to supper and learn that his old man had found out. How would he face it? If only he hadn't done it!

But he'd lied, and had had to go on telling more lies until now he was so damn mixed up in lies about it, that he didn't know what to do. He hadn't wanted to go to high school anyway. Well, it was the old man's fault. And if the old man did find out, all right. Studs Lonigan would let him know that *he* was his own *boss*. It was a black cloud always hanging over his head.

He shrugged his shoulders, because Wilson was going to declare war any one of these days, and maybe the war would get him out of it. He might be able to go. In a few months he'd be sixteen. Next fall, he might be doing his bit for Uncle Sam, and then all his troubles about school would be forgotten kid worries.

Praying in church, at Stations of the Cross, he'd learned something about himself, and about praying. Whenever he prayed for something he really wanted, and he could see the thing he wanted clearly in his own mind, he could pray good, concentrating on God and holy things. But when he just prayed in general, with no particular intention in mind, he just mumbled out the prayer words, and his thoughts wandered over everything, and he couldn't, not even to save his neck, keep them on God and holy things. Today, he'd asked God in his prayers to be on the side of America, if Wilson declared war, and let them fight and be a hero and not get killed or mortally wounded.

He remembered his history lessons from grammar school. We had, America had, the most glorious and bravest and noblest war record in all history. Old Glory had never kissed the dust in defeat. And now, maybe, yes, Old Glory would be flying victorious over the battlefields of the biggest war in history. But what would it be like in war times, because war times were the only important times in history? It was great to think that kids in the future might be reading about the times when Studs Lonigan had lived. They might even be reading of William Lonigan, the hero, just like he'd read about Hobson, the guy who had carried the message to Garcia in the war with Spain when America had set Cuba free from tyranny. He guessed he might still be too young, but he'd get there soon, somehow. He was prepared to fight, and, if necessary, die for his country. He paused under the elevated structure at Fifty-ninth and Indiana, and slowly, solemnly, as if taking an oath in the very presence of God, he muttered:

I pledge allegiance to the flag, and to the republic for which it stands. One flag, one nation, one people, indivisible, with liberty and justice for all.

He turned down the alley between Indiana and Prairie. He was going to be a soldier of his country. Suddenly, he trembled. If he was killed in action, it would be a hero's death, but . . . he thought of the Stations of the Cross in the church, slow, sad, solemn, the story of Christ on the Cross, the sad singing, all the statues draped, death, and dying, people going, soldiers going, never speaking again or seeing anybody they wanted to see and speak to, and leaving the people they loved like he loved Lucy, and he was afraid of war because there was so much dying in it. He hastily muttered a Hail Mary to the Blessed Virgin, asking her protection, and promising always to remember her, pray to her and wear her scapular.

He fell into marching step, as if he were an American soldier going off to war. He imagined himself going over the top with the American army, not stopping until they captured Berlin. He saw Private Lonigan as the soldier who captured the Kaiser. He saw himself with levelled gun forcing Kaiser Bill to cower into a corner and yell Kamerad, like a yellow skunk.

"Take that, you raping sonofabitch!" he said, swinging on the Kaiser.

"And that!" he followed, massacring the air with a good old-fashioned American right uppercut.

A passing laundry-wagon driver leaned out of his seat and yelled:

"Hi there, Jess Willard!"

Shame blushed his cheeks. He walked circumspectly. Well, after war was declared and Studs Lonigan was a brave and gallant soldier of his country, he wouldn't have to pretend, and he would make everybody and Lucy envy him and be proud of him, and recognize he was a somebody all right, and he'd win medals for bravery and have his picture in the papers, and maybe, years ahead, even in the history books.

Studs emerged from the alley and walked down to the northeast side of Fifty-eighth and Prairie. At the elevated station, a half block down, he saw people crowding excitedly around Sammy Schmaltz, the newspaper man. He started to go down there, but heard Red Kelly calling him from the other side of the street. He turned and saw Red waving in front of Frank Hertzog's shoe repair shop, about fifty yards or so down from the corner. Studs dashed across the street, dodging a truck that just missed him. The driver cursed him. Red said war was declared. They went inside the shoe repair shop, and stood outside the counter. Frank, a middle-aged man with a square face and a mustache, was carefully half-soleing a shoe.

"The extras are out now. And we're gonna cook the Kaiser's goose plenty. How about it, Frank? You know we can do it, don't you, because you're from Germany?" Red said, slurring and running some of his words together.

"I'm an American citizen now," Frank remarked without looking up from his work.

"Say, Frank, tell us what kind of a lousy country Germany is," said Red.

Continuing to work, Frank said that he had come to America because it was a democratic country with more opportunity, and because there was no compulsory military service.

"Yep, it's the land of the free and the home of the brave," Red said knowingly.

"We had to do it or the Germans would have come over and attacked us," Studs said.

"We got to save a civilization. You can see what the Germans are doing from the papers. Only they haven't told half of it. Why last week, I was reading a book by a Catholic priest telling what the Germans did in Belgium. You know what they'd do? A hundred or so of 'em would line up, and take a woman, or even a six-year-old girl or an eighty-year-old grandmother, like old Mrs. O'Flaharty, and they'd strip her and rape her one after the other, until she was dead. Then they'd go and do the same thing over again."

"The book says that? Does it describe the rapes?" asked Studs.

"Yeah."

"What's the name of it? I'd like to read it," Studs said.

"I forgot, but I'll take you down to the library and show it to you and you can read it there."

"I'd like to. You say it describes the rapes?" Studs asked.

"The Huns, they're not civilized . . . of course, Frank, you know I don't mean you because you're Americanized . . . but the Germans are brutes. Why, they're destroying Catholic churches, and Red Cross hospitals, and they sink ships without warning, letting helpless women and children drown. Look at the *Lusitania!* I tell you, they ain't civilized."

Frank's eyebrows rose, and he glanced at the two boys. He thought of other years, back in Bavaria, his fatherland. And friends and cousins, and the children of friends and cousins, boys of fifteen and sixteen like these, being taken off to war and killed. Why? His own brother, shot with Hindenburg's army on the Russian front! The world was calling them Huns, beasts, brutes, savages. These silly boys had picked it up like parrots, all that awful talk. He tried to work rapidly. He had come to America, haven of peace and liberty, and it, too, was joining the slaughter, fighting for the big capitalists. There was no peace for men, only murder, cruelty, brutality. He was choked with feelings and fears. His own name! His birthplace. His fatherland! He loved it, suffering Bavaria. America would be a war-crazy nation. He told the boys he was very busy, and asked them to return and see him another time. He went to the back of the shop to sit down and try and think and assimilate this terror.

"I want to go," Red said.

"Me, too," said Studs, leaning on the fireplug in front of the chain drug store.

Some of the passing people acted as if nothing had happened. Others had their heads buried in extra papers. Groups paused on the corner to discuss the declaration of war. From down the street, newsboys barked:

"EXTRA PAPEE! CONGRESS DECLARES WAR! EXTRY! WAR!"

"Yeah, I want to go," Studs said reflectively.

"I'm going to try and get in."

"But you're underweight and under age."

"I'll say I'm eighteen, and I can maybe put on enough weight by eating bananas and drinking water before I go down to enlist."

"Say, Red, that's an idea."

"What you say? We'll both join the Marines?"

"Maybe we'll get all the guys. We'll have a company from Fifty-eighth Street," Studs said.

"It'd be good if we all could become aviators, and have our own squadron," Red suggested.

"We'll have a swell time. And we'll bring Kenny Kilarney along, too."

"Say, he'll be a one-man circus in the war. . . . But did you hear, Kenny's got a job?"

"No kiddin'."

"Sure, he's deliverin' orders for Ortenstein and Vauss' drug store down on Garfield Boulevard. I wouldn't believe it myself if I didn't see him there."

"If he goes to war, he'll probably pull off some stunt like capturing all the rats in our trenches and sending them over to the Huns. That'll be the way we'll win the war," said Studs laughing.

"And I hear the hustlers are yum-yum in France, too," Red said.

"We won't do nothin' atall with those French chickens," Studs bragged lasciviously.

"If we save civilization and France, I think we'll have a right to."

"You know, I got to laugh, just thinkin' of what a guy like Kenny wouldn't pull in the war. He'd probably go over and cop all the German soup-kitchens, or he might nab Berlin from right under the Kaiser's nose, without the Germans knowing it was gone."

They talked of how they would come home in glory and victory, marching down Michigan Boulevard with their medals and souvenirs. And Kenny Kilarney would probably have the Kaiser's mustache, iron helmet and his iron cross, and he'd hold them up, shouting RAGOLIRON, as he marched out of step.

Kenny happened along, carrying a bottle of seltzer water for delivery, and singing, *Reuben, Reuben, I Been Thinking*. They told him about enlisting. He looked at them in that goofy surprised way of his, waved his arms, and sang, *I Didn't Raise My Boy To Be A Soldier*. It was so funny they had to laugh, because Kenny was a funny guy. They said he ought to go into vaudeville. He said that, all kidding aside, the idea was jake with him. He showed them how he would jam a bayonet up the Clown Quince's.

"Hey, there's that Jew punk, Stein. His old man speaks German. I'll bet he's a German spy," Red said.

Studs grabbed Stein, a neatly dressed, twelve-or-thirteen-year-old, four-eyed sissy. Bawling like a mama's cry baby, Stein asked what he had done. Kenny squirted seltzer water in his face. Stein shrieked to be let alone. Kenny appointed himself judge for a court martial and told them to hold the prisoner until he came back. He dashed away. While they waited, they tortured the kid with questions. Kenny quickly returned with a small American flag which he'd copped from the nearby five-and-dime store. Stein was sentenced to kneel down and kiss the flag. He demurred, but rough handling changed his mind. He knelt down and pressed his lips towards the flag which had been placed on the sidewalk. He was hurtled forwards by three swift kicks in the tocus. He was still bawling when Kenny grabbed his feet, and Studs and Red nabbed him under the arms. They gave him the royal bumps, slamming his can against the sidewalk. A stranger told them to let the kid alone. Kenny said that the kid's father was a German and that he had just yelled "Down with Wilson" and "Hoch der Kaiser."

MacNamara, the pot-bellied cop, came along twirling his club. He intruded to halt the punishment. They told him Stein had spit on the flag. Stein, stuttering and tearful, denied the accusation. MacNamara asked him his name. Stein replied meekly. The cop said you could expect anything from one with a name like that, kicked his tail, and told him to get home. He told the guys that they'd done right, but the next time to go back in the alley where they wouldn't cause such a commotion. He flatfooted along twirling his club.

Kenny turned his cap around backwards and sang:

Oh, say can you see, any bedbugs on me . . .

It was funny. Red pointed at the empty seltzer bottle on the sidewalk, and asked Kenny wouldn't he get canned on account of what he did with it. Kenny said no because he'd quit. He struck a Napoleonic attitude, and said:

"On to Berlin!"

They shook on it.

II

After he became a hero, and everybody knew of him, the story of the stunt they were pulling would be remembered and they would all be telling it. . . . Well, he would become a hero. . . . He would!

He casually leaned against a girder in the alley in back of the Fifty-eighth Street elevated station, cigarette drooping from the corner of his mouth, his cap set back on his poll, a mop of darkish blond hair showing.

"I wish Kilarney would shake a leg, wherever he is," Studs Lonigan said, as if he were not excited, and all this that was happening was just ordinary and everyday.

"He'll cop a bike, all right. That boy is a past master," Red said.

"Yeah," said Studs, secretly envying Kenny Kilarney's talents.

Studs itched to walk around a bit and do something—anything. Waiting like this got him. But he couldn't let Red see he was nervous or Red might think he was yellow.

They heard whooping down the alley. They looked and saw Kenny on a bike, coming towards them like a bat out of Hell. He clamped the bicycle brake, and leaped off. He was breathless and he laughed.

"How do you like it?" he asked, smiling goofily.

They examined the bike, a new one, with blue bars and mud-guard, and a bushel basket tied in back of the seat.

"Jesus Christ!" Studs exclaimed admiringly.

"Where'd you get it?" asked Red, also with admiration.

"Off a back porch at Fifty-sixth and Prairie," Kenny proudly said.

"That near? Maybe we better get away from here. Somebody might be following you," said Studs.

"Hell, no! I stopped in the alley right near there and tied this bushel basket on," Kenny said.

"Well, now let's get going. We got lots to do today," said Studs, nervous.

"You guys got any ideas on how we'll pull the trick off?" asked Red.

"Leave that to Uncle Kilarney," said Kenny confidently.

"Why? We ought to help," said Red.

"If you leave it to me, it'll be pie. I got the bike. All I got to do is find a banana peddler, and wait till he sells something and leaves his cart. Then, I'll just fill the basket and blow. If you guys come along, it'll be easier to catch you because you'll be on foot."

"But listen, Kenny! . . ."

"Never mind, Red. You guys meet me at Sixtieth and Prairie. Take a little time getting there, and wait. I won't be long. It's just a matter of finding a Guinea peddling bananas."

He shot off. They shrugged their shoulders, and walked slowly down towards the meeting-place.

"We won't be seein' much of this burg for a *long time*," said Red.

"I guess not," said Studs, melancholy at the thought of leaving. Did Red feel the same way? He didn't like to ask because he'd never had a friend he could feel sure of in talking about things like that. Everybody might feel that he was soft and yellow. But, gee, he was leaving the burg, and everything. He was game. He wasn't backing down. But he did feel a little, well, sad at the idea of blowing.

"Think your old man will put in a squawk when he finds out?" asked Red.

"Gee, I wonder. I'm afraid he might."

"I don't know about mine. I don't think he will, but I ain't positive."

"If mine does, I'll just raise all holy hell with him," Studs said.

"I guess the best thing to do is not to tell them. We'll just blow, and then, when we're sure they can't crab our act, we'll let them know. Anyway, Kenny's old lady will probably just say good riddance. He won't have any trouble," said Red.

Studs wished he had parents like Kenny's old lady. He seemed to do anything he wanted to without ever having any trouble about it at home.

"Say, Studs, what's happened about school?"

"I won't have to worry about it any more now."

"I know, but has your old man found out?"

"No! But if he does, Jesus! He'll throw cat-fits all over the house. I haven't gone in months, and last winter I got sixty bucks from him for tuition and books and blew it in," said Studs, laughing with a pride of achievement.

"He isn't wisened up then?" said Red.

"Not yet."

"Got any more cigarettes?" asked Red.

Studs shook his head. Red sniped a butt from the street.

"Too bad we can't get more of the guys to go," Studs said.

"Aw, they're yellow! They all said they would, and where are they? Tommy Doyle, today of all days, giving us that crap that he has to help his old man. Say, that bastard hasn't helped his old man or old woman do anything since he was an infant. That crap!"

"Yes," said Studs, thrilling with a feeling of his superior courage.

"And Weary Reilley, the tough guy, saying they can keep their war," said Red.

"His name ought to be Schultz or Hoffman, the way he talks," said Studs.

"Well, let 'em. We'll do our duty, and we'll have our fun, too. With Kenny around we'll have a hell of a time," said Red.

"And if we do get killed, it'll be for our flag, and you know, a soldier dying for his country don't have to worry about going to Hell. It's like a martyr's death," said Studs.

"We won't get killed. We'll just kill the Germans," said Red.

"What'll we join?" asked Studs.

"I'm all for joining the Marines," said Red.

"Me too, the devil dogs," said Studs.

"There's where that screwy big elephant Jeff lives," said Red, pointing to a three-story apartment building next to a vacant lot between Fifty-ninth and Sixtieth on Prairie Avenue. "The punks all over the neighborhood are digging trenches," said Red, pointing at trenches which had been dug in the vacant lot.

"It'll be nice coming around on leave in devil-dog uniforms before we go across," said Red.

"Yeah," said Studs, thinking of how he would go to mass in his uniform, receive everybody's congratulations, even be seen by Lucy. And he'd go back and see Battling Bertha too.

"We'll be among the first from the neighborhood to go. Lee Cole was the first. But that'll be something, because we're younger, and not even expected to fight," said Red.

"Yeah," said Studs, a sense of martyrdom and nobility plunging extravagantly within him.

"I'm kind of anxious to get the thing settled, and sign on the dotted line," said Red.

"Me too," said Studs.

They sat on a fence at Sixtieth and Prairie Avenue in front of the home where that punk from St. Patrick's, Morrie Regan, lived.

"Say, maybe we can get in just as we are," said Red.

"We hadn't better take any chances. I only weigh a hundred and ten pounds, and Kenny's lighter. How about you?"

"I'm about one nine," said Red.

"We better eat the bananas," said Studs.

"You're pretty anxious," said Red, as Studs got up and walked in front of him.

"Kind of," said Studs, running his words together.

"I can understand it."

"Suppose he gets caught?" said Studs, glancing north.

"Kenny never gets caught."

"Hello, fellows. . . . Say, got a fag?" asked Three Star Hennessey.

"Go on home and wash your face," Red said.

"Don't be a heel," said Hennessey.

"Why don't you go to school? The truant officer will be nabbing you, and your old man will kick your ears off," said Studs, with the superior sneer warranted by age and size.

"Say, what you guys doing today?" Hennessey asked.

"Nothin'," said Red with obvious mysteriousness, and winked at Studs.

"Hey, punk, blow!" Studs commanded.

"Aw, come on, Studs, what did I ever do to you?"

"I'll give you just about five seconds to remove yourself from sight," said Red.

"This place is free. I don't have to, if I want to stay here."

"No?"

"No!" whined Hennessey.

"For the last time. . . . Blow!"

Hennessey stood there gritting his teeth. Red kicked him in the tail. He bawled.

"Need another invitation?" asked Studs.

"You don't own this sidewalk," Hennessey sniveled, snot running from his nose.

Red slapped his face. Studs booted him one.

"If you don't blow now, I'll kill you, you little. . . ."

Hennessey ran, yelling back wait till he got his gat.

Kenny rode up whooping, with a basket full of bananas. They congratulated him again. He imitated the way the dago peddler had shagged him. But there had been no one on the street so it had been a cinch. They went to Kenny's basement.

"Here goes," said Red, peeling his first banana, as they sat on boxes.

"Well, Kenny, how'll you like it in the trenches?" asked Studs.

"Me, I'll be a general by that time."

"General Kilarney," said Studs; they laughed.

"This ain't so bad," said Studs, starting on his second banana.

"Nope," said Kenny, swigging water from a milk bottle.

"Wait till we get over there. You'll be so funny, the Germans will have to laugh at you. Christ, when we get to Berlin I'll bet you'll steal the Kaiser's mustache," Red said.

"I'll be a soldier of America," Kenny said melodramatically.

"I'd like an iron cross to bring back," said Studs, his face stuffed with banana.

"I can just picture Kenny. When he goosesteps, it'll be better than Charlie Chaplin," said Red.

Kenny mimicked the goosestep.

"How do you feel?" asked Red, after Kenny had finished the comedy.

"All right," Studs valorously said.

"I'm O. K. too," said Red, slowly reaching for another banana.

"I never felt better. These things agree with me," Kenny said, biting off almost a half.

"Me too," said Studs, not to be outdone, as he jammed half of a banana in his mouth.

"Wait till tonight when we go around the poolroom and say: 'Well, boys, wish us luck!'" Red said.

"Christ, will they be surprised," said Studs.

"They won't believe us," said Red.

"Here, have another, Red," said Kenny, tossing him one.

Studs took the milk bottle and filled it slowly at the faucet. He looked at the bananas stacked in the basket.

"Jesus, you certainly got enough," he said.

"Need 'em, I'm only a bantamweight," Kenny replied.

Red took a gulp of water. He set the bottle down and cursed.

"What's the matter, son? Gettin' you already? That's no way to be a soldier," said Kenny.

"I just drank too fast," Red said, biting a hunk.

"Say, Kenny, your janitor will like us, dumping these skins all over," said Studs.

"He's only a Hunky," said Kenny.

"You won't win a war on that stomach, Kelly," kidded Kilarney after Red had belched.

"I'm all right. It's only that I drank that water too damn fast. How about you, Studs?"

Studs nodded, reaching towards the basket.

"Kenny, show us how you're going to bayonet the Clown Quince," said Studs.

"This is serious," said Kenny.

He told a dirty joke. It was a scream. In the midst of laughing, Studs hiccoughed.

"Take a drink, Studs," said Red, fighting his hiccoughs.

"I'll be all right," said Studs, not liking the tone of Red's voice.

"Well, here goes for another," said Red, reaching for the basket, and looking at Studs, so that Studs would notice him. Studs grimly took another also.

"Maybe you better let up for a while, Studs," said Red as Studs nibbled.

"No, I just think we've all been eating too fast," Studs answered.

"Jesus Christ. Say, why the hell do we have to eat bananas to go to war?" Kenny suddenly said.

"You got to. You won't make the weight," said Red, nibbling.

"You don't get me, fellow! I just always think of Kilarney's comfort," Kenny said.

"You know what General Sherman said. . . . War is Hell," said Red.

"That was General Sheridan," snapped Kenny.

They had an argument over which general it had been.

"Say, is there a can here?" asked Studs.

Kenny pointed.

"I'll bet Studs fell in," Kenny said, after Studs had remained absent for about five minutes.

"It's got him," Red said.

Studs came out in about fifteen minutes, his face white.

"Sick?" asked Red.

"I'm all right," said Studs, taking a banana.

Red went to the can. He took a long time too. Then Kenny.

Studs looked at the basket, over half full. They ate more and more slowly.

"I won't eat any more of those goddamn things," Kenny suddenly said.

"Come on. You want to get in. Well, you gotta have the weight."

"I'll stay home if it means eatin' all that crap," Kenny said.

"Come on, Kenny. We can't go on without you," Red pleaded.

"Jesus, Kenny, won't you do that much for your country?" said Studs.

"My country can have me, but I don't see why it makes me eat bananas till I bloat like a balloon," said Kenny.

"Well, I told you. You have to be a certain weight, or you can't be accepted. Listen, after it's all over you'll be glad. Think of it, going to France. Say, we'll have a hell of a time. And you'll come back a hero," said Red.

"Come on, Kenny. We need you with us. And we ain't beefing," persuaded Studs.

Red handed Kenny a banana. Kenny took it with a pout. They nibbled their bananas, and sipped water, almost by drops.

"Say, it's gettin' late. We better be going," said Studs.

"I was thinkin' that too. Only there's more bananas. And we don't want to get rejected," said Red.

"I'm going," said Kenny.

"Come on, just a few more. We want to make sure," said Red.

"But listen, Red, if we don't get in, we can come back and try it again," said Studs.

"Not this boy," said Kenny.

They sat there, each taking another, gazing at it long. They finally agreed to go. They left the basket, still about half full, and the basement floor was a litter of banana peels.

"How you feel?" asked Red.

"Ask me another, wise guy," said Kenny; they laughed.

"It wasn't so bad," said Studs.

He saw that Red was white. Red noticed that Kenny was pale. Kenny observed that Studs didn't look so hot. They walked very slowly. It was a job, climbing up the back stairs of the elevated station, to gyp the elevated company. On the train, they did more hiccoughing than talking. People noticed them and suppressed smiles. Suddenly, Kenny lit for the rear platform. Studs and Red followed. They stood by themselves, looking at the tracks as if sightless, while the train sped downtown. They got off at State and Congress and found a Marine recruiting station, with a picture of Uncle Sam pleading, and pointing to a Hun in the background. Over it were the words: "He Needs You."

"I guess Uncle Sam needs us all right," Red said.

Studs nodded.

"Kilarney only needs some Pluto Water," Kenny said.

Their smiles were sickly.

"Well, here goes," Red said.

He stepped up to a beefy-faced, hard-boiled sergeant. Studs and Kilarney stood by him.

"We came to join up."

The tow-headed sergeant took one look at them, and laughed. They hiccoughed, almost trembled.

"Sure, we're keepin' a little date with the Kaiser," Kenny said.

The sergeant let fly a gob of tobacco juice.

"G'wan home, children, and get your diapers pinned on!"

They trooped off.

"The bastard," said Red.

"We should have socked him," Studs said, and Red nodded.

"If we did, all he would have had to do was touch my belly. I'd have blown up like a balloon," Kenny said.

"We could have mobbed him, and cleaned him too, only for the bananas," Studs said.

"That's what I thought. As soon as we feel better, I say we come down and lay for him. We'll get him," Red said.

"How about the navy?" asked Studs.

"That's an idea," Red said, without interest.

They started out for a naval recruiting station. On the way they passed a burlesque show with advertisements flaunting pictures of semi-nude girls. Studs had money. They went to the show.

III

Aloof and alone, his stomach like a lump of lead, Studs stood on the sidewalk by the vacant lot near Fifty-eighth and Indiana.

In the prairie, the Indiana punks were in two trenches facing each other, and exuberantly warring with sand-filled tin cans. The nearer trench was a wide hole, partly covered with a piece of tar paper, and protected by earthworks of sand, heavy stones, and grocery boxes. The farther trench was long and narrow, and connected by a communication trench with a shallow reserve trench. In front of it was a deep hole, dug as an observation post.

Studs wondered where they could have collected so many cans. He sneered. Only for that goddamn recruiting sergeant, he wouldn't have to watch punks in short pants have an imitation war. He couldn't forget that lousy, tow-headed marine. They ought to go back and jump the bastard.

"G'wan home, children, and get your diapers pinned on!"

He belched. And last night had been just like a nightmare. They ought to go back, all right, and jump him.

Andy Le Gare and Danny O'Neill rose from the farther trench, holding, between them, a five-gallon oil can that was heavy with sand. They maneuvered into position to heave it. Dick Buckford rose from a nearer trench, and whacked Andy in the arm with a can. Andy let out a yell, dropped the can on his foot, and dove back into his trench amidst a tin-can shower. O'Neill retrieved the trench mortar, and scrambled to safety. Studs laughed. He wished he'd been in the trench and had such a chance to plop goofy Le Gare.

He felt like joining in the battle. But, hell, it was only playing at war, and he wasn't a kid in short pants any more. And they wouldn't take him in the army. A lot of nerve that goddamn sergeant had had.

And then when he'd gotten home, with an awful bellyache, he had all that trouble. They never made any least effort to try and understand him. His old lady still nagging him to study for the priesthood. And Fran, a great big pain she was. And the old man! Let him yell. He'd told them he didn't want to go to school. Now they knew. Father Mahin from Loyola had called up to ask what had happened that he hadn't been to school for so long, and the old man had also learned about his having blown in the tuition money. All the damn yelling they'd done over it. And just when he had that bellyache.

He felt like blowing, going on the bum. He could just hop a freight and enlist in some other town. Then when he went to war, and they'd learned that he'd died a hero's death, how'd they like that? The old man would be plenty sorry, and it would serve him right. And Father Gilhooley would say a solemn high mass for him at St. Patrick's, and they'd all be there in tears, and maybe his old man would even cry. And then, maybe Lucy Scanlan would be proud she'd known him, and maybe she'd cry too.

But he didn't want to die. Well, maybe he wouldn't. Maybe he'd enlist and become a hero, and not get killed but would return as Lieutenant, or Major or Colonel Lonigan with medals all over his chest. And his picture would be in the paper, and when he came back they'd be pretty goddamn proud to see him.

Led by Ralph Borax, the enemy in the farther trench spread out in No-Man's-Land in front of their earthworks, and kept up a steady tin-can barrage, permitting Le Gare and O'Neill to get into position and heave their trench mortar. It smashed sand and wood down in upon the punks in the nearer trench. Andy jumped up and down, yelling with idiotic glee that he was smashing the German line. Dick Buckford plopped him on the ear with a can.

Studs laughed, but he couldn't keep his mind off that trouble at home. Anyway, the cat was out now. That was a relief. The worst that could come would be better than having that dark cloud of fear always hanging over him. The old man would probably cool off. He'd said plenty already about it being dishonorable. And the old lady had cried and babbled that they were disgraced, and that she'd never again be able to hold her head up, and that they'd have to move out of the neighborhood, because she could never again face the neighbors and parishioners. And Fran sticking her nose in too, as if it was her business. If she wasn't his sister, he'd kick her teeth in for her. And when he'd said he never wanted to go to school, and that he'd told them so that night he'd graduated, that hadn't meant anything. It was always the same. They all acted as if they were always right.

The punks argued shrilly. He laughed, forgetting his own troubles. Fat Malloy jumped up from his trench and yelled in his bullying loud-mouthed way:

"All right, you birds! Play square. We said the side that lost the toss-up had to be the Germans. And who lost? Tell me that! Who lost? . . . If we lost we'd have been the Germans. Play square."

"You guys ain't got any sportsmanship," Young Horn Buckford said, wiping his nose with his sleeve.

"You cheated in that toss-up, and we won't be no Germans," Andy yelled.

"If you guys was patriots you'd want to be the Germans anyway because you're getting licked. You wouldn't want the Americans to be licked," yelled O'Neill in a loud, squeaking voice.

"Come on over and try and make us be the Germans," yelled Andy.

They drove him under cover with tin cans. In the midst of the battle, he popped up and shouted:

"You guys would cheat your own mother."

Young Horn tried to rearrange the battered earthworks in front of his trench. O'Neill hit him in the shoulder.

"Hurrah for us Americans!" yelled Andy, again jumping up and down, and laughing like an idiot.

"Hey, Le Gare, watch out for the squirrels," Studs shouted.

No one heard him. The punks didn't even seem to know that the great and tough Studs Lonigan was watching them.

Studs was keen to join in the battle. He couldn't play punk games any more. He wished that Red and Paulie Haggerty and some of the guys would come along. Then they could all get in, and that would be different. It wouldn't be just him, alone, playing. Or else the bunch of them could bust the game up, and that would be fun, all of them kicking in the trenches, and when the punks got loud-mouthed, booting their tails around the block.

O'Neill crawled out from the reserve trench, and yelled that he was wounded and couldn't be hit. He went over by the side fence of the prairie, walked past the baby-buggy where Young Horn had left his baby brother, and came out on the sidewalk, as the battle continued.

"Hey, goof!" yelled Studs.

O'Neill came over to Studs like one in his sleep.

"Where you going?"

"Hospital," said O'Neill, showing a hand bleeding slightly from a scratch.

Studs shook his head quizzically, as he watched O'Neill enter Levin's drug store across the street. But he itched to get into it, or else break it up. He looked at his long pants. He stuck his hands in his pockets, and stood sneering.

Well, before the war was over, he'd be in it, and get the real stuff. And suppose he did get killed. All right, it would make him one of his country's heroes, along with those who'd died in the other wars to make America the great land that it was. And it would only serve his old man right.

Screwy McGlynn, the laundry driver, hopped from his wagon and joined Studs.

"That's why this country's great. These kids exemplify the unconquerable American spirit. They show in their way why this country can lick the world, and why our boys aren't going to stop, once they get started, until they march straight into Berlin," philosophized Screwy.

Studs assumed a mature man-to-man attitude, and nodded.

"Pretty crazy, but it's great to be a kid," a needle-faced stranger said, ranging himself alongside of them.

Studs tried hard to convince himself in his thoughts that he was not envying the punks out there fighting, and, hell, he'd grown past all that kid stuff. But he knew that he couldn't fool himself and tell himself lies, and that when he wanted something, he wanted it, and all the telling himself in the world that he didn't want it couldn't make him get rid of that wanting. The same way he tried to tell himself that he didn't really love Lucy, and that loving a girl the way he loved Lucy was goofy, because a big tough guy should only want to jump a girl, and think that all the rest and the love was crap.

"Kids will be kids," said Screwy.

"Yep, they will," a baker driver said.

"Yeah," the needle-faced guy said.

"No time in life like when you're a kid," the bakery man meditated aloud.

"You should have seen them bellyaching before it started. They both wanted to be the Americans. I thought they'd end up in a free-for-all fist fight," said Studs, a man in a man's world.

They haw-hawed, Studs the most loudly. Not one punk noticed Studs Lonigan laughing, a man in a man's world.

And smiling-eyed, curly-haired Lucy Scanlan, plump, pretty, flowering beautifully into young womanhood, came along.

Studs saw her. She saw him. Studs took out a cigarette and
lit it like an expert. He talked and laughed with the other
men, as if Lucy might have been in Africa. She paused on
the sidewalk, only a few yards away from Studs, watching
the battle. She didn't look at him. He tried not to look at
her. He watched her out of the corner of his eye. She might
be going to the store. He could go along, help her carry the
groceries home, go to the park with her, like last summer
on the day when they'd sat in the tree, and he'd kissed her,
and seen her blue wash bloomers, and she'd sung *In the Blue
Ridge Mountains of Virginia*, swinging her legs in the tree,
as if they two had been all alone together in the world. He
looked at her out of the corner of his eye, at her shapely legs,
and her growing girlbreasts, Lucy. Gee, she was even prettier
than she was last summer, and growing, too. And she wouldn't
bat an eye at him even.

Screwy spoke of playing pirate in Missouri, when he was
a shaver living only about a hundred miles from Hannibal,
that Mark Twain had written about. The bakery man spoke
of barefoot-boy days in Indiana. Studs listened and laughed
as they detailed their boyhood pranks. He looked at Lucy
cold. She looked back. Their eyes met. She turned away, as
if he were a total stranger.

The tin-can battle raged on, and after an attack was repulsed,
Andy again went batty, jumping and yelling that the Americans
were winning.

And Studs wanted to be a soldier now, marching away in
uniform, and become a hero, and then if he died, well, it
would serve her right. Because he loved her with the best
and deepest part of himself, and what did she care! And if
he came back with medals all over his chest, then she might
change her tune. He'd walk along Indiana in his major's
uniform, sword at his side, and she'd maybe come up and
say, very penitent and meek:

"Studs, I'm sorry."

And Major Lonigan would walk past her as if she was
a flea.

The battle raged.

Lucy walked on. Maybe on her way back, with her arms
full of groceries, she'd talk, and he'd help her carry them. Or
maybe he wouldn't. She'd say hello Studs, and he'd say hello,
or maybe not, and then let her go on with all her groceries.
And if she dropped them, he'd just laugh. She'd laughed
at him, not caring how he felt. He wouldn't care about her
feelings. He who laughs last, laughs best, and Studs Lonigan
was the kind of a guy who got the last laugh on everybody,

and he'd get it on her. He watched her go. She didn't look back. The hell with her. Only the image of her girlbreasts, underneath her dress, stuck in his mind. Lucy!

"Yeah, great sport," Screwy said for the sixth time, with nostalgia aching in his voice.

"Say, I see trenches like this all over," the bakery man said.

"You do?" the needle-faced guy said.

Studs wished the bunch had thought of doing this a couple of years ago. Would have been fun. It still would, if they'd all come around. Nope, punk stuff.

"Yeah, great sport," Screwy said for the seventh time.

In his mind, Private Lonigan, with a steel helmet, and in khaki, dodged star shells, crawled through the shell holes of Flanders Field, and flung a hand grenade into a dangerous German machine-gun nest. And with fixed bayonet, he leaped into the nest, and frightened all the Germans that were still alive into yelling:

"Kamerad!"

He led them back across the shell-torn midnight of No Man's Land, and turned them over to that same sergeant, who'd said:

"G'wan home, children, and get your diapers pinned on!"

The men from Studs' man's-world departed. He watched the punks, alone. He glanced towards Fifty-eighth Street to see if she was coming back yet. Mrs. Dennis P. Gorman, the lawyer's wife, stopped by him, and Studs perfunctorily tipped his hat. She remarked that it was very dangerous and rowdyish and disgraceful for those boys to play that way. She passed indignantly on.

War reigned in the vacant lot. And in the mind of Studs Lonigan. Suddenly, a randomly-flung tin can hit the young Buckford baby. It squawled, with irritating loudness. Young Horn rushed over and wheeled the buggy out on to the sidewalk. The punks gathered impotently around it, accusing each other of having thrown the can, while the baby continued to yell. Studs singled out Young Horn, who was a snotty kid with a head that seemed three sizes too big for his body, and told him he ought to be socked for leaving the baby where it could be hit like that. Young Horn shouted that it wasn't his fault. Women surrounded the baby, and slobbered baby-talk over it. Young Horn turned his back on Studs, and, poking one lady in the thighs, said:

"Hey, what the hell, that guy ain't hurt."

The woman continued to slobber baby-talk.

"Hell, lady, last week I had him down the block and you

know what he did, he fell out of the buggy on his bean, right on the stone, and it didn't hurt him none. Hell, lady, you can't hurt that guy's bean."

Dick Buckford dragged his kid brother aside, and told him to shut up and take the baby home. He kicked Young Horn in the tail. Horn shrieked. He got his face slapped, and the cooing women were appalled. Horn wheeled the baby buggy off. He turned, a hundred yards away, and yelled at Dick:

"Wait till I tell Mother on you!"

The punks continued the battle, but the spirit of fun was gone.

Studs turned and walked down Indiana towards Fifty-seventh. He wished he'd see Dan Donoghue or some of the old Indiana bunch he'd gone with from St. Patrick's. He felt like going over to Fifty-eighth and Prairie to see if any of the Fifty-eighth Street guys were around. But he waited for Lucy to come back, walking slowly down towards Fifty-seventh. He passed and re-passed, and re-passed her house, looking furtively at the gray stone building. And last year, she'd stood on the porch and blown him a kiss. And he'd been a damn fool, and proud, and when someone had scrawled those things about him loving her, he'd been just dumb. She'd stood there as it was getting dark and thrown him a kiss. He belched. His stomach still felt like lead from those bananas. He came back to the prairie, but the punks had gone home for lunch. The twelve o'clock whistles blew, piercing the scene. They made Studs very lonesome. When would she speak to him again? He wanted to kiss her again too. He shook his head, thinking that he sure did have his troubles. He didn't see her coming back either, and there was no one else around, and he couldn't go home and eat. And if he'd only get into the war, he'd be a hero. And he'd sat in the tree with her, and the way she'd swung those legs that were now so pretty and had such shape, and her lips that were now redder, and then, she hadn't hardly any breasts to notice, and now she was like . . . like a growing flower . . . and he wanted to kiss her again. He glanced at the deserted trenches. He went over and looked down into them. He jumped into the nearer trench, and flung a can. He inspected the other trench. His troubles still weighted his thoughts. He was sore, goddamn sore at the world. He'd pay it back too. He got sorer. He kicked in the trench, and tore down the earthworks.

He heard a laugh. He looked towards the sidewalk. Lucy Scanlan stood there laughing at him, holding her head high.

His face a blazing red, he walked out of the vacant lot

past her, and on over towards Fifty-eighth and Prairie Avenue. He tried to think of himself as a hero. He was a hero in his own mind. He was utterly miserable.

II

KILLED IN ACTION, NOVEMBER 11, 1918 . . . LESTER H. COLE.

CHAPTER TWO

A drunk in the jammed elevated car sang *The Star-Spangled Banner*. Studs tried to join in. The train rocketed along, and the song died feebly in the noise. A souse on the rear platform donged a cowbell. The train whistle emitted a piercing wah-jwah. A powerful roar came from the front of the car:

"TO HELL WITH THE KAISER!"

Studs was swayed with the crowd as the train pulled into the Fifty-first Street station. The platform was crushed with people, and when the conductor refused to open the gates and admit additional passengers, they blared protests and loud-voiced jokes. There was another drunken bellow when the train pulled out:

"TO HELL WITH KAISER BILL!"

A female body pressed against Studs. From the corner of his eye, he lamped the woman; her face was wrinkling, and she must be forty or over, almost old enough to be his grandmother. But she excited him as much as if she was a young jane. Perspiration beaded his broad, planed face.

He again tried to sing and was toppled sidewise in a wave of good-natured shoving. A fox-in-the-bush got his place beside grandma. Studs looked at the beard, lace curtains that must be dirty as a doormat. Hatred of fox-in-the-bush flared in him. He remembered his excited sensation as she wiggled against him. She'd been giving him the works all right, and he didn't care about her age, and he'd liked it. And that goddamn fox-in-the-bush had gotten his place. He wished he was alone with her; he'd bet she knew her onions, and could teach him plenty that he ought to know. Catching a quick glimpse of her ruined face, he was disgusted with himself. But he looked around, to see if he could get shoved against any other woman on the car.

The train passed Forty-seventh Street. He was all nerves

to be downtown and off the train. The whistle wah-wahed.
Kenny let out a long and funny wahooo that took down the
car. Studs glanced around for a woman, wondering how he'd
never before thought of the possibilities of getting against
one in crowded el trains. Suddenly everybody was laughing.
He looked to his right, and saw that Kenny Kilarney had
fallen into the lap of a young chicken and didn't want to
get up.

He heard the fox-in-the-bush squeaking that the war was
over. He imagined himself socking the guy. He was shoved
near him, and as fox-in-the-bush said something else to hot
grandma, Studs felt like asking why he didn't give towels with
his shower baths. A drunk in front of Studs ponderously muttered uh huh the war was over. Two girls near Red Kelly sang
Over There, making Studs lonesome to be in France. He looked
at the young janes, and thought that Red was a lucky guy,
and there was gold in them there hills. To attract their attention,
he started singing, *We'll Make the Hindenburg Line Look
Like a Dime*, very loudly.

The train stopped at the Indiana Avenue station, started,
switched onto the express track, took the curve to go north
again, and quickly gained momentum. The passengers were
thrown every which way, Studs saw that fox-in-the-bush had
grandma leaned forwards on him, and he was jabbing to
her a mile-a-minute. They meant business, but how could
any dame, even grandma, kiss a guy like that. Her tongue would
get lost in all the thickets on his map. He edged down towards
the janes by Red.

The train whistle wah-wahed. It roared downtown, over
the slums and filth of the black belt.

A drunk yelled that America had won the war. A long-faced
bozo shrieked that the world was safe for democracy. A
cabbage-faced woman with a brogue a yard long hollered:

"Bully for Wilson and Ireland!"

"Six cheers for the Scandinavians," whooped a jag.

"Aw, quit your kiddin'," Kenny innocently shouted back
at the jag, and people nearly busted their guts laughing.

They passed the Thirty-third Street station. It was crowded
with happy, singing dinges.

A monkey-faced mick blubbered tears, whining that Padraic
Pearse was dead, whoever that guy was.

The trainwheels clattered with the friction of steel, rolling
over steel rails. The whistle wah-wahed. The car grew more
and more rancid with alcohol and tobacco breaths, stale perfume, perspiring human odors.

Studs noted fox-in-the-bush, still barbering like an express train. He was envious, knowing she'd give the guy what he was after. He slowly squeezed nearer to the janes by Red, casually eyeing the train advertisement above the window. Chew Wrigley's Gum! American Family Soap made it cheaper to wash than buy new clothes. The latest war news was to be found in the *Chicago Daily Tribune*. Red, the lucky bastard!

The train rocketed onward. Studs became suddenly oblivious to its strains and jerkings. He thought of France . . . Doughboys marching, fighting, loving the mademoiselles. The Yanks were there rum-tum-tumming up everything. And if he was only one of the Yanks who'd come. He was seventeen, and just ready to try again, after that time he'd eaten the bananas, and everything at home was just grief. If he'd gone, he might be dead now. . . . But no, the Blessed Virgin would have protected him because he would have worn her scapular. And the next war we had, with Japan, or Mexico, or the Bolsheviks, he'd go and be a hero. If he was only a Sammy now, in Paris, celebrating the Armistice!

A fat, gray-haired woman in tears said that her son Allen had been killed, but that she was happy the war was over, because no more mothers would be brokenhearted over their dead boys. A gray-haired man tried to soothe her, saying her son had died saving the world, and everybody had to bear their crosses. Studs edged further towards the janes by Red.

"It hurts me . . . here!" the mother sobbed, pointing to her heart. The train whistle wah-wahed. The jag on the back platform steadily clanged his cowbell. Studs was halted getting near the janes. The crying mother made him think of Death that was terrible, and cold, and all maggots and putridness, and rotting, and awful on the battlefields or anywhere, even when you died after receiving Extreme Unction. And even if he wasn't Over There, he was alive, and might get in the next war. But he'd give any damn thing to be a soldier, laying up with a French broad right now in Paris. But he might have got killed, just before the Armistice whistles blew, and Death was an old man of ice, smelling lousier than the stockyards, or than a stiff pair of socks that have been worn a year, if anybody wore socks that long. And he had a swell time, shadowing soldiers in France, until they were cold and gray and stiffer than branches stuck to the ground in January. Anyway, he wasn't getting Studs Lonigan for a long time now.

The crowd took up singing, and Studs, swaying in the grinding car, edged nearer the janes. He saw that one was giving Red the works. The other smiled at him, and yelled:

"TO HELL WITH THE KAISER!"

Smiling, Studs accidentally on purpose bumped against her

and the quick brush against her body went through him like electricity. She said it was all kinds of fun celebrating the war, and he could feel her bad breath on his face, and smell it too. He didn't care. She had everything she owned pressed right up to him, yumyum, and she made him want it like he almost never wanted it before, and he knew he'd be able to pick her up and make the grade.

The train passed Twelfth Street.

"It won't be long now," said Red.

And Studs didn't want it to be long until they hit Congress Street, and she was pressed right into him, and he could feel the whole outline of her body, too, and she seemed to be breathing hot in his face, panting. It made him proud, a manly feeling. He asked where she was going.

"To hell, want to come along?"

"It'll be Heaven if you're there."

"You're a kidder."

She twisted against him and he felt that it was all set.

At Congress, the whole car seemed to jam towards the door simultaneously. He and Red lost the janes in the crush; just their goddamn luck.

He hoped he'd pick her up again, as he ganged along with the guys over to State and Van Buren. He looked frantically into faces, hurried the going, wanting to get her again, suddenly wanting Lucy Scanlan, but wanting her the more because she had everything a guy could wish for, and she'd go the limit, and what the hell if her breath was bad.

The Chicago loop was like a nuthouse on fire. The sidewalks were swollen with people, the streets were clogged, and autoists honked their horns, and motor men donged bells in vain. Tons of paper and confetti blizzarded from the upper stories of buildings and sundry noise-makers echoed an insistent racket. People sang, shouted until it seemed that their lungs would burst from their mouths.

Studs followed a guy playing a clarinet. A bag of water dropped on the guy's bean. He played on, and a fellow clamped him on the dome with a banana stalk. He played on. He was caught in a laughing crowd which followed a fat black mammy who paraded down the sidewalk, dressed in a washtub full of clothes, joyously singing:

> *Oh, Lawd, I'se happy!*
> *No mo' washin' fo' me!*
> *No mo' washin' fo' me!*
> *My two boys'll be comin' home soon!*
> *My two boys'll be comin' home soon!*
> *Oh, Lawd, I'se happy!*

He watched a sailor and a Marine scrapping. A pretty girl stopped the fight by kissing each of them. He clapped and catcalled with the crowd. If he was only in uniform. Everybody snickered as another sailor rushed forwards and threatened to fight if he wasn't kissed. She kissed him, and the other two demanded second kisses. Everybody laughed.

He was plumped on the head with a banana stalk, and went sick with a sudden thud of a headache. He shook his head, turned, and tripped the guy with the stalk, just as he had lifted it to club someone else. He grabbed the stalk, and circumspectly clubbed a little fellow. Ahead, he saw a guy parting a way by brandishing a blackjack. Somebody spit in his ear, yelling that the war was over. A drunk came up to him, seriously and methodically shook hands, and then seriously and methodically walked on. Another drunk rolled in dt's on the sidewalk, and a girl stuck her high heel in his guts.

Jesus, it was great! he thought.

He suddenly looked up through the noise and falling paper, and there was Old Glory on a flag pole, furled in the breeze, glinting the November sunlight—Old Glory that had never kissed the dust in defeat, and he could see it floating, flying over the trenches, ruins, corpses of the fields of France, again Victorious! Old Glory! His Flag! Proudly he told himself:

I'm an American.

He heard raucous feminine shouting. Turning, he saw a hysterical woman, her gray hair falling over her ageing face. She yelled:

"My son didn't die in vain. Thank God, my Willie is not dead in vain!"

He joined a snake dance which sang *There'll Be a Hot Time in the Old Town Tonight*. The snake dance dissolved, when a man on crutches, with two wooden legs, solemnly marched holding a small American flag between his teeth. He was cheered uproariously.

He bumped into the gang while they were gathered around a drunk who insisted that they all would hang the Kaiser to a sour apple tree. They tried to scrounge a drink but he said that now the Kaiser must be hung to a sour apple tree and Wilson must be crowned King of Germany and the League of Nations. They tried to scrounge a drink, and he said they'd get a barrel if they'd bring the Kaiser to him. A soldier dragged him off.

An insane-looking woman passed, holding a sign aloft:

FOLLOW ME TO THE KAISER'S FUNERAL HANS AND FRITZ HAVE THE FITS.

"WAHOOOOOOOOOOO!" they yelled under the leadership of Kenny Kilarney.

Studs lost the gang again. He didn't care. There'd never been a day like this in history. And he'd find her or another girl, and would he get it today!

He went on, head lowering as if he was a fullback hitting the line, feeling like he was a bursting boiler that was liable to blow the whole Loop to smithereens.

"WAHOOOOOOOOOOO!"

He fought his way into a store in a jam, copped a horn, crushed out, and blew the horn for all he was worth. A funny-looking egg pushed a wheel-barrow along, lashing an effigy of the Kaiser in it with a horse whip. Studs got behind the guy, blowing his horn, feeling swell that everybody was seeing him in the midst of things, hoping she'd see him, and rush out and grab his arm, hoping that Lucy Scanlan would see him and think that he was pretty much the real stuff.

He blew the horn out and joined in a mob that was making a center rush. A girl's dress and coat got torn off, and Studs fought to get a look at her. But she flung herself into the arms of a sailor and yelled for him to hurry up and take her with him where she wouldn't need the damn rags. Jesus, it made him hot.

He was jammed to the curb to watch a parade of hearses. The first hearse was black, and carried a sign:

THE KAISER'S COFFIN! KILLED BY THE U. S. A.!

A white hearse following it:

THE KAISER'S FUNERAL!

A third, black:

THE KULTUR INVENTOR DIED AT 2 A.M. HIS NEXT EMPIRE IS HELL!

Damn good stunt! thought Studs, trying to out-bellow everyone else, wishing like hell he had mightier lungs and stronger mitts.

A bunch of sailors came by, and he joined them. They cursed fiercely because they wouldn't get their shot at the Huns. One of them gave Studs his first slug of whiskey. It burned all the way down, made him sneeze and cough, with watering eyes, and they laughed at him. He slunk off, and even when out of their sight, seemed to hear their laughter. Shamed feelings blistered into oaths. He put his cap on at a crooked tough-guy angle, slung back his shoulders, scowled with intent ferocity, and clenched his fists. He saw a little girl with a flag, and, fed up, he snatched it, letting her bawl her eyes out.

He laughed, forgetting, as he spotted a funny drunk leaning against a department store window. Studs gave him a disdainful hello. The fellow mummed his fingers to his lips, drew Studs close, almost suffocated him with an alcohol breath, and whispered that he couldn't move because German spies had undermined the foundation of the building, and he alone was holding it up, and if he moved, it would come down on everybody. He, like Wilson, was a savior of Humanity. Red came along. Studs gave Red the wink. Red nodded. They each cut one of the drunk's feet from under him and he went down, his head snapping and cracking on the sidewalk. Blood oozed from it. A singing bunch of Marines stepped on the drunk as he lay there, and Studs and Red hurried away, afraid that maybe they'd killed the fellow.

They followed in the trail of five janes who were singing dirty songs and carrying a sailor on their shoulders. Studs wanted a uniform. Jesus! All the janes would be kissing him, and telling him to come on. He tried to think of himself in uniform, being kissed and grabbed by all the janes, carried about, taken to hotels, loved up by ten of them in succession. Goddamn it! He was nearly knocked down, and that brought him to his senses. Red grabbed him and said look at the funny bloke with the pig.

They went behind a fellow who dragged a pig along by a rope. There was a sign tied on the pig:

THE KAISER.

The fellow kept twisting the pig's tail to make it squeal, and it was funny.

They followed him over to Michigan Avenue, hoping to get near enough to twist the pig's tail. They spotted Kenny Kilarney on top of one of the lions in front of the Art Institute, flinging tomatoes into the crowd, and rushed over. Studs grabbed Kilarney's last tomato, and let it go. He was glad when it hit a soldier in the ear. They dashed down the steps, and bumped square into a girl as she went for a sailor with open arms, shrieking:

"Here I am, sailor boy!"

Studs stood next to them, watching them kiss, the girl's body straining, her lips pressing, her face going taut, tense, her arms and his arms tightening vise-like, their mouths opening, french-kissing in public.

"OOOHHHHHHHH!" muttered Studs.

Kenny grabbed his arm.

"Where to?" muttered Studs.

"We'll brown the Kaiser," shouted Kenny.

"And the Clown Quince too," said Studs, his mind painful with the thought of girls.

They stopped at a fight. It was Tommy Doyle. He knocked

a souse out. Red Kelly kicked him in the ribs.

"That's the Fifty-eighth Street spirit," yelled Studs, as they rushed on.

They ate in a restaurant and ran out without paying.

They saw a guy fall through a plate-glass window. He was pulled out, and laid on the sidewalk. They fought in a whole mob, that milled like cattle to look at the guy, as he lay bleeding and moaning.

It got dark. Studs saw the girl from the elevated train again. He rushed to her and said, "Hello," but she didn't hear him, and dove for a passing Marine. Another jane copped the Marine, Studs grabbed her and kissed her. She slapped his face, and stopped a soldier to kiss him. She simulated moans as the soldier kissed her.

"Come on, girlie!" the soldier said.

Studs watched them quickly disappear in the crowd, and he was hot and wanted it, and gloomy, and just like that his heart seemed to go out of the whole celebration, and he felt that he was only a punk to them, just as the kids around the neighborhood were only punks to him.

It was late when Studs climbed into bed. He was tired, but too excited to sleep, and the refrain of *Pack Up Your Troubles In Your Old Kit Bag* drummed in his head. He tossed in the bed most of the night, wishing the war wasn't over, wishing he was a hero, wishing, wishing he'd had the dough for a can house, or had copped off a broad downtown. He tried to keep thinking of that girl on the train, and of making her, over and over again. His head got drowsy, his eyes heavy, and he tried to think even more of her because then he might dream of her and something might happen in the dream

and

Dough-boy Studs Lonigan wearing a steel helmet, his bayonetted gun levelled, crossed No Man's Land Over There, one of the rum-tum-tumming Yanks who were advancing. Star shells flared. Shells fell all around him. Machine gun bullets whizzed by his ear. He stepped over corpses. He leaped into the German trenches and suddenly discovered that he was alone, and that the Germans, the whole German Army, brutes, every one of them looking like the fat man with drooping mustaches in the Charlie Chaplin pictures, came at him. They came slowly forwards, goose-stepping, bayonets pointed. He backed into a corner, prepared to pay dearly for his life, terrified into courage by abject fear. And suddenly, all of a sudden in a funny goddamn way that he couldn't understand, there were no Germans, only Old Man Death, wrinkled and creaky,

coming at him with a scythe to which there hung a skull
and cross-bones. And every time he breathed, ice floated out
of his mouth. Studs cowered, prayed to the Blessed Virgin
Mary. He turned and ran. He looked behind, and there was
Old Man Death coming, an even steadiness in his tread. He
realized that Old Man Death was The Rose of No Man's
Land, and he ran the swifter, it seemed for miles and miles,
and turned, thinking that he had escaped, and there was The
Rose of No Man's Land, still coming, even, steady, breathing
chunks of ice, carrying his scythe. Sweating, he turned and
ran through fields and towns back to the eighth-grade classroom of St. Patrick's Grammar School, and there he found
Lucy Scanlan in a nun's garb, teaching the class. He took his
seat. Down the hall, he heard the heavy steps of The Rose
of No Man's Land

and

then Studs Lonigan was in
the cockpit of an airplane, flying over France, surrounded
by German planes. He took a nose dive, and headed straight
into one German plane, waiting until he could see the aviator's
face. It was the face of grandma. He shot once, and down the
plane went in flames. He climbed a cloud, and above it,
headed for a second plane, saw that the aviator in it had the
face of the girl on the elevated train, shot one machine-gun
bullet and smiled with ecstasy while it went down in flames.
He looped the loop and went for another German plane,
controlled by an aviator with the face of Lucy Scanlan. He
shot it down in ecstasy with one machine-gun bullet. He shot
down another, and another, and another, and Ace Lonigan
ruled the sky. He turned around, headed for the landing field,
tired, as he coasted downwards, gently bringing his plane
to the ground. He was met by Father Gilhooley of St. Patrick's parish, President Wilson, and Abe Lincoln, all of them
holding aloft a phallic-shaped medal. He got out of the plane,
prepared to accept his glory

and

Studs awoke, and outside it was a gray
November morning. He was lassitudinous in a mood of
let-down, already lonesome for yesterday. He hummed *Over
There* and nostalgia crushed him. The thought that the war
was over struck him almost like an unexpected club on the
head. All along, he'd thought he'd get into it and become a
great hero, and back when it had started, he'd been excited.
But after eating those bananas, it had got more natural, and
he'd gone along doing all the things he'd been doing, just
the same. But it had made life more exciting, and then, in

a way, it had all been worth yesterday. Now, he'd have to figure out what he'd do with himself. He could go to work for the old man, or try and get a job, or go back to high school and become a famous football player. He knew he could, but he couldn't stand school. He wondered what the hell he could do for himself. He lay in bed a long time.

Finally he got up, washed and went to breakfast. The old man asked him what he was going to do, and Studs said look for a job. Fran butted her nose into the picture and said she didn't believe him, and thought he'd go and hang around those awful bums in the poolroom. His old man said he didn't want him hanging around no poolroom. The old lady said he should go back to school and get educated and maybe study for the priesthood. They gave him a pain. He was glad when the old man gave him a buck and left. The old lady slipped him a half a buck. He went out at eight-thirty, determined to go downtown and look for a job. When he got to the el station, he couldn't do it. He hung around, hardly able to wait for the guys, so they could talk about yesterday, and maybe find more excitement.

III

Mrs. Lonigan and Mrs. Reilley, each carrying a black prayer-book, walked home from Sunday mass. Mrs. Lonigan observed that there were two cavities in the front of Mrs. Reilley's mouth. Mrs. Reilley perceived that Mrs. Lonigan was thinner and bonier than she had been when they had last met, and that a few of the strands of hair falling from under her hat were gray.

"And how is your Frank? I never see him about the neighborhood," Mrs. Lonigan asked.

"My Frank has not been feeling up to snuff these days, and he doesn't be runnin' in the prairie with the lads. He does be a quiet boy, and he often comes to me and says 'Mother, sure I don't care to be keeping company with the likes of them that's always at that poolroom on Fifty-eighth Street.' Sure, he's a sensible boy, and he knows full well that the curse of God has been put on the likes of them, the tinkers, that's always to be seen in that poolroom," Mrs. Reilley said, with a pronounced brogue.

"Is he working?" asked Mrs. Lonigan, as the two mothers glanced pointedly at each other.

"Sure, the lad and his father have had a great talk about that only this last week, and the lad's father thinks that as

*soon as the boy is up to it, we'll be sending him off to learn
something technical, because there's money to be got there."*

*"Of course, you can't place a boy of that age under too
great a strain."*

*"And aren't them the very words I was telling me old man
this last week."*

*"My William went to Loyola for one year, and he made
a fine record for himself. But we decided to keep him out this
year and let him help his father with the business, because
Patrick has so much to attend to. We're leaving him rest
awhile first, because he is only young and growing. But after
Christmas, Mr. Lonigan will be starting him in, and he'll
finish up his credits at night school. He's going to start at
the bottom to learn the business, but it shan't be just as a common laborer," said Mrs. Lonigan.*

*"Well, me and the boy's father expect to see the day when
the lad is an engineer," Mrs. Reilley said.*

*"Only recently my husband and I were talking about all
the boys our William knew in school, and Patrick was saying
that your Frank must be a great comfort to you, he was always
such a good boy."*

*"And sure, only last night, I was saying the same words
to me old man, telling him how you and Mr. Lonigan must
be proud of your boy, him such a fine upstanding lad, and not
at all the likes of them that's to be found at that poolroom,
morning, noon, and night."*

*The women parted, looking at each other in a way that
women have. And in each mother's heart was the gnawing
of fear and disappointment because of a boy threatening to
go wayward.*

CHAPTER THREE

I

"You guys complaining that there's nothing to do ought
to just stop and think about all the poor chumps who got
to work on a day like this. Think of some goddamn Hunky
swinging a pickaxe, chopping up the street with his fanny
dragging to the ground, swinging away with that goddamn
pickaxe, thirsty, his underwear dripping, wishing it was all
over and he was sitting in the shade of the old apple tree,"
Benny Taite said, tilting himself backwards on a chair in
the corner of the poolroom, and looking at the boys seated
about in a circle.

"Benny, can that crap. You make us hot and tired, just hearing about it," said Red Kelly.

"I got a job swinging a pick for the city, and I worked one day. Was my can draggin'?" exclaimed Tommy.

"That was your record for work, wasn't it?" said Kenny Kilarney.

"It wouldn't hurt Taite there to try that for a couple of days. It might make a man of him," kidded Studs.

"Sure, Taite, tell us where you got all that pep of yours?" said Red.

"I inherited it from my grandfather. He didn't work for forty years, and I'm out to break his record," Benny dryly said.

"Say, for Christ sake, let's do something," Studs said, suddenly restive with inaction, while the boys were laughing.

"Exercise your tail on that chair you got. That's what days like this were made for," said Taite.

"What time is it?" said Studs.

"Two o'clock," said Red.

"Lonigan's waitin' for supper again," said Kenny; they laughed.

"Let's go over to the park," said Studs.

"Walk a block and a half in this sun? Not this sundodger," Kilarney said.

"Oh, by the way, fellows, I forgot to tell you that I saw Paulie Haggerty," Red said.

"Is he still chasin' that jane of his?" asked Studs.

"Married her. I think it was a shot-gun wedding," said Red.

Kilarney suddenly changed their astonishment to amusement by melodramatically lamenting that poor Paulie preferred double wretchedness to single blessedness.

"You know, fellows, getting your ashes hauled is one thing, and getting married is another. You can joke all you want about marriage, but it's sacred, a sacrament of the Church, and when you're married it's serious, for life. Paulie's too young for that, he's only seventeen. He might be ruining his whole life. . . . Well, he can't say that I didn't warn him because I did, plenty," Red Kelly said.

"Hey, Kelly, why don't you hire a hall?" Kilarney said.

"Kilarney, you couldn't be serious about anything, could you?" Kelly said, good-naturedly.

"He must be cured," Studs said, butting in on Kilarney's rejoinder.

"He said it cured itself, but he can't kid me, and nobody can tell me that a dose cures itself without even a doctor. And if you ask me, he's playing a damn rotten trick on Eileen.

She was a sweet girl, coming from a decent family and a good home. She falls for him, and what does he do but knock her up, and I suppose dose her. Paulie is a pal of mine, and I'd stick through hell with him, but he certainly did act like a rat with Eileen."

"Hell, Red, that jane is five years older than he is, and don't tell me she didn't know what he was doing. She chased him all over the neighborhood, and now she's got a ball and chain on him. Christ, he'll even have to go to work," Taite said, burlesquing his last sentence.

"That's not so. It was a lousy trick, and she comes from a decent family and doesn't deserve it," Red said.

"Red, she's a terrible spider, and she spun a web around Paulie, my pal Paulie," Kilarney said, extravagantly.

Weary Reilley entered, with his right hand bandaged. They asked him if he'd been knocking brick buildings over.

"I just tangled holes with some flukey-looking wiseacre down at Sixty-third and the Grove. He thought he was tough, so I sent him home with a handful of teeth and a puss full of blood. But I damn near broke my hand to hell on him and had to have three stitches put in it. Anyway, I learned something. Instead of breaking my dukes any more on some rat's face, I'm getting me a nice pair of brass knucks."

Studs thought of how he hadn't had a fight since hell-and-gone. But once he'd cleaned up Reilley. Nobody else in the neighborhood had. He supposed, too, that he'd have to tangle again with him. Reilley always tried to get even. Well, Reilley wouldn't be as hard this time, with his dukes on the fritz. They kept asking Reilley questions and praising him. Hell, had they forgot what a battler Studs Lonigan was?

"Say, who in hell is going to give me a fag?"

"Kilarney, don't you ever smoke your own?" Red responded.

"O.P.'s satisfy me."

"Some day other people will get wise to you," kidded Red.

"Fellow, you know what Barnum said?"

Studs handed Kenny a cigarette.

"Thanks, chump," kidded Kilarney.

"Hey, Kilarney, think you'll ever amount to much?" asked Taite.

"Sure! Why I even went downtown yesterday to look for a job."

"How was the show?" asked Doyle.

"Good bill at the State and Lake."

"I guess then we'll all have to go looking for a job tomorrow," Red said.

"What about you, Reilley, have you been thinkin' of getting

a job and desertin' our cause of late?" asked Taite.

"There's plenty of chumps workin' already," Reilley said.

"That's what I'm trying to suggest to my old man. But he goes on a soap-box every morning at breakfast and threatens not to give me any more dough," Studs said.

"My old man tried that once, and I blew. He knows better than try it again. He's got enough dough and did enough work for the Reilleys for a long time to come. If he cracks wise about it, he knows I'll just tell him all right fellow, and blow. I can get me a gat and pull a stickup when I need the kale," Reilley said, causing them all to admire him.

"You know, boys, sometimes I think it would be a good idea to go on the bum," Doyle said.

"Not me. I know where I can find my pork chops," Studs said.

"If you did go, you might meet Davey Cohen. Hell, he's been gone three years, ever since that time we gang-shagged that little bitch Iris, and she told him no soap because he was a hebe," said Red.

"If somebody hasn't croaked that kike by this time, they ought to. I don't like kikes," Weary said.

Studs finally tired of the gassing and sitting around, so he drifted over to the Washington Park boathouse. It was a long, low, open structure, bounded on two sides by shrubbery. He picked out a cane chair and rocked rapidly. There were few people around, some old men and women who talked too much in loud, cracking voices, Coady, the red-faced, flat-footed park cop who always eyed the lads with suspicion, and a couple of dinges. If the guys had come, they could have ganged the dinges. Niggers didn't have any right in a white man's park, and the sooner they were taught that they didn't, the better off they'd be. He looked around; no chickens.

A coatless fellow rowed effortlessly by on the lagoon. If he had a dollar for deposit, he could get a boat and row around, maybe pick up a chicken by the stone bridge, and fool around with her until it was dark, and then take her over to the wooded island.

Rocking away wasn't his idea of a picnic, so he went out-side, and plumped down under a shady tree behind the bushes that stood in front of the boathouse. He fell asleep thinking about girls. Suddenly he opened his eyes, feeling stiff; he didn't know where he was. He heard sounds, voices, the shouts of children, footsteps, the hum of automobile motors as if in a blur. He rubbed his eyes, sat up, and realized that he'd been sleeping.

He was moody, trying to recall something sad that he'd

been dreaming about. He couldn't remember it, and started thinking again of picking a chicken up, and making her. The fact that later on he'd have to go home for supper dropped in his thoughts like a soggy towel. The old man would probably be on the war-path again. He didn't mind work, he guessed. It was the looking for it, having to learn things about it and seeming like a goof while he was learning. He mightn't even mind working for the old man, but it was only the idea of it, the old man still trying to be his boss. The old man seemed to understand less and less every day and he couldn't be natural with the old fathead. Treated him just like a kid in short pants. If things got too hot at home, he had that gat he'd gotten from Young Hennessey. He'd take it and blow. Weary wouldn't be afraid to. He could do anything that skunk could. But robbing was dangerous. Jail, getting pot-shotted by cops! It was more fun thinking of pulling off a stick-up.

He pillowed his head in locked hands, and looked driftingly through the stirring leaves at the almost cloudless sky. The wind waved branches, the sun glinted on the leaves, and the sky was big and round and far away. He was lonesome, wanting things, a girl, Lucy, wanting that and something more and he didn't even know what it was. Always these days, no matter what he was doing, he wanted to be doing something else, and he couldn't think of much else for long, but girls, Lucy, and girls too, and he was always wishing, looking at girls on the streets as if they were the thing he was always wanting, thinking every morning he might meet Lucy again, or some girl who would be what he wanted and might help him find out the thing that was always bothering him without even knowing what it was. Must be going bugs! Doyle, Red and the guys didn't seem to have troubles like that. He looked through the leaves, with wind creeping in them, waving branches in groups. Looking and shuttering aside his thoughts, he felt pleasant and happy. And a girl could make him so much happier!

"Hello!"

It was a big guy, maybe thirty or even older, who had sat down by Studs without his knowing it. The fellow looked like a bag of mush, with soft skin, almost like a woman's, and a squeaky, weak voice. He made Studs uneasy.

"It's a ripping afternoon!"

"Yeah!" Studs said coldly, thinking that the guy was goofy all right.

"You come over to the park to find the girlies. There's plenty of them here, nice buxom nursemaids, you know, who would like a strong young boy like you."

What the hell was he driving at? Something fluky about him all right!

The fellow stretched out, and his thigh, very casually, seemed to touch Studs' knee. This slight contact made Studs want to vomit, just as the sight of oysters did.

"You like the girlies?"

"Oh, yeah," said Studs, feeling more and more uncomfortable, wondering if he ought to blow, or take a chance and sock the guy, even if he was heavier, or what?

"Boys your age generally do. If you don't there must be something wrong with you. How old are you?"

"Seventeen," Studs answered, not knowing why he even answered the guy.

"You're old enough to play. . . . You know?" the guy said with a wink as he gave Studs a soft but knowing little poke.

Studs knew he must be blushing.

"You shouldn't be ashamed of it. It's only natural to do that."

"Say, what's the idea?" Studs tensely asked.

"Oh, nothing! You needn't worry. I just like to try to be friendly with young boys, talk over their problems with them, give them advice."

Studs glanced aside. The fellow's leg kept rubbing against him. It made him feel like he might if he'd drunk something like toilet water.

"Playing, you know, is safer than fooling around with the girlies, because you can pick up diseases from them. Most of them have diseases."

"Yeah, I know," Studs said, trying to be hard.

"You have to be careful all the time."

Studs felt like telling him a lot of bull, but he couldn't think up any story. The guy clogged up his tongue.

"You know, there's better and safer ways," the fellow said, his hand ever-so-lightly running up Studs' thigh. Studs noticed how queer and tight the fellow's face got. He felt himself being pawed.

"Listen! What's the idea!" Studs said very excitedly, sitting up.

"Now, sonny, be calm! I'm only going to be a friend to you. I wouldn't try and hurt a clean decent-looking boy like you."

"Yeah!" jerked Studs menacingly.

He stood up with his fists clenched, but indecisive. The guy arose, slipped into the bushes and disappeared.

Studs woke up. The guy was fruit, the first one he'd ever

met like that. He was sorry he hadn't hauled off on him. He walked into the path, and looked up and down. Then he looked in the boathouse, but couldn't find the guy. He returned again to sit down under the tree.

He was ashamed of himself, of his thoughts, his body, of the way life was. He heard birds chirping and the winds above him in the tree leaves, pure like Lucy, and he looked up at the waving bushes, first one group of bushes flaunting, then another, then all of them whipping back and forth, and through them he could see patches of sky. He felt as if somebody had rubbed him all over with horse manure.

He got up, and walked about, moody, not wanting to go any place, not wanting to go back and sit around the pool-room with the guys, feeling all clammy.

He got home for supper late, and the old man was crabby. He didn't say anything at the table. They noticed that he was acting queer and kept asking him what was the matter.

"Nothing," he said.

II

After supper, Lonigan called Studs into the parlor for a talk. He said all right, a bit surlily, and stopped off in the bathroom to get his thoughts collected. He felt that maybe this was going to be a showdown with the old man, and if it was, he'd let him know that Studs Lonigan was going to be his own boss.

The old man sat in his rocker, an ancient piece with a plush cushion that the old lady had been trying to get out of the parlor for years. Studs entered with a scowl of determination on his face. The old man gave him a sharp look, as if to scare him. He told Studs to sit down, his manner authoritative, and he dabbled away at lighting his stogy.

"You're going on eighteen?"

"Yes."

"I wonder if you agree with me that it's about time that you begin to figure out what you're going to do with your life?"

"Well . . . I looked for a job today."

"Where?"

"Oh, a number of places in the Loop," Studs said, wishing he had told the old man to mind his own damn business.

"Do you want to go back to school or don't you?" the old man asked, nodding ironically.

"I don't like school," Studs said with uncertain firmness.

"Well, what do you want or like?"

"I'll get a job one of these days."

"Yes. You've been doing that for over a year, and it's cost me a buck a day. What's the matter with you? Are you sick? Tonight at the supper table there, you didn't even bat an eye and had a face a yard long. What's wrong? Are you sick or in trouble?"

"Nothing. I'll get a job."

"Take the chip off your shoulder!"

"I ain't got any on it!"

"I can't understand you. Here I'm willing to give you a hell of a lot better chance in life than I ever had, and you won't take it. You just mope along . . ." the old man stopped short and shrugged his shoulders, a gesture of weariness. Studs waited to see what would come next.

"Well, as they say, you can bring a horse to the trough, but you can't make him drink!"

The old man whewed as if expressing the difficulties of thinking down into disconsolate depths.

"Maybe you're better off without an education, and a lot of book-learning. It might make you into a high-hat snob like it did Dinny Gorman. You don't need an education like that to be a success. I didn't."

Studs wanted it to be over so he could get out of the damn house.

"What you need is hard work, and I'm going to give it to you. Tomorrow you can come with me, and I'll put you to work."

Remembering what Weary had said of his old man, Studs felt that he'd be yellow if he took this. And he felt his courage ebbing.

"I had to work a damn sight harder than you'll ever have to. . . . And I'll be damned if I let you become a poolroom bum!" Lonigan said with sudden energy, banging his right fist into his left palm.

"I'm not a poolroom bum," Studs unconvincingly replied.

"I don't want you to become one!"

"I'm not!" Studs countered like a pouting child.

"I'm your father, and it's my duty to see that you amount to something and turn into a decent citizen. And, by God, I will. You children are all your mother and I got. We worked hard for you, and we don't want to feel that we done it all for nothing. You owe us something in return, and all we are asking of you is that you amount to something, be decent citizens, give us the right to be justifiably proud of you. We don't want to have to hang our heads in shame because of any of our children when we walk down the street. And, by God, I'll see that we don't have to!"

Studs was sore, but words just choked up in him.

"You understand now. You come with me in the morning!"

A dangerous pause.

"I can find a job, maybe tomorrow," Studs said, immediately perceiving that his words had weakly fizzled.

"I told you what you'd do!" the old man half-shouted.

"I'll find my own job!" Studs said swiftly and breathlessly, as he jumped to his feet.

"For once, you do what I say! In the morning, you start turning over a new leaf. . . . And, yes, you might as well stay in tonight so's to get a good night's sleep. You'll need it in the morning."

"I'm my own boss!"

"Why, you goddamn little . . ."

A red flush from the slap he got appeared on Studs' left cheek. Uncontrolled tears welled forth. He wanted to hit back. He was afraid of his father. He sniffled without will.

The old man dropped back to his rocker, held his head in his hands. Studs looked at him, imagined himself smashing the old bastard's face till it bled and swelled. He stood impotently.

"You heard me! Tomorrow! Now get the hell out of my sight before I give you the trimming you deserve, you dirty little whelp!"

"Patrick! What's happened?" the old lady said, coming to the entry way, as Studs, still bawling, turned to go.

"William! . . . *William!*"

"I'm leaving here!" Studs said, brushing past her.

"Did you hit him?" the mother demanded.

"And I'll hit again. After all I done for him, the dirty little ingrate, defying me! All right, go on, get out, and don't come back. I don't ever want to see you again!"

"Patrick Lonigan! How dare you! Striking my son, my own flesh and blood! Ordering my precious first-born baby out of my home!"

"Mary, you don't know what you're talking about. Don't tell me what I'm to do in my home! And don't be wastin' your sympathy. What he needs is to get the tar kicked out of him. And if he wants to live here, he'll do what I tell him!"

In his room, Studs was proud of himself for having defied the old man. Glad, too, that his father and mother were having a big blowout. He cried; well, he was so goddamn sore, he couldn't help it.

"You ought to be ashamed of yourself!" Fran said, stopping in his doorway.

"Mind your own goddamn business!"

"How dare you curse me!" she said, shocked.

"For Christ sake, shut your trap!"

She rushed into the parlor, and shrieked in a high-pitched voice. It was like a nut-house now. He slipped into his old lady's room, and copped five bucks from her pocketbook. He got his rusty old gat from its hiding place at the bottom of his closet. He put on his cap, and went to the bathroom. He saw that his eyes were red from crying. He tried to hide the redness with Fran's powder. He was ashamed of himself.

"My son . . . my son!" his mother muttered, trying to block his path at the front door.

"I'm going!"

"William, your father just lost his temper. Go in and tell him you're sorry and. . . ."

"I can take care of myself!" he said, viciously slamming the door.

"You don't know what you're doing to Dad. Come back," Fran begged, pursuing him in the hallway.

"Take your lousy hands off me!"

His parents called him from the window. He didn't look at them. At the corner, he turned, and saw his old man coming out of the building. He ran, ditching the old man by running through alleys and gangways.

III

With dew-soaked feet, Lonewolf Lonigan tramped across the ball field at Washington Park. He suddenly wheeled around, thinking that he had heard approaching footsteps. He looked in back of him; darkness. He gazed all around at the surrounding blackness, the extended shadows of bushes on the edge of the park suddenly losing themselves in an awfulness of night. To his right, and several blocks away, was the illumination of the park refectory. The lights of a passing automobile showed like fleeting electric pinpoints and vanished.

To get rid of the thoughts he was having about himself and the darkness, he whipped out his gat, and pulled the trigger, the hammer clicking.

How could he get bullets? Where did burglars go for their ammunition? He could see himself walking into a joint, looking tough, saying in a hard-boiled way:

Three rounds of cartridges for a forty-four!

Well, soon he would have a forty-four, instead of a twenty-two!

From Cottage Grove Avenue, he heard the muffled echoes of a street car. The air was cut with the unhuman shriek of ungreased automobile brakes that had been suddenly applied.

The sounds faded deeply into all the surrounding silence. He heard many crickets.

Lonewolf Lonigan stopped, stricken with indecision. He could see himself captured, shot . . . killed.

If he hadn't gone off the handle! He could have gone to work for the old man and it mightn't have been half bad. Right after graduation, he'd wanted to. And the old man had been right in what he'd said. He had been wasting his time. But it was the way he'd said it, the bossy way, disregarding all of Studs' feelings, treating him the same way as if he was only thirteen or fourteen, that caused it all. If he was working though, the old man couldn't pull a stunt like that, because he'd be independent.

He couldn't remember ever having felt like he did now, with only his feeling of being alone, as if all the loneliness of the night and the sky were inside of him, crushing out everything else. It was a snaky feeling like maybe some one would have, or Robinson Crusoe might have had, being alone on a desert island. He had burned all his bridges, and gone from everything, and he was a man alone forced to fight by himself, an enemy of society, a burglar and robber—well he would be one after he pulled off his first stickup. And he would. He'd pull it off, and make his getaway. His old man might have called the police by now, after going around Fifty-eighth and not finding him there. He guessed he'd been wise not going around. But it had been slow as hell, with nothing to do all night. He'd been so nervous and excited that he didn't even know what picture he'd seen in the movie. It was tough too, that he wouldn't be able to go around Fifty-eighth with his gat, and show 'em what he did and could do. But it would be dangerous. He'd have to blow town tonight, because his old man might even have his picture in the paper, and dicks might even be looking for him at the railroad stations. He might never come back either, and they'd be searching for him all over the country. Or he might come back sometime, and rob his father and leave a note signed:

THE LONEWOLF!

Fun, thinking of all the things like this that might happen. But it was getting late, and he'd have to get busy. He clenched his fist, emphasizing firmness to himself. He stopped and drew out his handkerchief, and wrapped it around his face. He bent down on one knee, waited with drawn gun. He jumped up with a levelled gat, threatening the darkness.

"Stick 'em up fast. . . . Come on! Hand over your jack quick or I'll drill yah!" he said in a cool, collected voice.

He snatched, as if taking money, and ran, turning repeatedly to pull the trigger. He dropped behind a water fountain, and shot. Suddenly, he dropped his gun, and clutched his left shoulder. He pressed his upper lip over his lower lip, and grunted, fighting off an apparent effort to moan. He picked his revolver up and swung the butt of it down, like he was cracking a copper's skull. He ran, with simulated staggers, turning again and again to shoot.

Suddenly, he remembered that Martin had often played like this in the back yard. But he wasn't playing. He was just rehearsing things, so he would have all his plans down pat, and know what to do in every emergency.

He jerked off his handkerchief, and lit a cigarette. He was calm now, and he ought to pull the job off right away. He walked on across the park. He'd do it, and not get caught. If he did? Even so, he might be let off because it was a first offense, and then, the old man would see he meant business, and if he did go back home, the old man would change his tune. But he wouldn't be caught. He wouldn't ever see his old man either, and he'd let him do the worrying. Studs Lonigan was the wrong guy to monkey around with.

He paused by the bushes on the eastern edge of the park, and looked back across the park to the southwest. Out there, in back of the darkness and shadows were all the things he was leaving, his home and family and friends and Lucy. It was his last goodbye to everybody, everything, even maybe to all the fellows, the best pals in the world. Goodbye!

He put his hands before his face to ward off branches, and dived through the bushes. He came out of the park at Cottage Grove, and started to scuttle across the street. He saw a cop down a little on the east side of the street walking towards him. He had to cross the street calm, not arousing any suspicion. He felt as if the cop could see he was a criminal. He walked across, going slower than he had intended so as not to make the cop suspicious, fearing he'd hear the cop call him to halt, touching his hip pocket to be sure his gat didn't stick out, then touching all his pockets so it wouldn't look fluky to the cop. His shoulders slumped unconsciously after he got across and down Fifty-third out of the cop's sight. A close one, that!

He walked towards a fellow at Ellis, and wondered if he ought to stick him up. He passed him at a swift pace. Too bad he hadn't taken a pal along. It would be easier. But no, he was going to be Lonewolf Lonigan, taking his own chances, pitching his own game in his own way.

He turned towards Fifty-fourth Street, and, spying another cop, went on to Fifty-fifth. Tough luck! He had to go over a block, and on a street with car lines where there'd be more people to see him. He turned south again, and spotting a fellow and a girl coming north, pulled his cap peak lower and went by them with his head down, hoping he made them afraid of him. He stopped and, rubbing his hands in dirt, smeared his face a little; made him look more desperate. And goddamn it, he was going through with this stick-up tonight.

He found a place in back of a telephone post at Fifty-sixth Street in the alley between Kenwood and Kimbark. He stood hunched, trying to figure all his plans out clear. He'd step up to a guy with the gun drawn, talk fast, get the dough, blow. Nope, the guy might yell and set up an alarm. Have to tap the guy on the bean with the gun butt, just enough to knock him cuckoo, but not kill him. If the guy was too much trouble, all right, kill him. Before they sealed a coffin lid over him, he'd knock plenty of guys out of his way like that.

The wanting for home blotted his plans aside. But no, he had to be brave. Could postpone it until tomorrow? Yellow? He took his handkerchief out quickly and tied it around his face, leaving only his eyes revealed. He crouched. His heart pounded. His hand, touching the gun in his pocket, quaked. But when the time came, he'd be just as cool as . . . a cucumber.

He heard the sound of an automobile. Far away, there were the dying echoes of a girl's voice. A black cat ran before him. Still he would take his chances. He'd overcome bad luck too. A fellow was coming along . . . the steps got nearer. In a few seconds . . .

"Stick 'em up!" Studs said in a husky, strained voice, as a big fellow stepped into view.

The man stopped short, and his hands went over his head. Studs leaped before him, the gun pointed by a trembling hand. The realization that it was just like a movie holdup flew through his brain.

"Don't . . . m-move . . . or I'll . . . drrrr . . . drill you."

The victim smiled with self-possession.

"Son, you better put that toy away!"

The gun fell. He turned and ran lickety-split down the alley, hearing diminishingly, the echo of hearty laughter.

IV

At two o'clock in the morning, Studs Lonigan walked breathlessly along Fifty-eighth Street. A large man with shoulders bent, and something of a pot-belly, approached him.

"Bill?"

Studs stopped.

"Come on home, Bill," the man said with kindness.

Studs walked beside him.

"Bill, you don't ever want to be doing a thing like this again. Your mother's heartbroken!"

Studs was glad to be going home.

IV

Davey Cohen risked his last two bucks in a crap game around the Toledo docks. He stood, rattling the dice in his right hand, holding fifteen bucks in the left one; he had twenty dollars in his pocket.

"Come on, baby needs new diapers!" he said, shooting, trying to act natural and unafraid, when he was goddamn near crapping in his pants; there were plenty of big tough babies in the game. He'd like to get their dough, but if he did, he knew what would happen.

He looked at the dice: seven. He picked up the pot of eight bucks. He threw ten down. If he lost ten or fifteen bucks, it wouldn't look like he had much, and he could slip off. The money was faded, and Davey rattled the dice in his right hand.

"Shake 'em, Jew!" crabbed a big, beefy-faced Lakes sailor.

"I'm shaking," Davey replied apologetically.

Seven again. He picked up five and left fifteen on the ground.

A bruiser complained about the dice. Davey held them for inspection in the palm of his hand.

"I know they ain't loaded. But use these ones. Them damn things is jinxed!"

Davey's first roll with the new dice was a seven. He coughed sharply and laid twenty bucks down.

"You damn kike, you got too many horseshoes," a sorehead said as Davey raked in the pot.

"I'm shakin' fair, brother. They're just hot for me this time. The dice get hot for a guy like this maybe once in his whole life."

"They get too damn hot when I lay my sheets down."

"Want to finish my turn and try 'em yourself?"

"Shake!"

"I was just lucky tonight," Davey said, picking up the winnings of the last pot.

They glowered at him. He said so long. He walked slowly away, trying to feel that it wouldn't happen. He'd get away, get a swell meal, have a high-class woman for the night. Then, he'd buy a new suit, and ride back home on the cushions.

*It would sure be swell, seeing Paulie Haggerty, Studs, Red,
Tommy Doyle, all of the old guys, the best gang in the world.
Hadn't seen them in three years. It sure would be great.*

*He knew that he was being followed. As soon as he had
a chance, he'd run. He walked along, as if he wasn't quaking
with fear. He glanced back. Two of the bruisers were drawing
close to him. He started to run. He tripped. They coldcocked
him, and left him unconscious. They weren't letting a runty,
hook-nosed kike get their dough.*

*The two bruisers fought over the dough, and one of them
was laid out.*

*When Davey came to, feeling the bump on his head, he
cried like a baby. Christ, wouldn't he ever get a decent break?*

CHAPTER FOUR

I

He could hear the old man in the parlor, happily telling to
the old lady that this summer sure, they'd have to step out
a little, and go out to Riverview Park, and have a good time,
like they'd been planning to for a long time. And Fran was
in her room, singing a new song about west-side chauffeurs
who kiss 'em where you find 'em and leave 'em where you
kiss 'em.

Studs studied himself in the mirror. He tipped his first straw
hat at a rakish angle. He felt his face and looked closely where
he'd shaven off the down. He stood back, erect, and pulled
down the sleeves of his gray suit, holding them with the last
three fingers of each hand. He arranged his blue tie. Quite
a guy, he thought. But maybe he ought to have a loud purple
silk shirt, the kind Pat Coady and Percentage wore. He would
have gotten one, only if he had, he'd have had his tail kidded
off. Later on, he would, and damn tootin', he was quite a
guy.

Pretty well off too at seventeen. Hell, Dan Donoghue and
the others from the Indiana gang he'd graduated with from
St. Patrick's were still only high school kids. He was earning
his own living, making good dough, and his old man had
changed his attitude towards him. He really wasn't so bad,
and he'd only been saying the truth in that scrap they'd had.
Great, all right, to be earning your own dough. He took his
wallet out, counting the twelve single dollars from his first
pay that he'd stuffed into it. And, some day, he'd be a full-
fledged painter, on a scaffold, spreading on paint just as nice

and easy as old Mort Morrison did now. There was a good guy; all the fellows he worked with were white, and treated him decent. And, yes, the time would come when he'd step into the old man's boots; then, though, wouldn't Fran change her tune?

He whistled as he walked towards the front door.

"Have a good time, Bill, old boy, and don't take any wooden nickels," the old man called from the parlor.

His mother rushed to the door, made the sign of the cross before him, kissed him, and told him to be a good boy.

He walked along, whistling. He stopped at the corner of Fifty-eighth and Indiana. If he walked down to Fifty-seventh, he might just bump into Dan or Helen Shires, talk about old times, let them see how he was all dolled up, bowl 'em over by flashing his roll. And he could maybe see Lucy, and speak, and she'd say how swell he looked, and he'd say what are you doing, and he'd say come on, let's take in a show, and he'd have a blowout with her, and not go around the poolroom, and he'd kiss her good night on the steps. Now, he'd have the dough to take her out regularly. Girls liked a fellow to take them out and show them a good time. Swell to be earning your own living.

Hell, he was out of their class now. He took a few steps across Indiana Avenue. He paused, looked down to see the street in a fading spring twilight. Buildings he knew, a few automobiles parked along the curbs, some kids playing across from O'Brien's house. The tumble-down wooden buildings near Fifty-eighth on his right, where Mush Joss lived. The row of two-story gray bricks where Lucy lived. Where they used to play tin-tin on nights like this, and sometimes with everybody giggling, he'd kiss her. He wanted to put his arms around her and kiss her again. Aw, hell, he had the dough to get all the girls he wanted. He turned, and walked slowly down Indiana Avenue on the west side of the street. Maybe he'd see Dan. The last time he'd stopped in, Dan had been studying. Let him!

No curtains in Lucy's house. The lights out. . . . Moved. He looked in. Funny, he hadn't heard from Fran or anybody that she was moving. Where? There was the house empty, and he could remember seeing her around it so often, on the steps at this time of day when they'd come home from the park, and she'd blown him a last kiss, on the steps yelling for him when he fought Weary, looking out the window one day smiling in that way of hers when he had passed by. She had even perhaps moved to another city. Perhaps never, never again would he see her! All his hopes were gone, like they'd dropped into a sewer, and what if he had dough in his kick, and looked swell, and was wearing his first straw katy! Through the window there was growing darkness, no furniture. There were plenty of girls to be gotten, and perhaps he might never see her, or would see her only far far ahead, when it was all too late.

He walked down to the corner, absorbed. Without realizing it, he stood by the mail box, opening and closing it. If anybody saw him, he'd look crazy as a loon.

"Hello, Studs!" said Andy Le Gare, entering the corner building.

"Shut up!"

Studs walked west on Fifty-seventh to the alley, and then turned around. It wouldn't look fluky now, if he just turned back and walked by her house again. Look like he was just on his way somewhere. He didn't want to go anywhere. He glanced at the empty house, desolate. Across the street kids played hide-and-go-seek, their voices and shouts seeming far away. He and Lucy had passed the crossroads of life now, their paths had cut away from each other. In that movie the other night the same thing had happened to the fellow and the girl, only they'd found each other again, in time.

Aw, what the hell! Let it go! He was sitting pretty!

He was aware of it being very quiet, lonesome, the sad part of the day. A dog barked. A horse and wagon clattered by on the rough, unpaved street. There was the noise of automobile brakes. The kids. The dog barked again. Quiet.

He went over Fifty-eighth Street. There was the tailor shop run by Cohen's old man. A dry goods store in place of the old Palm Theatre. A shoe repair shop where Schroeder had had that ice cream parlor they'd raided. The alley. The chain store, and the five and dime. The neighborhood was still much the same, and yet it was different without her. Every block, every store was somehow connected in his mind with her. It was as if she was like God, and her spirit was in everything in the neighborhood, only it wasn't any more. Suppose he had gone to war, and been killed. They would always remember him as a hero, and now maybe. . . .

He stopped to get a drink of water at the fountain in front of Sternberg's cigar store straight across from the drug store at Fifty-eighth and Prairie.

Some punks he didn't know stood at the fountain, and as that snotty, loud-mouth little hebe, Phillip Rolfe, drew near, they squirted water square in his puss. Studs laughed. Phillip shouted irritatingly. They squirted again, and, dodging, Phillip bumped into him.

"Get out of my way!" he said, missing a kick.

"Aw, it wasn't my fault!"

"Shut up!"

An old man limped stiffly along, shouting swear words at the top of his cracked lungs. The laughing punks egged him on, and he cursed them. Studs laughed.

"Hey, grandpa! Button up. You're losing something," Rolfe yelled, everybody laughing; the old man heaped foul curses on them. Funny! Studs watched him struggle along, followed by the punks.

A truck was coming, and on an impulse he dashed before it. Had to cut that out. Might be mashed someday, if he didn't.

He looked at his shoes, and leaned down to run a finger across the right toe. But it had been scuffed. Didn't like that. He noticed the sharp press in his trousers.

He walked on towards the poolroom, wishing he was going out with Lucy, a girl. Maybe they'd all go to a can house. He was afraid to do that; no, he wasn't.

He smiled at Sammy Schmaltz the newspaper man, hoping Sammy would comment on his new lid and clothes. Sammy was too busy selling papers.

Self-conscious, he joined a gang before the poolroom, and smiled deprecatingly when they kidded that he was all dolled up. Then they went back to kidding Paulie Haggerty, the married man, they said, who was too young to stand the gaff.

"Yeah, you guys just ask my wife if I ain't the goods!" said Paulie.

Studs envied him. He could stand up and say there was one girl who was all his, every inch of her. And every night with her, he could get it, as much as he wanted.

"Hey, Haggerty, does your wife wash your diapers?" asked balloon-bellied Barney Keefe.

"Ooph, that's a hot one," Fitz, the poolroom pest, said, as they laughed.

"You know, Barney, you look almost human these days, even with your false teeth," Paulie replied.

"He just bought new knee pads today too," Kilarney said.

"Lookat the can on that one!" Slew Weber said, pointing as Elizabeth Burns passed.

"Hey, Haggerty, shield your eyes. You're married," Barney said.

"A married man has more experience."

"Listen, she lays for every punk in the neighborhood. She's a fourteen-year-old bitch," Kelly said.

"But she's all right. I speak from experience," Doyle said.

"I wouldn't kick her out of bed," Slew said.

"Weber, your age limit is from eight to eighty," Barney said.

"Let's do something," Paulie said.

"Let's!" Studs said, forgetting his moodiness.

"Hey, lads, look!" Pat Coady said, pointing.

They saw Barney tagging after Elizabeth Burns.

They laughed, and when Barney came back, unsuccessful, they kidded his pants off. Barney retorted by kidding Paulie, telling him a married man had to keep his feet from smelling and take regular baths.

"Let's do something," Studs said.

II

Studs glanced around the saloon. He watched a big bloke at the rail spitting into a spittoon. Some of the birds at the bar, like that red-faced guy in khaki at the end, looked tough. Suppose there would be a free-for-all fight? Might get mashed. He imagined himself in a brawl, fighting like a demon.

"Dempsey's too damn small to take Willard," Kelly said.

"My dough's on Dempsey," Studs said.

"Say, Willard's sixty pounds heavier," said Red.

"And that sixty pounds is crap," said Barney.

"A good little man can often trim a big guy," Studs said, hoping they'd think of himself.

He took a sip of beer and ate a pretzel, because the beer didn't taste as bitter with the pretzel.

"Barney, what you gonna do after Prohibition?" asked Coady.

"Become a nun!"

"No kiddin', Barney?"

"Get married like this punk," Barney said, wiping his chin with his coat sleeve.

"Who'd have an old man like you?" asked Paulie.

"Listen, punk, there's plenty of stuff left in Barney Keefe!"

"Horse," said Paulie as they loudly reminded him of Elizabeth Burns.

"Come on, Barney, tell us what you're going to do after Prohibition?"

"What am I gonna do after Prohibition. . . . What am I gonna do after Prohibition. . . . What am I gonna do after Prohibition? Ask me something brighter!"

"Isn't Prohibition a goddamn bright idea," Red said.

"Like hell," Fitz, the pest, answered seriously.

"I'll tell you what I'm going to do . . . I'm going to stay drunk," Barney said; they laughed.

The beer began to make Studs a little dizzy. He didn't like it, didn't want any more. He saw Lucy in his head, and suddenly she spun around, and his head whirled like a merry-go-round. They ordered more, and Studs grunted he'd have another with them.

Slug Mason joined them. He was a bruiser over six feet, broad-shouldered, a leathery, stupid face, and hands like steel cranes. He looked like a brute to Studs.

"After the first of July, they're planning on deporting all you Irish along with the bullshevicky. The bullshevicky kill you with bombs, and the Irish with the whiskey breath," Slug Mason said, changing all his ths to ds, dropping the h from his withs, and slurring the pronunciation of most of his other words.

They laughed.

"Say, Slug, didn't you have a tryout with the Sox?" asked Fitz.

"Long time ago when they had Ed Walsh. Nineteen eleven or twelve. But I was supposed to be there at twelve, and for three days, goddamn it, I couldn't wake myself up that early," Slug said.

"Early to bed, and early to rise, makes a man healthy, wealthy, and wise," Kenny said, apropos of nothing, and raising his mug aloft; they laughed.

"You punks ought to be home in bed," said Fitz.

"A guy going to bed early never meets a regular guy like myself," Barney said.

"Say, Barney, do me a favor. Lose your head back there in the can," Pat Coady said.

"This Lothario, Haggerty, better be early to bed and early to rise, or that wife he's got will knock his tail off," Barney said, ignoring the crack.

Slug talked about women. Everybody bragged how much he had had. Studs felt out of it, because he hadn't had so many girls like that, only Iris, and that Hallowe'en in 1918, when they had gang-shagged some bum they had picked up on Wabash Avenue. Red Kelly bragged, and Studs, even though drunk, knew Red was throwing bull all over the place. He wanted a girl. But he felt so lousy, he couldn't keep thinking of it. His belly seemed bloated; he was dizzy in the head. He could only sit straight by exerting all his will-power.

Charlie Bathcellar joined them. He told them he'd just closed a deal, selling the poolroom to a Greek. The guys were sorry, and got sentimental. Suddenly Charlie remembered that Paulie's wife had been around, almost in tears, looking for him. They laughed, kidding Paulie. Slug told Paulie he was handling his woman right. They had to be trained, and when they were trained right, they were as meek as a lamb, and if they weren't, they were female tigers. Once you let them wear the britches, they'd never take them off, and you were a goner. Paulie drank on it with Slug.

"But fellows, you know, my wife is a good kid," Paulie suddenly said.

"She looked awfully blue," Charlie said.

"She'll get over it," Paulie said.

"My old woman did. Just treat her a little tough, and when she squawks, slap her down. They like that," Slug said, in his way of pronunciation.

"You guys drop the skirts. Here's the only solace for mortal man," Barney said, raising his mug aloft.

"Sure, but try and keep it from having the old sailor freeze on a windy night," Slug said.

Paulie's head fell to the table. Barney laughed, and said it was one punk drunk under the table. Slug said Barney didn't have any belly; it was a barrel down there.

Slug suddenly saw that Studs was getting pale and glassy-eyed. He said they better get the kid some air, and, lifting him, supported him outside. The whole gang followed. He helped Studs along, the two of them looking like Mutt and Jeff.

Paulie staggered in the rear. In tears, he said that he loved his wife. He asked Kenny if he didn't think she was one damn swell woman. Kenny answered that she was homelier than Maggie in the Jiggs cartoons.

"Come on!" challenged Paulie, putting up his fists; tears splattered down his face.

Paulie swung wildly, belaboring the air, while Kenny laughed and shadow-boxed out of his reach.

"Please fight me," sobbed Paulie, dropping his hands to his sides.

"No, but I'll play you a little casino."

"Well, come on then, you bastard!"

They sat down on the sidewalk, and Kenny started dividing rocks between them. Paulie said these were stones, not cards. Kenny seriously said they were cards. Paulie said he'd fight over it. Kenny leaped up, and ran ahead. He watched and kidded while Slug held Studs, who was vomiting over the curb.

"I love my wife," Paulie shouted, as he staggered in the rear, his coat slung over his shoulder, his hat askew, his hair plastered down his forehead.

He caught up with the other guys, and sobbed that he was worried because he thought that he still might have that dose of his, and he was afraid that if he had any kids, it would make them blind, or even nuttier than Kilarney.

"Blah!" mouthed Kenny.

"Say, for Christ sake, will somebody drag that puppy home to his she-bitch," Barney complained.

Paulie mumbled it was no fooling. He was worried because it might even mean that he'd have kids like Kenny Kilarney. He fell down. They had to carry him, and he wouldn't shut up.

III

"I'm drunk!" Paulie said emphatically, as he floundered beside Studs.

"I'm weak," Studs said.

"I'm drunk, Studs."

"Didn't it give you a headache," Studs said, feeling his head, glad he had vomited it up.

"Christ, Studs, I'm drunk!"

Studs belched.

Paulie complained, too, because of that dose and having kids like Kilarney. He said he loved his wife. Studs wanted to mention Lucy, but he didn't get a chance. Paulie talked a leg off him. He left Paulie, and walked slowly home, his head pounding. He felt proud of having been drunk, and sorry, and rotten. He worried lest he would wake up the family. He started walking on a crack in the sidewalk, back and forth, to prove to himself that he could walk straight. And if anybody was up, they might smell his breath.

Getting in, he fumbled with his key, and it seemed like he was as noisy as an earthquake.

"That you, son?"

He stood still, like an apprehended burglar. His mother said she'd worried because it was late. He said he was all right, and had only been talking with some of the fellows. Luck! He quickly tumbled into bed, into its soft whiteness, protection from his headache, and thoughts, and everything.

V

Studs Lonigan, Tommy Doyle, Red Kelly, Benny Taite, and Kenny Kilarney acted slightly aloof, while a gang of blood-thirsty kids swirled and milled about them reiterating the cry of "Let's go!" Clubs and sticks were brandished. Three Star Hennessey gritted his teeth, and slashed the air with a straight razor. Weary Reilley casually and publicly examined a twenty-two revolver. Kenny Kilarney put on a pair of brass

knuckles, and permitted the punks to examine them. Studs
Lonigan gripped a baseball bat, and swung as if stepping into
a pitch. He said that when he cracked a dinge in the head,
the goddamn eight ball would think it had been Ty Cobb
slamming out a homer off Walter Johnson. Red Kelly un-
sheathed a hunting-knife, and vowed that he was ready. Andy
Le Gare tried to tell everyone that in close fighting they should
kick the niggers in the shins. Tommy Doyle said the niggers
were never going to forget the month of July, 1919. Studs
said that they ought to hang every nigger in the city to the
telephone poles, and let them swing there in the breeze. Benny
Taite said that for every white man killed in the riots, ten
black apes ought to be massacred. Red said that the niggers
had caught Clackey Merton, from Sixty-first Street, down in
the black belt, and slashed his throat from ear to ear, and
plenty of niggers had to be slashed to pay for the death of
Clackey. They lamented that Clackey was a victim of the riots.
Fat Malloy started telling how the Regan Colts were marching
into the black belt and knocking off the niggers. Andy said
well the Fifty-eighth Street guys were going to do the same
thing.

Young Horn Buckford suddenly appeared and breathlessly
said that there was a gang of niggers over on Wabash Avenue.
Studs, Red, Tommy, Weary, Kenny, and Benny Taite led
the gang along Fifty-eighth Street, over to Wabash. For two
hours, they prowled Wabash Avenue and State Street, between
Garfield Boulevard and Fifty-ninth Street, searching for
niggers. They sang, shouted, yelled defiance at the houses,
and threw bricks into the windows of houses where they thought
niggers lived. They were joined by other groups, men and
kids. The streets were like avenues of the dead. They only
caught a ten-year-old Negro boy. They took his clothes off,
and burned them. They burned his tail with lighted matches,
made him step on lighted matches, urinated on him, and sent
him running off naked with a couple of slaps in the face.

Back around the corner at six o'clock, Studs and Red talked
of how they would get a bigger gang together after supper,
and go north of Garfield Boulevard until they found niggers.
They described what they would do to them. They walked
down to the el station and bought a paper. The headlines said
that with the militia out, peace and order were being restored
in the riot-stricken black belt. They cursed, and said they
would get the niggers in spite of even the whole United States
Army. They would avenge Clackey Merton, the kid from Sixty-
first Street, who had been killed down in the black belt.

CHAPTER FIVE

Studs walked with Paulie and his Eileen towards the park, and he and Paulie gassed about the good old days. But it seemed stiff with her there, smiling politely at everything they said, even the things they kept exaggerating and making more than they actually had been, in order to make her think that they'd been great guys.

They talked about what the boys from Fifty-eighth Street had done in the race riots last month, and she acted horrified, but Studs guessed it was only put on. They told each other that the niggers needed a couple more riots.

Crossing South Park Avenue, Paulie took her elbow. Studs envied him, because she was his girl, his woman, and she slept with him, undressed in front of him, and he could do whatever he wanted with her body. It was something, having a woman all the time. When you walked down the street, with her on your arm, everybody could see she was yours and gave it to you whenever you wanted it. And you could bring her around to meet your friends, and let them see you got it, and they'd look her over, and envy you, seeing she had nice legs, a swell figure, enough meat on her in the right places. Maybe he did kind of wish he had a woman of his own, as nice and as hot as Paulie's with a good figure, and good-looking clothes like the blue suit she had on. Studs fell behind, pretending to pick up something, so he could get a look at her. She was hot-looking all right, with plenty of meat on her, nice tocus, slim ankle, and the fragment of leg between dress and ankle was the stuff too, fleshy and shapely. She was gorgeous to look at, to touch, to. . . .

It was swell out, just cool enough, with the park air smelling sort of cool; and the trees were green and leafy, their shadows falling in solid black now as it got dark. He looked at her again, then up at a tree, and in back of him; she must be catching on that he had to keep looking at her. What a sweet piece she must be!

She told Paulie about the new set of dishes she wanted; he didn't seem to be interested; Studs thought that part of things should be taken care of by the wife, and she shouldn't bother the guy about it. Same way at home, the old lady always had to tell the old man what she'd buy, and he didn't want to hear it.

"Going to have a football team in the fall, Studs?" Paulie asked, ignoring her as she harped about dishes.

"I think so. Looks like it will be pretty good."

Maybe Paulie would say something to let her know he'd be captain and quarterback, and that he was one damn sweet football player. Next fall, she might even come out to one of the games and see for herself how good he was.

"You're not going to play, Paul?" she said, entreating.

"No."

They walked along on the path that led from the entrance, and curved around to the left, past the boathouse.

Studs used to like to talk to Paulie; now, with his wife around, there didn't seem anything to talk about, and it didn't mean much; it was like stabbing in the dark to reach something when there was nothing to reach. Paulie was different.

"Think you'll be getting married?" Paulie asked, and Studs saw that his wife smiled condescendingly.

"No," Studs said, luckily checking himself from putting a "hell" first; he'd just thought that it had its advantages, but then the way it kept a guy from his pals, the arguing, the kids later on, the time to come when your wife wouldn't be a hot hunk any more; there were both sides to it.

"You'll tumble some day," Paulie said in the voice of experience.

"No danger," Studs insisted, dismayed by her steady smile.

"It's always the ones talking like you who fall the hardest," she said, smiling sweetly.

"You'll fall!" Paulie said confidently.

Studs enjoyed being the center of conversation like that. If it kept on, Paulie might say something like, how's Lucy, or, why don't you marry Lucy? Of course, he'd answer he didn't want to, but he didn't know if he did or not. And he'd shrug his shoulders don't-care-like when Eileen would ask who Lucy was, and Paulie would say she was a nice girl, Studs' girl. The whole business suddenly seemed goofy. Still, he waited to hear Paulie mention her name.

"Yes, Studs, some morning you'll just wake up to find yourself married."

He forced another laugh. He tried to think of himself settling down with a wife. Himself getting up in the morning, kissing her, sitting down to be served breakfast, eating supper with her; himself coming home one night and telling the family he was going to be married, looking Fran in the face when he said it. He was glad he wasn't going through that kind of thing yet. But having a woman! Fellows saying Studs' woman. That was all right. Thinking about it, at least, was. They'd kid him, but it would only be fun and half jealousy on their part. Himself coming home in winter, she taking his shoes off, putting his slippers on, sitting and watching him with love while he read, doing things for him, and then, when it was cold out, going to bed, he taking her clothes off, she taking his off, getting all warmed up together. That would be better than hanging around the poolroom. But then, if she nagged! He had time, and there were both sides of it.

"Why so quiet?" asked Paulie.

"Ope, just looking around, and thinking about the team we'll have in the fall," Studs hurriedly answered, feeling, though, as if Paulie had seen right into what he'd been thinking.

They sat on a bench near the circle with the fountain, where the path curved.

Studs noticed a doodish guy on the bench across from them. He was classily dressed, the kind of a bird who'd go over bigger with girls than fellows.

"Gee, it's a swell night," Paulie said.

"I think I'll be dashing along," Studs said.

"Hang around a while," Paulie said.

He sat on the edge of the bench. Maybe they wanted to be alone. He wanted a girl, Lucy, a girl to be sitting with him on a bench, under the trees like this.

"Dear, it's perfectly grand here."

"Swell," Paulie said, looking up at the trees that roofed in the gathering darkness.

"Yeah," muttered Studs abstractedly, raw with thoughts of himself and Lucy in the park, himself all open so that every thought and word seemed like they were touching an open cut inside him.

"Many's the times we had in this park, huh, Studs?"

"Yeah," Studs said, observing that the guy seemed to be looking at her, wishing that Paulie would speak of some of the fights he had had.

He glanced down at Paulie, and saw that his wife had her legs crossed, showing her leg almost up to the knee. No wonder the guy looked. Couldn't blame the guy; hell, her legs were worth seeing all the way up. If he sat alone on a bench and saw a girl like her with legs crossed, he'd look for all he was worth. . . . But Paulie was his friend, and she was Paulie's wife. He liked Paulie and liked to stick with him; it was his duty to a friend to tell Paulie, and, if necessary, help him sock the guy. Anyway, he didn't like the bastard's looks. Some of the guys might be in the boathouse too, if they needed help, but they wouldn't. Studs turned to tell Paulie, but saw that he was on to it.

"See anything green?" asked Paulie.

The fellow didn't answer.

218 THE YOUNG MANHOOD

"Hey!" snarled Paulie.

"Paul!" she begged, touching his sleeve.

"Hey, you, I said: 'See anything green?' " Paulie said, rising and brushing his wife's hand aside; Studs jumped up.

"The grass is green," the fellow said, smiling good-naturedly, an expression of almost sick friendliness on his face.

"Buddy, there ain't room for all of us around here!"

"Yeah, fellow, shove on while you're all together!" Studs said.

"Paul, please . . . please, don't go fighting; he hasn't done a thing to you," she pleaded, pulling at his coat.

"Shut up!" he snapped at her.

"It's healthier in that direction," Studs said, pointing with his right hand.

The fellow, taller than Paulie, started to slink away. Paulie swung, catching him unexpectedly in the jaw from the side. The fellow staggered, then made a start to run. Paulie caught him, and jerked him around, for Studs, who drove him a fierce uppercut. The fellow punched and kicked back.

"Oh, you will, will you!" Paulie said, his wife screaming as her husband's fist drove into the bastard's mouth. It bled. He went down, and they kicked him. He went off, holding a handkerchief to his face.

"Brutes!" she said.

"Listen, bitch!" Paulie said.

A fellow asked what was the matter. Studs said the guy had monkeyed around with his pal's wife. The fellow said it was good for him. There was a lot of damn mashers like that, and they all needed a sock in the puss.

"And you listen to me. Any goddamn time you sit like you were then, showing off everything you own, there'll be trouble. My wife ain't acting like a whore in a public park when I'm around. Get that straight, and don't forget it!"

She cried, denying his accusation.

"You're a goddamn liar!" Paulie shouted.

"I'm going to the boathouse," Studs said, embarrassed; he left without them noticing him.

None of the guys were around. He noticed, too, that no niggers were in sight. He spied a lonesome-looking chicken sitting up towards the front. Maybe she wanted to be picked up. He sat near her, and kept giving her the eye. She was pretty, a baby-faced blond. She sat impassive. He could just go up and talk to her, say let's take a walk, and get her over on the wooded island. And he'd go back to the poolroom, and tell the lads what a lay he had, describing how it all went off, and knock them cuckoo wishing they'd been that lucky.

She met his eye, icy, not a hint on her face. Sometimes they were like that in pretense, making it a game where you worked for it. He lit a cigarette, nonchalant, as if he were just as unaware of her presence as she seemed to be of his. He looked out at the water, black, except where the boathouse lights and stretches of moonlight lay over it. He tried to think up something clever that he might say to make an opening. He could just see her smiling at his cleverness, if only he could hit upon some good crack. He watched two couples rowing away from the landing. One of the girls laughed loudly. He arose, and casually sauntered to her side, glanced at her while she looked uninterestedly ahead. He said hello. She didn't respond. He got nervous, and greeted her a second time. She looked up at him, as if he were so low that he crept on the ground.

"Like to go oaring, cutie?"

"I should say not," she said, turning her back.

He felt like he might just go crawl into a barrel, and sink his head. Blushing, he left the boathouse. Just a goddamn bitch trying to be swell! He wandered back on the grass, wondering if he might take in the movie at the Prairie Theatre. Dirty it was, jumping the poor bastard, when you couldn't blame him for looking at something offered to him on a platter; she knew he was looking. If that jane, bitch, in the boathouse had a husband, he'd be the same way and want to start swinging. Just natural to look at a girl's legs. He was sorry, a bit ashamed of himself; but that uppercut he'd given him, it had been beautiful, timed just right. Remembering the thrill of landing it was even swell.

He crossed the bushes in back of the bench where they were. He saw them in each other's arms, and heard her say to Paulie:

"Honey, I love you!"

Made him want a girl! Put his arms around her, draw her tight so he could press into her, feel her hardening herself against him, feeling her quiver and shake with excitement because he touched her, wanted to know her. No girl had ever said she loved him like she'd just told Paulie. The Great Studs Lonigan, the battler . . . no girl ever seemed to think so. He wanted one, maybe he even wanted to marry one . . . maybe, perhaps, Lucy. . . .

He met Elizabeth Burns crossing the drive from the Fifty-eighth Street entrance.

"Say, aren't you afraid being over here alone in the dark?"

"Nobody would hurt little me," she giggled.

"You need protection," he said, taking her arm.

He walked her around the south bend of the lagoon, and over the stone bridge to the wooded island. They found a spot right near the tree where he and Lucy had been. She didn't offer him any resistance.

He was tired, drowsy, walking back with her, their clothes all rumpled. She was too much for him. Never would get enough. What a bitch! But before he had got so tired that it hurt him, nice, and he'd looked up at the sky, blue, big, so many stars like jewels, feeling perfectly at peace. Only she wanted an army. And what she didn't know at the age of fourteen wasn't worth knowing. They walked slowly towards Calumet, not saying much. At the corner of Calumet, her old man, a big bastard over six feet, jumped out with a horse-whip.

"Get home, you whore!" he said, roughly pushing her aside. He snapped the whip, bearing it down on Studs' shoulder. Studs was so surprised that he stood stock still. The old man lashed him three times, before he ran. Old Man Burns followed him down the street, cursing him, lashing him with the horse-whip till it stung and burned. Strangers stopped to laugh. He felt that he couldn't run much farther, and he ran, gasping, his side paining sharply. He couldn't stop, and Christ, that whip. He dashed recklessly in front of automobiles and got across to the park side of South Park Avenue. He turned and saw the old man flaunting his whip on the other side of the street, yelling:

"I'll teach you whose daughter you're monkeying with!"

He flung a rock, and ran through the bushes on the left-hand side of the tennis court. Old Man Burns didn't follow him.

SECTION TWO

1922

VI

Holy Mary, the Mother of God, the Virgin of Virgins, Mother most Powerful and Merciful, Morning Star and Health of the Weak, Comfortress of the Afflicted, Mother of God, Mary who had herself gone down into the valley of the shadow of death . . . she, Blessed Mary, she would understand the burden of distress and naked sorrow that lay on the heart of a poor mother whose precious baby son lay at death's door; she, whose only begotten Son had been crowned with thorns and crucified to save all mankind, she would understand, she would sympathize, she would intercede at the throne of God Almighty, the Creator of Heaven and Earth; she would beseech that if it be the will of God, to Whom all things were possible, that he spare the life of Mrs. Haggerty's son, Paul.

Mrs. Haggerty, stout and shabby, her eyes raw with tears, dropped her tenth dime into the slot by the candle rack before the altar of the Blessed Virgin. She gazed adoringly and with tears of hope at the waxenly expressionless face on the blue-robed statue of the Mother of God. Her face accumulated intenseness, and the lips on the waxenly expressionless face seemed to move, miraculously, in calming words.

Mrs. Haggerty lit her tenth candle and placed it in a holder that it might burn as a prayer of entreaty.

She prayed in a church wombed in quiet. A jangling street car passed outside, and its racket was like a rough, uncouthly handled instrument lacerating the churchly hush. The beat of marching feet thundered on the ceiling. From outside came the shouts of school children, boys and girls. The swinging door in the rear was jammed back and forth; feet scraped on the aisles. A boy knelt before the center altar, and his face became wistful in prayer. Mrs. Haggerty looked at him with maternal eyes.

And only five years ago—life was short—Paul had been a boy like that, innocent; and his steps had mingled with the feet of other boys and girls as they marched out of the schoolrooms upstairs. And he had romped and shouted as the children without were now doing.

HAIL MARY, FULL OF GRACE, THE LORD IS WITH THEE, BLESSED ART THOU AMONGST WOMEN, AND BLESSED IS THE FRUIT OF THY WOMB, JESUS . . .

Mary, please spare me a mother's agony, please, oh, please, save the fruit of my womb, my Paul, my precious baby son.
. . .

HAIL MARY, FULL OF GRACE. . . .

CHAPTER SIX

I

Mike stared out of the poolroom window. His face was a gaze of primal obtuseness. An elevated train rumbled out of the Fifty-eighth Street elevated station. An automobile whizzed by.

"Hello, Mike!" said Slug Mason entering, his smeary-lipped mouth cracking in a smile.

Mike greeted Slug with an idiot grin. Slug lit a cigarette, shoved his hands in his pockets and leaned back on his heels.

"Smoke?" asked Mike, holding out his greasy, sweaty paw.

"Say, it looks like there's gonna be some sun out this morning," Slug said, with faulty pronunciation, as he studied the street outside and the blue September sky that was slowly being shattered with sunlight.

Mike lit one of his own cigarettes.

"Jesus, was we all cockeyed las' night . . . but say, Mike, I fixes the lads with some flaming jazz-babies!"

"Push-push," mumbled Mike, lust, like thick, ugly sweat, oozing from his eyes.

Slug beamed patronizingly.

"Push-push!"

"Yeah, Mike, I'll bet you know your stuff."

II

"Wheeeee!" shouted Young Rocky Kansas as he crashed through the narrow entrance door, removing his jacket coat.

"Wheeeeeeeee!" echoed skinny, toothpick Harry Pochon, following upon Young Rocky's heels past the shoe-shining stand, which stood where Charlie Bathcellar had had his barber chairs.

"Time on table number one, Greek!" Young Rocky shouted.

"Come on, time on, you dumb Greek bastard!" parroted Pochon.

Mike's face clenched with hate. Slowly, he turned and went to the counter. He punched a card on the time clock.

"These eighteen-year-old punks needs their snouts punched in to teach 'em a lesson," Slug said.

A slow gleam of assent was born on Mike's face. He shrugged, and placed a hat on the cleaning block. He commenced to brush the hat.

Slug watched the youngest Sullivan girl trip stiff-leggedly by.

"Nice," Mike babbled, with clumsy, pawing, emphatic gestures. They laughed in mutual understanding.

III

Bob Connell entered, wearing a loud gray summer suit with bell buttons. Big Rocky Kansas followed him, walking muscle bound and like a tame bear. He was a bushy-browed lad of about twenty-one, with broad shoulders. He smiled with intoxicating good-nature, and, sticking a cigar in his bucolic face, ranged himself alongside Slug. Slug ignored Bob's cloying salutation; he said Rocky looked like a politician, smoking that cigar. They heard the click of the pool balls. Big Rocky yelled hello to his kid brother.

"Say, last night, Gleen Reaves and me had some red hot mamas dated up. Cost us five bucks at Kling Hing Lo's Chop House. But, boy, did those broads know how to sock. Say, fellahs, I tell you, I never danced with the broad who socked like mine did. Why she dry . . ." Bob said with enthusiasm, cutting off his words, and answering the call from Young Rocky.

"Say, that punk has only got fifty cards in his deck," Slug said, pronouncing his ths as ds.

"Hell, he is only young, sixteen. He hasn't lost his cherry," Big Rocky said.

"Look! Look!" Mike said, pointing at a passing broad.

IV

"Well, Studs, you're a man now," grinned Slug.

"That doesn't mean nothing," replied bleary-eyed Studs.

"Say, you're right there. It's true," Slug said.

"Most things are just plain crap to me," Studs said.

"Ain't they though?" said Slug, saying "though" as if it were "dough."

"My head!" said Studs, feeling his right temple.

"Well, you was polluted last night," Slug said.

Studs nodded agreement.

"Say, Paulie's in bad shape. He was prayed for in Church this morning."

"He's a good lad."

"Gee, I hope he pulls through. But he's in a tough spot now," said Studs.

"He's down for the count, huh," said Slug.

"Let's get a coke and take a little walk," Studs said, as they walked out.

V

"And was I blind last night!" reiterated eighteen-year-old Ellsworth Lyman.

"You were soused to the gills," Wils Gillen said, causing Lyman to smile with the pride of achievement.

"Ellsworth was so drunk he went around with tears in his eyes, sobbing the blues, because he couldn't stop breathing," said Darby Dan Drennan; they guffawed.

"I don't remember that, but I do remember a guy getting

tough with me around Sixty-third, and I was all set to knock his teeth down his throat. But he was so yellow, I didn't have the heart to lay one on him."

"When Lyman called him, he folded up like an umbrella," Gillen said.

"I can't stand a guy with a yellow streak down his back," Lyman said.

"Well, by God, Ellsworth, you were snaky last night," said Wils.

"I guess I was," Ellsworth proudly said.

VI

"Jeff, you're falling away to a ton!" Red Kelly said.

"Yeah, don't fool yourself! I just dropped seventy-five pounds," Jeff replied, handfuls of fat on his cheek, chin, and neck wiggling into a smile.

He rolled along the poolroom, a lumbrous, slightly limping, waddling barracks of flesh.

"Hi, boys!" he said with excessive good-nature.

"Boys, here's Jeff, the baby elephant!" yelled Pochon.

"Say, Jeff, I thought you'd already joined a freak show," Young Rocky said.

"Say, Hippo, Man Bleu is gunning for you, and promises that he won't do anything at all but lose his fists in your goddamn fat puss," Lyman yelled.

"I ain't done nothing to him," Jeff protested.

"What, another chump you took in?" asked Kelly.

"Man gave him five bucks to get him some punch boards. He ain't seen the elephant since," Lyman said.

"He's not gettin' gypped. He'll get them. They were just delayed at the factory. Just got 'em yesterday. In fact, I came around to see if he was here now."

"B.S.," Young Rocky said, lip-farting.

"Jeff, you ain't got the heart of a snake, have you?" said Kelly.

"Commere, Red. I got a funny story to tell you," Jeff said.

"Jeff, the first ton is the hardest, ain't it?" said Gillen.

VII

"Arnold, where'd you get the shiner?" Stan Simonsky, nephew of a baseball magnate, asked.

"Oh, a fight last night," Arnold replied.

Stan, plump and medium-sized, stretched on his toes to examine Arnold Sheehan's black eye. Arnold was taller, and well built; his face was crude in features, with heavy dark brows, and a long nose. He wore a loosely-cut black suit with flashy pin-stripes, a checkered gray topcoat, an almost pearly gray fedora, and black tie.

"Drunk again?" asked Stan.

Arnold nodded.

"Every time you get snozzled, you get a break, don't you! Two weeks ago you were maggoty and got your dose, and you're still limping from getting shoved down those elevated steps last week. You better stick to malted milks, Arnold."

"Just hard luck! I was dancing at the Bourbon Palace, and got in a scrap over a broad I was trying to make. I wasn't so drunk, though. You should have seen Weary Reilley. He was tossing sugar bowls all around Kling's Restaurant."

"Some day that guy's gonna get worse than you'll ever get."

"Say, Arnold, what'll you take for your shiner?" Kelly hollered over to him.

VIII

"You were pretty gone last night," beefy Tommy Doyle said to his cousin Les.

"Yes, I was," Les modestly said.

"Your old man should have seen you."

"Don't worry. He's tipped many a bottle himself," Les said, smiling like a cherub.

Tommy shook his head in expression of indefinite amusement.

"Hell, I might just as well get drunk. I don't see why I got to rot away in that rut, working on an electric for the Continental Express Company. Gee, I'm never going to amount to anything, and I might as well have a little fun . . . . Say, Tommy, I sure do wish I'd gone to school and gotten an education," Les whined.

"You don't know when you're well off. I'd like to have a job paying the dough you get."

"Well, I wish I had an education. Look at where Joe O'Reilley and Dinny Gorman are. Now if I was a lawyer, I might be getting somewheres."

IX

"You know Dot Gorman. She's older than us guys, see, but lemme tell you . . . she's keen. *KEEN!*" funnyface Young Duffy orated for his own benefit.

"She ain't so much. She's horsefaced and stuckup," Denny Dennis said.

"Say, your taste is all in your mouth," funnyface Duffy said.

Goofy Nate Klein called Duffy aside.

"Listen, punk. Dorothy Gorman is a friend of mine. She's too nice a girl to be talked about in a joint like this. If you know when you're healthy, don't mention her name in this place again. And don't call her Dot. Get me?"

"I didn't say nothin' against her. I was just complimenting her. . . ."

"I told you that if you don't want your friends taking up a collection for flowers for you, don't mention her name in this joint again!" Nate said, hard-boiled.

X

"You know, I just went into the bedroom with that broad last night, and everything went out like the lights," Studs said.

Tommy Doyle cracked a joke about what should have happened.

"Lookat the punks. They ain't washed under the ears yet," sneered Slug, gazing surprisedly around the poolroom.

"They look goofy in their ding-dong pants," said Studs.

"Monkey suits," said Slug; he pointed at the twenty-two-inch-bell-bottoms on Phil Rolfe's carefully, precisely, exactly careless black suit. Phil turned his light-complexioned, insipid face towards them and smiled. He was wearing a blue shirt, collar attached, a soft, wine-red knit tie, and a light brown hat.

"Pull up your skirts," said Stan Simonsky.

"Hi, kid," patronized Phil.

"Hey, Rolfe?" yelled Red.

"What you say, Red," replied Phil with aplomb.

"Hey, punk, where's your rubber knee pads?" Studs sneered.

"Did you get that out of a joke book?" he asked, but he blushed slightly.

Phil walked away from them, towards a table in the back.

"Hey, Studs, I haven't eaten today. Can you loan me two bits. After a while, I'll shark some guy in a pool game, but Christ, I'm starved!" said TB McCarthy; TB was thin, consumptive-looking, with jaundiced cheeks that seemed to be shrivelling and hollowing away. He wore a spotted, unpressed, shabby, brown suit.

"Get out of here, heel."

"Muggsy mooching again?" said Red.

"Jesus, Red, I haven't eaten today," said Muggsy.

"Well, McCarthy, there's lots of horse manure in the alley," said Slug. All the other guys in the bunch guffawed.

XI

"Thanks, kid, and I'll have the liquor back to you at three-thirty this afternoon. And I guarantee that it's bonded," Jeff said, taking three and a half dollars from funnyface Young Duffy.

"Sure now that it's good stuff?" asked Duffy.

"I wouldn't sell it to you if it wasn't," Jeff convincingly replied.

Jeff struggled and puffed towards the door. Everybody got in his way and he had a hell of a time squeezing past them.

XII

"All I hope is that that dope starts her like nobody's business," Wils Gillen said.

"It did for me when I had the scare about Elizabeth," Ellsworth said.

"Well, if it don't . . . Holy Jesus!"

"You'll either have to join the navy or else . . . marry the pig."

"Marry her, a Midway Garden bum?"

"If it don't, I know a doctor. I fixed up Sadie Prevost with him when she was knocked up by all you guys. She's all right, only to raise the dough she had to go out and hustle. She did so well hustling that she's in the business for good now," Darby Dan Drennan said.

"She sacrificed her amateur standing, huh?" said Ellsworth.

"If it don't, it's the marines and see the world, boys," Wils said.

"Anyway, Wils, no matter how tough a hole you're in, remember that you'll always be better off than poor Paulie Haggerty," philosophized Darby Dan Drennan.

"Now ain't that something," said Wils.

XIII

"Sure, I'm good," Young Rocky said, hanging up his cue.

"You made some good shots," Bob Connell said professionally.

"Hang around with me, brother, and you'll learn how to shoot pool," Young Rocky said. His eyes opened in wide interest. "Let there be light and there was light. Let there be Louisa Nolan's Dance Hall, and there was Three Star Hennessey."

Three Star Hennessey, a pimply-faced runt, wearing a cheap blue suit with flapping bell bottoms, ambled towards them.

"Spats and all," said glassy-eyed Swede Larsen, looking at Hennessey's pearl gray spats.

"Goin' to the jig this afternoon?" asked Connell.

"If he didn't, Nolan's would close up."

"Say, Hennessey, is it true that you go down to Castle Gardens and dance so that you can pinch pocketbooks?" Swede asked.

"I combine business with pleasure . . . but, say, who'll loan me a buck until tonight?"

"Scrouging dough again, huh, Hennessey?" said Young Rocky.

XIV

"What?" Fat Malloy bellowed.

Long-faced Jawbones Levinsky adjusted his horn-rimmed glasses, stuck his hands in his topcoat pockets, and sneered.

"Gypp was overrated."

"For Christ sake!" exclaimed Malloy, belligerent and nonplussed.

"Well, what did he ever do?"

"What did he do? Didn't he make a seventy-yard drop kick?"

Jawbones' right hand pushed outwards in a gesture of disdainful unbelief.

"Listen, Jew! I SAY THAT GYPP MADE A SEVENTY-FIVE-YARD DROP KICK AND YOU CAN FIND IT IN THE RECORD BOOK."

"What record book?"

"Why, you damn fool kike, the record book. What the hell record book you suppose, the one on volley ball? What the hell do you go to an A.P.A. college like the U for if you don't understand English?"

"Think I fall for that stuff?"

"Why, you lowdown Jew! Say, get this straight and don't forget it! George Gypp of Notre Dame made a seventy-five-yard drop kick," Malloy said, clenching his fists, and shoving a bull-dog mug forward.

"Hell, you're just another one of these synthetic Notre Dame alumni. . . . And you can't even pronounce the name correctly."

"YOU LOUSY KIKE! I OUGHT TO PUNCH THAT FACE OF YOURS FULL OF HOLES. . . ."

Departure became the better part of Levinsky's valor.

XV

"You're exonerated, then?" said big Gannon, a park cop.

"Yeah," Joe Moonan answered; he was a classily dressed, angelic-faced dick.

"How did it happen, Joe? I never got the story straight."

Joe told how he had caught the kids shooting craps down near Twelfth Street, and had yelled at them. They had run after he called to them to halt, and he pulled out his gun, intending to scare them. He had been aiming to shoot over their heads, but somehow, he didn't know how, and was sorry it happened, he'd hit one of the kids.

"It sure caused a stink, didn't it? But anyway, I'm glad they exonerated you."

"It was all accident. And what the hell, the kid was just a goddamn alley-rat. I don't see why there was so much trouble about it."

XVI

Jim Doyle stuck a fat cigar in his face, and rubbed his right hand over the alderman he was starting to develop.

"Now, Lonigan, remember and always vote Democratic," Jim said, buttonholing Studs.

"Sure, the old man's a good Democrat," Studs said.

"It's only a left-handed mick who'd vote Republican. Hell, Lonigan, if the Irish only would stick together and realize that the Democrats are their party, they could run this city. And if they don't, well, the Jews and Polacks will be stepping all over them."

"Sure."

"Too bad you're not in my precinct. . . . Anyway, a vote's a vote."

"You precinct captain now?"

"No, I just help out Old Rubenstein."

"Oh!"

"Well, congratulations, old man, and so long."

Jim turned back and handed Studs a cigar.

XVII

"Say, Vinc, remember the girl you kissed at Sarah Windlemann's beach party last month, Mary the Wop?" Runt asked.

Vinc Curley, tall with an enlarged and elongated head, and a mouth chronically opened like a fly trap, gaped at them, visibly remembering and curious.

"I haven't got the heart to tell the guy what she's got," Runt said, giving Young Rocky a knowing eye.

"But, Runt, it's only fair to tell him," Young Rocky said after due reflection.

Young Rocky studied a cold sore on Vinc's lip. He looked dolorous, and placed a hand on Vinc's shoulder.

"Vinc, I hate to tell you, but you're my pal. . . . Mary the Wop has syphilis."

"Yeah, the dirty bitch!" Runt said with feigned hate.

"And . . . fellows . . . have I got it too?" Vinc asked after a long pause.

Balefully, they nodded affirmation. He asked what it meant, what he should do. They answered with mysterious remarks about something gotten in drug stores, called G.O. 45. They told him it was very serious, and made the skin maggoty, caused it to moulder, and might even lead to blindness, deafness, dumbness, and his arms might even fall off, his eyes drop out, and his toes fall apart. Terrible thing! And he had better get it taken care of immediately.

"Vinc, old pal, they'll put you in quarantine, and we'll miss you," Runt said, slowly extending his hand.

Young Rocky sliced Runt's elbow, warning him not to risk contagion by shaking hands with Vinc.

Vinc bolted out of the poolroom.

XVIII

"Tough about Paulie Haggerty, my old buddy," Hennessey said.

"Say, just what is wrong with him?" asked Lou Bruner.

"Every goddamn thing. Clap, gonorrheal rheumatism, his heart is shot, his lungs are gone, and he has ulcers of the stomach. The guy has just drunk and jazzed himself to death."

"Jesus Christ!" exclaimed Lou.

XIX

"Yes, I said the Republicans, they went and steal the election from Cox by crookedness," Andy defiantly declared.

"Where did you get all that inside dope?" asked Darby Dan Drennan.

"My father told me. And he ought to know. Doesn't he belong to the Ku Klux Klan?"

"Fellows, his old man wears a nightshirt and burns fiery crosses in empty prairies," said Darby Dan, guffawing.

"He don't neither."

"His old man rides around in bed-sheets on a horse," said Darby Dan.

"Where does he keep the horse?" asked Pochon.

"He ain't got no horse."

"Does he belong to the Ku Klux Klan?" asked Drennan.

"Yes," Andy proudly said.

"Then, he's got to have a horse."

"He doesn't need no horse," Andy shouted above their laughter.

"If he hasn't got a horse, how can he wear his nightshirt and go riding?" laughed Pochon.

Andy stuttered.

XX

"Whenever you think about girls, you know, wondering if they are all they're cracked up to be, more decent and better than guys, think of this angle! Think of the keenest broad you know sitting down to take a great big healthy. . . ."

"What sweet thoughts you have," Swede said, interrupting Young Rocky.

"Guys talking like you do, just don't rate."

"Is that so, Hennessey? Well, lemme tell you that since I came here from Kansas City two years ago, I've dated up

"Curley hasn't got a marble in his bean," Young Rocky said.

"Horse."

Charley Josephson, a silly-looking runt of seventeen, rushed in and asked what was biting Curley. They told him the joke they had pulled on Vinc. He said he'd been in the drug store at the corner, and Vinc had come in, red in the face, and all excited, demanding G.O. 45 right away to rub on his lips.

"Curley hasn't got a marble in his bean," Young Rocky said as they all roared.

XXI

"Well, Conrad's a classic," Mose Levinsky, poolroom intellectual, said.

"What is a classic? Define it," said Big Syd.

"A classic is a book that lives."

"Now take a book like Robert Herrick's *The Common Lot*," said Big Syd.

"It's a good book, but it isn't a classic," said Mose.

"Say, you guys act like you thought you were too good for the human race," said Red Kelly, passing them on his way from the can.

XXII

"I'm getting along," Hoppy Shanks said, lighting a cigarette.

"The job you got sounds O.K.," said Loeb.

"I make forty bucks a week. My room costs me six and

my meals about four or five a week, because I'm cutting down on 'em. I'm salting fifteen and twenty every pay day," said Hoppy.

"That's pretty good. I wish I had a decent job."

"I worked hard for this one. I don't believe in loafing around like some of these guys do. When you're not working, you got time on your hands, and keep hanging around wondering what time it is, and what you'll do. Hell with that for this boy. I'm playin' the game smart."

"Say, Shanks, can you spare two bits? I'm flat, but I'll be able to pay you back this afternoon," Mush Joss asked.

"Haven't got it, Mush."

Mush passed to another group.

"That bastard hasn't worked since Noah got piped on the Ark," said Loeb.

"I wouldn't give him my dough. Him and McCarthy try and scrouge on me every time I see them."

XXIII

"Andy, are the Irish hundred-per-cent Americans?" asked Connell.

"No, because they believe in the Pope," Le Gare answered.

"All right, punk, keep religion out of it," ordered Red Kelly, who had come over to see why they were having such a good time razzing Andy.

"Say, if the Klan is so tough, why doesn't it come around looking for the Irish some night when it's out riding in nightshirts like kids on Halloween?" asked Darby Dan.

"They know when they're healthy," said Red.

"I'll bet Andy's old man has a horse looking like Sparkplug in Barney Google," commented Eddie Eastwood.

"Why don't you come around with the Klan if they're so damn tough?" Drennan said.

"If they did, you would all run home and hide behind your mother's apron string."

"Blah!"

Andy issued a blanket challenge to fight anyone his size and age who was present.

"Gawan home, and come back on a kiddy-car, wearing your sister's nightgown and we'll fight you," sneered Drennan.

"Don't insult my sister!" Andy said, knocking Drennan down with a punch.

Drennan sat on the floor holding his jaw; Andy stood over him, defying him to get up and fight like a man. George the Greek told Andy to get out and not come back.

"Keep your old poolroom!" Andy yelled from the doorway in a sulk.

"No, Andy, take it along with you," Hennessey answered.

XXIV

"Paulie's dead!" Benny Taite yelled, rushing in excitedly, disrupting everything.

"Poor Paulie!" Studs said, next to Taite in the center of a stunned group.

"You know, years ago, I warned him to take care of himself, and not be a damn fool with the molls. But poor Paulie, every time he saw a skirt he lost his head and didn't know what he was doing," Red Kelly oracularly said.

"You know, I can't really believe that he's gone," said Studs.

"He was my old buddy," Hennessey said.

"A better lad never walked Fifty-eighth Street," Kelly said.

"Death is a funny thing, all right," Tommy Doyle said.

"We all get called at some time," Les said.

"Yeah, it's a funny thing. You never know who it's going to slap down next, and you never think much about it until one day, it puts your best friend out for the count," Red philosophized.

"It's awful, a tragedy," said Phil Rolfe.

"He had the priest, didn't he?" said Red.

"Shrimp said that a priest named Doneggan was there when he died," Taite said.

"We'll have to take up a collection for flowers," suggested Red.

"Jesus, he's one poor bastard who ended up behind the eight ball," Slug said.

"He can't be dead. Why he was so young, he never lived," said Bob Connell.

"Say, punk, how old are you?" asked Kelly.

"Sixteen," said Hennessey.

"Punks like you should be seen and not heard," Kelly said.

"Poor Paulie," sighed Les.

XXV

"Say, let's give the Greek the finger on this game," said Lyman.

"O.K.," said Young Rocky.

Lyman aimed to shoot the fifteen ball for game in slop pool. He missed, and poked the ball in a pocket with his cue.

"Pay up!" he hollered.

"I will like hell," said Young Rocky.

"You lost," said Lyman.

"Gimme! Gimme!" said Mike to both of them.

"See him," said Lyman.

"That bastard is trying to cheat me. I won," said Young Rocky.

"Come ona, you fellahs, what's a the matter?" asked George, coming over.

"I won't pay. He shoved the game ball in with his cue."

"Pay up, you tight heel. I made it fair and square," said Lyman.

"You're a liar!" said Young Rocky.

"Don't call me a liar!" said Lyman.

"No! Well, it's double," said Young Rocky.

"Come on outside," said Lyman.

"Here! Pay, pay, pay!" said Mike.

"I'll brain you guys with a cue," threatened George.

Lyman and Young Rocky grabbed their coats, and dashed to the door, followed by an expectant group. At the door they turned and yelled in unison.

"Finger! Finger Greek!"

They laughed and walked away, arm-in-arm.

XXVI

"Quarter after one!" said Slug, standing with Mike at the window.

They heard the click of the cue balls from the back where Stan Simonsky was practicing. An elevated train rumbled. An automobile whizzed by. A heavy-footed, well-formed girl passed.

"How you like it?"

"Push-Push!" mumbled Mike.

VII

It was Saturday night. A cardboard picketing sign, letters turned downwards, lay in a corner of the small, disorderly bedroom. Mr. Le Gare looked at it. He felt like a dead man who had returned to life.

Blacklisted!

No hotel in the city would hire him. He had been a waiter all his life. What work could he do now?

When he had told his family, their faces had dropped. They were discussing it now in the dining room. They had opposed his striking, picketing the Shrifton Hotel, and serving on the strike committee, acting as treasurer for the union. They said nothing; but their silence was more criticizing than anything they might say. He had supported them for years. Now they were irked, lest he be a burden to them. Well, by God, he wouldn't.

But what else could he do?

He had been sold out, and made the goat. Most of the other waiters had crawled back on their knees, begging for their jobs at any salary, under any condition. Yellow Scabs! They had betrayed him, betrayed the cause of the American working man. They had betrayed themselves. The rankling of defeat and disappointment grew upon him until he cursed, using the filthiest words he knew.

The blacklist meant the dust heap, the garbage can, for a man his age. And his sons, daughter, wife, didn't understand; it was tragedy, living with people who couldn't understand what a man was doing. Only Andy stuck by him. But Andy didn't have a very good brain, poor boy. Andy, whose brain was not so good, alone of his children had been loyal. But Andy did not understand either.

He wasn't a fool! He wasn't! He had been right. And they needn't have lost the strike, if only they had all shown unity, courage, heart. But they, foreigners, Syrian busboys, fat Dutchmen, foreigners, hadn't been interested in strikes. They wanted Shrifton's crumbs. They wanted their tips. They had come over, not to make America their home, but to milk it as well as they could, and go back. They had their stocks, and some of them owned buildings. They served the rich, and tried to think that they were rich. All waiters, almost, did that; aped the rich, and thought that some day they would be rich. Scabs!

Suddenly, he laughed with twisted joy. They had sold themselves for nothing. Girls were cheaper and most of them were on the blacklist too.

He could see it so clear. They could have won if only . . . Some day all the American working-men would strike, and even the waiters would have to then, and then too . . . they would win, and men like himself wouldn't be made goats. He clenched his weak fists, wanting to fight back. But there was no fighting left in him.

Others before him had been blacklisted, and had known his bitterness. Others had been betrayed. But it wouldn't, couldn't always be thus. All that bitterness and defeat would not die. It would gnaw the souls of men. It would fester. It would spit poison. It was only with bitterness and poison that the workingmen, even the waiters, would beat the Shriftons. He vowed

that his defeat would not be in vain. He would pass the bitter-
nss of it on, help to make for that day when he would be
dead, but when the bitterness of workingmen would rise above
the brim, and then, the Shriftons would be blacklisted. He
felt a brief exaltation. It drowsed and died.

"Hello, Dad," Andy said.

He looked at his son whose brain was not very good.

"Don't worry, Dad. Maybe I'll get a job next week and help
out."

Tears grew in Mr. Le Gare's eyes.

CHAPTER SEVEN

I

His life was much the same as it had been last week or last
year. It was a week now since his twenty-first birthday, and
his life was much the same as it had been last week or a
year ago.

The old man owned a new building on Michigan, near the
Carter School, and the Lonigans lived on the third floor south.
Studs emerged from the building and walked along, taking
loose, easy strides, strides that he considered self-confident.

He had made his decision while shaving. Now, it caused
him to have a sense of impending unpleasantness. It would
be a wasted evening, and tomorrow he would regret having
let a night slip by him. But that wasn't the right attitude to
show. Sometimes, he wished that he wasn't a Catholic, and
didn't have to meet the responsibilities of a Catholic. But that
wasn't the right attitude either.

The Carter playgrounds surrounding the school were rimmed
by an iron picket fence. Walking along, Studs had an
impulse to touch each picket as he had used to do. But he
walked along like a guy of twenty-one who wasn't a clown.
He paused at a spot along the fence which stood almost opposite the third base of the indoor diamond in the northeast
corner of the grounds.

Remembering, remembering many things, he nodded. And
Paulie was dead now. He had never thought that on his twenty-
first birthday, first day of manhood, that his old friend, Paulie,
would die. Life was funny and unpredictable.

He looked at the rambling, tan-and-gray school building
that stood in the center of the grounds facing south. The sky
over it was red. It all made him lonesome. The sky red, the
empty buildings, the playground he had known so well as

a kid, with nobody now in it. He looked at the batter's box on the diamond. Paulie had stood there batting right-handed in a piggy game, cursing Young Coady for twirling the ball on the day he'd cleaned Red Kelly. He could almost hear Paulie's voice:

"Come on, you goddamn punk, or I'll fling the bat at you!"

And right inside the fence from where he stood was the spot where they'd had the fight. Paulie had placed the stick on his shoulder and Red had knocked it off, and they'd tangled. And the fists of Studs Lonigan had won him respect.

Suddenly, he was lonesome, lonesome to be a boy again.

He looked at his clenched fist. It was pretty big, considering his size. He was only about five six, but he was broad, and he was still tough, and able to spot a lot of guys on weight and take them.

But still he couldn't get himself to believe that Paulie was dead. He had stood right inside the playground, and Studs could almost see him, mushy-faced, a bit fat, big fanny, wearing a red-trimmed, gray baseball shirt. The first to go, and all shot to pieces with clap, and drink, and dissipation.

Poor Paulie.

Studs lit a cigarette. He wondered why the good guys like Paulie went, and the louses like Weary Reilley didn't. He shrugged his shoulders and told himself he ought to snap out of it. But when he looked at the playground, with the sky red over it, and remembered so many things, and thought that Paulie was dead, out in Calvary Cemetery, he was lonesome, lonesome to be a kid again. He walked on towards the corner, along a sidewalk he'd walked with Paulie many times. Even though he was sad about Paulie, he couldn't help being a bit proud, because he was twenty-one and strong, and yes, tomorrow in the football game, he'd show his strength. He'd done his drinking and jazzing too, and still, he was strong and tough. He was the real stuff.

He'd never realized that he was growing up and changing. There had been signs on his body, but they, too, had come gradually. Each day he had grown stronger, bigger, with more hair on him. He had changed, though, slowly day by day, gotten to hanging around the poolroom, worked with his old man, and then, well, he wasn't doing the things he'd done as a kid. Now he was a man. Well, he was! He felt a little goofy, remembering how, before coming out, he'd looked at himself in the mirror, and assured himself that he was a man. But he was. And there were many years ahead of him, drinking, jazzing, poker-games, plenty of things. And he had dough. With the birthday present from his old man, he now had four hundred bucks in his own name in the bank. He was pretty goddamn well off.

A girl came toward him. He liked her looks. He had confidence in his walk. He was well dressed too: gray Stetson, conservative gray topcoat, well-fitting sixty-five-dollar Oxford gray suit, good cut, the trousers wide enough so that he didn't look like a hick, but not ringing bell bottoms. The girl passed him. He passed her, and turned over Fifty-eighth Street.

But the evening was all wasted, because he had made his decision and would stick to it.

He walked towards the poolroom thinking about a lot of things. He saw young Cooley, and motioned him over, calling him a dope.

"Droopy, when you gonna let it alone?" he asked, not knowing why he did it, and laughing to see the hurt, shocked look on the kid's face.

He walked along. He had let himself get into the wrong attitude. Well, he didn't have to go tonight. But he did. He didn't like to admit it to himself, but he was afraid. Well, it wasn't yellow. It was a different kind of fear. It was fear for his soul if something did happen to him.

He just felt all off kilter. Maybe afterwards, he would feel different.

II

Studs had what Father Gilhooley always called a feeling of gratification. Red, Tommy, and the guys had kept trying to talk him into going with them, and he had resisted all temptation.

He walked up towards the church, taking his time. There wouldn't be a crowd there. He thought of himself as having already gone to confession. He saw himself saying his penance, saw himself kneeling in the confessional, talking through the screen to Father Doneggan, running through the catalogue of his sins, commandment by commandment. He tried to put himself into a contrite mood. He wanted his act of contrition after confession tonight to be a perfect act of contrition, as if it were his last confession.

Studs walked slowly; nervous, he lit a cigarette.

The thought of Paulie dead out there in the cemetery still hung on him. The thought of another, a waiting grave out in Calvary Cemetery, hung more heavily.

Already this football season, he had read of five or six different fellows being killed in football games. When he had been a kid, he remembered having read about how a fellow named Albert at the U of C had been killed. In Thursday's

paper there had been something about a fifteen-year-old kid
who'd had his skull fractured.

A voice within Studs, as if it were his conscience, kept assuring him that he was yellow.

He seemed to keep seeing that kid he had read about in
Thursday's paper, before him, prostrate, moaning, blood from
his cracked head dropping to mix in the dirt, moaning, deathmoans persisting, ringing out as if in prophecy of his death,
and of the death of everyone that he knew. He seemed to see
Studs Lonigan in place of the kid with crushed head. He seemed
to hear the deathmoans of Studs Lonigan.

He walked slowly.

The night was crisp. A mist swung down low. It was not
the kind of a night to think of death. It was the kind of a
night to make one want to live.

He paused at the curb on Fifty-ninth, to let a truck swing
around the corner. He had a crazy impulse, that he couldn't
understand, to dive in front of the truck.

He crossed the street, walked on lazily.

He tried to examine his conscience. He hadn't broken the
first commandment. He had taken the name of God in vain,
fifteen, no twenty or twenty-five times a day, he guessed. Third
commandment. He hadn't missed mass. His thoughts wandered.
He realized that he was lonesome. He wondered what he could
do after confession. He didn't want to go home. He figured
he hadn't better go to a show. It might cause him to have the
wrong kind of thoughts after confession. He wondered what
the bunch was doing.

He thought of himself, out on the football field for tomorrow's game. The kickoff. Studs Lonigan running the first kickoff
back a hundred and three yards. He wasn't going to be hurt
either. But suppose he was. Well, he was going to confession
so he wouldn't be. He'd be afraid to enter that game tomorrow
if he didn't, because he had that kind of a feeling.

He got back to the third commandment, and walked slowly
towards St. Patrick's Church.

In the church, a low-ceilinged structure of boxed-in gloom,
he took a seat in the rear pew on the left-hand side. He bowed
his head, and said a few prayers to the Blessed Virgin
in preparation for an examination of conscience. Up forwards, near the side exit door, a woman arose, and waddled
a few steps forwards to the plushed entrance of Father
Gilhooley's confessional. Behind him, the door of Father
Doneggan's box clattered slightly as it was closed. He heard
a street car passing, and then the whistle of a railroad engine.

He riveted his eyes in a stare on the altar that was hallowed back in the center. He watched the flickering altar light above it. A man arose from the front, center, and did a St. Vitus dance down the center aisle, coming with twisted and painful slowness, dragging along the ruins of a paralyzed body. It was Joe, the paper-man. Studs knew him. He was all right, and not goofy to talk to, although he looked completely off because of the deadened nerves in the left side of his face. He came to church every morning, and received at least once a week. Poor bastard, he lived somehow on a few pennies made peddling the *New World*. Studs felt sorry for him.

The fellows had talked about going to the State and Congress. He wished . . . but a burlesque show was an occasion of sin. Couldn't be thinking of them and planning to go to confession. Not the right attitude. . . . Oh, my God, I am heartily sorry for having offended Thee, and I detest all my sins. . . . He heard the bang of a door from the confessional box of Father Roney, on the right-hand side of the church, just in front of the choir box.

For no reason at all, he glanced up at the low ceiling. He had to get himself into the right attitude. Feeling contrition was hard. He had to feel it deeply, with his whole heart and his whole soul. Oh, my God, I am heartily, heartily sorry. . . .

He had taken God's name in vain twenty-five or thirty times a day. He had been late for Mass on his own account, but they were only venial sins because he'd gotten in before the Consecration.

He looked behind him. Four and five people in the line before Father Doneggan's box. He turned and glanced off from his right towards Father Roney's box, five and six people in two lines.

An old man walked down from the altar, where he had been praying, and on back towards the rear, his heels rattatting on the rubber aisle.

A feeling of fear came over him, fear of being injured in the football game, fear with a sudden realization that Hell was a place of torments, endless torments in a fire that never ended, the monotony of its hissing flames, a sudden fear of life. He wanted to be outside in the fall night. He wanted to get it over with. He couldn't get himself to arise and join one of the waiting lines before Father Doneggan's confessional box. He heard the swinging doors of the entrance, and heels on the marble steps leading from the vestibule. He heard the closing of a door in back of him, then, the closing of a door of Father Roney's confessional. He had violated the fifth commandment by anger towards others, maybe . . . maybe . . . maybe. . . . His eyes were again attracted by the ceaselessly glowing altar light. He had violated the fifth commandment by anger. . . .

Suddenly, he found that he had lapsed into dirty thoughts. He labored through an Act of Contrition, trying to make it a perfect one. A feeling of death was in him, and went from him to the gloomy church, and the autumn night without. He just couldn't seem to be able to get through the commandments.

Suddenly, he just raced through them, estimating his sins, in violation of each commandment, and arose. He took a place in line, his back to the altar, before the left-hand door of Father Doneggan's box. There were four ahead of him. He waited.

The door on the other side opened. Art Hahn, a tall, slim fellow, blond, several years older than Studs, emerged. A woman entered the box. Art smiled at Studs, as he passed him, down the aisle, and Studs pointed toward the exit door. Art nodded. Father Doneggan was quick in everything he did. Studs soon got inside the stale-smelling box. The slide opened, and he saw, dimly, the blond priest inside the wire screen. He confessed his sins, said the Act of Contrition, was absolved and received a penance of nine Our Fathers and nine Hail Marys.

Outside, Studs and Art lit cigarettes and went north along Indiana Avenue, the street along which Studs had, in his day, always come to and from school. The past came back into his thoughts. The day that Paulie had been licked by Johnny O'Brien. The day in winter that he had clipped a truck driver on the ear with a snowball and they had all been shagged. He felt as if tomorrow he would be going to communion with the boys' sodality at the eight o'clock Mass. But what the hell!

Studs asked Art how he happened to be going to confession.

"I'd never think of playing football without receiving communion. You never know what's going to happen to you in a prairie football game like that one we've got scheduled tomorrow. And I always play safe."

"Yeah," said Studs, feeling good that he wasn't the only guy who'd felt that way.

"Why did you go—same reason?" asked Art.

"Oh, I just thought it was about time that I'd receive. And then I thought I'd do it for Paulie Haggerty."

"Say, that reminds me, I ought to be offering up my communion for Paulie tomorrow too," said Art.

Studs suddenly recalled that he had intended to make it a general confession for his whole life. And it had skipped his mind. He was afraid all over again, because of that slip.

He saw himself killed in the football game. But he was offering his communion up for Paulie and Paulie in Purgatory, if he was there, would pray for him to return.

Jesus, what the hell was happening to him, getting like he was.

He went down to the Elevated to get a Sunday-morning paper, vowing to himself that he wouldn't stop at the poolroom. He did, and found Bill Donoghue there. He told Bill he'd gone to confession, and they played several games of straight pool. Studs won. Then they had coffee in fat Gus the Greek's restaurant, between the Elevated and Prairie Avenue. They talked about the old days when they were kids at St. Patrick's. Studs had a good Saturday night, and got home about a quarter to twelve. He told his old man that he should tell his mother not to get him breakfast, he had gone to confession. Lonigan beamed.

VIII

Worry did not sit well upon a jolly, red, robust face like Mrs. Sheehan's. But she had a premonition. Last night in a dream, she had seen her Arnold lying dead in a football uniform. Oh, if only sons would heed their mothers, there would be less trouble, fewer broken-hearted mothers in this world. And how much happier a world it would be!

She remembered that Saturday in Rockford; how she had sighed with such relief when Arnold came home and said he had played his last game with the high-school team. She had had her premonitions in those days, too, when he would be playing, and she knew that he would have been maimed for life or killed, but for her prayers. A boy could only trifle so much with the Grace of God, though. She felt it in her that Arnold would be carried home, perhaps dead.

She took a chair by the parlor window, and prayed. She looked out across the street at the leafless trees in the graying October Sunday. Down at the other end of the park, he was playing; perhaps at the very moment, he might be injured, dead. She knew, knew in her mother's way, that something would happen to her oldest boy.

Arnold was her favorite child, her first-born. Her four girls gave her no trouble. They were well-raised, and she could trust them; only sometimes she worried that they couldn't have more clothes. But their father was only a motorman. The youngest lad, Arthur, he was an altar boy, a bright, fine, innocent lad who always obeyed. And Horace, he worked in a gambling house, but he was steady, and brought money home to her regularly, and he didn't drink like Arnold. Arnold, her baby, he worried her. He was the most generous of her children, when he had it to give, with a heart of pure gold. Only he had gotten in with the wrong sort. With the Grace of God, he would settle down.

Her premonitions would not down, and her prayers were not completely self-comforting. Hers was a mother's agony.

CHAPTER EIGHT

I

Watching himself in the mirror, Studs hitched up his football pants, carefully arranging the cotton hip pads around his sides. Wished he had better ones. Wouldn't be much protection from a boot in the ribs. He touched the schimmels under his blue jersey, and put on his black helmet. Every inch a football player!

He thought of himself going out to play with old street pants, a jersey, and football shoes. Dressed that way, tackling so hard he'd knock them cuckoo; jumping up ready to go on, no matter how hard he was slammed. No use to be senseless and play without sufficient padding. Only it was swell thinking of being reckless that way, having the crowd recognize such gameness.

He flexed and unflexed his arm muscles. Even with the drinking and carousing he'd done these last couple of years, he was still pretty hard and tough. He slapped his guts. They were hard enough, too, and there was no alderman yet, or not enough anyway to be noticed. And there never would be, because he'd take care of himself before that ever happened. He'd never have a paunch like his old man had. Iron Man Lonigan! The bigger they are, the harder they fall. He lit a cigarette and sat on the bed, thinking proudly of his body, good and strong, even if he was small; powerful football shoulders, good for fighting. And this afternoon, he'd prove that it was a good body, and that there was heart and courage inside of it.

But there wouldn't be any girls out there for him to be playing for. Other guys had girls. Wished he had a girl, Lucy, a girl coming out only to see him play . . . Goofy! . . . But he still loved Lucy even if he hadn't seen her in about four years. And if she was coming out there to see him play, because she loved him, he would play much better, and instead of being in it just for the fun and the glory, and to show them all what he was made of, he'd be playing for her also. And he wanted to. Christ sake, he was getting like a clown, all mush inside. He tried to laugh at himself; it was forced.

Smells of the cooking Sunday dinner came tantalizingly from the kitchen. His mother came to the bedroom door, and said that she had a bite ready for him.

"I can't! I'm going to play football," he snapped in uncontrolled exasperation.

"I certainly don't think much of a game that deprives you of your food," she replied.

Jesus Christ! Couldn't she understand anything!

She nagged and persuaded. He got up, and walked towards the door, with her following, still wanting him to eat. He said that he couldn't play with a belly full of food, and as she dipped her hand in the holy water fount on the wall, and showered him, he slammed the door. The father, hearing him, called that he wouldn't have such vulgar language used around the home; but Studs was gone.

He went down the steps two and three at a time, thinking why they always had to be like that, never open to reason and sense, wanting you to do whatever they wished in everything. Felt like leaving home, and living in a room by himself; some day he'd have to, if they didn't keep from trying to run everything he did.

It was humid and sunless. He liked the click of his cleats on the sidewalk. He felt so good, and in such condition, that he had an impulse to run. He checked himself, and took his time. Studs Lonigan was going to use his noodle, and conserve his energy. He was a wise guy, and in everything in life he was going to be that way, always with a little stuff left in him for a pinch.

Jim Clayburn's dude father came along, dressed in snappy gray, wearing a derby, and tapping a cane on the sidewalk. With his gray bush of hair, his face looked soft, almost like a woman's. Must have been something of a sissy and teacher's pet in his own day at school, just as Jim had been. He bowed stiffly to Studs, and Studs nodded, hoping he noticed the football outfit. Jim was studying law now, clerking for a measly ten or fifteen bucks a week. Well, by the time Clayburn, with all his studying and kill-joy stuff was in the dough, Studs Lonigan would be running his old man's business, and be in the big dough too.

He saw Tubby Connell and Nate Klein flinging passes in the street in front of the poolroom. Nate muffed one, and Studs told him to get a bushel basket. He lit a cigarette and laughed at Nate's scenery; an old-fashioned square black helmet that must have come down from Walter Eckersall's day; tight green jersey with holes in the sleeves; pants so big that he swam in them; shoes turned up at the toes because of their size. He looked more closely at the shoes; they were spiked baseball ones. He told Nate they'd never let him play in those, because he might cut somebody to ribbons. Tubby said that Klein was wearing them to show that he had the Fifty-eighth Street fighting spirit.

"This ain't tiddledy-winks; the guy I cut up will be a Monitor, and that's his tough tiddy," Nate said, hard-boiled.

He and Tubby disregarded Studs' advice to save themselves, and went on fooling around with the ball. Studs turned his back to them, and let his hand fall on his hips; his helmet was over his right elbow, and his blond hair was a trifle curly. His broad face revealed absorption. A middle-aged guy with a paunch doped along; Studs hoped that the guy had noticed him, wished he was young like he was, and able to go out and play a game of football, still full of the vim and vitality of youth. A quick feeling of contrition came over him. Suppose he should get hurt? Suppose he should never come back alive? His mother would always remember how he had slammed the door in her face. But damn it, couldn't they be reasonable?

"Hello, Flannel Mouth! How's the brother?" asked Studs, as Young Fat Malloy showed up.

"He'll be there, and he was saying that if you guys lose your first game of the season, he was going to kick your tails around the block to hell and gone. And don't think he can't! He may be a little runt, but let me tell you, Hugo was one of the toughest sergeants they ever had in the army."

"I know it," Studs said, thinking that it was another case of a good little man.

"Look at Klein, that crazy hebe! He's liable to break his neck trying to catch that football!" Fat said.

"Yeah, he's that way because he got gassed in the war."

"But he has guts. You know, Studs, you guys ought to have a crack team this year. And with a good coach like Hugo, you oughtn't to lose a game."

Studs nodded. He thought that maybe, this year, they would all get to working together like a well-oiled machine, and then, next season they could join the Mid-West League. He saw himself flashing through that semi-pro circuit like a comet, and getting himself signed up to play in the backfield with Paddy Driscoll on the Chicago Cardinals.

There was excitement; a wild fling of Nate's nearly hit a baby being wheeled along. The father crabbed like hell, but finally pushed his buggy on. Nate told Studs that wise guys like that bird needed to be punched full of holes.

More players came around, and a gang of them started over to the football field in Washington Park.

II

Wearing a large white sweater, and his old army breeches, bow-legged Coach Hugo Zip Malloy stood with arms folded, his tough mug intent, as he watched the Fifty-eighth Street Cardinals clown through signal practice.

"Come on over here, you birds, and sit on your cans a minute. That's what they're for," he yelled, regally waving his short right arm.

The players dragged over and planked themselves down, facing him. Strangers collected to gape at them. He glared at the strangers.

"Everybody not associated with the team, please fade!" he commanded; some obeyed; others dropped backwards a few feet, and then commenced to inch forwards again. Courageous gawkers stood in their tracks.

Kenny Kilarney suddenly appeared, and did a take-off on a college cheer leader:

> *We ain't rough!*
> *We ain't tough!*
> *But oh! . . . are we determined?*

"Say, Monkey Face!" Coach Hugo said to Kenny.

"No hope for him," Bill Donoghue said.

"Now I want you birds to listen to what I tell you!"

"But say, Hugo?" Bill Donoghue called.

"That's my name."

"Would you mind taking the cigar out of your mouth so we can see you?"

"Sonnyboy, the playground is on the other side of the drive, in back of me," Coach Hugo replied.

"Another thing, coach? Don't you think we ought to give Klein a rising vote? He hasn't been hurt yet this season?"

"Jesus, wouldn't the squirrels make mince-pie out of you?" Coach Hugo said, darting a no-hope look at Bill.

"Now, when the clowns get finished pulling the whiskers off their jokes, I'll talk. . . . And by the way, can't you guys leave the cigarettes alone for a minute. It takes wind to win a football game, and you don't get wind eating them coffin nails!"

"You tell 'em, coach, I stutter," said Shrimp Haggerty, lurching drunkenly into their midst; he was thin and sallow, and dogged out in classy clothes. He wore a black band on his top-coat sleeve.

"Haggerty! The other team needs a couple of mudguards. Go on over there," Coach Hugo said.

"Now that the children have finished throwing spitballs around, teacher will talk. . . . Haggerty, get the hell out of here before I have to throw your pieces away! . . . "

Haggerty saw that Coach Hugo was really sore. He staggered away, singing.

"All right, you birds, keep your dirty ears open! I ain't gonna repeat myself! You're goin' out there now for your first crack of the season, and you're gonna play a man's game. There's only one way to play it. Play hard! Hard! Get the other guy, before he gets you! Knock him down! Let them drag him out! If you don't, you might be the unlucky chump that's dragged out. And if any of you birds are carried off that gridiron, cold, don't expect me to break down and weep for you like I was your old lady! Because you won't get knocked cuckoo if you keep your heads up, and play hard! It's the soft guy that gets knocked silly in this game. And if there's any soft babies on this team, the sooner they get it in the neck, the better off they will be, and we too! You guys got to go in there and hit hard, hit often, and every time you hit, make the guy you hit think he's collided with a battleship. Don't worry about giving the ambulance drivers work; they got wives and kiddies to support, and need it. . . ."

"Hey, Hugo, what undertaker's giving you a rakeoff?" interrupted Arnold Sheehan.

"Sheehan, step into the second grade. You're too bright a boy for first. . . . And now, you birds, you're goin' in that football game in about a minute. If you want to win it, you got to do it yourself. I can't win it for you. That's your job, and if you want this game, you'll have to get it by fighting" (he slammed his right fist demonstratively into his left palm). "I watched you guys go through signal practice. You stunk! If you go into this game like that, it'll be like the Fort Dearborn massacre. And get me, if you guys don't fight, you can get an old lady to coach you. I won't. All right, snap into it. And, oh, yes, a final word. If any bird on this other team starts dirty work . . . give him the works!"

The team arose. Nate tore forwards. The others walked slowly towards the football field, Coach Hugo making up the rear.

"Say, coach, that's a ripe husky bunch of boys you got there. Tell 'em to try center rushes, and they'll win as easy as taking candy from a baby. Now, when I was a kid. . . ."

"Say, fellow, will you do me a favor?"

"Sure, glad to, coach!"

"All right. See that automobile drive. Well, walk across it, and keep on going until you lose yourself in the lagoon."

Coach Hugo roughly yelled gangway, as he went through a crowd, and stepped over the ropes. He clapped his hands together, and yelled to his team:

"All right, you guys, show me if you got any guts in your veins."

III

C
Nate Klein

L G		R G
Harold Dowson		*Carroll Dowson*
LT		RT
Red Kelly		*Dan Donoghue*

FB
Hink Weber

| L E | LHB | RHB | RE |
| *Weary Reilley* | *Arnold Sheehan* | *Art Hahn* | *Jim Nolan* |

QB
Studs Lonigan

waited, while the ball was put into position for the kick. It fell off the little mound on the forty-yard line four times, so a Monitor stretched himself out and held it in position.

Referee Charlie Bathcellar, wearing an astrakhan coat and a new derby, importantly signalled the two captains. Studs felt a thrill of pride as he signalled the readiness of his team; hundreds of people were watching, saw that he was captain. The whistle blew. A thin fellow in street pants and an old red jersey booted the ball on a line. Studs muffed it. The Fifty-eighth Street Cardinals formed disorganized interference. Studs scooped the ball up on the go, and thundered forwards, head down as if he were bucking the line, knees pumping. One Monitor clutched at his left sleeve. Another pulled at his pants from behind. A third dragged at his jersey from the right side. A fourth leaped to make a flying tackle around his ears. The whistle declared the ball dead. Nate Klein and a Monitor player were in the center of the field, bucking each other with arms folded together chest high.

The Cardinals lackadaisically took position in a balanced line formation. The defensive Monitor line crowded together, both tackles kneeling down inside of Dan Donoghue and Red Kelly. Hink Weber told Kelly not to play standing up. Red knelt down. Hink told him to crouch low so that he could charge. Red gave Hink a soreheaded look, but squatted in a weak position.

"Signals," Studs yelled huskily, leaning with hands on knees, eyes on the ground.

Studs tossed a lateral pass to Arnold Sheehan, who went through a mile-wide hole at right tackle. The fellow in the red jersey, Jewboy Schwartz, plugged up the hole. Arnold started to pivot, and Jewboy Schwartz got him while off balance. Three Monitors piled on, and Arnold groaned.

"Watch that piling on!" Weary yelled, rushing up.

"We ain't piling on!" Jake Schaeffer, the big Monitor captain, retorted.

"Well, he was down, wasn't he?"

"He might have crawled."

Hink Weber drew Weary back to avoid a fight.

Arnold limped, his face twisted with pain. Nate angrily asked if they had played dirty, because if they did—the works. Taking short, ziggedy steps, Coach Hugo appeared. Arnold was helped to the sidelines, and as he sat down, Fat Malloy told him that he'd played a swell game.

Weary Reilley switched to left halfback, and Tubby Connell took Weary's end. On the next play, Studs slapped the ball into Hink's guts as Hink thundered at center, hitting like a ton of bricks. He fell over Nate Klein. Getting up, he just looked at Nate and shook his head. Nate said he had been holding out his man, hadn't he? Weary Reilley was tackled by Jewboy Schwartz after a three-yard gain. When the players picked themselves up, Nate Klein was stretched out, ostensibly hurt. Coach Hugo strode importantly onto the field, followed by Fat Malloy, who lugged a water bucket. Fat rushed to Nate, and doused him.

"For Jesus sake!" Nate protested.

"Well, you were out, weren't you?"

Nate groaned weakly, rose to tottering feet, and moved dazedly, with his head hanging as if his neck were broken. But he told Coach Hugo he would stick in the game and get those bastards. Coach Hugo called it the old ginger. Nate floundered into position over the ball, and his face became a mirror of jungle ferocity.

Hink Weber punted down the field, and it was the Monitors' ball.

Studs took a defensive position, twenty yards behind the scrimmage line, and placed his hands on his hips. People in the crowd might notice how collected he seemed to be. He might get his chance to be spectacular. A fellow might break

through, and Studs would stave off a touchdown with a flying
tackle. Jewboy Schwartz started around the end, outran Tubby,
who was boxed in, dodged Weary's lunge with a side leap,
graceful as an antelope, and tore towards Studs. Studs dashed
forwards a few paces, arms encircled outwards and tensed
himself. Schwartz came, fast. Five yards from Studs, Jewboy
Schwartz performed a feint with his right foot. Studs lunged.
Schwartz would have been free had he not slipped, and Studs,
in his lunge, caught Schwartz's foot. Jewboy dragged Studs
along, and slipped free, but Dan Donoghue was up to make
the tackle.

They patted Studs' back for such nice work. Studs' glow
of pride quickly faded. He had been out-smarted, and the
fellow would have been free to make a touchdown if he hadn't
slipped. He was only wearing street shoes. With cleats, he
wouldn't have slipped. Studs waited in back of the scrimmage
line. Next time, the guy might make a monkey of him. If
he was playing the other half, he might not break through
as easily because Jim Nolan and Dan were better than Red
and Tubby. Studs' confidence seemed gone. The Jew was
too speedy and clever for him. No, goddamn it, he'd leave
his feet next time before that feint! Nail him! Studs moved
forwards a few feet with the pass from center. Dan smeared
the play for a loss. The teams lined up and Nate staggered
into his place as defensive center.

The game see-sawed through the first quarter, slow, argu-
mentative, marred by fumbles. On the last play of the period,
Studs took a punt, ran forwards, swinging the ball from side
to side for effect, running forwards, thinking he was making
a long run, hearing cheering from the side, and . . . Jewboy
Schwartz dove into him, his shoulder smashing Studs in the
solar plexus. Studs went down with a thud, and lost the ball.
His guts pained; he gasped. He slowly picked himself up, a
sick expression on his face. The whistle saved him from having
to call time out.

IV

Early in the second quarter, Jewboy Schwartz broke loose,
and fleeted down the side line. Studs ran over, left his feet,
smashed through the air as Schwartz sidestepped, and picked
up speed again, rolled over offside four times in a histrionic
effort to show the crowd that his try had been fearless and
desperate, sat up and yelled to get him. Schwartz was over
for a touchdown.

Studs' shame and disappointment was lessened a little when

he heard Tommy Doyle call that it was a good try. The kick for extra point was missed. Hink and Weary walked by Studs, into position. Hink said that they would have to slow the Jew up with some rough tackling. Weary declared that if he got his guts slapped a couple of times, he'd slow down because Jews were yellow. Nate ran awkwardly to Studs and started bawling him out. Studs told Nate to freeze it. Nate megaphoned to all of them that they had to fight now. Studs waited, hands on knees, worrying himself, forgetting the crowd, thinking that they had to win, had to stop that fast Jew.

The Cardinals pepped up and shouted after taking the ball to the Monitor thirty-yard line on four plays. They were going over now, but on the next play Art Hahn went through tackle, and he was stopped by Red Kelly who stood in his way. Nate yelled to Red that it wasn't a sanitarium, and Red told him shut up while he was all together. Weary yelled to can the beefing and play football. Studs flung a pass. Jewboy Schwartz picked it neatly out of the air, and ran in the clear. Studs, playing safety, went for him without confidence, left his feet in a blind dive, opened his eyes as he encircled the Jew's slippery, powerful thighs, clenched them, tumbled him down. Hearing a cheer, he realized it had been neat work. He jumped up, forgetting that it had been lucky in the glory of being cheered. He walked casually away. The thrill of leaving his feet, rushing through the air, hitting him, dragging him down so nicely, lingered. He wanted to do it again. Weary patted his back, and called it a sweet tackle in the most genuine words he'd uttered to Studs since their fight. Studs felt good again. But, boy, that Jew was built like steel. Light and fast, and hard as nails. They'd need a club, or a tank to put him out. Still, the memory of that tackle, a split second of keen release and thrill, hung with him.

Jim Nolan recovered on a bad pass from the Monitor center. Hink Weber took the ball on the first play, and ran forty yards down the left side of the field for a touchdown. He kicked the point after touchdown. The Fifty-eighth Street Cardinals talked to each other like happy children.

Jewboy Schwartz took the kickoff. His own men got in his way, and Weary tackled him. There was a pile on, and Weary jammed his knee into Schwartz's groin. They got off, and Schwartz lay there, moaning and rolling, with both hands gripping his crotch. Schaeffer rushed to Reilley and told him to cut it out. Weary snarled back that he didn't like people to talk with their tongues; fists spoke a harder language. Hink pulled Weary aside, and again avoided a fight.

Jewboy Schwartz tried to play. When he had to punt, his kick went weakly to Art Hahn. He limped off the field, and at the half, the Fifty-eighth Street Cardinals led 7 to 6.

V

Between halves, Coach Hugo Zip Malloy told his team they weren't hitting hard enough. He promised to buy a drink for every one who laid out a Monitor so that the guy stayed out. He told Austin McAuliffe to go in at quarter and unleash their trick plays, because Austin, a thin, weak-faced, red-haired chap, was a scientific player. Studs took Art Hahn's half, Arnold was to go back in, and Weary was to play end in place of Tubby. Bill Donoghue was to take Kelly's tackle.

Jewboy Schwartz was back and returned the kickoff twenty yards. Weary grouped the team together after the play, and said this time, they had to put that Jew out for keeps. Studs took his position at defensive half, keen to be more in the game, tackling, running the ends, bucking the line, smearing passes. Only they couldn't let the Jew get loose. Austin was a poor safety man. But they'd stop him dead now. He waited for the play, suddenly wishing he'd gone to high school and been a star like Dan had. Studs smashed in with the play, but Dan nabbed Schwartz behind the line. Schaeffer carried the ball on the next play. Arnold Sheehan was clipped from behind, and Schaeffer got twenty yards before Hink sliced into him from the side. Arnold went out with a wrenched knee, and Art Hahn came on the field. Nolan recovered a fumble. Austin called a trick play. The ball was passed from Austin to Studs to Hahn to Nolan, and eighteen yards were lost. Austin called another trick play, a quarterback sneak, and he circled backwards, running wide. Tacklers closed in on him. He outran them to the sideline for a twenty-five yard loss. Hink punted.

Schwartz took the ball on first down and came flying through tackle without interference. Dodging to break into the open, he was hit simultaneously by Studs, Weary, and Hink. He arose groggy.

"They'll be picking up the kike's pieces now," Weary said, walking off with Studs.

Schwartz started a wide end run. Nolan smashed in, and made a flying tackle, catching Jewboy by the heels to dump him on his head. The crowd could hear the thud. He lay unconscious. He was revived and insisted on playing. Jewboy dropped back to punt. Weary and Nate Klein broke through, and piled into him blocking the kick. He got up with a bloody nose, and a hand slightly scratched from Nate's spikes. There was a row, but Hink Weber sent Nate to the sidelines to borrow another pair of shoes.

Hink took the ball through the line. Schwartz dove for him, and was stiff-armed on the chin, his head jerking back as he flopped. Hink scored another touchdown.

Hink kicked off to Schwartz. Five Cardinals hit him. He was out again, bleeding from the mouth, his upper lip crusted with congealed blood from his nose. A Monitor yelled that he was dead. Jake Schaeffer helped carry him off and walked back onto the field in tears, vowing he'd get the sonsofbitches. Weary recovered a Monitor fumble, and Schaeffer piled on him.

"What's the idea?" Weary challenged, arising.

"Play football, and quit squawking. You half killed my buddy!"

"And I'll kill you too, kike!" Weary said, clipping Schaeffer on the jaw. Before he knew what hit him, Schaeffer got two more clouts, and went down.

"Get up and fight, louse!" Weary sneered, hovering over him.

Both teams started swinging. Spectators and substitutes rushed onto the field. The three cops, at the game, struggled in vain. One of them whistled loudly. Another fled to call for reinforcements. Hugo Malloy parted through the crowd with a billy. Three Monitors went for Weary. He laid two of them cold with punches, and picked the third up and tossed him four yeards away. Studs caught him as he stumbled, and he went down. A fellow stepped on his face. Nate Klein kicked him, and was smacked in the eye from behind. He slunk towards the edge of the crowd. Weary shoved about, swinging when he had to, trying to find Schaeffer. He caught him, and let him have both guns. A billy came down on his shoulder. He wheeled around, getting force, and belted the guy with the billy, flush in the mouth, closed in, and gave him the knee. He kicked the guy for good measure.

A park cop grabbed Weary. He wriggled loose, slipped behind him, and gave him a rabbit punch. A bruiser, guard on the Monitors, slugged wildly at Studs. Studs ducked, in desperation at the guy's size, and swung blindly, landing in the guts. The ham's guard dropped, and he whittled down to Studs' size. Studs let an uppercut go from his heels and caught the fellow under the chin. The bruiser fled. Slug Mason came into action, pumping with both fists. He caught two guys, and crashed their heads together.

"The cops!" somebody yelled.

The cry was taken up. The mob separated in all directions.

Police reinforcements came across the park, and clubs were swung, as everybody ran. Studs, running, passed a group carrying Schwartz.

"You bastards, come down to Forty-seventh Street!"

Studs turned and thumbed his nose. An opened pocket-knife zizzed by his ears. He ran.

"Swell work, Studs!" said Fat Malloy ranging alongside of him. Shots in the distance were heard.

Studs came out of the park at Fifty-sixth Street, out of breath, his side paining.

VI

The poolroom was crowded. Rumors spread quckly. Talk went of arrests, broken heads, people dead. Studs passed along from one excited group to another, liking it all, the praise, the talk, the excitement. He came upon Arnold Sheehan, who had a sprained ankle, a twisted knee, and a shiner. He had been sitting down, and when the fighting came close, he had arisen and hobbled along the ropes. It had been just his luck to get sloughed in the eye. Weary tried to stir Studs up to go down to Forty-seventh. Nobody was interested. Fifty-eighth Street had won the game and the fight anyway, they all said. Nate came to tell Studs how he'd gloriously gotten his shiner. Young Rocky Kansas interrupted to tell how he had mashed in a big baboon. Studs knew they were liars. Guys always lied like that about how they fought, how they drank, how they jazzed. He told of hitting the big guy, and lied, too, saying he had knocked the guy cold with a punch. It was like being on a glorious jag, a little bit like it had been on Armistice Day.

He heard Dan Donoghue near him ask Danny O'Neill what he thought of the game.

"Most of them don't know how to play. They tackle high, can't block, don't even know how to play their position."

"Well, they are uncoached, but don't you think it was a fair bunch for an uncoached team?" asked Dan Donoghue.

Studs frowned when O'Neill superciliously answered yes. Remembered the punk when he ran around with his stockings falling and snot running out of his nose. Uncoached! Ought to slap his teeth! Seemed to think his was gold, droopy punk!

"That Schwartz is a player. I never tackled anybody as hard to get in my high school career with Loyola and I played against some tough men," Dan said.

"He was good. But some of the guys, Kelly, McAuliffe, and Klein, for instance, were jokes."

"What do you think of Studs?" asked Donoghue.

Studs tensed. Waited. Oughtn't to care what the punk thought. Waited.

"A bit slow, but he knows what to do, leaves his feet when he tackles and handles himself well."

"Studs is a natural-born football player," Donoghue said.

O'Neill wasn't so bad. Heard too that he was a high school star. Studs sidled to them.

"Now that you're a star on the team at the Saint Stanislaus high school, what did you think of our . . . amateur game?" Studs asked, fatuously.

Before O'Neill could answer, the rumor spread that Schwartz had died on the way to the hospital. Everybody gabbed and shouted at the same time.

"Will anything be done about it?" Studs asked Kelly.

"They might hold us for manslaughter."

"Why? We played a fair game. The fight was afterwards."

"Well, they might, only, of course, we'll get out of it, and anyway, besides, we were in the right. We can get drag through my old man, who's sergeant down at Fiftieth now, and your old man knowing politicians, and some other guys the same way," Red said.

"We can get enough witnesses," said Studs.

The rumor was still being discussed when Studs left for home. If they did throw them all in the jug! He saw himself in the pen for a manslaughter charge. But they couldn't get him. He'd played a clean game.

He realized how tired he was, and his shoulders drooped. But it had been a great game, and a great fight, and he could feel proud of his part in both. He'd showed them all. He remembered that first clean tackle he had made, leaving his feet, the way he smashed into the runner, that sudden rush of his body through the air for a split second, and bang, the guy was down. Hundreds of people, too, had seen it. He was nostalgic to be still playing, making tackles like that.

Dumb, too, not to have gone to high school. If punks like O'Neill could make the grade, what couldn't he have done? He cursed, though, realizing that they would lose their permit to play in Washington Park, and that they couldn't get up a good team to travel, particularly after a fight like this; because if they traveled and didn't have a big enough mob along, they'd get the clouts plenty somewhere. Damn Reilley! And just when the scrap had started, he had been getting into top form, he felt. But the fight, too, had been a wow. The way he had hit that big yellow bastard. Only, gee, he might have been a bigger star in the game than even Schwartz, if it hadn't started.

He stuck his shoulders back, and forced himself to walk briskly. Proud of himself and his body. In his prime right now.

He became aware that it was dark, and an autumn mist was settling over Fifty-eighth Street. Street lights were on at the alley between Indiana and Michigan. There were lights in windows. He heard the scrape of shoes in back of him, and the rumble of an elevated train. Down at State Street a street car was going, the bell donging. An automobile passed. The lonesome part of the day.

If Lucy had seen it, him! Well, what if he did admit to himself; he had played and acted like a hero!

That poor bastard Schwartz, game, had to grant that, lying dead in a hospital or morgue. It could have been him, perhaps. No, he knew he wouldn't die that way; he knew that he had some kind of a destiny to live for, and that he would live until that destiny was fulfilled. Maybe he would be a damn important guy later on, politician or something. That poor Jew bastard in a morgue. On the impulse, he mumbled a prayer for the guy!

The street around him seemed gloomy, and he was gloomy too. He couldn't get the thought of that dead Jew out of his mind. He didn't feel so cocky. He felt now like he wanted something in life, and didn't know what. That game and fight now, it had been swell. But there was something more he wanted than the glory of it, and he didn't even know what it was. Funny that he kept coming back to thoughts like this.

IX

"Money's pretty tight right now," Lonigan said.

"I know, Paddy, I wouldn't come to you if I could go any-wheres else. I'd borrow on my insurance only I can't, because I had to do that when Ann had appendicitis," Lonigan's brother, Joe the motorman, said.

"How old is Tommy?"

"Twenty," Joe said deferentially.

"You say he stuck this guy up and spent the dough, and you got to make it good?"

Joe nodded.

"He can't get off on first offense?"

"The Jew is sore, and threatens to press charges if he don't get his money back. You know these Jews, always wanting their pound of flesh."

"Joe, you should have watched him."

*"I tried, Paddy, but I was working every night on the cars.
I did all I could, and it was a great sacrifice sending the boy
to high school. But now, Paddy, I think the kid has learned
his lesson. And I can't stand by and see my boy go to the pen.
That would ruin his life sure."*

*"A bad business! You should have watched him more.
You know, Joe, when a boy goes wrong, it's not only his fault.
It's also the father's. I tell you that, Joe, because it's the truth,
and we got to face the truth even though it hurts."*

"I know, Paddy," Joe said with almost miserable weakness.

Lonigan meditated. Joe waited. Both brothers looked alike,
but their difference in economic status was written into their
countenances. Lonigan was stouter, his face full. Joe had a
frustrated, harassed look.

*"All right, Joe. I can do it this time. But I can't if anything
happens again, because I got lots of expenses, with my two
youngsters still in school."*

"Thanks, Paddy. The kid's learned his lesson, I'm sure."

*"I'll give you a check for a hundred bucks. But take it
from me, what you ought to do is pound some sense into him
with a horse whip."*

*"Paddy, I think he's learned his lesson. . . . But how is
your oldest boy?"*

*"Oh, Bill is a fine kid, working with me, learning the
business, a clear-headed, ambitious lad. Bill is all right;
he's turned out fine, and I'm proud of him."*

CHAPTER NINE

I

"Now, William, please come to our December formal,"
Fran said.

"Bill, I'd give anything to see you in soup-and-fish," Lonigan
said, boisterously spraying Martin with saliva as he laughed.

A blush spoiled Studs' efforts to appear noncommittal.

"A lot of fellows you know, Dan Donoghue, Johnny O'Brien,
scads of them will be there, even that awful brother of Geral-
dine Malloy's," Fran said.

"Now, Frances, you needn't go bothering William. There's
time enough for him to be getting a girl. Nowadays, all a girl
wants is to get a fellow and have him spend all his money
on her. William works hard for his money, and he'll have time
enough for girls. He's young yet," the mother said.

"Mother, please don't be so ridic," Fran said.

"My goodness mercy, the language you use. I was saying to Mrs. Reilley only the other day, that the way our young ones are talking, we soon won't be able to understand a word they say," the mother said.

"Bill, don't let 'em fool you. I'll bet you'll be a real sheik, and have a winning way with the ladies. Chip off the old block, you'll be. Now when I was young . . ."

"Father, please!" interrupted Fran in a tone nasty with boredom and disgust.

Lonigan looked hurt.

"Yes, to hear him talk! If I hadn't married him, he'd still be a wall-flower," the mother said.

"Is that so?" said Lonigan.

"I'll bet Martin will be a sheik and not need any encouragement when he gets a little older," Loretta said.

"Aw, go hop in the bowl," Martin said.

The family paused from its supper to look aghast at Martin.

"Why, the idea!" said Fran in dudgeon.

"Martin, where do you hear language like that?" Lonigan sternly asked.

"He won't get a girl ever if he talks like that," Loretta said, amused.

"Now, see here, young fellow! I never want to hear you talking like that inside this house, and above all at the family table, blessed be God," Lonigan commanded.

"You children are the life of me! I don't know where you get your talk and your ideas," the mother said.

"If you would send him to a refined private school, like the one Catherine Hovey's brother goes to, he wouldn't talk like he does," Fran said.

"I won't go to that dopey school," Martin protested.

"Listen! If you want to sit at this table with your mother and sisters, you're going to use civilized, refined language," Lonigan said.

"All right, but gee, can't all of you let me alone?"

"He takes after him," Fran said, pointing at Studs.

Studs was inwardly proud. He was always being told his kid brother was just like he'd been, and plenty tough.

"Nobody asked for your two cents' worth," Studs said.

"Why, William Lonigan, you're not going to talk to me in that tone of voice!"

"Children, please!" interjected the mother.

"I give him up. I don't care what he does any more. I don't want him at our dance, disgracing me. If he chooses to be a bum, let him! I wash my hands," Fran said like a martyr.

"You've been doing that for years, I hope it's final," sneered Studs.

"Don't worry. It is. You have a positive hatred of acting like a gentleman. Go your own way! You might wake up some day and be sorry," she said.

"Swell," Studs said sarcastically.

"That'll be about enough," Lonigan boomed.

The table lapsed into a hostile silence. To break it, Lonigan asked Loretta how she was coming along at school.

"Fine, Dad."

Studs ate quickly. Hell, he didn't want to take his time, and listen to all the talk that went on.

"What are you studying?"

"Oh, Latin, and Advanced Algebra, and Christian Doctrine, and History, and . . ."

"You're going to be a smart lady, I see."

"Martin! Haven't you been told before not to set your knife against your plate like that. Put it on your plate. You're not eating with African cannibals," Fran said.

"Oh, all right!" Martin pouted, putting his knife across his plate.

"I thought I said there's to be no more of this!" Lonigan said.

"Well, there wouldn't be, if someone would teach him some manners," Fran said.

"Aw, mind your own business," Martin said.

"Fran, please!" said Loretta.

"Well, he could at least eat in a civilized fashion," Fran said.

"Martin, who do you ever see eating like that?" Lonigan asked.

"Him!" Fran said, pointing at Studs.

"Say, keep your trap shut."

"You're not going to snarl at me," she said. She jumped up, and flushed out of the room. Lonigan impotently looked from one to the other.

"I do wish you'd treat one another like brother and sister," Mrs. Lonigan said. She arose and followed Fran.

"Bill, you know your sister's a little nervous and you got to make allowances for her," Lonigan fatuously said.

Fran returned with the mother, frowned, and sat down, preserving an air of armed truce.

"Well, I had an offer of ninety thousand for the building today," Lonigan said.

"You took it?" asked Fran.

"I should say not."

"But, Father, this neighborhood is deteriorating all the time.

The best people in it are moving over to Hyde Park or out in South Shore. Soon I'll be ashamed to admit I live around here."

"Young lady, you're wrong. The niggers will be run raggedy if they ever try to get past Wabash Avenue. This is a good, decent neighborhood full of respectable people, and it will always be so. Didn't you hear Father Gilhooley talk about the new church he was building on this street? What did he say? Didn't he say Michigan was going to be a boulevard straight through. Then, this building will be worth twice as much. Why this neighborhood hasn't even commenced to grow yet, the way it will, and property values have hardly started to rise in it."

"But, Father . . ."

"Young lady, this is my business."

They finished supper with little talk. Studs left the table and washed his teeth. He put on his hat and coat. He looked at himself in the mirror. He wasn't a bad-looking guy at all. He heard footsteps in the hall, and turned away. He remembered how Fran had once caught him at the mirror, and had razzed him about being conceited in a snotty, superior way that she had.

"Bill, come here a minute!" Lonigan called as Studs turned the knob of the front door.

He was smoking in his rocker. Studs noticed that his belly seemed to stick out more and more every day. He plunked down on the piano stool.

"Bill, you know, Father Time is beginning to catch up on your mother and me. You kids are all we got, and . . . we'd kind of like to see more of you, have you all stay in and spend a quiet, happy evening with us. That isn't asking a whole lot. You're young and want to go out and be a regular fellow, and we don't object. Only there's always another night. And you know, Bill, you'll never have another mother. She sits up night after night worrying about you. It would just tickle her heart pink if you would, now and then, go up, kiss her and say, 'Mother, I'm going to stay in with you tonight.' "

"I'm just going to a show. I'll be in early."

The phone rang. Studs was glad it was for him. He went out of the parlor and Lonigan picked up his newspaper to read about the Grand Jury quiz of some aldermen implicated in a school board graft. It was Dan Donoghue calling to say that he had found out for certain that Jew Schwartz would be all right, except that he had been ruptured and wouldn't ever be able to play football again. Studs asked Dan about a show, but Dan had a date. He noticed Martin sitting by the crystal radio-set with the ear phones on, keeping time on the floor. Loretta came out of the bathroom with a copy of *True Story* magazine in her hands. She stopped, shaking her shoulders and doing a little dance when she saw him. He left, shouting good-bye.

II

Off the drear and rock-bound coasts of Alaska, that frigid land where men gamble their lives and souls with the dice of death, and sin for love and gold, the good ship *Mary Ann* braved all the monstrous terrors of the deep. Rolling, tipping, tossing, swaying, swerving, straining through the black and mysterious night, it tacked against a pelting rain, a howling wind, and huge waves that washed over it like evil spirits from out of the bowels of the unconquerable seas.

Captain Arnold, of the good ship *Mary Ann*, was a bulky man with cruelty stamped on a vicious, unshaven face, and a heart more ruthless than the stormy seas. He commanded his seamen with the iron hand of a tyrant. With each order, he gave them a curse, a kick, a blow. One of his sailors was Morgan, a smaller man, with the milk of human kindness in his soul. He gave Morgan an order, and slapped his face, sneering like a fiend out of hell. Morgan received the slap unflinchingly, but defiance struck the kindliness from his eyes.

Captain Arnold turned, and staggered across the rolling deck, with waves washing foamily past him, into his cabin. While the door was opened to admit him, wind and water gushed in, a flickering candle almost died, and a whiskey glass tumbled off the table, to crash. In a bunk, Captain Arnold's timid Indian wife cowered like a small and frightened rabbit, her baby girl in her arms.

"Christ, he's a mean-looking brute," Studs Lonigan whispered to Slug Mason, as Captain Arnold's scowl revealed his fangs.

"You said it."

There was conversation, glowering hatred on the Captain's face, naked fear on the countenance of his wife. With wild animal ferocity in his eyes, Captain Arnold pointed demonstratively at the cabin door. The little Indian wife strained her baby girl more tightly to her bosom, huddled herself into a corner of the bunk, and shook her head. Her mouth opened in a scream as he approached her. He clutched her arm, and brutally yanked her out of the berth. He tore the baby from her, and dropped it in the berth, flinging her aside with such force that she catapulted against the cabin wall. Wrenching her arm, he pulled her out of the cabin, dragged her through the high, icy waves, and shoved her amongst the crew of out-cast sailors who worked like demons amidst falling spars. A wave knocked her down, and she rolled to the edge of the ship. He struggled towards her, pulled her to her feet by the hair, and forced her back amongst the men. A falling spar cracked her head, and she fell. He commanded his sailors, while she lay unattended in a puddle, prey of the washing waves. Morgan staggered back to the cabin with her in his arms. He gently placed her in a berth, gave her whiskey, and carefully covered her with warm blankets. Through the long and stormy night, he tended her.

And came the dawn, calm and peaceful over the waters by the rock-bound coast of adventurous Alaska. The Indian wife lay at death's door. With her last forced words she begged that Morgan save the baby daughter from its heartless father. Captain Arnold entered the cabin, tore off his sou-wester, and guzzled whiskey. With a face as unfeeling as the sea, he watched his wife die.

"He's a bastard all right!" Studs muttered.

Morgan shook his head sadly as he gazed upon the tragic face of the dead woman. Gently, he covered it with a blanket. He turned and looked into the animalistic eyes of Captain Arnold, and saw a fiend in human form. An overpowering rage stirred him. He punched Arnold's jaw. Taken by surprise, the captain's head snapped back. He stumbled backwards to the wall. Arnold rushed at the brave, impetuous Morgan and stunned him with a blow. He grasped Morgan in his arms and hurled him into a corner. The baby cried. Captain Arnold, his powerful arms threatening, heavy-footedly approached. Morgan saw a murderous intent written on that beastly face. He clutched a club from the floor and when Captain Arnold was upon him, he leaped up, and crashed it on Captain Arnold's head.

"The little guy has guts," Slug said with his mispronunciations.

Captain Arnold staggered backwards in a daze. Morgan clubbed him, until he toppled like a heavy, dropped sack of potatoes. He looked at the prostrate form of Captain Arnold, fearing that he had killed him. He took the baby, hustled out of the cabin, and escaped in a lifeboat.

Years passed, and much water ran under a crumbling wooden bridge. Seventeen years later, Morgan, now known as Jerome because he feared that he had murdered Captain Arnold, owned a general store in Flamingo, Alaska, where men still gambled their lives and souls with the dice of death, and sin for love and gold. Tenderly reared and named Gloria by Morgan, the baby girl had become a beautiful wild flower of Alaska. Not the faintest suspicion that she was a half-breed clouded her pure and innocent mind. She had been sent away to school, and on the day of her expected return, the Law came to Flamingo. The commanding officer of the contingent of soldiers was Lieutenant Ames Dubois, a cynical Southern aristocrat and Don Juan.

Morgan, now Jerome, feared that the soldiers might discover him to be the murderer of Captain Arnold. Morgan's friend, the half-breed Durer, feared them because he was engaged in fur-trading enterprises which they might halt. Durer loved Gloria, the wild flower of Alaska, but she reciprocated only with the affection she would have borne a brother. An even greater fear developed for both men when Lieutenant Ames Dubois captivated Gloria's innocent heart. For they perceived that the officer was only a trifler. And Gloria was young, and as lovely and as innocent as the flowers and sunshine of the springtime.

Then one day, a strange ship put into the harbor, apparently for repairs and supplies. When the captain strode into the general store like a self-confident bully, Morgan, now Jerome, recognized him. He recognized Morgan, now Jerome. Morgan, now Jerome, was relieved of the fear that he was a murderer only to have it supplanted by the fear that Captain Arnold might demand his daughter, and tell her that she was a half-breed. Smiling, and just as innocent, she ran into the store, and back of the counter to the rear, girlishly pecking a kiss on the forehead of Morgan, now Jerome. The captain asked who she was, and Morgan, now Jerome, replied that it was his own daughter. The captain nodded his head sceptically.

But he bided his time.

And one day while Morgan, now Jerome, lived harassed with his new fears, gold was discovered. Gloria quickly persuaded Ames to go out with her and stake some promising claims. As they journeyed, Ames attempted to climax his pursuit of Gloria, and ruin her. She resisted girlishly, suddenly touching the deeper and better chords of his nature.

"Pretty broad, all right," Studs mumbled.

"If the guy gets her, he's gettin' something," Slug said.

Ames changed from a trifler and a Don Juan into a genuine lover. She promised him her hand. They sacredly sealed their newly awakened love by a kiss under a snow-laden spreading chestnut tree. Happy as two larks, they staked some of the best claims.

In the meantime, Morgan, now Jerome, and Durer had gone

out to stake ground. On their return, the happy news of love was broken. In the midst of the congratulations and new-found joyousness, Captain Arnold nefariously revealed to Gloria that she was a half-breed.

"He's a rat, all right!" Studs whispered.

His interest was completely absorbed. He was, and he wasn't and he was Ames. He felt that that rat, Arnold, would crimp up all the plans. Ames had to get the girl. Usually in the pictures the hero did. But it was exciting, and wracking waiting, and he was strung tight.

Ames and Gloria walked moodily off by themselves, their faces saddened with this new rift that had been cast, like a menacing cloud, between them. He pleaded with her that this new revelation, that no revelation, could chill the ardor of his love for her.

Just like Studs had so often pleaded with Lucy in his mind.

She was stunned, and it did matter to her. One small tear crawled from her eye, slid down her cheek. And another. Gloria wept. Ames' tender solicitations and persuasions were vain. She turned and walked slowly away, and Ames' face gleamed disappointment as he watched her disappear beyond the snow-laden spreading chestnut tree where they had sealed their love with a sacred kiss.

Gloria returned home, and quickly packed a few belongings, determined that duty demanded that she go off with her father, no matter if he were a vicious brute. Durer, discovering her note, followed. Ames returned to the general store, and he too set out to apprehend and save his beloved. In a threatened icefloe, Captain Arnold set sail with his daughter. The ship was jammed in an ice field. The crew deserted. Captain Arnold and Gloria were alone on the ice. Separately, Durer and Ames stumbled and fought their way over the slippery ice. Heavy, blinding Alaska snow fell. Ames slipped into the water, and clung tenaciously for life to the precarious ice.

In the cabin of the ship, Arnold looked with eyes of lust on Gloria. She was his daughter. But he was a brute.

Like a bastard, Studs watched, hoping that Arnold would be successful, and rape her. No, he didn't. He thought of himself as Ames, coming to the vessel in the nick of time.

Arnold trapped her in a corner, and imprinted a long and filthy kiss upon her unsoiled lips. She squirmed free. He trapped her in another corner. She dodged under his arm, her sleeve ripping, and fled behind a table. He faced her with eyes of lust.

Studs could just see him grabbing her, flinging her on the bunk, and . . .

Outside, in an Alaskan blizzard, Ames crawled back onto the ice, inch by inch. Durer reached the ship, staggering from his exertions. He busted into the cabin, just as the powerful arms of Captain Arnold encircled the girlish waist of Gloria. Arnold flung her aside, and her left breast almost, but not quite, fell out of her torn dress. The dent where her breasts commenced, and about half an inch of warm bare flesh were revealed.

Durer punched Arnold. Arnold fell. He rose and drove Durer to the other side of the cabin. Durer charged, and with a punch knocked Arnold back three feet. Arnold lifted the table, and brought it down on Durer's head. Durer toppled.

His shirt torn, his unshaven face a mask out of Hell, his hairy arms and chest visible, he moved, like a gorilla, upon Gloria. Ames regained the ice, and staggered into the face of the Alaskan blizzard with the courage of desperation, born of the flames of a powerful love. He fell, arose, fell, arose, rushed undauntedly onwards. Arnold drew the exhausted dishevelled Gloria near to him. Ames staggered through the cabin door, snow flying from his clothes. He leaped upon Captain Arnold, and the men fought, knocking each other down, driving each other back and forth across the cabin, while Gloria stood trembling with her hands flat on her cheeks. The men clinched, and Captain Arnold attempted to gouge Ames. Ames knocked him into the wall. Rebounding, he grasped a club. Ames dodged low, and twisted his wrist. The club dropped to the floor. The men went down, and rolled over and over, punching fiercely. They arose. Arnold hurled a chair at Ames. Ames ducked, and the chair broke against the wall. They staggered at each other. Ames warded off Arnold's blow, and connected with a last punch, into which he put all of his ebbing strength. Arnold fell unconscious. Durer shook his head, regained consciousness. They bundled Gloria in warm blankets, and carried her back across the ice, in the Alaskan blizzard. Arnold remained to die a villain's lonely death in the ice-jammed ship.

Back at the general store of Morgan, now Jerome, the three friends enjoyed a happy and delicious dinner which Gloria had prepared. After dinner, she sat on Ames' knee, and the men smoked. Suddenly, Durer arose and said goodbye. He walked out and away to a new village, singing but with a heart painted in the deep dyes of sorrow and unrequited love. Ames and Gloria saddened as they looked out the window to see him disappear. But love overpowered their sadness. They walked out into the glory of an Alaskan twilight, with the fading sun glowing over the snow. Under a tree, in the snow, before the setting sun, they kissed.

And under an Alaskan sunset, Studs Lonigan kissed Gloria, and kissed Lucy.

He made his exit with Slug, wishing there were more of it.

III

In front of the Michigan Theatre Studs guessed that he'd get coffee an' with Slug near the show, and then go straight home. Slug wanted to go down to Fifty-eighth first and see if the lads were around. Studs said all right he'd go along, but he didn't want to be out late because he needed rest; hadn't had a decent night's sleep all week. They crossed Garfield Boulevard, and walked south on Indiana Avenue. Studs felt close to Slug, as if Mason were his best friend. They seemed to understand each other, and when they were alone, they didn't say much; but there seemed to be something deeper than words could express between them. Studs wondered did Slug have the same kind of thoughts that he had.

Exciting picture, full of action; peachy fight at the end, it was. And the broad had been a knockout. When Arnold went at her, her boobs had almost fallen out. If they only let the boobs really fall out in scenes like that. If they could show everything in movies. Wished that she had gotten her clothes wet; they would have stuck to her body, and it would have been the next thing to seeing her stripped. Would be plenty of delights marrying a jane like that. He kissed her; married her; went to bed with her . . .

"Good picture," Slug mumbled.

"Yeah."

"Have one," Slug said, offering his pack of Camels to Studs.

Studs wondered what it would be like, hunting gold in Alaska. Yukon Lonigan in the gold fields. Taking a roulette game in Flamingo, Alaska, for a buggy ride. Shooting his way out to keep the gold he'd won. The picture made him want things like that, big dough, travel, broads as gorgeous as Gloria. The things he did, had no comparison with such a life; hanging around the poolroom, now and then a small-time crap game or round of poker; benders on Saturday night, and maybe a couple of times during the week; sometimes a can house. Nothing like it. And he could see himself returning from Alaska, with endless stories to tell, and his jeans sagging with dough. Knock everybody for a row then!

There were lots of things in life he'd been missing. He was doing a lot of the things he dreamed of doing when he'd been a kid. He wanted more and felt that somewhere there was something else for him in life, and it was the ticket that would satisfy the feeling he always got from the movies, from seeing a nice jane on the street, sometimes from walking in the park in summer and maybe looking at the sky, sometimes when walking home from work in the sunset.

Maybe if he married Lucy, it would turn out happy. Or someone like Gloria. If she and Lucy were the same girl! But what about when she would get old, and he'd want younger broads, and she had him tied home like a trained monkey in a zoo, and there'd be regiments of squawling brats coming along; he hated kids. He could just see himself parading in the hall in the middle of the night, carrying a bawling baby, and maybe having the baby let go in his arms. But having a decent girl, who was your wife, must be different than being with whores or bums you took over to the park. Slug said all broads were the same. There had to be more to it than that, more than it was like in a can house, hurrying through with it and being disgusted afterwards. But was it worth having a jane sink the hooks into you, and handcuff your dough? He didn't know, but on summer nights when he saw guys out with their broads, he felt different about it than he pretended when he was with the guys.

"Like the broad I fixed you up with last Sunday night after the football game?"

"Yeah."

"Nice, huh?"

"Yeah."

"Say, wouldn't I like that broad in the pictures," Slug said with all his mispronunciations.

Hell, what right had he to think of a broad like her? She wouldn't even spit on him.

They passed the white-tiled Methodist Church at Fifty-sixth and Indiana. At Fifty-seventh, Studs kind of wished that Slug would not turn but that they'd walk down to Fifty-eighth past her old house. But he didn't have any special reason to give for wanting to go that way, and walked with Slug when he turned east on Fifty-seventh. They turned by the Crerar Presbyterian Church on the corner of Fifty-seventh and Prairie, and Studs remembered one Sunday night when they'd been kids; how they'd gone to services there, put slugs in the collection box, and laughed until a sappy-faced usher kicked them out. They saw a group on the corner. Studs determined he wouldn't hang around long. He wondered too, if he didn't marry, would he be an old soak like Barney Keefe. He wanted to be something big in life. But look at what his fat, loud-mouthed old man was! Or Dinny Gorman, the high-hat wind-bag of a politician! It got him all right.

"Lonigan!" Barney Keefe exclaimed with drunken exuberance.

"Keefe!" Lonigan replied with pumped boisterousness.

"Lonigan, you pig-in-the-parlor-mick!"

"Keefe, you drunken flannel-mouth."

Slug complimented the boys for being polluted. Baby-faced Mickey Flannagan faced them, stupefied, swaying like a reed in the wind.

Studs told them that Schwartz from last Sunday's game would be all right. They said good.

"Flannagan has his guts pickled in gin," Keefe said.

Mickey mumbled. Slug caught him as he fell forwards, and set him against the fire plug.

Barney pulled out a bottle, and held it aloft;

> Past the teeth,
> Down the tongue,
> Look out, stomach,
> Here I come!

They laughed. Kelly grabbed the bottle. Barney beefed like hell. Taite and Les tried to get a sip from Kelly, but it was all gone.

Mickey mumbled for them to watch his match trick. He fumbled through his pockets and came out with a box of safety matches. He hiccoughed. He lit a match. It went out. He lit another. The flame quickly died. He repeated until they asked him what the trick was. He pawed out a match and lit it. It went out. That was the trick.

"Look out there, Flannagan, your guts are rising!" Keefe said.

Mickey belched.

"Here's the Bad News Twins," Studs said, seeing Mush Joss and TB McCarthy approaching.

Muggsy, looking like the con, round-shouldered, a cigarette drooping from the corner of his mouth, tried to scrouge two bits off Keefe.

"So long, boys. I'm going home and sleep," Studs said, yawning.

"Hang around. The Alky Squad is here, and something might happen," Slug said.

TB tried to hit Studs for a quarter. Studs told him to get away.

"Flannagan, you lousy paper salesman, give these mooching bastards a quarter. I can't stand their sight," Keefe said.

Flannagan fell on his face, mumbling incoherently.

Kelly suggested a poker game at his house. Studs said he had to go home. He went with the boys. Flannagan was left draped around the fire plug. Muggsy and Mush rolled him, and had a meal. Stepping out of the Greek Restaurant, Muggsy wished now that they could pick up a bum broad and take her back with them to the basement where they slept. Muggsy said it was the best meal he'd had all week.

Studs left Kelly's at three o'clock. He walked along with his eyes heavy. He bumped into a building, and realized that he was asleep on his feet. What a chump he'd been! He'd be pooped tomorrow, and only have a couple of hours sleep. And he'd lost eight bucks.

X

Davey Cohen pulled up the collar of his thin overcoat. He climbed a hilly street of Jamestown, New York, in the rain. He spewed up a racking cough, and spat. He entered the public library for shelter. A girl looked askance at him, and he felt as if he were an interloper. A blue-covered book lay before him. He read the title. The Collected Poems of Heinrich Heine, *translated by Louis Untermeyer. He opened the book, just to pass the time, and read the preface. He read the facts of the poet's life, saddened at his fate, proud that he had been a Jew. A quotation from one of Heine's letters excited him:*

"When the harvest moon was up last year, I had to take to my bed, and since then I have not risen from it . . . I am no longer a divine biped: I am no longer a joyous though slightly corpulent Hellene, smiling gaily down on the melancholy Nazarene. I am now only an etching of sorrow, an unhappy man—a poor sick Jew."

Words that might have been tortured from Davey's own consumptive being. For what was he, too, but an etching of sorrow, a poor, sick, and homeless Jew.

He turned the pages and came upon Monolog From A Mattress. *He could visualize the Jewish poet, twisted in body, unhappy in mind, expressing crucified thoughts from his mattress grave. The deepest poignancy of his whole life trembled within him.*

                    For the rest—
That any son should be as sick as I,
No mother could believe.

It washed gloom into him. Might he not die on a mattress grave from con in the charity ward of a hospital if he did not die in a prairie or doorway. Just like Heine, who suffered so many years ago in Paris, exiled. He was like an exile from Chicago. He thought of Heine, "who has all the poet's gifts but love," Heine, "a twisted trunk in chilly isolation." Day after day he lay:

Slightly propped up upon this mattress grave
In which I've been interred these few eight years.

So unhappy that he envied a dog! How many times hadn't Davey Cohen, hungry, cold, knowing he was useless to the world, walked along the streets of strange towns, envying the dogs that people owned, knowing that the dogs were better fed than he, that some people thought more of them than any human being did of him. He thought of dusk coming upon the poet on his mattress grave, another day of life robbed from his twisted body. Outside, in the rain, dusk came too, robbing Davey of another miserable day. He read and re-read Heine's monologue, and then, other poems. The library closed, and the hours had seemed like minutes.

Davey slipped the book under his coat, and left. Rain slapped his face. He was back in the world now. He felt himself an "etching of sorrow, an unhappy man—a poor sick Jew." He coughed, a sharp sword-like pain slicing through his lungs. He spat blood.

He was hungry.

CHAPTER TEN

I

Studs Lonigan arose with the ringing of the alarm clock, and rode to work on a crowded surface-car which ran backwards. As if through a mist, he saw the familiar unremembered faces of the other passengers. A man with an indistinct face and the sleek uniform of an army officer stared at him with contempt. Studs tried to recall that somewhere he had seen that face before. He crossed the aisle and eyed the man with an expression that was both questioning and conciliatory.

"Say, Chauncey, we're going backwards, and I got to be at work."

"All the cars in Alaska go this way."

In a shock of surprise, Studs saw from the window of the moving car that they were passing through expansive, flat fields of snow.

He returned to his seat, and his disappointment dissipated when he realized that he was an adventurer, journeying to fight for love and gold. And the army officer was Lieutenant Ames Dubois. With the pride of ingenuity, he outlined a plan of action. Ames would be returning to Gloria. After seeing her, he would lead his soldiers out on an expedition to shovel snow. And Gloria would be awaiting her lover, Studs Lonigan, in a little Alaska love-nest. She would be prepared for him, without a strip on, and she would give herself unto him, body and soul, until it hurt. Then she would show him where the gold was in them there Alaska hills, and he would become a billionaire. He would return to Fifty-eighth Street with his fortune, and he would go round to the poolroom of George the Greek, escorting glorious Gloria, who would wear pearls in her ears, diamonds on her fingers, and rings on her toes. And every night for a century, glorious Gloria, stripped, would give herself unto him, body and soul, until it hurt. He glanced across the aisle at Lieutenant Ames Dubois, thinking what a chump that boy was.

The car jolted as it was jammed into an unexpected halt. Studs looked up into the face of Ames Dubois, and the countenance of the conductor; he knew that he knew the conductor and hated him like poison.

"Lonigan, take your goddamn tree off the tracks!" they jointly demanded.

"My tree?" Studs asked in surprised apology.

To the amusement of all the passengers, he was ejected from the car, and landed in unwet snow. He found no tree on the tracks, and when he looked up, the car was in motion, and Weary Reilley, the conductor, stood on the rear platform thumbing his nose.

Studs ran, flagging after the car, and pleading in shouts for them to wait. He was outdistanced and he stopped to catch his breath. A sense of loss swept him with oceans of sadness, and he was more sad than any man had ever been. He peered around him, and saw the same monotonous desolation of snow on every side, with neither sight nor sign of a human being. He had lost glorious Gloria forevermore, and he was poor, and miles upon miles from his home in Chicago that he should never have left. And when he did return, after walking the whole distance without shoes, he would have neither love nor gold.

You're no good! You're not a man. You never will be, you yellow Lonigan louse, a voice within him, as if it were the voice of conscience, sneered.

He dropped a dejected head, and set out upon that thousand-mile journey back to his home, without any shoes on his feet. He already could hear the crackling, sarcastic laughter with which he would be greeted. Suddenly, he was amongst buildings which resembled the houses and apartments in the 5700 block on Indiana Avenue. And in the sky, like a rising sun of the spring time, he saw the beaming face of Lucy Scanlan. In a voice as sweet as candy, she sang to him that she still loved him in a cosy Morris chair, and that if he wanted her, he must go and touch the tree. He confidently strode through a recognizable gangway, and came out upon a street which was fronted with a park of huge oak-trees. He crossed the street, but the trees receded and disappeared with his approach. He chased the vanishing trees across fields of grass, encouraged and hopeful, only because the face of Lucy Scanlan still shone in the sky like a rising sun of the spring time. He came upon a bent, gnarled oak-tree, and knew that it was the one, because the face of Lucy Scanlan blew kisses down upon it, and it sang *In the Blue Ridge Mountains of Virginia* with the voice of Lucy Scanlan. He touched the tree gently with the second and third fingers of his right hand

and suddenly . . .

the boy Studs Lonigan sat nervously in the eighth-grade room of St. Patrick's school, wishing that school would let out, because he had just touched something that was the secret of love and happiness and he couldn't remember what it was, or where it was, and he had to go out and find it again before it was too late.

"William Bastard Lonigan, you were late for school this morning," Sister Battling Bertha said, wrinkling the toothless face of a crone.

"I wasn't. The bell rang before I got here," the boy Studs Lonigan replied, and a six-foot-four pupil in short britches named Slug Mason guffawed.

"Sister, he played poker last night and lost eight dollars and when I asked him for a penny because I was starving, he wouldn't give it to me," TB McCarthy said, turning a sickly yellow face upon the schoolboy, Studs Lonigan.

"All I did last night was go to bed with Lucy, only we didn't sleep much. Ha! Ha!" the schoolboy Studs Lonigan said.

William Bastard Lonigan, by your gambling and immoral

thoughts, words, deeds, acts and wishes, you have spilled the consecrated blood of the Sacred Heart of the Crucified Jesus, and you have put gray hairs upon the heads of your father, mother, God the Father, Son and Holy Ghost, and all the communion of saints in Heaven and on earth. You will go to the gallows for your sacrileges, and God will send you special delivery to Hell to burn forevermore in a lake of brimstone!

She descended on him like a cyclone, and vigorously shook his head.

"Oh, how I hate to get up in the morning," he sang.

"Get up!" she commanded, slapping his face, while the entire class laughed at Clown Lonigan. . . .

and . . .

Studs Lonigan opened eyes that were heavy with sleep to find his mother gently shaking him. He sat up in bed, yawned, rubbed his eyes with the sleeve of his pajamas.

"Goodness, didn't you hear the alarm, son?"

"Gee, Mother, it was the funniest darn thing. I dreamt I got up with that clock, and was riding to work," he said boyishly.

She suddenly flung her arms around him, pulled him to her thin bosom, and kissed him, declaring that he would always be her baby. He was embarrassed.

"You must hurry now, son. Breakfast is all ready."

He sat on the edge of the bed half asleep, tiredly stretching. He opened his eyes; he'd fallen asleep sitting there. He looked over and saw that Martin was up, and in the bathroom washing. It got him sore. Martin returned to the bedroom.

"Say, what the hell's the idea? You know I have to be out of here earlier than you. You're just too damn wise a punk, ain't you?" Studs said, arising, and raising his hand as if to slam his kid brother.

"I'm going to Communion this morning. It's first Friday," Martin whined, drawing back.

"You could have waited until I was washed. I got farther to go than you. Why didn't you wake me?"

"Yes, wake you! The last time I did, I got a clout in the ear."

"One of these days, I'm going to slap some of that wiseness out of you, punk!"

"You do, and I'll . . . kill you," Martin shrieked, almost in tears.

Studs advanced a step.

"Don't touch me, you big bully!" Martin hollered.

The mother rushed into the bedroom, and enfolded Martin in maternal arms.

"Is he hurting my darling little child?"

Martin fought to break free. He blushed. Studs busted out laughing.

"If I wasn't going to communion, and it wasn't a sin to lose my temper, I'd tell you what I think of you, you big bum! You just wait until tonight, and I'll tell you."

The mother pressed a wet determined kiss on Martin's cheek.

"Can't there ever be any peace in this home?" Lonigan futilely protested, as he stood in the doorway with his suspenders hanging from his trousers, and his belly falling out.

Studs felt more awakened after he had doused his face in cold water. Shaving, he wished the day was over. He knew how pooped out he would feel in the afternoon, and how he'd only be able to get through his work by doping himself with cigarettes and coffee. Tonight he'd get some decent sleep.

A plate full of pancakes and a cup of black coffee were set before him on the kitchen table. He gulped the coffee down black and asked for another.

"Son, I don't want to nag you, but I'm worried about your health. You never get enough sleep and every morning you gulp down black coffee like that. Coffee is not good for your kidneys. You know the human body can stand only so much, and no more. A boy your age, doing the kind of work you do, has to get his proper rest. If you keep on like this, you'll be getting into consumption at twenty-five."

Studs hadn't listened to her, and with his mouth stuffed with pancakes, said that he was all right.

"Bill, always remember that the wise guy knows that he can always have another night, and doesn't try to do everything in one evening," Lonigan said.

The mother looked at the clock, and dashed in to awaken the girls.

"Bill, a man's health is like Humpty Dumpty. Once it is gone, nothing can repair it, not with all the money in the world, or all the king's men and horses. It can't be repaired like an automobile."

Studs felt like throwing the plate of syrupy pancakes at his father.

An uproar started in the girls' bedroom, and Fran was heard threatening to pull Loretta's hair out if she ever again wore her stockings.

"This family will put me in the nut house yet!" Lonigan said, wincing. He arose and went to stop the quarrel.

Studs was almost finished when Lonigan returned.

"Bill, you know, girls and women have to be handled with kid gloves and jollied along. So when Frances comes out to breakfast, kid her a little. You know, say, Good morning! How is the charming slim queen on this bright and sunny morning?"

Studs' face sank. He arose from the table. His father told him that if he'd wait, he could ride to work with him in the Ford. Studs said it was no use of having to go out of the way, he could take the street car. He was glad to get out. But he was damn tired.

II

"Kid, I'll be damned if my old lady didn't go and get sick again," Mort said, from the other side of the small vacant dining-room in an apartment building where they worked.

"Yeah," said Studs, brushing over the cream-colored paint with measured strokes. He yawned.

"You know, a young chap like yourself who's footloose as the winds don't know how well off you are," Mort said.

Studs yawned. He dipped his brush, tapped it against the side of the pail, drew it down the center of the wall.

"Sometimes when you get married, you don't know what you're being let into. You see a girl, a nice sweet kid, and she's cherry. You think, now I'll be happy with her, and we're just cut out for one another. Well, one thing and another happens, and first thing you know, you're married. You take her on a honeymoon, and there's nothing at all in life like those first nights. Now, take my wife. She was just as pretty as a picture. I'll show you a picture of her took when we was just married. And then our kids came along, and we thought things was going to be nice and smooth, and that we'd find comfort in the kids and someone to take care of us in our old age. And then eight years ago when our last youngster was born, my wife, she gets what they call a milk leg, you see, that's some kind of a clot that makes your leg swell up, all out of shape, and her heart goes back on her, and now the doctor says that she's got to be careful and any kind of excitement might be the finish of her."

"That's tough," Studs said, feeling that he had to say something.

Mort had told him the same story before, almost every day that they'd ever worked together. He went on painting, evening off the last coating. His arm was tired. He wasn't at all interested in the damn work. He liked to look at it when it was finished, and see that it was a good job, and he always took

pains to do a good job because he couldn't stand to slop on
paint and leave it any old way. But goddamn it, he hated to
think of going on, painting walls day after day after day, risking lead-poisoning too, until he got old and a big belly like
his old man, and then to go around bossing other guys who
painted walls day after day after day. Goddamn it, yes, there
was something more to life. There had to be. He jerked out
a watch: a quarter to three.

"Every night when I go home, I don't know but maybe
I'll find my wife dead. I tell you, kid, married life ain't all
it's cracked up to be, and don't let anybody kid you that it
is."

"No danger," Studs muttered with over-exaggerated confidence. He yawned.

"It's not that I'm complainin', because I ain't. My wife
has been the best in the world, but it's just that life doesn't
turn out the way you want it to."

Their brushes swished and slapped as they worked. Studs
yawned. Ten to three. Would it or wouldn't it be a good idea
to get married? Everybody did, and had kids. He guessed
that maybe you couldn't help yourself about it when the right
broad came along. That was what love was. Five to three.
Love was B.S. Suppose now he got married to Lucy and the
same thing happened to her that had happened to Mort's wife.
But it wouldn't. Things weren't going to happen to him that
way. He had luck, a lucky star, four aces stacked for him in
the cards. Well, he did. He had to have them. He did. Three
o'clock. He yawned. He whistled.

"As I was sayin', I don't know why the Lord should of
visited us with all the misfortunes he did. Sometimes, I fear
maybe it's because I sown my wild oats when I was your age,
or else because I drank now and again. Oh, sometimes too
it's maybe, I feel, because of something I done in a previous
life. Say, kid, do you believe in reincarnation?"

Studs didn't hear, and Mort repeated the question. Studs
thought it was all crap, but hell, he was too damn tired to
argue, so he said he didn't know.

"Well, I sometimes wonder if that's why we were punished.
But I tell you it isn't fair. I done the best I could. . . ."

Studs yawned. Seven minutes after three. He was going
straight home for supper, and then, maybe, he'd read his
newspaper and turn in early.

"But I always come to this conclusion. No matter how bad
off you are, there's always somebody in a worse boat. Now
take my brother. He's lived in poverty all his life, and would
you believe it, he still has a place with the can in the backyard.

I always tried to help him out, but charity begins at home. That's what I always figure, no matter how bad off you are, there's always somebody who's worse off. Now take him. About six years ago he was living at a place down on Bishop Street, and one night a rat bites the baby and it dies. Maybe I shouldn't be complaining. But goddamn it, when any night you come home to supper, and you might find a dead wife, it gets you."

Three-fourteen.

"That's why I always say to a young fellow, look before you leap. You never know what's gonna happen, and when you got a wife and love her and got to sit day after day and see her grow old and lose her looks, yes, sir, look twice before you leap."

Three-sixteen. Studs went to the can and smoked a cigarette. It knocked off twelve more minutes. He worked slowly. Mort's voice went on in an unpleasant drone, complaining that it wasn't enough for his wife to get sick, but that damn it if he didn't go and get lead-poisoning because he knew he had it.

III

"Well, I hope the old lady is feeling up to snuff," Mort said, as he, Studs, and Al walked to the street car line.

"Tonight all I'm doing is sleep. I was playing poker till three this morning and I'm all pooped out," Studs said.

"I know what I'm going to do tonight," smiled Al.

"You ought to. You're a newlywed."

"Wrong again, Mort. You guys noticed these crossword puzzles in the papers. They got a contest, and they give real dough to the winners, thousand bucks first prize. Well, I'm working them and trying to get me them prizes. They'll fix me up jake with a nice new Ford and something to spare," Al said.

"They're goofy," Studs said.

"Now wait a minute, Lonigan. There's money in them. And I won't be losing out. Suppose I don't get a sou out of it. Look at the self-improvement, the words and things you learn. Say, when I finish all the puzzles in this contest, I'll be knocking you guys for a row of tongue-twisters and the things I know. Take all I learned already. Now do you know the name of a battle fought in England in the year 1066. Well, there was one and it was called the Battle of Hastings. All kinds of things like that, knowledge, you learn. These puzzles are an education in themselves."

"Well, I leave you boys here," Mort said.

"Poor devil!" said Al, after Mort had gone his way.

"He got some tough breaks all right."

"Yeah, he gets my sympathy."

"He's white too," said Studs.

"Don't I know it? I worked with him for five years now. You ask your old man. He knows Mort. Mort's worked for him for years. But, Jesus, he's a tank. He's got a crying jag on all the time. But then, with all his trouble, you can't blame the guy. He's got to drink to forget . . . but here's my car. So long," said Al.

"Don't swallow that dictionary," Studs yelled.

IV

The street car was crowded with home-going workers, a swaying mob of begrimed Hunkies, foreigners, who jabbered in broken English and their own tongues, and smelled of garlic. Studs was relieved when he alighted at Fifty-ninth and State. On his way home, he paused at the corner of Fifty-eighth and Michigan, and decided that since he was a little early for supper, he might as well take a stroll over to the poolroom. He met Red Kelly at Fifty-eighth and Indiana.

"Tired, Studs?"

"I feel like a rag."

"We played on after you left 'til daylight. I cleaned up twenty bucks."

"I would have been better off going home."

"Say, I'll be damned, Studs, if you ain't getting an alderman," Red unexpectedly said, giving Studs a friendly poke in the belly.

"Only a little," Studs said apologetically.

"Better look out, Studs, or you'll be getting like Barney Keefe."

"I'll get it off before that happens," Studs confidently replied.

He felt his belly; just a little bit fat, not any more than Kelly himself had. He was just afraid of getting fat himself. Studs knew he'd be able to watch himself and exercise the fat off before it got serious.

A noisy, excited crowd was talking in front of the poolroom. Studs saw a squad car parked at the curb, and a cop standing importantly by the doorway. He started to move out of the crowd and see what was up, but noticed Joe Thomas, dressed in his bricklayer's clothes, step before the cop and ask what was the matter. The cop grabbed Joe, and called inside. People edged forwards, and the cop told them to get back, while Joe crabbed that he hadn't done anything. A tough-mugged dick appeared from inside the poolroom and talked with the cop. He grabbed Joe by the arm and dragged him inside, heedless of Joe's protests. Studs guessed it must be serious, and edged back in the crowd. He kept asking what had happened, and nobody knew, people saying it was a raid, a murder, a fight, a stabbing, a shooting, a chase after a robber. If it was serious and he tried to get in, he might be held for questioning, and he might, by accident, find himself giving one of his pals away. But none of them ever violated the law, except by drinking or going to can houses. He wondered.

With an air of mystery and authority, six lantern-jawed detectives emerged from the poolroom, putting their guns away in holsters beneath their coats. Talking, they clambered into the car, and shot off. The cop walked on. Studs rushed with others of the curious crowd into the poolroom. Everybody talked at once, and amidst all the gabbing, he finally pieced together the fact that nothing had happened. The dicks had just suddenly showed up with drawn guns, and lined everybody against the walls, and asked them useless questions. Then they had left. Most of the guys took it as a joke. George the Greek crabbed, because he said his business was getting a bad name. He declared, with many reiterations, that from now on, no more drinking, and rough-housing would go in his poolroom.

When the place quieted down, Studs shot a couple of rounds of poker dice with George. He won six bits' worth of chips, good in trade. He moved away from the counter, and stood in a group of punks who were raking Rolfe over the coals. He looked at Rolfe's outfit, a darkish gray topcoat, opened to reveal a blue herring-bone suit with blue-bordered handkerchief showing from the pocket, a blue English broadcloth shirt with collar attached, brown tie and black brogans.

"Phil, is that so that the only thing you read in the paper is Gallicoe's column on what the well-dressed man wears?" asked Swede Larsen.

"Phil, they tell me that with all the sheiking you do, you still don't know what it's for," Ellsworth Lyman said.

"Bug House Fable Number 999; Phillip Rolfe giving a penny to a starving blind man," said Young Rocky.

"I just see you boys shoveling out dimes like you were John D.," Phillip sharply retorted.

"Studs, it's nigger date night tonight. *It* has a date," Tommy Doyle shouted, passing along.

"It wouldn't do a lot of you guys any harm if you invested a dime in a second-hand joke book," Phillip said, walking off.

Skinny Joe Thomas asked Studs how about a game of pool. Studs said he thought maybe he could take Joe.

"Always ready to give you the chance. We'll play fifty

straight pool, and I'll spot you ten. And just to make it interesting, we'll play for half a buck, if you say so?"

Studs nodded, hating to take the handicap and admit that Joe was better than he was. But Joe had it on him with the cue, and if he refused the spot, he'd just look like a stuck-up sap. Joe reached with his cue, and set off ten beads on Studs' side of the marking wire stretched above the table. Lagging for break with the ivory, Studs lost, and had to break. He chalked his cue, and took careful aim, planning just to graze off the eight ball on the right of the last row of the racked triangle of balls. He hit the ivory too hard and with poor aim, cracking seven balls loose from the rack-up. Joe sank three shots, and missed an easy one, but left Studs sewn up.

"That was just luck," Joe said, his buck teeth showing in a good-natured, chinless smile.

Automatically chalking his cue, Studs studied the table, roving slowly around it to survey the balls from varying angles. He frowned in concentration. He heard Tommy Doyle remark that it was Studs' can. He bent over the table, and took careful aim, calling the three ball in the left-hand side pocket on a sharp cut. He was aware of a silence amongst the spectators. He shot, the three ball rolling straight into the pocket. He smiled, with a sense of relief. He made a run of ten, and as he sank his shots he saw himself as a careless, chance-taking pool shark. He missed a set-up before one of the lower end pockets. He set the balls back on the table in a line up from the spot, and pushed ten beads more on his side of the wire. He could not check a smile when he heard Doyle tell Joe that this time Studs looked like he might give him a run for his dough.

Three Star Hennessey sauntered in and oozed out a greeting to the gentlemen present. Doyle hopped on him about his spats and bell bottoms. Hennessey replied that they kept his feet warm, and everybody haw-hawed. Joe kidded with Hennessey as he made a difficult bank shot. He knocked six in and left Studs sewn up. Studs nettled his eyebrows and called a double bank.

"So, you're smoking Melachrinos now, Hennessey?" Joe remarked.

"The best is none too good for Mrs. Hennessey's son, John," Three Star said.

"Robbing the broads again," Studs remarked, trying to pull Joe's stunt of kidding while he made difficult shots; he fizzled the shot, and left the table open for Joe.

Joe ran off twenty and was ahead of Studs. Studs nettled his brows. He felt his confidence ebbing away. On his next inning, he slammed the eight ball into the side pocket. He had position on an easy shot, and hoped the guys would think he played for it, instead of getting it by accident.

Hennessey and Rolfe started ragging each other in their loud-mouthed punk manner. Studs, unconscious of everything but the balls before him, ran the table, feeling a sense of skill and power as he made ball after ball, planning shots ahead, putting english on the ball to get position, feeling a complete mastery. Joe set the balls back in a line up from spot.

"I only need to make two more to break my high-run record," Studs said to Tommy Doyle, as he chalked his cue.

"You're hot tonight, there, Hoppe," Stan Simonsky said.

"Looks like he's got my number," Joe said, undismayed.

Studs bent over, and pushed the cue through the crooked index finger of his left hand, aiming at the end ball that was frozen against the back rail. The ball seemed suddenly unclear to him. He was nervous. He felt like a mechanical man without control over the cue. He wanted to break that record.

"Well, anyway, louse, I don't snatch pocketbooks," Rolfe shrieked.

The punk's voice drummed in Studs' ear. He stood up, and rechalked his cue. He took a puff from the cigarette which he had placed on the wooden edge of the table, trying to steady himself. He bent over, and again took aim.

"Any goddamn time you catch me snipping purses. . . ."

The damn . . . Studs miscued. His shoulders dropped in a droop of relaxation, relieved from the strain, even though he was disappointed. Those two snotty drug-store cowboys had taken his mind off his game.

"Hey!" Studs yelled at them, sore.

"G'wan, rat, frisk some more nickels off working girls," Rolfe yelled.

"Say, Rolfe, you goddamn Jew, if you don't close that trap of yours, I will," Studs barked, throwing everyone into a waiting silence.

"Jesus, Studs! I'm sorry if I disturbed you," Phillip apologized, blushing; Hennessey quietly smirked at him.

"One more bat out of you while I'm shooting, and it'll be curtains for you, punk!"

Studs couldn't regain his form. Joe walked away with the game, and won a second game with ease. Studs handed him a buck, and paid for the time with some of his chips. Joe said it was tough, going so good, and then suddenly losing your form. Next time, he might have better luck. Studs smiled weakly, but a sudden hatred of Joe stirred in him. Joe was almost chinless, not good-looking, a nice guy, but he had nothing on his side except his ability with the cue. No reason for jealousy and hatred. But Studs hated him for winning, hated to lose or be second fiddle at anything. He was even glad when Joe remarked that his rheumatism was bothering him again.

He started out and met Arnold Sheehan limping in the doorway. He asked how tricks were. Arnold said he had a job with a construction gang for the city, and was on the wagon. He was going to start working as soon as his knee, twisted in the football game last Sunday, was better. Studs said swell.

He walked along amidst the six-o'clock confusion of Fifty-eighth Street, with people pouring out of the elevated station, elevated trains rumbling almost continuously, kids barking as they sold the *Saturday Evening Post*, Sammy Schmaltz yelling his latest papers, people hurrying in front of and by him. It made him nervous. And he thought how he had just been going so good, ran the table for the third time in his life at straight pool, had been on the verge of breaking his record run. He remembered the feeling of power he had had, running the table, his eye, brains, arm, all of himself concentrated on the balls, all clicking together like a coordinated machine, and the thrill that went with each shot as the balls were smashed, cut, banked, eased into the pockets. A feeling that, in its way, was like the one he'd had making that first clean tackle of Jewboy Schwartz in the football game.

He saw the dumpy figure of Helen Shires ahead of him, and caught up with her. She looked mannish, with a shingle bob, a simple felt hat, almost like a man's, plain blue suit with shirt waist and blue tie. Not good-looking any more. She'd been almost like a pal with him when they'd been kids. Some of the old feeling for her came back. But she hadn't turned into much. Wouldn't be a bargain in bed now either.

"I'm glad to see you again, Studs; haven't seen you in ages," she said.

"How are you, Helen?"

"Fine. Working in an office, stenographer. I hear you're still working for your dad," she said, and he nodded, lighting a cigarette.

"I saw Loretta the other day and she has certainly grown into a sweet young girl."

Not much for them to say to each other. It made him sorry they had changed and drifted apart, because he could remember how she had been such a pal, just like a guy you liked a lot.

"Seen any of the old bunch?" she asked, after the silence between them had grown uncomfortable.

"Bill comes around once in a while and we go to a show together. He has a pretty good job, repairing adding-machines."

"And how's Fran?"

"All right."

He wanted to talk about old times, and have them just naturally talk about themselves, and maybe Lucy.

"I saw Jim Clayburn. He's studying law," he said.

He told her about last Sunday's football game and the fight.

"You're just the same as ever, aren't you? Haven't changed, even to the fighting," she said in a complimentary way; he was pleased, and looked at her out of the corner of his eye. Might date her up at that and make her; she probably could be made, and every jane a guy made was another notch in his belt. But he liked her and wished they could be as they used to be.

"What's your sister doing?"

"She's in high school. She's a flapper now," Helen said.

"You haven't changed either, Helen," he said, but it was a lie. She wasn't the old Helen. And she looked sort of whipped, too. Maybe it was because she wasn't good-looking or something.

They stood awkwardly at the corner of Fifty-eighth and Indiana. Finally they said they'd have to be trotting along. Studs said they'd have to get together some time, and she replied vaguely. He watched her walk mannishly along, her dumpy figure swaying a trifle. He wished. . . . He went in the drug store and bought copies of *Snappy Stories* and the *Whizz Bang* to read after supper, since he wasn't going out.

He felt moody over having seen Helen, noticed the way she seemed whipped, and wasn't the old Helen. And then losing that game too. He yawned, tired. He remembered what good times he and Helen and the old bunch used to have roasting marshmallows and baking potatoes in a bonfire nights over by the foundation when the Prairie Theater was just being built.

XI

A hollow roar, like heavy thunder splitting the sky in a storm, boomed over the neighborhood. People near Fifty-ninth and South Park Avenue heard falling glass, and in some cases, their buildings, and the very bedrooms in which they slept, quaked. Inside of five minutes, a crowd was collected in front of a low, two-story, red stone house between Fifty-ninth and Sixtieth on South Park Avenue. Two policemen stood before the crumbled steps, and the long wide porch before the building was splintered and half-wrecked.

The crowd was steadily enlarged by people of all ages who displayed the signs of hasty arousal from sleep; men with trousers and coats pulled on over pajamas, kids with tousled hair and sleep still in their eyes, surprised and half-dressed women. There was much talk and speculation, and amongst them there was a general consensus that the bomb had been placed there through the machinations of real-estate people who desired that Abraham Clarkson, the leading colored banker of Chicago, should sell his property and cease living in a white man's neighborhood. Most of the excited and gaping people present also eyed the wreckage wth approval, wishing that it would have a proper and fearful effect. But they knew that the bomb would teach no lessons and inspire no fear. For Abraham Clarkson had been bombed before, and he had stated defiantly that he would move from his home to another one only in a casket. It was nerve for the nigger to say that and go on ruining a white man's neighborhood, living amongst people who didn't want him. Secretly, many of those present wished that he had been killed. Some of the Catholics wished only that it had wounded him, un-mortally, for didn't he always give Father Gilhooley a hundred dollars in the annual Easter and Christmas collections. The crowd increased. After about three quarters of an hour of gaping, it slowly dispersed. Red Kelly walked off arguing with Tommy Doyle, Red insisting that it was the fifth time that the jigg had been bombed, Tommy contending that it was only the fourth time.

CHAPTER ELEVEN

I

"Papee! Box score!"

Studs Lonigan laughed at Sammy Schmaltz like a drunken apparition.

"Which one?"

"There ain't no box scores on Christmas Eve," Studs said, continuing to laugh.

"Papee! Latest papee!"

"Merry Fourth of July!" Studs bellowed, with an uncontrolled wave of his hand; he staggered over to plaster himself against the bellied front of the Fifty-eighth Street elevated station. He saw Phillip Rolfe and bellowed a command for him to come over.

"Say, are you a fag?" Studs sneered.

"You're drunk, kid," Phillip replied, taking Studs' arm. "The boys said you've been home laid up with the flu for several weeks. Do you feel all right now?"

"I'll bet you are a pansy," Studs said, brushing Phillip's arm aside, and eyeing him with curiosity, as Rolfe inched backwards.

"Why do you punks wear those goddamn monkey suits? You can't keep them pressed when you get on your knees," Studs said, studying Phil's bell bottoms.

"They're the rage, kid," Phillip said, walking away.

Studs fell back against the building. He coughed. He saw people passing as in a dream, and imagined himself just walking up to them one by one, and laying them cold.

"Hey, Jew, commere!" he commanded.

Smirking, Jawbones Levinsky halted a respectable distance from Studs.

"So you're the goddamn Jew who's prejudiced against the N. D. football team."

"Yeah," said Levinsky, quickly dodging a right haymaker.

Studs chased him half way across the sidewalk. Strangers watched with amusement. Levinsky stopped on the other side of the alley, which ran parallel to the station, and laughed. Studs floundered like a listing ship, and again plastered himself against the station bricks. Mr. and Mrs. Dennis P. Gorman, passing, saw Studs and clucked.

"Everybody's a bastard!" Studs mumbled to himself.

"William!"

"Thought Studs Lonigan die influenza. Plenty left in Studs Lonigan, get that, you bastards! Whoops!"

"William!"

The sharp, aggravated feminine pronunciation of his name slowly wormed itself into his drunken consciousness. He looked in the direction of the voice. He saw Fran leaning from the front of a closed car that was parked at the curb. He lip-farted.

"William! . . . Come here!"

He threw his shoulders back, and almost toppled sidewise in his effort to walk straight. He stood before her, swaying, his leering face smudged, his clothes spotted with dust.

"The idea! You're a perfect sight; you ought to be ashamed of yourself, disgracing the whole family by your drunken boorishness. And you just out of a sick bed!"

"Whatjahsay?"

"It's shocking, disgraceful!"

A slick-looking tuxedoed young man, with a talcum-powdered shaven face, leaned sidewise from the wheel.

"Fran, we'll have time to drive him around for a spin in the park and let him get some air."

"Huh!" Studs nastily exclaimed.

"Then, a cup of black coffee might help sober him up."

"Who in the name of all holy hell wants to get sobered up. . . . Sobered up, huh there, Droopy Drawers? Christ is born, and I'm celebrating," he whooped.

"William Lonigan, you'll stop that uncouth, blasphemous talk this minute and get in here!"

"Whoops!"

"Fran, he's drunk. Let me handle him!"

"What's that, Charley?"

"William, don't be so disgusting! You're not funny."

"Sure thing, Charley!" he said with an insulting laugh; he almost fell on his face.

"William. . . ."

"I'm just about ready to haul off on a skunk that I see!"

"William!"

"You're the bastard I'm talking to!" he said, stepping forwards.

Fran slammed the car door, and it shot off. Studs stumbled after it, cursing. He fell in the street. A traffic jam was caused, while he struggled to his feet, and staggered back onto the sidewalk. Slug Mason grabbed his arm, and said, with his familiar mispronunciations:

"Studs, you crazy bastard! Here we all hears that you was in bed with the flu, and what does I do but find you trying to take a nose dive in the gutter."

"Like tuxedoes?" asked Studs.

"What's that?"

"Sure," Studs said, trying to light a cigarette.

Slug lit it for him.

"Say, who took your stick of candy away?" Studs asked Les Coady, as Les lay crying against the poolroom window with tears running down his bucolic face.

"Studs, I'm no good!" Les said heavily.

"You need another drink," Slug said, pronouncing it "anoder."

"I'm only a common ordinary wagon man for the Continental Express Company; I never got a chance. I'll never amount to nothing. I'm rotting away like I was dead, a common ordinary wagon man."

"You better come with me tonight, and get yourself a fast and furious jazz," Slug said.

"Slug, go down to the drug store, and buy him a lolly pop!" Studs said.

Les ran a gloved hand across his teary face, streaking it.

"And I almost went and studied to be a priest. I'm no good," he whined.

Inside the poolroom, a crowd was gathered around the telephone booth, where Red Kelly was cursing his girl. The gang laughed boisterously. Slug took Studs and Les to the can, where they secretively had a drink. When they came out, TB McCarthy tried to scrouge a nip and two bits from them. He was so insistent that Studs handed him a quarter, but said that if he ever asked again, a certain louse named McCarthy would get his consumptive face pounded full of holes.

"Yeah, up your back, Charley," Red yelled, slamming the receiver.

He came out, and led Vinc Curley to the rear of the poolroom, telling him, as a friend, to stand there a minute. He returned to the first pool table, where Funnyface Duffy and Swede Elston were shooting a game of pool. He grabbed the balls from the table, wound up like a baseball pitcher, and hurled them at Vinc's bean. They missed Vinc, and crashed into the wall. Red was grabbed. Vinc stood dumbfounded. Studs ran down, and pulled the dumbsock aside. Vinc, blushing, misunderstanding, asked Kelly why he would do such a thing to a good friend of his; and they roared. George the Greek nearly went into a fit of apoplexy, sobbing about his business. Vinc, still perplexed, drew Studs aside, and asked him why Kelly would do a thing like that. Studs told Vinc to soak his head. He drifted off, and saw Mush Joss stemming a buck from Les; he asked Mush if he and Muggsy were making the rounds again. Slug insisted that they go to Burnham. They all went to the can and killed the gin they had. Slug again suggested that they go to Burnham. It was a good idea.

As they crowded towards the door, Vinc clutched Studs' arm, and asked him if he wanted to go to confession.

"Got your car?"

Vinc nodded. Studs said sure they were all going to church. He told the guys and they shoved Vinc out to his car. Some of the guys crowded into Vinc's car, and the others got into Nate Klein's taxicab.

"All right, Vinc, you bastard, drive."

"But I got to go to confession. Are you guys going?"

"Sure, but listen, Vinc, we're goin' to have a nice little harmless party, and we're going to confession out in South Chicago."

"But that takes gasoline."

"Vinc, you crazy idiot, drive and shut up!" Studs said.

Nate honked for them to get going.

"But listen," Vinc said hesitantly.

"Get going, Curley, or we'll throw you out of the car," Tommy threatened.

Vinc was cowed, and he started up, following Nate's cab over to South Park Avenue, and then south.

"Hey, Vinc, look out or you'll get run in for blocking traffic," Mush Joss said as the car crept along.

"I'm driving all right. They can't arrest me," Vinc replied about a minute later.

"They don't allow parking on this street, Curley," Studs said.

"Say, Curley, for Christ sake, move!" Benny Taite yelled.

"Benny, I wish you wouldn't talk like that in this car on Christmas Eve. It might make bad luck and cause an accident," Vinc said.

"His old lady certainly must have dropped him hard when he was a baby," Red said.

"Come on, Vinc, for Christ sake, we don't want to get run in for mopery," Tommy Doyle said.

Two minutes later, he said: "Tommy, what did you mean by that last thing you said?"

"Whoops, we passed another block," Studs shouted.

"For Christ sake, chloroform that idiot," Doyle said.

"Step on it, Vinc," Studs said.

"Why, Studs, I never drive over fifteen miles an hour."

"Hey, Vinc, let me drive!"

"Why, Red, I couldn't. Didn't you know I wouldn't even let my grandmother drive this car?"

"Cheer, boys, we passed another block!" said Mush Joss.

"Hey, Vinc, I'll give you a stick of candy if you'll go twenty miles an hour," Studs said.

"I don't like sticks of candy, Studs," Vinc laconically replied.

"Let's take the car away from him, and throw him out on his ear," Red said.

"We hadn't better. The goddamn fool will yell so much we'd all get pinched," said Taite.

Studs whispered that it would be good just watching Vinc with the whores out at the Cannonball Inn.

Vinc shot the car up to twenty, and after two blocks of silence, asked if he was now going fast enough to satisfy them, because it was the fastest the car had ever been driven.

"Vinc, you're Dario Resta," said Studs.

"Say, Curley, does your mother love you?" asked Mush.

"Why, Mush, I thought you was my friend, and I never thought you'd talk about my mother."

"Christ, I never saw an idiot like it," Doyle said.

"What was that you said, Tommy?" asked Vinc.

"I was talking about the bald-headed sailor."

"I don't think I know him. Does he come around Fifty-eighth Street?"

"Hey, Vinc, please don't drive so fast. You'll make me sea-sick," Studs said after they had guffawed.

"Is that so? I was afraid, Studs, that I was going a little too fast," Vinc replied, slowing the car back to about fifteen an hour.

"Yes, Vinc, you better be careful so we don't have an accident," said Tommy.

"That's all right, Tommy. Don't worry. I had this car a year now and I never had an accident."

"Say, you horse's ass, drive!" Studs said.

"Why, Studs!"

"Whoops, another block," said Taite.

II

"We're here," Studs whooped, as the car drove into a dreary parking yard.

To the left, there was a low, rambling structure, lit by a small electric sign: CANNONBALL INN.

"But, fellows, what place is this?" Curley asked, still sitting at the wheel after all the others had gotten out.

"Church," Doyle snickered.

Studs and Slug pulled Vinc by the shoulders. He yelled. Slug told him to shut up and get out of the car, if he didn't want a foot jammed through his teeth. Vinc got out, and followed them, as they lurched towards the narrow doorway of the inn.

"Studs! Studs! Just a minute," Curley yelled.

"Shut up!" Studs replied, looking back at him.

"Jesus, Studs, see what he wants," Doyle said, when Vinc continued yelling that he wanted to ask Studs something.

Studs waited. Vinc put his hand to Studs' ear, and whispered:

"Studs, there ain't anything wrong in going here, is there?"

"No! Come on in, Vinc," Studs said, in fake friendliness.

"Well, Studs, if you say there's nothing wrong or sinful about going in, all right."

They entered a narrow saloon. Four tough-looking eggs leaned against a long bar.

"Merry Christmas, Spike!" Slug said to the beefy-faced burly bartender.

"Same to you, Mason. I see you brought the boys along to have a good time," he replied.

The gang lined up for a drink. Vinc asked for pop. The

bartender's thick lips popped open with surprise. Slug gave him the wink, and he nodded.

"Well, here's how, boys!" Slug said, lifting his small gin glass.

"And may it never get weaker," Studs added, downing the stuff.

"And here's to you, Vinc, you fuzzy wuzzy," Red said.

Vinc drank. He coughed, sputtered, lowered a face of boiling redness, hiccoughed. The bartender gave them the wink as they laughed.

"Say, are you sure that was pop?" he asked, when he was again able to talk.

"Sure thing, Charley."

"This guy's a friend of ours, Vinc. He wouldn't fool you," Benny Taite said.

"Well, it's awfully strong pop. Maybe I better have root beer."

"Don't handle it."

Vinc asked for a glass of water. They paid up. Vinc laid a dime on the bar. The bartender sneered, and said it was a half a buck. Vinc drawled that was awfully expensive for pop. He asked Studs if it was right. Studs nodded. Curley paid reluctantly.

Slug led them to a door in the rear of the saloon, and rapped three times. A slide opened, and an eye peered out. The slit closed, and the door was opened. A greasy, pimply-faced fellow with hollow cheeks wished them a Merry Christmas out of the side of his mouth, and told them to have a good time. They heard music as they crossed a dim hallway, and entered another door which led them into a gaudy cabaret with colored lights. A miscellaneous assortment of males were scattered around the tables or belly-dancing with girls in teddies and chemises. They saw the guys who had come with Nate and there was confusion and kidding while two ham-faced waiters placed two tables together. Girls quickly clustered around.

"Say, let's see the snake room first," Slug suggested.

They ordered drinks, and Slug talked to one of the bouncers. He told the girls to wait, and they all said yes, dearie.

They followed a bouncer with cauliflower ears along an aisle of tables, out a doorway, and down a narrow, dim hallway. They heard a mingled echo of moans, curses, indistinct sounds.

"It's as soundproof as we can get it," the bouncer said.

He opened a door. They were struck by an alcoholic stench,

and drunken exclamations. The lights were shot on and they saw a bare room where drunks were crowded all over the floor.

The gang laughed at one drunk who snored in a corner, his belly rising and falling, his mouth wide open. Other drunks rolled on the floor, raved, and one sat playing with his toes, his shoes beside him.

"Like a booby hatch," Slug said, with a smile.

"Say, are they sick?" drawled Vinc.

"Don't mind that chump," Slug said, when the bouncer looked curiously at him.

A thin guy crawled towards them on his hands and knees, bumping others, falling over one bloated fat fellow. He told them he had to crawl because he was having a terrible time with his feet; every time he tried to walk, his left foot got ahead of his right one. He braced himself along the wall, and with effort. He walked in zigzags, and then turned, and told them to judge for themselves if his right foot didn't always keep getting ahead of his left one.

"Siddown!" the bouncer said.

The guy crawled away. A fellow who had been sleeping suddenly lifted himself from the hips, and heaved; he fell back in his own vomit. Two guys in a corner tried to drown out the room by singing *She's My Lulu*.

"Jesus, let's go. That odor will kill me," said Studs.

A blond boy of about eighteen let out an insane shriek, and dashed towards them, stepping on the face of an unconscious drunk. He fell on his knees before them, and loudly begged that he be saved from the snakes. It was funny. He arose, clapped his hands to his ears, and yelled. He fell before the bouncer, and repeated his entreaties to be saved from the snakes; pointing dramatically in back of them. He crawled to the wall, still shrieking. The bouncer jerked out a blackjack and neatly put him to sleep. His face was pale and sickly in the artificial illumination.

A husky fellow rolled over to them, and yelled he'd been rolled.

"Fade!" the bouncer commanded.

"Give me my money back, you sonofabitches, or I'll. . . ."

The bouncer cracked him in the jaw; he fell on top of a sleeping Polack.

"Mother! Mama! Your little boy needs you. He's sick. Mama in heaven, Mama," a fat fellow moaned on his knees in a corner.

"Jesus, they're blind," Slug said with a laugh.

"We got to do something with them," the bouncer said, turning off the light, and shutting the door. Two bouncers, with padded shoulders, passed, carting a drunk along the hall-way.

"Boys will be boys!" Red said.

"Makes you want to puke," Studs said.

"Say, Studs, why do they do that?" Curley asked, innocently.

"Shut up!"

"Say, Red. . . ."

"Curley, you talk too goddamn much," Red interrupted.

The bouncer explained, in answer to Red's question, that they dumped them out in the morning.

"Say, most of the guys who work here look like they bought their faces at a second-hand auction," Studs said.

They returned to their tables. The girls were there. Slug whispered to a big, angular-faced, high-cheeked, blond Polack in pink teddies.

"Gimme the dough now," she said, pronouncing her words as Slug did.

He whispered to Studs, Doyle, and Red. They handed him some change. He slipped two bills to the Polack broad.

"Hello, Vincent," she cooed, draping herself on his lap.

"Say, how did you know my name?" he asked, as drinks were set down on the table.

"Vincent, a little love-bird whispered it in my ear."

Vinc turned from the girl and called to Shrimp. Haggerty was busy telling the girl on his lap that he got tired of his wife, and needed a change. Vinc yelled to him. He turned.

"Do you want to go to the Michigan with me tomorrow afternoon, and see the picture?"

They roared. Studs told his girl that the goof had water on the brain; born that way, and no hope.

The jazz blared. Arnold, Studs, and Shrimp belly-danced with their girls. The Polack led Vinc onto the dance floor. He protested that he couldn't dance. She said she'd teach him. She rubbed against him. His face looked as if it were on the verge of being consumed by flames.

When he came back, he was kidded. He couldn't understand them. He suddenly called Mush Joss to say the other day Mush had said he had lived in the neighborhood a long time. Vinc said well he would bet ten cents he had lived in the neighborhood longer than Mush.

"You wouldn't bull me," said Mush.

"Come on, big boy, kiss me!" the Polack said.

"And kiss your maidenhead good-bye, you, you goddamn fathead," Studs said.

"But, Studs. . . ."

"Daddy, don't you like to love?" the girl asked him.

"Don't do that," Vinc protested feebly, as she placed his hand on one of her wobbly breasts.

"Dearie, you don't know what loving I'll give you," she said.

"Take your hand away. Why, I wouldn't even let my mother touch me there," Vinc said, convulsing them.

She made a little moan. He threw her off him; she landed on her can. Two bouncers grabbed Curley and they carted him to the door by the seat of the pants and the collar. He got a clout in the jaw, and landed outside.

"For Christ sake, what the hell kind of a fluke is he? Does he want me to beg him," the Polack said.

"That's all right, girlie, come on over here," Slug said.

"I never had one as goofy as that. All kinds of crazy people come to me, and want all kinds of things done to them, but I never had any guy as goofy as that."

"You know, I got four sisters, and they're all the most decent girls in the world. You know, my four sisters are as pure as a lily," Arnold Sheehan bragged drunkenly, and the girl on his lap curled her lips.

"Sing 'em, Sheehan!" Slug said.

"They're as pure as a lily. I shouldn't even walk on the same side of the street with them, after I come here. And anybody that says my four sisters ain't pure as a lily has gotta fight me," Arnold said, pounding the table.

"My two sisters are as pure as yours," Studs said.

"Say, are all these guys queer?" the Polack asked Slug.

"Polluted. The boys is out for a good time," Slug laughed.

"Well, why don't they shut up talking and prove themselves upstairs. A man only proves himself in a bed. No girls are pure and those that pretend they are are just yellow. They all want it, and they get it too, and they pretend like hypocrites," the girl on Arnold's lap said.

"Sally!" the girl with Shrimp remonstrated.

"I don't care. I'm sick of these guys coming here and telling me I'm a whore and not as good as their goddamn wives, and sisters, and sweethearts."

"Sally had a fight because she wasn't getting enough towels. She's cranky tonight," the girl on Shrimp's lap said.

"Hey, cut it. The show is starting," Slug said.

XII

Los Angeles, Cal.
Dece. 25, 1922

Dear Dan:

I thought I drope you a few lines to let you know how we all are, and what a very fine Xmas we had an I hope yours was just as marry as my. Well Danny you know we are all settle out here now and it seem different from are last when my father was living. But you know when he lose his job because he was a union man and they give the double + it break his heart and he was a man of sixty year and you know how that just kill him of broken heart. And we miss him but we had a marry Xmas like we know he would want us to and we had sun shines only we all miss my dad lots and it was very hot it was 81 not so bad is it for Dece. I gest its kinda cold in old Chi today but I gest you enjoy it anyways. It looks grate to see all the flower in bloob in Dece and the trees and grass as green as ever. We had lots of rain a cupple of weeks ago and it sure did come down hard when it rain here it is in Nove or Dece. And Dan, but after that seson is over we don't see any rain all summer until the nex rainny seson. Well Dan in one of your letters you send me you told some me one said in about two mor month you won't get letter frome me but don't let that wurry you because you will always me hear frome the only one that won't get a letter from me is the one that don't answer letter I send them. You my bes pal Danny O'Neill you are and a cupple other are the only one that have send me at all. I have sent a gril a number of letters to and I have got only one answer to them and I dont know what is the matter with him I mean Hoppy Shanks. I thought he was one of my best Pal. but Dan I gest you are the only true Pal I got and I'm sure glad its you. I've been writing a gril in Chi. I gest you know her. Her name is Catherine Heving and she sure is a fine gril and I got quiet a number of letters frome her. Well Dan I gest your getting ready for bed while I'm writing this little letter but I gest I can't think of any mor so good night. You Pal.

Andy Le Gare

Happy New Year
P.S. Dan and please tell Stutz Lonigan that Andy Le Gare

294

wish him a Marry Xmas and a Happy New Year Tell hime
I wanted a send him a card but Dan I couldn't send him one
wishing him a Marry Xmas and a Happy New Year when I
never know his address because Dan I am always ready to
say Stutz Lonigan is the bes whitest guy of the older guy who
hang around that pool roome den of iniquieties and the only
one of them guy who treat me decent when I was a kid and
I like hime and want him to know that I wish hime a Marry
Xmas and a Happy New Year and so Dan you please dont
forget to tell hime that.

CHAPTER TWELVE

I

"Now, Mary, compose yourself! No news is often good news,"
Lonigan said feebly to his wife who sat with her bowed head
lowered in tears.

"He's not worth crying over, getting drunk and acting
like a pig!"

"Frances, after all, Bill is your brother, and this is Christmas
day," Lonigan said in a conciliatory manner.

He stared out the window at the snow flurrying lightly through
the sunless Christmas day. There was a catch in his throat;
the whole family had received communion at five o'clock mass,
except Bill.

"A curse must have been put on him," the mother exclaimed
between wails.

"Mother!" Lonigan muttered, unable to say any more.
He arose and patted her head. She sobbed that he was her
boy and she had suffered a mother's agony bringing him into
this world.

"Oh!"

"Don't worry, nothing has happened to him except that he's
probably drunk as a pig!" Fran said; she strode nervously back
and forth across the parlor.

Mrs. Lonigan drew some rosary beads out of her apron
pocket, kissed the crucifix attached to them, blessed herself
with it and commenced whispering her rosary.

"Well, maybe I had better notify the police, at that," Lonigan
said, continuing to remain slumped in his rocker.

"Dad, he has his name and address in his wallet. I'm sure
that if anything serious happened to him, we'd have heard
about it," Loretta said.

Lonigan looked gratefully at his youngest daughter.

"I warned you all along to make him go to Loyola and get in with the right kind of fellows instead of with drunken poolroom bums," Fran said; her father winced.

"God, what can we do? If people we know saw him, I'll never again be able to set foot in St. Patrick's church with my head up," the mother mourned.

"And what will I do? Shamed and disgraced before Michael so that I couldn't look him in the face last night. My whole evening was ruined. I was so disgraced that I could have wept," Fran complained.

"Fran, please!" Loretta exclaimed.

They were thrown into silence as the key clicked in the front door.

"Now, folks, let me handle this!" the father said, showing a sudden sense of confidence and control.

The mother rushed to the hall as Studs was heard walking to the bathroom. She flung herself on him, and sobbed:

"My son! My son! My precious first-born baby son!"

"Mother!" Fran indignantly called from the parlor.

He heeded their summons and walked into the parlor, limping, with his clothes filthy, his face bloated, his eyes bloodshot.

"Well!" he exclaimed, with a slight shrug of the shoulder.

"Bill, isn't this a fine how-do-you-do on Christmas morning?" the father said accusingly.

"Yes, William, Merry Christmas!" Fran said sarcastically.

"Jesus, Mary and Joseph, what did Satan do to my son!" the mother cried, throwing her arms dramatically over her head, looking vaguely at the ceiling with haggard, red eyes.

"Please, Mother!" Loretta pleaded, showing presence of mind.

Lonigan looked from son to mother, pain in his face. Fran's lip turned with contempt. Martin quietly entered the parlor; he was ordered out, and stood listening in the hallway.

"Mary, most holy Mother of God, what did I do to earn this misfortune?" the mother yelled.

Loretta looked hopelessly from one to the other, striving to calm them with her glances; she smiled weakly but with sympathy at Studs.

"Never as long as I live will I feel towards him again as a sister, or recognize that he is my brother!" Fran said with appropriate melodrama.

"After all I've done for my children, and suffered!" the mother exclaimed.

Fran went to her bedroom, and returned with Studs' Christmas present of six pair of silk stockings.

"Till my dying day I'll hate you . . . you . . . you brute!" she said, returning the present.

Studs accepted them without a word. He was tired and pooped. His head ached. He could taste vomit all the way up from his guts. He could hardly keep his eyes open.

They looked at Fran, shocked, hurt. In a wearied voice, the father asked her please not to do a thing like that. She retorted that her ears still burned from the vile, unmentionable things he had called her and Michael last night. The mother pulled a faint. Fran blamed Studs for it. Loretta ran for water. Studs stood helpless in the center of the parlor. The father excitedly told everyone not to get excited. He patted the mother's pale cheeks.

"Close your trap!" Studs finally barked, tired of Fran's accusation that he was murdering his mother.

"Jesus, Mary and Joseph!" the mother cried, coming to and sitting up, her words drowning Fran's querulous voice.

"Are you all right, Mother?" Loretta solicitously asked.

"Don't worry about me. I'm only a mother!"

The father asserted that he would take charge of things, and asked Bill to wash up and have a talk with him. He drank a cup of coffee, and sat in the dining-room trying to read his crumpled copy of the morning newspaper, while Studs washed up and changed his clothes. He drifted into thinking of what he would tell Studs, and was quickly precipitated into nostalgic memories of how he had gone on benders in his own day; and how, once, right after he had popped the question and Mary had said yes, he had gotten blind as a bat and almost kicked over the apple cart trying to start a scrap with a whole room full of her relatives. He had made his mistakes, plenty of them. Ah, some of those Saturday nights. But that was no excuse for Bill. He had had no chance in life. His father had been poor and a heavy drinker, and he and his mother, Lord have mercy on their souls, had always quarreled and bickered. Bill had a good home, a good example set for him, a place made for him in life, all that a young man could ask for. His own mistakes should serve as a beacon light to guide the boy, Bill, along the right way. That solid old maxim: Do not as I do, but do as I say, it was sound sense. And he hadn't drunk stuff like young fellows drank nowadays. It was rat poison, that killed people like flies. If the young fellows kept up drinking stuff like that, they'd all be dead by the time they were twenty-five or thirty. And then too, except for a few times, he'd always known how to keep his liquor under his belt. Ah, yes, he must point out to Bill the vanities and pitfalls that beset a young man, make it serve as a lesson to him. He had to guide Bill so he wouldn't make the same sorry mistakes that all the young fellows in this jazz and Prohibition age were making.

Studs entered, smiling sheepishly; he was cleaned up and had on a fresh suit and shirt. Lonigan's planned talk faded from his mind, and he was only aware that there was a deep common bond between him and his son; after all, he and Bill were the men of the family, and when he dropped the reins of responsibility, Bill would have to take them up. And Bill was the one who took after him the most. A real Lonigan. The others took more after their mother.

Melancholy misted his thoughts. Ah, he was growing old and life was moving along, he thought; he glanced towards Bill. Father and son faced each other with averted eyes.

"Bill, it was too bad, too bad this unfortunate thing had to happen," Lonigan mourned, shaking his head in sadness, and then emitting a drawn-out and soft sigh of regret.

He stuttered and hesitated as he tried to say that he didn't mind a young fellow drinking a little and having a good time, but that there was a limit, and he hoped that it wouldn't happen again. He told Bill what great confidence he was placing in him. He hoped Bill would not destroy that confidence completely; last night he had shaken it severely, yes, severely.

He stopped talking. Father and son sat in silent misery. If only they could get a grip on the right words. They couldn't, and were keenly aware of their smokes.

"Yes, Bill, it's a great disappointment and it's nearly broken your mother's heart," Lonigan said, arising.

He asked Studs to be more careful in the future and said that they would forgive this mistake, but that it shouldn't happen again.

II

In Nomine Patris, et Filii, et Spiritui Sancti. Amen.

A street car grated by. The swinging doors of the church were shoved to admit influxes of worshippers. The new arrivals clustered about the two tables near the holy water founts at the end of the center aisles, paying their ten cents pew rent, causing coins to be weakly clinked together. The ushers led a few lucky persons to the last vacant seats towards the rear of the aisles, while many others joined those who stood in the back and down the side aisles. Those parishioners who had rented pews by the season or annually marched proudly to their reserved places towards the front. Feet were scraped on the rubber floor covering. A man coughed.

Father Doneggan, clad in gold vestments of joyousness, bowed profoundly before the gilded golden altar with joined hands, and sing-songed:

Confiteor Deo omnipotenti, beatae Mariae semper virgini. . . .

Studs Lonigan knelt crushed in a pew towards the rear on the Blessed Virgin's side of the church. He was aware of the perfume scent and presence of a girl beside him, and her squirrel coat was brushed tantalizingly against his knee. He bowed his head to pray, and thought that the Mass was sacred, the unbloody sacrifice of the body and blood of Jesus Christ, Our Lord, the symbolic repetition of His Holy and inspiring life, and he would have to hear Mass in the right and proper spirit. He shook his head to ward off the threat of sleep. He mumbled the words of the Our Father by rote, and looked forwards as Father Doneggan bowed down over the altar, and prayed rapidly:

Oramus te, Domine, per merita sanctorum tuorum quorum

Unwittingly, he wished that the mass was over. He had let himself in for it, coming to high mass. Anyway, Father Doneggan always hurried through his masses, and it wouldn't be as long as if Father Gilhooley or Father Roney were celebrating it.

He heard the swinging doors, and the scrape of feet, and then, another street car. He glanced around to his right, and saw Young Rocky yawning. He watched Mr. and Mrs. Dennis P. Gorman proceed down the center aisle to their rented pews, past Austin McAuliffe, the usher who stood in the aisle and smiled as they approached. Over to his right and a couple of pews down, he saw Arnold Sheehan's twin sisters, and he thought of how Arnold had bragged of them last night. They weren't as good-looking, or as well-dressed as his sisters. He smiled, seeing the Nolan family marching down the center aisle to their pews; they were built like steps, first the old man, then the mother, then the three boys in the order of their sizes. He smiled again, remembering that joke he always sprung on Jim Nolan; "Every time your old man saves a couple of hundred bucks, he brings another Nolan over from the old country, and gets him a job on the railroad."

He heard the choir singing:

Kyrie eleison!
Kyrie eleison!
Kyrie eleison!

He had to keep his mind on the mass particularly because he had acted like such a bastard last night on Christmas Eve. He prayed. He watched Jim Clayburn go by him, tall, erect, dignified in a conservative black suit. Jim turned and pointed to a pew seat a couple of yards in front of Studs, and Studs stared at Jim's thin, white face, set above a high stiff collar. A man genuflected and took the pew seat pointed out to him. Jim strode back, smiling a weak recognition at Studs.

Studs looked at the lighted altar. Standing in the middle of it, extending his hands, then joining them, Father Doneggan intoned:

Gloria in excelsis Deo, et in terra pax hominibus . . .

Studs knew that he was singing the praise of Almighty God, but couldn't remember just what this part of the mass was called and what it symbolized. Hell of a Catholic he was. He mumbled Hail Marys. Again he listened:

Quoniam tu solus sanctus. Tu solus Dominus . . .

After his prayer, the priest bowed down to kiss the altar, and again turned to face the people and chant:

Dominus vobiscum . . .

The choir replied:

Et cum spiritu tuo.

Studs closed his eyes, opened them. Covertly, he rubbed spittle on them in order to remain awake. He shuddered with a sudden shock, as if of electricity, when the squirrel coat of the voluptuous blond next to him rubbed against his leg, just above his knee. He started saying another Hail Mary, but his thoughts were distracted before he concluded, and he wondered what had happened last night. There had been that raid. Jesus Christ, he'd been afraid. He had been so goddamn shaky that he'd jumped from the second-story window, spraining his ankle. It hurt now. But he was proud of his stunt, escaping from the Law, perhaps being the only one who had. It was something they'd remember around the poolroom and the corner for a long while.

He gazed around the church to see if any of the boys were present. Seeing none of them, he guessed that they must all have been picked up, and were enjoying Christmas Day in the can. He knelt forwards and slumped his shoulders, because kneeling erect was tiring. He grimaced with a sudden pain in his ankle, and had to maneuver his right leg. He felt that she was looking at him, thinking he was a clown. His expression became serious and circumspect. He felt her eyes upon him. He would impress her. From the corner of his eye, he saw a finger on her rosary beads, a soft finger, soaped in whiteness, the long nail polished and shinily pink. He sideglanced and saw her thin face, powdered, neatly rouged, a long straight nose, wide lips, an expression of calm sophistication. The squirrel coat touched his leg. Imperceptibly, he let his body edge a fraction of an inch towards her. He heard the mumbling sounds vaguely as Father Doneggan bowed over the altar and silently uttered the prayers in preparation for the reading of the holy gospel. He yawned. His mind returned to last night. He almost fell asleep, and as if he were coming to his senses, he heard Father Doneggan swiftly chanting:

Sequentia sancti evangeli secundum.

He felt a sudden elation as if he had realized one of his dreams, because he was, he knew it, on the verge of doing just that. He always, each day when he got up, and every time he went to church, had the feeling that maybe he might meet a girl, the girl he knew he would some day meet. And now this girl next to him, maybe she was the one. He quickly palmed his hands together, and tried to pray, and to look like he was praying, with proper seriousness. More aware of her than of the ceremonies, he pattered out the unthought words of the Our Father. He arose with the people, and stood like one in a dream. He sat down, hoping now, maybe, he and she would sit with their thighs against one another. He saw, in surprise, that Father Doneggan stood by the altar rail with a black book in his hand. He arose for the reading of the gospel, determined to listen:

The shepherds said to one another: Let us go to Bethlehem, and see this thing which is to come to pass, which the Lord hath showed us. . . .

He leaned his weight on the back of the pew in front of him. He tried to keep her face in his mind, but he forgot what she looked like, and had to side-glance to recall the features on her thin handsome face. He stared straight ahead at the priest, whose reading made disturbing indistinguishable sounds to him, and the image of her face thinned out, and then, it suddenly bloated with fat, as if he was seeing her in one of the crazy mirrors at the Fun House in White City. He looked at her again. There was an icy quality about her, too. It made him afraid she was too proud for him to make her love him, but no, it would be different and she would go for him as he did for her. Me for you, baby, he told himself. He determined once again to put exterior thoughts from him and hear mass in the right way. He forced himself to listen:

And the shepherds returned, glorifying and praising God for all that they had heard and seen as it was told to them.

After the gospel, Studs sat down with the other people and perfunctorily blessed himself as the sermon began. The sermon seemed like a drone to him. He recalled the phrase from the gospel, "glorifying God," and a mood of repentance struck him with a sorrow that was almost abject. He said an act of contrition, trying to make it rise from a penitent heart. This was the first Christmas morning since he had made his first Holy Communion upon which he had not received. Glorifying God. Doing what he had done on Christmas Eve. Drunk, in a whore house, watching a filthy performance by two of the lowest women there could be, going up with a whore. . . . Oh, my God, I am heartily, heartily sorry for having offended Thee, I am not worthy. . . . He had come home stinking from drink, looking like a sow, worse than the prodigal son, spoiling everybody's Christmas day at home. Oh, my God, I am heartily sorry . . . and he had been in bed with the whore. The noise of the raid, the disappointment in that moment of discovery, came back, and recalling how it had just been before the moment, hot desires flushed his thoughts, and he wanted a woman, and her presence next to him made it worse, and if only the raid had been pulled off two minutes later. . . . Oh, my God . . .

He listened to Father Doneggan's description of the manger, where the Christ Child had been born, that conception which was the most important single event in all the crowded history of mankind.

His mind floated and he thought of her next to him in a way that decent girls shouldn't be thought of, and he wished that there was one more person in the pew so that he and she would be squeezed together, and Jesus Christ, he felt like a plain low-down ordinary sonofabitch.

"And there was the Christ Child in that humble manger, a child of poverty. Christ, our Lord, could have come unto man, a king in proud kingly robes, a monarch greater than all other earthly monarchs. But no, he came as the foster-child of a poor and humble carpenter. He came unto man in humility. And, my friends, that humility of Christ, our Lord and Savior, is one of the many lessons that we should learn

on this great and joyous feast day that is celebrated throughout Christendom."

She was sitting straight up. Was she listening? Did her mind wander? Did she think of him, want to meet him, know him? Had she ever heard of him? Perhaps she had been maybe to a dance and had met Dan Donoghue there, and she had heard Dan say something about Studs Lonigan, and she had asked who Studs Lonigan was. And after Dan had told her, maybe she had said, or at least thought, that she would like to meet Studs Lonigan. And now she was kneeling next to him, and afterwards, going out of church, maybe they would talk, and then he would walk home with her, and arrange to take her to a show this evening. He quickly covered a yawn with his right hand. He put his hand down because he didn't want her to notice the nicotine on his fingers. He glanced about him with an air of put-on seriousness, and saw Tommy Doyle's mother in a pew across the aisle to his left. He looked to the rear, and saw the people standing, and by Father Doneggan's confessional, the beaming red face of Father Gilhooley. Father Gilhooley was probably happy, thinking of what a collection he would get, and of how so many parishioners had received Holy Communion. So many, but not Studs Lonigan.

Father Doneggan blessed himself at the completion of the sermon, and turned back towards the altar.

Studs determined that he would be more attentive. He would have to be, or it would be just the same as not having heard mass, and that, after last night, would be flying too flagrantly in the face of God Almighty. His belly was upset. His head throbbed. He was almost overpowered with thirst. His back was heavy. His ankle pained. He had just about ruined himself . . . like a goddamn fool. He had to smile, remembering Vinc Curley, and that snake-room full of drunks.

Credo in unum Deum. . . .

Somehow, somehow inexplicably, her thigh seemed to brush against him, and it seemed to remain pressed an instant longer that it would have if she had done it without intention, and maybe, maybe it meant she wanted to break the ice. A nervous tremor signalled through him, an exultation flowed from nerve to nerve, and that pressure, like a deft finger, made him feel as if he were on the verge of great happiness and excitement. The pressure relaxed, and a sense of sin came into his thoughts like vomit. He silently muttered an Our Father. The future seemed opening up to him like a new land, and he could see himself and her going together, making each other happy,

surprising everybody who knew them, making the guys all
jealous, and he could hear them saying, she must have been
stewed when she picked him, she's the keenest girl in the parish,
she's hot, boy, Studs got himself a woman and I don't mean
maybe.

And he would take her places, and the future was before
him like a new land, and he felt like Columbus might have
felt when he discovered America.

Father Doneggan kissed the Altar. He turned and saluted
the people:

Dominus vobiscum.

Et cum spiritu tuo.

Oremus.

The choir sang the appointed psalm. A sense of solemnity
came upon Studs. He bowed his head as Father Doneggan
reverently lifted the paten before the crucifix. Studs' head
remained bowed. A vision of Heaven, with God enthroned
in red on a golden throne, came to him as through a mist.
He was unaware of the sacred progress of the mass, and he
knelt with his head still bowed, filled with vague thoughts of
adoration, until he heard the choir:

The shepherds were watching, the whole night through,
Under the starry sky. . . .

As a boy, he had sung the song in the children's choir at
five o'clock mass on Christmas morning. The feeling of Christmas, a feeling of joy and reverence suffused upon him, and
he remembered boyhood Christmas days, with the snow coming
down as he dashed to five o'clock mass, wearing high, laced
boots like those lumberjacks wore in movies, kicking chunks
of ice with them, hoping to meet Lucy, meeting Dan and Bill,
hunching his face forwards and hurrying into a raw wind.
He remembered himself, Dan and Bill running to church
to be there on time. He remembered them singing, with Lucy,
standing with the girls, singing, now and then seeming to
dart a glance at him, and TB McCarthy in front of him, goofily
singing:

The shepherds were guzzling the whole night through,
Under the beery sky. . . .

Jim Clayburn came towards him with the collection box,
a small, square, wooden container attached to a long pole.
Jim pushed it by Studs, smiling a trifle, and Studs dropped

in a Christmas envelope, containing five dollars. Studs noticed that the box was packed with bills and envelopes. He hoped she'd noticed that he was making a good offering. She put in a dollar bill.

The offertory bell sounded a warning that the Canon or Sacrificial part of the Mass was beginning. Heads bowed, and hands beat on chest.

Sanctus, Sanctus, Sanctus. . . .

Studs muttered the words of the Act of Contrition over and over again. He wished last night undone, like he had almost never wished for anything. The bell, the sudden feeling of change in everyone at Mass, the knowledge that he was to witness the greatest of mysteries, the changing of bread and water into the body and blood of Jesus Christ, the memories of other masses, other Christmas days, catechism lessons, all converged in him. He was lonesome, and contrite, and adoring. He felt himself a part of the great and powerful Catholic Church, built upon the rock of Peter, a member, however unworthy, and he vowed to be more worthy. He thought of how, ever since the Last Supper, the mystery of the mass had been celebrated, and God, through Jesus Christ, Our Lord, had given himself to the faithful for their redemption. In ancient Rome, in catacombs, in the Middle Ages in great cathedrals, in Ireland in caves when the priests were hunted, and the British had put a price on their heads, today all over the world, this same Mass, this same sacrifice was being celebrated, and pride in the Church mounted in equal proportion with his cumulative feeling of shamed unworthiness. . . .

Vere . . . Quia per incarnati Verbi mysterium . . .

The Latin words blended into the mystery, and Studs would have given anything to have received Holy Communion on this Christmas Day. He prayed sincerely, saying Our Fathers and Hail Marys, his mind filling again and again with visions of heavenly rejoicing about the shining thrones of the bearded and powerful Creator of Heaven and Earth, of other Masses, of the Church through the ages, the Popes celebrating Mass in Rome centuries ago, missionaries celebrating in far-off heathen Asia. . . . I believe in God, the Father Almighty, Creator of Heaven and Earth. . . . Envy flashed in his thoughts, and he wished that he were in Father Doneggan's place, celebrating the Mass, exercising the greatest and most mysterious powers that man could have, and that only could be exercised by him who was consecrated in the priesthood.

He thought that perhaps his mother had been right, and that he had had a vocation, and that he should have studied for the priesthood. Perhaps he had scorned a vocation, and that was the reason why he was always feeling that there was something more in life that he could never seem to get, and couldn't even name. Perhaps his heedlessness to the call from God Almighty meant that he would be unhappy all his life.

Adeste fideles! Adeste fideles!
Regem angelorum.
Venite adoremus, venite adoremus
In Bethlehem.

The tune of the Christmas song ran through his mind, again drawing it back to boyhood, and boyhood Christmas days, and that Christmas morning that he had come home from five o'clock mass, and had been given a ten-dollar gold piece by his old man, and in the afternoon, he and Dan Donoghue had gone to a show and seen Salome, and in the picture, Theda Bara as Salome had done the dance of the seven veils, stripping off veil after veil, and the scene had suddenly changed before the last veil had come off, and they had been so damn disappointed. He was sad because he had grown up, and because the years passed like a river that no man could stop. Oh, come let us adore, oh, come let us adore, Christ, Our King. He had all the old feelings he had used to have on Christmas day, feelings he could not find words for, feelings that ran through the songs sung in church on Christmas. . . .

Pater noster, qui es in coelis. . . .

Again, the bell knelled through the hushed church. Studs bowed his head in unison with the people, and tapped his breast. His thoughts were vague. His body and mind seemed separated, his mind swimming away free and in a sea of melancholy, his body heavy and sluggish like a dragging weight.

He listened to the choir singing, a sweetness and strength in their voices and in the song:

Agnus Dei, qui tollis peccata mundi. . . .

He watched Father Doneggan bowing his head low and silently reciting the prayers in immediate preparation for the reception of Holy Communion. Through his mind there ran a communion song:

> *Oh, Lord, I am not worthy,*
> *That Thou shouldst come to me.*

But speak the words of comfort,
And my spirit healed shall be.

He felt like a plain, ordinary low-down bastard. He vowed that he would receive Holy Communion next Sunday. But he knew he would always be sorry for having done what he had last night. And he thought of her next to him, and tried to wish she and he were engaged, and going to Communion together this morning, and. . . . He bowed his head as the bell rang for the Domine non sum dignis.

Mass would soon be over. He wanted it to be, and he didn't want it to be over, because maybe if he didn't work fast now, he would never see, or never get a chance with the girl who was next to him. And he was tired. The church seemed to get more and more stuffy, and he was almost falling asleep. He kept side-glancing at her, and he wanted her more and more with every glimpse. He faced the altar, all his confidence shattered, and wondering whether or not she was thinking of him, or even secretly laughing at him. He tried to regain his confidence by assuring himself he was Studs Lonigan, and that Studs Lonigan had done things, was real stuff, and tough, too.

He arose for the last gospel and people commenced leaving the church. He heard her whispering pardon me, the voice striking him will-less. She had to repeat it. He turned. She smiled, and he didn't know what to make of her smile, whether it was friendly or sarcastic or what. She passed him, and was gone. It was like a toppling of thrones, a toppling of something inside of him. Maybe she was gone out of his life, just like Lucy. He tried to remember her voice, with its quiet but confident tones. He tried to remember her face. He tried to feel he would see her again, and that with her everything would be different, and there would be no more jazzing around, drinking, can houses. Maybe next Saturday night when he went to confession, she would be there and remember him, and he'd be reformed by her, and . . . He yawned. Felt rotten, goddamn it. He had been a complete, undiluted, unadulterated, all-around chump. And he was sorry, very sorry.

Deo gratias. . . .

He walked out of the church, while the choir sang:

Oh, come, let us adore Him! Oh, come, let us adore Him.
Christ, our king. . . .

He shoved forwards, passing people, but when he got outside, he couldn't find her in the crowd. People wished him a Merry

Christmas and he hardly heard them. But he would, he would, by Christ, he would see her again, and she would know him, the real Studs Lonigan that nobody had ever known.

He met Tommy Doyle, and they looked at the people pass until Tommy got tired. Studs dragged along with Tommy, still wanting to wait as a last hope that she might be outside, that she might even be waiting for him. Tommy told Studs how they had all been thrown in the can, and asked how he had gotten away. Studs told him. Tommy marvelled. He said Red's old man had gotten them out. Studs felt lousy, but hurried Tommy along, despite his sprained ankle, because he was hoping they would pass her on the street. They stopped for a coke at Fifty-eighth and Indiana Avenue, and then went over to the poolroom, because Studs wanted the fellows to know how he had escaped during the raid. But he didn't think that he had ever felt so low in his whole life.

SECTION THREE

1924

XIII

It was dreary February weather. The children were all out, and Mrs. Lonigan had the dinner dishes finished. She rearranged a few chairs. She emptied an ash-tray. She straightened her son's dresser. She pottered about until there was absolutely nothing to do. Then she picked up the New World *and read the news. Lonigan laughed over the funnies. Cigar ashes dropped onto his shirt, and some fell on the floor. Mrs. Lonigan cautioned him, and hustled in with the carpet sweeper. He said she should not worry because ashes kept moths away and were good for a rug. She said ashes did nothing any good. She put away the carpet sweeper, returned, and looked through the society section of the* Chicago Daily Tribune. *He glanced at his watch. She asked the time, and he answered that it was a quarter to four. She remonstrated aloud with herself that it was too late to go to Benediction. She suggested that they take a little walk and get a nip of air. He yawned and said he was too tired and thought he would take a nap. She picked up the funnies and arranged them neatly with the other sections of the Sunday paper. When Lonigan awoke, it was dark out. Mrs. Lonigan was preparing supper, and Martin was in the parlor playing* The Sheik of Araby *on their two-hundred-dollar electric Victrola. Lonigan went out to the kitchen, his face wide with a yawn, and remarked that spring would soon be bursting forth, and that he would have to be taking his sweetheart out a lot like the good old days. He pinched her cheeks. She told him not to be bothering her while she was fixing the meal.*

CHAPTER THIRTEEN

"I'm your buddy, Hink. I'll take care of you," Shrimp Haggerty drooled; he tottered forwards to clutch at Hink Weber's arm as Hink reeled by the curb edge. Mush Joss feebly grabbed for Hink's other arm, Hink strained and muttered incoherently, while he dragged them about.

Nate Klein alighted from his cab and joined Studs, who stood in front of the poolroom with his hands sunk in his overcoat pocket.

"Weber is aiming to take a nose dive in the gutter," Nate said with a silly laugh.

"Yeah. But say, Nate, I thought Mush Joss was in the navy?" Studs asked.

"He deserted, second time, the boys were saying."

Hink shook free of his care-takers and floundered into a precarious balance. He swayed as helplessly as a baby in the center of the sidewalk, with his shoulders bent and his nodding head lowered.

"How goes the cab racket, fink?" laughed Studs.

"Well, Studs, I ain't got no complaints. I wasn't working for a long time, and then I got me this job, and now I'm also lined up with a can house, and get my split on anybody I bring there. That reminds me. The next time you boys want a girl, let me bring you there. The girls are all young."

"Sure. How about you? Ever take part of your split out in trade?"

"Do I? They got a seventeen-year-old blond there who's as low as a broad could be, but say, Studs, she knows her stuff," Nate said, lasciviously.

Studs watched the blind meanderings of the three drunks. Nate laughed and wisecracked.

"Nate, it looks like hell to see a guy like Hink so goddamn helpless. Christ, look at him, and he's such a powerful fellow,

with a beautiful physique. Say, they could make a statue out
of that boy's body," Studs said reflectively.

"Hell, Studs, we all get that way now and then; he'll get
over it."

"Say, and you know Shrimp is looking bad these days.
He's getting skinnier than a rail."

"Yeah, he's hitting it up."

"His wife takes plenty from him. Christ, he's drunk every
day, and she goes out and works for him, and they got that
kid. I wonder why the hell Shrimp married her. He doesn't
seem to give a damn for her," said Studs.

"You know how it is, Studs. A broad won't come across
and a guy gets hot for her, so he marries her to get it. Then
after he gets it awhile, he gets tired and wants something else
to change his luck. It happens that way in the best-regulated
families," Nate said.

"I guess so, but how come you're blowing so quickly?"

"Work, my boy. I ain't booked a thing tonight yet," Nate
said, leaving.

"I see you're sober tonight, Studs," well-dressed Phil Rolfe
said, stepping out of the poolroom.

"I got to lay off the stuff. I drank too much of it already.
Got a heartburn, and I want to watch my guts."

"Doctor's orders?"

"No, I just figure I better cut the stuff out for a while."

"That's the smart thing to do; it makes a pig out of you
when you get blind."

Studs watched Shrimp and Mush laboring to lift Hink from
where he had fallen on his face. Studs assisted them and then
returned to his post by the window.

"It's chump stuff, drinking that way, and it doesn't pay
a guy nohow," Phil said; he trotted on.

Hink broke loose from his buddies and wandered towards
Calumet Avenue, babbling; pedestrians gave him a wide berth.
While Shrimp and Mush laughed, he let out a big heave, and
some of his vomit splashed the silk stockings of a passing girl.
She walked on indignant, muttering that it was perfectly disgusting, while Shrimp and Mush flirted with her. Studs looked
at her leg.

They dragged Hink back, and got him inside the poolroom.
Studs walked off towards the park. Like a pig in a gutter.
It was queer all right, the way people always drank. You were
calm and sober, and wanted something to do, excitement,
wanted to cut loose. So you warmed your belly up with a
few drinks, and it made your head a little giddy. Everything
seemed suddenly rosy or funny, you were happy, you forgot

everything that was bothering you. People laughed at what you said, and you laughed at your own jokes too. Everybody looked at you. You were proud of yourself, proud because you couldn't even walk straight. You weren't afraid of any sonofabitch and his brother—sometimes, not even of Johnny Law. You didn't care what you did, told everybody what you thought of him, kicked in windows, raised all holy hell. It was a glorious feeling, but you kept wanting more to drink, and kept wanting to talk more and tell the world who you were and what a great guy you were, make everybody just pay attention to you. And soon, the lights went out. Everything was black, and all you knew about was a kind of torment the same as when you went under gas to have a tooth pulled. You acted like a clown, became so helpless that you couldn't walk, puked, sometimes got puke all over yourself, made a pig out of yourself. Pig Lonigan. A wave of self-disgust swept through him. It wasn't worth it. The stuff was generally strong enough to corrode a cast-iron gut. It was canned heat, rot-gut, furniture-varnish, rat-poison. When you drank it, you took your life in your hands, and even if it didn't kill you, it might make you blind, or put your heart, liver, guts or kidneys on the fritz for life. And after you went on a bat, you woke up the next morning with a hangover. You were so jumpy you couldn't be satisfied with anything. You had sweats, a general feeling of tiredness and were ashamed of yourself for having been a fool. Your head throbbed with lines of pain running clean through it, and you had to put ice packs on it. Your guts were upset and heaving, and you couldn't eat. You were so damn thirsty that you couldn't drink enough water. You had to dope yourself with bromos, bicarbonate of soda, black coffee, aspirin, and cokes. It ruined your whole goddamn day, and you tasted bum gin and moonshine for three days.

He crossed over into Washington Park. It seemed funny to him now, how it was something to brag about, like copping a cherry, and how back in the sixth grade, he and most of the kids had thought drinking was a horrible disgrace. He didn't know why he had drunk so much of the world's liquor in his twenty-two and a half years. He had just started drinking because all the guys did. But he was on the wagon. Yes, and for good . . . maybe.

Suddenly, he sensed that spring was in the air. He could smell it. He breathed deeply, changed his slouchy walk into a brisk one, and looked around him at the dark shadows, the naked shrubbery and trees. He crossed the park drive, and walked around the patch of shrubbery on the right-hand side of the walk that curved to the boathouse. He could see the lagoon, steely, dark, glittering here and there with the moon and stars. The world, the night, the park, spring that was going to come, it was all new. He felt as if he were discovering them for the first time in his life, as if the sense of budding things, of leaves coming out on the branches, the gradual warming and laziness in the air, the grass bursting green through the cold, hard, wintry earth, as if all these were inside of him. He wished that it were spring already. He determined that it was going to be a different spring and summer for him. He was fed up with the old stuff, and he had let himself go far enough already.

He stood by the lagoon watching while trifling waves swished into the thin line of pebbled shore. He glanced up at the sky and was quickened with surprise and elation because it was so clear, with such clean clouds, and a moon which seemed like frothy ice or frozen snow. And he had never realized there were so many stars in the sky, some of them blue like signal lights far, far off. They were all over the sky like jewels flung on a dark carpet and they made him wonder about life, and what it was and why people had such curious feelings. But he guessed that God had made life and the stars just as they were so that people would wonder like that, and marvel at His handiwork.

He had a feeling of freshness and cleanness, even if he, too, had often been drunk like a pig. Pig Lonigan! And the thought of the spring that was coming made him happy. He thought how he would walk about in the park, with the trees and smells and sky and shadows and people, young girls in summer clothes, looking like Lucy had looked just so soon after graduation. Spring was like new life to the world, and he was going to be a new person in this coming new spring. And that girl. He had seen her a couple of times at church, but she had not batted an eye; she didn't know who he was, or if she did, she didn't show it. But he knew, he had faith that she was going to be the center of his new life in this coming new spring, and he was going to be a different Studs Lonigan, not a pig, stinking with lousy gin, and rolling helplessly in the gutter, like he'd seen Hink Weber doing. Some day he'd see her, meet her, speak to her, tell her how he had been in the park this very night, and of the things he'd thought, and how she had been in them so much, as if she were the trees and flowers of the new spring growing inside of him. He suddenly remembered Lucy. Hell with her! The other girl was keener. Lucy had had her chance. She could be sorry when it was too late. But he would learn from losing Lucy, and he wouldn't sulk with foolish pride and bashfulness, and be afraid of this girl. He would even every so often treat her coldly, acting as if he didn't care, because the minute a girl was too sure of a guy, she'd tire of him like Lucy must have gotten to feel. He'd learn from experience, learn about women from Lucy. He wondered what her name was.

He walked on and sat on a bench by the stone bridge around past the south bend of the lagoon. He pulled up his overcoat collar, and thought of how it was funny that a guy never took time off to think of what he was doing, and think about life. When he was home, he never did, but always listened to the radio, played a Victrola record, read a story in some magazine like the *Argosy*, or looked at the newspaper. Once in a while he would lie down, but then he would think of something he wanted to happen, getting girls, drinking. Often, since he had knelt beside her at Mass on Christmas day two years ago, he'd thought of her, of knowing her and loving her. And when he went out, he hung around so goddamn much, restless, wondering what to do, and hardly ever satisfied when he did do something, gassing, goofing clowns like Curley and he always kept wondering what time it was. And all along, he had known there was something missing. But this spring it would all be different and he would be better off from every viewpoint, all because he was going to meet her, and, yes, go with her. He remembered when he licked Weary Reilley, that other day when he had sat with Lucy in the tree, and that day when he had gone home from work with his first pay, how on all those times, he had felt that life was going to start being different for him. This time, though, it had to be. It would. He looked across the lagoon at the wooded island which was on a small hill, half hidden in shadows, with bare trees ranged backwards at intervals from the bank.

He tossed aside the cigarette he was smoking. Most painters smoked and drank too much. He guessed those heartburns he got were from too much smoking. He was going to cut down. Under no considerations would he smoke more than a package a day. He was suddenly afraid that he had a bum heart. Suppose he wouldn't live long, and even a long life was short. He was going on twenty-three now, and look how quickly time seemed to have passed. He thought of himself being cut off early.

He slowly calmed his fears, because he was sure that it was not too late for him to start taking care of his health. He'd exercise, get the fat off, because if he let it go, he'd have too much on and fat would be dangerous and maybe make his heart worse, and you looked like hell with an alderman. Everybody kidded you. And she wouldn't want a guy who stuck out in front like a balloon. He would exercise every day, go on the wagon, even watch his eating. Many a guy had dug his grave with a knife and fork, just as that writer in the *Questioner,* Cathcart, had said. The hell with boozing, whoring. It was the crap. Didn't pay. Ended you up behind the eight ball.

He felt chilly, and started back to Fifty-eighth Street. He looked at the trees which spread before him, like corpses, with the wind saddening through them. Nice. He was glad, too, that he had taken this walk. And he was going to stick to· his determinations, fight not to break them. By God, he wouldn't! He shot his butt, realizing that he had determined to cut out smoking. Well, it hadn't been breaking his intentions, because he hadn't realized that he was smoking. He felt more different than he had ever felt before. He felt that he had will power, and will power was the main asset needed in every walk of life. Over near the drive, he was again aware of the wind sweeping through the shrubbery. It was a sad song, and it seemed to sing through him. It made him sad, but it was a pleasant sadness, because he knew he was different from all the mopes at the poolroom, he was going to do different things and be more than they. He could see himself, meeting them thirty years from now, himself thin, in the pink, not looking his age, them fat, red-nosed, failures, like Barney Keefe, envying him, and saying Studs you haven't changed a bit, you look swell, say how in the name of Christ do you do it? He was glad he had seen Hink. It had been like having ice-water thrown in his face to wake him up. It had made him think. Pig Lonigan! Not any more. It had made him learn his lesson in time, before he ruined himself like poor Paulie Haggerty had done, and his brother Shrimp Haggerty was doing.

Kelly came out of the poolroom as Studs slouched along. He asked Studs about doing something. Studs shook his head, and felt superior to Red. It was the first exercise of his new will power.

"Hell, Studs, if you go home now, your old man and old lady might have a fit of apoplexy or heart failure, they'll be so surprised," Tommy Doyle said.

"I'm turning in and getting some sleep."

He went towards home. At the corner of Fifty-eighth and Michigan, he saw a nigger and his black girl ahead, walking arm in arm. He thought of how in this new spring time, the new man Studs Lonigan would be walking about in the evening with her on his arm. Suddenly, he sneered, thinking that the goddamn niggers had their guts, invading a white man's neighborhood, and sooner or later they'd have to be run out.

Lonigan was glad with surprise. He and Studs talked about business for a half hour. He turned in with the mother. Studs and Fran talked, and he promised to go to the Wednesday evening Lenten services at St. Patrick's next Wednesday. In bed, the father said to the mother that he was gratified because Bill was getting some sense now, and settling down. He took the credit for it.

XIV

Phil Rolfe was one of the best-dressed cake-eaters at an afternoon dance given on Washington's Birthday at a hall near Englewood High School. A sizeable, lively crowd was in attendance. Amongst them were a number of fellows and girls who rated in the south side high school fraternity and sorority world.

Phillip spotted Loretta Lonigan. He thought that she was pretty, with her dark hair, and small but compact figure, and her gray serge dress, trimmed with collar and cuffs of hand-drawn handkerchief linen. Damn keen girl, even if she had a big nose like her brother, Studs. She smiled as he approached her between dances.

"I see you haven't forgotten me?" he said, smiling with all his talcum-powdered, stacombed charm.

"Why, Phil Rolfe, how could I forget you, ever?"

"Shall we dance?"

"I'd be delighted to."

Phil placed his right hand with effective masculine firmness in the small of her back, and crooked his left arm with his palm flat against hers. He held his head high, his thin shoulders straight and erect, and danced in calculated and precise rhythms.

"Say, Loretta, you're a swell dancer. Where have you been all my life?"

"And, Phil, you are too. And you have a nice line."

They talked about the music, dances, the people present, places to go. As they glided into a corner it seemed that Loretta let herself go tensely against him. He thought maybe she would sock it in. But he had to be careful. She was a nice girl. She might get sore. Had to handle nice girls with kid gloves that way, until you broke down their resistance. And her brother was tough. They turned gracefully in and out of the moving crowd, and Phil whistled the tune of Frivolous Sal *as the orchestra played it. She smiled up at him with white,*

*even teeth. He commented again on some of the people present
and she laughed. He strategically manipulated his body until
he had it against her. Her curly bobbed hair brushed his
cheek. She wondered would he think her awful, and try to
get too fresh if she shimmied. Fellows often did. But he was
so cute. And a girl had to do something about that, and if
she didn't shimmy, she might do something worse. In a corner,
she took a chance. Phillip figured she was a nice sweet girl,
and he'd have to date her up some time.*

CHAPTER FOURTEEN

Goodbye, Arnold! Studs silently thought.

Amidst exuding flower odors, Studs and Tommy Doyle
blessed themselves, and knelt down. Their eyes suddenly met
and their heads bowed in a mutual expression of surprised
regret. They muttered prayers to themselves for the repose
of the soul of their dead pal, while behind them, they could
hear a choked feminine sob, and the loudly whispered remarks
of Mrs. O'Neill that it was God's will, and that Arnold was
in Heaven, and that we must all resign ourselves to the Will
of the Almighty.

They rose, and looked lugubriously down at the unbelievably
dead body; the prominent ashen face with the beard marks
apparent despite a close shave and talcum powder, the black
hair, thick and wavy, the stiff arms folded in front with a
white pair of rosary beads draped between them, the well-
built torso sedately clothed in its black death-suit, black tie,
white shirt, black socks, and black patent leather pumps. And,
pressed against the white satin lining of the coffin lid, they
saw their card, statement of the spiritual bouquet they had
all chipped in to send. And as he gazed abstractedly, Studs
found himself expecting Arnold to smile, hear him tell a
funny story, ask if anyone wanted to get a bottle, laugh and
say that it was only a joke he was playing on everyone because
he wasn't really dead after all. But Arnold would never again
speak, never again tip a bottle to his lips, never again make
a broad he had picked up at the Midway Gardens dance hall.
The finality of Arnold's life made a sudden gash upon Studs'
thoughts. He wanted to talk to Arnold, get to know him better
than he had, take in a show with him; and knowing that he
never could do these things, he had the vaguest kind of a
feeling that whenever anyone you knew and liked died, a

part of yourself died with him. It made him think of church on Good Friday, with the statues draped in sorrowing purple, with the odor and feel of ashes everywhere like a pall, and of Ash Wednesday, and the priest's words when he thumbed your forehead with ashes:

Remember, Oh, man, that thou art dust and to dust thou shalt return!

They heard another muffled sob, and turned to face Mrs. Sheehan, who sat on a camp chair near the gray casket, dressed in black with her robust face paled and compressed.

"I'm very sorry," Studs muttered, feeling helplessly inarticulate.

"Mrs. Sheehan, I am very sorry for your great misfortune," Tommy Doyle said, as if learned by rote.

"I know, boys, I know," she gasped, dropping her head and permitting them to stand awkwardly before her. They edged, self-consciously, past a double aisle of crepe-hanging women who sat on camp chairs. Mrs. Dennis P. Gorman grabbed Studs' sleeve near the edge of the parlor, and whispered that he should remember her to his dear mother.

They saw Mr. Sheehan standing, lost, by the front door. He was a ruddy, full man, with stooped shoulders, a clipped mustache, and a half-bald gray head. They expressed condolences. He seemed not even to see them, and they smelled his rancid whiskey-breath.

"God, it's sad," Studs said, as he and Tommy walked through the hall to the rear.

"Poor fellow, it's knocked him groggy," Tommy sorrowed.

They passed through the dining-room where a small group was gathered around one of Arnold's twin sisters, a pretty black-haired girl who was distraught.

They heard the guys talking in the kitchen. Horace, Arnold's grown brother, stood in the doorway.

"Jesus, I'm sorry Horace," Tommy said.

"I know! It's tough, Tommy. You know I think it's broken Dad. He acts just like a broken man, interested in nothing, hardly ever seeing anybody. I doubt if he'll ever get over it," Horace replied, emphasizing his feeling with slow shakes of the head.

"And Arnold was getting on so well," Studs said.

"Well, all we can do is make the best of it and call it life," Horace said reflectively.

A thick veil of tobacco smoke hung over the kitchen. Jim Doyle stood by the kitchen sink, a cigar pasted in his round, jolly face, and he greeted them, called them hoods. They saluted in return, and sat down near Red Kelly. Studs noticed a girl in a corner, shabby, faded, blowsy, looked like a two-bit whore; her face seemed familiar. He frowned, and wrinkled up his forehead trying to think; he realized that she was Paulie Haggerty's widow, Eileen. What a bitch she had turned out to be!

"Well, Studs, what's new?" Red Kelly asked.

"Not much."

Horace passed around cigars. Biting off the end of one, and lighting it, Studs remarked with a certain air of importance and maturity:

"Well, Red, I never expected to be here on an occasion like this."

"Studs, when I heard it, you could have slapped me down with a feather. It's very sad, too. It's hit the poor mother hard, very hard. Arnold was her favorite, and he was always a little reckless, you know, a nice guy but a crazy bastard too when he was drunk, and that always caused her worry. And think of it, here he was sloughed off in the very prime of life."

"Poor Arnold, the guy did run in bad luck," Studs said.

"Like that time he was pie-eyed, and got stabbed by a shine; then he no sooner got his wounds healed up than he gets a dose."

"Say, was he oiled when the accident happened?"

"No, he was on the wagon again. He had gone back to work for the city. Remember how he got canned from the job for being oiled and then went back?"

"Yep, that's right."

"He was riding home from work last Saturday, on a city truck, standing on the tail gate, and hanging on to a rope. The rope broke, and Arnold fell off. He cracked his skull. They took him to the County Hospital. He never came to, but in a coma he kept muttering for his mother. By luck a priest was gotten and he received Extreme Unction before he passed away. But when his mother got there he was dead. You know, Studs, it just goes to show that some people are born lucky, and others always live under an unlucky star," Red said to Studs, who hadn't been listening to him, but had rather been looking about from face to face, and smoking his cigar as if it were a ceremony.

"Jesus!" Studs suddenly exclaimed in expression of his reaction to the whole situation.

"Yep, that's the way it is; you're here today, and gone to-morrow," Tommy Doyle said.

"And just think, I saw him at church last Sunday, feeling so swell, and dressed up like a lighthouse," Red Kelly said.

"Life is sure funny," Tommy remarked.

"And it always seems to get the guys who are white, and not the sons of bitches. Take a bastard like Weary Reilley. He's a rat clean through, and he couldn't do a decent trick if he tried. He goes around smashing guys he can lick in the mug, smacking girls to make them come across, and he's even hit his helpless father. Well, now, nothing ever happens to him. I tell you, it's one of the oddities of life and one of the mysteries of the Will of God that a guy who's white almost never gets the grapes," Red said.

"Reilley's a skunk," Studs said, kind of hoping that Red would mention how he had cleaned Weary as a kid.

"Too bad!" said Tommy.

"Where was the fire sale, Muggsy?" asked Studs as Muggsy McCarthy entered the room. He was more slumped and hollow than ever; but he wore a new dark gray suit.

"Muggsy, you look prosperous," Doyle remarked.

"Boys, I'm working for the city now," Muggsy said almost unnaturally exuberant.

"So you got in the political game, huh, Muggsy?" Tommy Doyle asked.

"Yeah, my old man took me back home and got me the job. I'm off that damn crap. There's nothing to it, hanging around all the time with not even a son in your jeans. How you like the suit, boys?" Muggsy asked.

"I think I'll get me into the political game," Tommy said, while the boys examined Muggsy's suit, and kidded him.

Like an apparition, Barney Keefe stood in the center of the room, and pointed at drunken Irish Mickey Flannagan; everybody laughed.

"And you, bitch! The last time I saw you, you passed out in a saloon over at Twelfth and Halsted, and the boys all took you on while you were dreaming of the birdies of the springtime," Barney said, pointing at Mrs. Haggerty; she smiled feebly and apologetically.

"Yeah, Tommy, you never know when you're called," Studs said, profoundly feeling the uncertainty of life, sensing a sudden fear lest he be the next of the boys called, buoying himself up with the feeling that he was strong and well and taking care of himself and wouldn't need to worry about death for a long, long time.

"Hey, Barney, where you think you're at," Red said, sore because Barney was keeping up the horseplay.

"I thought I came to a wake, but seeing all you flannel-mouth Irish here, I guess it's a saloon or a poolroom," Barney said. They laughed.

"Hello, Studs," Phil Rolfe ingratiated, while the boys still laughed at Barney's wit. Phillip rolled the cigar in his mouth. Studs acted as if he hadn't heard the greeting.

"Yeah, too bad, but we all got to go sometime," Phillip said, finding a chair in back of Studs.

The room snapped into rigid quiet with the appearance of Mr. Sheehan. He ignored the remarks politely directed at him. Red arose and offered him a chair. He looked around and walked out.

"Just like a ghost," Red dolefully said.

"Hey, Barney, you rat, when you going to sober up?" Mickey asked from the fogs of inebriation.

"Can it, Flannagan, before we toss you on your ear," Red said.

"I'll sober up when I put a lily on the grave of every pigs—t Irishman here," Barney said.

"Come on, you guys," Red repeated.

"Say, Studs, you know, isn't it a shame. You know, Arnold, he was my friend," Vinc Curley said.

"Say, Goof, dry up," Studs said. Vinc looked at Studs, hurt.

"I remember the time that Arnold and I got pie-eyed in a black-and-tan joint. You know he went for a high brown, Georgia Brown, and, boy, I thought we'd get our throats slashed from ear to ear," Benny Taite said.

"Hey, Benny, is that the only thing you can think of now that Arnold is dead? You can't think of anything else, can you—the time you might have seen him coming home with a present to his mother or something?"

"Gee, Red, I didn't mean anything," Benny said.

"Well, those aren't the kind of breaks you want to be making at a time like this," Kelly snapped.

Everybody laughed as Kenny Kilarney came in with that goofy, boyish smile on his thin face, just as it always was.

"Boys, this is Timothy O'Shea," he said, pointing his finger at the character with him.

"Hi, boys!" Timothy O'Shea said like a prizefighter accepting well-earned applause. He swam in a huge, flowing overcoat, and had a rough, wide, surly face. He pushed his dirty fedora on the back of his head, and smiled.

"Say, boys, excuse me a minute!" Timothy O'Shea said, going to the sink; he relieved himself.

They were too surprised to speak. He took a seat. Horace came with the box of cigars. Timothy O'Shea and Kenny each took two.

"Hell, you guys are all hoods. I'm going," Jim Doyle said.

"Sit down, Jim, and tell us about the political outlook for next fall," said Studs.

"Democratic landslide."

"What do you think of the mayor, Jim?" asked Red.

"He's a Sunday School mayor," Jim said.

"Bill Dever, oh, he's all right, Bill is, if you know how to take him," Timothy O'Shea said.

"You know him?" Jim asked hostilely.

"Sure, him and my old man is like that," Timothy O'Shea said, crossing the second and third fingers on his right hand and holding them up in indication of closeness.

"Say, Jim, say?" Curley called.

"You in the political game?" asked Doyle.

"Sure! Me, I'm in everything. Christ, yes," Timothy O'Shea said.

"Listen, Jim, I wanted to ask you if you wanted to go to the Tivoli with me some night this week?" Curley said.

"Hey, Curley, did anybody ever tell you that you were a pest?" said Jim; they laughed.

Fat Malloy arrived and glad-handed all the boys. Studs said he acted like he was a pupil of Jim Doyle's.

"You know, fellows, I hate it, having to think that Arnold's gone from us like this," Les said.

"Yeah, Les, you'll have to drink more to make up for what he won't, huh?" said Tommy.

"Say, Kenny, where in hell you been keeping yourself?" asked Studs.

"Out of the pen," Kenny said.

"Same old Kilarney. But tell me, are you working?" Red said.

"Sure, everybody."

"Say, any drinks in the joint?" asked Timothy O'Shea. No one answered him.

"Hell, come on, Kilarney. I thought you said there'd be some sparkling waters here. Come on, this joint is a hell of a wake," Timothy said.

"Brother, we got respect for the dead," said Red.

"Sure, you run a wake like you were all Jews. If I hung around I'd have to drink noodle soup. Come on, Kilarney," Timothy O'Shea said, leaving, his huge coat swinging after him.

Kenny followed him and left a roomful of soreheads.

"If it wouldn't have been disrespectful, I'd have socked that ignorant ape of an Irishman," Kelly said.

"Kenny was always cockeyed, and didn't have sense about serious things," Tommy said.

"Leave it to Kenny to find a guy like that for a wake where tragedy has occurred," Kelly said.

"Same old Kilarney," Studs said.

They talked. More came, and some went out. Finally, Studs and Red left, re-expressing their condolences before departing.

"Studs, let's get a drink."

"I'm on the wagon, Red," Studs said.

"How come?"

"I'm taking care of myself these days."

"Come on, one drink won't make any difference."

"Nope, not tonight, Red."

They walked silently towards Fifty-eighth Street. Across the street, the park seemed gloomy with its deserted tennis courts, and the bare, black trees and shrubbery behind them.

"Say, Studs, I think it was goddamn funny they didn't ask any of us to be pall-bearers," Red said.

"I suppose his old man is sore. Thinks we were always responsible for his drinking. Notice the old man didn't say much to us?"

"Yeah, and the first time I met Arnold just after his family moved in the neighborhood, he was looking for a bottle," Red said.

"It's fluky, all right."

"I feel sorry and I understand how his folks might be feeling, and I offered them my condolences. But Jesus Christ, we were Arnold's best friends, and we'll miss him too. I tell you, Studs, it's an insult to all of us!" Red protested.

Studs wasn't listening. He couldn't get the memory of Arnold out of his head, and it gave him a feeling of awe and fear. He had just seen death, death with something terrible, final, about it. It made him suddenly leery of even living. He determined all over again that he was going to take care of himself.

"I suppose old man Sheehan must feel bad. You know, he sees us living, and his son dead, and it must have hit him. But we didn't kill Arnold. He shouldn't act that way towards us. But then I suspect it might be Horace. Come to think of it, he hardly ever comes around the poolroom, and when he does, he doesn't have a lot to say."

"Yes," Studs said, not feeling so badly that he hadn't been asked to be a pall-bearer.

"Arnold was a prince, though. That's why I'm going to the funeral, even if his family did act that way, and not ask even one of his best friends to stand by him in his last journey," Red said.

"I'll miss him. He was white, all right," Studs said.

"Say, Studs, sure you won't change your mind and have a drink?"

"No, Red, I'm really starting to put myself into decent shape."

"What the hell, you're in good shape, aren't you?"

"But what I mean is get hard, and get this little bit of belly I got off, and then next season we can get the old team together and play football again."

"That's not a bad idea. Remember that fight with the Monitors?"

"Say, that reminds me, remember that kike they had who was so fast and who nearly got killed? I forget his name, but you remember him?"

"I think it was Schwartz."

"Well, I'll be goddamned if I wasn't out to a game in the park last fall and he was playing, and just as fast as ever."

"But we stopped him," Red said.

"Yeah, we did," Studs said, hoping Red would mention one or two of those tackles.

"But come on, Studs," Red said; Studs shook his head no.

"I was thinking I'd join the Y, and go swimming there and fool around the gym a couple of nights a week. What do you think of it?"

"I might too."

"I'm going over this week, want to come along?"

"Maybe. Pick me up at the poolroom."

They had coffee an' in the Greek restaurant. Studs went home, and turned in early. Lying in bed he felt as if he had again conquered himself, and was already started on the road to making himself as healthy as the guys whose pictures he saw in the physical culture ads in magazines. He thought that every day in every way he was going to get harder and healthier. But he couldn't get Arnold from his mind, and the words of a song the guys sang kept running through his head.

Did you ever think, when a hearse goes by,
That some day you and I will go rolling by. . . .

XV

I hate to see the evening sun go down. . . .

Mickey Flannagan's head fell onto the table, and a glass, half full of gin and ginger ale, almost toppled. Slug Mason looked at the high-brown singer; she was dressed in a shimmery blue gown with a slit down the side, and she rolled her abdomen with agonizing slowness as she sang in the center of the glassy dance floor. Slug whispered that he'd take a baby like that on, even if her skin was purple. Red Kelly countered that he personally had too much self-respect to go monkeying around with low niggers. Barney Keefe sneered that Red was BS, and that it was always the same, a guy wanted a woman, and everything else was crap.

Feeling tomorrow just like I feel today.

Stan Simonsky said he had to laugh when he thought that Studs and Les had gone tonight to the . . . Y.M.C.A. Slug said he couldn't understand what had happened to Studs. Stan added that he hoped Studs wasn't losing his guts.

Barney told them to shut up while they heard the song. The black girl repeated the chorus, her voice throbbing with a mixture of despair and innuendoed sex. The house applauded.

A six-piece Negro jazz band went into action, producing an evil orgiastic jazz. The dance floor of the Sunrise Café on Thirty-fifth Street quickly crowded, and it became like a revolving wheel of lust, the dancers swaying and turning, every corner and floor edge filled with dancers who moved sidewise, inch by inch, socking their bellies together in quick rhythm and with increasing frenzy. The fellows watched. Their faces went tight with hostility every time a white girl went by with a Negro. They saw one beautiful blond girl with a coal-black, sweating nigger, and they said nothing, only because there were too many shines in the place. Slug said what the hell he was going to dance too. He left, and soon he was socking with a black girl. The others followed Slug's example, and Red Kelly sat boiling sore, alone with Mickey Flannagan, who slept peacefully, with his head on the table. Red looked about at the empty tables. Then at the dancers. He saw Stan socking with a skinny yellow bitch. He thought the jazz would drive him nuts; the thick-lipped singing and shouts of the niggers grated until he was ready to jump. And the place was like the stockyards; he thought they ought to use a little perfume anyway. He called over a nigger waiter, paid his share of the bill, and got up while the dance was still going hot. As he walked towards the exit, he noticed the snottily suspicious glances he got from niggers, and Christ, how he'd have loved to have gotten a couple of them out on Fifty-eighth Street. At the door, there were four dicks, their faces drawn, waiting, as if they were expecting trouble. As he left, two white girls entered, laughing, with loudly-dressed buck niggers. The doorman told him to come again. Yes, he thought, he'd like to come with a machine gun. He took a cab to a white can house.

CHAPTER FIFTEEN

I

Studs' eyes were attracted by a framed picture of the Sacred Heart of Jesus, around which was written the verse:

> *Heart of Jesus, my true friend,*
> *Make me faithful to the end.*

He wanted to substitute the word healthy for faithful. He looked at his feet where he had just dropped the evening's copy of the *Chicago Evening Journal* that he'd been reading. He'd come across a squib telling of how a thirty-seven-year-old man had dropped dead of heart trouble at the ball game. He thought that he had been having pains in his heart, and down around his stomach of late, and he was gloomy and worried, because maybe he'd be having heart trouble and dropping dead, or having to have an operation for appendicitis, or be suffering from ulcers of the stomach or something like that. Maybe his plan to condition himself was just too late, and it was too bad for him. Health was the greatest gift and wealth that any man could receive or have, and when health was gone, all was gone.

He might be dead any day. He might drop dead in the street. He might have already torn all the lining out of his stomach with rotgut gin.

He wanted to live to be a hundred. He could see himself celebrating his hundredth birthday, with everybody he now knew dead, and his great-grandchildren and his great-great-grandchildren surrounding him. He could see himself at a hundred, hale and hearty, having his picture in the newspapers and telling the reporters, while they took his picture, that he attributed his health to careful living, and explaining how when he had been twenty-two he had laid out a plan of careful living and exercise for himself, and he'd followed it conscientiously for years. He could see himself a hundred years old, walking erect without a cane, not fat either like his father was, coming back to the old neighborhood, looking at all the old buildings where Lucy and Helen Shires and Dan Donoghue and Red Kelly had lived, going over to Washington Park and sitting by the lagoon, or in the boathouse, walking over to the wooded island, looking at the tree where he and Lucy had sat, or at the spot, if the tree was gone, going all around to see the old sights, thinking about all the things he'd done as a kid so long long long ago, and the things he was doing now, thinking about Lucy and Helen Shires, and the girl who sat next to him at Christmas mass and who maybe would be his wife. And maybe when he was a hundred and did that, he might still be having as much as ten years to go. He wanted to live longer than any man in the whole world had ever lived. And goddamn it, he would.

He wanted to be strong and healthy and never turn into a weak-kneed, unhealthy guy. And he would. He got up, and shadow-boxed clumsily around the room. He tensed his stomach and felt it to see if his exercises and training had hardened up his guts. He couldn't tell. He still had something of an alderman. Well, that would go. And he would have a long time to live. He'd only worried unnecessarily about his heart and his stomach. He dressed, ate supper, and then left. He was going over to the Y tonight, and Red and some of the guys were coming along. He walked along, confident and happy, feeling, too, that he wouldn't be hanging around, wondering every few minutes what time it was, and what they'd do.

II

"But it's a pretty long walk, Studs," Les said.

"It'll do us good. It'll be exercise."

"I get plenty of exercise wrestling freight for John Continental."

"Come on, a little more won't hurt you. I get exercise, too. And if we go by street car, we'd have to go down to Sixty-first, and then transfer at Cottage Grove."

"It'd be quicker."

"Come on," Studs said, as they entered the park.

"Say, what'll we have to do?"

"Sign up, pay the fee, and then we can use the gym and swimming pool."

They walked across the park, saying little. Studs tried to think of himself as a prizefighter or some kind of an athlete putting himself in condition to come back. It made it appear more interesting and important that way. It was as if he was somebody in the limelight, a celebrity, and the world was interested in his success and failure. And now, suppose he was a fighter, would it be best for him to call himself Studs Lonigan, Young Lonigan, or K. O. Lonigan?

"Say, aren't Y. M. C. A.'s dopey places?"

"I guess they got all boy scouts in them, but we're going there to swim and use the gym and get ourselves in condition physically."

"Then, what do we do?"

"What the hell! Don't you like to be healthy?"

"Sure, I guess so."

"Puddles here," Studs said, skipping and leaping over a stretch of watery ground.

"I knew it would be best not to come this way."

"We're near the hills now. Then we'll be past the puddles."

Les laughed to himself.

"What's the comedy?" asked Studs.

"I was thinking what would the teameos I know at the express company think, if they knew I was going to a Y. M. C. A. . . . Jesus, them turkeys down there would ride the pants off me."

"You don't have to tell them, and if they do find out, what the hell's the difference? Tell them to go to and stay put."

"But they'll find out. Down there at that express company they find out about everything a guy does. They got the best grapevine in the world."

"There are a lot of bastards like that in this world. I'd like to see them all in hell too."

"Cigarette, Studs?"

"No, thanks."

"Jesus, you're doing this thing right."

"If I plan to do something, I don't see any reason to do it half ass," Studs said.

"I wonder why Tommy and Red and the guys didn't come along. They all promised to."

"Hell, they're mopes. And they're going to a goddamn shine cabaret, and maybe get slashed with a razor," Studs said.

"They never think of what's going to happen to them."

"They're mopes."

They crossed the hills on the far side of the park, went over the drive, along a path, and out at Fifty-fifth and Cottage.

"It's only down a few blocks and over on Fifty-second Street."

"That don't irritate me none," Les said.

They turned east on Fifty-second Street.

"Hey, Shrimp doesn't look so good, does he?"

"He's hitting the bottle every day. I don't think he's been sober since New Year's. He's wasting away to a shadow," Studs said.

"Yeah, poor Shrimp's wasting away to a shadow."

"He can drink the whole gang of us together under the table," Studs said.

"He certainly doesn't look any too good. I'll say that," Les said.

"He's ripping his guts out with rotgut," Studs said.

III

Feeling out of place at the Y entrance, they paused in momentary indecision. Studs acted casual. Les was nervous, and blushed.

"Studs, this joint looks phony to me," Les said.

"Yeah."

There was a drugged sanctimoniousness about the sappy-looking birds seated in the lobby. Studs felt that there wasn't a man or a regular guy amongst them. The desk was at the right of the rectangular lobby, and a blond young man, with a pinhead mustache, stood behind it.

"I suppose we should ask this dope," Studs said, approaching the desk.

"All I can say is that I don't like the looks of this joint," Les said.

"Sure, everyone in the joint was probably a boy scout when he was a punk. What can you expect? But we came here to use the gym and swim. We don't have to worry about all these mopes."

As they passed a lounge, a small little chap, with a wax-like mustache and stacombed hair, stopped before another guy who was reading the *American Magazine*.

"Hello, old man!" the chap with the wax-like mustache said.

"Why, George! Gee, George, I'm pleased to see you."

"I wonder what museum those eggs came from," Studs quietly said to Les.

"This one," Les answered.

The clerk directed them to the office of the Membership Secretary. As they entered the office, the vacuous-looking, pale secretary rose and said:

"Good evening, fellows!"

He heartily shook hands with them. They took seats at his direction.

"You gentlemen, I presume, are desirous of becoming members."

They nodded.

"Well, we're always pleased to have the right kind of members. And were you intending to reside here with us?"

"No."

"You're Christians, I assume?"

"Irish," said Les.

"And if I may ask, what is it that prompts you to join us?"

Studs said for the use of the gym and swimming. He told

them of the salutary effect of exercise and sports, and what fine fellows they had in the organization. They were given membership blanks to fill out, and their dough was collected. They were told they'd have to be examined by the doctor, but the doctor was not around. They went down to the lockers to undress for a swim.

"That guy's clammy," Studs said.

IV

"You know, I don't think I've ever gone swimming before at this time of the year," Les said.

"I did," Studs said.

"I always hate the first splash. Hitting the water for the first time makes me nervous."

"All you have to do is just dive in and it's over with."

"I know, but thinking about it in advance makes me nervous."

They came to the pool, and heard shouting and splashing. Inside, they paused, and looked around, seeing many naked guys. A tall fellow made a big splash as he dove from the board at the deep end of the pool. Studs said that guy didn't know how to dive. . . . They moved around to the diving board. Studs said let's go, walked to the end of the board, stood on his toes, rocked a moment, and leaped, turning over as he went down, arms first, making little splash.

"Nice one, Studs," Les yelled.

Studs came up, puffed, and took a few strokes. He about-faced and swam the crawl stroke back to the pool edge. Holding to the railing with one hand, and splashing water with the other, he told Les it was swell, to come on in. Les said he would, he was just standing there a minute. Studs let go of the railing, and pushed himself away from the pool edge. He turned on his back and floated, the pool sounds and muffling shouts sounding vague in his ears. He turned over and swam speedily to the shallow end of the pool, turned around without stopping, and returned swimming as swiftly as he could, but tiring with each stroke, so that his breath came more irregularly, and his arms seemed to grow heavy. He puffed noticeably, and his arms were leaden as he climbed up the ladder, and out of the pool.

"Go ahead. Make the leap, and it's swell."

"I will. I was just watching a minute."

"That almost pooped me. I got to get better wind than I got," Studs said.

He patted the fat around his belly.

"This has to come off."

"There isn't much there."

"It's more than there should be."

A big splash was made, and water was thrown up against them.

"Why don't that bastard learn how before he starts diving. He's like Moses parting the waters," Studs said.

"You're a good swimmer," Les said.

"I used to swim a lot as a kid."

"So did I, but you're better than I am," Les said.

"Well, here goes again. Coming?"

"All right."

Studs ran off the board, and let go, again doing a neat dive. Les followed, diving more awkwardly, splashing heavily.

"Nice," Les yelled, coming up, and swimming alongside of Studs.

"Let's race," Studs said.

"You can beat me."

"Oh, come on, anyway."

They raced, Studs let Les gain, then, with full confidence, he took even powerful strokes to draw alongside, and then ahead of, him. They stood up in the shallow water.

"I'm glad I came."

"It's good," Studs said, shaking his head.

"Race back?" he added.

"What's the use. You beat me."

Studs turned, jogged out to the deeper water as he moved, done, swam under water, and came up near the middle of the pool. He turned and saw Les coming towards him. He swam to the deeper edge, followed by Les, and climbed up the ladder. He took another dive, went under water for about six feet, came up and moved swiftly, exulting in a feeling of complete bodily freedom. It was swell. The water was just right, lukewarm, and he took rhythmic strokes, gaining a confidence in his physical powers, feeling removed from the world, clean. It was like losing all the gripes that had been piling up within him. He felt, too, that he still had a good body. After a few months of this, and then the summer, he'd be hard as nails. And whores and whore houses, and booze, all that were like sins of the past. He swam until he was tired and gasping, with his arms again heavy and laden, and his back weary as if it were crushed down with weights. He was spent. He climbed out of the pool, thinking how it had been fun spending himself. He lay down wet on the slippery tile, covering his eyes with his arms.

"Gee, this is swell," Les said, lying down beside him.

"Uh huh," Studs said.

Guys talked, dove, swam, ran around the tile flooring. It all seemed far away.

"Yes, hell, it's much better swimming this way than with suits."

Studs looked up, as if he were just awakening. He and Les sat up.

"Come on, let's take another dip before we call it quits."

They dove in, swam the length of the pool, and then went down to the lockers to dress and go out.

"I had a swell time," Les said.

"Yeah, and it's good for you."

"The guys don't know what they missed," Les said.

"They're all mopes."

XVI

"Say, Mister, could you help me to get a bit to eat?" Davey Cohen begged, touching the sleeve of a well-dressed bucolic-looking fellow in front of the Circle Monument in Indianapolis.

Davey watched the fellow move away. Hadn't even batted an eyelid. He was so goddamn hungry that he couldn't get any hungrier. And it was the cheapest damn town he'd ever struck. He sat down on the steps of the Monument, and reflected that the old burg was only about a hundred miles away. He could grab a freight, and tomorrow he'd be in Chicago. He hadn't been back home since 1916. It would be swell seeing the old bunch. Yes, they were a damn fine bunch of guys, Paulie Haggerty, Kenny, Red, Tommy Doyle, Studs, all of them. He'd go back and just pop around Charlie Bathcellar's poolroom, if it was still there. He guessed it was a fixture in the neighborhood and would be there. They'd be glad to see him, and he'd be glad to see them, and they'd talk about old times, and about what had happened to him, and to them, since he'd gone on the bum. He ought to go back and maybe get a job. If he did that, and watched himself, his health would pick up. Hell, he was digging his own grave, living like this. And Vinc Curley. He wondered if Vinc was as goofy as ever. But he was too hungry to think of that. He went around and around the Circle Monument, mooching until he finally got two bits. He walked off towards a cheap restaurant singing:

"Gee, but I'd give the world to see
    that old gang of mine,
I can't forget that old quartette,
    that sang 'Sweet Adeline'
Goodbye forever, old fellows and pals . . ."

CHAPTER SIXTEEN

I

"Say, Studs, if I knew you were coming around tonight, I'd have had the boys hire a band to meet you. Where you been keeping yourself?" asked Red Kelly.

"Oh, I've just been catching up on my sleep."

"So I heard; the boys were saying that you're living hygienically."

"You must be another one of these guys who's been working cross-word puzzles."

"Say, listen, Studs, how about coming along with me tonight to that meeting at St. Patrick's?"

"What's doing?"

"Don't you remember, Gilly announced it at mass last Sunday."

"Oh, yeah, the club they're going to have for young people."

"I was thinking I might as well go there."

"That'll be all blah. Every damn time they've tried that stunt in this parish, it's flopped."

"I just thought I'd see what was going to happen."

"All the church ushers, Larkin, McAuliffe, Al Borax, and maybe even Jim Clayburn will run it and think up some committees to put themselves on. Then they'll pass the plate. And all the punks will be up there, smelling after young broads. You can have that crap for yourself."

"But look here, Studs; I was thinking that if a couple of guys like us went there, we might be able to make something out of it besides a dancing school for the drug store cowboys, or a hall where those goddamn church ushers could try and pretend that they're Father Gilhooley," Red said.

"Say, Red, are you planning to go into politics?"

"Well, if I ever do, an outfit like this wouldn't hurt me none," said Red.

Studs nodded his head, smiling knowingly.

"Come on, Studs."

Up there, he might see that girl, and he was still Studs Lonigan, and all the punks and everybody would treat him with respect. They always did. They knew they had to. Let them try kidding him! O'Neill had the other day, and he'd shut up when he'd been told, because if he hadn't, he knew what was coming to him. And going back around St. Patrick's made him think of the old days when, goddamn it, he'd had such a swell time.

"All right," Studs said, feigning disinterest.

"I really think we ought to go. This time they're organizing the thing to raise money for the new church. After all these years and all this talk, Gilly's really going to build it. And there's no reason why St. Patrick's shouldn't have as fine a church as any in the city. This is a good neighborhood and a good church. There's plenty of good Catholics, Irish, in it, people like your old man and mine, and we ought to have a church. There's enough dough in the parish, too, and Gilly's the boy to raise it. But it's a worthy venture, and we ought to try and do our share."

"Red, you're getting the gift of gab. If I'm not careful, you'll probably be selling me real estate out in the middle of Lake Michigan," Studs said, starting with Red towards St. Patrick's.

He could feel it in his bones that tonight he was really going to meet her. And there were things about him that nobody knew, and that he'd once thought Lucy would notice, but hadn't, and she would. Well, Lucy could go plumb to—and then stick her head in the bowl. Tonight was going to be his night in a big way. He'd get her, and maybe marry her. Why not? He tried to remember what she looked like. She was blond. She was slender but with enough meat on her. Her face, eyes. . . . He couldn't remember.

"St. Patrick's is a coming parish, Studs. And the new church is going to make it. It's going to stop all this wild talk about the jiggs moving around here and running the neighborhood. Gilly is a smart man, and what he said last Sunday in church is the goods. Michigan Avenue is going to be made a boulevard. Property values around here will skyrocket. The new church will clinch the matter. You watch, it'll make people stay here, and the new ones of the right kind with money will move in and buy property. Gilly knows his stuff."

"That's what my old man thinks. He won't sell the building because he thinks it'll be worth more in a few years."

"He's got a head on his shoulders, too."

"Oh, yeah."

"And a young guy from a good family in this neighborhood, now he's got a good chance here in politics. You know,

we all laugh at Jim Doyle and kid him about being assistant
precinct captain. But he's got the dope. He's got a good paying
political job now on city construction work, and he's going
to get along. You see, Studs, we're younger than Jim, and we
still got some wild oats to sow, but sometime we'll have to
settle down. That's why I was saying a young fellow in this
neighborhood can get along in politics."

Studs kind of wished that he'd finished school and studied
law. He could see himself as alderman of the ward some day,
maybe even Mayor Lonigan. They walked a stretch without
talking.

"Say, Weary Reilley damn near killed a guy in a scrap
around Sixty-third and University the other night. You know,
that bastard is riding for a fall. He's got into the habit of thinking he's tough, and he has to act tough to keep up his rep,
and well, you know what happens to such guys. There's always
somebody just a little bit tougher."

"He's got plenty coming to him."

"I never was afraid of him as a kid. Neither were you, Studs.
You cleaned him, I remember."

Studs nodded with pleasure. They stopped for a Coca-Cola
near the church, and then went to the meeting in the basement
auditorium of the parish. Upon entering, Red commented that
there was a pretty good crowd. Studs shook his head in agreement and remarked that every drug store cowboy in the neighborhood was present. He and Red circulated from group to
group, acting superior, feeling that they deserved being noticed
the way the punks noticed them. Without realizing the drift
of his thoughts, Studs found himself remembering how they
all used to come down to the same place when he was a kid,
for singing practice for church, and for elocution lessons.
A jane named Miss Cobb had been their elocution teacher.
They'd all have to recite, and reciting, they'd have to stand
up straight, heels together, feet out, the right foot straight,
the left foot, half sidewise, a goofy position, and then recite
things like:

> *Where are you going, young fellow, my lad,*
> *On this glorious morn of May?*
> *I'm going to join the colors, Dad,*
> *They're needing men, they say.*

It was goofy, and he'd always hated the singing too, but
maybe because his own voice wasn't so hot. Preparing to
sing at five o'clock mass on Christmas, they'd practice a
half hour right after the afternoon bell rang at one o'clock.
Christ, he used to hate it. He sang to himself:

Holy God, we praise Thy name!
Lord of all, we bow before Thee!
All on earth Thy sceptre claim,
All in Heaven above adore Thee!

For a moment, he felt as if he were a kid again, and then the song blew out of his mind, and he felt just lonesome and sad in a vague way without anything clear in his mind, and he hoped some of the guys from his class would be there. He realized that Phil Rolfe was talking to him.

"Say, Jew, this ain't a fish peddlers' convention," Studs said.

"I can come here, can't I? I just met Father Doneggan. He said he was glad to have me," Phil said.

"Well, don't sell him any fish," Studs said.

"Jesus, we better get the doors locked all right," said Red.

"Maybe they got rat traps in back of the stage," Studs said, pointing to the stage up in front, the same stage on which he had received his graduation diploma. Young Rocky called Phil to tell him something.

Big Nodalsky, who had turned into a tall, dark, sheiky guy, with greased hair parted in the middle and sideburns, greeted Studs.

"You're looking good. You haven't hardly changed a bit, Studs."

"What are you doing?"

"Managing a dancing school and taxi dance hall down town, and giving lessons. But I expect to get lined up for a dancing act with Orpheum. But say, ever see any of the old boys?" Big Nodalsky asked.

"Once in a while. Monk McCarthy's brother, Red, is studying for the priesthood, and Monk has a political job and doesn't come around mooching any more."

"Muggsy was always funny. He was smart but he'd never do anything, and he was always getting in trouble. But say, remember Cudahy? He's got a job with Sloan's Deerfield, the mail-order house."

"Yeah, and I see Bill Donoghue once in a while," Studs said.

"How is Bill? What's he doing?"

"He's got a job repairing adding machines."

"Good old Bill, and what about his brother, Dan?"

"Dan runs a movie in his uncle's chain up in Madison, Wisconsin. He gets into town now and then, Bill says, but I hardly ever see him."

"And Tubby?" asked Nodalsky.

"Haven't seen Tubby in a couple of years. The last I heard

of him, he was a glazier's apprentice."

"Jesus, those were the days, weren't they, Studs?"

"Yeah, they were. You were in the same room with our class, weren't you?"

"I was in seventh grade when you were in eighth, but, say, I wonder what happened to Battling Bertha?" asked Nodalsky.

"I think she died."

"She was hard-boiled all right; the year I was in eighth grade, I remember one day she got tough with Johnny O'Brien. He was a grade behind me. Well, he hauled off on her. Yeah, he socked her."

"I think I remember hearing something about that when it happened."

"There'll never again be days like those."

"Nope," said Studs.

Studs' eyes roved. Plenty of girls, most of them young flappers, Loretta's age. Only a couple of years ago they were kids. Now they were all painted up, and Christ, he'd bet a lot of them knew more than you imagine.

"Say, Studs, remember the time, the year after you graduated, when you, Weary Reilley and some of the other lads from your class came around in the afternoon and ran through the hall like a tornado. It was funny; and Goofy Cudahy yelled out, 'Jesus, the Germans are here!' It was funny. But Bertha gave him the clouts," Nodalsky said, both of them laughing.

Austin came up with a glad hand. Red followed, and asked when the meeting was going to start. He answered right away. He said he was glad to see Red and Studs up to the meeting, because they wanted to make a go of this club, and they needed fellows like Studs and Red. Studs was pleased to have Austin say this, but then, he reflected, what the hell! Austin was still a goddamn boy scout. Austin shot off to greet Dorothy Gorman.

Studs, after considerable hesitation, walked over to Father Doneggan and said hello.

"Well, how are things, Studs?" Father Doneggan asked.

"Oh, pretty good, Father."

"Glad to hear it. And how are Dad and Mother?"

"They're fine."

"Say, Studs, it's good of you to come up tonight! I meant to tell your brother to ask you, but didn't get around to it. I want, you know, to get a few of you older fellows with good heads in this organization to give it stability. We've got to weld a lively club together and still have it sensible, and we'll need fellows like you, Studs," Father Doneggan said.

Studs smiled. Nice to have Father Doneggan say that.

But he didn't know what a wild bird Studs Lonigan had been. Well, no, he was right, fellows like him and Red could be useful, if the boy scouts and church ushers or the punks just didn't go ahead and ruin it.

Big Larkin called Father Doneggan, and Studs watched him shoot nervously away. Father Doneggan was a regular guy. Studs would even bet that he'd have a drink with a fellow.

II

Larkin called the meeting to order. The males sat on one side of the hall, separated from the females by an aisle. Larkin leaned o the table, and jutted his mushy, red, almost womanish face forwards.

"Now, fellows . . . and . . . ah . . . ladies," he commenced.

There were a few titters and smiles. Vinc Curley let out an unexpected horse laugh. Everybody looked pityingly at him.

"We are . . . ah . . . here to form a St. Patrick's Young People's Society for various . . . ah . . . reasons. First and foremost, we want to . . . ah . . . get behind Father Gilhooley in his effort to raise funds for getting this parish . . . ah . . . a church, a beautiful church that will be second to none in the city and that . . . ah . . . none of us need be ashamed of. And then again, we want to . . . ah . . . establish a permanent organization. But . . . ah . . . before we do that, discuss our plans and procedures . . . ah . . . we'll hear a few words from Father Doneggan."

He smiled respectfully at Father Doneggan who rose, and, with swishing cassock, walked forwards. There were a few perfunctory and self-conscious claps.

"I am here to speak for Father Gilhooley, and to deliver to you his message, expressing his fondest hopes that this organization of the young people of St. Patrick's parish will be a most gratifying success, as I know, and as he knows, that it will. He asks me to state, in his name, that he promises to cooperate with you in every way that is feasible. Now, you people all know that for years it has been the fondest dream of your pastor to give the people of this parish a church of which it can be justifiably proud. When he came to this parish in the very first year of this century, there was not even a church, and he celebrated his first mass in a store building down the street that had been kindly donated to the purposes of God by a generous parishioner. He has built this present church building, housing the church, school, and the auditorium in which we are now gathered; and he has also built the sisters' home and the priests' house. All of these buildings are now free of debt, thanks to his diligence, energy, and intelligent handling of church moneys. Now, he is prepared to open the drive for funds which will enable him to realize his dream, the dream of every good parishioner of St. Patrick's. If all the parishioners support him according to their means and ability, as I am confident they will, he will continue with his present plans, and in the space of a few short years, St. Patrick's new church, bigger than the present, one of the most beautiful houses of worship in this city, will be not merely a plan or a dream, but a living actuality. And one of the principal reasons that your pastor sponsors the formation of this proposed young people's society is that he solicits your aid in the realization of these plans."

Studs saw her, and Father Doneggan's words became a distant hum of distraction. She sat quietly, confidence in her manner, keen, with blond bobbed hair. He could see that her face was thin, proud. She looked like she'd be a hard dame to make. He didn't want just that. She would be hard to win. But there was a broad made for every guy, and she was the pattern cut out for him. He looked at her, unobtrusively, trying not to give himself away, as she sat, still, straight, wearing a green and red plaited flannel dress. He was hot for her, hotter than he'd been when he knelt beside her. He wanted the meeting to be over, so he could have her notice him, notice how people spoke to him. Hoped Fran knew her and would be talking to her, and he could just go up to Fran as if to ask her some question.

He looked back at Father Doneggan, heard him say that the organization they were forming would be a chance, also, to cement old friendships, and establish new ones, and to provide for a decent, satisfactory social life for the young people, with clean dancing and fun.

Father Doneggan was applauded at the conclusion of his talk. His face touched with redness, he sat down. Larkin arose and stood behind the table, leaning clumsily on it with closed fists.

"Now the first thing that concerns us is to get organized. I think we all agree to that," he said dully, speaking first quickly and then pausing to hem out "ahs" as if he were struggling to catch his breath.

"And then the first task in getting organized is to elect a permanent chairman who will conduct meetings until we have our constitution with duly elected officers under it."

Her silk-stockinged legs were crossed, showing up to the knees. She seemed bored. He acted bored, but he wished that some sort of a debate would start so he could say something and make her see he was different from Larkin and the church ushers.

"Mr. Chairman, I have one suggestion and one motion to present to the house. First, I would suggest that a temporary secretary be appointed to keep the minutes of this meeting," Red Kelly said, arising.

"That's an excellent suggestion, Mr. Kelly," Larkin replied.

"And I would suggest in order to save time that the chairman we elect appoint this secretary. Later on, when we have a constitution, we will elect one. Now I move that nominations for a permanent chairman be placed before the house."

"I second Mr. Kelly's motion," said Austin McAuliffe.

Larkin was nominated and elected chairman, and he appointed McAuliffe as temporary secretary. A pencil and several sheets of paper were procured, and Austin took a chair at the table beside Larkin.

"Now, the next thing that we need is a constitution," Larkin said, without omitting the "ahs."

"Mr. Chairman, I think that it would be wise before we made any definite move about the constitution to have a little discussion so that we could be clear in the purposes and aims we wish to embody in our constitution."

"Well, I think that we all have that in mind and know more or less what we want, but if anyone wants to say anything about it, he can have the floor."

"You got a line like a Philadelphia lawyer," Studs said to Red in amazement and admiration as Red sat down.

Adele Rogers, who had turned into a flapper, arose, swung her shoulders from the weight of a raccoon coat and said she thought they ought to run a dance. Larkin said of course they would, but that would be worked out after they got the organization settled. Dick Buckford proposed a baseball team, and that likewise was tabled.

Austin McAuliffe, smiling and polite, asked for the floor, and said that if he may, he would like to say a few things.

"We know, in general, what we want in a constitution. There must be provision for the way to conduct meetings, elect officers, the payment of dues, the minimum number of meetings each month, the organization and conduct of social affairs and such things."

"How much will we have to pay?" Vinc Curley interrupted.

Austin concluded his suggestion by proposing that there be a committee appointed to draft a constitution, and a time limit be set upon them so that they could get going. Red asked that the floor be left open for a brief period to solicit sug-

gestions on the constitution before the chairman appointed
a committee. Studs saw through Kelly, realizing that Red just
wanted to shoot his mouth off. There was a debate on whether
dues should be twenty-five or fifty cents a month. Studs tried
to think of something to say so he could pitch right in and
impress her. His mind empty of ideas, he watched her from
the corner of his eye. He hoped he would be put on the committee. Finally, the committee was appointed. Red was on
it, but not he. He was sorry, and yet glad, because he didn't
want to be bothering with a lot of crap, and having to meet
Larkin and McAuliffe and draw up a damn constitution. But
an appointment might have made her realize who Studs Lonigan was.

III

"Let's go!" Studs said to Red, while chairs were being folded
up and piled along the walls, amidst confusion and a preten-
tiously affected masculine show of energy. Studs wanted to
hang around, but he was losing his nerve.

"Hell, Studs, there's no hurry. And there's a lot of nice girls
here. We might as well dance."

Martha Curley played *Frivolous Sal* on the out-of-tune piano.
Studs watched the dancers spread over the large floor. He
saw her standing alone. He took a step to go over and ask
her to dance. He decided he wouldn't be too much in a hurry.
Making them wait was a good technique. He was interested
only in her, dancing with her, so he acted as if he was interested in everything. He moved from spot to spot and
watched Larkin waltz with Dorothy Gorman. Larkin kept almost a yard between them and acted as if he were being reckless. And Dorothy had always been plain, almost homely.
Her face looked muddy. He guessed that because of her old
man she had forgotten how to laugh, and only smiled in a
half-interested way. He wondered if Larkin was too thick to
realize that any regular guy would be laughing at him. He
saw Phil Rolfe and Loretta going as if they were dancing
slow-motion. The kike could dance, though, and he guessed
that was what pleased young kids like Loretta. He didn't like
her dancing with the Jew, felt like telling her. But after all
it wasn't his business. He minded his business, and felt it
was the place of everybody else in the family to mind theirs
about him. Austin came by with Lillian Stone, taking short,
choppy, graceless steps, keeping over a foot away from her.
All church ushers danced alike; if a broad just danced close
to them, they'd die of stage fright. Danny O'Neill whirled
past him with one of the wild Dolan girls. Both of them were

good dancers; it was nice to watch them. But Christ, any guy could waste his time learning how to dance.

She was still standing alone. Funnyface Duffy approached her. He got turned down. Hell, she wasn't a wet nurse to punks. He felt as if her refusal of the goof established a bond between them. He wanted this dance to end, because he knew that he'd dance the next one with her. Fran Reilley was a hot girl. Aggravating. Just like his own sister. Whatever you said about them, the two of them could get about anybody they wanted and wind him around their fingers like a piece of old string. And Loretta was going to be the same way. He felt proud that he had two such good-looking sisters. And they could take care of themselves too. He saw Weary's kid sister, Jane, almost laying against that loudmouthed Young Rocky, who turned frequently, and placed his thigh between her legs with each turn.

After the dance Red said:

"It's hell dancing with a broad as tantalizing as Fran Reilley. She knows she's got everything and it just teases your pants off. She eggs you into thinking you can get away with murder, and then pulls herself away and goes right on talking as if she didn't even think of what she was doing. Then she starts it all over again. Christ, Studs, she drives you into utter misery."

"Yep, Red, she's luscious."

"The guy who gets her is getting his jack's worth. Only nobody will do it without the ring. She knows how to play her game," Red said, half in tribute.

"Hello, fellows," Larkin said, offering a limp, sweaty hand that made Studs feel as if he was grasping a chunk of contaminated meat. He greeted Larkin with condescension.

"Gee, I'm glad you came, because we all want to get behind Father Gilhooley in the drive to raise funds for the new church."

Studs and Red gave each other the wink.

"Studs, how's it going?"

"Nothing to complain about," Studs replied disinterestedly.

"Well, I hope that now we'll be seeing a lot of you, and Kelly, too."

"That goddamn fat slob," Studs sneered, as Larkin walked away.

Another dance started. Studs hesitated about asking her. Fran came up to him and demanded that he dance with her. He saw that she was with a sappy-looking guy he didn't know. The bird was taller than he, but he'd take him on. He saw himself meeting the guy out on the street, asking him, Are you tough? and letting him have something he wouldn't forget

THE YOUNG MANHOOD

very easy. He danced a bit woodenly, and Fran made it worse, because she kept leading him. She made a dirty crack about Fran Reilley. Studs guessed good-looking broads were that way about other broads. After the dance, she told him he wouldn't be a bad dancer at all, if he got more practice. She went off to join Fran Reilley and some other girls. He looked around until he saw the girl walking towards the other wall with the sappy-looking egg. He felt she'd notice him if he kept looking at her, and he might seem like a goof. He watched Austin join the group around his sister, Fran. Austin talked. He heard them laugh. What the hell could they see to laugh at in anything Austin said?

"Hello, Studs! Say, I'm glad to see you, just like old times," Johnny O'Brien said, smiling, shooting his arm up as if a button had been pressed, and giving Studs the collegiate handshake. Studs remembered that Johnny had been a fat, husky kid. Now he was thin, pale, a bit lifeless. Johnny asked him what he was doing. Studs told him.

"I'm over at the U. Belong to Kappa Psi now. Come on over some time, and I'll introduce you to the boys. Fine bunch of brothers, they are."

"Say, I hear they're anti-Catholic at the University. First thing you know, you'll be losing your religion," Studs said, kidding to make talk; he saw that the sappy-looking guy was walking away.

"Well, some of the professors are. You know, they believe in evolution and teach it in their classes, and say things against the church, but, of course, that doesn't affect me. And the fellows in my frat, say, Studs, they're all swell fellows. I'd like to have you meet them."

"You're all dressed up like Joe College," Studs said, letting his glance wander. She was dancing with Larkin, smiling at something the mush-face said. Somebody ought to take a picture of the guy. Johnny continued speaking.

"Now, you take this suit. As I said, it's new, first time I wore it. Had it made to order at Jerrems, seventy-five bucks. That's the way I believe in getting clothes, if you want to be really well-dressed. Pay for them and get clothes that fit properly and make you look distinguished. You can always tell what kind of a guy a fellow is, and how he rates, from the clothes he wears. A lot of guys you know have enough suits to change every day in the week, and they pay nothing for them. You can't take them out in the rain. Not me, I'd rather have a few suits, but good ones like this one I'm wearing."

Johnny excused himself and shambled over to Big Nodalsky. Studs watched him give the college handshake, and thought

what a heel O'Brien had turned into. He wondered if Lucy
would hear about the society here, and come out to a meeting.
He could see the other girl, himself with her, dancing, everybody
taking it for granted that he and she were going together,
and Lucy seeing it. Himself treating Lucy with cold formality.
He'd dance with her once or twice, and talk about general
things. That would be all. See how she'd like it. He wondered
what her name was. He could find out from Larkin. He knew
he wouldn't ask that mush-face. She was dancing with Austin,
and they seemed to be getting along all right. An old, not-
belonging feeling came upon him. He felt like going. He felt
that it was just nerve, expecting to make the grade with her.
Let her go. If Austin and Larkin were her speed, well, she
wasn't his kind. He'd go. He watched them dance. He accidentally caught the eye of Martha Curley and she smiled. He
turned towards the piano and saw that Dorothy Gorman was
playing.

"Don't you dance?" asked Phil.

"Why?" Studs asked, snottily.

"I just noticed that you hadn't been dancing. I wondered
because I heard you were a pretty good dancer."

Studs guessed it must have been Loretta. They must have
talked about him. He wondered what Loretta really thought
of him. He didn't really know 'her. He looked at her on the
floor, young, pretty, lively. She had grown that way, into a
pretty girl, without his even realizing it, as if one day she was
just a kid, and then the next, she was the kind of girl he saw
dancing.

"I suppose you're selling dancing shoes," Studs told Phil.

"Studs, I'll bet the hebe is the kind that takes St. Patrick's
day off," Red said, joining Studs.

"And Jewish Easter too," Studs added.

Phil went off to dance. Studs saw that she was again alone.
He ambled slowly towards her, hoping no one would spot him,
because he became suddenly as shy and speechless as a boy.
With a forced effort of courage, he asked her if she'd like to
dance. She thanked him but said that she was very tired. He
walked away, sore. He tried to whistle. He felt he had to do
something. He motioned to Martha Curley. She came towards
him. They danced. Martha had used to be a nice girl, and full
of life. She seemed tired and faded, and she was only about
a year older than he. Girls had to grab their husbands off quick,
he guessed. Martha said well, well, and they asked how each
other were. She said she hadn't seen Studs in quite a long time.
Studs said he hadn't seen much of her either. She guessed they
must attend different masses on Sunday. He asked her if

she was working. She said no, she was just a home girl. He danced past the girl; she was dancing with Young Rocky. He couldn't miss seeing how close their bodies were pressed against one another.

After the dance, he told Red he was going. Red was unable to persuade him to stick around. Walking along Indiana Avenue, he thought that if he had danced with her, she might have remembered him, remembered that she'd smiled at him at mass. If maybe she'd gotten a good look at him, she'd have remembered. But he never could have told her all that he'd thought of her since then. But maybe, maybe, if he had danced with her and things had gone right, maybe he might have, at that. He would maybe have said something like:

I never thought I'd find you here!

No, well, you never know what you can expect, she might have answered.

You're more than I could hope to expect at a place like this, he might have added.

They would have talked, told their names, laughed at jokes he would have been able to think up, and he would have walked home with her. At her door, he would have said, how about a show tomorrow night, and tomorrow he'd be taking her to a show. And they would, yes, go together. What the hell did he care if the gang would try and kid him. He wasn't just a hood, and just going to turn into another Barney Keefe, or Mickey Flannagan.

It was all a goddamn pipe-dream. He was just filling himself full of the stuff, only if the thing had turned out different! He'd missed his chance. He thought of her in her green and red dress, and her cold aloof face and expression. Haughty jane. And he wanted her. He thought of going with her until finally she'd say yes and no one would be home, and he'd kiss her, and they'd. . . . All a goddamn pipe-dream!

"Jesus Christ, here comes the Fifty-eighth Street Alky Squad," he said with a laugh as he met Slug, Mickey, Barney, Tommy Doyle, Les, and Shrimp at the corner of Fifty-eighth and Indiana.

"We need another recruit," Slug said.

Studs chipped in with them. They bought paregoric in the drug store and drank it. They formed a drugged and stupefied line against the side of the drug store building. Studs was so helpless that Red Kelly had to take him home.

XVII

Martin Husk Lonigan poked Crabby Konetchy's books out of his arms.

"Pick 'em up!" Crabby commanded.

"What? Huh! I don't know what you're talking about."

"Well, you will know, if you don't pick up the books you knocked out of my arm."

"What's he sayin'?" Husk Lonigan said to his pal, Pete McFarland.

"What you say, Koney?" kidded McFarland.

"I said pick 'em up!"

"He said to pick something up," Pete said.

Husk Lonigan looked up and down the street.

"There ain't no girls around to pick up."

Pete laughed.

"Gonna pick 'em up?"

"Who was your servant last year?" asked Husk Lonigan.

"You knocked 'em out of my arm."

"What?"

"You did."

"You're a liar," Husk Lonigan said, sneering and looking quite like his brother Studs.

"Who's a liar?"

"You, if you said I knocked your books down."

"Aw, smack him, Husk," said Pete McFarland.

"Try it!"

"Oh, you want to fight?" said Husk, again sneering.

Crabby punched Husk's nose. They fought, and Crabby gave Husk a bloody nose and a shiner. Husk picked up the books.

CHAPTER SEVENTEEN

I

"I'll get you a girl if you want me to," Fran said, taking the three bucks from Studs for the ticket he was buying to her sorority's dance.

"I'll get a girl."

"All right. Only if you want me to, I'll arrange a nice date for you," she said, sitting cross-legged on the piano bench.

"Yeah. I suppose with some fishface."

"Why, William Lonigan!" she exclaimed, and he smiled so she wouldn't get sore.

345

"You'll have a good time. And if you don't think you can dance well enough, you can practice with me."

"No, thanks."

He left and went over towards the poolroom.

Christ, now he'd let himself in for it and where would he get a girl. Lucy? Hell with her. The girl from the parish. How could he? He didn't want her. Let the punks have her. If she wanted punks and guys like Larkin, let them have the bitch. To hell with her! To hell with them all! He didn't have to go because he gave Fran the three bucks for a ticket. He could get out of it by just not going.

But he could see himself at the dance, togged out in new raiment, knocking them all dead, with a broad as keen as that blond. Everybody would wonder who he was, and everybody who knew him would be cockeyed with surprise, realizing that they had been totally wrong when they thought that Studs Lonigan was just one of the hoods in the Fifty-eighth Street Alky Squad. He could see himself at the dance, getting blind and tough, asking all the goddamn boy scouts and sweet boys in the place if they thought they were tough, and then laying one on them. Walking up to some bastard who had a Joe College handshake, messing the dope's manly vaseline locks, twisting his nose, and if he batted wise, giving him the works. Himself cleaning out the goddamn dance, with the blond seeing it. Lucy seeing it, and the blond and Lucy walking up to him, protesting.

And he would look at both of them with his lips curling into a sneer, and say:

"That for you, sister!"

Fran would be sore, and go up, Jesus, like a balloon. But it would be funny. He saw Phil coming along, singing.

> *Oh, I loved her in the morning,*
> *And I loved her at night,*
> *But last night on the back porch,*
> *I loved her best of all.*

"Where the hell you singing?"

"Sunday school."

"You look it."

"No kiddin', Studs, is Fritzie ready yet?"

"I don't know. She was dolling up. Why, you going out with her?"

"I'm taking her to the Tivoli."

"Oh!" said Studs.

"Fritzie is a fine girl. She's the nicest girl in the neighborhood. And don't think I don't appreciate it."

"Should I pay you for that?" Studs asked.

"I'm serious. I mean it, Studs."

"She must be stewed going out with you. You must have sold her the whole line."

"Studs, I'm serious in saying I respect her, and I'd fight anybody who doesn't."

"Who the hell could you fight?" Studs asked, bursting into laughter.

"Say, Studs, what you got against me?" asked Phillip.

"No kiddin', aren't you going to sing in some Sunday school?"

"Honest, Studs, I want to be friends with you."

"Sure, shake!" said Studs, a veiled note of sarcasm in his voice. They shook.

"Well, I better hurry. I don't want to be late."

"So long, Dopey Dan," Studs called.

Loretta could find better pickings than that kike. Well . . . he shrugged his shoulders.

He supposed Phil would be taking her to the dance. He didn't want to go to the goddamn thing. But he could see himself there, and surprising the whole damn bunch of them. Hell, he could do anything they could do.

He wondered how Lucy had turned out, and was she pretty and keen. She was a hell of a lot nicer than that blond. Christ, maybe that blond was only a bitch after all. Maybe she put out even to the punks. Come to think of it, she looked a little hard-boiled. The kind of a broad who knew a hell of a lot. She could probably be plenty hot all right. He thought of how funny it might be, say, in a couple of years, if he and the boys all went to a can house, and who should he see and pick, but her, the blond.

Lucy. He repeated the name, Lucy Scanlan. Lucy Lonigan. Mrs. Lucy Lonigan. Mrs. William Lonigan. He ought to call her up and see her, take her to the dance. He would telephone and act as if he thought, hell, he might as well see her again for old time's sake, and if she wanted to, why they'd go to Fran's sorority dance. Make it just natural.

He'd take her in a cab, and they'd walk through the hotel lobby, he in a new suit, she dressed up like the nuts, and people would spot him, and think there's a guy who's got a hot woman, and the punks with their seventeen- and eighteen-year-old broads, they'd all look at the woman Studs Lonigan rated. And he'd maybe see Dan Donoghue. Hadn't seen Dan since Hector was a pup. And then let the guys around the poolroom give him the horse laugh for going to a swell dance. Slug would look queerly at him, and feel his head, wondering if it ought to be examined. He'd say they better get Studs a bottle and bring him to see a new whore to change his luck. Let them. He liked them, but they would never be anything but hoods. They were all right, but he was cut out for better stuff than being a hood. Damn tootin' he was.

He bought a slug from the cashier in the chain drug store at Prairie and walked back to the telephone booths. He found her number in the directory. He dallied, turning the directory pages to figure out what he'd say. He felt as if everyone in the store were watching him, and knew what was going on in his mind.

He'd sure let himself in for something. He took a booth and was relieved when he got the busy signal and his slug came back.

"Wasn't she home?" asked the pretty cashier, when he set his slug down.

She handed him a nickel and smiled.

"Better luck next time."

He felt a sudden pride, because it was as if he did have a girl all his own, his. It gave him a feeling he'd never had before. She thought he had his girl, a girl who cared only for him, turned down other guys, waited for him to telephone her, went out only with him, his girl. Lucy would be his too. She'd always liked him. She still must. She knew what he really was, and she'd told him she did, and Helen Shires had said, after they'd quit speaking long ago, that Lucy still did care. He laughed at himself, defensively. Studs Lonigan of the Fifty-eighth Street Alky Squad, talking like that.

He joined Slug and the boys in the poolroom.

"We was just gettin' some Jamaica ginger," Slug said.

"Count me out."

"Say, after that night las' week, I thought you was still the same old Studs," Slug said.

"Yeah, listen, that goddamn paregoric made me sick and jumpy for three days."

"You just got to get used to it."

"Say, Studs, I'll bet some flossie's got you," kidded Tommy Doyle.

"No, I just got to work tomorrow."

"I admire Studs. He's got more will power than I got," Les said.

"You singin' the blues again?" asked Slug.

"Well, he has. Jesus, there's nothin' in drinkin' all the time," Les said.

"Les, hire a hall," Shrimp Haggerty said wearily.

"We'll have to be shippin' you over to that Bug Club in Washington Park," Slug said.

Studs was tempted to get drunk, but finally determined that he wouldn't succumb to temptation again. Not after that paregoric hangover he'd had.

"Come on, let's take in a movie," he suggested.

"Hell, I saw three this week. Come on, we'll get Jamaica ginger and we'll be a movie," said Slug.

"You'll have to count me out, boys," said Studs.

"Desertin' us?" said Doyle.

"I don't feel like it tonight."

They gave Studs up and left.

He kind of wished that he'd gone along. Stan Simonsky came in, and they played rotation pool. Studs won. He and Stan went to a movie. He was determined he'd call up Lucy, too, tomorrow, and take her.

He went home around twelve, feeling confident.

He was going to show the boys something! He counted the days until the dance.

"Hello, Bill."

"Hello, Dad."

"Say, I hear you're going to your sister's dance. I'll bet you cut a swath there. Now when I was your age, I never missed any of the big shindigs. That's why your mother fell for me. I was a dandy, even if I do admit it."

"Maybe I won't go. I thought I'd buy the ticket to help her along."

"You don't want to be a stick-in-the-mud. And there you might meet some fellows who can be valuable to you. You know, meeting the right kind of friends, useful ones, is what counts in this world. And the fellows who will be there, now they're the kind that will count later on. They'll be having their homes, their businesses, their buildings. You'll know them and when they'll want a decorating job, right away they'll think, I'll let Bill Lonigan do this for me."

Studs picked up a newspaper and casually glanced at it without knowing what he read.

"I hope you'll be taking that Lucy Scanlan girl. I remember her. She was a fine girl, a fine decent girl, just like your own sisters."

Studs left the room. The old man looked hurt.

II

Studs had a feeling of uncertainty as he got off the elevated, and walked towards Louisa Nolan's, a dancing school over a store near Sixty-third Street. He resigned himself. Only twenty days to the dance, and if he did a little dancing before then, he'd make a better impression on Lucy and everybody. And the punks always seemed to get something here; he could too, and broads were always broads. He spied a group of fellows before the place, and as he passed them to go through the wide-doored entry, he felt that they were giving him the once-over. He started up the broad stairs with slow casualness. The way the gang of guys had looked at him, made him wonder would he get into a fight. It was a windy March Sunday, and the gang would be around the poolroom, because they had nothing else to do. If he got in a real jam, a punk would call them up and it wouldn't take long for them to get here. And Studs Lonigan could take care of himself. Only whenever a guy went to a place where he wasn't known, he had to be ready for anything.

He paid fifty cents and entered, handing his ticket to a bald-headed, narrow-faced man who looked as if he belonged ushering in a Protestant Church. A mixed, talkative crowd was spread over the shabbily-carpeted lounge. Studs was ill at ease because so many of them were strangers to him who were known here, while he wasn't. Strangers coming into the Greek's poolroom and seeing him and all the fellows perfectly at home, would have felt the same way. He saw a sign pointing up a stairway to the check-room. He went up and checked his hat and coat. Two kids with familiar faces looked at him with a glimmering recognition, but he was unable to place them and did not speak. He perceived that the upper floor was a bare balcony and returned to the lounge.

"Come up here to ankle around?" asked Wils Gillen, his face brightening with surprise.

"Oh, I thought I'd look the place over and watch you punks."

"You want to watch the lads strut their stuff, huh, Studs?"

"Christ, most of them here look like kids," Studs said, glancing around.

"Sure, we get the girls from Park High in first year, and train them. After we break them in, there's nobody can complain of their style and technique. Right now we're putting them through their spring training, so that when summer comes they can all do their stuff over on the wooded island in Jackson Park."

"So that's what you guys do! Ruin nice girls," Studs kidded.

"Leave it to us."

"What, do all the girls up here put out?"

"If you don't succeed, try again. But there's Elizabeth and she's easy stuff."

Studs smiled as Gillen hastened towards a mushy-lipped

kid, with a ravishing figure. Music started and there was a
crush towards the dance floor. He saw Hennessey with a
luscious blond in wine-red, and after them, Young Rocky leading a baby-faced thing. He moved to the edge of the rectangular dance floor, and watched the couples pass. In the center,
he saw a group of six couples doing the Polack Hop, holding
partners by the shoulders, skipping contortedly from side to
side, and then skipping on one foot sidewise. He shook his
head. That wasn't dancing! He saw Three Star Hennessey,
and the blond in red, wantonly socking it in, in a corner.

"Hello, Studs," said Ellsworth Lyman, interrupting him
from watching.

He watched Lyman move away and grab off the dance with
a dark-haired Irish kid, who looked like a knockout. He approached a homely but husky Swede. They walked to the dance
floor. From their first step, her big feet got in his and her own
way.

"Do you come here all the time?" she asked with an accent.

"Me? No," he said.

"Nice music," she said.

He nodded. He felt as if everyone in the place knew him and
were watching him, perhaps laughing behind his back, and
thinking that all he could get for a dance was a dumb Swede
pig. An expression of lust settled on her face, and she socked
with him shamelessly.

"Hello, Studs, how come you're here," yelled Three Star
passing him.

Studs did not reply. The Swede had got him hot, and she
had her uses, even if she was so damn clumsy.

"Like it?" she said.

After the dance, they walked off the floor.

"So long," he said.

He felt like dancing with her again, but hell, she was easy
meat. Maybe he'd get something better. If not, he could always
try her again.

"Hello, Studs, Hydrox. How you Ben Turpin?" Noel Morton
said.

"Oh, hello," said Studs, looking up at Noel, who was about
six foot one, and loose-jointed. His baboonish, loose lips broke
into an unassuming and friendly smile. Studs looked his outfit
over and kidded him because his suit coat hung so low that
most fellows could have worn it for a top-coat.

"Gee, I never expected to see you here."

"I thought I'd see what the place looks like."

"Well, how you like us? Think we're swell people?"

"Half of the broads here look like jail bait."

"They are. But sometimes, when they're young, they're sweet."

"Yeah, and it's sweeter too, laying in a can after you make 'em," said Studs.

"He who hesitates is lost, as I said to my old boy friend, Jess Dempsey," said Noel, dashing off.

"Hello, Studs."

"Hello, Weary. How goes it?"

"Oh," said Weary, shaking his shoulders in a gesture indicating that there was nothing to say.

"How come you're here?" asked Weary.

"Hell, I heard the punks around the poolroom gassing about the place, so I thought I'd see them in action."

"Listen, we'll have a crap game in the can in a little while. Come on and get in. Buddy Coen and the guys will be around. You know him, don't you?"

"No, but I heard about him."

"Well, the lads probably know you by name too."

Studs felt more at home now. He was not talking with punks.

"I got this hop. See you later."

Studs watched Weary go over to a sexy-looking dark broad in a black velvet dress. They moved among the dancers. He envied Weary because the guy danced so well. He wanted to meet the lads. They probably heard that he was the guy who'd once licked Weary Reilley. He wished some of the broads who knew Reilley knew who he was.

A tall girl, with long blond hair and a purple dress that made her figure sylph-like, stood a few feet away. Studs was wordless looking at her. She turned. It was Helen Shires' kid sister, Marion. And only a few years ago she hadn't known enough to wipe her nose, and one summer, too, they'd thought she was going to die from infantile paralysis.

Like Fritzie. Hell, she was practically a woman, she had everything. She was young, girl-like and woman-like, full of spirits and fun, and gay, with small straight breasts you almost ached to touch, nice figure, pretty as a picture, nice to see, like sunlight, like spring, like a flower blooming, like Lucy had been just before she'd moved from the neighborhood. He saw the same thing in Marion Shires that he'd seen in Lucy that day when the punks had been having their fight with tin cans in the prairie. He perceived that she was gazing at him.

"Say, aren't you Helen Shires' sister?"

"Why, yes. You're Studs Lonigan."

"You've grown into a fine-looking lady. I hardly knew you."

"Thank you."

"How's Helen?"

"She's fine. She's working downtown."

"I haven't seen her in a long time."

"Times change," laughed Marion Shires with disconcerting self-possession.

Studs figured the punks must break their necks over a girl like her. He felt suddenly proud, though, of his sister Fritzie. She didn't come to a hole like this. She was too decent.

"I never expected to see you here," said Marion.

"Oh, I don't come here regularly. I was just looking the place over."

"So am I. Like it?"

"I suppose the kids have a good time."

"Mr. Experience. But aren't you going to ask me to dance, or am I one of the . . . kids?" she asked as the music started.

"Why, it'll be a pleasure," Studs said, trying to be gentlemanly.

They walked to the floor, and danced. She lay against him with her head tilted back. He tried to hold himself in, because, after all, she was Helen's sister, and she was only a kid. Hell, he'd expect a guy to be white to his sisters, and if they weren't, he'd sock them. After the second piece, he couldn't do that. He gave her what he guessed she wanted. Suddenly she drew back, and her face seemed to go cold.

"You still live on Indiana Avenue?" he asked, figuring that she was a damn little teaser trying to make a monkey out of him.

"Yes."

"I suppose you're going to high school?"

"Englewood. I'll graduate this year."

"So is Loretta."

"Yes, I see her a lot at dances."

He was glad when the dance ended. He told her it was very nice to have danced with her, and asked to be remembered to Helen.

The little teasing bitch, somebody ought to cold-cock her, he thought. He looked at her surrounded by four cake-eaters. He saw O'Neill go up to her and could tell by the sudden disappointment on the punk's face that she had refused to dance with him. He smiled. The Swede pig he'd danced with edged towards him. He moved off as if he hadn't seen her. He watched a guy with a bald head and pince-nez glasses shine up to a wrinkled faced Polack. Made him realize that the joint looked like a freak show. Next to him, a kid, she couldn't be more than fourteen, was oogle-eyeing a high school punk.

Young Rocky rushed up, glad to see Studs. He remarked about all the keen janes there were for the dance. Phil Rolfe joined them, saying it was a surprise to see Studs Lonigan present. Studs was condescending. They toddled off after a jane. The punks sure felt their oats, and strutted their stuff. He felt that he'd come to the wrong place. He should have gone to the Midway Gardens or Trianon where the bunch was older. It was robbing the cradle here. Hennessey tried to mooch two bits off of him. He told Hennessey to try it on some of the broads. Hennessey said he was known here and didn't try to pinch pocketbooks. Studs realized that Hennessey was goddamn proud of being skillful at robbing pocketbooks; he hated the louse.

Studs stood, posing and watching with a smirk of superiority on his face. He liked to see them pass, see their faces. The youngest Bleu kid, dark, tall—hell, almost six feet—went dancing by, his nose up in the air as if it were severed from his face; he kept glancing all about him as he danced, looking, Studs guessed, for everyone to notice him. The kid he had only came up to his shoulder, and she looked damn young. Christ, he'd be robbing the cradle here. Weary winked as he went by, crudely socking it into a plump girl.

A fake collegian, one of these guys who bought college boy suits on the installment plan, danced by like a whirlwind. Noel Morton followed, turning in a speedy succession of circles, his coat tails flying behind him as if they were affected by strong winds. The jazz was fast and full of sex. Studs' blood thumped. His feet worked. He turned, and saw a kid, she couldn't have been a day over sixteen, making eyes at him. An awfully sweet-looking kid, with large black eyes. It was pretty just to look at her, her body half-formed, thin, so touched with energy. She smiled as he took a step towards her. They walked to the floor. She clung close, followed every step with lightness, and it would have seemed as if he were dancing with himself, if she had not held herself so tight against him. She chattered steadily, telling him about a movie she had seen. Then she said that her name was Nellie, and explained that it was her first time up here. She described a crazy woman with an accent who taught her history at Park High, and talked all the time about ouija boards, so funny. When they drew into a corner, she heated him up with a twisting little wiggle. It made him feel like a bastard. Christ, she was younger than Loretta, and seemed so damn innocent. A kid coming into it all. He tried to draw away from her, but she squeezed more tightly, and her breath came down hot on his cheek. He looked down at her, and her responding smile was tight and forced, almost painful. He felt like a bastard, but he couldn't control himself, and they danced sidewise, socking and shimmying the whole length of the floor. At the end of the dance, she was limp and perspiring. She said she was going to hold the eleventh dance open for him.

He bumped into Weary again, and Reilley asked him to come on back to the crap game. Weary stopped to talk to some guy a minute and Studs waited. They walked back. The music began and dancers passed them. Weary suddenly stopped, frowned.

"Why, that sonofabitch!" he said, standing with hands on hips. Studs saw June Reilley, dancing with a slim fellow, who was about two inches taller than Weary. She seemed to see her brother, and a look of fright came swiftly on her pretty dark face. She seemed just like the kid he'd danced with. It made him wonder, was something happening to girls with this jazz age. Weary motioned for June to come to him. She said something to her partner, and they danced over towards Weary and Studs.

"What are you doing here?"

"Why . . . Why, I was dancing. There's nothing wrong with my dancing. . . . You come here and dance, don't you?"

"Nobody told you you could. You go on home, and do it quick. If you ever come back here, I'll slap your little face. You've got no right here. Hear me!"

A great big baby tear rolled down her cheek.

"Go on!"

"I won't. You have no right to make me, or tell me what to do. You're not my boss and I don't have to do what you tell me to. I won't go."

A crowd gathered. Her tall dancing partner edged out of sight. June broke into uncontrollable tears.

"I'll tell you once more to leave or get dragged out of here!"

"I won't," she said, sweet and cute, as she cried and stamped her right foot.

He took hold of her arm. She walked off, crying.

"Where did Bain, that bastard, go?" Weary said.

"Who's that?"

"The louse who was dancing with her."

Weary ran about, looking, followed by a small crowd. Finally he gave it up.

"I'll get the bastard," Weary said.

He and Studs went to the can, in back of the stage. Twelve guys stood in a circle shooting craps. Buddy Coen, a wiry little guy with a snotty face, said hello to Weary. He and Studs were introduced. The game went on with a big ox shooting.

"Come on. Shake them dice!" Buddy said.

"I'm shaking."

"Well, shake 'em harder!" Buddy said.

The guy looked at Buddy and shook. He won his pot. Buddy, running the game, took a ten-percent cut on the dough. The guy handed Coen five bucks.

"Five. Five bucks. Who'll fade. Come on, you cheap skates!"

Studs handed him two dollars.

"Three bucks!"

A little fellow, whom Weary had called Razz, faded another dollar. Somebody else took the last two. The fellow shook and made his seven. He shot the ten. Studs took five of it. The guy won. He shot fifteen.

"Shake 'em this time, you!"

"I'm shaking."

"Well, see that you do!"

Weary frowned at the guy, and faded ten of the fifteen. Studs took the other five. The guy made his point.

"Now, let's see them dice!" said Buddy, holding the pot.

"They'll be all right!"

Buddy took a step forwards. Weary crowded in. Three husky micks stood by the ox who held the dice. Weary grabbed the dice from the guy. He, the big ox, and three other fellows edged backwards.

"You sonofabitch! Loaded!"

Weary pumped his right into the ox's eye. Two fellows jumped Weary. Buddy Coen swung and brought his knee into a groin. A fellow went down moaning. The ox swung at Studs. Studs ducked. He hit the wall and winced. Studs swung. The ox dropped, and Buddy kicked him in the head. He moaned, and crawled towards the door. Studs jumped on the back of a guy tackling Weary and got a stomach hold. Studs followed the group out, chasing the bunch who'd cheated in the crap game. The dancing stopped and everybody swirled about, a milling crowd. Girls screamed. Studs ran downstairs with Weary and Buddy, but the guys got away. He learned that they were from Sixty-third and Halsted. Buddy and some of the other lads shook hands with Studs, told him he was white and had guts. Studs felt good, like a hero. Coen gave him ten bucks back from the pot he had held just before the fight started. They chipped in for a bottle, and Studs went back to dance. He found Nellie. She said the fight was terrible.

"They were rats. They got what they deserved. Every one of them should have had his teeth kicked in," Studs said.

"My, what language!"

"Thataboy, Studs," said Phil Rolfe, passing him.

Studs felt like he belonged there, and it made all the difference in the world.

"You must be a terrible fighter."

He shrugged his shoulders a trifle. He didn't want to brag or talk about it a lot, but he was pleased with what she said. He started talking, against his will:

"Well, what I do is keep in good condition, and then, if any trouble starts or I have to fight, I can take care of myself."

"That's very sensible."

"There's a lot of things I can take care of," Studs said in innuendo.

"Yes," she said knowingly.

"Sure."

"For instance?"

"Well, girls and . . ."

"I'll bet you could, at that."

"You can't keep a good man down," he said.

She smiled an invitation.

After the dance he left her, and decided that he wouldn't, couldn't be the bastard to take her cherry. But he was tempted. He'd never been first with a girl. He wouldn't, and anyway, she was just jail bait and he could get into all kinds of trouble.

The liquor came, and he went back to the can with Weary and some of the boys. He took a swig. It was pretty strong, and he had to fight to get it down.

"Good stuff," he said.

"Sure it is," said Weary.

"To those bastards we cleaned! May they walk under a street car and forget to wake up," Buddy said, raising the bottle.

He drank and they laughed.

"Say, Lonigan, where do you hang out, Fifty-eighth Street?" asked Coen.

Studs nodded.

"Well, drop around and see us any time. We can always get a bottle, and maybe some janes, and can have a little party, or else a game. You know! We got a white bunch around here, and we always like to have more white men with us."

Studs thought that Weary glowered a bit at him. If he came, he supposed he'd have to tangle again with Weary sooner or later. Anyway he would. Goddamn it, he'd take Weary again. He was in condition, and he'd stay that way.

After the dance, he found Nellie waiting for him. She took

his arm and started walking away with him. It was too much. If he was a bastard or not, he couldn't help himself. He looked at her. He was proud he was going to get something so sweet, even if he was a bastard for doing it. If he didn't, somebody else would.

XVIII

"Why, Marty O'Brien, how are you?" Patrick Lonigan asked, seeing Mr. O'Brien in front of church after ten o'clock mass. Mrs. Lonigan and Mrs. O'Brien greeted each other.

"Hello, Pat. Glad to see you," O'Brien said, shaking with Lonigan.

"What are you doing back in the old neighborhood, Marty?"

"Oh, we just thought that we would come down here to church, today. You know, it's nice to see the old sights now and then," Marty said.

"Yes, I suppose the old place is the only place for many of us," said Lonigan.

"I'm sorry I cleared out, but glad, because I see what's happening."

"Well, Marty, I don't know if I would be so pessimistic. To be sure, the jiggs have got on Wabash Avenue, and a lot of Polacks and Wops have come in along the southwestern edge of the parish, but still I wouldn't be so pessimistic. I got a building now on Michigan and I think it's going to be worth plenty more than what I paid for it. Particularly since Father Gilhooley is going to build the new church."

"Pat, I don't want to sound discouraging, but if you ask me, I'd say this: the whole neighborhood is being ruined, and quicker than you think. You mark my words, it's going to be so full of black clouds that a white man won't belong in it. Fifty-eighth and Prairie is going to look like Thirty-fifth and State with them."

"Golly, I don't think so, I hope not, Marty, but if it does, well, I'll be out. I'll turn a neat profit when I sell my old building. But if that does happen, it'll be a crime."

"Crime or no crime, those kike real-estate bastards are getting in, and what for? I'll tell you: to sell to niggers, that's what for."

"That will be a crime. We ought to do something about it."

"That's what I thought, but what can you do? That's why we moved."

"That will be a crime, and what with the new church Father

Gilhooley is going to build. Goddamn it, Marty, they'll never get Michigan. We won't let them!"

"Well, mark my words . . . but how's business, Pat?"

"I can't complain; things are running smooth enough. I'm worried about unions. You know, them damn unions are robbing me, twelve and fifteen dollars a day. Why, no painter or plasterer is worth that, but they got to get it; but how's business with you, Marty?"

"Fair."

"Say, you'll have to come up and see us some time," Lonigan said.

"And come and see us, Pat!"

Marty gave Lonigan a card with their new address printed on it. They went to their car and drove away.

CHAPTER EIGHTEEN

I

Studs observed that the Scanlans had a lamp in every corner, floor-lamps, table-lamps and lamps on the piano. The parlor contained so much furniture that it seemed overcrowded. He wanted to light a cigarette but restrained himself for fear that he might spill ashes. He looked at a rose-green pottery lamp set on the table near the heavy blue velvet drapes. He moved over to sit on a large overstuffed davenport that was upholstered in dark blue velour. He touched it, studied it. The Scanlans must have spent more dough than the old man on furniture. They'd always been well off, but the old man wasn't tight. He'd been awfully decent, too, slipping him a ten-dollar bill just before he had left to come out here and call for Lucy. He looked about the parlor again, wishing that Lucy would shake a leg. Doggy house all right! Mrs. Scanlan entered. Studs jumped to his feet, smiled, and asked her how she was, simultaneous actions performed with the feeling that he knew the book of etiquette by heart, and the determination that he was going to carry the evening off. Mrs. Scanlan shook hands with him. He saw that she had changed, and it made him feel a little bit sorry. She was gray, and much stouter, and she didn't seem to have any pep. When she commented on how pleased she was to see him, and on what a fine young man he had grown up to be, it seemed almost as if it was only a tired voice without any body behind it. She sat down. He sat down after her. She asked if his mother and dad were well, and he said they were. It was hard trying to talk to her. But all girls were the same, didn't care how long they made a guy wait. Thought it was their privilege. Fran and even Loretta were that way. It was hard to think of anything to say to Mrs. Scanlan. He hoped Lucy would hurry up.

"Lord have mercy on me, I suppose I wouldn't even recognize the old place, if I was to go back there now. Five years is a long time, the way the world does change nowadays," Mrs. Scanlan droned monotonously.

"It hasn't changed so awfully much. Some of the old people, like the O'Briens, have moved away, but many of them are still in the parish."

"Have the Shires sold their house yet?"

"No."

"Ah, they were fine people, even if they were on the other side of the fence. What I always said to my girls, and what I still say, is that if many Catholics lived as upright lives as the Shires family did, they would need have no fear of meeting their Maker on the Day of Judgment. That oldest girl, Helen, she was a bit of a wild one, but a fine, decent girl. I suppose now she's settled down."

"Yes, she's working downtown," Studs said.

"My Helen was saying she saw the O'Brien boy downtown, and he was saying the niggers were getting in there. Isn't it a shame?"

"There's some on Wabash Avenue. That's why my father sold his building, and got one on Michigan. But they won't get any farther. Father thinks property values will go up and the property will be worth a lot more after Father Gilhooley builds the new Church."

"You know, William, I never felt the same about any place I've lived in as I did about our home on Indiana. I wouldn't have sold it only for the girls. That neighborhood, there, it was just like home. I lived in it for over twenty years, and raised my family and buried my husband from it. But after he died, I did feel kind of sad like he was always coming back, and I felt it was bad luck to stay living in a house when one of yours has died in it. I've always heard that said."

Studs smoothed his hair back. He wanted to look groomed when Lucy walked in.

"Your sister, Loretta, the one that always played with my Helen, she must be a grown girl now, too. I can remember when they were just tots together, and my Helen had such long red curls. I used to braid her hair every morning. But you know, my Helen, she had scarlet fever, and they had to cut off every inch of that lovely hair, and it's never grown back like it used to be. It's bobbed now. Loretta, she must be the young lady, and the youngest boy—what was his name?—he must be a big strapping lad too. My, my, how time flies."

"Martin, you mean, he's a little bit taller than I am," Studs said.

"Well, life is strange . . . but here's my Lucy now."

"Well, well, so we meet again. How are you, Studs?"

Studs arose and smiled sheepishly as he shook hands with her. His old feelings arose so strongly that he saw her as through a mist. No use kidding himself, his feelings hadn't changed a bit. He'd always like Lucy.

"You haven't changed a bit," she said, standing before him, with a self-possession that dismayed him and aroused envy.

"You have. You look even sweller than you used to," he gulped.

"I'm wrong. You have changed. You've picked up the blarney," she said, smiling and pointing a finger at him in the old teasing manner.

He was only gradually able to see the attractive, sweetly plump young woman before him. He perceived the same devilishness in her eyes. He noticed how her lips and cheeks were still red. And she knew how to dress.

She wore a green crepe, low-waisted dress, the semi-full blouse forming a broad, tight band around her hips; and the skirt fell about three inches below the knee. The ensemble effect was flaring and there were silver rose-buds on the shoulder straps, which were matched by high-heeled silver pumps.

"No kidding, you do look swell!" he said with embarrassment.

"Enough of that, now," she said in a tone which was almost maternal.

"You know, it seems only like yesterday that you two were only children. Now you're a grown up young man and young woman. Ah, 'tis strange, life," the mother said.

Studs came out of a feeling of paralysis sufficiently to suggest that maybe he'd better call a taxi. She said they could pick one up outside.

"You know, Lucy, I'm right. William does take after his father. All of the children, except maybe the youngster, what's his name, do," Mrs. Scanlan said, studying Studs.

"Oh, Mother!" Lucy said impatiently.

The mother's face dropped. Lucy got her wrap, a large square silver and gold cloth shawl with black thread through it and bordered in white fox. She threw it over her shoulders. She looked like a knockout. The mother muttered maternal benedictions upon them as they left.

"Poor mother," said Lucy as they walked along a street of

apartment buildings, toward Sheridan Road. They heard a
Victrola record from an open window, and Lucy started snapping her fingers, and singing:

> *Don't mind the rain,*
> *It's bound to come again,*
> *For when the clouds go rolling by . . .*

It was like a picture that Studs wanted never to forget. The
warm spring evening, the promise it offered to him, a mist in
the lush air, Sheridan Road ahead, with traffic lights, people
crossing the street, automobiles going by, the Victrola, Lucy
singing, so pretty that he wanted to look at her, touch her,
kiss her, love her, take her arm, say something to her of what
it all meant, and of how all along he had really wanted nothing
like he had wanted her. And he couldn't say anything, because
it all stopped him. He guessed that when you felt like he did,
you just had too many feelings to tell them to anybody. And
it made him feel like a louse, him still not completely cured
from the dose that little bitch from Nolan's had given him,
taking Lucy out when he had a dirty disease. He wasn't at
all worthy of her. He felt as if he wanted to crawl before her
on his hands and knees, and kiss the hem of her dress.

"Poor mother, she's never been happy since we've moved,"
Lucy said.

"My folks like the old neighborhood. I suppose they would
feel the same as your mother if they left it."

"How about you?" she said, looking at him as if she could
see through his mind.

"One place to sleep is as good as another," he said, indifferently shrugging his shoulders.

"Cynical," she said in a dismaying tone.

He hailed a Yellow Cab on Sheridan Road, and helped her
in, the mere touching of her arm affecting him like electricity.
He tried to give directions in an assured and suave manner and
felt like a clown. He sat beside her, liking the perfume smell,
and the clean new smell of her clothes.

"You know we sold our building and moved over to Michigan. There's niggers on Wabash now," he said, trying to make
conversation.

"Yes, isn't it awful . . . those niggers."

"I suppose there'll have to be more race riots to put them
where they belong," he said.

"That would be just perfectly horrible . . . but exciting."

They became silent as the cab rolled along. The silence grew
upon Studs. He guessed he better talk, not give her reason to

think that he was so damn dumb that he couldn't even open his mouth.

"The O'Briens and some of the other old parishioners have moved out," he said.

"Yes, I saw Johnny. He's made a frat that rates high at the university," she said.

He glanced out of the window at the lake in the spring night. He looked at Lucy. He wanted to put his arm around her.

"You weren't at the Zeta Dance?" she asked.

"What?"

She repeated the question.

"No," he muttered.

"You don't go to many dances?"

"Oh, once in a while."

"I see Dan. He does a lot of stepping out when he's in town," she said.

"I see Bill once in a while," said Studs.

"Bill, he was so funny."

"He still is."

"Say, Studs, have you a cigarette?"

He gave her one and smoked himself. It put him more at ease. He edged an imperceptible inch towards her.

"This is going to be a big dance."

"Fran talked about it enough."

"She works so hard for her sorority. I suppose Loretta will be there. She's gotten to be such a darling."

"She's a good kid," said Studs.

The bumping of the car pitched her against him. She stayed there. That perfume smell, and the smell of her clothes made him want to kiss her even more than he had been wanting to.

"With my sister and your sister grown up, I feel like the older generation," Lucy said.

"Yeah," he said.

He put his arm around her. He quickly and clumsily, on an impulse, kissed her.

"This is awfully public," she calmly said, completely disturbing him.

He looked at her, her face now vague in the cab.

"You work fast," she teased, pursing her lips as if she were waiting for another kiss. He kissed her again.

"You're fast," she said.

He tried to hug her more tightly against his shoulder. She stiffened.

He seriously puffed at his cigarette. Remembering the afternoon in the park, in the tree, swinging her legs, himself looking through the leaves at the park lagoon, neither of them speaking, swinging their legs, her singing *The Blue Ridge Mountains of Virginia*. It couldn't have been so many years ago. It wasn't all gone. He wished she'd sing that song now.

"They're having a hot Benson band tonight," she said, breaking his mood.

He was in for it, a chump. How in hell would he act? Jesus Christ. Already, he felt as if he were an entirely different Studs Lonigan from what he'd ever been, and they wouldn't even know him around the poolroom. They rolled nearer and nearer to the Loop, and he felt like he was being taken to his doom.

II

Entering the hotel, Studs tried to appear calm and natural, as if he belonged in places like this, and was the kind of a guy who could bust right into any kind of a joint, no matter how swell it was, and act like he belonged there and knew what to do. They passed across a pillared lobby that possessed an indefinable atmosphere of lacy ornateness. Studs felt that everybody was looking at him, ready to laugh if he pulled a boner. He knew that he was blushing. He walked by an old man lounging in a chair, half asleep, his somnolent face making him look like he was dead on his feet. He threw back his shoulders. He thought of himself as youth, and hoped the old man saw him and thought so too. He spotted several loudly dressed Jews, and they seemed to be looking at Lucy. She was worth looking at, and they should be envying him, but let them crack wise or dirty!

They turned to their left, and up a marble stairway with gilt banisters to the Blue Room.

"All the dances that count are being held here this year," she exclaimed.

"Yeah!"

He could just tell that she was able to see right through him, see that he was out of place and without confidence. Maybe she was just silently laughing at him, and later she would laugh and talk about him behind his back. If she did, let her, he thought, in a cursing mood. If she was that way, she could go plumb to——. He wished it was over or that he hadn't been chump enough to let himself in for such a thing. He knew he would make a fathead out of himself. And he was too old for this cake-eater stuff. He determined that if trying could do, he would carry himself through it with . . . dignity.

A lanky effeminate fellow, with blond marcelled hair, stood collecting tickets. Studs handed him the ticket, his face set in a challenging sneer. Let that sap bat out of turn. The fellow pointed to the right, and stated in an affectedly refined voice that the checkroom was in that direction. He started taking his coat off as he walked towards it. Placing it over his arm, he realized that he hadn't paused first to take Lucy's shawl. She handed it to him, and said that she would go and powder up. It was bull number one for him, bad way to start the evening off. Girls got sore when fellows pulled little boners like that; Fran always talked about them, and she didn't like fellows who were so dumb. All girls, he guessed, were the same way. After checking the wraps, he went to the lavatory. He shook his head with surprise. Building cans like palaces nowadays. Two fellows stood smoking by the washbowls. They looked like boy scouts to Studs. The kind of fake gentlemen that Fran would like. They all looked alike, and talked alike, and shook hands in the same Joe College way. Johnny O'Brien was getting that way too. They were all like a walking book of etiquette, and the only thing they needed was a good hard mash in the puss.

"Jake has a keen woman with him tonight," said one of the young fellows by the washbowl, as Studs washed his hands.

"I don't like her."

"What did she do, two-time you on a date?"

"That mama wouldn't two-time anything in pants. She's a tramp and anything from eight to eighty goes with her. If you ask me, Jake had plenty of guts, plenty of guts, bringing her to a dance like this, where there's all kinds of decent, respectable girls."

"Jake must be hard up if that's the case. Only whatever you or I saw, I know I'd never kick her out of bed."

"I never could understand Jake anyway. He always does things like this."

"Yeah, he is kind of unconventional."

They passed on out. A white-coated shine started brushing Studs' suit. He was a pest. Studs handed him two bits and told him to lay off. Studs dallied over a cigarette, because he didn't want to face the crowd. Finally he shot the cigarette aside and walked out with the air of a guy who was making a big decision.

The groups, spread across the long, narrow, and gaudily upholstered lounge, disheartened him. They talked in muffled voices, strolled languidly up and down, stood and sat about. He was afraid of it all, afraid he might act like a clown. But it seemed warm, gay, because there was such a number, so many good-looking young girls. He was glad he'd come, and he wanted to, was determined to, become part of it. He went forwards as if he had nothing to do, hoping he'd recognize some friends. He'd never seen so many hot-looking women in his life; and he had one of the hottest ones of all here. His

elation subsided as quickly as it had arisen. Hell, it was all
artificial. They were all trying to put on the dog, show that they
were lace-curtain Irish, and lived in steam-heat.

He waited for Lucy in a corner, near the entrance, feeling
lonesome, watching more couples coming, envying the guys
who came with laughing girls, because he knew they were
going to have a good time, and he wasn't. He saw Lucy coming
toward him and his mood vanished. Maybe she did like him.
He noticed her high-heeled silver slippers, and the silver rose
buds on her shoulder straps. He realized that she didn't see
him, as she walked forwards, half-smiling, seeming very happy.
He hoped she was that way, because of him. She was damn
keen all right. Plenty of bastards were going to wish they were
in his shoes tonight.

"Here you are. I've been looking for you," she said in a
very friendly voice.

He said yeah. She babbled that the dance was going over
big and would make money. It tickled her so that she could
hardly wait to see Fran. Fran would be so thrilled because
she had plugged so much for it and took such an interest in
the affairs of the sorority. Studs listened, shifting his weight
from foot to foot. When she finished chattering, he answered
yeah.

"Everybody is here," Lucy said.

"Yeah," Studs said, wondering what the hell she meant by
everybody, a lot of these goddamn two-bit jellybeans around
the place.

The music started up. He suggested dancing. She nodded
but said to wait until a few others went in. If she was one of
the first on the floor, she'd feel like she was on exhibition. He
put his hands in his pockets, and waited. He took them out,
and let them hang at his side, figuring he guessed he might
as well not put them in his pockets. She said he had a nice-looking suit on. He said it was the first time he had worn it. She
said it was in good taste and in fashion. He folded his arms, self-
conscious of his hands. He unfolded his arms and let them hang
at his side.

They followed the other couples towards the ballroom. Studs
was afraid he wouldn't dance well, and was too excited to
say anything clearly to her. But he felt quite proud that others
could see him with Lucy, see how well-dressed she was. A
spine-shivering solo from the saxophone broke into his attention.
It made him sad and want to be reckless. He walked down the
steps with her, and saw the dancers inside, wheeling, and spinning on the glossy floor in dim lights.

The Blue Room was square-shaped, with French windows

on two sides, a vaulted ceiling, and pillars in the center of the floor. The decoration was in a blue motif. He danced a little stiffly. The mere touching of her in the dance postures made him want to crush her to him, squeeze her against him almost to the point of breaking her bones, tell her that goddamn it, she had to be his woman, and there was no other side to the question. It made him gloomy. Some said a dose could never be cured, although his doctor said otherwise. Maybe even if she did love him and would marry him, he'd never be able to. A sudden vision of him ruining her for all times came to him like a nightmare. They swung into a patch of colored orange light, and then passed the tuxedoed orchestra, which was playing wildly on a dais. She let herself go against him, drew back. He wanted her close against him, wanted to feel her belly hot against him. He didn't have the nerve.

The lights brightened, and the music stopped. Following the example of other fellows, he clapped perfunctorily. A fat blond girl smiled at him. He smiled back, not knowing who she was. Must be a sorority sister of Fran's. It was pleasing, though, to have people he didn't know remembering him.

"Studs, you dance nicely," Lucy said.

He tried to take the compliment modestly, but wondered if she was only pulling his leg, the way janes always enjoyed pulling a guy's leg. He guessed, though, he did dance well enough to get by. And he wanted Fran, everybody to notice it. If he and Lucy went together, he'd learn how to dance as good as all the cake-eaters, even Rolfe. He saw Rolfe with Loretta at the other end of the room. Fritzie looked sweet in her new black velvet dress; too sweet for Rolfe.

The music commenced, and he tried to dance more swiftly, like so many of the guys did, and they got out of step and Lucy almost tumbled on the floor. She smiled, then laughed. There seemed to be a twinkle in her eye, the twinkle in the eye of the old Lucy, and he was reminded of the way she'd smiled at the party at his house on the night of their graduation.

"You trying to win a race or go to a fire?" she asked.

"We better not go so fast," he said with gravity.

He passed Rolfe and Fritzie, holding his head erect. His face was grave, and he nodded curtly. Phil smiled back at him, and then bent down to say something to Fritzie. She smiled sweetly at him.

"Penny for your thoughts?" said Lucy.

"I was just noticing my kid sister."

"Oh."

She turned and smiled at Fritzie.

"I'll bet she'd like to hear you calling her your kid sister. She's a young lady now."

He went outside of Carroll Dowson and Fran. They smiled at him; he nodded back.

"You know a lot of people here," he said to make conversation, noticing how many couples she greeted.

"Oh, you meet everybody, here and there," she said with intended casualness.

"Yeah, it's tough being popular."

"Now, don't you go getting sarcastic," she said, but not angrily.

Christ, he felt that he was acting and talking like a goddamn dingbat. Well, if it was so, he was only getting what he had bargained for. He looked into Lucy's face, and away, and felt again the desire to crush her to him.

Fran and Dowson joined them after the dance. She bestowed an approving glance on Studs and told Lucy that she looked lovely and darling. She said with enthusiasm that the dance was way over, and that they'd clear at least two hundred dollars on it.

"Thinking about playing any football this fall?" Carroll asked, shaking with Studs.

"Maybe," said Studs.

"If you do, let me know."

Studs asked Dowson how his brother was, and Dowson said all right. He was here some place with Gertrude O'Reilley.

They talked until the music for the next dance was heard. They again waited for others to go in first and then followed.

"Everybody is here," she said in a very natural voice, as if her body was not tight against him.

"Yeah," he said, looking at her, hoping she'd say something else, some hint about the way they were dancing, and that it meant something to her. Colored lights were played across the floor. Silly words were in his head. He was silent.

"Oh, there's Mike!" Lucy exclaimed.

"Mike who?"

"Don't you know him? Mike Crowley. He's such a cute boy."

"Hello, Mike," Lucy called.

"He's a darling boy," she told Studs.

Studs looked after him. He was a big, dumb, but decent-looking young chap, and the girl with him seemed eighteen or nineteen, a plain-looking girl with a wide, Dutch face.

"He's only a boy, but he's so darling. He's the captain of St. Ignatius football team, and everybody says he's a fine player and that some day he'll be a famous college football player."

"Oh," said Studs, looking again after Mike Crowley, wanting to meet him, wanting Lucy to remember that he'd been and still was a good player.

Studs told her he had just seen Dan Donoghue on the floor. He danced towards Dan, good old Dan. It made him feel better and more confident than he had all evening. Dan smiled with surprise, but Studs knew he was glad to see him, and said he'd never expect to see them together, and Studs liked it; particularly, because Dan linked him and Lucy together as if it was very natural and expected. After the dance, Dan and Studs walked off the dance floor together, and Dan's girl and Lucy strolled just ahead of them.

Studs asked how everything was going, as if it was a question of grave import. Dan said he couldn't complain, and asked Studs how it was riding, and Studs said he couldn't complain either. He asked about the old fellows, and Studs said he'd seen some, and he hadn't seen others. Dan said to tell them all he'd been asking for them.

They grouped together in the lobby. Studs felt as if he belonged, one of a talking group. Good old Dan. Dan was no cake-eater either, and if Dan could enjoy these dances, well, he could. He'd take Lucy to more of them. He looked at her as she laughed with Dan's girl, Catherine Marie Boylan. He envied everybody who knew her. He wanted the dance to be over, and the two of them to be alone in a cab, because it would mean the chance he'd been waiting for all his life, ever since they had sat in the tree. If he didn't make the most of it, win her, maybe he might never have another chance.

Studs and Dan exchanged dances. Catherine Marie was only a kid, but damn pretty, with chestnut hair, round face, blue eyes, athletic figure.

"I feel as if I know you," she said on the dance floor.

"Yes."

"Dan's spoken so much of you."

"We went to school together."

"I know, he thinks a lot of you."

"First down ten," Dan said: Studs had bumped Catherine Marie into him and Lucy.

Studs smiled, but his confidence was severely shaken. He danced rottenly and had nothing to say. Different from Dan and Lucy, they were talking so naturally. Some guys were just built that way, and could break into any new place. He wasn't and couldn't. Hell, he didn't belong with all these broads. They were not his kind. He couldn't talk about dances, and didn't know the people they talked about and knew.

"Oh, there's Perc Byrnnes," Catherine Marie said.

Studs said nothing, because after all, she was his old pal Dan's girl, and he didn't want to make a snotty crack. They waited between pieces. A heavy but soft fellow with a thin girl in blue on his arm approached them. Catherine Marie greeted them effusively. Studs didn't like the way the punk seemed to have polish rubbed all over him, the way shoe polish was lathered on shoes. Catherine Marie introduced Studs to Perc Byrnnes and Vivian May Corrigan. Studs shook hands with the guy, feeling that he was holding a handful of crap.

"And how are you?" Perc Byrnnes said with a soft, solicitous discomfort.

"I'm rarin', Perc."

The Corrigan girl asked if he were Loretta Lonigan's brother. He nodded. She said she knew Loretta.

"I must congratulate you the way your sorority has put the dance over. It's the most successful dance of the year," the Corrigan girl said to Catherine Marie.

Studs looked quickly at Byrnnes, and then back at the Corrigan girl.

"Isn't it gorgeous?" Catherine Marie Boylan said.

He was glad when the music started up again. All he wished now was that he was drunk with Slug and the boys and that they were all here. He had to smile at what they'd do.

"Oh, I'm sorry," he said, clutching her tightly. He had collided with a couple, and she'd almost been knocked off her pins.

"It was my fault," she said, laughing.

Returning to the lounge, he unobtrusively wiped his perspiring face. He wondered how in the name of Jumping Jesus Christ a regular guy like Dan could stand all this crap. Dan excused himself and said he'd see Studs later. He and Catherine Marie walked off. Studs watched them pause to speak with that Byrnnes clown.

During the next dance, Lucy told him that Dan was going steady with Catherine Marie. Her father was a broker on La Salle Street, and she rated. She was awfully sweet, but young, and in Loretta's class at high school. Dan and she were awfully attached. It made him wish that people would be saying Studs Lonigan and Lucy Scanlan were awfully attached to each other. At the intermission between pieces, they were joined by Phil and Loretta. Phil adopted an air of equality in greeting Studs, and asking him how he liked the dance. Studs ignored Phil and told Fritzie she looked nice. The music saved Studs' patience. After the dance, Fran and Carroll Dowson joined them in the lounge. Harold Dowson came up. He introduced his girl, a pugnosed thing named Gertrude O'Reilley. She was the niece of Joe O'Reilley, the lawyer whom Studs' old man admired so much. Fran stood watching him with studied approval. He didn't like it.

"You're comporting yourself fine. I'm proud of you. I never knew it was in you," Fran said, dancing the next one with him.

"Yeah."

"Now don't get nasty. I'm only telling you what's true. All the girls in my chapter have been saying nice things about you."

They were noticing him! He hoped Fran would tell that to Lucy.

"And you're dancing well. Only there's one thing. Please be careful about the way you acknowledge introductions."

"I can take care of myself."

"Now please don't get bull-headed," she said.

He frowned sullenly. She accused him of trying to disgrace her on the floor.

"Cut it out," he said.

"Won't you please speak more loudly. The orchestra leader didn't hear you," she said.

"Well, I didn't ask you for any opinions."

"You're simply incorrigible."

In the lounge again he stood in a chattering crowd, feeling useless. Lucy whispered that she was having the next one with Frank Dolan, who was stagging it. He watched Lucy walk off with Frank Dolan, a big broad-shouldered guy. He might be big, but, well, Studs Lonigan wasn't afraid of him. He could see himself whittling the big fake down to his own size.

"Jesus, how come you're here?" asked Fat Malloy with contagious good fellowship.

"My sister talked me into it."

"That's right. It's her sorority."

"Say, do those bastards call this a good time?" asked Studs.

"Well, it is in a way. I mean there's all kinds of fine girls, and it's swell. Most of the broads rate high, and I don't mean maybe."

"Well, Fat, I don't like most of the guys around here. They're fakes."

"A lot of them are. There's one guy here named Perc Byrnnes, and he's the biggest fake in the joint. He's got dough and his old man lets him have a big Lincoln, so he thinks he's the reincarnation of Jesus Christ!"

"I met him."

"Well, I'm gunning for that boy. The first time he cracks wise to me, I'm just going to up and let him have one. He's a foul ball! But say, Studs, come on in the can," Fat said, smirking.

"By the way, what girl did you take?" Fat asked in the lavatory.

"Lucy Scanlan."

"Say, she's a fine girl."

"Yeah," said Studs, proud.

"Drink," Fat said, pulling out a bottle.

Studs drank.

"Your dose must be better?"

"The doc says it's clearing up all right."

"Say, how did you get it?"

"I got it from a sixteen-year-old bitch named Nellie Cullen. I picked her up at Louisa Nolan's. I've met plenty of lowdown whores but she's the filthiest bitch I ever came across, and she's only sixteen."

"You ought to find her and crack her one in the teeth."

"I tried, but she never went back there while I was looking for her."

"Say, I heard about the scrap you got into at Nolan's."

"Yeah."

"You know, those lads around Sixty-third and Stony are plenty tough. Plenty. And I hear you made a hit with them."

"They're all white. I was around with them a couple of times. But you know, I'm not yellow, but hell, I don't go around inviting trouble. Christ, when they get drunk, they see a guy they don't like, and they walk up and clout him, or else if it's in a restaurant, they just toss a sugar bowl at his head. And Buddy Coen. . . ."

"I know Buddy."

"I like him, but, Jesus, he gets drunk all the time, and then picks out the biggest cop or dick he can find and pokes him. If I have to fight, I will, but that's too much," said Studs.

"They're tough hoods."

"Say, know a guy named Frank Dolan?"

"He's another one of these flannel-mouth Irish who thinks he's society stuff."

"Can he go?"

"A fart in a windstorm would blow him over."

"I didn't like his looks."

"We'll drink on that," said Fat.

They killed the bottle.

Studs and Fat walked back. Fat was only a punk, and he acted like an equal and old-time buddy of Studs. But Studs liked him. He was a godsend now.

Dolan walked up and thanked Studs, calling him old man. He nodded to Fat. Fat frowned. Studs was introduced to several couples but missed the names. He almost had to laugh when Fat Malloy acknowledged introductions the same way Byrnnes did. The dance suddenly seemed to Studs like a bunch of ten-year-old kids playing they were in a secret society. He looked at Lucy. Goddamn it, she'd got him. He looked at her hair, black curly hair, her face, round, young, always breaking into a laugh and a smile. They could talk and make up for all these years. He felt like a bum and a louse too. She was too damn good for him, with a dose, all that stuff. But with her, well, she'd got him. Guys said love was all the crap. When a girl like Lucy got you, it was different. He wished, Jesus Christ, that things had turned out different after that day in the park, and all these years hadn't been wasted. He wanted to say something to her. Maybe in the cab, the time would be set, and the right thing would just come to him. He felt goofy, not at all like the Studs Lonigan everybody knew. He wanted the next dance to begin. He wanted to be just alone with Lucy. Lucy said that her old friend Morris Smith wanted the next dance. Smith smiled fatuously. Studs said all right. He watched them disappear, thinking how he'd like to take Smith and Dolan on together and lay them out cold. He didn't hear while Malloy talked half drunkenly. He watched a punk cooing with a little flapper. Silly. Goddamn it. Lucy had got him. When the dance ended, he anxiously watched the couples coming out. Fran Reilley bowed to him. Dan winked. Byrnnes gave a silly grin. Phil and Fritzie waved. They came, walking slowly, talking as if they were sincerely interested in each other. Studs' fists clenched. He was surly when Smith thanked him for the dance. Lucy seemed to notice it.

"You know, Studs, a girl likes to dance with different fellows. Variety is the spice of life," she said, during the next dance.

"I didn't say anything."

"I know that old dark look of yours."

He tried to smile. He wanted it to be over, and him and Lucy to be alone. He wanted to kiss her and love her. Waltz music and colored lights made him sentimental like a mooncalf punk. He could hardly wait to be alone with her.

III

Studs was glad when he and Lucy left a large group in front of the College Inn and got into a cab. He didn't mind the nine bucks he'd forked out at the place, but the people weren't his kind, and he was glad to be away and alone with Lucy at last. She babbled about how successful a dance it had been.

"I guess it made money," he said without interest.

"Didn't you enjoy it?"

"Oh, yeah."

"You certainly sound awfully enthusiastic."

"There were a lot of mopes there."

"Why, they were all nice fellows."

"Nice mopes, I say."

"I see that you're still a . . . tough guy."

He wanted to expand his chest and say yes, he was, and he was going to be tougher after seeing those dingbats at the dance. But he said nothing. He felt as if she were slipping through his fingers, and that he ought to say something to catch and stop her before it was too late. He looked at her, wanting her, all of her, and she was like something beautiful in a mist. She smiled at him. Maybe no, he wasn't losing her.

"You're just the same, Studs . . . just like a little boy."

She edged towards him, patted his cheek, took off his hat, ran her hands through his hair. She kissed him. She was in his arms. Suddenly, he was french-kissing her. He dug through her dress and touched her breast. She froze up, turned her face away.

"I'm not that kind of a girl."

He tried, crudely, determined, unthinking, to pull her to him again.

"Please be careful," she said cuttingly.

He looked out the window. He saw the lake. He grabbed her hand. He kissed her. She opened her mouth on the next kiss. He felt under her dress.

"I won't hurt you. Come on," he said huskily. He didn't even think of his dose, all he had in mind was Lucy.

"I can't . . . no . . . not here. If Mother isn't home, maybe. . . ."

"Why not?" he said.

"I can't . . . it'll be awful . . . I'll ruin my clothes . . . please wait till we get home," she begged.

He believed her. They kissed, and he felt her all the way home. She got out of the car rumpled, and rushed into the hallway. He paid the bill.

She opened the inside door, and stood holding it, blocking his entrance. She pursed her lips for him. They kissed. He tried to push open the door.

"No," she said.

She pushed his hat off, and when he turned, closed the door on him. He watched her go upstairs. She didn't look back.

He walked slowly out and away.

"That goddamn teaser!"

He felt that he'd been a goddamn chump, but realized what a bastard he'd been, trying to make her. He couldn't get her out of his mind.

XIX

July 19, 1924
Los Angeles, Calif.

Dear Danny:

Well, O'Neill, I mean of course Danny old pal received your letter today and just think it took all that time from 18 to 28 to arrive to me I don't know what kept it so long Cause you know right well I would ans. it just as soone as it would arrive to me like I'm doing now I'm very sorry to hear that Arnold Sheehan die good old Arnold he was a card and wish to you to express my sincere sympathy to his folks for me because I always like them and I know how they feel because I feel the same way when I lose my father and he was the best man in all the world to me and there never a better father live anywhere You said you once had a pal name Andy but let me tell you still have that pal if I got anything to say about it. Acorse I sure felt kind of bad over you not writing figure I had said something in one of my letter that you didn't like so stop writing. So you might know how glad I was to hear from you first letter I received from any one in Chi for a long time indeed. So old Mike Higgins is back there again in one place then another thats hime all over with he sure has seen a lot of this good old United States let me tell you that we sure had a strange meeting know him the first time I saw him Can't forget that boy and blives me he has change in every way got a he mans voice and quite tall and take it from me none of the fellows there will make a full of him now and I don't mean maybe and I don't mean even the older guys like Stutz Lonigan. I never like them any way they always want to make a full out of us and I sure wouldn't let them try and make a full out of me anymore if I was back in good old Chi only Stutz now he was all right and work for his father and not like Red Kelly and the rest of them and I wouldn't maybe want to have any trouble with Stutz but if I was back in good old Chi and they others tried to make a full of me they sure would have a fight on their hand and I don't mean maybe Oh so Mike Higgins said Iwas setting on tope of the world Hu well not quit the tope yet Dan not until I get to be a real saxophone player get my shelf a nice little sport mondle Buick 1924 about six months ago and it sure is a dandy and I don't mean maybe had the

*Saxe for little over a year and I'm sure getting good even thow
I say it myself playing now in a six peace dance Orchestra
                          do
and I sure. . . . like it. I will start om a Clarnet in about two
mor weeks and learne to play that. And then when I will be
able to play about five insturments well then I can say I'm sitting
on the top of the world there to stick Have not had any time
for ball sence I've been going in the past year about forgot
how to play. Glad to hear that you are still at the Con Ex and
I want to say, you got the righ kine of stickia a fellow never
gets no where going from one job to another look at the time
I lost doing that but never again fore me I haven't been in
a pool roome sence I've been out here Cause if I was you know
how har would be guess I don't have to mention it. And also
Dan that's why I respec Stutz because he got stickia too like
you only I don't think he ought to waste his time away in that
old Greek pool roome the Greeks they only want to cheat you
of your har earned money and make a full of you too Dan Well
the White Sox lost to Pilly to day but they are still in first
division and I expect to see them stay there and if they cant
win the pennet why they sure can beat the Cubs thats there
meat don't expect to the Cubs to be in second at the end of
season doing good if they are in the fourthe by then. As fore
me being a native son in a way I am and in a way I'm not
but take it from me you made a good guess when you said
McAdoo I had McAdoo writen all over my face and sure did
hate to see hime lose out frome now on I'm sopponting Daves
I don't kno where you get that Wilson son in law at he is the
best man of the lot and that is why they did not wan't him Cause
he is for the labering man and my dad if he was alive would
want the man that was for the labering man to get in and so
do I and as for your pick Walsh is a good man I amit so is
Ralston but this Underwood he is rotten as can be to much
a raitcal and not a good enough American to suit me and I
don't think very much of your Choce in mentioning him cause
he can't compare with McAdoo and the rest good Americans
And as for Woodrow Wilson why he is my Idee the graest
Presendent the United State ever had like my dad said baring
none. But sence it is a over lets forgot McAdoo Underwood and
the rest but Wilson and then saport Daves for the nex
Presendent do you agree with me this time cause I don't belive
you did the last time. Well old boy it was quite late when
I got home tonight so I guess I better Close for the percsent
Hoping I received a reply on the letter very soon I remain*

your Pal

Andy Le Gare

P.S. Glad to hear all the folks are well as for me well I hope you can read this Miss Lady writing so small what say By the way when you see Stutz Lonigan do say I send hime my regards and hello because I like hime but not the other older guys By the way my new number is going to be R F D #. 18½ or 869 Alhambra Calif.
no not in the country the city Ha Ha.

CHAPTER NINETEEN

I

"Here's Shanty Irish Lonigan!" Barney Keefe said.

"Hello, False Face," Studs retorted.

"Hey, Barney, why don't you go to work?" Shrimp Haggerty kidded, as the gang commenced strolling over to Washington Park. Barney did not reply, and Shrimp smiled. Shrimp spotted a baby-faced thing with bobbed hair hobbling along on the other side of the street on high heels, and he declared that it was a pretty nice beetle.

"Yoo-hoo!" Tommy Doyle called.

"You dropped something," Les shouted.

Studs had an impulse to try picking her up, but he had been kidded so much because of what had happened the last time he had robbed the cradle and had made Nellie Cullen that he didn't. The sight of the flapper, the sight of any girl, even his sisters, drove Lucy back into his mind. Just before he had left the house, he had surprised Loretta in the hallway, when she dashed out of the bathroom in only a chemise, her left breast sticking out. Last week, by accident, he had seen Fran without a strip on. Such things were driving him almost cuckoo. He had just called Lucy up before meeting the guys and tried to get a date with her, and for the third time since the dance she had given him the go-by. All over again, he tried to convince himself that she was nothing in his young life. She did mean something to him. Goddamn it, he was going nuts without her, thinking of her all the time. He could see that she was only a teaser. It didn't matter what she was. He remembered dancing with her, talking to her, holding her in his arms, kissing her, their tongues touching, digging his hand under her dress and touching her breast. He loved Lucy. He wanted—yes—to marry her. Red asked Studs what was the matter, was he thinking hard, worrying about his dose, what? Studs said there was nothing and that the dose was cured. Red congratulated him. Shrimp suggested getting a bottle and celebrating. Les said it would be all right by him.

"Say, Les, don't you and Shrimp ever have the curiosity to find out how it would be to stay sober for one night?" Kelly asked.

"What the hell! All the tanks here couldn't get drunk on one measly bottle."

"Sorry, Haggerty, but the Alcohol Squad is A.W.O.L. this evening," Stan Simonsky said.

"It's swell out," Studs said, looking at the twilight sky, wanting to forget things by talking and looking at the sky; only the sky made him remember all the more. A song came to him. Blue and broken-hearted—Blue because we're parted.— There was a time I was jolly—You know the reason, I'm melancholy. The words only half-expressed his feelings. And he had had them ever since the dance. He had had them all his life.

"Say, you know, I think I'll join the Navy," Shrimp said, looking pointedly at Barney.

"Last week, Shrimp was joining the Marines," Doyle said.

"Hell, Haggerty, with that caved-in chest you got, and with your guts pickled in alcohol, and a leg and a half in the grave, the Navy wouldn't even take you for punkin'," Barney sourly said.

"I'm organically all right. I'm just tired of hanging around here, without any job, so I thought I'd join up, see the world, building myself up physically so I wouldn't end up with a balloon belly and false teeth like Keefe," Shrimp said.

"I'm laughing," Barney snapped.

Studs wasn't interested in the gassing and kidding.

"If I was like Studs now, with an old man who's well heeled, and gives him a good job, and has a business to leave him when he kicks the bucket. But, hell, all a guy can get is a thirty-five or forty-dollar-a-week job. You won't find me wearing my can out that way," Shrimp said, giving Barney the eye.

"Yeah, you should be a painter too, and in summer time climb a ladder so much that your pants rub blisters on your tail, the way it happened to me last summer," Studs said. They laughed.

But Studs wished that Lucy would realize—see—that he could take care of her, give her things, make them . . . happy together. Why did he have to be such a goofy damn fool with sloppy feelings?

"Haggerty, better go back to that wife of yours, and let her take care of you. She might love you, even if her taste is all in her mouth," Keefe said.

"Shrimp is right. Now take me, what have I got to look

forward to but always wrestling freight for the Continental Express Company?" Les whined.

"Will you bastards quit singing the blues? You're young, and there's plenty of gash in the world, and the supply of moon goes on forever," Simonsky said.

Studs wished he had someone to talk it over with. He had almost talked with Fran or Loretta. But he had never been able to talk about things like that with anyone. If only things were the same with him and Helen Shires as they used to be when they were kids. Then he could talk about it with her.

"Haggerty, if you get in the Navy, you'll end up like Mush Joss in the jug after deserting three times."

"Mush was always a bum anyway," Shrimp said, and he got the horse laugh.

"Mush was a funny guy. You know, he was a damn swell baseball player, and if he kept on he'd be in the big leagues now. He played a good game for one year with the Carmelites High School. Then he left school because the family didn't have the jack to send him, and he just went to hell," Red said.

"Studs, you know, I'm pulling Keefe's leg. The bastard thinks he's getting a job as sewer-pipe layer down at Grant Park. And today I spoke to a guy I know who's assistant foreman and he told me I could count that job mine. Watch me get him," Shrimp said in confidence.

"Yeah, I think I'll join the Navy. No flunkey job for me. If anyone comes along, Barney can have them," Shrimp said, looking at Barney; Barney whistled.

"Well, I been thinking I'd get into the political game," Doyle said.

"You goddamn Irishman. Because your brother is assistant precinct captain without pay, you think you'll be assistant to Brennan, or Barney McCormack, the state senator. Every election day they let you stand in front of the polls looking like Jesus Christ, and wearing a tag, begging everybody to vote for a bunch of Shanty Irish crook politicians, and you think you're an influence," Keefe said.

"Sic 'em, Keefe!" Kelly said.

They crossed over to the park. The trees and grass were deep green, and they made Studs think of the trees on that day as a kid, when he licked Kelly. People were walking, they seemed contented, as if nothing was bothering them. The only way he would have that feeling was if he could get Lucy.

"Lonigan, that rat Haggerty can't kid me! He's pulling his own leg. That bastard thinks he's going to be sewer-pipe layer, and I was speaking to a friend of mine who's an assistant engineer down at Grant Park, and he told me I got that job sewn up. That skunk ain't puttin' nothing over on anybody but himself," Barney quietly said.

Studs smiled. He wasn't able to appreciate things like he had used to. Goddamn Lucy! He shouldn't let her be bothering him; wasn't he young, healthy and tough, didn't he have something to look forward to, hadn't he even bought himself a couple of stocks that the old man said were hot stuff?

Only. . . .

"Well, what are we going to do?" Studs said, feeling restless.

II

Shorty Wolfson, a young chap the size of a bantamweight who worked as a lineman for the telephone company, boxed with Eddie Eastman on the grass in the park. He tore into Eastman and cracked his jaw. Eastman lay down white. Milt Rosensplatz, the referee, counted ten.

"You're pretty good. There's a yellow streak all the way down your spine," Studs said.

Eddie tried to justify himself, and they told him to get away with that BS.

Wils Gillen and Swede Elston boxed like two clowns. Wils grimaced, swung, missed, fell on his face. He jumped up, rubbed his glove across his nose, hunched himself, cocked his hands. Swede toe-danced backwards out of danger. They missed haymakers, and clinched. They made faces at each other for a three-minute round and didn't land a blow. Studs told them not to box another round, because they were liable to break their hands on a tree.

Rosensplatz, the husky, flat-footed Jewboy, and Big Nose Jerry Rooney, from Johnny O'Brien's class at St. Patrick's, put on the gloves.

"Let there be light and there was light! Let there be Louisa Nolan's, and there was Three Star Hennessey! Let there be nose, and there was Rooney!" Young Rocky said.

"What battlers these boys are," Studs said, as they jabbed cautious gloves at one another.

"These punks are all the same. They can all fool around with fourteen-years-old girls, and not make the grade, but they got sawdust in their guts," Kelly sneered.

"Hey, Rooney, when did you get so good?" asked Doyle.

"I feel like I might go a round with one of the punks," Tommy said.

"Me too, but we don't want to hurt them," Studs said.

"A good stiff punch might wake 'em up, and they'll quit flogging the dummy," Doyle said.

"Hey, punk, I'll box a round with you," Red said.

"No slugging," O'Neill replied.

Red and O'Neill boxed. O'Neill fought defensively, jabbing with straight lefts, blocking Red's lunges. He caught Red on the nose with a left jab.

"Think you're tough!" Red said, his nose bleeding.

"It was an accident," O'Neill apologized.

"Better cut it out, Red, you're getting sore, and you don't want to kill the punk," Doyle said.

"Think you can fight me! Think you're tough!" Kelly bullied, while Wolfson unlaced his gloves, and Studs held a handkerchief to his nose.

"We were just boxing," O'Neill said.

"You better say that," Red said, walking over to the drinking fountain by the boathouse.

"That isn't anything. Red's nose always bleeds easy," Studs said, thinking Red was slipping, remembering how he had given Red a bloody nose in their fight, feeling proud because he knew he was able to stand the gaff when Kelly couldn't, glad Red had been shown up.

Doyle boxed with O'Neill. Doyle rushed, and O'Neill again boxed defensively, jabbing with his left, blocking, trying an occasional jab to the guts with a right cross.

"Hey, for Christ sake, I said I'd box with you, not run a foot race," Tommy beefed, stopping, hands at side, breathing rapidly.

"I am boxing."

"You mean you're trying to win a track meet," Doyle said, still winded, as he held his gloved hands up to be unlaced.

"Hey, I'll box with you!" Studs said to Rolfe.

"That's not my racket," Rolfe said.

Rosensplatz and Morgan were going to box next, but Milt acceded to Studs.

Jack Morgan was an unassuming, well-built, twenty-year-old kid. He waited calmly while the gloves were laced on Studs' hands. Studs felt good. He decided that he'd go easy with Morgan, and just show them that he wasn't through like Doyle and Kelly, but was the old Studs Lonigan. Just let the kid know he had the gloves on with Studs Lonigan.

Morgan faced Studs with hands out in the classical boxing stance. Studs crouched low, and waved his arms in Jack Dempsey fashion. He heard encouraging words from Fat Malloy, and it made him more strongly confident. He thought of himself a little like Jack Dempsey would be when going into the ring. He circled and swayed, pulled two feints, frowned for effect, set himself to let go with a left, and was stabbed in the jaw by a left jab.

"That boy's fast," Fat Malloy said professionally.

Studs lumbered in, and got stung with another left jab. He feinted, swayed, and let loose with a roundhouse right. Morgan stepped back and Studs looked foolish.

"Clever boy," Doyle said.

Studs didn't like the way Morgan looked at him, calm, unafraid, never changing his expression. He frowned to scare him. He feinted with a left, and got another sharp left jab, and before he knew it a right cross that gave him a headache. He momentarily saw wavering black dots. He forgot trying to box like Jack Dempsey. He rushed, and hit Morgan with a solid right. They clinched, and he tried to shove Morgan around. His arms were pinned, and he got a snapping short one in the ribs. Studs rushed again, took and gave a punch, they clinched. Breaking, he got Morgan with a wild right on the side of the head, and everybody was pepped up and yelled. Morgan's face was unchanged, and he waited, poised on his toes, left out, right cocked. Studs realized the kid could take it. No more giving him a break. He had to show some stuff, or be shown up. He rushed, and got four jabs for the punch he landed. Coming out of the clinch, he got an uppercut. Studs missed two rights, and received another stiff jab. He lost his temper, and slugged, not knowing what he was doing. Morgan slugged back punch for punch, until Rosensplatz said time was up.

"How about another round, kid?" Studs said, trying to hold in his temper and appear unaffected.

He wanted more. He knew he had been outfought and outboxed, and he had to come back. Everybody was pepped up too, but it was dark, and anyway, O'Neill had to take his gloves home. Studs shook hands with Morgan and said patronizingly that he'd been given a good workout. Morgan smiled taciturnly.

The older guys walked off. Studs was winded. His arms were leaden. His back ached. He had a headache and cuts inside his lip and jaw. He hoped they'd suggest sitting down on a bench or in the grass.

"There's little difference in the world between sparring with gloves on and fighting with your fists. If I was using my fists and really trying, I'd have massacred that snotty little punk, O'Neill," Red said.

Studs agreed. Hated O'Neill for having taken the gloves home. Still he felt that he couldn't have gone another round.

"The punks took you guys," Barney said.

"So says you! You toothless, dried-up Irish bastard!" Red said with venom.

"That Morgan kid is clever. He could make a monkey out of punks like O'Neill," Red said.

"He slugged, too," Doyle said.

"He gave me a good workout. He's clever. I think I'll put the gloves on with him again. With a little coaching, he'll be a sweet young fighter," Studs said.

He waited for them to say he'd outpointed the kid. Well, he had, Studs thought, trying to lie to himself. One of his punches was worth six of the kid's. Their non-committal remarks hurt him.

"I'm not in the best condition, and I think a few more workouts like that will do me good," Studs said.

"Yeah, he is good. He got in some nice lefts," Red said. He continued: "But I still say it's totally different, just boxing good-naturedly with gloves, and going to it with fists. That's why I told that snotty O'Neill so. I don't want him to think he can get tough now, because if he does, I'll slough him," Red said.

Studs agreed. Doyle said that if he had ridden a bicycle, he could have caught O'Neill. Barney sneered at them. Studs was glad when Tommy suggested they sit on a bench on the short walk near the boathouse. He brooded, and the whole thing about Lucy came back to him.

"You know, boys, the goddamn shines are getting too frisky coming around here," Red said.

"You Irish oughtn't to kick. You and the niggers can both look up to a snake," Keefe said.

"I came around the boathouse last Sunday, and it stunk with niggers. You know, it's so bad, that a decent girl can't walk alone here any more for fear a nigger might rape her. They ruin the park. When they come over here, you need a gas-mask if you want to stick around. . . . Why, you can tell they are inferior to the white race by the clothes they wear. Those goddamn loud clothes, wearing pearls in their bell-bottoms, purple suits, pink shirts. They're worse than the Polacks. You know, you can tell an inferior race by the way they dress. The Polacks and Dagoes, and niggers are the same, only the niggers are the lowest. That's why I say we ought to get the boys together some night and clean every nigger out of the park. They're all yellow and if we do it once, they won't come back. We can get a few billies and clubs, and if they try to use razors, make them just wish they hadn't."

Barney told Red to hire a hall. Shrimp agreed with Red, and Barney kidded him, saying he'd run if he saw a mammy coming after him. Doyle said that it always turned out the same way. If you give a nigger an inch, he always took a mile.

Studs wished there was something distracting to do, wished he could get Lucy out of his mind. He was pooped and felt that he was slipping because of what Morgan had done to him. The cuts inside his face hurt. Finally they walked over to the Bug Club.

III

They saw a crowd at the Bug Club near the hills by the Cottage Grove side of the park. There was one large circle, many smaller groups and numbers milling about.

"Well, I say that the world is coming to an end," Studs said, pleased when people from various groups frowned at him.

"The Bug Club will save the world, and drive everybody to drink or hell," Red shouted.

Smirking, they edged into a group, and saw, in the center, a well-fed, hefty, elderly, Jewish man shaking an Eversharp pencil at malcontent debaters.

"I should believe that. Rosenblatt here should tell me that I should think that. I should believe that Rosenblatt knows more than Einstein. I should think he can explain the theory of relativity in one sentence. Yah!" a sloppy fellow bellowed at the well-fed Hebrew.

"Friend, I shall explain the basic principle of relativity in one sentence that even you can understand."

"And I tell you I'm the traveling salesman that made Mary heavy with Christ. Yah."

"Relativity is a theory which assumes that, on a high basis of probability, there is no hitching-post in the universe."

Red lip-farted, and Slug said they were over his head. Red added that they were over the head of the human race.

"Friend, look at Orion up there in the sky. . . ."

"I should think maybe they got a hitching-post for mules like Rosenblatt up there."

"Finklestein, you're impossible!"

"Rosenblatt, get some monkey glands."

Jim Doyle brought them to hear Bishop Boyle in another noisy group. Bishop was a witty little Irishman, always kidding, and all right; he had a son a priest, and he was smart.

"Sure, Bishop, Jesus Christ was a bum. A hobo, with no place to lay his head. Why shouldn't he have been one when he wouldn't work and produce?"

"Arkwright, you're wrong there. Jesus Christ was the first communist."

"That guy talks like an atheist," Studs said, as Red emitted more lip-noises.

"He doesn't know whether Christ was crucified or killed with a second-hand book," Barney said.

"Sure, he's one of those liberal-minded fellows with no faith, who wants God to prove his existence by hiding behind every tree," Bishop Boyle said with a brogue.

"If I could see God behind a tree, I'd believe him."

"God made the tree; isn't that, my friend, sufficient proof? Or is the incomprehensibility in your anthropoid skull too dense to perceive that one fact of experience?" Bishop Boyle said.

"I'd like to see God. I'd like to tell him a few things. I'd like to say, 'God, why do you create men and make them suffer and fight in vain, and live brief unhappy lives like pigs, and make them die disgustingly, and rot? God, why do the beautiful girls you create become whores, grow old and toothless, die and have their corpses rot so that they are a stench to human nostrils? God, why do you permit thousands and millions of your creatures, made in your own image and likeness, to live like crowded dogs in slums and tenements, while an exploiting few profit from the sweat of their toil, produce nothing, and live in kingly mansions? God, why do you permit men to starve, hunger, die from syphilis, cancer, consumption? God, why do you not raise one little finger to save man from all the turmoil, want, sorrow, suffering on this human planet?' That's what I'd say to God if I could find him hiding behind a tree. But God is a wise guy. He keeps in hiding."

"You could make a better world, couldn't you, fellow?" Red Kelly yelled.

"Red, hell with him. He's a crazy radical," Studs said.

"Friend, if I had the powers attributed to Bishop Boyle's God, I certainly would not have created as botched a world."

Bishop Boyle tried to explain that the ways and purposes of God were mysterious, and that man suffered because of the fall of Adam. The atheist, a starved-looking little man, said it was disgusting, and walked out of the crowd. Red grabbed his arm.

"Fellow, are you healthy?" Red asked.

"I do not understand you, friend."

"If you want to preserve that health, lay off the Catholic Church."

"Yeah, keep your trap padlocked while you're all together," Studs said.

"You hoodlums cannot abrogate my rights of free speech."

"See this!" Red said, showing a closed fist.

"I'll have you arrested if you dare touch me!"

"It would be worth going to jail to punch in your filthy blaspheming mouth!"

"Yeah, blow!" Doyle said.

The atheist slunk off. Red said it was the only way to talk with fellows like that. They had no brains, were ignorant and filthy-minded, and you couldn't argue with them. The whole human race should treat them the same way.

"I don't see why they let these radicals congregate here and speak like that," Shrimp said.

"The cops used to clean them out, but they got an injunction. I'd like to have been the judge. I'd have made them all go to work," Red said.

They listened in on a political argument. A Single Taxer was defending Davis, declaring that the Republican Party was corrupt, that La Follette was trying to destroy the Supreme Court, and that also, when the last war had been declared, La Follette had proven himself to be a traitor to his country. A six-foot-four giant was defending La Follette's progressiveness. A communist was saying, in a foreign accent, that La Follette was a class betrayer. Red got into the argument and spoke for Davis, but he didn't get tough because the communist and La Follette man both looked pretty big.

They wandered to another group. Jim Doyle said there was Father Kroke, who thought he was God. He pointed to a skeleton of a man over six feet, not weighing more than one hundred and twenty pounds, whose hollow eyes and face contrasted with a full Jesus beard and seemed ghostly.

"I suppose, Father Kroke, that you're the second coming of Christ?"

"Say, this guy's belly must have the same feeling for a meal that mine has for gin," Shrimp said.

"Hell, if he got a meal, he'd die of indigestion," Red said.

Father Kroke tried to say something, but stuttered so badly that no one understood him. Red told him to say it in Greek. Jim Doyle said the nut had taught himself Greek and nine other languages. Red countered that he'd never taught himself how to earn an honest dollar.

"I ask you to believe me because it is a revelation. I was an atheist, too, and talked as you do now. I did, until one night when the Blessed Virgin came to me in a vision, and her spirit flew through my whole body. . . ." Father Kroke said, stuttering on almost every word.

"She must have been pretty hard up, huh, Father Kroke?"

Father Kroke explained that mankind had been led away from the true Christianity by Anti-Christ, the Pope of Rome, and he had been called by God to guide it back to the simplicity of the early Christians, and to reestablish the Church of God on democratic principles. The American Church was, in basic doctrine, the same as the Catholic, only priests were elected by the congregations, and the doctrine of papal infallibility was branded a lie. It had only a small membership but it was growing. Next Sunday, he would say mass in the park by a nearby tree, if one member of the church was able to procure the wine for sacramental purposes, as she had promised.

Slug remarked that the guy had plenty of marbles missing. A fellow at Slug's side said he was a paranoiac and also thought himself descended from Robert Bruce. Slug gave the guy a queer look. The fellow said, last Easter, Father Kroke had tried to say mass by a tree in the park, and that lightning had struck the tree. Red said it was an act of God. Studs said that nut thought he was the Pope and laughed. Jim Doyle said he was a real nut. Came from a good family, and his father would give him anything if he would work, and cut out all this insanity. But he was too far gone, and had let himself be disinherited. He lived by begging, and picking things out of garbage cans, and had no place to sleep. Sometimes, when he could get an extra dime, he walked downtown and slept in an all-night movie.

Studs goosed Father Kroke. He jumped and quivered. The mere touch of his bony body disgusted Studs.

"Father Kroke, the Holy Spook did that to you!"

"If the person who did that to me will step up, I shall be perfectly within my rights as an American citizen in slapping him," Father Kroke excitedly stuttered.

"Satan has his eyes on you, Father Kroke!"

"Yes, Satan tried to put obstacles in my path all the time, but God is behind me."

Father Kroke took up a collection, and four slugs and two pennies were dropped in his filthy straw hat. Father Kroke limped away from the Bug Club, a hunched living corpse in ill-fitting, hand-me-down clothes.

They went to the big circle. Jim Doyle told them about the chairman, Pat Gilroy. He was a corpulent, medium-sized, bald-headed man in white flannels and blue coat, and he had been running for Congress in the district east of the park ever since Noah put the Ark in slow speed. The Democrats let him run on their ticket because they didn't want to waste time and money on a certain failure. He'd pull off a hundred votes anyway, at the next election. Jim said he was also another crazy radical.

Gilroy declared that he was not trying to use the chairmanship of the Bug Club for personal aggrandizement by trying to get votes. He then told the crowd that the next speaker was a man they had been waiting to hear all evening, a man whose talks were always a delight and benefit, a man of solid intellectual integrity and conviction, who would have many interesting and original words to say on the question of race prejudice which they had been discussing and listening to all evening— John Connolly. Jim told them to listen because he was a brilliant fellow, and King of the Soap Boxers. Red sarcastically described it an honor. Studs suggested shouting him down. Jim said Connolly was tough.

Connolly stood in the center of the circle, a tall, handsome, physically impressive man with dark hair. He spoke in a deep, convincing voice remarking that the previous speakers all seemed to have been debating whether a Yiddish junk-man, a Pullman porter, or a flat-footed guardian of a hundred million city ordinances were the lowest example of the human ape. He did not propose to continue such inane blather. On the contrary, he would present certain aspects of urban growth which were relevant to the question of race prejudice in Chicago. These factors also were not mere hearsay, but plausible ideas presented by members of the Department of Sociology at the University of Chicago, and developed from the work they had already done on a community research programme. He explained that the City of Chicago could be divided into three concentric circles. The innermost of these circles was the business or downtown district, the Loop, where the principal stores, offices, and commercial houses were located, and where most of the high-class legal gypping went on. The second circle housed manufacturing and wholesale houses, slums, tenements, can houses and other haunts of vice. The outer circle made up the residential districts and it could boast of the most fog houses because the sky pilots and camouflage artists always found sweet pickings amongst the well-to-do whose gypping was high-class and within the law. When the city expanded, it expanded from the center. In Chicago, thus, expansion spread out from the Loop. The inner circle was pushed outwards causing corresponding changes in the other concentric circles. The Negroes coming into the situation as an economically inferior race, had naturally found their habitation in the second circle. Since they had located in the slums of the black belt, the city had been growing into a bigger and better Chicago. The pressure of growth was forcing them into newer areas. Furthermore, some of the Negro booboisie had gotten into the big gypping process, and like their white brothers, they did not like to live in stench, and sandwiched in between a whore house and the junk shop of Isadore Goldberg. With their economic rise, the Negroes sought more satisfactory housing conditions. Besides, the black boys were happiest when engaged in the horizontals. That meant an increasing birth-rate amongst them, and another factor necessitating improved and more extensive domiciles. All these factors produced a pressure stronger than individual wills, and resulted in a minor racial migration of Negroes into the white residential districts of the south side. Blather couldn't halt the process. Neither could violence and race riots. It was an inevitable outgrowth of social and economic forces.

A young fellow booed.

"Some waffle pup in the audience is aching to get his puss slapped. Now the next one of you cheap wise guys who heckles is going to get the smile slapped off your mugs, and if any two or three of you want to try it, the same goes for you. If you want to go home with your snotty faces in a sling, just try getting wise. Otherwise, keep your traps closed like your mothers warned you to!" Connolly bellowed.

After the applause, he continued speaking.

"Slug, I'd like to see you tangle with that louse," Kelly whispered.

Slug said he had nothing against him, and liked a fellow who took nobody's sass. Red said he couldn't understand an Irishman being a nigger-lover. Studs supposed that the guy would let a nigger jazz his sister. The next speaker, a small, untidy Jew, monotonously said that according to anthropology, which was a new science they were studying at the University of Chicago, they had proven as a scientific truth that no one race is superior to any other race. Studs asked Red what he was trying to say. Red said he was trying to prove that a Jew was a white man. The audience called for time.

Excitement started outside the circle. The gang rushed to it. They found a cop arguing with a kid. The cop pulled a gun. Connolly, by a quick twist of the policeman's wrist, took the gun and warned him not to try shooting off more than his mouth. The cop barked loudly. Connolly told him to keep cool. He sent the kid away, handed the gun back to the cop, and told him to be careful or it would go off. He walked away, followed by an adulatory crowd.

IV

"He's a real guy," Slug said as they walked towards Fifty-eighth Street.

"He'll get his. Those wise radicals always do. You can't go against the human race," Kelly said.

"He's got guts," Slug said.

"He was in jail during the war for being a pacifist. And a

few years back he went out to agitate at a coal strike in Colorado, and the police kicked out a couple of his front teeth. But even though I know he's wrong, he's a smart man," Jim Doyle said.

"If I'd been that cop, I'd have plugged him," Red said.

"He's just over the heads of you hoods," Jim Doyle said.

"Sure, he thinks he's too good for the human race," Red said.

"He isn't yellow," Studs said, thinking how big and tough Connolly was, and how small he himself was. He thought of how Morgan had baffled him. He admired and envied and hated the big fellow.

"All those guys read too much. When you do that you get lop-sided. Now I was reading some stories by a Frenchman named Balzac. . . ."

Haggerty punned the word.

"He was an atheist, and because he was, he wrote stories that are so filthy they make you want to puke," Kelly continued.

"Dirty stories?" asked Shrimp.

"And how," Red replied.

"Maybe I'll read them," said Shrimp.

"But, anyway, I suppose the French are a pretty filthy race, and that's why this guy wrote such stuff," Red said.

"Look at all the American soldiers who got the syph," Shrimp said.

"Me for Paris," Slug said.

"Boy, I'll bet that with a little dough you could get all you wanted there," Red said.

Tommy wondered how long it would take Slug to know as many whores in Paris as he did in Chicago. Shrimp said they needed some liquor. Studs wanted some. He couldn't get things off his mind, the humiliation he had suffered, Lucy. He wished he'd been a hero in the war or even killed.

When they got tired of hanging around Fifty-eighth Street with nothing to do, they got drunk on Jamaica ginger. Their drunken attention was caught by a passing Negro hot-tamale-man. They slugged him and took the wagon. Red wheeled it and they marched down the street towards the park. They each had a hot tamale and debated what to do with the rest. Red caught a passing shine. They tossed him into the fountain by the curve in the boathouse path. He struggled to get out of the slippery fountain, and was shoved back, and pelted as long as they had hot tamales. Studs passed out. He was carried home, and they left him to sleep all night on the back porch.

SECTION FOUR

1926-1929

XX

St. Patrick's new church was a half block long, and several hundred yards wide. It was cruciform in shape, a squat box of dull red brick with a dome rounding out of the center. The nave was expansive, giving an illusion of tremendous size. It was segmented by impressive marble pillars, overhung by the hollowed dome of glass, and lined with oak pews. The floor was stone. The main altar, imported from Italy, was a huge slab of marble, set back in a hollow, and flanked by two altars that formed the horizontal sides of the cruciform. At the side altars, there were weakly conventional statues of St. Joseph, and the Blessed Virgin Mary. Above the altar were circular windows of stained glass with the half-distinguishable figures of Christ, Mary, St. Patrick and other saints, trumpeting and flying angels with the face of Donatello's "David," baby angels, sheep and retreating snakes. On the left towards the front, there was an altar shrine to St. Anthony with a marble statue of the saint. The stations of the cross dotted the church with cheaply emotionalized statuary representations of the suffering and death of Christ. The choir box, with a ten-thousand-dollar organ and gilded pipes, was overhead in the rear, and next to it, a small gallery with tiers of pews. The edifice was built in no specific architectural style. It was a loot of traditions.

At eleven o'clock on the second Sunday in February, the year of our Lord nineteen hundred and twenty-six, the first services, a high mass celebrated by his eminence, the Cardinal Archbishop, were conducted. Parishioners, former parishioners, visitors, sightseers, all attended mass, and every pew in the church was occupied, with an overflow crowd along the side, in the aisles, and in the rear. In his eulogistic sermon, the Cardinal Archbishop decribed the occasion as the greatest day in the history of St. Patrick's parish. He lauded the untiring zeal, devotion, foresight, energy, and courage of the pastor, Reverend Father Gilhooley, and the unstinted loyalty, generosity, faith, and cooperative spirit of the good people of the parish. Years afterwards, this day of rejoicing and victory

391

*would be remembered by all who were so fortunate as to be
present. For was it not a day celebrating the opening of a new
and beautiful house of worship to God Almighty, the consecration of a church that would stand almost until eternity
as a tribute of art and beauty to the lasting glory of God, and
also as a memorial record of the religious fervor of the people
of this parish. After the Cardinal Archbishop, Father Gilhooley
mounted the marble pulpit, and expressed his own brief words
of gratification, pride, joy, and appreciation.*

It was a great day.

*And standing in the rear of the church were four new and
totally edified parishioners. Their skin was black.*

CHAPTER TWENTY

I

Sally, a buxom human heifer, leaned forwards over the cashier's counter, and handed Dapper Dan O'Doul the autographed
picture of Ramon Novarro, which she had procured by sending
money and stamps. Her blue energetic eyes flashed, and she
continued leaning forwards with the front of her dress sagging,
permitting Dapper Dan to get an eyeful.

"Isn't he keen?"

"He's the nuts," Dapper Dan said, arranging his precisely-
tied silver-and-red cravat.

"That bastard hangs around all night, peeping down Sally's
dress," Studs said.

"Still raining. Christ, this weather," Red said, looking out
the door to see the rain bouncing on the sidewalk like silver
dollars.

"Say, will that broad come across?" Studs asked, resting
his elbow on the radiator.

"Dapper Dan is sure trying hard enough," Doyle said.

"These young punks around here are worse than O'Neill,
and that goof, Young Rocky, who went to New York," Studs
said.

"They call O'Doul the Kodak kid. He hangs around the
drug store all winter posing, and he kodaks on the beach in
summer time, combing his hair as if he was having his picture
taken, and never even getting his feet wet. He's a lulu,"
Tommy Doyle said.

"That goddamn rain," Kelly said.

A customer, hastening in hunched and wet, had to shove
to get by the gang because they were choking the doorway.

"Hey, Dapper Dan," Studs called.

"Studs, it doesn't shave yet," Red Kelly said, as O'Doul stood before them.

"Listen, O'Doul, does she say you're handsomer than that movie actor whose picture she's got there?" Studs asked; the older guys laughed in O'Doul's face.

Sally heard, and laughed; Dapper Dan blushed. Red cursed the weather. Slug said O'Doul ought to wipe the milk from behind his ears with toilet paper. Studs sidled over to Curley and whispered to him. Curley looked at Studs, blankly.

"Go on!" Studs prodded.

Vinc pouted at Studs. He sulked over by Sally's desk.

"Say, Dan, Studs asked me to ask you if you got that topcoat all paid for?"

"Vincent, you're not even as funny as a hearse," Dapper Dan said; the older guys laughed, and Sally gave them the wink.

"Studs, why did you ask me to ask that when you knew he would get sore, and he's my friend?" Vinc gravely said, causing another barrage of laughter.

"Vincent!" Sally coquetted.

"Hey, Cowboy, Curley's competition for you. Watch your step!" Tommy Doyle said.

"Studs, is Curley becoming a lady-killer?" Fat Malloy asked.

"Vincent, won't you even talk to poor little harmless Sally?" she cooed.

Vincent said he had to ask Malloy an important question. Fat roughly asked what. Vinc said that with everybody all talking all at once he had forgotten it, but if he had a minute to think, he'd remember again. Studs yelled for him to beware of brain-fever.

"All right, Vincent, you'll be sorry some day, if you put Sally on the shelf," she tantalized.

Studs looked at the time: eight-twenty.

Malloy told Vinc to wake up, the girl was stuck on him. They shoved Vinc towards the desk.

"Vincent, you're perfectly horrid, you always act so high hat, and never speak to me. Why, you treat me like I was a bug or something."

"When did I do that? I never said you was a bug."

"Hey, Fat, tell him to cut it out before we all laugh ourselves into a nut house," Studs said.

"I don't remember when I said anything like that," Curley said, twisting himself around the counter.

"Tell him to let it alone," Studs told Tommy.

"I'll bet if he had let it alone, he wouldn't have so many marbles absent from his brain," Slug said.

Studs suggested doing something. Slug said they might if the rain would stop. Tommy said they could go down to the poolroom at Fifty-fifth Street. Red said it would be nuts going down there in the rain. They said it was too bad that the Greek had closed up the poolroom.

"Here comes Society Brand, the Clothes Peddler," Fat Malloy said. Phil Rolfe entered, pulling down an umbrella. His greeting was ingratiating. He remarked that it was raining. Fat told him not to crap them, the sun was shining bright.

"Say, Society Kid, you look like the rage," sixteen-year-old, skinny Pete Webb said, as Phil unbuttoned his yellow slicker.

"Like the suit, boys?"

"It's the nuts, Phil," Pat Carrigan said.

"Listen, any time you need one, come down and see me. I'm at Sankey, Hatfield, and Cohen's, on Adams Street. We handle straight Society Brand stuff, give perfect fit, and have a reasonable budget plan. Here's one of my cards."

"Say, Phil, I was waiting to see you," Curley said, leaving Sally.

"Hello, Vincent," Phillip said.

"Want to go to the Michigan tonight?"

"Gee, Vincent, I'm sorry, but I got a date. We'll make it some other night."

He walked over to Studs, smiling. He ignored the grunted greeting he got, and mentioned that he was selling suits, had some swell buys, and suggested that Studs drop in on him the next time he was needing clothes. Couldn't get a better suit for the price anywhere in town.

"Leave it to the kikes," Tommy Doyle said, after Rolfe had gone over to the group around Pat Carrigan and Pete Webb.

"They're all the same. I'm your friend, fellow . . . but business first," Red said.

Studs looked at the clock: eight-twenty-seven.

"Jesus Christ!" he exclaimed, bored.

Slug mentioned seeing the girlies. Tommy said that after the last four nights, he'd had enough for a while. Slug kidded that he must be getting old. Studs said no more for him for a while. Slug kidded that you never could get enough of it.

"Say, I'll be damned, if the Jew isn't selling Curley a suit," Red said.

Tommy yelled for Vinc not to buy a suit. Phil protested that he wasn't selling anything.

"Oh, say, Davey Cohen's back," Red said.

"How is he?"

"He hasn't grown hardly an inch since he left, and he looks

like hell. I tell you, if he hasn't got the con, I'll eat it on State and Madison at high noon."

"What'll we do?" Studs asked, observing that it was eight-thirty.

"What do you say, Doyle?" asked Slug.

"How about you, Kelly. Any bright ideas?" asked Tommy.

Slug called Vinc over and asked him if he wanted to go to a can house. It merited some more buffoonery. Phil button-holed Vinc again, and warned him not to let the barbers get his goat. Studs sneered, and moved more closely to them. He overheard Phil telling Curley that a new Sankey, Hatfield, and Cohen society suit would make a man of him, make him at-tractive to all the girls. Vinc said he'd think about it, and prop-ositioned Phil again about the movies. Phil said he couldn't because he had a date with Fritzie Lonigan. Studs frowned and ambled back with Doyle and the guys by the radiator. Slug said that the punks had caused the poolroom to close, because they'd always hung around, and never spent any jack. Phil got razzed as he left.

Studs looked at the clock: eight-thirty-four. He watched the second-hand sweep around once. Another minute gone. Car-rigan hurt the feelings of Dapper Dan O'Doul by telling him he could never succeed in outsheiking Phil Rolfe. Phil was the one and original.

"Jesus, let's do something. I can't stand the sight of these goofy young p——s and their goddamn gab," Studs said.

"Wait a couple of minutes, and if the rain stops, we'll walk down to the Michigan," Red said.

Malloy spoke loudly about the way Phil rooked in all the boys, telling them to come down, pay their first deposit, get the suit on the budget plan, and then not pay any more. He said that he got his commission anyway and didn't care. He had rooked Rooney in that way and Rooney could tell them how he had been dunned and forced to pay.

The store manager interrupted Fat, and asked the crew to leave because they were blocking the door and injuring busi-ness. They sulked. Everybody wondered what to do. It was still raining heavily. Vinc got in Studs' way, and Studs booted his tail. Studs looked at the clock in the window: eight-thirty-nine. Studs hated the manager, wished he'd clouted him. Get-ting kicked out of the store because of the punks!

Finally they went to the show. Coming back with the boys for coffee an', Studs noticed that Dapper Dan was still mushing around Sally. He laughed. He wondered out loud if she could be made. He consumed his coffee an' quickly and said good-night to the boys. He stopped for cigarettes, and asked Sally what she was doing after work. She said her boy friend came and got her every night. He left. Another goddamn night wasted, and the movie had been punk too.

II

After supper, Studs walked out of the dining-room with Loretta. He side-glanced at her, this girl, his sister. She was smaller than he, hardly more than up to his shoulder. Everyone said she looked like him. Well, she did. All four of them looked alike; they had the same broad brows, the same complexion, the same eyes. Only the girls had dark hair, and he and the kid brother had lighter hair, brown.

"Say, I saw Phil last night," Studs said, not knowing how to commence, feeling what the hell business was it of his anyway, but still believing that he ought to say something.

"Yes, I was to College Inn with him."

"Have a good time?"

"I had a perfectly grand time."

He couldn't but wonder how far Phil, how far any guy, could go with her. They said any girl could be made by the right guy, and maybe so, but, Jesus, he hoped that that kike was not the right guy. All those punks were always talking about making girls. He wondered how much of it was just crap talk.

Hell, for years now, he'd hardly spoken to her about anything much. He'd lived in the same house, seen at breakfast and supper, talked a little bit now and then, but almost never about anything that was important. She was his sister, and she was a stranger. But goddamn it, she could find someone better than a cheap kike.

"It seems to me that you could find better fellows to go with than Phil Rolfe," he said, making his tone of voice doubly nasty because he felt that he was butting his nose where it didn't belong, and also because he didn't know his sister or know how she would feel or act about anything important to her.

Her mouth popped open; she was too surprised to speak.

"You're a good-looking girl and you could go with a lot of nice fellows, without having dates with a Jew."

"He's not a Jew. He's preparing to become a Catholic. He told me so last night," she said.

"They wouldn't let him in the Church, not a Jew like him," Studs said, losing his temper because of his lack of conviction.

"You have nothing to say about what I do or whom I go with," she said, her voice almost cracking into a sob.

"Well, if any guys like him start fooling around with my

sister, I might show what I got to say," said he.

"You're a perfect beast. I hate you!" she said.

Her face relaxed; she cried. She turned and walked away. He was sorry.

"You leave her alone!" Fran yelled at him.

She talked to Loretta. Studs, passing back through the hall to the bathroom, heard Fran saying the same things as he had said, only in a different manner.

The father called Studs into the parlor.

"Bill, I know how you feel. I'm proud of you, proud that you would stand by your sisters. Only Bill, you know women are like a delicate instrument. You have to handle them with care. You got to be diplomatic," Lonigan said in preparation for an outburst of platitudinous parenthood.

"All right," said Studs.

"Bill, I had something else to tell you. Wait a minute. Don't go yet," Lonigan said apologetically.

"Yeah," Studs answered with annoyance as he half turned towards his father.

"I was thinking that maybe next summer I'll be taking myself and your mother back to the old country, and letting you manage things."

"All right."

"I got the business going fine. I just got that new hotel contract, and the way it looks, I'm gonna get that school contract. Of course, it's costing me a little. You know when you want a school contract, well, you have to see the boys you're getting it from. But I think I'll have that sewn up just as neat as you'd like in a week or two. Well, when those two are finished, I think I'll take a rest and let the mantle of responsibility fall on your shoulders."

"That's good. When will we start on that hotel?"

"In about a month. It's a hundred-thousand-dollar job. And that school one, there's going to be real gravy."

"How you getting it?"

"Barney McCormack and I came to a verbal understanding today. He can fix it with the right fellows who are letting out the bids. Of course, it'll only be fair to repay Barney for his favor, but I tell you, it's real gravy for us, Bill."

Studs left. His sister Loretta followed him out. He was conscious of her walking behind him, her heels clicking on the paving. She walked fast, flung her head proudly to one side, passed him. She kept a few yards in front of Studs. He was sorry he'd had the damn squabble with her. He was right, though, in trying to tell her but he hadn't gone about it the way he might have.

He watched her. She was a pretty kid, and decent. He felt as if always, even though they'd said little to each other, they'd had sort of a bond between them. Now that was broken, and he liked her and she was a pretty kid.

She walked in front of him as far as Fifty-eighth and Indiana Avenue. He wanted to talk to her, and tell her to forget it, but he could just see himself doing that.

She turned down Indiana. He walked on over to the corner. The contracts the old man had gotten would mean dough, but lots of work. He hated everything about the goddamn work. Sometimes he felt like taking all the damn paint he could get his hands on and dumping it in the river. But it meant dough and when the old man kicked the bucket, it would be his.

"Jesus Christ!" he said, expressing an unclean and sudden disgust.

From force of habit, he walked past the drug store on down to where the poolroom used to be. Looking at the empty, light-less place, he suddenly came to and realized that the poolroom was gone. He wished it wasn't. He went back to the corner of Fifty-eighth and Prairie.

III

Studs and Tommy Doyle leaned against the side of the drug store building, watching the punks. They were in old clothes and football outfits.

"Jesus, I'll bet they make a fine bunch of players," sneered Studs, wishing that he were in football togs.

"I'll bet they'll play that touch football so they don't get their hair mussed," said Tommy.

"If they get up against a good tough team, they'll be sweet," said Studs.

"Hello, Studs," said Phil, who was in football regalia.

"What the hell do you play?" asked Tommy.

"I'm one of the halfbacks," said Phil.

"Sure, he's the All-American-Half-Ass," said Studs. Phil turned to say something to one of his teammates, acting as if he hadn't heard Studs' crack.

"OOPH!" Studs exclaimed, seeing Dapper Dan O'Doul in a football outfit.

"Jesus Christ, him too," said Tommy.

"You know they got their suits from Gorman. He's running for judge, and they're Gorman Boosters," said Studs.

"Well, they sure ought to make him lose the election," said Tommy.

"Here comes that kike pest," said Studs.

"Got a nickel or a butt, Studs?" Tommy mimicked.

"You got Father Abraham there down to a 't' that time," said Studs.

"Hello, boys," Davey Cohen said with ineffectual cheerfulness.

"Got a cigarette, Tommy?" said Studs. Tommy held out a pack and winked.

"Say, got another there, Tommy?" Davey asked.

Studs winked back. Davey took a cigarette.

"Boys, I saw Helen Shires," said Davey.

"How is she?" asked Tommy.

"Is she married?" asked Studs.

"I heard she's a Lesbian," said Davey, laughing sardonically.

"What the hell's that?" Studs asked.

"She's like a fairy only in love with women. I don't know if that's true, but that's what I heard," said Davey.

"Oh!" said Studs.

He remembered that show he'd seen at Burnham. He was disgusted. His disgust turned to a fierce but silent hatred of Davey. All his old liking and respect for Helen from the old days returned. It couldn't be true. It wasn't.

"Tell us the dope about her," said Studs.

"Well, I just heard it, that's all, she was living with another girl, and that, well, a guy I know who knows her girl chum, he says he was up to their apartment, and that he saw plenty."

Davey bummed a cigarette off Studs and told Lesbian stories that he'd heard on the road. He was happy. And he hadn't been happy much since he'd returned. He had that cough. And the guys weren't the same. They didn't accept him as one of the boys. He knew it, and needn't kid himself. He was a little sick Jew now, a sick tormented Jew. He could see the way they looked at him, talked. And he was down, broke and sick. They weren't sick, and even the ones who hadn't any dough were able to raise more than he ever could. All he had was what he bummed. His kid brother had a good job, and once in a while gave him a half buck, but not often. Now, he was telling them stories that interested them, and he felt like it was the same as the old times when he was one of the boys, in with them, a battler who could go with the best of them; and goddamn it, he had been able to go with the best of them—once.

"That's queer, all right," said Studs.

"It ain't natural. They ought to take and shoot girls like that, they ain't natural, and they're a disgrace to the human race," Red Kelly said.

"I'll bet she must be awfully unhappy if that's true," Les said naively.

"That thing is against the natural law," said Red with un-shakable self-conviction.

"Well, of course, I feel they can't help it. I think maybe they're born that way, or they are made that way because of something that happens in their life," Davey said, apologetically.

"B.S.," Red said.

"I suppose you'd like to kiss a girl like that," Tommy sneered.

"That's worse than having a nigger. Think of it, a girl comes from a self-respecting family, with a decent old man and old lady. She had a decent home, a chance for an education, an opportunity to meet decent fellows, and to become a fine, decent girl. And what does she do, but become worse than the hustler of a nigger pimp? And you try to say she can't help it! Why girls like that ought to be made to live with pigs," Red proclaimed.

"I wonder if much of that stuff goes on?" said Studs.

"Plenty, if you ask me. Only I said I just heard that," said Davey.

"She was always a tomboy as a kid," said Red.

"Yes, it wasn't natural for a girl to be like a boy," said Tommy.

"She was a swell pal as a kid," Studs said, nostalgically.

"Say what you want to, but the finest and most decent girls are Irish Catholic girls," said Red.

"No jane is decent if she meets the right guy," said Slug.

"Well, I don't know that I agree with you there, Slug," said Red.

"Say, it ain't a matter of what you call decency. It's all a matter of the right guy coming along at the right time," said Slug.

"No, sir, you get a good Catholic girl, who has a decent home, the right kind of parents, and fear of God in her, like Studs' sisters, and they're decent, they're fine, they're amongst the finest things you can find in life," said Red.

Studs felt proud of his sisters.

"And when girls don't, there's only two things to do. The old man to give her his razor strap, and the old man or brother or somebody to give the clouts to the guys that try and fool around with her," said Red.

"Well, boys, let's go to a show," said Studs.

"All right."

They walked off. Davey trailed after them, and asked if anyone had enough to lend him to come along. They didn't answer him.

"Studs, I can pay you back tomorrow," said Davey, half pleading.

"Sorry, Dave, all I got is enough for the show and coffee an' afterwards," Studs said.

Davey watched them straggle down towards Garfield Boulevard. He was sorry that he had returned. He had no pain in his chest, but he felt that he had. Only a poor sick Jew. He thought of Heine, whose poem he'd read in the Jamestown library.

"That Jew moocher," sneered Studs.

"Yeah," said Slug.

"Say, he's the kind, his kind, that sold out Wabash Avenue to the niggers. If it wasn't for the Jews, this would be a better neighborhood than it is. But anyway, with the new church, it will pick up," said Red.

"I know my old man is beginning to wonder if he ought to sell his building after all, and clear out," said Studs.

"Well, I tell you, once the kikes get in a neighborhood, it's all over," said Red with unanswerable argument.

IV

Davey Cohen bummed a dime off Joe Coady. He hung on Joe's neck talking, telling him about bumming, about anything, just to talk. Joe finally blew. Davey could see that he'd bored Joe. He suddenly hated Coady. Joe was only a punk. Once he'd been only that, and Davey'd been one of the big guys, and one of the toughest of the tough—well, he had—around the corner. Now, he was a little runt, cadging nickels and dimes off kids he'd formerly protected and been a hero to. He hoped, Jesus, some day—But it was pretty much crap to hope. He felt convinced that he had that pain back in the chest. He stopped in the Greek Restaurant for coffee.

Christy, the waiter, was at the last seat by the counter, writing, with a book at his side. He came forwards, and said hello. Davey got a cup of coffee.

"Gee, I wish I was back in California," Davey remarked, putting sugar in the coffee, and stirring it.

Christy said that he'd gone to an American high school out on the coast.

"I like the climate. Jesus, it's a grand place," Davey said, wishing pathetically that he were there, forgetting that when he had been on his uppers in Los Angeles, he'd wished that he'd been in Chicago.

"It's nice out there," Christy said.

Christy was a tall, heavy-set, full-faced Greek in his forties. His hair was thinned out, and there was a bald spot on his head.

"The broads out there, they're thick as flies around a garbage can, and they're all like rabbits. Say, that place is paradise for a guy if he's got a little jack," Davey said.

"That's the movies," Christy said.

"Plenty of them are hot, nice."

"I know girls go there. They want to be like . . . like Mary Pickford. They are poor girls, no money. They get no jobs. They become what . . . whores. Yes," Christy said.

"I know it. Say, there's girls like that all right out there. They'll go the limit, do anything a guy wants for a meal. There's girls like that in any big town."

"It's this country, capitalism."

"I know how it feels to be out of work, in a strange town, stony," said Davey reflectively, taking a sip of coffee.

"And in Los Angeles, they have fanatics. Christians," said Christy.

"Sure. All kinds of bugs. There's more fake saviors there than any place in the world."

"Christians. Love your neighbor as yourself. Christians," sneered Pete.

"And what the hell did they do to get their God but steal Him from the Jews," laughed Davey.

"And the Catholic Church. Yes. It has perverted the great philosophy of Aristotle."

"I don't like the Catholics none. They're hypocrites and idolators," said Davey.

"Jesus, He was great. Great men like Lenin and Savonarola and Socrates. Christians, they drag him in the mud. They don't love Jesus, or follow his example. They are afraid. They have a God of fear. That's religion . . . fear."

"The Irish made a shanty Irishman out of Christ," Davey said.

"Yes, Jesus was a noble man. The Christians, Catholics, they put Him in a sink of superstition."

"Yeah, Christy," said Davey, kind of agreeing with him, feeling that agreement got him even with the Irish bastards like Lonigan and Kelly.

"And America, this great country. It's all cheap journalism, selling. Everything is sell, and what do people get. Things they can't use. Automobiles. Radios. Cheap clothes. The capitalists kill workers, pay them starvation wages, and why? To sell all these things, junk. America was a good country. It isn't now. America is capitalism. It bleeds the world."

Davey didn't know what to say. Maybe he agreed. Goddamn it, people didn't need as much as they had, when others, now himself, had to go without things, be sick, possibly die from want of care.

"America is a country for the parvenu rich man. No art,

it's all journalism. America, you have one poet, you don't know him."

"Who's that? Longfellow?"

"Whitman. I'm translating him for my countrymen to read. Perhaps they will appreciate his greatness more than his own countrymen."

"Christy, what do you think of that German-Jewish poet, Heine?"

"A great spirit too, like Nietzsche. He was a great spirit, a great lyric poet."

"But wasn't Nietzsche pretty much of an anarchist?"

"Nietzsche was a great genius. Too great for people like Americans with Sinclair Lewis and all their journalism," said Christy.

Christy waited on another customer. Then, Davey told about how he had picked up the book of Heine when he was on the bum, and how much he'd liked it.

"Yes, he was a fine lyric poet."

"You know, Christy, I like to talk with you, because, you know, hell, I never got a break. It makes me think there are things in life after all," Davey said, sentimentally.

"Yes, but the fine things in life, they are obscured in America because of greed. In America you have greed, capitalism. There are, boy, two countries in the world. Greece and Russia. Greece is the world's past, Russia the future of the world."

"You know, I wonder. Look now at all the things about Russia you read in the newspaper."

"Don't believe the newspaper, American journalism. That's the trouble with Americans. They believe the newspaper lies all the time. The newspaper is an American's bible."

"The papers are pretty yellow."

"You want to read, read Plato's *Republic*. That's what Russia is going to become, maybe. A government and land of justice."

"Well, maybe bolshevism is not so bad as it seems," said Davey.

"Bolshevism is going to be justice for the workingman. He will no longer be a slave, work ten, twelve hours a day and have his children starved and underfed. He will have opportunities. Bolshevism will not allow greed, not allow capitalists to steal all the money to crush people, kill them in wars, to waste their toil on jewelry for silly women and silly wives. Russia is trying to make a decent world. America is trying to make a world for greed, capitalists, crooks, gangsters, criminals, and kill the working-man, make him a slave."

Davey sipped his coffee. He liked Christy, and maybe some

of the things Christy said were true, but, hell, Christy was a Greek. He didn't get the idea about America right.

"In America what have you got? . . . politicians. Crooks and liars. You have that man in this city, Gorman, running for judge. What does he know of . . . justice? A noble word, and you make it like a whore in America."

"I guess Gorman is a shyster, but all the boys around here are for him."

"Yes, what do they know? Silly boys. They have no education. They go to school to the sisters." (Christy folded his arms, and made a face of mock piety.) "Sisters, sanctimonious hypocrites. They pray and pray and pray. Fear! Crazy! What can they teach boys? To pray and become sanctimonious hypocrites too. Silly boys, they grow up, their fathers want to make money, their mothers are silly women and pray like the sanctimonious sisters, hypocrites. The boys run the streets, and grow up in poolrooms, drink and become hooligans. They don't know any better. Silly boys, and they kill themselves with diseases from whores and this gin they drink."

Studs came in.

"Or else they are sent to the capitalist war and they get killed, for what? Like the last war, they get killed to make more money for Morgan and the bankers."

Studs looked quizzically at Christy.

"Why did America fight? Because of money, money for Morgan and the capitalists. Why, even the Kaiser in Germany, he had a better government, better laws for the workingman than America."

"I guess the war was for money all right, but I think Wilson was a great man, the greatest American we ever had."

"Why, then, did he want war to save the bankers, and why did he keep Debs in jail?" asked Christy.

"Who's he?" Studs asked.

"He was a great man," said Christy.

"He was a socialist," said Davey.

"Oh, he was against religion and the home," said Studs.

"How come the boys aren't back?" Davey asked.

"Oh, they went drinking beer after the show. I thought I'd go home for a change. Jesus, I've been hitting the bottle too goddamn heavy lately," said Studs.

Davey hoped Studs hadn't heard much of the talk. He didn't want them to think him completely cracked.

Christy looked at them, two boys. He went back to work on his translation of Whitman into Greek.

"What the hell was that goddamn Greek talking about?" asked Studs.

"Oh, lots of things. He's radical," Davey said in a very low voice.

"Well, if he doesn't like this country why don't he go back to Greece or Russia?" asked Studs.

"He's a nice fellow, a white Greek. Only he's a little bit radical. He's a poet," said Davey.

"For Christ sake! I suppose he writes about the birdies and the stars, and my heart in love," sneered Studs.

A song of several years back jingled in Studs' mind, *Don't Bite the Hand That's Feeding You* . . . The first line kept returning to him:

> *If you don't like your Uncle Sammy* . . .

The song hit the nail square. Studs had an image of Uncle Sammy in his brain, tall, thin, angular, kindly, a trifle bucolic, but with powerful Abe Lincoln or Slug Mason mitts. He had a picture of him steady in his mind, this thin, tall, kindly, bearded man in red, white and blue clothes, his eyes sad with sorrow caused by the ingratitude of all the foreigners who had come over here and been ungrateful to him. But he was a powerful man. He had licked the Kaiser and he could lick the world. It made Studs feel like saying to Christy:

"Why, you lousy Greek sonofabitch, get the hell out of a white man's country."

"Say, is that Greek an American citizen?" asked Studs.

"Yeah," said Davey.

"A hell of a lot of nerve he had, being an American," said Studs.

He had that image of Uncle Sam again, and it made him think of how, as a kid, he had used to see cartoons with Uncle Sam in them in the newspapers, and he used to wish that Uncle Sam was a real man, the same to America as God was to the world. It made him wish that again, and wishing that, he was wishing he was a kid again. He had a heartburn. He felt his stomach. Getting more and more of an alderman. He felt rotten. He wasn't sleeping so well, and some days, he got all pooped out at three or four o'clock.

"Say, remember the fun we used to have as kids?" he said to Davey.

"Yeah. It was the nuts. Jesus, wouldn't it be swell to be like that again, no responsibilities. Remember the time you licked Red Kelly?" said Davey.

"Yeah, and Paulie had that trouble in the piggy game with that punk, what was his name?"

"Young Dennis," said Davey.

"That was it."

"And I remember the day you licked Weary Reilley. That was a battle," said Davey.

"Were you there? I didn't think you were," said Studs.

"Yeah. In front of Helen Shires' house. Sure I was," said Davey.

"I didn't remember you there. But that was a fight, the hardest fight I ever had," said Studs.

"Say, Studs, could you stand me to another cup of coffee?" Davey asked.

Davey got the coffee. He asked Studs if a piece of pie would be all right, too. Studs said yes. He was thinking of the old days.

When Davey finished, they went outside. Hink Weber was on the corner, and he had a wandering look about him. Davey rushed up to Hink, put out his hand, and said hello. Hink didn't notice him.

"Hello, Hink!" said Studs, more ordinarily, feeling a sense of triumph that Hink had not batted an eye when the Jew had tried to put the rush act on him. Hink scarcely raised an eyebrow, but did not speak. He walked on, like a somnambulist.

"Jesus Christ!"

"Say, what the hell, Hink never used to be high hat like this, did he?" asked Davey.

"No. Jesus, he looked queer tonight."

"Yeah, he looked awfully strange. Did you catch that look in his eyes?" asked Davey.

"Yeah."

"He didn't look drunk to me. He looked crazy," said Studs. "I wonder was he drunk."

"Jesus!" exclaimed Davey.

"He's been acting queer of late," said Studs.

"Yeah," said Davey knowingly.

"He hasn't been around much of late, but when he has, he's been acting sort of far away," said Studs.

"That's too bad, all right," said Davey.

"I'm sorry, all right," said Studs.

"Me too," said Davey.

Studs had gas on his stomach from the coffee an'. He knew now he wouldn't sleep. It worried him.

"Well, I guess I'll be moving along," he said.

"So long."

"Poor Hink!"

"Poor Hink!"

"Say, I just thought: we oughtn't to say anything about it, huh?" said Studs.

"I guess so."

"So long."

Davey hung around, a bit chilled, waiting to see if anybody else would come. He hated to go home. He thought how swell it would be if a broad came along, and he met her, and they went to her room, and she warmed him, and ummmmm, Jesus Christ! He wanted a lot of things. Poor sick Jew! He wished the guys would come. They didn't. He tramped disappointedly home.

XXI

At the supper table early in 1927, Mrs. Lonigan sighed that she was glad because soon it would be time for Father Shannon, the missionary, to be coming back to the parish to conduct the first mission in the new church. And she was anxious to hear what he would say about it, and how surprised he would be, and pleased to be conducting a mission in such a magnificent house of worship. Lonigan reflected aloud that Father Shannon was as brilliant and as educated as any Jesuit.

Mrs. Lonigan, her hair graying, looked over her brood, her two stunning daughters and her two sons; Loretta, a fine girl with an excellent high school education at St. Paul's swell school for girls; Frances engaged to be married to that well-to-do Dowson boy; Martin, a growing boy, innocent and fine, attending the Carmelites high school, and, she hoped and prayed nightly to God, preparing himself to answer the call to the priesthood. She saw the day, in a mother's day dream, when he would celebrate his first mass at St. Patrick's parish. There was only William, her baby. She prayed to God, too, that he would settle down. She was worried. Oh, God, would He only put grace into William's heart at this next mission. William was a good boy, with no harm in him. It was only bad companions.

"You children will have to make the mission," she said, covertly looking at William as he forked a piece of steak.

"Yeah," Studs mumbled, chewing.

"I like Father Shannon. He's a swell priest," Martin said in the changing squeaky voice of adolescence.

The father thought a better word than swell should be used to describe a great man like Father Shannon. Mrs. Lonigan said he was a holy man, and what a pride he must be to his old mother, if she were still living. Loretta said he was a darling. Fran said he was brainy. Lonigan told Fran that Father Shannon might say a word or two about those books by that man Sinclair Lewis that she was reading. She said she was not taking them seriously. She only read them because a couple of her girl friends who thought they were sophisticated were reading them, and she had gotten them to look at, only so they wouldn't be able to think that she was old-fashioned, or not up to the times in things. Mrs. Lonigan said that some books were like bad companions.

"Please, Mother!" Fran said.

"You're going to make the mission, William?" the mother said.

He was sure. Martin said he was also. The mother said she wanted them to because she and their father were going to make the mission for the older people, and if the whole family did the right thing, their home would be blessed by God.

"Sure, we'll take it in a couple of nights," Lonigan said.

She said every night they would. Lonigan said that missions were not meant for guys like himself who weren't sinners. She said he must set a good example for his children. He nodded, not to get her going. She was getting more religious every day, and it was a good thing, but she was filling the house with holy pictures and holy water, and hell, they weren't sinners, and did all their duties to God and the Church, and she didn't need to harp on it. He looked at Bill, with a father's love and pride. Only, he hoped, God, he hoped, that the mission would affect Bill, make him sort of settle down.

The daughters arose to get the coffee and dessert from the kitchen. Mrs. Lonigan told them how holy Father Shannon was. Lonigan expanded, rubbed his spreading belly, and agreed.

CHAPTER TWENTY-ONE

I

"Sure, Father Shannon is regular. He won't jump three feet every time he hears a hell, and he doesn't try to scare people into loading their pants with any hell-fire and damnation sermons. He talks man-to-man, using psychology," Kelly said.

"I like Father Shannon," Les said, while Red frowned at some passing niggers.

"He seems to be working wonders with you hoodlums," Red said.

"Us hoodlums! What about yourself?" Doyle retaliated.

"I sure like him," Les said.

"He's certainly different from Gilly. He knows human nature. And he doesn't always harp for money. Still he gets it," Tommy said.

"The way Gilly harps on the dough, you'd think no one ever gave a cent. Like a couple of weeks ago, when he told people they should quit putting pennies and nickels in the collection box," Studs said.

"Of course, he has to, with the debt on the new church, and so many well-to-do parishioners moving out of the parish before it's up hardly more than a year," Kelly said.

"Hear Ye! Hear Ye! Hear Ye!" burlesqued Barney Keefe; they certified that he was sober by smelling his breath.

"Coming to the mission, Chu Chu?" Studs asked.

"Yes, but not with you hoodlums. The mission is for sinners and louses like you guys, not me. I'm holy," Barney said; Red frowned as two more niggers passed the corner.

"Listen to the bastard talk, when his war cry has always been: 'Let's get a bottle.' " Red laughed.

"One of these days, I'm going to sue all you heels for defamation of character and slander," Barney said.

"Tell me, Barney! Is that the right spirit to have when you're making the mission?" asked Red.

"Get away from me. Woe! Woe! Woe! You're all the occasion of sin," Barney said.

"Seems to me you guys ought to be more serious," Stan Simonsky said.

"Of course, Stan, we're all Catholics here. If there were outsiders around, we'd talk different," Red said.

"Talking of people needing the mission, though, now this bastard Lonigan doesn't need it at all. Not after the way he went for that blond at the Rex last week," Doyle said.

"How about Les here? Drink isn't his temptation. He's a temptation to gin," Studs beamed.

"But, fellows, Father Shannon is showing us what's what," Les said.

"I know I wish I was as smart as he is," Doyle said.

"Remember Tuesday night, when he was talking about atheists, and said the Bible says that any man who says there is no God is a fool. And then he said that if anyone says there is no God, let him just go outside and look at the moon, and after looking at it, try to say that the moon made itself. Listen, if some of those atheists over around the Bug Club heard that, they would have squirmed in their seats, and if they aren't already too vain about their puny human knowledge, they'd come to their senses, and quit thinking that they were too good for the human race," Red said.

"Between us and that fireplug, I'll bet, too, that when he was young, he was no sissy," Stan said.

"Sure, he knows the ways of the world. He had his wild

oats, I'll bet. That's why he knows so much about human nature," Red said.

"Oh, hello, Hink," Studs said.

"I just heard you guys talking about that priest. Sure he
has his good times. All priests do."

"Say, Hink, I was hoping you'd be around. I wanted to
ask you to come along with us to the mission tonight. Father
Shannon is different from any one you ever heard speak, a
brilliant, educated man, and he'll make you understand the
Catholic philosophy," Red said.

"What do I care about the Catholics' side of it?"

"You wouldn't be so radical, then, about our religion,"
Red said.

"I'm not interested," Hink said snottily.

"Honest, Hink, he's the real stuff," Tommy said.

Hink walked away from them.

"There's something queer about Hink. He's not like he
used to be," Studs said, and he offered one more of his many
repetitions of the experience that he and Davey had had with
Hink the previous autumn.

"And, Christ, nearly every night he's rolling all over the
street drunk," Stan said.

"Hink is a white fellow. But there's something wrong with
him. I think it's in the family. His brother Slew is in the sanitarium now. Remember how he always looked first for the
suicides in the paper, and remember how he would chase sixteen-year-old girls, and hang around the Bug Club, talk like
they did over there, sit around the park all day stripped to
the waist taking sun-baths. I tell you I think a brain disease
like paranoia runs in their family. It's too bad," Red said.

"What the hell's that?" asked Barney.

"It's a brain disease that unbalances you, so that you won't
associate with people, don't care about them or even yourself,
think you're too good for the human race, and talk about
people like Hink does about priests and the Catholic Church,"
Red said, causing doleful shaking of heads.

"Say, Slug, come on to church with us tonight. You don't
want to miss it," Studs said, as Slug shambled up to them.

"You guys must want the pillars of the church to crumble,"
Barney said.

"Tonight, Slug, the sermon is going to be about guys who
get nooky," said Doyle.

"I don't want to hear about it. I just like to get it. And I
know all about how to get it," Slug said, with his Polack pronunciation.

"Come on, Slug!" Studs persuaded.

"Hell, I'd do everything the wrong way in church, and then when the priest was talking, I'd maybe fall asleep, and start snoring, and get thrun out of church on my tail," Slug said.

"You won't fall asleep when Father Shannon talks," Red said.

"Not me. Say, I wish it was over. I ain't had anybody to get a bottle with me all week," Slug said.

"Don't tempt us this week, Slug," said Doyle.

"Listen, you bastards, if you're making the mission, it means you should get there on time for the rosary that's said before the sermon. What are you trying to do, miss the rosary? Come on!" Barney said.

Slug nodded, watching them depart.

"Another black skunk," Red said, pointing to a young Negro ahead of them.

"Boy, they've been coming into the neighborhood fast, and so soon after the new church was built," Stan said.

"I see some at the mission every night," Studs said.

"They're ruining the neighborhood. That's why Jim and I have been trying to convince the old lady to sell the building before it's too late. Property values are going to pot here. You can tell it, when there's a saloon on Fifty-eighth Street, and beer flats all around, and flats and buildings being made into rooming-houses. And down on Garfield Boulevard the other night, why a hustler even tried to pick me up," Tommy lamented.

"If we had a pastor like Father Shannon, instead of Gilly, that mightn't have happened. He wouldn't be the kind to build a beautiful new church, and then let his parish go to the dogs. He'd have seen to it that the good parishioners stayed, and that the niggers were kept out. He'd have organized things like vigilance committees to prevent it," Red said.

"That's what my old man has been saying," Studs said.

"It was the Jews who did it. And he would have settled those profiteering shonickers. It's a lousy thing, if you ask me, Jews ruining a neighborhood just to make money like Judas did. It's all greed all over again, the greed of the Jews," Kelly said.

"Why don't the Jews all go back to Jerusalem where they belong?" Tommy said.

"And why don't you Irish go back and sleep with the pigs in the old country," Barney said.

"Chu Chu, you can't be serious for a minute," Stan said to Keefe.

"Speaking seriously, something will have to be done pretty quick if the neighborhood is going to be saved," Red said.

"It's too late now," said Tommy.

"What I want to know is this: Will the mission convert Doyle to work?" said Barney.

"No danger," said Les.

"He worked all summer warming his fanny in the boathouse," Red said.

"And don't think I didn't put in long hours," Tommy boasted.

"Say, fellows, I got a letter from Shrimp," said Red.

"That tb rat," Barney said.

"He's a good fellow," Tommy said.

"Yeah, a snake in the grass. I had a job as sewer-pipe layer all fixed up a couple of years ago. And that louse queered it thinking he could get it. It was muscling in, and I lost it, and he just queered both of us," Barney said.

They laughed, and Red said anyway, Shrimp didn't like the Navy at all.

"I hope he falls overboard into the mouth of a shark," Barney said.

"Say, by the way, did all you guys know that Rolfe has been converted, and is making his first communion Sunday?" Stan said.

"That's the dope," Studs said.

"It was your sister, Studs, who did it," Red said.

"I suspect that guy. Him being a Catholic is too much for me. He's full of so much B.S. that I doubt how much he means it," Tommy said.

"If he gets your sister, Studs, he's getting a damn fine, decent girl. My opinion is that she's much too good for him," Red said.

"All right, you guys, step on it! You're going to church, not to an employment agency. You're too late for the rosary now, anyway," Barney said.

II

St. Patrick's church was packed, and hushed. Father Shannon, a plump, bald-headed priest, emerged from the sacristy door on the right, pushed the back of his right hand to his mouth as he emitted a half-cough, genuflected, facing the altar, and proceeded to climb into the marble pulpit. He laid his beret beside him and faced the audience of young people, his soft, mushy, almost womanly face, half-distinct. He stretched his arms, and smoothed down his cassock. His bald head shone as it was caught in candle flickers. He emitted another cracked cough. In a quiet and confident voice, he said, while blessing himself:

"In the name of the Father, and of the Son, and of the Holy Ghost, Amen!"

He paused pregnantly, and dramatically. In a calm modulated voice, he exclaimed:

"My text for tonight's sermon is: 'Stand, therefore, having your loins girt in truth, and having on the breast-plate of justice, and your feet shod with the preparation of the gospel of peace.' Epistle of Paul to the Ephesians, sixth chapter, sixteenth verse.

"In the words, then, of the stern and austere Saint, Paul himself, I come and say unto you boys and girls tonight: 'Stand, therefore, having your loins girt in truth, and having on the breast-plate of justice, and your feet shod with the preparation of the gospel of peace.' "

His voice lowered almost imperceptibly:

"This evening, I shall have serious things to say, words of more serious import than those which have been, or will be contained in any other sermon or talk of this mission."

He smiled.

"Hence, I am constrained to ask that those of you who have the habit of sleeping through sermons, will kindly refrain from snoring. You know, there is a commandment of Jesus Christ, our Lord, which dictates that we must all love our neighbor as ourselves. Snoring, when your neighbor may be trying to hear what I say, or, God bless the mark, when he himself may be trying to sleep, is not what I call loving your neighbor."

He leaned on his arms, chest forwards, and smiled, while there were ripples of laughter.

"I stated that I have serious things to tell you. But don't, in the name of God, think that because I have said that, that I am coming here like a black-faced (he frowned dourly and hunched his shoulders) old man of gloom with crepe hanging from my shoulders. Because I am not (he smiled). I was young once myself, even though many of you may doubt that because of this billiard ball I have."

He touched his bald head; he waited until the self-conscious, restrained laughter subsided.

"I know what it means to be young. I know that Satan rides about through the night, like a witch in Sleepy Hollow, planning traps and temptations with which to beset the young. I know that when you are eighteen, nineteen, twenty-one, even twenty-five, you cannot be expected to live the kind of life that a crabby, old maid aunt would desire you to live. I know that you want good times, I believe, uncategorically, that you should have good times. (His pitch rose.). . . . But I do say that they should be clean good times, clean fun, decent pleasures that will not rob you of your soul, your mind, even your body and your health. Thus, I want you to realize that I am coming here as your friend, attempting to understand you, and to be sympathetic with you in the problems you must face, and the temptations which you must resist."

He paused, permitting his eyes to rove about the church.

"I fail to see any sleepers. That, I take, as a good augury."

He waited again, while there was a quiet outburst of laughing.

"My young friends, modern youth (his voice became explosive) in that quest for joy and amusement and fun, which is the perennial quest of youth, has drunk deeply from the muddy fountains of sham sophistication. Modern youth, therefore —and I do not exclude many Catholic boys and girls of this nation—must, under the pain of serious and eternal consequences, eject this soiled, germ-ridden, sin-ridden sham sophistication from its minds and its souls. And the sooner young people realize that the only lasting purgatives to perform this task of spiritual catharsis are the Sacraments and teachings of Holy Mother Church, the better off they will be, the better off this great nation will be, the better off this world will be.

"Today, we live in a world (he sneered and his voice sharpened) that is debauched with paganism of the vilest kind. For in pagan Greece, and even in pagan Rome, there was a measure of spiritual and intellectual accomplishment that is lacking in our own times. We live in an age of growing laxity, of sin (his face and voice intensified), ugly sin that is the cancer destroying immortal souls that have been made in the image and likeness of God Almighty. Our modern jazz age of freedom and untrammelled unconventionality is characterized by immorality, vice, disease . . . spiritual cowardice. Today, there are afoot movements started by vicious men and women who philander with the souls of youth in order that they will receive their paltry profit, and their cheap, ephemeral notoriety. I refer to such movements as jazz, atheism, free-love, companionate marriage, birth-control. These, and similarly miscalled tendencies, are murdering the souls of youth (he slapped his hand on the pulpit)."

(His voice broke into lamentation.) "Oh, how closely, how closely, my young friends, does not hell yawn to the youth of America!

" 'Weep, oh, weep for Adonais!' if I might quote that misguided poet, Shelley."

(His voice became calm and normal.) "I travel through this great, wide-flung country extensively. In the course of every year, I go from coast to coast. I contact these tendencies. I see their evil effects, the young people they ruin, the homes they wreck, the sadness they cause in the hearts of God-fearing mothers and fathers. I see how (his pitch rose) those seats of the godless—the universities—those iniquitous incubators of vice, cheapness, and trash—the movies; (he sneered) those imitation Anti-Christs, modern authors whose books perfume the vilest of sins—how all these take their toll in lives, in souls. In short, my young friends, I can perceive clearly (with dolorousness) oh, how clearly, Satan is making a powerful offensive, with all his artillery and machinery of stratagems, bribes, craftiness, seductive lies and promises, upon this so-called modern world of ours.

"And speaking of books, what do I mean? (His tone sharpened.) I have no fear of naming names and titles, and condemning where condemnation is due. And if I met the authors of the books I shall mention, I should tell them to their faces (his voice rose, almost to a shout): 'Your books are vile. In order to make a sale for them, you fill them with spiritual poison, with all the resources of your filthy and putrid minds. For thirty pieces of silver, you sign your names to oozing immorality. You are worse than dogs! You are the vilest of the vile, the most vicious of the vicious, lower than snakes, you rats who write books to rob youth of its shining silvered innocence!' That's what I would say to them, if, God forbid, I were to meet them face to face. (He vigorously smashed his hand against the pulpit.)

"What books do I mean? For one, there is a scurrilous novel, *Elmer Gantry*, a book that belongs in no decent household, a book that no self-respecting Catholic can read under the pain of sin, a book that should be burned in a garbage heap. In that novel, what does the author do? He mocks the most sacred profession that man can enter . . . the cloth, the service of Almighty God. Do you think I am afraid to tell you what kind of a man the author of *Elmer Gantry* is? (His voice grew in fearlessness.) Well, I am not afraid! I shall tell you. . . . He is a liar. I say (bellowing), he is a liar, and I am prepared to tell him so to his face!"

He paused, and surveyed a church taut with silence and interest. His voice dropped and he continued evenly:

"And in Denver, there is a puny little man, whose mind would have to be seen through the lenses of a powerful microscope. A man who has sullied the sanctity and justice of the courts . . . one Judge Ben Lindsay. And what does he preach? (He sneered.) . . . Companionate Marriage! Companionate Marriage, another of those masked fads that rise from a cesspool of spiritual cravenness (sneering). Companionate Marriage!

That is his sugar-coated, seductive term. This little man, this human atom, this intellectual midget, what does he preach—at a profit (with rising voice)? I'll tell you in straight language without any fake pretence of those abused words, liberality and tolerance. In simple words, this human rat, like the anarchistic, atheistic Bolshevists in unhappy Russia, says (his arms flung out in a gesture): 'Away with the holy bonds of Matrimony!' Jesus Christ (his head bowing), our Lord, said 'What God hath joined together, let no man put asunder!' Mother Church, after nineteen hundred years of tested wisdom and experience, achieved with the guidance of the Holy Spirit, Mother Church says that you must be married by one of God's anointed representatives, and that unless you are, you sin when you take unto yourself a man or woman as husband or wife. And Judge Ben Lindsay (with a sneer) says that this is all nonsense. It is not modern. It is old-fashioned. Away with it! (His cassocked arm again swung outward in a demonstrative gesture.) He tells the youth of America to go out, flirt, taste sin, ruin their souls, experiment, and that if it does not succeed, try again. He advises young men to take a girl, a pure, innocent, decent, perhaps even a Catholic, girl, and live with her in violation of one of God's Holy Commandments. Try her out! Ruin her! And if she doesn't powder her nose the right way, or burns the toast in the morning, or you stub your toe getting out of the wrong side of the bed, and think she is the cause, leave her. You are then incompatible. Leave her a ruined girl, unable to look her mother or her God in the eye, unable to find a decent young man who would want her! Incompatibility! Another of those masked, ambiguous, lying phrases used to clothe the intent of Satan who skulks in the bottom of low and depraved mentalities, like that of Judge Ben Lindsay.

"And only recently, I conducted a mission in Baltimore. Baltimore, founded on principles of religious liberty and tolerance. Baltimore, that splendid city that was once the refuge of Catholics who risked death and exile for the sake of their faith. What books do you think the Catholic youth of Baltimore was reading? The books of that fake sage of Baltimore, that man who profits by telling youth to read Nietzsche. I refer to H. L. Mencken. Who is H. L. Mencken? He is a noisy, vociferous, and half-baked little man. What does he say? He says: 'Read Nietzsche!' That was what the ill-fated Leopold and Loeb read in this city, almost in this neighborhood. That is what the Germans who started the last war read. That is what H. L. Mencken says to youth. And they read him, and think themselves (sneering) smart. So I said to them from the altar of God: 'Do you think that smart? Do you think it smart to mock at all the things that are sacred to God and man? Do you think it is smart to blaspheme? Well, get it out of your heads! It is a cheap and easy sin! It is blasphemy! And woe unto him who is guilty of blasphemy! Woe!'

"The writers I have named are merely a few out of many. There are others, and amongst them, there is the biggest windbag of them all . . . H. G. Wells. That Englishman who preaches evolution, who says that man came from a monkey. And on what evidence do such false prophets preach evolution? On the evidence of science? That is a lie. I'll tell you the evidence. A slab of shin bone and a half a skull was found in China. These half-baked pseudo-scientists gave it a confounding and terrifying name—Pithecanthropus Erectus. Then they went to a zoo and saw a monkey eating with a fork. Because of that, and because of—pardon me if I mispronounce it—Pithecanthropus Erectus, they say that man came from a monkey and is only an animal. In their insane egotism, they think that all men are made unto their own image and likeness. (Snickers.)

"And the universities, miscalled seats of learning, temples of truth, are full of such men. Over here on the Midway, you have one such university. Recently, I conducted a mission in another part of the city, and a Catholic girl came to me and said: 'Father, what am I going to do? I'm given these kind of books to read in my courses, and if I don't read them, I'll be flunked. And they present fallacies contrary to my faith.' I told her what to do. I told her what every Catholic student should say in such circumstances. I told her to take the books back to her professor and say that Father said she should tell him this: 'I am a Catholic. I will not read these books and endanger my holy faith. They are full of half-truths, paradoxes, lies, and the men who wrote them are either ignorant, or else they are liars. You must put a stop to this sort of thing. You must stick to what you know, to the limited field which you have studied, and stop talking about or recommending books on morals and theology, because you are ignorant and biased.' That is what every Catholic student in a godless university should do.

"Another class of people contributing to the sham sophistication which I have mentioned is a bunch of snivelling old maids who do not care how many souls they ruin, as long as it permits them to get their hatchet-faces plastered all over the newspapers as forward-looking women. And what do these snivelling old maids advocate to earn the dubious honor of being forward-looking? (A pause.) Birth control! The deliberate murder of human souls, in defiance of the laws of God and Nature. I'll tell what the birth control of these snivelling, hatchet-faced old maids means. It means this (he banged his right fist into his left palm): It means the legalization of sin, disease, promiscuity, the destruction of the Christian home; and the Christian Catholic home is the backbone of this, or of any civilized, nation. But what do such irresponsible old fools care? What do they care if they incite to the murder of innocent, unborn babes? What do they care if they turn this nation into a state of debauchery which would make pagan Rome look virtuous by sheer comparison? What do they care if all men live without even the decency of the beasts of the field? What do they care so long as their long, hatchet mugs are in the daily newspapers, with a description of forward-looking and modern, under the photographs?"

He paused, and slowly wiped his perspiring face with a large handkerchief. He coughed. He recommended in an even voice:

"Ah, my friends, the mind of America is being ruined. For the youth of a nation is that nation's future. And our youth is being contaminated. And there is only one way, one method, of fighting this ruin and contamination. There is only one hope for America. That hope lies in the Catholic young men, the Catholic girls of this nation. They must be the leaders. They must offer the strongest resistance to sin and blasphemy. They must fight the untruths spread by these cheap little half-baked, second-rate anti-Christs. When they, when you, meet someone defending birth-control, this must be said in answer: 'Birth control solves nothing. There is only one answer—that of the Catholic Church. It is not Birth-Control that we need but . . . Self-Control!' When you meet someone advising you to read the latest book, you must say this: 'I am unashamed to say that I will not expose my mind and my soul to such trash. I read only good books, decent books, and no books by windbags and publicity-seekers like Sinclair Lewis, and H. G. Wells. I read books like those of G. K. Chesterton, the foremost living writer of this century. No, I don't read psychoanalysis, either. I read psychology, the true psychology, the rational psychology by the foremost psychologist in the world today— Father Maher.'

"For, my friends, your minds and your bodies are vessels of the Lord, given unto your keeping. They must not be abused. They are not tools for the indiscriminate enjoyment of what the world calls pleasure. There is one commandment which, above all, you must not violate. God says, clearly and without equivocation: 'Thou shalt not commit adultery!' If you do, the torments of Hell await you for all eternity! That is clear and unmistakable.

"Today, sad to state, I come here as a priest of God, and I have to confess that the youth of this land neglects that commandment. On every side, they are encouraged. Books! Filthy movies. Newspapers. The doctrines in universities aimed to destroy morality. Men who cater to the purposes of the devil, and expose youth, tender girls and immature boys, to the danger of this sin, all because it is profitable, because a dirty, soiled thirty pieces of silver can be collected. Such men, I say, are worse than Judas.

"And what are the results? One result is this: today in America, there is a type, a class of young men, a recognizable young squirt. This squirt spends the money that his father earned and saved after long years of honest toil. He has an automobile. He has been miseducated at a godless university. He is fast, modern; he talks smartly, dresses smartly, acts smartly. He is always on the loose for a girl. He meets an innocent Catholic girl. She is pure and sweet and good, like Longfellow's Evangeline. But as young girls often are, she is attracted by his clothes, his talk, and his automobile. He has what they call a line. He gives her a lot of soft soap. So Mary has a date with him. He is pleasing, and spends money. She thinks he is a nice boy! Like the spider, he is weaving his web. He takes her out again, and drives toward the country. He pulls out a bottle and has a drink. He offers it to her. She demurs. He looks at her as if she were a zoological exhibit. He can't understand, because all the girls he knows drink. He laughs and asks if she is afraid. She shows her fear. So he tells her: 'Come on Mary, don't be a wet blanket. Once won't hurt!'

"Cursed phrase; 'Once won't hurt.' That first time seems so harmless and so easy. It seems to have such little effect. And it leads straight down the road to perdition and ruin. With it, he plays on Mary's vanity. He convinces her with soft-soap talk that once won't hurt. Then, he takes her to a roadhouse. There, they meet other couples. It is what they call a wild party. Everybody but Mary drinks. She is teased, and told not to be a kill-joy. Once hasn't hurt her. Once more won't, they tell her. Rather than spoil the party, Mary takes a second drink. Before she knows it, she is drunk. There is dancing, immoral animalistic dancing and petting. Then, there is another automobile ride. Mary goes home, pillaged of her most precious treasure, robbed (he smacked his right fist into his left palm) of that gift which is a girl's finest possession—her virtue, her honor, her chastity.

"This is not an exceptional occurrence. Pray God that it were! It is ordinary, and happens every day. It is the way in which Catholic girls, girls like those of you here, girls like

the sisters and sweethearts and old schoolmates of you lads
here, are ruined, and dispatched along a path that can only
end in misery, both in this world and the next. You girls who
are now listening to me! If you have not already met such
temptations, you will. And, you fellows, your sisters will meet
them. For if these squirts had their way, there would not be
a decent girl left in this country.

"And when you girls do meet with this temptation what
are you going to say? Are you going to agree that . . . 'Once
doesn't hurt?' Or are you going to say: 'See here now, what
are your intentions? I'm a decent Catholic girl, and I do not
intend to fling myself away on any rat because he has a funny-
looking suit of bell bottoms and an automobile. Before I ride
in any automobile of yours, I want to know why you want
me to go, what intentions you have, what kind of a person
you are?'

"And you fellows, if you find some cake-eaters trying to
take advantage of your sister, what are you going to do? Are
you going to shrug your shoulders, and say that you are not
your sister's keeper, or turn your head the other way to avoid
trouble? I know of one such case. It happened in Marion,
Ohio. The sister of a young Catholic fellow was ruined, and
died giving birth to an illegitimate baby. And the spineless
brother answered my questions this way. He said: 'Father,
it would have been such a mess. Father, I believe that each
person has the right to live their own life.' Well, let me tell
you this: God won't agree to such a principle on the final Day
of Judgment.

"If there is an ounce of decency and red blood in a young
fellow, he'll not do that. When any one of these jazz-age, drug-
store cowboys starts trying to fool around with his sister, he
won't mince his words. He'll say: 'See here, now, what do you
mean, trying to ruin my sister?' That's what he'll say. He'll
tell him to get out and stay out. And he'll punch his yellow nose
in for him. Because that is the only kind of treatment these
wise young squirts merit.

"Why, if I had a sister, and one of them started monkeying
around with her, I'd grab him by the coat collar, and I'd say;
'See here! You're not honorable! You're not decent! Are you
going to let my sister alone?' And then I'd let him have one."

Father Shannon paused, and again mopped his face. He
glanced from face to face in the church. He spoke with calmness again.

"Remember these words! Years ahead, I want you, when
you're my age, and I'm dead, to pause and think, to remember
what Father Shannon said in his missions at St. Patrick's. And

I want you to remember this statement particularly. . . . Sin doesn't pay.

"And I am willing to bet anyone here a hundred dollars that then you'll nod your head, and think that, yes, Father Shannon told you the truth. And of all sins, that which pays the least, is a sin of the flesh. Ah, you boys and girls, you don't want to ruin yourself, body and soul. You don't want to disease your body so that a decent person will shun you as he would a leper. Your bodies are young and strong now. You don't want to wreck them with disease and over-indulgence. There is nothing as fine as the sight of a good strong boy or girl, whose body and mind are clean, pure, decent. And the ideal of retaining such a body and such a mind is both noble and practical. It isn't as hard as sin. I know, because I've seen hospitals where people were rotting away with disease as the result of their sins. One day, my young friends, they had bodies like you had, and the chance that you still possess. And they forsook that ideal. You want to remember the words of Thomas a Kempis: 'For they that follow their sensuality, do stain their own conscience, and lose the favor of God.'

"When the devil tempts you, as he tempted such people, you want to say to him: 'Satan, No! No! No! you cannot have my body and my soul!' You young fellows, you don't want to be fools, and go skulking, like thieves in the night, into brothels, consorting with the lowest kind of human beings, exposing yourself to diseases that can ruin your lives, and blast the chances of a successful and happy marriage with that sweet little girl whom you love. Ah, no, you don't want to do that. Because it doesn't last! And it doesn't pay. It's not pleasure. It's not fine. It's not decent! It's not manly. You don't want to be that kind of a fellow. If you do, you're not choosing the brave course. You're being a coward and a fool.

"And you girls! I know many of you. I know your fathers, mothers and brothers. And, yes, some of your sweethearts too. I know that I've never met finer girls than you anywhere. That's why I'm saying that you don't want to be riding around in automobiles with fast young fellows, petting and necking, drinking, smoking cigarettes. You want to preserve that fine chastity you have, those fine, beautiful bodies God has given you, and later on when you marry that decent boy you love, you'll go to him clean and honorable. Worthy of the love he offers you, worthy to be the mother of his children, just as your own mothers were worthy of Dad."

He paused.

"And there's one thing all of you should not do, if you want to avoid these evils. That's drink. Once does hurt. Once starts you off, and you're in grave danger. Drink destroys character and will power, and stultifies the voice of conscience. It is the precursor of all sins. It poisons the body. Today in this country there are scores and hundreds of young people in every city whose hearts, livers, stomachs, vital organs have been ruined by drink. They are dying in their prime. Why? Because they didn't believe that once would hurt. You know what Shakespeare, the greatest genius who ever lived, said of drink: 'Oh, God, that men should put an enemy into their mouths, to steal away their brains.'

"You don't want to do that. Because it is you, your kind, your class, to which America looks. And if America is to avoid that drastic, terrible fate which befell the proud and mighty empire of Rome, it is you, and others like you, who will have achieved the victory. I can't save America. My generation cannot. But yours can. That is why Mother Church counts on you. She knows that today she must fight one of the greatest battles she has ever fought. She faces a world where materialism drives out the laws and will of God and Nature, where sin is rampant, where money is poured into the coffers of vice, making it rich and powerful, where great industries are built up only to pander to lust, where books, theatres, movies, universities, are all aligned on the side of godlessness, and where all these forces together constitute a mighty propagandistic effort to take her sons and daughters from her and give them into the hands of Satan. And her fight is your fight. . . . (A pause:) Now, how are you going to fight? What are you going to say?

"Unless I am wrong, you're going to say this: 'Get thee behind me, Satan!' You're going to be manly and womanly, clean, upright, decent, and you're going to stand four-square in the front line trenches of Mother Church in her ceaseless war against the world, the flesh, and the devil. You're going to be soldiers of righteousness, and you're going to say: 'Jesus Christ, my Savior, has walked down the aisles of time, a white-robed figure of virtue and strength. And His Church has followed Him and His doctrine. With it, I take my stand. I shall not bargain away my soul, my honor, my right to be a member of that holy Church for a paltry night's pleasure, for filthy pieces of silver. I shall not be another Judas!' "

He wiped his face.

"Shakespeare laments: 'Oh, that we should with joy, pleasance, revel, and applause, transform ourselves into beasts.' You're not going to do that. No! I know it. I know that the young men and the young women of St. Patrick's parish are going to stand defending the gates of Truth and Righteousness, armed with Grace.

" 'Stand, therefore, having your loins girt with truth and having on the breast-plate of justice, and your feet shod with the preparation of the gospel of peace.'

"In the name of the Father, and of the Son, and of the Holy Ghost, Amen!"

There was rustling and straining in the pews.

"And now, I want to ask you all to follow me in a prayer to Mary, asking her protection and aid in the struggle of the Catholic youth of this land for the triumph of virtue."

He recited the prayer slowly, and the young people sing-songed it after him, verbatim.

"O Victorious Lady! Thou who hast ever such powerful influence with Thy Divine Son, in conquering the hardest of hearts, intercede for those for whom we pray that their hearts being softened by the rays of Divine Grace, they may return to the unity of the true Faith, through Christ, Our Lord! Amen!"

He climbed down from the pulpit, genuflected in front of the Blessed Sacrament, and disappeared through the sacristy door. An altar boy came onto the altar, cassocked, and lit the candles for Benediction of the Most Blessed Sacrament.

III

"Say, wasn't that a sermon!" Les exclaimed.

"It was a knockout," Studs said, watching the people gush from church, looking at the girls coming out with an attitude of almost futile hope and expectancy.

"It was even better than the sermon he gave Tuesday night," Red Kelly said.

"Sure it was, if it only teaches you guys something," Barney said.

"People who live in glass houses shouldn't fling bricks," Stan said.

"Me, I'm an old man. He was talking to youth, and you bastards might still technically classify as youth," Barney said.

Studs scanned the faces. Maybe that girl would be coming out, but it seemed that she had moved away. Lucy. He wanted them to see him there, calm, nonchalant. But he realized that he wasn't so much to look at any more. Getting fatter all the time, had an alderman, was twenty pounds heavier than when he'd taken Lucy to that dance. Then he had been a damn good-looking guy, and he hadn't danced so badly either.

"I like what he said about these bastards monkeying around with a guy's sister. Like the time at Nolan's, and that bastard,

Guy Bain, was trying to lay it into my kid sister on the dance floor. Remember, Studs? Well, I got him," Weary Reilley said.

"He knows his apples," Les said.

"He didn't hand it to the sheiks much, did he?" Tommy said.

"And neither did he to those people who think they are too good for the human race like Young O'Neill who goes to the University. He knows better than make the mission. He'd get his ear full," said Red.

"Isn't he making the mission?" asked Studs.

"He's an atheist," Red said.

"I always thought he was goofy," Studs said.

Studs watched for a girl. Still plenty of them in the parish. He hated guys with a girl. Goddamn it, he needed a girl, he wanted the feeling a guy would have, having a girl that was his only. He edged over to listen to the punks razzing Curley, because he wanted to get closer to the crowd. He listened with a supercilious expression on his face. The razzing suddenly turned on Jerry Rooney because he had a big nose. Studs touched his own nose. . . . Well, Rooney's was bigger. Young Horn Buckford rushed to Studs from another group, and said he would let Studs prove it. Studs curtly asked him what?

"Listen, I was telling these dumbbells that there's a fellow named Cardigan who beat Locke of Iowa running backwards. Remember you told me about it. This Cardigan beat Locke in the hundred yards, running backwards, and he made a backward dive over the tape to nose Locke out. Remember you told me, Studs?"

"You heard Father Shannon, didn't you? Well, for Christ sake, leave it alone before it's too late."

"Hink wouldn't have a leg to stand on after that sermon," Tommy said, as they trailed back to the corner.

"He sure laid it on thick," Les said.

"That's the only way to do it," said Red.

"Well, then, let's see if you guys cut out the bottle after the mission is over, and quit adding to the revenue of whore houses," Barney said.

"Say, Barney, at a time like this, when we're all making the mission, there's no place for kidding. I know we all done things, but the flesh is weak, and that's why we're making the mission. It's to help us be more decent. We all know he told us the truth, and we all know that at times we've been pretty filthy bastards. But we're going to try not to from now on," Red said.

"Yeah," Studs added, as if with deep reflection.

"He didn't tell you nothing I ain't been telling you for years," Barney said.

"This is serious," Red crisply said.

They had coffee an' in the Greek restaurant. Coming out, Studs told about hearing Christy talk with Davey.

"Why don't he go back to Ireland where he belongs," Barney said.

"I think we ought to boycott the restaurant until Gus gets rid of him," Red said.

"We'll make the punks do it too," Studs said.

"We don't want radicals like that in this neighborhood. Father Shannon showed just what they are," Kelly said.

"Well, finished with religion yet?" Slug asked, coming towards them.

"Gus is not there now. But I'm going to speak to him tomorrow. If he wants our trade, he'll get a Greek waiter in there who isn't radical," Red said.

Slug told about the beer he had in Colisky's saloon down the street. Barney said all the boys would be back having it on Sunday night. Red said not this time, and asked the boys how about it. They agreed. Slug said that for him, seeing was believing, and that he had never given that religion stuff a go because you couldn't live up to it.

Red was still trying to explain religion to Slug when Studs started home. He saw Phil kissing Loretta in the hallway, and walked back towards the corner. It was a clear fall night. Even the Jew had a girl to kiss. Aw, hell, it was all the bunk. He turned back from the corner and took his time. Phil came along, whistling gaily. Studs started whistling in a don't-give-a-damn manner.

"Say, Studs, wasn't it swell? He's the best speaker I ever heard," Phil said.

"You got what he said, didn't you?"

"Sure. Why?"

"Well, now, don't try any monkey business."

"You know I wouldn't, Studs. You know I think too much of Loretta, and she's too fine a girl. If I did, she'd probably give me the gate. And anyway, I wouldn't because I think too much of her, and I'm not a sonofabitch."

"You got your warning," Studs said, walking on.

IV

"I saw Gus last night. He gave that radical bastard his pay when he came down tonight, and he's through. There's a new man in there. I told Mike we'd boycott the place, and that if that wasn't enough, wreck that bastard," Red said.

"Good stuff," Studs said.

"How was the church tonight, boys?" asked Slug.

"Not so good. Father Shannon only gave the short talk

tonight, and his partner, Father Kandinsky, gave the sermon. He's a bit dull," Red said.

Slug muttered an "oh," as if he understood. Tommy remarked that there wasn't as many as last night, and that no priest drew them like Father Shannon. Les said Father Shannon was an artist.

"Whenever he gives a mission in this town, there's a lot of people, particularly girls, who are Father Shannon fans, and travel all over the city to hear him," Studs said.

"He's worth hearing," Tommy said.

"Notice how the girls and women go for him," said Red.

"My old lady thinks he's a saint," Tommy said.

"Mine too," Studs said.

"Speaking of women, I know a new girlie that sure can guarantee to keep the sailor warm when it's zero outside," Slug said.

"Save it, Slug," Red said.

"Jesus, you guys must have got religion," Slug said, shaking a puzzled head.

"Studs went to confession," Red said.

"Yeah, Foul-Mouth Lonigan has got to keep his mind pure until Sunday morning. But then, I'll bet the bastard makes up for it," Barney said.

"Nix, Keefe," said Red.

"Sure, go ahead. I'll tell all of you, you have such filthy minds that I'm risking my immortal soul associating with you," Barney said, getting laughs.

Slug said he hadn't gotten the dope about Studs straight. Red explained that Studs had confessed his sins, and that he had to keep his soul in the state of grace by not committing any new sins between now and Sunday morning when he received Holy Communion.

"You mean he told the priest about all the parties we have been having?"

"Yeah."

"Wasn't the priest jealous?"

They tried to explain it to Slug, but he finally went back to the saloon for a drink. Red said that Phil Rolfe had meant things and was really baptized. Studs said sure, he went the whole hog. Stan said he was sweet on Studs' sister. Studs nodded, frowning. Tommy said he hadn't realized Phil was so intelligent as to really accept the faith. Red said to wait and see how much he accepted it before tossing bouquets at him. You should never trust a Jew.

"For Christ sake, Fat, where you been?" asked Studs.

"Hell, I moved out of this nigger neighborhood," Fat Malloy answered.

"Where you living?"

"Out near Sixty-seventh and Stony."

"My old man's thinking of selling the building, and buying one out somewhere south," Studs said.

"You belong in a white man's neighborhood," Fat said.

"What you doing, Malloy?" asked Doyle.

"Down at the water works with my old man."

"I been thinking of going into the political game myself," said Tommy.

Fat pulled out a poem about gonorrhea. Studs said he went to confession. Fat said he was sorry. The other boys looked at it privately. It turned Studs' mind to girls. He started home to avoid the occasion of sin. He stepped on sidewalk cracks to keep his mind off women. Christ, he wanted one. He remembered how, as a kid, he used to count the cracks on a sidewalk as he walked. Those days. A girl walked ahead of him. Young. He liked young girls, something about them when they were just budding, when they were the age Lucy had been that day the punks had had the tin-can fight, the age that that bitch, Nellie Cullen, had been. But it had been nice with her, even if he had been dosed. Jesus, he wanted a girl that age again. Like the one in front of him. He would take her over to the park, kiss her, gradually work her up, pat her head, kiss her hair, her eyes, nose, mouth, ears, neck, feel her back and her boobs on the outside, stick his hand inside her dress, french-kiss her, grab under her dress. . . . He came to realizing what kind of thoughts these were. But he hadn't done it willfully. They had been temptations, not sins. They had come on him without his being aware of them. A sin had to be a grievous matter and have sufficient reflection and full consent of the will before it was mortal. He hadn't thought of having these thoughts or willed them. They had just snuck up on him. He couldn't keep his eyes off the girl. He wanted to swear, do something. And he had to keep himself in the state of grace all day tomorrow, until Sunday morning. He counted his steps, and avoided landing on the cracks in the sidewalk.

V

On Sunday morning at the eight o'clock mass, St. Patrick's Church was jammed with young people. Father Shannon, in his brief sermon, said it was an edifying sight indeed to see how successful this mission had been, to see so many young men and young women doing the honorable, courageous thing by marching up to the altar to receive their God. It was the kind of a demonstration that made himself and Father Kandinsky, and also Father Gilhooley and his assistants, take renewed heart and courage, because they realized that they did not labor in the Lord's Vineyard in vain, did not sow seed on fallow ground.

Three priests and over twenty minutes were required to give out Holy Communion. Studs went to the altar rail with a free conscience. He had gone back to confession again on Saturday, even though everybody had kidded him. He was certain that way that he was in a state of grace, after the thoughts he'd had Friday night. All the hoods received and Phil Rolfe knelt amongst them receiving his first Holy Communion.

In the afternoon, the church was crowded for the formal closing of the mission. Father Kandinsky delivered a short sermon, lauding them for their good works and intentions of the past week, and telling them about the mission collection that would be taken up before they left the church. He followed it with a short exposition of the sins in violation of each commandment, but he said little exciting about the sixth commandment. They lit their candles, and followed him, word by word, in a renewal of their baptismal vows. They received the Papal Blessing and Plenary Indulgences, and Benediction of the Most Blessed Sacrament followed. After it, the mission was over.

On Sunday evening, the boys gathered around the corner. Slug suggested a drink. They refused. They hung around, gassing, and smoking, looking at the drug store clock, wondering what the hell to do. Again they refused to drink with Slug. They hung around. Slug kept insisting that one beer wouldn't hurt them. They went down the street to Colisky's saloon and had a beer. They had another. Before they realized it, they were drinking gin. They got drunk and raised hell around the corner. They hung around until Slug talked them into going to a new can house, a small place. They went and had the girlies, and gypped them out of their pay. It was a big night.

XXII

A disturbing sense of loneliness caused Danny O'Neill to close the copy of The Theory of Business Enterprise *which he was studying for one of his courses at the University. The elation of intellectual discovery and stimulation, the keenness of feeling mental growth within himself, the satisfaction of having uncovered additional proofs to buttress his conviction that* the world was all wrong, which he had derived from his reading, suddenly eased.

He looked out of the window of the Upton Service Station on a corner of Wabash Avenue in the black belt where he worked. He felt as if he were in a darkened corner of the world that had been trapped in a moment of static equilibrium. The light on the corner seemed only to emphasize the dreariness of the scene. Across from him was the box-like carburetor factory that stood now darkened like a menace of gloom.

He had gone to services one night during the mission last week, and afterward, he had waited for Father Shannon. He had asked the priest if he could talk with him about the faith, because he was a University student who had lost his religion. Father Shannon had curtly replied that he was, for the present, very busy. The incident had crystallized many things in Danny's mind. It had made him feel that it was not merely ignorance and superstition. It was perhaps not merely a vested interest. It was a downright hatred of truth and honesty. He conceived the world, the environment he had known all his life, as lies. He realized that all his education in Catholic schools, all he had heard and absorbed, had been lies.

An exultant feeling of freedom swept him. God was a lie. God was dead. God was a mouldering corpse within his mind. And God had been the center of everything in his life. All his past was now like so many maggots on the mouldering conception of God dead within his mind. He jumped up, and went outside to stand on the gravel service-station driveway, and shook his fist at the serene and brilliant March sky.

He opened his book, but after a few more pages, closed it a second time. He was too lonely, too aware of almost complete rootlessness to study. Everything of value, all his ambitions, had turned, churned on him, curdled. He remembered himself as a boy, one of the neighborhood goofs. Around the corner he was now more of a goof than ever. His nostalgias for past experiences in the neighborhood seemed to have died too. He hated it all. It was all part of a dead world; it was filthy; it was rotten; it was stupefying. It, all of the world he had known, was mirrored in it. He had been told things, told that the world was good and just, and that the good and just were rewarded, lies completely irrelevant to what he had really experienced; lies covering a world of misery, neuroticism, frustration, impecuniousness, hypocrisy, disease, clap, syphilis, poverty, injustice.

He tried again to study. He envisioned a better world, a cleaner world, a world of ideals such as that the Russians were attempting to achieve. He had to study to prepare himself to create that world. A few more pages, and he again closed the book.

His sense of loneliness seemed to grow upon him. The air compressor behind him suddenly whirred, and he jumped with that fear that is caused by unexpected distraction in a moment of over-sensibility. He sat down again. He opened a book of readings in English literature, and read The Garden of Proserpine. His realization that death was the end terrified him. Then he was lulled, and he imagined a world when the last human had died, a world of tall grass over the gravestones of humanity, with winds sweeping the grass, through which the sunlight spread to reflect colors perceivable by no eye. Death seemed like a sensuous falling into sleep. But it was not so. It was the last slap in one's face, a final defeat, disgusting, disintegrating, insensate. His courage ebbed. Who was he to dream of doing things? What did he know? What had he accomplished?

He wanted to be a writer. He didn't know how. He wanted to purge himself completely of the world he knew, the world of Fifty-eighth Street, with its God, its life, its lies, the frustrations he had known in it, the hates it had welled up in him. The mere desire gave him a sense of power. Without his having seen the man enter, an old Negro, hunched, the weary price of work in his creased face, stood before him holding a gasoline can. He bought four cents worth of kerosene. They talked.

"You all is white and young. You is not black, you all has a chance in dis worl'."

"Someday you will, too, maybe."

"Ah, no, not in dis worl', son!"

He watched the Negro slowly leaving, a wistful snapshot as he crossed the station driveway, and turned down Wabash Avenue. He was returning with the kerosene for the lamps. He lived in one of the hovels along Wabash Avenue. He gave O'Neill a sense of the misery of the world, perhaps the unnecessary misery in it.

It would all go in a newer, cleaner world. He seethed with sudden dizzying adolescent dreams and visions of this new world. He, too, he would destroy the old world with his pen; he would help create the new world. He would study to prepare himself. He saw himself in the future, delivering great and stirring orations, convincing people, a leader, a savior of the world. He became aware of the clock. It was fifteen minutes past his closing time. He hurriedly closed up the station, and walked to the elevated at Twenty-sixth Street. Riding home, tired, he felt that people didn't realize they were riding home with somebody who was destined to do big things. His dreams

*again collapsed on him like a tire gone suddenly flat. He re-
peated and repeated a line from Swinburne's poem:*

"Even the weariest river winds somewhere safe to sea."

He was a disillusioned young man.

*He wanted to get coffee in the Greek restaurant. But he
might meet some of the guys. He hated them. He didn't want
to see them. And Christy, whom he had always talked to in
the restaurant, was gone. He didn't know why. The new waiter
had just said he had left. He walked home, carrying a brief-case
full of books. Studs Lonigan, Red Kelly, and Barney Keefe
passed on the other side of the street. They called him goof
and told him to leave it alone. He didn't answer. Some day,
he would drive this neighborhood and all his memories of
it out of his consciousness with a book. He swerved again
from disillusionment to elation.*

CHAPTER TWENTY-TWO

Studs and his father stood in the parlor and the early morning
sunlight glared through the unwashed, curtainless windows.
They looked around at the covered furniture. The room had
an appearance of disruption.

"Bill, I'd rather let the money I made on this building go
to hell, and not be moving," Lonigan exclaimed, with wistful
regret.

"Patrick, are you sure all your things are packed," Mrs.
Lonigan said.

"Yes, Mother," Lonigan said, very gently.

It seemed to Studs that his mother wiped away a tear. She
turned and went towards the back of the house to ask the girls
if they had all their things packed.

"Hell, there is scarcely a white man left in the neighborhood,"
Studs remarked.

"I never thought that once they started coming, they'd come
so fast."

"You know, Bill, your mother and I are gettin' old now,
and, well, we sort of got used to this neighborhood. We didn't
see many of the old people, except once in a while at Church,
but you know, we kind of felt that they were around. You know
what I mean, they were all nearby, and they all sort of knew
us, and we knew them, and you see, well, this neighborhood
was kind of like home. We sort of felt about it the same way

I feel about Ireland, where I was born," said Lonigan.

Studs didn't like the old man to let himself out like that because how could he reply? The old man and old lady were taking it hard.

"Yeah, it used to be a good neighborhood," said Studs.

"Well, Patrick, we're going to have a new home," Mrs. Lonigan said, returning to the parlor.

"Yes, Mary, but no home will be like this one has been to us. We made our home here, raised our children, and spent the best years of our lives here."

"Sunday in church, I watched Father Gilhooley. Patrick, he's getting old. He's heartbroken, poor man. Here he built his beautiful church, and two years after it's built, all his parishioners are gone. He's getting old, Patrick, poor man, and he's heartbroken."

Studs stood there, looking at nothing, feeling goofy, vague, as if he was all empty inside.

"We're all getting old, Mary; it won't be long before we're under the sod."

"Patrick, don't talk like that, please."

"Goddamn those niggers!" Lonigan exploded.

"I guess it was the Jew real-estate dealers who did it," said Studs, believing that he ought to say something.

"Mary, remember that Sunday, a long time ago, when we came out here in a buggy I rented, and drove around. It was nearly all trees and woods out here then, and there wasn't many people here," the old man said.

"Yes, Patrick, but now are you positively certain that you're not leaving anything behind?" Mrs. Lonigan said.

"Nothing, Mother! And remember when we bought the building over on Wabash. That was before you were born, Bill."

Studs walked over to the window. He saw two nigger kids twisted together, wrestling in the street. They went down squirmingly. He remembered how, coming home from St. Patrick's every night, they used to wrestle and rough-house like that, and Lucy and the girls, not meaning what they said, would call them roughnecks, and then they would go at it all the harder. Funny to think that was all gone, and here he was twenty-six, actually twenty-six, and next fall, he'd be twenty-seven. He lit a cigarette.

"Out there there'll only be about ten buildings in our block, the rest's all prairie," Lonigan said.

"It'll be nice, though," the mother absent-mindedly exclaimed.

"Mary, you know it's not like it used to be. We're not what we used to be, and it'll be lonesome there sometimes."

"It's a shame. This was such a beautiful neighborhood. And such nice people. A shame," Mrs. Lonigan said.

"Well, there'll be nice people out there south, too," said Lonigan.

"I wish they'd hurry up," Fran said nervously, as she joined them.

"They ought to be here any minute now. The movers said they would be here at seven-thirty. Let's see now, it's seven twenty-five, no seven twenty-six," Lonigan said.

"Well, I wish they'd come. OOOOh, I can't stand the sight or thought of this place and this neighborhood any more. OOOH, to think of all those greasy, dirty niggers around. Every time I pass them on the street, I shudder," Fran said.

"Yeah, they look like apes, and, God, you can smell them a mile away," said Lonigan.

"Dad, they're coming in here, aren't they?" said Studs.

"Yeah, a shine offered the highest price for the building, so I let it go. But he paid, the black skunk."

"And this is such a beautiful building," Mrs. Lonigan said.

"Well, they can have it, only I hate to see how this building and the neighborhood will look in six more months," said Lonigan.

"Yeah, I guess the damn niggers are dirty," said Studs.

"I know it. Did you ever look out of the window of the elevated train when you go downtown and see what kind of places they live in? God Almighty, such dirt and filth," said Lonigan.

"Sometimes, I almost think that niggers haven't got a soul," said Mrs. Lonigan.

"There's quite a few were in church last Sunday," Lonigan said.

"Yes, and coming out, did you see how they were trying to talk to Father Gilhooley, and he trying to edge aside from them. Poor man, he's heartbroken, simply heartbroken," said Mrs. Lonigan.

"Well, well, well! How's the little fairy queen? Is she ready to move too?" Lonigan said. Loretta smiled back at her dad.

"Dad, Phil is going to come over and help us move," she said.

"Now, that's fine of him. You know he's Jewish, and I always made it a point to never trust a Jew, but I finally am convinced that he's one white Jew, if there ever was one. And accepting the faith, well, I suppose we oughtn't to call him a Jew any more. He's on our side of the fence," said Lonigan.

Loretta smiled.

"He's a fine boy. He's got manners, and he was willing to

be an usher in the church," said Mrs. Lonigan, looking at Studs.

"Yes, Father Gilhooley, I guess, is proud he's made a convert," said Lonigan.

"And he is so polite and thoughtful. Every time I come into the parlor when he's here, I notice that he stands up. And before he smokes in my presence, he asks my permission. I think he is a fine boy," said Mrs. Lonigan.

"Well, it's seven twenty-nine, they ought to be here," said Lonigan.

"Martin, now you're only a boy. Don't you go trying to lift and carry any of these heavy pieces," said the mother.

"No danger," said Studs, smiling at Martin, who was now a tall, skinny, awkward young boy, a trifle loutish in appearance.

"I'm all right," Martin said in a falsetto voice.

The bell rang. Loretta rushed to the buzzer and pressed it. In a moment, she came back with Rolfe, who was dressed in old clothes. He politely said hello to everyone.

"Well, Phil, we're all set," said Lonigan.

"Yes, Mr. Lonigan, I see that you are, and it's a fine day for moving too!"

"Phillip, it was awfully nice of you to come and help us," said Mrs. Lonigan.

"It wasn't any trouble, Mrs. Lonigan, I was glad to help you."

"Here, I must get you a cup of coffee," said she.

"Please don't, Mrs. Lonigan, I had my breakfast. I'm not at all hungry."

"It won't be any trouble, and I can fix it in a jiffy," she said, rushing out, as Phil graciously protested.

"I suppose you're glad to be moving, Mr. Lonigan."

"Well, Phillip, as I was saying, we're getting old, Mrs. Lonigan and me, and we kind of felt we'd rather not live with a bunch of damn smokes."

"Yes, I know how you feel. They ruined the neighborhood," said Phil.

Mrs. Lonigan called him from the kitchen.

"Yes, I wish they hadn't of gotten in, and they wouldn't have, if all the property owners got together. But I'll tell you this much, they'll never get out where we are going. That's certain. It's nice out there, too."

"Phil, Mother is calling you for your coffee," said Fritzie.

"Hi, there, Martin. All set?" smiled Phil, turning to go out to the kitchen.

"Say, Bill, he's a good decent, clean-cut boy," Lonigan said. Studs nodded.

"Dad, the movers are here," Fran called.

"Well, let's go."

The movers commenced taking things down. Studs took a large rocker, and carried it slowly downstairs. It was tedious work. His arms and back got tired. When he set it down in the alley, he was breathless, and all pooped out. Jesus Christ, and he was only twenty-six. Goddamn it, he felt rotten. In rotten condition. He touched the soft, unnecessary flesh about his abdomen and stomach. Goddamn it!

He walked slowly back, wishing the moving was done. Upstairs, the old man, mother, and two girls were standing in the parlor.

"Well, Mother, take a last look around and say goodbye," the old man said.

"Yes, Patrick."

"Now, you and the girls go ahead out there."

"No, Patrick, I'm afraid you'll forget something."

"Not on your life."

"I had better wait until everything is moved."

Studs picked up a lamp. It was lighter. He carried it down towards the back. Loretta and Phil followed him. He paused at the kitchen sink, and got a drink. Turning, he noticed Loretta squeezing Phil's hand, and telling him not to hurt himself lifting anything big.

He walked downstairs with the lamp. Yeah, he was kind of sorry to be moving. So were they all. Well!

XXIII

It was a Saturday night. Husk Lonigan had the dough from the first pay he had earned since starting to work for the old man. He, Pete McFarland, Crabby Konetchy, and a couple of other fellows from their old gang at St. Patrick's wanted a woman. But they were leery about going to a can house. They stood around the corner of Sixty-third and Cottage Grove, telling each other how they wished they would pick up some broads. Husk finally got bored and suggested some liquor. They chipped in and bought a quart of moon. They walked down to Jackson Park and sat on a bench drinking it, talking about girls, each trying to pretend to the other that he had already lost his cherry. They followed two girls and couldn't make the grade because of their lout-like approach. The booze gave them more courage and they took a taxi down to Twenty-second Street. They walked around lost, but feeling romantic and adventurous. A pimp picked them up, and took them to

*a can house. It cost two bucks, and the women wormed two
bucks extra out of Husk, who was afraid and unable to talk.
It was over quickly, and they were disappointed, because there
didn't seem to be hardly anything to it.*

*Riding back to Sixty-third Street, they acted like men, and
with bravado and hard obscene language, minutely discussed
their experience. They killed their stuff, and, scarcely able
to walk, they bought another pint of cheap moon and staggered
back to Jackson Park. They coughed as they drank the bitter
stuff, but would not be outdone. Husk suddenly pitched forwards, bawled like a baby, and muttered prayers. He passed
out, still mumbling prayers that were interspersed with incoherent curses. They carried him around, and once, he started
coughing and spit up some blood. They let him sleep on a bench
for about half an hour, and still they couldn't bring him to.
They soaked their handkerchiefs in water, and sponged his
face. Konetchy went over to Sixty-third and Stony Island and
came back with black coffee in a milk bottle. Trying to pour
it down Husk's throat, they spilled it all over him. Finally,
they rushed him frantically to a hospital. It cost ten bucks
to have his stomach pumped. The doctor said he would have
died if they hadn't brought him. Husk was left in the hospital,
and the gang departed, humble, but still with a feeling that they
were adventurous and the real stuff.*

CHAPTER TWENTY-THREE

Ooph, the last of the Mohicans! Studs thought to himself,
as he came out of the Fifty-eighth Street elevated station and
saw Sammy Schmaltz.

"Say, Schmaltz, who won the ball game?" asked Studs.

"Studs!"

"You're still around, I see."

"Yes, I'm always here."

"How's business?"

Sammy shrugged his shoulders, and said he sold some
papers.

"All the old people are gone, huh?"

"Doyle, he still lives around here. Oh, one or two."

"They hang around?"

Sammy had to turn and sell a racing sheet to a nigger.

Studs walked towards Prairie Avenue. In the cigar store
on the right-hand side of the elevated station, he saw a group
of niggers hanging around, talking with a sweaty brown-looking,

sporty bastard who leaned forwards on the counter. He saw pearly white teeth flash in a coal black smile.

Niggers passed him on the sidewalk. They nearly all looked alike, as if they were the same person. The corner, their old corner, looked like Thirty-fifth and State. A gang of young niggers were gathered around the fireplug talking, kidding, laughing. He tried to frown. Suppose they should get snotty or try to mob him? He suddenly thought of himself fighting ten or twelve niggers, standing with his back to the wall, swinging, laying them down one after the other with a punch, as guys sometimes did in the movies.

He went into the drug store. There was a pretty, white girl at the cashier's desk. He walked over to the soda fountain to get a coke. But the niggers used the same glasses. His stomach almost turned as he thought of himself using the same glass as a nigger did. He bought a package of cigarettes, and stepped outside.

A loud, irritating Negro laugh struck him, rubbed him up the back. He turned to see a dude, with baboon lips, twisting and bending forwards as he laughed.

"Hi, there, Mistah Morgan!" a loose-jointed, middle-aged Negro said to another passing Negro.

"Hi! Brother Jones," the second replied.

A handsome, light brown, well-built girl passed. Studs looked at her. So did the Negro lads on the corner. He wondered if she was a whore. He'd like to have her. He remembered how a couple of times he'd been to nigger can houses, but the girls he'd had had been too black and bony. One like that was nice, even if she was black.

He felt uncomfortable on the corner, and walked west towards Indiana Avenue. The street was changed. There was another chain store in the block. The garage was still at the corner of the alley. There was still a dry goods store where the old Palm Theater had been. He remembered how they'd used to sneak in the side doors, years ago when he'd been still in grammar school. He tried to remember some of the pictures he'd seen, with Maurice Costello, Fatty Arbuckle, John Drew, Broncho Billy, Charlie Chaplin, Mary Pickford. He couldn't remember them well, except for Charlie Chaplin.

He lit a cigarette. Hell, it hardly seemed that they had moved five months ago. Now, too, there was no place to hang out. Sometimes he went to Sixty-third and Cottage Grove, and sometimes to Sixty-third or Sixty-seventh and Stony Island. No other corner would ever be the same. Christ, and what wouldn't he give to have just one more night, with all the guys back again, and Arnold Sheehan too?

There was a greasy-looking Jew in the drug store at Fifty-eighth and Indiana where Levin had been, and where once, on the day he'd licked Weary Reilley, Helen Shires had treated him to a chocolate soda. He looked north down Indiana Avenue, and slowly crossed the street and walked down, past the vacant lot, past the three-story building where Red O'Connell had lived. Red was a skunk, a no-do, no-work, crapping sonofabitch. He'd used to hang out down at the poolroom around Fifty-fifth the last Studs had heard of him, and he and a bunch of guys like him would be there, shooting their mouths off, selling the buildings around there and even real estate out in the lake with their line. He passed the wooden house, set back from the sidewalk, where the O'Callaghans had lived. On past the apartment where the Donoghues had lived. He stopped at the gray stone brick, Lucy's old house.

He had stood there that summer night, and she had blown him a kiss, and he had gone home carrying his handkerchief, as if he kept it there, and never again had things been the same, and funny, time had passed, and here he was, and Lucy was married. He hoped to Jesus Christ she'd get fat as a pig, have ten kids, and a husband who'd kick the Christ out of her, dose her, and blow out. He looked at the house, with lights behind shaded windows. Niggers now lived in it, and the house was probably stinking because niggers always stunk, and it was dirty because niggers were dirty. He tried to whistle. He heard some vague sounds, and stood convinced that they were human voices, and somehow he felt as if he was hearing Lucy, and Dan and Helen Shires, and all of them talking once again.

He turned back towards Fifty-eighth, cut through the vacant lot, where they'd played, into the alley, out on Fifty-eighth Street and over to Michigan. He crossed Michigan and looked at the playground, dark and gloomy, with the school building half visible. It was misty, an autumn mist, a night like many nights he'd known around the neighborhood, when they'd all get together in the poolroom or at the corner, Slug and Red, Tommy and Les. And they'd goof around, listen to the punks, or go to a show, or get a bottle. He turned around, and walked back. The same railing stood by the grass plot, in front of the corner buildings at the northeast corner of Fifty-eighth and Michigan. Sometimes as a kid he used to jump back and forth over it. He vaulted over it. He vaulted back. He put his feet together to make a standing jump over it. He looked at the railing. He didn't jump, might not make it that way. He was stiffened up, heavy on his feet. He felt his belly. Jesus, was he going to get a belly like the old man?

He walked back to Indiana. On the east side of the alley between Michigan and Indiana, there was still that row of shacks. Poor people had lived there. He looked in and saw a dirty, disrumpled Negro home, lit by a kerosene lamp.

A buck nigger came along. Studs took his hands out of his pockets and tried to look tough. The nigger passed, singing.

He wondered where the guys were. He turned and walked south along Indiana towards St. Patrick's.

He started singing:

> *"Gee, but I'd give the world to see*
> *That old Gang of mine,*
> *I can't forget that old quartette,*
> *That sang, 'Sweet Adeline.'"*

Goodby forever, old fellows and pals. . . .

He stuck his hands in his pockets. He took them out, and swung them at his side. He lit a cigarette. The night was swell, that mist, the moon, just a little bit damp, all like some mystery or song or something. He thought of Lucy, and of that girl he'd knelt next to at mass. Wonder what had become of her. Was Lucy happy? Hell, things were all funny. He guessed he, too, might as well get a girl and marry. What the hell else was there to do? Red Kelly had his girl. Sooner or later a guy married . . . if he could find somebody to marry him.

Ahead of him, he saw the lights of an elevated train appear, disappear. He heard the echoes from the train.

A long time ago, he had walked along the same sidewalk with Lucy. He stopped under the elevated structure, just south of Fifty-ninth Street. A train rumbled overhead. Sometimes they'd played shinny, or had fights here. He moved on past a row of apartment buildings. In his time, they'd looked new and modern, with lawns and trimmed bushes in front of them. Now they seemed old. The niggers, all over again, running down a neighborhood. He heard a Victrola record going:

> *I hate to see de evening sun go down,*
> *I hate to see de evening sun go down,*

An elevated train blotted the song out momentarily, then he heard it again:

> *St. Louis woman, wid her diamond rings. . . .*

He walked on. Niggers living in all these buildings, living

their lives, jazzing, drinking, and having their kids, and flashing razors at each other.

He crossed Sixtieth, and, quickening his pace, he saw the sisters' convent, and the east side of the church grounds, with a bare flag-pole half distinct, in the center. And the school building. He looked at it, a long, low building, now like a shadow, its shape distorted because of the night. Christ, how many times had he come here? They used to play pompompullaway in the yard at lunch hour. He'd run through, stiff-arming anybody who came near. They were afraid of him. Damn tootin', they were. Studs Lonigan had been something to be afraid of. And one day, he remembered Battling Bertha giving TB McCarthy the clouts. He remembered TB covering his face and yelling to be let alone, then thinking suddenly that she was finished, he'd raised his face, and she'd been bringing her clapper down, and it had got him in the nose. He had yelled like hell, and his nose had bled. And in all those days, he'd sat in the chalk-smelling room, looked up at the desk where Bertha sat in the right-hand corner of the window, he'd watched the sun coming through the window, and it would seem to come in lines, and show up all the dust. And the way Bertha would say with respect: William Lonigan, now perhaps you can diagram the first sentence. He'd had a drag with her, and she usedn't to give him the clouts as much as she had the others, because his old man always gave the sisters a turkey at Thanksgiving and Christmas. He still sent one to the sisters.

He passed along the iron picket-fence. He noticed a light in the sisters' convent. He looked at the old building, from the front, the steps leading up to the wide wooden doors. He'd stood here, too, after mass on many mornings.

He was still doing it. With this building here, looking the same, things couldn't be changed, and it couldn't be so many years ago, it couldn't. This building gave him confidence. Everything was all the same as it used to be, and he wasn't fat and worried about his health, and it couldn't be different, and all that couldn't be gone. He stood in a trance.

A street car passed. An old nigger in overalls walked wearily by him. He looked to his left at the new church, standing now huge and high. He remembered how the parish had talked of it. And it was a goddamn beautiful church, and what was it for now—a handful of black bastards.

He turned and walked away. At Sixtieth and Calumet, he paused to watch two young nigger kids wrestling. Three classily-dressed young shines minced past him. He walked right along behind them.

"I swear, ah'll tear your eyes out, Gloria, if you all start making those oogle eyes at my big man."

"What does I care for that big black bastard you got?"

For Christ sake! He followed them. They slackened their pace. He walked by them, and one of the fairies said hello. A second one said he looked lonesome. A third asked if he had any chickens on the block. He was momentarily tempted to take a chance out of curiosity. Self-disgust rose, changing his mind. He turned and told them to blow. They laughed, and he walked on, hearing their voices and laughter behind him, feeling that he was being talked about. It was almost as if he were being humiliated, undressed, in public, and he hastened.

Automobiles were coming in all directions at Sixtieth and South Park. He wanted to get across the street. He dashed in front of the cars, dodged, and just landed safely on the other side. He was out of breath, but he was proud of himself. It had been taking a chance. His guts were still there, and he was still the old Studs Lonigan, ready to run risks. If he hadn't had guts, he wouldn't have taken the risk of his life, dashing in front of the cars. Damn tootin', he was! He drifted through the park. The wind was powerful, and he heard it beating steadily through the empty trees, scraping and rustling the dead leaves. It was dark, with scarcely a star in the sky. Dark, lonely in the park. It had used to be his park. He almost felt as if his memories were in it, walking about like ghosts. He turned to go and look at the lagoon.

Ahead, he saw a stout, squat fellow searching on the ground, repeatedly lighting matches. The sight was funny, almost like a shot from a movie comedy. He suddenly imagined that the guy had lost a valuable ring, money. It was perhaps something happening in real life, like one of the detective stories he had been reading recently. Studs Lonigan the sleuth would find it.

"Lost something?"

"Lonigan!" the fellow said with a curious lisp, as he looked up.

Studs laughed at Barney Keefe, who faced him, wearing pajamas and a bathrobe.

"The sonsofabitches!" Barney said.

"You drunk?" asked Studs, perceiving that Barney did not have his false teeth.

"No!" snapped Barney.

"Well, what the hell's this?"

"I'm sick!"

"You look worse. What the hell you doing out here in that outfit?"

"Oh, Doyle and them bastards came around, and I was sick, and they said come on, they'd take me for a little ride, because Doyle has his old lady's car, and they promised to give me a drink of some bonded stuff. And the wise bastards left me here and threw my false teeth some place around here. But there's nothing funny about it," Barney said, because Studs had to laugh.

Studs found the false teeth. Barney cursed all the way back to the park exit. He hailed a cab, and gave Keefe the fare.

He walked back, because Barney had said that the boys always met by the stone bridge in the park. He knew they'd be back. He found them seated on a bench. They all laughed when he told them how he'd met Barney.

"The jiggs drove us over here," said Tommy.

"How's everything been going?" Studs asked.

"Oh, so-so. You heard about my cousin, Les?" asked Tommy.

"Why, no, what happened?"

"He's in a sanitarium."

"How come?" asked Studs, surprised.

"Oh, drink. His heart is on the kibosh from that bum gin he'd been guzzling," said Tommy.

"Jesus, I'm sorry to hear it. Is it serious?"

"It almost was, but I guess he'll be all right."

"Les ain't drank his last yet, thank God," interjected Joe Moonan, the dick.

"But Shrimp is in a bad way," said Tommy.

"Yeah? Where's he at?"

"He was dishonorably discharged from the Navy and he's down in Fort Wayne. That's where he comes from, you know. Yeah, he's dying by inches," said Tommy.

"It's too bad. What's up with him?"

"Con. I guess he got it from too much carousing around."

"Jesus, first Paulie, and then Shrimp."

"How you feelin', Studs?"

"Pretty good," said Studs, wishing he wasn't worried about his health.

"You're looking good," Tommy said, although it was too dark to see how Studs was looking.

"Slug been around much?" asked Studs.

"Sure. He's always around. He'll be here tonight."

"I'd like to see him."

"You heard about Hink, didn't you?"

"No?"

"They put him in the nut house."

"Jesus, I'm sorry to hear that. Christ, that's too bad. He was kind of queer, though. I remember seeing him several times when he didn't act like he was all there. But say, Joe, how are you these days?" Studs said.

"Oh, I'm all right. Since Thompson got elected again, I feel better, because that goddamn Dever wanted the force to be honest," Joe said.

"He made the boys work for their dough," kidded Tommy.

"Wait till your brother Jim gets on the force, Tommy. He'll work. They'll make a flatfoot out of him goddamn quick."

"When you getting a jane, Lonigan?" asked Moonan.

"Hell with that crap," Studs said.

"Come to think of it, Studs, you never ran around much with girls," Tommy said.

"Jim's getting up in the world, huh?" said Studs.

"Yeah. He'll be on the force in a month," Tommy said.

"Seen any of the other boys?"

"Red. He's still around. He's out with his jane tonight. He's been going around with her more than he used to. I think he's already put the ring on her finger since he's got to be a bailiff in Dinny Gorman's Court," Tommy said.

"That stuff's crap," Studs said.

Tommy said also that Davey Cohen had just come out of the county hospital and he looked bad; lungs.

Slug came around. He and Studs greeted each other.

"Say, listen boys, it's getting late, and this ain't no place to be hangin' around all night. What you say we go to Cooley's saloon, huh?"

"Sounds like an idea," said Tommy.

"Gee, things are changed," Studs said, getting into the cab.

"Yeah, the old neighborhood is shot."

"The boys are all getting separated."

"You know, I was thinking, it might be a good idea to get all the boys together, and have a blowout party, say, New Year's Eve. Red's been thinking about it, and he's willing to make the arrangements and collect from the boys," Tommy said.

"Count me in on it," said Studs.

"How you like the car? My mother finally put out and bought it."

"Pretty nice."

"The Doyle Cab service," Moonan said.

"Well, I'll tell Red to call you up," said Tommy as they drove to Cooley's saloon.

Studs got the blues from gin. He suddenly left the boys. He staggered back to the park, and over onto the wooded island. He looked for the tree where he and Lucy had sat on that afternoon so long ago. He couldn't find it. He staggered about frantically, and finally got out of the park at Cottage Grove. He fell asleep on the car and rode out to South Chicago. He didn't get home until three o'clock. He felt lousy.

XXIV

Les's old man and his sister, Mrs. Doyle, went to the midnight show at the Prairie Theater on New Year's Eve. He was a wizened man, with a bloodless, wrinkled face, humped shoulders, and quivering hands. She was a full-bodied woman, who breathed in gasps when she did much walking.

"Well, Mike, sure and another year's passed," she said.

"Ah, yes, Margaret," he said.

"There won't be many another year for the likes of you and me, Mike."

"Ah, no, Margaret. But God forbid that we should be dead before next New Year's."

"Well, Mike, I only have one more boy to see married to a nice girl, and it's me baby Tommy."

"And Les is my only worry, Margaret. He's a hard-working boy, but after him being so sick, I hope he doesn't drink tonight."

"And I do be worried about my Tom. He's a good boy, only it's bad companions. Now that my Jim is on the force, and Tommy has his job with the city, he might be settling down."

"Sure, Margaret, let us hope. It's the New Year."

At Prairie, Nate Klein staggered up to a passing white stranger, and told him to go take a pee-pee-pee for himself in his hat. Nate told the street that he was going to the party.

"And Lord Bless me, I was afraid for a minute that that was me Tom."

"Ah, and I thought it was my Les."

She walked rheumatically across Prairie Avenue, holding onto her brother's arm.

"I do be worried because my Tom has the car, too. That car has a curse upon it," she said.

"Now don't worry, Margaret," Mike said.

At the midnight show, they saw sixth-rate vaudeville, and a weeping, five-months' old movie.

Coming out, they yawned, and complained that it was too late for people their age to be up. They walked home slowly.

"Mike, I hope that my Tom is all right. I have a feeling."

"Now, Margaret," he said, without conviction.

CHAPTER TWENTY-FOUR

I

A voice within Studs, that wasn't his voice, and that perhaps maybe might have been the voice of conscience, said reiteratively, as if in a hoarse accusing tone:

You're nothing but a slob. You're getting to be a great big fat slob. Nothing on the ball any more. Slob! Slob! Fat slob! Double slob!

"I'm drunk. Happy New Year. Whooops!" Studs yelled loudly: he staggered backwards and forwards with the utterance of each syllable.

Slob! Slob! Double slob!

He looked at the street. It seemed familiar. What was the name?

The voice said:

You don't know your fanny from a hole in the ground!

He ran to escape that voice that kept hammering at him, in his heavy, heavy, twirling head. He ran, thinking he was running straight, and with form. He halted after about a hundred yards and thought that he'd run a block.

He knew the street as well as he knew his name. His name was Lonigan, the great Studs Lonigan.

Slob Lonigan! that voice said.

He stared bleary-eyed up and down the street. There was a light mist, and the street lamps seemed lopsided.

An automobile passed. Studs eyed it intently.

"Hey, where's . . . fire?"

He looked at three-story buildings. They seemed like he knew them and had seen them before. Where, oh, where is my wandering street tonight? Where, oh, where can it be?

The street rolled under him like a ship in a storm. His head spun like a top that was in perpetual motion. The street went up, whoops, and slow, slowly, evenly, it went down, whoops, just like a see-saw.

He shoved his hat on the back of his head.

He stared across the street, and it went up, whoops, and it went down, whoops, and the building came towards him, whoops, like a railroad engine coming forwards on a screen, growing nearer and nearer. Whoops! The building stopped. That was funny.

You're drunk, you clown, drunk as a lord.

He walked, like a paralytic, head down, his body loose, his nervous control deadened. He raised his feet high, as if in a caricature of Germans in a movie comedy doing the goosestep. He halted, threw out his chest, tossed back his head, and almost fell over backwards. His hat slipped to the sidewalk. He turned around in a circle, wondering where, oh, where was his wandering hat tonight.

He saw the hat lying as big as a balloon on the sidewalk. He pulled out a stick that had somehow and somewhere been stuck in his overcoat pocket, and held it over the hat as if it were a fishing pole. He jerked with both hands, like a man dragging in a huge fish, and he tottered backwards for about three yards before he gained a precarious balance. He looked at the end of the stick. No fishee; no hattee! Whoops!

He laughed, and tossed the stick away. He snuck up on his hat, tiptoe, shshing his right index finger to his lips. He circled, continuing to shsss his finger to his lips. He quietly snuck three feet from the hat. He dove for it, clumsily, like a green football player falling on the ball. He lay on the sidewalk. It was cold. Struggling, and by degrees, he achieved his feet again.

Slob Lonigan! Slob Lonigan! You're no goddamn good any more. Got an alderman. Alderman on your gut, and couldn't even get yourself a decent girl. Slob! Slob! Double slob!

"Who's a slob?" he shouted.

You're a slob, the voice said.

He hauled off on the air, and went for a head-first dive in the hard, cold dirt by the walk. He lay there and looked at the world go around. The buildings spun about as if on a swiftly propelled merry-go-round. An automobile coming along went uphill and then downhill. Whoops! He arose, and ran around in circles in the middle of the street, trying to catch the buildings.

A taxi came skidding along. It stopped.

"You goddamn fool, get off the road!"

Studs uttered some inarticulate sound which seemed like uuuuhhhh.

The driver jumped out, and asked what did he say. Studs cursed him. The taxi driver pushed Studs back over the curb, and drove away. Studs fought to his feet, and rushed in the middle of the street, yelling after the vanished taxi.

Studs staggered, and draped his arms tightly around a lamppost. He vomited.

"I'm sick. I want Lucy. I love Lucy. I want Lucy. I want Lucy," he cried aloud, a large tear splattered on his cheek. The vomiting caused a violent contraction and pressure, as if a hammer were in his head.

"I'm sick! Lucy, please love Studs!" he cried.

A light flurry of snow commenced. Studs tenderly kissed the cold lamppost, which suddenly seemed to be Lucy.

"I always loved you, Lucy!"

Tears rolled down his drunken, dirty face.

II

Weary Reilley went to the Bourbon Palace to get a pickup to take to the party the old boys from Fifty-eighth Street were throwing. There was a huge crowd at the dance hall. He moved about, and danced with several girls. One of them wouldn't sock it in. Another couldn't dance well enough to please him. A third laughed as if she were an idiot. The fourth girl was pretty in a chubby way with brown eyes and a quiet manner. He guessed, though, that here was a case of still waters running deep. She was his meat. She weighed about a hundred and twenty-five pounds, nice figure, got a guy hot just looking at her, straight, small hard breasts, nice legs, meat on them and on the thighs. Just his speed! He danced three successive times with her, and she seemed to like him. At first she drew back when he got her in the corners, but then she laid it right up to him, and they socked it in plenty. That made him sure that she was what he wanted. She had everything. He was going to give it to her like she'd never gotten it before. Dancing with her, he thought of what he would do to her, direct, crude images of brutalized sex.

"You're a pretty good dancer," she said.

"You're keen too," he said, working against her. "Shake that thing," he added.

"That's not . . . nice," she said, blushing as her eyes dropped.

"Come on, sister!" he said, aggressively.

She smiled, and let herself go against him.

"Do you come up here often?" she asked, hanging on his arm, and walking off the floor at the conclusion of the dance.

"I haven't got time for it," he said.

"Umm. Swell people. I suppose you go to the South Shore Country Club."

"No. There's too many pigs, and no-do's around here."

"Am I to take that as a compliment?"

"You're the real stuff, girlie."

"You'd be surprised."

"Meaning which?" he said, looking unflinchingly into her dark eyes.

"Maybe I'm not."

"I can take care of that."

"You're not confident, are you?"

"I pick my women, baby."

"Just like that! You're not what they call an . . . egotistical."

"Listen, want to go to a party?"

"Oh, I couldn't."

"How come?"

"Why, I don't even know you!"

"Come on, never mind that. This damn joint is too crowded. There's too many no-do's here. Come on, baby, and can the stalling. You don't want to be wasting your time with these imitation Valentinos up here."

"But what will my girl friend say?"

"Hell, she can find some guy to look after her, and if she can't, that is just tough."

"But. . . ."

"Listen, Irene. You know you want to come, and you're just playing around before you say yes. I don't like that stuff."

"You're a frank fellow, I see," she said.

"Come on," he said, grabbing her arm. They walked down the stairs to the cloak rooms.

III

The party was held in a suite of three rooms at a disreputable hotel on Grand Boulevard in the black belt.

"Here, Pat, have a drink of my stuff," Red Kelly said to Carrigan, as they stood in a corner of the crowded room.

After drinking, Pat Carrigan coughed and grimaced. He smiled that broad, happy, good-natured, chubby-faced smile of his.

"Ah, good stuff," he said, rubbing his belly.

"Damn tootin'."

"Where'd you get it?"

"Never mind. It's good stuff."

A jazz record was put on the portable Victrola.

"Here now, Red. Have some of mine," young Carrigan said.

"Don't care if I do."

Pat handed Red the bottle, and Red took a big drink. Pat

tried to take as big a drink, but couldn't. He put the bottle aside, coughing and sneezing.

"You'll learn how to take it in time," Red said.

"Say, I had too much already. Jesus, I'm drunk as a loon. I'm drunk, Kelly. Drunk," Carrigan said.

"Sure, I know how it is."

"But why shouldn't I be drunk? Ain't it New Year's Eve?" argued Carrigan.

"Don't crap me now."

"Hey, Leach, commere."

"What the hell you want, you drunken Irishman?" Shorty Leach sourly asked.

"What day is it?"

"What's this, a joke?"

"I'm trying to tell Kelly here what day it is, and he won't believe that it's New Year's Eve."

"Jesus, that's tough tiddy. Give me a drink," said Shorty.

"Sure. Happy New Year," said Carrigan, handing him the bottle.

IV

"Don't say that I'm not a lady, you bastard," the exotic dark girl said.

"But say, kid. The ladies do it, and so do the birds. Don't you know that song, I love the birds, and the bees, and the trees, because they all do it too," Wils Gillen said.

"Well, don't say that I ain't a lady," she said.

"You know what I think you are?" said Wils.

"What?" she muttered, slobbering over the small glass of gin she had in her hand.

"I think you're a man."

"Look at me, then!" she said, laughing raucously.

"I'm from Missouri, kid. Show me!"

"Goddamn you, I will!" she said.

She ripped off her clothes.

"Now, you sonofabitch, do you believe me?" she shouted.

"Yeah, I guess you are."

"Now, you goddamn dirty skunk, show me that you're a man."

"I always aim to please."

"Come on over here, and show me. I had plenty, and I'm particular. Particular, I said. You got to prove it to me," she said, looking him over with a sneer.

"You got the right telephone number this time, girlie."

V

"Hey, Swede, don't. Lay off that bitch. She's got a dose."

"Listen, you ain't a man till you got it," Swede said.

"Well, don't say I didn't warn you."

Swede took the pig into one of the bedrooms.

VI

"Say, Dan," said Vinc Curley.

"Yeah," said O'Doul, as he stood in a corner, sheiked out, and unrumpled.

"Want to go to the Tivoli tomorrow afternoon?"

"For Christ sake, hop in the bowl."

Dapper Dan turned his back. Vinc looked puzzled.

VII

"Say, kiddo, listen! Give Doyle here a break!" Slug commanded.

"You know. I can't," Slug's blond jane protested.

"It ain't nothin'."

"I don't mind you, dearie, when I'm this way because I love you, but nobody else. That goes!"

"Come on, kid. I won't hurt you," Tommy Doyle said, his drunken face full of lust.

"No!"

"Go ahead, and do it, or it's the gate!" Slug said, shoving her.

She looked at him with eyes of meek protest.

"Hear me!" snapped Slug.

She went into a bedroom with Tommy.

VIII

"I'll tell you why I'm drunk," Shorty Leach said, letting the tears stream down his cheeks.

"Sing 'em! Sing 'em!" Joe Moonan said.

"You didn't know my girl, Pearl. Well, I love Pearl. I love her."

Joe vanished. Shorty buttonholed Les, who looked thin and pale.

"Here, kid, have a drink and brace up," said Les.

Shorty took the bottle and drank.

"I love Pearl. And she's out with Jack Morgan tonight. Now Morgan stole my girl. He's a nice guy, and I always liked him, but he's out with Pearl, and I'm crazy about her."

"Sing 'em, kid!"

"Have you ever been in love? Well, I have. You know I was out riding with Pearl. And she took and held my head in her hands and she looked into my eyes, and she said: 'There's something about you that makes me crazy.' That's what she said. And I tell you, if you've never been in love, you don't know how I felt. And then I looked out at the moon, and she did, and Jesus, I've never had a feeling like that before. And I thought she was straight, and now she went out with Morgan."

"Here, kid, have a drink, and brace up. The first hundred years is the hardest."

Shorty drank.

"But I tell you I wouldn't be drunk if I was with Pearl because I love and respect her too much. I love that girl," sobbed Shorty, putting his head on Les' shoulder.

IX

"Whoops!" yelled Studs, standing in the doorway.

They wished him Happy New Year. Slug handed him a bottle, and said bottoms up. Studs drank. The New Year bells rang. Everybody drank, and shouted, and a naked girl rushed from one of the bedrooms to kiss everybody. They had to hold Vinc while she kissed him.

"Whooops! It's 1929!" yelled Studs, raising an empty gin bottle with an unsteady arm.

X

"Where you going, Joe?" asked Red.

"I can't telephone here with this noise, and I want to call my mother. I do every New Year's."

"Wish her a Happy New Year for me," said Red.

Moonan went out.

XI

Vinc heard a moan. Then, he heard a girl sobbing. He rushed through the opened door of a bedroom, and turned on the light. He saw Benny Taite and a girl.

"Is there anything wrong?" he said, breathless and embarrassed.

"For Christ sake, who let you in, monkey face?" the girl asked.

"You goddamn idiot!" said Taite.

Taite went at Vinc. He socked Vinc. Vinc lost his temper, and rushed Taite like a bull, socked him, knocked him down, and stood over him yelling:

"Come on! Come on!"

A crowd gathered. Some of them laughed. Red dragged Vinc off, and told him to get the hell out of the place.

"But he hit me!" said Vinc.

"I told you to blow!"

"He hit me. And I paid my money. I won't."

"Will you shut up, you bastard?"

"Gimme my money back, or I'll call the police," whined Vinc.

"Let me handle the mutt," said Slug.

"Listen, seal your trap and there's the door," Slug said.

"I'm gonna tell my mother!" he said, surlily from the door.

Taite sat in a corner nursing a shiner.

XII

Mickey Flannagan slept in the corner with a stupid expression on his face. He snored. Barney Keefe folded his hands, and placed a soggy Merry Widow in them.

XIII

"Daddy, you're a man. What a man! Daddy!" the exotic dark girl said to Wils Gillen.

"As Napoleon said, don't give up the ship," Wils said.

XIV

The blond girl rushed from a bedroom yelling that she'd been raped. She opened a window, screamed that she'd been raped, and threatened to jump.

Red pulled her back. She stood looking about the shocked group, her face distorted and insane. Tommy appeared, asking what the hell was eating her.

"He! He! He!" she shouted, missing Tommy's head with a gin bottle; it ricocheted off the wall, and hit Mickey in the bean. He continued to sleep.

Slug walked over to the girl amidst a tense silence. He slapped her face. She cowered.

"One more bat out of you and you won't have to jump!"

XV

Shorty Leach sat fully clothed in a bathtub of water, droning:

The pal that I loved, stole the gal that I loved, and took all
my sunshine and joy;

Nobody but he was a buddy to me, since we played on
the floor with our toys.
I just can't believe my old pal would deceive. Gee, but I'm
heartsick and sore,
The pal that I loved, stole the gal that I loved, that's why
we're not pals anymore.

XVI

"I shouldn't be drinking. I'm sick. I just came out of the hospital, and the doc he says to me, 'Les, cut it out, or you'll be picking daisies!' "

"Shut up, fool!" Barney mocked.

"But I don't care. There ain't nothin' in life for me. I'm just a goddamn expressman for the Express Company. I ain't got no future."

Tears rolled down his thin, red face; he drank.

"Listen, heel, what's the idea of holding out?" said Keefe.

"Here, pal!"

"Barney, I had a vocation to be a priest. I should be a priest. And look at me! Look at me! Look at me!" Les said, while Barney guzzled.

"I am looking!"

"Ain't I a wreck?"

"Sure, you're the Wreck of the Hesperus."

"Barney, I might be dead next New Year's. The doc said so. He said: 'Kid, lay off the liquor.' But why should I? I'm nothin'. A goddamn teameo for John Continental. Here, gimme a drink," he said, snatching back his bottle and drinking.

Les sneered, looking at a lamp.

"That goddamn thing, I don't like it!" he said.

He kicked it over.

Barney pulled out a little bottle and raised it aloft, saying:

"To myself; good men are scarce."

XVII

There was a sharp rap on the door and a command to open up. Two burly, monkey-faced cops entered.

"What the hell do you call this?" one said.

The other drew a gat. A girl fainted.

"Call the wagon," said the cop, holding the gat on them.

"Who's running this party?" asked the other cop.

"We all are," said Carrigan.

"All who? Speak up, you birds!"

"What the hell, Officer. It's New Year's. We're just havin' a little party," Slug said.

"Yeah, so I see," said the cop ironically.

"Pipe down, you!" said the cop with the drawn gun.

"Me?"

"Yeah, you!"

"Say, what's the idea?" Slug asked.

"Stand back, or I'll shoot."

"Drop that gun, and talk!" Slug commanded.

"Just a minute, Officer," Joe Moonan said, appearing, and flashing his star. Red followed, showing his bailiff's star.

He and Red talked to the officers, and Red told them his old man had been a sergeant.

"Sure, this is just a party. You know, all the boys having a good time," Joe said.

"Well, we got a complaint, and we had to come."

"Want a drink, Officer?" Red asked.

"Sure."

Red gave them a couple of drinks.

"And say, listen, you know, Moonan, kind of ask the lads to pipe down on the noise. We don't like to be gettin' calls like this."

"Sure."

"Here, take this along," Red said, handing one of them a bottle of gin.

XVIII

"Say, Slug, that goddamn broad in there has made a wreck out of me. Jesus, I'm a wreck. Christ sake, please help me out," Wils said.

"Sure thing, kid," said Slug disappearing.

"I just wanna lay down and die," Wils said, dropping on the floor.

XIX

"Come on, let's play football," said Nate Klein, squatting.

Red yelled to cut it out.

"Sixteen, nineteen, twenty-four, Fifty-eighth Street. Cardinals hike!" he yelled, springing against the wall.

Red and Weary grabbed him from behind, and told him to cut it out. He struggled free, squatted, flung himself at the wall again. He bounced back, moaning, holding his hand. Red took him into the bathroom to soak it in hot water.

XX

"Come on, it won't hurt you," Weary coaxed.

"I better go," she said.

"Irene, come on. Don't pull that stuff," he said sharply.

"No. I've never drank. I'm not that kind of a girl."

"Listen! Don't kid me!"

"Please, I'm afraid of you," she said, drawing back.

He took her in a corner, kissed her, pushed her head back, and poured the gin down her throat. She coughed.

"Please, take me home!"

"Come on, we'll dance."

He dragged her, half-willing, to the Victrola. He put on a record and yelled for them to pipe down. They danced, and Weary shimmied. She stood in the center of the floor, an abandoned look on her face, her abdomen pressed forwards, her arms loose, her head flung backwards, shimmying.

XXI

Mickey Flannagan lay in a corner, still out.

XXII

"I got mine from that broad," said Mahoney.

"I thought she was a virgin?" said Fluke.

"She was!"

"Well, how did you do it?"

"I got her blind. She's out."

"Where is she?"

"She's in the second bedroom. She passed out, and I carried her there. She's out like a light."

"Mind if I try my luck?"

"Go to it, Fluke," said Mahoney.

XXIII

"Come here, bitch!" Studs said to one of the pigs.

"After a while," she said.

"Come on, bitch!" said Studs.

He pawed at her. She gave him a shove, and he was so drunk that he stumbled backwards. Taite laughed at him. The girl ran into the bathroom. Studs staggered to the door, and tried to open it. It was locked. He pounded the door.

XXIV

"Listen, Irene is my broad. Don't you be monkeying around her," Weary said to Dapper Dan O'Doul.

"I was only dancing with her."

"Listen, rat, you're all together. I you want to stay that way, don't monkey around her," said Weary.

"I'm sorry."

"You heard me!"

XXV

Barney crawled on his hands and knees looking for his false teeth. Slug gave him a slight boot in the tail. They laughed. Barney cursed. Everybody laughed again.

XXVI

"Let's drink this one for poor Shrimp Haggerty," said Les.

"Yeah!" said Studs.

"Poor Shrimp is dying in Fort Wayne. I'll be dead, too, maybe by next year," said Les.

"Yeah!"

Les raised the bottle. Tommy Doyle grabbed it, and told Les he'd better lay off.

"All right, Tommy, but will you and Studs drink to poor Shrimp, our dying buddy?"

"To our buddy Shrimp, may he be guzzling with us next year," said Tommy, drinking.

"Yeah," muttered Studs, taking the bottle.

He raised the bottle and drank, most of the gin pouring down his chin and shirt.

"Studs is so drunk we'll have to hold his head while he drinks," said Tommy: he laughed.

XXVII

"Jesus, Joe, let's get some of these guys out of here. This is getting to be too much of a goddamn mess. If we don't, something's going to happen," said Red.

"Yeah," said Joe.

"Hey, punk," Joe said.

"What's the matter?" O'Doul asked.

"See the door? Blow!"

"But I ain't doing nothing!"

Red told some other punks to blow.

"Some goddamn thing is gonna happen if we don't get some of these drunks out," Red said.

"Tommy, can you get Les out? He's sick and needs air, and we want to cut it down. Then you and him come back," said Joe.

"Sure. Les is my cousin. I stick by my cousin Les."

"All right, do it, Tommy."

XXVIII

Three of the girls staggered away drunk.

XXIX

Studs floundered over to Irene like a listing ship.

"Come on, bitch!" he muttered, clutching her arm.

"All right, Lonigan, hands off!" Weary commanded.

"Aw, gimme the bitch!" Studs said.

Weary socked Studs in the eye with a right. Studs went back against the wall, and bounced off, his eye swelling. Weary caught him in the nose as he rebounded. He grabbed Studs by the coat lapel with his left, smacked him in the eye with his right, and then gave him a last one on the button. Studs sagged to the floor, and lay there, his nose bleeding profusely.

XXX

"Please let's go. Everybody else is gone," Irene said.

"He's here," Weary said, pointing at unconscious Mickey Flannagan.

"Please?"

"Have another drink!"

"Then will we go?"

"Sure!"

"Promise me?"

He nodded. She sipped from his bottle.

"Now get my coat," she said, shrinking, as she saw the expression on his face.

"Oh, please! Please! Please! I'll scream. . . ."

"Commere, goddamn you! And shut up!"

She cowered with fright. He tried to kiss her. She fought off his thrusting mouth with her hand. He knocked it aside, and pressed his lips against her shaking forehead. He encircled her with his arms, and dragged her towards the bed where Mickey lay. He flung her towards the wall, and rolled Mickey off. She ran to the door. He tackled her.

"OOOH, my ankle!" she sobbed.

"Will you come across now," he said, towering over her, while she sat on the floor, holding her ankle.

She screamed. He grabbed for a pillow slip, and tore a strip off it. She hobbled out of the room on her sprained ankle, screaming. He caught her from behind, and as she twisted and tore, he got the pillow slip tied around her mouth. She raised her hand to tear it off, and he twisted her arm. He could see the pain on her face:

"Will you come across?"

She nodded.

He released her. She tore the rag off her mouth. He smothered her scream with his hand, and she hit and scratched. He gave her an uppercut, and she toppled to the floor. She started to rise unsteadily, and he was on her, holding her mouth, using his other hand to ward off her scratching hands. She slumped back limp, breathing heavily. Her hair was down. Her dress was torn.

"Please. I never done it before. Please, lemme go. Please!"

"I won't hurt you. For Christ sake, cut out the stalling."

"Honest to God, please, I never did this. Please. . . ."

"Can that! You're comin' across if I have to kill you!"

"Please . . . you might act like a . . . gentleman."

"Come on, for Christ sake!"

He half smothered her scream. He stuck his knee in her stomach, and slapped her viciously with his left hand.

"Oh, you will, will you!" he said, punching her jaw after she again flashed her teeth.

He carried her unconscious to the bed.

XXXI

Her face was black and blue, and her coat thrown over her torn dress. She winced with each step, sobbed hysterically, shook all over.

"Now don' try that game on a guy again!" he said, shoving her out the door of the suite.

He left the bloody sheets soaking in the bathtub. Coming from the bathroom, he saw Mickey Flannagan stagger out and he smiled.

He was awakened by the cops, who had been let into the suite by the night clerk.

"This is gonna be a tough rap to beat for you, fellow!"

"You ain't got nothin' on me."

"No! She's beat up pretty bad!"

"She was drunk and fell down!"

"Maybe you can prove that alibi."

The other cop came from the bathroom with the dripping, bloody sheets and asked what about them.

"I don't know nothin' about them."

"Where did you get your puss scratched?"

"I had a fight."

"Yeah!"

"Yeah!" said Weary, challengingly.

"Listen, everybody isn't a helpless girl. Watch the way you talk."

"Listen, they sent you to get me. Here I am. Call a cab, and

I'll pay the bill. But don't try pullin' nothin' on me!" Weary said with clenched fists.

"Shall I let him have it, Joe?" asked the other cop.

"Don't soil your mitts on him."

Weary sneered. He walked out with them. As they went through the door, he made a gesture and said:

"She ain't got no kick. She only got that much!"

XXXII

The dirty gray dawn of the New Year came slowly. It was snowing. There was a drunken figure, huddled by the curb near the fireplug at Fifty-eighth and Prairie. A passing Negro studied it. He saw that the fellow wasn't dead. He rolled it over, and saw it was a young man with a broad face, the eyes puffed black, and nose swollen and bent. He saw that the suit and coat were bloody, dirty, odorous with vomit. He laughed, the drunk stirred as the Negro said:

"Boy, you all has been celebratin' a-plenty."

He searched the unconscious drunk and pocketed eight dollars. He walked on.

The gray dawn spread, lightened. Snow fell more rapidly from the muggy sky of the New Year.

It was Studs Lonigan, who had once, as a boy, stood before Charley Bathcellar's poolroom thinking that some day, he would grow up to be strong, and tough, and the real stuff.

XXV

There was an inward, self-absorbed expression upon the black face of woolly-headed, fourteen-year-old Stephen Lewis, as he walked along Fifty-eighth Street. He thought of an awkward black girl named Eliza May Smith. He spotted a tin can on the sidewalk, and kicked it, thinking that he was the hero of a high school soccer game, and that Eliza May Smith, pretty as a picture, was watching him. Suddenly he paused, fearful. He couldn't remember now, gosh darn it, whether his mother had told him to get butter or sugar. He stood as if petrified, with his eyes popped open, the whites showing. He scratched his head. He proceeded slowly, racking his brain.

At the corner of Fifty-eighth and Prairie, he stopped to watch some older fellows shooting craps. He listened to their language, watched the dice, gazed large-eyed at the money. Some day, he would be big enough to stand on the corner and shoot craps for real money, and he'd win and buy some-

thing pretty for Eliza May Smith. He went on because he had been instructed to hurry home. In the chain store, he ordered sugar. A clerk left a half-pound of butter on the counter, and continued to fill an order. Stephen copped it; he had both butter and sugar. He paused a few more minutes at the crap game. He went on, kicking a tin can, imagining himself to be the hero of a high school soccer game, while Eliza May Smith, pretty as a picture, watched him.

1929-1933

Judgment Day

Deliver me, O Lord, from eternal death in that tremendous day when the heavens and the earth shall be shaken, when Thou shalt come to judge the world with fire. Seized am I with trembling, and I fear that approaching trial, and that wrath to come. O that day, that day of wrath, of calamity and misery, that great and bitter day indeed, when Thou shalt come to judge the world with fire.

FROM DEVOTION TO BE SAID AT THE BEGINNING
OF THE MASS FOR THE DEAD.

SECTION ONE

CHAPTER ONE

I

"Red, I tell you, when I saw poor Shrimp Haggerty laid out in the coffin, I got a damn snaky feeling," Stan Simonsky, riding backward by the window, morosely said, turning to Red Kelly beside him.

"I used to tell Shrimp, Lord have mercy on his soul, I used to warn him that with his health and condition, he shouldn't do as much carousing and drinking as he did," Red Kelly oracularly said, and he and Stan glanced unobtrusively at Studs opposite Stan.

Twisted partially sidewise, Studs Lonigan captured quick-appearing and -disappearing glimpses of flat Indiana plains and isolated farm houses, in the early drizzling twilight. Buildings, tumbling shacks, barns, dotting the landscape, heralded the approach to a small town, and he commenced to see thin puffs of smoke snaking from occasional chimneys. The train clattered over a wetted road where, beyond the closed train-gates, an impassive, overalled man leaned on the handle-bars of a bicycle, waiting next to a Ford automobile. With decreasing speed, they were carried down the center of a small-town street that was set against a background of sooty clapboard buildings. Among the dribbling of people on the narrow sidewalk, Studs singled out a schoolboy, who was staring dreamily at the train with open-mouth wonder, his strapped books flung over his shoulder. Whisked along, the train swept by a paved street, flanked with stucco bungalows, and Studs thought that the hick villagers, stopping to gape at the train, might have caught a load of him from the window, wondering who he was, and where he was going. If they had, he was a mystery to them, and being a mystery to others when he knew himself so well, stuffed him with the feeling of being important.

The train crawled through a station and a mustached man, lazily pushing a station truck containing a few mail sacks, reminded him of many such characters from movies. He did not catch the town name lettered above the station window, and as the engine picked up speed, he saw scattered wooden houses standing at the other end of the town like so many lonely sentinels. And then again, the altering picture of flat farmlands, dreary and patched with dirty snow at the end of February, houses, barns, silos, telephone posts, steel towers connecting lines of strung wire, with a row of wintry trees in the distance, bare like death, and appearing to speed as swiftly as the train travelled.

The car clattered over a small bridge, affording him a momentary sight of a thin stream of steely-colored water. The engine emitted a piercing and desolate whistle that seemed to puncture the countryside with echoing loneliness, and he was reminded of how, as a young kid, he had heard train whistles at night, even ducking his head under the covers because of them.

"Say what you like, our gang from the old neighborhood was the best damn gang of lads you'd want to see anywhere on Christ's green earth," Muggsy McCarthy, sitting beside Studs, exclaimed with gusto.

Hearing McCarthy, Studs wondered where the guy got that *we* stuff. In grammar school, he had been TB McCarthy, the goof, and often they used to hold his arms behind his back, and let the punks sock him. And around the Greek's poolroom, he had been a mooching clown with only about fifty cards in his deck. Now he was trying to spread out the bull and act like he had been a big shot among the boys back in the old neighborhood. But then, what the hell, all that was past, and Muggsy had turned out better than anybody thought he would, and he was just another guy getting along with a small-time political job, and everybody tossed out a little crap now and then to make himself feel better.

His mind drifting from their talk, he thought of how this trip to Terre Haute had broken up the monotony of living in one place all the time. The world was full of places and things he had never seen and would probably never see. If only, when he'd been younger, he'd bummed around and seen something of the world, gone through many towns and cities, and even villages, like the one they had just passed, seeing the stores and movie shows, and houses, listening to the people talk, meeting the girls. He might have made girls all over the country, and like a sailor leaving a girl in every port, he could have left a sweet little lay behind him in every town of the good old U. S. A. And one of them might have been prettier and keener than Catherine, and he might have liked her more than he did Catherine. She might have been an heiress for whom he would have cared more than he had once cared for Lucy. And if he had, the fellows would often say to each other, I see where Studs Lonigan copped off a bim whose old man is lousy with dough and is he up in the world now!

The train shot up an embankment and rattled along parallel to a cement road. Below, he saw a large and shiny automobile, probably a Cadillac, racing even with the smoking car, shooting ahead, slowing down and falling back at a right turn to a road that cut through the dreary fields, regaining its lost speed, darting forward until he could see only the back bumper and rear end. They whisked past a deserted and probably unused station platform, and he looked vacantly out at fields that were being covered with the lengthening shadows. It was funny that he should be riding home now from the funeral of Shrimp Haggerty, and so many things should have been changed from what they used to be, and from what he had expected them to become. But since his kid days, there had been many years, all piled on top of one another, and now, each year, each month, each week, each day, every hour, every minute and every second even, carried him further and further away from them, just as if he was on a moving express train which was shooting him forever away from some place where he very much wanted to be, and all the while carrying him nearer and nearer . . . to his own death. He was going on thirty now, almost a third of a century. If he was going to die when he reached sixty, it meant that half of his life was already gone. If he would be called before sixty, it meant more than half of it was already spent.

Outside, he watched the fields, bare, wet, slipping into the gathering darkness as if they were dropping off into emptiness. Night growing over them was like a coat of gloom being buttoned on, and it was like a coat of even heavier gloom being spread over, buttoned tightly down on, his own thoughts. And the sky seemed to be heavier, to be pressing down close to the earth as if from the force of tremendous tons of lead. Stan was right. Seeing Shrimp Haggerty so wasted, like a bag of old bones, would make anybody feel a little snaky.

The dim light of a solitary farm house whisked before him, and again he heard the long, piercing engine whistle. Winter had never seemed so dreary to him as it did now, not even on some of those sunless days, when, as a kid, he had walked alone through Washington Park with the ground hard and chunky, the snow dirty and crusty, the trees and bushes stark and bare. From the train, the land here looked harder, the patches of snow dirtier, an ugly sight. He wondered how the people in these parts, cut off from the rest of the world, could stand looking at the earth on such days as this one, hearing nothing but silence or the wind, except for the passing trains and automobiles. He thought of how his father and mother would so often sit home in the evening, and not have a word to say, and asked himself how the farmers and their wives ever had anything to say to each other. Living like they did out here, their minds must, he felt, always be on such things as death.

He chuckled to himself thinking how glad he was that he lived in a big city like Chicago.

II

"What's on your mind, Studs?" Joe Thomas, riding backward across the aisle, called over.

"Nothing much. I was just looking out at this Godforsaken country and wondering how the hick farmers around here can even manage to stay awake," Studs replied, an apologetic strain in his voice.

Joe's thin and sharply-featured face broke into a buck-toothed smile which annoyed Studs. But when he closed his mouth again, Joe seemed like a guy who had been kicked all over the lot and was, in everything he did, excusing himself for being alive. Poor bastard! Studs recalled how sore he had once gotten because Joe had cleaned him in a game of straight pool, and he was sorry now for that forgotten feeling of a long time ago.

"Taking in the scenery, huh, Studs?" Stan Simonsky said listlessly.

"I hope you don't call that dreary stuff outside scenery. Now, if you want to talk about some real scenery, take Niagara Falls, where I went on my honeymoon. The way the water pitches down over the cliff! And you know, the spray comes up over a hundred feet where you stand by the railing, and you think it's raining. Buckingham Fountain they got down in Grand Park looks like a piker alongside of it. That's scenery and the glories of nature, and not these hoosier mole hills they got around here," Muggsy said with mounting enthusiasm.

"McCarthy, you'd go over big on a rubber-neck bus," Stan said.

"Monk McCarthy is a poet and he don't know it," Studs said.

"Studs may be kidding you, boys, but not me. He's been mooning over that jane of his," Red said.

"I was just looking out the window," Studs said, flushing guiltily.

"Well, fellows, say what you will, here's something that's got cards and spades on the joys of nature, and the joys of love also," red-faced Les exclaimed, looking at Joe Thomas opposite him, and fishing out a partially filled bottle of moonshine.

"All right, tank, give us break," Red said as Les drank.

Smacking his lips, Les handed the bottle to Joe.

"With mud in your eye, Irish!" Joe said, drinking.

Joe passed the bottle over to Red, and wiped his lips with a shiny blue coat sleeve. Watching Red drink, Muggsy exaggerated his impatience. Studs lit a cigarette while the bottle moved to McCarthy.

"Still smoking a lot, huh, Studs?" Red said, as if delivering a mild reprimand.

"I've cut down a lot," Studs said, Muggsy distracting his attention by taking a drink as if he were putting on a vaudeville act.

Muggsy handed the bottle to Studs.

"I'm on the wagon these days," Studs said with a note of piety in his voice.

"Not a lot here," Stan said, eyeing the bottle he had taken from McCarthy.

"Kill it, Stan. That's always an act of merit," Les said.

While Stan drained the bottle, Kelly glanced self-assuredly at Studs.

"Studs, you know, ever since you got the attack of pneumonia after our New Year's Eve reunion, you haven't looked like your old self. I'm saying this as a friend and warning you that you better watch yourself, and watch the smoking, too. A number of our pals have passed away in their prime because they didn't take care of themselves. Shrimp and his brother Paulie, and Tommy Doyle. Tommy Doyle was as healthy as any one of us here, and he just ruined his heart carousing. I think it ought to be a lesson to us."

"I do watch myself, Red," Studs replied defensively.

He guessed that Red was showing off and if he didn't watch himself with the way his head was swelling up, it would break open. His face, too, was all puffed out like a balloon, his alderman stuck out in front of him and he didn't look at all like the old Red. He was getting to look and act like a politician, all right. But he was getting along. The camel's hair coat he had folded over the seat hadn't been picked up at no fire sale.

He noticed Stan, medium-sized, chubby, dark, his face no longer pimply as it used to be. His clothes were old, the coat sleeves frayed, and Studs knew that he had come to the funeral at Red's expense. Poor bastard, he looked down in the mouth and he sure hadn't gotten the breaks. Married. No job. His baby born a cripple. It was funny the way some of the old boys had died, while others like Red had gotten on, and Stan had run into stiff luck. And here he was, not so much to write home about. He puffed at his cigarette, enjoying the memory of how as a kid he had once cleaned up Red in a fight over in the Carter School playground.

"Gee, fellows, I sure was sorry to see our old buddy Shrimp Haggerty go like he did. He must have suffered, too, sick for well over a year with the con," Muggsy said, nodding a saddened head.

"Poor Shrimp. He drunk himself under the sod. He was an alcohol fiend," Les said.

"Well, Les, nobody can accuse you of not having done your damnedest to pull off the same stunt. You drunk enough in your time to put yourself picking daisies alongside of your cousin, Tommy Doyle. And that time you went to the sanitarium, we all thought you had sure gotten yourself the works. And here you are, as hale as ever, and still doing your share to keep Al Capone in business," Joe Thomas said, causing Les to beam.

"You know, boys, speaking straight from the shoulder, it does kind of get you the way so many of our old gang passed away. Arnold Sheehan, the Haggertys and Tommy, Hink Weber who killed himself in the nut house, Slug Mason beating the Federal Government Prohibition rap by dying of pneumonia, all our old pals. Lord have mercy on their souls. Here today and gone tomorrow, nobody ever spoke truer words," Red said.

"Tommy Doyle always used to say that when he went to a wake, little thinking that soon others would be saying it at his wake. Poor Tommy," Les said, while Kelly sucked contentedly on a fat cigar.

"And the only one of the old gang who got his just deserts was that bastard Weary Reilley. When he got that re-trial he should have been re-sentenced for life, instead of ten years. That poor girl he raped at our New Year's Eve party is paralyzed for life. Reilly was one first hand skunk," Red said vindictively.

"And you know at that party, he was a bastard, socking me when I was so plastered that I couldn't stand up. He knew I licked him when we were kids, and he wouldn't have had the guts to sock me if I was sober," Studs said.

"That's right, he broke your nose, didn't he, Studs?" Red said innocently.

"Yeah. And it was the rottenest trick he ever pulled, getting me when I was maggoty drunk," Studs protested.

"And Reilley came from such a decent family. He just about ruined them, too, I hear, with the expenses of his two trials," McCarthy said.

"The family wasn't so nice in court during the first trial.

His old lady cursed the poor paralyzed girl and spit in her face, and the sister, Fran, was so keen and such a teaser, she called her a whore," Red said.

"Weary was a tough bastard, knocking the bailiff down in court after being sentenced on his last trial," Stan said.

"I licked him when we were kids," Studs growled.

"Well, I never was afraid of him and even to this day I'd like to tangle with the skunk," Red said.

"You know, it was rotten of him, waiting for me until I was so cockeyed I couldn't see straight, and then swinging on me," Studs said.

Noticing McCarthy from the corner of his eye, Studs could see that it wasn't the same old Muggsy. Fat in the face, looking well-fed, wearing decent clothes, but still as hunched as ever. And he was the guy they all had expected to be first to kick the bucket. Life was funny, all right.

"Say, Muggsy, how's your health these days?" he asked.

"Never felt better in my life, Studs."

"I'm getting to feel better right along, too," Studs said.

He yawned. The jarring of the car seemed to get on his nerves, and he felt cramped. He arose and squeezed by McCarthy.

"Don't fall in, Studs," Joe said.

III

Studs shoved back his shoulders and tried to walk down the smoking-car aisle like a big shot. He swayed a trifle, and noticed a beefy man with bulging neck and jowls, his puffed face stupid in sleep. Red Kelly would be looking something like that in fifteen years, he thought, smiling. In the next seat two tough-looking but pretty girls sat, and one of them spoke in a loud voice.

"And I sez to him, say, chump . . ."

They did not return his hopeful glance, and he tried to think of an especially witty crack to make on his way back. His glance caught two men, one with a shiny face and stuffed appearance, who was earnestly speaking to the other, a gaunt and thin fellow.

"It is the duty of sales specialists like you and me, Joe, to sell confidence . . ."

Might be something in the idea. Moving on, he wondered if the people in the car noticed him, asking themselves who he was and what he was, and wondering if he might be more than they were. Toward the rear of the car he spied two middle-aged people, evidently a man and his wife, who faced each other blank and bored. Waiting for the undertaker, he thought to himself. In back of the woman, who was riding forward, there was a well-dressed young fellow, with a much better build and healthier appearance than Studs, who puffed on a briar pipe and read a thick, black-covered book. Studs sneered, thinking that this fellow was maybe like the guys who used to jaw at the Washington Park Bug Club, saving the world when they had to eat from the pickings of garbage cans, nuts who went crazy from reading too many books, the same as Danny O'Neill had become by going to the University of Chicago, and losing his religion. Guys like that, as Red always said, thought they were too good for the human race.

He entered a cubby-holed door marked MEN. In the lavatory mirror he saw the image of his pale and pasty face with hollow cheeks. He shook his head from side to side, thinking of how the New Year's Eve party in 1929 had been the ruin of him. Weary Reilley pasting him when he was drunk, and then someone ditching him, letting him lay in the gutter and catch pneumonia. The guy, whoever he was, who had left him like that, in the cold and snow, he was no pal. Hell, he wouldn't have done that even to a nigger or a dog, he whined to himself. He thought of how he used to worry over getting an alderman, and now, he'd be happy if he could regain some of the twenty pounds he had lost since the party. Funny, all right, he told himself, grinning dejectedly into the mirror.

Returning along the aisle, he saw the two salesmen seated with the girls, telling them jokes. Quick workers, he thought. He couldn't carry things off like that. Must be something lacking in him. But then he just wasn't a bull artist the way most drummers were.

"Now, just as I was saying, fellows, we're older than we used to be. Take Chu Chu Keefe. He and Mickey Flannagan are the same as they always were, and the last time I saw them, they were as cockeyed as ever. They're both swell fellows, regular, but you come to a time in your life when you realize that there's no place for everything. Barney and Mickey, the only thing they got a place for in their lives is booze and female bums. Drunk and whoring all the time, with no ambition. And as I said, speaking straight from the shoulder, there's something more than that in living. A man gets married and settles down some time. Of course, he doesn't become a mollycoddle and let his wife wear the pants for him, and he drinks with the boys once in a while, but still he does a little settling down, and tries to figure out what the whole thing is all about," Red Kelly orated as Studs returned.

Kelly was just showing off, Studs thought.

"Red, I think you're right. Since I got married, and saw how in these times the breaks can go against a guy I've begun to think a little the way you do," Stan said.

Studs lost interest in their talk. Quickly, he thought that he was getting too mopey and the guys would notice it if he didn't jack himself up and quit mooning as he had been. He determined, he wished, he tried to make himself believe that some day he was going to be a much bigger shot than Red would ever become. He sat up erectly and looked at Red. He wasn't going to act like a dope.

"Say, Red, some day I'll bet that you're going to be sheriff or alderman, or even mayor, a real big shot," Les said.

"Well, Les," Red replied, biting on his cigar, rolling it around with his lips, "I'm in the political game now, and a fellow doesn't get into that for nix. Naturally, I'm aiming to go as high as I can, and to get out of it whatever I can." He paused. "You know, boys, the stuff about politics and political issues that you see in the newspapers, well, between us, it's mostly so much crap. Politics is a game you got to play, and you got to get what you can out of it. If you don't, you're a chump, and the next fellow that comes along takes the pickings while you hold the bag. That's what happens to these honest reformers. They are sincere and think they are doing the right thing, but they don't play the game and string along, and in the end they make the next election twice as hard for the party that put them in. That was the trouble with our last Democratic mayor, Dever. He was an honest man, but he didn't know the game of politics. And, well, there's one thing boys that you can lay it on the line on, and that's this . . . Red Kelly is in to play the game, and get all the legitimate getting that comes his way."

"In hard times like these, I guess it's best to get what you can."

"You said it, Stan, because even then, there's none too much, but you watch! In the primaries, it's going to be Thompson and Cermak, and this spring will be a Democratic one. Cermak and the whole ticket will get in. Thompson is dead politically, and he deserves it. He's a demagogue, and he goes campaigning down in the black belt, kissing nigger babies and playing up to the shines. Any man who does that ought to be run out of town on a rail. The jiggs in Chicago are dynamite, and if they ever break loose, it's going to be hell to pay. And right now the dirty nigger-loving Reds are playing up to them to stir them up, and Thompson, kissing nigger babies, is playing right into their hands."

"Let the niggers just get tough. We'll hang them up on every

telephone pole in the city, just the same as we did in 1919,"
Studs said.

"I agree with you, Studs. We ought to give them the same
kind of medicine they get in the South and not even let them
sit next to a white man in a street car, let alone vote," Red said.

"I don't like niggers none, either," Muggsy said.

"They smell pretty bad," Stan said.

"But getting back to politics, boys, this spring is only going
to be a preview to the presidential election in 1932. Then we'll
have Democrats all the way from the White House to the street
cleaners on every block. And there'll be better times, too,"
Red said with smug pride.

"Somebody better get in and do something, because I
tell you, it's goddamn tough," Stan said.

"Well, Hoover is nothing but the tool of the international
bankers, and he's the guy who put the country on the fritz,"
Red said.

"That's just what Father Moylan has been saying on the
radio," Muggsy said.

"There's a man for you. Boy, what Father Moylan doesn't
say about the bankers, and the Reds, too," Kelly said.

"Yes, boys, things have been happening these last few years
that you'd never expect to happen," Stan said.

"Well, all I know is that I wish I had a job," Joe Thomas
said.

"Look at me, fellows. After all the years I put in the service
of the Continental Express Company, what am I doing? Working as an extra, getting a few hours work every week with Long
Johnny Continental," Les said whiningly.

"Say, Studs, by the way, how is your old man weathering
the depression?" Red asked.

"Petty good," Studs answered, figuring that there was no
use in advertising about his old man's business.

IV

"You know, I honestly got the creeps when I saw poor Shrimp
in that coffin, looking so wasted, just like a bag of bones,"
Stan said.

"Such are the mysterious ways of life," Red pronounced.

Remembering the pallid yellow corpse of his old friend,
Shrimp Haggerty, lying in the small parlor in a blue suit, the
heavy odor of flowers, the gray-haired mother sobbing, the
father like a broken man in a dazed fog, hardly seeing anybody,
not hearing what was said to him, arising to walk to the casket
and stare at his dead son, turning away to pat his mourning
wife, Studs felt pretty damn low. He was afraid, afraid of

death, of his friends dying, of the day when he would be stretched out in a coffin and people would be sitting at his own wake saying how sorry they were that Studs Lonigan was dead. He remembered back on a night just before his twenty-first birthday, when they had all gone to see Paulie Haggerty, trying to cheer him up and make him think he wasn't dying. And Kenny Kilarney had pulled such a dumb stunt, kidding by saying that soon they would all be Paulie's pall bearers. Without meaning it, he had made Paulie feel so damn much worse. Just like Kenny! And a few days later, on his twenty-first birthday, they had all been in the poolroom when Benny Taite had come in with the news that Paulie was dead.

Yes, he felt pretty damn low. He heard the voices of the fellows, and he looked emptily through the dusty train window. The moon was riding high now across the sky, a half moon that seemed almost like a fire of whiteness and silver, and the growing early darkness seemed itself to be sorrowing, to be carrying through it an unseen and awful sadness, and it made all the world seem to Studs like a graveyard. He wished that he could see his old pals, Paulie and Shrimp, Arnold Sheehan, Slug Mason, Tommy Doyle, Hink Weber, talk to them. If he could, it would make him feel less the fact that he, too, would one day be dead. He tried to tell himself that they were still alive, but only living in some other town, and that some day they would all come back and have a regular reunion. The train whistle cut in upon him, a deep puncture of sadness into his thoughts. He could not shake this sadness or shutter it from his mind, and it put its fingerprint upon every thought that popped up. He didn't want to talk to the fellows while he felt like this. He wanted just to sit and think. Suddenly, he saw himself as a lonely and unhappy adventurer riding upon this train, to some dangerous and unknown end. Another farmhouse light stabbed the darkening obscurity, and to Studs, for the moment that he saw it, it was like some supernatural and all-seeing eye. The train rumbled over a crossroad, spanned by the track, and he saw the headlights of an automobile coming forward. He turned from the window, fearing to look out now and continue thinking, because if he did, they would be convinced for sure that he had become a mope.

"Les, I agree with you. We'll never have the old days back again. But, as I was saying, what's gone is gone, and a guy can't always be thinking of it. He must be thinking of what's ahead for himself, where he's going," Red said.

"I know this, too," Studs said, cutting in on a defensively apologetic remark of Les', "I know that my old man and old woman have never felt the same about our new neighborhood as they did about the one down at Fifty-eighth Street."

"And my aunt, Tommy Doyle's mother, she seems to feel just the same way, Studs. All she does, these days, is to sit at home and brood. She keeps saying, every time I see her, how there were such good people around Fifty-eighth Street, and she will hardly even leave the house, except to go to church. She just mopes around all day. And my brother Joe, who collects rent on her buildings on South Park, he can't hardly get a red cent out of the niggers living in it. Half of the time he doesn't even try because what's the use?"

"Damn it, you know, I can't get over seeing poor Shrimp, Lord have mercy on his soul. I can't get over the snaky feeling I got looking at his corpse," Stan Simonsky interrupted.

"When I die, I want to go out like a light," Studs said, trying, by speaking of death, to rid himself of the clinging fear of it.

"Me, too, Studs, only I want to have the priest first."

"All the boys from our gang who were Catholic had the priest. They were lucky at least in that," Les said.

"Me, now, all I wish is that this damn train ride was over," McCarthy said.

Studs, again not listening closely, had a sudden vision of a screeching collision, the cars smashing, turning over and dumping off the tracks and down the siding, the passengers, himself included, being pinned under the steel, moaning, crying and begging for help, gritting their teeth to be brave and bear their injuries, or crying forth in misery and cowardice, many of them dying before they could be rescued, or before, anyway, those who were Catholic had a priest. He saw himself dying without the last rites, his insides smashed and hanging out, his skull fractured. He went pale, and looked aside so they wouldn't notice him. He heard Muggsy still complaining that he wanted the train ride over, and he wished that he could be as lighthearted now as Muggsy seemed to be. He wanted to act and talk and be like the old Studs Lonigan.

"What's the matter, Monk, don't travel agree with you, or are you getting hot for your old lady?" Stan asked.

"Tickle Joe, Les," Muggsy said, pointing at Thomas, whose head had dropped forward in sleep.

"Let the poor guy sleep. With losing his job, and that rheumatism that has been bothering him these last couple of years, he's had one hell of a time," Kelly said.

"Say, Red, remember the time we tried to enlist?" Studs said with a forced smile, still the prey to disturbing thoughts.

"How could I ever forget it?" Red said, and the others laughed.

"And the time we went to Burnham, and tried to make goofy Curley lose his manhood," McCarthy said.

"And when the joint was raided, I jumped out of a second story window and escaped, even if I did sprain my ankle," Studs said nonchalantly, hoping that they would remember and speak of some of his past exploits.

"Those were the days," said Les.

"And just think, we're almost all of the old gang that's left," Muggsy said mournfully.

"Hey, Muggsy, you're a married man with a kid. Does your wife know about your past?" Studs grinned, and they laughed.

"That's all right. It never pays to tell a woman too much," Muggsy replied.

"Don't you wish you were single, Muggsy?" Studs said, wanting to keep up the kidding, because it made him forget many things.

"And I ain't sorry none, and I'm glad that I got my kid. She's beginning to talk now, and she says daddy just like she meant it."

Studs saw Stan's lips twitch, and his face cloud while Red gave Muggsy the razzberry. He wished that the subject hadn't been brought up. Stan was a good guy, and the poor bastard had gotten it plenty tough, no work, and a crippled baby.

"How about yourself, Kelly, when are you going to begin populating the world with little Red Kellys?" Stan asked, forcing himself back into the laughing fellowship.

"Sure, Red, don't tell us you ain't doing your duty," McCarthy kidded.

"I ain't saying nothing, boys, and I'm just letting nature take its course," Red grinned.

"If Les, there, ever gets married and has any kids, the first thing they'll say to him, if they are chips off the old block, will be 'Come on, pops, how about a bottle?' " Muggsy said, causing Les to beam.

"Les has no idea of sliding down the middle aisle while he hardly works two days a week," Les said.

"Studs, there, is going to be the next," said Red.

"I ain't saying nothing," Studs said, blushing, enjoying the crack, and thinking that they were all swell fellows, all right, and that their gang had, after all, been the best gang of regular fellows a guy could want to pal with.

"But say, boys, I meant to tell you the story about George the Greek who used to own the poolroom. He saved up all his dough and went back to the old country to act like a big shot, and the first thing they did was shove him in the army," Red said, everybody laughing.

"I never did like Greeks," Studs said.

"Me neither. Like that waiter Christy in the restaurant who was a Red. They ought to take bastards like him who don't appreciate this country and send them all back on the first boat. We got too many foreigners here anyway, and that's why there are so many Americans like Stan and Joe here out of work," Red said oracularly.

"Yeah, I guess you're right, Red," Studs said.

"You know, fellows, I was just thinking of how life is a funny thing," Les said absently.

"Is that what you call Bug Club Philosophy?" Red remarked with a mild jeer.

"Well, I was just thinking about poor Shrimp, and the boys who passed away before him," Les said.

Studs again turned to the window. He asked himself, and he asked the foreign darkness outside the window, would he be the next to go? Would he be stretched out in a coffin next, with the boys around saying poor Studs, as they said poor Shrimp? Christ, no! He didn't want people feeling sorry for him like they did for Stan and Joe and for all their dead buddies. He wasn't going to be poor Studs. He was going to be healthy and outlive them all, and be more successful, too, than Red Kelly ever would be. And he would marry Catherine. He wasn't going to crack up for a long time, mister, and when he came to his last day, he would leave behind him a long life, good times, and the name Studs Lonigan in bigger letters of success, mister, than many imagined. He vowed this to himself, but vow or no vow, he still saw himself stretched out in a coffin, with the boys coming, looking down at his cold and waxen face, kneeling, praying, going out to the kitchen to talk about the old days, and about poor Studs.

The train swept overhead through a town, and below him Studs saw, as if they were part of some warm life that he did not know, people moving in rainy streets, automobiles, lighted signs, and windows and stores and lamp-posts. And if he was dead, maybe Lucy would be there. But the hell with her and all that.

He didn't care, and he was alive, and he was going to marry Catherine. She was a damn swell kid, who would really do anything for him, go to Hell for him, and he really cared for her, and she would make him a good wife. Red was married and coming along. So would he. And tonight, goddamn it, he was going to pop the question. He was coming back, Studs Lonigan was.

The fellows were still talking. Let them chin, he told himself, still emptily staring out the window as the train passed through the industrial belt surrounding Chicago, a passing scene of factory chimneys, squalid and dimly lit streets, houses in rows like barracks, and then stretches again of country lost in blackness. He felt dirty and nervous, and he made up his mind right then and there that he was going to pull together. He wanted to get back to Chicago quickly to start on it, too, make a fresh start, regain his health, fight an uphill battle and show the world that Studs Lonigan could be somebody. He was conscious, acutely, of the gratings and strainings and clatter of the train, the squeaking windows, and again he heard the piercing, siren-like train whistle. He did not hear Red Kelly gently remark:

"Studs must be in love. He's moping so that he doesn't even hear us talking about him."

CHAPTER TWO

I

Chewing on a toothpick, Studs vacantly stared through the bay window, seeing the fat and loose-faced proprietor waddle from behind the horseshoe-shaped marble counter, and cross, against a background of hustling waitresses and people eating at white-clothed tables, to the counter case in front of the window. He noticed the sag in the man's broad trouser seat, and then he watched the dark, sexy-looking waitress scurry with a large tray of food. Three fellows, toward the front and close to the wall, were leaning across their food in talk and suddenly stretched back and laughed. Studs glanced in their direction. Three regular lads having supper, and then out to make a night of it! Where to? Show? Dance? Party? Canhouse? Speakeasy? There was a quality of warmth and friendliness, not for him, in the sight of these people eating fifty- and seventy-five-cent suppers, and he wished he were back inside, eating the meal he had just stowed away. He read the slanting line of enamelled lettering across the window, merely to waste time. . . .

MARCEL'S RESTAURANT

Still a half hour before he'd meet Catherine. Chilled, he turned up his coat collar and about-faced. He saw that Dearborn Street, lined with tall and old flat-sided office buildings, with lighted windows seeming like pieces of yellow paper pasted against a dark setting, had only partially dried from the mizzling rain, and the raw snap in the air seemed to stab through to

his bones. A few people walked down the deserted street, an
automobile sputtered, turned a corner, and an elevated train
rumbled by at Van Buren Street. Perhaps it was a south-bound
train. It would stop at Fifty-eighth Street, and shines would
bolt down the station steps to the street that he had once known
so well. One night, a year ago, when he had nothing to do, he
had gone walking in the old neighborhood, feeling very much
like a stranger who had no right to be there. Shrimp's funeral
brought things like this to his mind, and kept them there.
If he ever walked along Fifty-eighth Street again, Shrimp and
Paulie and Hink and Arnold would all seem to walk with him
like ghosts.

He halted on the opposite side of Van Buren Street to look
at the ordered rows of black and tan oxfords in the window
of Hassel's shoe store. Used to have more clothes than he
had now, he thought, his eyes straying from shoe to shoe
until he fastened upon a pair of black brogans with narrow,
perforated toes. But he oughtn't to spend five-fifty on shoes
when he still had two pairs that would do him for a while.

At Jackson Boulevard he stood on the curb irresolutely,
while several automobiles shot past him. A tall fellow stared
at him. Telling himself that the lad was constructed like a
power machine, Studs attempted to appear unobtrusively firm
in returning the glance. The fellow's stare was unrelenting.
Studs crossed the street, and walked by the Great Northern
Hotel, stopping to study a news photograph of Lindbergh and
his wife in flying outfit with a plane behind them. He thought
that Lindbergh was a fearless-looking brute, all right, and
tried to imagine what it would be like to be the hero of the
nation and to have been the first man to fly alone across the
Atlantic, winning twenty-five thousand dollars, a society wife,
and undying fame. Lucky boy! Realizing what Lindbergh was,
he began to feel measly and insignificant, and turned away
from the picture.

Maybe if he had gotten into the war he might have been
an aviator, and when the prize was offered he might have com-
peted with Lindbergh, beat him across the Atlantic, and become
more famous than the hero of the nation. He began to feel
joyful, seeing himself, Studs Lonigan, as Lindbergh, instead
of the Studs Lonigan that he was at the moment. Then the
world would have known what he was, what kind of stuff he
was made of! Damn tootin', it would.

Two tall youths approached him. From force of habit, he
clenched his fists, and his body tensed for action. He saw that
they were wearing smart and expensive clothes, with gray
stetsons, and their faces were bright and shiny. Doggy fellows,

he murmured to himself. The fellow on the outside in the gray coat, was talking in a highbrow accent. Studs guessed they were collegiate or just out of college. He turned to stare after them, noticing the cut of their beltless overcoats. The one in the gray coat laughed in a refined low-pitched way. Boy scouts in long pants! His fists again automatically clenched.

Walking on, seeing the lights of Randolph Street before him, he wondered if they were college football players. That was what Studs Lonigan might have been. Even if he did admit it, he had been a damn good quarterback. If he only hadn't been such a chump, bumming from school to hang around with skunky Weary Reilley and Paulie Haggerty until he was so far behind at high school that it was no use going. It wouldn't have been so hard to have studied and done enough homework to get by, and then he could have set the high school gridiron afire, gone to Notre Dame and made himself a Notre Dame immortal, maybe, alongside of George Gypp, the Four Horsemen, Christy Flannagan and Carrideo. How many times in a guy's life couldn't he kick his can around the block for having played chump?

"Lad, I just hit town and I'm on my uppers. I've been carrying the banner all winter, an' I'm hungry," said a seedy man, taller and huskier than Studs, shivering without an overcoat.

"Sorry, but I haven't got anything," Studs replied in a voice of controlled and even cautious surliness.

"Christ, lad, only a nickel or a dime for a warm cup of coffee. I'm hungry!" the bum said, doggedly following on Studs' heels.

Wheeling around, Studs snapped, "Listen, fellow, I haven't got it." He perceived a craven look come into the man's face, and frowning, his own courage mounted. "For Christ sake, can't you understand English?"

The bum turned and zigzagged along in the direction of Van Buren Street, while Studs watched, still flushed with his own bravery. The fellow had the advantage of weight and height, and was in at least as good physical trim as he was. He could have sloughed Studs. It must have been something of the old Studs Lonigan left in him that had led to his not taking sass, risking a fight. He imagined himself fighting with the bum on the darkened and almost deserted street, a long and gruelling battle, slugging back and forth, both of them staggering and bloody, until Studs would put every ounce of spirit and energy into a last haymaker, and the bum would tumble backward, fall over the curb into the street, and know that he had met a better man. Hands on hips, he sneered, and watched the bum diminish as he pursued a ziggedy course along the sidewalk. Studs turned and continued, himself fighting like Jack Dempsey used to. He began to feel that Christ, he could have spared a dime. But then, if the bum needed money, why didn't he work for it? He knew that in thinking this he was just trying to convince himself that he had done the right thing, when he really acted like a bastard over a measly dime. There was plenty of guys in the red now, meeting tough luck, out of work and not able to get anything. Some of his own friends, too—look at Joe Thomas, and Stan, and then there was Les almost in the same boat. Plenty of guys, all right, broke, begging, and how could he have known whether this fellow was one of them, or just a regular bum? He shrugged his shoulders, deciding that he had plenty of things of his own to worry about without bothering over every bum who came along the street.

At Madison Street, he halted to permit the passage of a west-bound surface car, reading above a window in the center of the car: MADISON & WESTERN. He had hardly ever been on the west side, and he wondered about it. It was probably like a city in itself, and it had its gangs and bunches and poolrooms all over, fellows just like their own bunch from Fifty-eighth Street, fellows just like himself, like Red and like Slug and Weary and all the old boys. He slouched onward, hearing the rumble of the elevated trains, several blocks distant, and then, from a nearer street, the shrieking sirens of fire engines, and the high-powered roaring of fire-engine motors. He wished the fire were along his way to meet Catherine, so he could stop and watch the excitement. If it was a big one, he might see the flames bursting out of the windows, and even watch the walls of the building crumble, making noises like booming cannons. But that was a goofy thing to hope for.

He increased his gait to a brisk walk, because Catherine was almost never late, and since he was going to pop the question tonight he oughtn't to annoy her by making her wait for him. The idea of proposing worried him; his body became tense and his breath seemed almost to jerk out of him. It was a serious business, and maybe he ought to think it over more. He reduced his pace unconsciously. He felt somewhat the same as he might have if he were going to a dentist's to have a tooth pulled, wanting to postpone what had to be done to some other time. Suppose he should make a fool of himself? After all, he was really a stranger to her. He was really a stranger to everyone else in the world also, and they really did not know what went on inside of him, and how he felt about many, many things. He wasn't sure that he would want to live so intimately with anyone as he would have to do with Catherine if he married her. Maybe he should not have made the date with her tonight, coming all the way downtown instead of getting off at the Englewood station, and letting Stan bring home his small grip. But if he hadn't done this, he would have nothing to do but go home and sit around watching how bored his old man and old woman seemed to be, or else going out alone. And these days he hated to be alone, and when he was alone, he worried and puzzled over too many things, and stewed over his health. And did he, now, really want to marry Catherine?

There was Lucy. And there was that girl he had knelt next to at a Christmas morning mass at St. Patrick's. He had wanted to get next to her, and he had used to hope that he would. As he remembered her, and as he remembered Lucy, they had class, the same kind of class that girls like his own sisters or Weary's sister, Fran Reilley, had. There was an air about them, about the way they talked, walked, the things they said and did, their clothes, everything about them that Catherine did not seem to have. Catherine would make him a damn good wife, he knew, but still, well, there was something common about her, something that would have kept her from being in the same group with girls like his sisters, from being bid to their sororities, something that was there even if he couldn't put his finger on it. She was decent, he was sure she would say yes when he popped the question, and she was the kind who would make a goddamn swell wife in some ways. Yet when he was with her, and met his sisters, he was ashamed of her. Thinking of Lucy, or that other girl, he kind of felt sorry for Catherine.

He turned the corner on to Randolph, the Loop noises bursting upon him with a sudden increase of volume, the elevated trains from Lake Street, the clanging of a street-car gong on Dearborn, the humming movement of the automobiles, the parade of people along the sidewalk, snatches of their talk, their feet scraping over the sidewalk. He felt as if he had left a place that was cold to come into one that was warm. He heard the jazz band of a nearby, second-floor Chinese dine-and-dance restaurant break into snappy music, and he glanced at the many and brilliant electric fronts of the shows along both sides of the street. Keyed up, he was glad to see people, he wanted to talk, to do something, to see Catherine, too. He felt that his body was now like some kind of a nervous instrument with strings like violin strings that had been plucked and tingled.

"Plenty of seats inside. No waiting. *Follies of 1931* with all-star movie cast. No waiting, folks."

Studs stopped to look at the six-foot, red-headed doorman of the Greater Artists Theater, who wore a long, purple, gold-braided coat and bluish-gray trousers with a wide purple stripe running down their sides. He saw a baby-faced girl, giving the fellow a come-on glance, and he thought that the lad was the kind to knock a girl's heart six ways from Sunday, even if he had a flunkey's job and was all dressed up in a monkey suit. He felt small, all right, looking at the fellow. And as he walked by him, he looked at the slender silken legs of a passing girl. He almost collided with a tall and haughty blond, and, mumbling an apology, he noticed that she had a long, grayish coat which made her look like the works. He turned to watch her disappear with her fellow, and to note the way she wriggled from behind. What did fellows have to do to make keen and classy broads like that one go nuts over them? Some guys did, too, and such broads would eat dirt for them. He had never had one gone like that on him, though, and he wished that he had. Catherine, he kind of felt that she would go nuts over him if he gave her the chance, only she wasn't the type, and he felt kind of sorry for her. She just lacked the kind of class that such girls had.

He stared quickly from face to face as he walked, liking the sight of so many people, of so many girls. He realized how he had come to feel so differently just by turning off of Dearborn and coming onto Randolph, where there were lights and people, and where there were so many girls to look at, many of them walking as if they were movie actresses, hot babies, as he could see by just glancing at them as they passed by. On Dearborn, he had felt out of the picture and all alone, and now he didn't. And there was something, mmm! He looked after the girl, a cold but desirable blond. He recalled Slug Mason's philosophy, that all broads could be made by the right fellow, but that the right fellow always treated them rough. He spotted a pock-faced girl, very stout, who hung on the arm of a thin, weasel-faced lad, and he figured that maybe Catherine was not so bad. She was a little bit plump, but so had Lucy been, so were lots of girls, and she had some stuff, and had a nice handful to her. Sometimes when she was dressed up, she looked plenty worth the getting. Gazing around, seeing so many couples, he was anxious to meet her, to walk back this street with her, and be in this same picture so that other fellows could see him, see him as part of this picture of fellows going out with their girls.

He walked the last block between Wabash and Michigan impatiently, but again the doubt about proposing came to his mind. He determined that he would pop it. He decided that he would wait a little longer, get the lay of the land better, and then if he was absolutely sure that she would say yes, buy the ring, and have it to slip on her finger then and there. And if he did pop it, would he or wouldn't he be putting his foot in for something that he wasn't bargaining for? Often when he was with her, he didn't have anything to talk about, and he had a queer tense feeling. It made him uncertain whether or not he was a sucker, wasting his time taking her around. And then, with business rotten for the old man, even though he had dough saved in the bank, mightn't he wait until the hard times were over and he was more sure of being able to support her? Christ sake, he didn't know what the hell to do, and there she was standing on the steps of the public library, and now she saw him and was smiling, and he was goddamn glad to see her.

II

Returning Catherine's pleasing white-toothed smile, Studs realized, as if it were a discovery, that she wasn't hard to look at. She was short and fleshy, but not so fat. Not seeing her these last few days, he had gotten to thinking that she was fatter than she really was. She had thin lips, a stubby nose, black eyes, a round, full-cheeked face, and she was wearing a new black coat with fur-trimmed collar and cuffs. He knew that he was damn glad to see her, and he was sure, from the way she had pursed her lips up at him and her smile, that she was glad to be seeing him.

"Well, stranger, how are you after your long trip?"

"Pretty good."

"You must be tired after the train ride."

"Not so tired," he said lightly, adding, "What have you been doing while I was away?"

"Same as usual. And oh, yes, I've gone on a milk diet. I'm going to lose ten pounds," she said, causing Studs to think, pleased, that she could shed that weight without hurting her figure a lot. "I started on it yesterday, and do you know, Bill, all I've had was orange juice yesterday, milk for lunch, and milk and two pieces of dry toast for supper. . . ."

Studs' mind drifted, as it so often did when she began to talk like this. He thought, with pride and growing self-confidence, that he had a girl of his own, and he was taking her out, just as so many other fellows were out on dates with their girls. There had been many nights back in the old days when he'd wanted a girl, and didn't have one. The punks would come into the poolroom, all togged out in their drug-store cowboy uniforms, talking and bragging about their broads and their dates. Listening to them, he'd feel superior, crack wise. And now he knew that behind his sneers he had wanted the same thing that many of them had had, a steady girl. He wouldn't have admitted it to the bunch, or hardly, even, to himself. But still it was so. And now he had the girl, Catherine, beside him, and he was getting to feel pretty sure that she was the right one for him.

"This morning, Mother said to me, 'You won't persevere on that diet of yours. You'll do just as you did all the other times that you went on it. I know you, my girl. I know how you have a sweet tooth, and you like to eat too much.' And I said, 'Mother, oh, won't I! Won't I!' And she laughed at me. But I just smiled back at her, because I knew that this time I was going to carry it through, and I said, 'Mother, you better do all your laughing now, because when I finish this diet and lose ten pounds, it's going to be my turn to laugh back, and will I laugh!' And when it is over, I'm going to take her out and make her watch while I stand on the scales. And then, will I laugh!"

He was beginning to feel much the same as he had sometimes felt with Lucy Scanlan. He took Catherine's arm, and he almost imagined that times had not changed, and that those fifteen years or so since he had been Lucy's fellow had not gone by, and Lucy Scanlan and Catherine, they were one and the same girl, and he was the same old Studs Lonigan, only knowing more what he wanted than in those days when he had only been a dumb punk. And he had as much ahead of him to hope for now as he had then, because now he knew more, and was a man, and he had done with his days of fooling around and ruining himself sowing wild oats.

He wished they could meet Lucy now. Last he had heard of her, she was married to an accountant, and they were not getting along so well. They had three kids, and Lucy was fat, getting fat as a pig. Just to think of her now so badly off, and to look at this girl, Catherine, who was younger and prettier and not washed out, that was revenge on her for the way she had hurt him and made a fool out of him. Now she was paid back, and if she could only see him this minute so that she would know it, and it would cut deeply into her, as it had into him, and she would see that she had made a mistake, and get to thinking that maybe she would be a hell of a lot better off if she hadn't given him the run-around.

And still he would always love Lucy, who had sat with him in a tree in Washington Park, kissing him, shy, swinging her legs, talking about little things that meant more than the mere meaning of the words, swinging her legs with her blue-wash-bloomers showing a little, a girl at the stage when she is starting to get breasts and a figure, and she is gay and laughs, and has imps in her eyes, swinging her legs, singing *In the Blue Ridge Mountains of Virginia.*

All the street and Catherine and all the scene about him had a meaning that it had never had before, a meaning just the same as Lucy in Washington Park had had a meaning, and the meanings were the same. He felt . . . like a lot of songs like *My Wild Irish Rose,* and *In The Blue Ridge Mountains of Virginia,* and *Valencia* and *Rose of Picardy and Chérie* and music and a lot of songs.

"When I came home tonight, I said to Mother, 'See, you thought that I had no will power? For lunch, I only drank a glass of milk. Now what do you think of that?' And she smiled as if she had to force herself to believe me, and she said that she was surprised that I was able to go this far. She doesn't think I can keep it up much longer. And Dad at the supper table, he just laughed at me and tried to tease me. Dad, he's such a sweet old darling, but he is a great teaser, and ever since I can remember he has always teased me. But I resisted his effort to tempt me, and I only had a half a bowl of tomato soup with a few bread crumbs in it, and a glass of milk."

Studs shook his head.

"Well, aren't you going to say anything?" she said, staring at him.

"Why, yes . . . That's swell."

"My, my, what enthusiasm," she laughed.

"I meant . . ." he said, trying to be convincing.

She freed herself from his grasp, and moved to a shop window. Tagging after her, Studs thought that, gee, they had taken a long time to walk a block.

"Look at that dress. It has a high waist line, and high waist lines are coming in and oh, dear, I'm much too short for them. Isn't that awful now? Men never have such troubles over their clothes as girls do. And that's such a pretty dress. Oh, it makes me almost sick. And you can see that they are all going to be longer too. Look, Bill, at that gorgeous black crepe. It's only twelve dollars. Clothes are dirt cheap now."

She pointed, Studs mumbled agreement, a sound which seemed to remain stuck in his throat and to be cast out only as a reverberation of breath that failed to become a word.

Just how was he going to pop the question? Because, he knew now, without any doubt at all, that Catherine was the right girl. And he could see the two of them, after they were married, walking along Seventy-first Street on a hot summer evening, old friends of his seeing Catherine on his arm, Studs Lonigan's woman.

The traffic lights delayed them at Wabash Avenue. Studs, with a feeling of manly responsibility, firmly clasped her elbow.

"But, Bill, you haven't told me a word about your trip or the funeral?" she said as they again stepped onto the sidewalk.

"Oh, it was all right," he said laconically.

"All right! I wouldn't say that that's a good way to describe a funeral," she smiled.

"It was a good funeral," he said, embarrassed.

"Were many people there?"

"Well, there wasn't too many, and still it was not so awfully small, either. And, you know, I felt sorry about poor Shrimp."

"I didn't know him, did I?"

"No, he used to live around Fifty-eighth Street," Studs said.

"From what I've heard of Fifty-eighth Street, I would say it must have been some neighborhood," she remarked.

"It was," Studs said proudly.

"I wouldn't need to be told that, not after the way I have heard you and Red Kelly rave about it. And say, isn't his wife rather sweet?"

Studs wanted to tell Catherine that Red's wife was not as sweet nor as pretty as she was, but the words choked up on him, and Catherine continued, "And Red, he just thinks the world of her, doesn't he? He thinks there's not another girl that can even be compared with her. Of course, though," her voice seemed to become wistful, and Studs wondered if she was fishing for him to say something, "that is the only way he should feel about her, since he married her, because marriage is a serious business, and people, when they start thinking of getting married, have to feel that way about each other." She looked up at him, and he wondered was she hinting and giving him his chance. He noticed that she suddenly turned her eyes aside to stare at a passing girl who wore a long black coat. And hadn't she pronounced the word marriage a little queerly?

"Well, she's his wife," he said.

Lacking words, still not sure what she meant and whether she meant anything more than her words, he looked at her, and she still glanced away. He held his eyes on her, hoping that she would turn and see in his eyes all the things that he did not seem able to put into words. And she looked back, and for a quick moment their eyes met, and she seemed to understand him, and she smiled, very sweetly, he thought. For about five more steps they looked at each other that way, her eyes seeming to be misty, and they seemed to want him to understand things, tell him things, they seemed to tell him that he might go ahead and dare to speak. They walked on, looking ahead, and crossing State Street she took his arm and nudged him.

"Well, for once we have the lights with us," she said.

"Let's get some candy," he said, out of sudden impulse to talk, and nodding his head to a chain candy-store window piled with tempting chocolates.

"Now don't tempt me. I'm dieting."

"That's right, and you've sworn off candy for Lent, haven't you?"

"And mister, do you realize that this is going to be my first show in Lent, and the only reason I'm breaking my resolution on shows is because when you telephoned me, you seemed so anxious to see one!"

If a girl like Catherine didn't like a fellow, she wouldn't break a Lenten resolution to be with him, he prided himself.

"Of course, we could do something else, if you really don't want to go," he casually said, feeling that he should say something like that.

"Booby, of course I want to go. You men!" she said, treating him with an air of gratifying condescension. "And anyway, I'm doing other things, not eating sweets, I go to mass every morning, to services at church three nights a week, and I'm receiving Holy Communion every Sunday during Lent, so that a little celebration for your return won't hurt a lot . . . Will it?"

"I guess not, since you're doing so many other things," Studs said as if he were seriously answering an important question with a valued answer.

"You don't talk a lot, do you?" she remarked after they had walked on a few more paces.

"Well . . . I talk when I've got something to say, and when I haven't, . . . what's there to say. I don't believe in talking just to hear my own voice like some fellows I know," he said, enjoying a vision of himself as a strong man whose words always meant something, wanting her to catch that same impression of him. In an afterthought, he realized that she often did a lot of chattering, and he regretted his remark, fearing it would make her angry.

"But who, for instance?" she said, smiling.

"What?" he asked, not sure that he understood what she meant.

"What fellows talk to hear the sound of their own voices?"

"Well, lots of fellows. There are fellows like that who could sell you Lake Michigan or the Masonic Temple," he said.

"For instance?"

"Oh, lots of fellows."

"I know, but who?"

"Oh, well." As he thought, Red Kelly's name popped int
his mind, and he did not want to be talking about a friend o
his behind his back. "Well, Red Kelly does," he said agains
his will.

"How does he do it?"

"Oh, well, he likes to talk a lot," Studs said in a fidget
manner.

"About what, besides his wife?" she asked, and Studs fel
that she was making a dirty dig.

"Oh, well, he likes to let everybody know he's in politic
and expects to be a big shot."

"I always felt that," she said, squeezing his arm. "And he
isn't so much as some people I know."

Studs' cheeks seemed to be hot, and he was both happy and
nervous. He found it hard to look at her, and he was happy
for the excuse to enter a cigar store and buy a package of cigarettes. He loitered in the store, finding change in his pocket
and lighting a cigarette, and he was happy as he dallied.

"Bill, I do wish you wouldn't smoke so much," she said as
he stepped out of the store.

"Yes, I guess I better cut down, but there's no use in throwing
one away after I just lit it."

"But, Bill, you really do smoke too much and I know that
it isn't good for you. Now, why don't you, for the rest of
Lent, give up smoking as a sacrifice? It will be so good for your
health, too."

"It's a good idea," he said evasively.

"I do wish you would!"

"I will. But of course, though, after you've been smoking
for years, it's kind of hard to give it up all at once, and it's
much better to cut down gradually and by doing it that way,
I should be more successful."

"Bill, I know you can do it if you make up your mind to,
because you have the will power."

He liked to have Catherine talking about him this way. She
was showing him she liked him. She spoke the same way his
mother and sisters often had when they tried to get him to
do something for his own good. But when they did he was
bored, and when Catherine did it, he liked it. She squeezed his
arm, and as they crossed over to a show he was sure that tonight
he was going to pop the question.

III

Studs steered Catherine into the Charlus Restaurant on Randolph Street. A tall and attractive hostess in a silken black dress flashed a business smile upon Studs and led them past rows of tables with fresh linen tablecloths, to a quiet corner. Just above the brown stained panelings in back of their table for two there hung an elaborately framed oil painting of a nymph who was semi-nude behind a trailing of gauzily painted white veiling. Hanging their coats on a hook, he gazed nonchalantly about the crowded restaurant where people spoke in slightly subdued voices. If anybody among them was watching him, he wanted them to see that he acted as if such restaurants were natural to him.

A waitress, whose white dress and apron gave Studs a sense of cleanliness, approached, waiting patiently for their order.

"I'll just have a glass of warm milk," Catherine said, smiling across the table.

"Warm milk, coffee, and a hamburger sandwich," Studs ordered.

He stared absently about at a lank, thin fellow seated nearby and across from a blond girl who was beautiful enough for the movies. She laughed at what the tall thin fellow said, and her eyes were for him. That guy was in luck having such a dame.

"Gee, will I feel good when I finish my diet and lose those ten pounds," Catherine said.

"I should imagine so," he said, still fretting over the question of proposing.

Studs puffed nervously on a cigarette.

"I'm beginning to feel a lot better than I used to," he said, fearing that she would remind him of his promise to cut down on his smoking.

"Gee, Bill, I'm so glad. At times I worry about your health and I wonder if you are taking the best care of yourself."

"I'm all right, and I'm going to be all right," he said.

"I know, Bill. I know it. But, Bill, you must take care of yourself, and cut down on your cigarette-smoking, too, like you promised me tonight you would."

"Was I smoking?" Studs said, looking with an attempt at feigned surprise at the burning cigarette between his fingers. "Can you imagine that! I had the cigarette lit and was smoking without thinking I was doing it."

"Bill, you should watch that and realize. And Bill, I don't want you to think that I'm nagging you, because I'm not. I'm not nagging you, am I, when I say you should watch about your smoking cigarettes?"

"No, you're right and after I finish this one, I'll watch myself," Studs said.

The waitress set their orders before them, and Studs squashed his cigarette in the glass ash tray. He began to feel that he had no guts because here he was delaying asking her after he had made up his mind.

"Catherine?" he suddenly blurted out, his nervousness seeming to choke his breath and force the syllables of her name out of his mouth.

Sipping at her milk, she looked at him, opening her eyes widely.

"How did you like the picture?" he asked, feeling foolish.

"Good, I always like pictures with a happy ending. Sad pictures send you away feeling blue and most of them are so foolish. For a while I thought that Ralph Hardwyne—isn't he a handsome actor though?—was going to lose out and not win back his wife, but I sighed with relief when he did."

"I thought it was a pretty good picture. Good acting, too."

"I don't like books either with unhappy endings. Life is sad enough without people writing sad books."

He lit a cigarette after finishing his sandwich and coffee. He delayed speaking and tried to seem as if he felt natural and normal. They looked at one another, their sympathies conveyed with glances, feelings that they did not trust to words.

"Why don't we get married?" Studs suddenly asked before he realized what he was saying.

Their eyes met again in the effort to convey intangibilities of emotion.

"Do you really want to?" she smiled, her voice very natural.

"Why not?" he said casually.

"But you don't sound very anxious or enthusiastic. You must be joking with me, or you wouldn't be so matter of fact about it."

"I mean it," he said in a strained voice, leaning toward her across the table, his facial muscles grown rigid.

"Honest?"

"Why should I be saying it if I didn't mean it?" he asked, leaning back again in his chair. "I've been thinking about it for a long time now, and today on the train I decided that I was not going to wait any longer, or put it off. I made up my mind then and there."

"You really care for me that much, Bill?" Catherine shyly said, her manner and voice thrilling him into an elation, causing her, because of his sudden uprush of feeling, to recede before his eyes, as into a veil of vagueness. An image of Lucy stirred in his mind. Lucy, pretty and seventeen, with her firm girlbreasts showing under her dress, her head tossing mischievously, waving and shaking her black curly hair. A lump came into his throat, and the image, persisting, made him feel all the mystery and all the attraction he had once felt, seeing Lucy one day on Indiana Avenue. He was aware of Catherine's knees touching him, and he wished that she were Lucy as Lucy had been that day.

"You know, Bill, I care for you, awfully," she said, her knees still against him.

"Me, too," he said, embarrassed with this confession of emotion, and determined to be casual. He couldn't, he told himself, give his hand away completely to a girl, because then it would be like it was with Lucy. He told himself he cared a hell of a lot for her, and Lucy was gone away, and she was going to be a better wife for him than Lucy could have been.

He screwed out his lips, and glanced around the restaurant, as if there were something interesting to see.

"All right," he said, turning back toward her.

"All right what, Bill?"

"We're engaged."

Outside, she slid her arm in his, glanced up at him, brushed her shoulder against his, and as they managed to wander in zigzags along the sidewalk, slowly toward Michigan Avenue, her shoulder continually brushed against him.

"Bill?" she said coyly.

"What?" he answered.

"When will we be married?"

"I haven't been working so regularly partly because business isn't any too good these days, and my dad does not get as many contracts as he used to in the good times. But I'll be able to work now, because I feel much better, and I think that business is going to start picking up. I'll save, but of course I have been saving money for some time now, only we ought to have a nice little nest egg," Studs felt goofy using such a word, "to start with, and maybe I'd say that we ought to figure on the end of this year or early next year," he said, his tone and manner suggesting the weight he was placing on his words, and the importance he was striving to give to his statement.

"Mother will be so glad to hear the news, because you know, she and Dad, they like you. Gee, dear, I'm so happy, and, honey, I can hardly wait to tell them."

That was the first time she had ever called him dear or honey. They approached Michigan Avenue, now deserted, the Public Library building standing dim and dark on the corner, a news vendor, standing by a fire in a wire basket, calling out the morning papers.

"Honey, tonight let's walk down to Van Buren and get our train there."

"All right," he answered, as if it were an important decision.

He turned her on to Michigan Avenue. Behind them the avenue was brilliantly lit, and the street seemed like a fog of electricity and mist between the massive piles of stone. Ahead of them, way down at Twelfth, they saw the lighted advertising signs in the distance and the warm mist deflecting the electric rays.

"Isn't it grand, dear? And you know, I don't think I'll ever forget tonight and this walk," she said.

"Yes," Studs said, still striving to keep a lever of control on his excited feelings.

"And we'll have a cosy apartment all our own, won't we? Let's go looking for apartments next Sunday."

"We'll have lots of time for that."

"I know, but it'll be fun."

"We'll have lots of time for that."

"But Bill, maybe your mother will be angry and not like our engagement," Catherine said after they had walked along silent for nearly a block.

"She and my dad both like you, and they are kind of expecting me to get married, and say, anyway, I'm not a kid anymore."

"I like them," she said, squeezing his hand, "and I like their son too."

"Well, that's me, I'm their son, William," he said with intended humor.

"And you know we're engaged, and you haven't kissed me. Now is that right, or is that the way it is done in the movies?" she laughed.

"Well, we're in public," he said, serious in self-defense.

"There's a big park across the street," she said, nodding toward the expanse of Grant Park.

"Come on, let's take a walk," he said, anticipation hidden behind his level voice.

She clutched his arm firmly.

IV

Ahead of them was the wide, cement driveway, flanked with brightly lit electric lamps, and in the distance, surrounded by a waste of hard, snow-patched earth, the Buckingham Fountain, with the lively spray of water drenched in colored lights. Strolling over the bridge to the right of the Art Institute, he saw these objects in the panoramic scene before him, as if for the first time. A high-powered automobile shot by and he watched its moving red tail-light until the car swerved onto the right.

"Gee, a few years ago there wasn't any of this here, and just think, when I was a kid, the Masonic Temple was the biggest building in town," he said, stimulated by the sudden and surrounding sense of the city's growth which he was experiencing.

A stiff lake wind blew against them, and they heard, from the railroad tracks below, the approach of a train.

"Isn't it so, and you know I can remember when North Michigan was not at all built up like it is now. They certainly have built up Chicago, and with the World's Fair coming in a couple of years, it's certainly going to be the most wonderful city in the world."

The railroad engine chugged under them, and a flurry of hot cinders struck Studs' face, causing him to grumble.

"What's the matter, Bill?"

"Oh a chunk of cinder hit me," he said, wiping his face with his handkerchief.

"Yes, isn't it a shame to have smoke in such a beautiful city. I was reading an editorial in the paper only the other day about it, and my boss, Mr. Breckenbridge, was speaking of it, too."

"Yeah, the I. C. ought to hurry up with the rest of its electrification programme. Look," Studs said, showing her the soot-streaked handkerchief.

"It's not right to have a smoke nuisance spoiling a beautiful city like Chicago," she said as they strolled on.

"You know, I haven't seen any other big cities, but I guess there isn't any of them to match Chicago," Studs said.

"Me for Chicago every time. That's what I say. And Mr. Breckenbridge, my boss, he's been all over, in the big cities like Indianapolis, and New York, Detroit, Cleveland, Minneapolis, all the big cities, and even in Toronto and Montreal in Canada, and he says the same thing. He always calls it Chicago Beautiful, and says there isn't another city like it in the world. It has the real city spirit he says, and he's interested in the plan they have, the Chicago Plan, to make it even more beautiful. He keeps saying that instead of there being so much graft, the money should be spent in improvements, particularly now in bad times when everything is so cheap. He even dictated a letter I typed the other day, showing how if the city would do that, there wouldn't be so many men out of work."

"It's a good idea. And say, I never imagined that it was so

nice down here as it is," Studs said dreamily, looking ahead
in fresh amazement at the spraying waters of the fountain.
There was something about the fountain, lit up as it was, something beautiful.

"And look at the Lindbergh Beacon," Catherine said, seeming to catch a sense of Studs' mood, and pointing northward
in the direction of the line of bluish light sweeping the sky.

"Nice," he said.

"And wait until we have The Century of Progress in 1933.
Won't that be grand! Mr. Breckenbridge says that by then Prosperity will be back and everyone will be making money again
hand over fist."

"I hope so," Studs said, wondering how his health would
be in two years. Would he even be alive? Two years ago, Shrimp,
Tommy Doyle, Slug, lots of people now dead, had been alive,
and in better health than he was now.

"And won't it be just grand, Bill, dear, for Mr. and Mrs.
Lonigan to go to the Fair? We'll see everything and go on
all the rides, won't we?" she said gaily, snuggling her arm
through his.

"There'll be lots to see, too," he said.

"And we'll dance. We'll go some night for supper and dance.
It'll be fun."

He felt her arm curled under his elbow, and began to get
anxious. He wanted her in his arms, and he ought to kiss
her, and she wanted to be kissed. Suppose he should be a chump
over the way he went about it? And how far would she let
him go? He remembered how he had made a chump of himself in the cab, that night he had taken Lucy to his sister's
sorority dance. And his anxiety seemed to increase.

He looked ahead feeling soft, and the dazzling rays of the
fountain seemed, somehow, to be part of his mood. And his
feelings about Catherine and the spray were like so many
diamonds lifting and falling, and to him, Catherine was like
a diamond, and his feelings were like the fountain, so many
diamonds rising and falling that way in the light, and the
light was Catherine. And was he thinking like a chump, or
wasn't he?

The lake breezes had sharpened, carrying in their rush the
smell of the waters. And behind them he heard the dry-sounding
clatter of a train. He felt himself to be walking in a different
world from what was back there, where the train had passed.
Even the dirt, hard and cold beside the walk, it seemed more
than dirt frosted from the long winter.

"Dear?" she said, her voice prolonging the sound so long

that Studs felt as if it had slowly melted on her tongue like chocolate candy.

"Yes," he answered expectantly, a vision of their future marriage, their first wedding night, a honeymoon to Niagara Falls, and many other nights of promise in his mind.

They turned to the right, crossed the outer driveway, hastened toward the lake. Studs reduced their pace to stare southward at the squat hugeness of the Chicago Memorial Stadium, standing, he guessed, maybe like some Roman ruins in the mistiness.

He took her arm and led her forward, thinking of how he felt like a new man, wishing that they were already married. He realized that he was chilled, and turned up his coat collar. Worry about his health fell over his thoughts, smothering them like a wet blanket. He felt, as if in a prophecy, that he would never live to have the things he had just been thinking about. . . . Oh, Jesus Christ! he silently exclaimed with pity for Studs Lonigan.

"Dear, we hadn't better go any farther. You might catch cold."

"I'll be all right," he tersely replied, not wanting her to think him weak or afraid or anything.

"No, let's turn back."

"Come on!" he insisted, and she glanced up at him with an expression of meekness, her eyes seeming to shine.

She again took his arm, and he clamped his elbow tightly against her hand.

There seemed to him to be a lot of meanings in their walk, their touches, the silence between them. Again, as when he had been with Lucy a few times, there had seemed to be ahead of him things that he wanted very much. Always in his life, he had believed, felt, knew, that it was going to be Studs Lonigan's destiny to get something he wanted and needed to give him a happiness he hadn't known but only wished for. It had always seemed ahead of him, and now he was on the verge of catching up with it. It had been, he guessed, a feeling like always being so thirsty that he could never get enough to drink, or like eating a fruit that he could never suck all the juice from, and now, he would. With Catherine, he was going to get everything that he wished for, all that he deserved. And, as he stumbled through these thoughts, he seemed to carry in a corner of his mind a fragmentary sense of the buildings standing along Michigan Boulevard with all their soaring suggestions of power. And in all those buildings, he suddenly realized, there were men with money and power and everything they wanted, men with

names that everyone knew and respected. Men who were suc-
cesses. And he could be like them. A man could have anything
in this life that he wanted if he had the guts to go after it,
and the faith and belief that he could succeed. Some day he
was going to do it for both himself and for Catherine, and
to show everybody what there really was in Studs Lonigan.
And he would lay it all before Catherine, and say that he
had done it for her and for himself, and to prove that she had
been right in having confidence in him and marrying him. He
knew that she was really going to understand him and see
the real stuff he had in himself.

He felt her arm pressed against his side, through his
overcoat, and they heard muffled voices from the city behind
them. The lake odors were pungent, and the wind rubbed
their faces like a brush with sharp fibrous hairs. They heard
the rolling waves and the crashing waters against the wooden
breakwaters and stones, the recession of the undercurrent,
and far out Studs watched the glimmering red lighthouse
signal, blinking. Down to their left, the lights of the Municipal
Pier were strung like floating lanterns. Again, he told himself
that from this night on, Studs Lonigan was starting. He was
going down the field, hitting the line like cement, bowling over
anything and everything that got in his way, Studs Lonigan
was. He saw now that even with the many good times he
had had, much of his past life had been foolish, much of his
time had been wasted, and he had almost wasted himself and
his health. He had nearly put himself in the same boat with
the Haggertys, Tommy Doyle, and Slug, Lord have mercy on
their souls. Now he saw. Now he was ready for the real fight
of his life, and he would have Catherine at his side, just as
his old man had always had his mother.

Suddenly he became weak and limp with the let-down
from his thoughts. His throat seemed to have tightened up,
obstructing speech. Feeling the necessity of doing something,
he lit a cigarette in the wind. The wind, colder and stronger
than it had been over near Michigan Boulevard, wrapped their
coats tightly about their knees. Smoking became too difficult,
so Studs tossed his cigarette away. They bent their heads and
shoulders forward, hastening. Suddenly, she stopped and
tugged at his arms. As he turned, she closed her eyes and turned
her head up at him. He kissed her, the touch of her lips seeming
like an exaltation that he would never forget. He gripped her
tightly and they clung to each other in an embrace made awkward because of their coats.

"If someone in an automobile turns a headlight in our direction, they'll see us," he said when they had freed them-

selves; he was shy and embarrassed and he breathed rapidly.

She smiled.

"Let them!" he said gruffly, feeling reckless and pulling her to him with awkward haste.

"You know what?" she asked, after recovering her breath.

"What?" he asked, the word gushing out of his mouth.

"I love you!"

They walked swiftly to the lake and stood on the jagged breakwater rocks, his left arm encircling her waist. Foaming with noisy whitecaps, the waters came in with a rush, pounded, dragged outward to the visible wall of darkness and mist. A path of moonlight, like a gleaming aisle, slanted over the water, away from them. Listening to the waves, and perceiving their merciless and resilient strength as they smashed into the breakwater and lifted, he felt how weak he himself was, how weak, perhaps, anybody must feel standing here. He felt that for years, and forever onward until the Day of Judgment, these waves would be pounding and smashing, day and night.

"It's cold," she said, shouting to be heard, shivering.

Speech, hearing her, seeing her, made him feel that anyway he was still alive, and that tomorrow morning he would probably still be alive.

He looked out over the waters, at the darkness closing over them. A dash of spray broke against his cheek. He thought that he might catch cold. Had to watch his health now. He peered down at the lights of the Municipal Pier. From behind, he heard faintly a screech from an automobile brake.

Fumblingly, he opened both their coats, drew her against him, feeling a sudden warmth and tenseness come into her. Held against him, she lost all shyness and kissed him with avid hunger, and he knew that he was keen on her all right and wanted her, and wanted to marry her.

"It's getting late, and it's too chilly for you here, dear," she said when she had regained her poise.

Turning, they climbed down from the breakwater and retreated rapidly toward the lights and the skyline of Chicago. He was tired and happy and determined. He wanted the future to come. He could hardly wait to get started now to show his real self, to make a success out of his life. He was happy with Catherine walking beside him. Catherine was going to be his and his alone, his woman.

CHAPTER THREE

I

"Why, hello, Studs."

Studs turned, surprised to find Pat Carrigan and a thin sickly-looking fellow with a familiar face on the platform of the Bryn Mawr Illinois Central Station.

"How's tricks?" Studs asked.

"Oh, so-so, Studs. Say, do you know Ike Dugan?"

"Yes, we met in South Bend at a Notre Dame football game last fall," Ike Dugan said.

"Sure. Are you through at N. D. now?"

"Him. He was just one of the synthetic alumni. He came next to me in breaking the record to see who could stay the longest in high school. It took me six years to graduate. It only took him five. If he'd gone to college, he'd have had gray hair before he became a senior."

"Studs, don't pay no attention to him. He's just trying to kid me," Ike said.

"Where you bound for, Studs? Date?"

"No, my girl has her bridge club tonight, so I thought that I'd go downtown and take in a show."

"Swell. We're going down to see *Doomed Victory*. I hear it's a swell gangster picture."

"Sounds O.K. to me," Studs said.

"Well, boys, here she is," Ike said as the train pulled into the station.

Studs followed them into the car, and they found seats together, Ike riding backward.

"Studs, did you hear about Stan? He's been living somewheres around here, and he was put out of his flat because he owed the rent. Poor guy is down in the mouth these days."

"The going is pretty rough for poor Stan," Studs said thoughtfully.

"Yes, but times is going to get better," Ike said.

"What, Ike, have you got a tip out of the La Salle-Street feed box?"

"I know, all right. I tell you, I know times is going to get better, and I'm not just guessing."

"Send a telegram to Hoover about it and let him in on the secret," Studs said.

"Ike, you're one of the original inside kids, aren't you?" Pat said.

"Fellows, I tell you, I know. Times is going to get better.

498

I'm making dough right now. And I have got a little inside dope," Ike said with a slick gesture of his hand and a knowing smirk.

"What, are you in the political game, too?" Studs asked.

"Fellows, I'm not kidding. Listen. I work for Imbray and I know. You know what's behind these stocks? Well, I'll tell you. All, or nearly all, the public utilities of the Middle West and the brain of a man like Solomon Imbray. What more security could you want?"

"If I had any dough, I'd spend it and see what I was getting," Pat said.

"Are you selling stock?" Studs asked.

"I'm not a salesman, but everybody in our company is privileged to sell it and if we do, we get a commission," Ike said.

"Got any real estate for sale out in the middle of the lake, Ike?" Pat asked.

"All right, kid me. But I'm no sucker. I'm kicking out my twelve-fifty a share and when I collect on it, I'll be collecting fifty bucks a share. And then, Pat, come around and ask me how about some real estate out in the lake," Ike said.

"Could I get it at twelve and a half a share?" Studs asked.

"No. That's only on our employee stock-purchasing plan. But Studs, it's cheap at twenty-five a share."

"I'd like to know more about it," Studs said.

"No. Me, I'm working for Imbray."

"What did you do, sneak into Solomon Imbray's office and read his private mail?" Pat asked.

"Well, listen, fellows, this is straight. If you buy Imbray stocks you're going to make dough."

"I don't know nothing about that and I ain't got any dough to be forking over anyway," Pat said.

"How come, Dugan?" Studs asked, leaning forward in his seat.

"Well, fellahs, old man Solomon Imbray has got a head on his shoulders. He's a smart man," Ike said.

"He ought to be. With all the dough he's made," Studs said.

"You're damn right he's smart. If you coast along with him, you're coasting along with a guy who's got a head on his shoulders. I know. I work for one of the Imbray companies, and I'm getting fifty bucks a week."

"That's good dough these days," Pat said.

"And you want to know what I'm doing? I'm sinking twenty of it in stock. We got a stock plan. They're floating a new issue called Imbray Securities at twenty-five bucks a share. Employees, we pay half for a share and the company gives us the other half. That means I'm picking up almost a share and a half a week. And when it's a company backed by Solomon Imbray, it's safe."

"Got any oil wells for sale, Ike?" Pat asked.

II

"This is the first sign I've seen of the depression that's encouraging," Studs said.

"How come?" asked Ike.

"No lineup outside the ticket window," Studs smiled.

"A couple of years ago, there'd have been a line a block long waiting to get in," Pat said as they purchased their tickets.

"Nice-looking place," Studs said, walking along the glittering foyer.

"Sure, these shows are swell dumps. Fit for a palace. Look at those draperies. They cost dough. Dough!" Ike said.

"Seats on the main floor. Aisle two. This way, please," a shiny, powdered attendant, in a maroon and gray uniform with many brass buttons, braided gold, and a long coat, announced formally.

"Jesus, that's a job for a pansy to have. Dressed up in a monkey suit like that," Studs said.

"Ike, you'd look the nuts with an usher's monkey suit on."

"The broads would give you the eye, too, Ike. They'd call you General Dugan," Studs said.

"I don't need that job."

"Sure, Ike's going to be a big shot out of the commissions he makes, selling shares of stock in the Jackson Park Golf course," Pat said.

"Boy, anybody in that outfit standing there and speaking his funny little piece, must feel like a clown if he isn't a damn pansy."

"Studs, a lot of the ushers in these shows went to college," Ike said.

"They look it," Pat said.

"Hell, I hate news reels," Pat whispered to Studs as an usher preceded them quickly along an aisle on the main floor, past many vacant seats.

The usher halted near the center, turned his flashlight on a row of unfilled seats, and they moved in to the middle of the rows.

"I hope we see something exciting in these damn news reels," Ike whispered.

"The thing I like best about news reels is that they're short," Studs whispered.

. . . . CALIFORNIA
BUSINESS ORGANIZATIONS AND FRATERNAL SOCIETIES DEVISE
NOVEL WAY OF COMBINING CIVIC SPIRIT AND FUN TO ATTACK DEPRESSION.

"Out on the coast these days, business clubs and fraternal organizations are doing some novel fighting against the bogey of Old Man Depression. And is it fun, boys! I'll say it is!"

As the announcer spoke, the camera flashed a view of business men shouting jubilantly as they pelted each other with eggs like a crowd of school boys in a snow fight. The next shot presented the sight of huge piles of eggs guarded by shapely girls in bathing suits who filled baskets and knapsacks with eggs for ammunition. A blond girl splattered an egg against the back of a departing warrior.

"Hot stuff," Pat whispered to Studs, while many in the theater laughed.

"Boy, that would be great fun," Ike whispered.

The laughter in the theater increased at the sight of a wobbling fat man, surrounded by enemies who subjected him to a merciless fire of eggs, spluttering and staining his white clothing.

"That's a shampoo, what's a shampoo," the announcer called with formalized enthusiasm as a detachment closed in on the fat man and broke his own basket of eggs over his head.

In a close-up, the fat man bawled like a baby, his hair matted, egg shells clinging to his face, his double chins dripping egg yolks.

"And watch this charge of the light brigade!" the announcer called as a crowd swept over the field of stricken eggs into the maw of a heavy fire. "We can't say that's not fun, and all in a novel manner which reduces the surplus of eggs, making it profitable for those who sell them. A new way of scrambling eggs, if you ask me."

Studs leaned forward, laughing. Wished he was in a fight like that.

NAVY BOMBERS GUARD AIR LANES

"Uncle Sam's latest bombers take to the clouds in a trial test of speed and endurance."

With purring motors, a winged formation of heavy bombing planes streaked evenly across low plains that were cut by a river. A closer shot revealed one plane riding against a background of clouds, and then the formation rode steadily above the Pacific Ocean.

"A comforting reception committee for unwanted guests at our coast line. The pick of the Navy's air fleet, Uncle Sam's latest bid for supremacy of the skies."

PITCHED BATTLE BETWEEN STRIKERS AND POLICE

"And now, here is a serious battle . . ."

Grim-faced men in working clothes and overalls with an interspersing of women in their ranks marched slowly along a high fence surrounding a factory in a mid-western town, watched by special deputies who stood at regularly-spaced intervals with clubs and truncheons ready. Above the geometrically patterned factory windows, two chimneys smoked.

"When non-striking workers attempted to relieve the day shift at this factory, they were attacked by strikers. And look at this for a sample of some real serious rioting," the announcer called in the same tone as if he were describing a heroic hundred-yard run on a college gridiron, and simultaneously with his words the screen presented men struggling and grappling, tugging, wrestling, raising a cloud of dust, and howling and cursing as they fought, groups coming together amidst flying bricks and swinging clubs, policemen breaking groups apart, shagging overalled men from the factory gates with raised clubs. A fleeing man in overalls was clubbed by a policeman, and as he fell groggily forward, a special deputy smashed him on the shoulder with a truncheon. He lay face forward in the center of the picture, blood oozing from his head, and the struggling crowd surged over his body.

Guarded by policemen with drawn guns, a sick-faced, injured, bleeding group of strikers sat dazed in the dusty street, and one full-faced policeman turned to smile into the camera.

"Poor bastards," Pat mumbled.

"This unfortunate riot resulted in the injury of scores. Two strikers and one deputy were taken to a local hospital in a critical condition with their skulls fractured. Not the best form of sport, I'd say, and it is to be regretted that such altercations occur and to be hoped that they are not repeated."

LOCAL CITIZENS BURY OLD MAN DEPRESSION

"And now, did anyone ever hear of a joyful funeral?"

A hearse drove slowly forward along the cartracks of a decorated and crowded street, its side strung with a large banner.

OLD MAN DEPRESSION DIED 1931. R. I. P.

A band playing the wedding march from *Lohengrin* trailed in the wake of the hearse, followed by a large and flowery float with flower girls throwing roses to the crowd, and a stately virginal girl in white seated on a bedecked throne.

THE QUEEN OF OPTIMISM

"Swell-looking dame," Studs whispered as boy scouts tramped behind an American flag.

A column of the local American Legion, with guns and steel helmets, marched in formation and then, at the head of a band of children, a dimpled girl of five or six carried a large sign.

OLD MAN DEPRESSION LYNCHED JOYOUSLY
BY THE SONS AND DAUGHTERS OF
CONFIDENCE AND HOPE

"Is that a happy funeral? Well, I'll tell the cockeyed world that it is. If all funeral processions were as gay, oh, death, where would thy sting be?"

MUSSOLINI REVIEWS BOY SCOUTS AT WAR GAMES

"And now, travelling to sunny Italy, the land of the olive and Il Duce, we see Italian Boy Scouts in war maneuvers."

A band of black-shirted boys of twelve and thirteen, wearing shorts and carrying wooden rifles like soldiers, marched along a road singing the Fascist anthem, *Giovi-*

nezza. The scene quickly changed, and the boys were shown charging through a weedy field toward enemy trenches.

"And now for the reward, parading before Il Duce himself."

Mussolini, in military uniform, stood stern-faced on a reviewing stand, returning a stiff Fascist salute to the boys marching in ranks below him.

"Bravo, says Il Duce, because he knows that they will some day grow up disciplined to fight and die for him and for Italy."

A hiss sounded from the rear of the main floor, and Studs wondered what the damn fool was hissing for. Mussolini couldn't hear it.

. . . BEAUTY CONTEST

"Girls and more girls and more girls from all over America and from six foreign countries entered this Beauty Contest in New York to determine the most perfect girl in the Universe. And Oh! Oh! is there pulchritude here!"

"Oh, mama!" Ike muttered at the view of girls in bathing suits marching slowly around an arc-lighted platform, with strips of lettered ribbon slanting across their chests.
"Control yourself, simp," Pat said.

"And here's Miss Estelle Cavendish, the winner."

A close shot revealed Miss Estelle Cavendish, dark-haired, seductive, her grayish bathing suit bringing out her brassiered breasts and her figure.
"She'd pass in a crowd," Studs whispered, he and Pat smiling.

"I consider it a great honor to be the winner of this contest to determine the most perfect girl in the universe, and I am very proud . . . and I'm glad," Miss Estelle Cavendish said from the screen in a cooing voice, a coy smile revealing her even white teeth.
"Thank you, Estelle, and so are we," said the announcer.

ANNUAL FETE IN SPANISH VILLAGE

"There may be wars or rumors of wars, depressions and

troubles and heartaches in other parts of the world, but sunny peaceful old Spain is still the same. For centuries, these Spanish peasants have celebrated their annual winter fete."

Spanish peasants, in local costumes, danced folk dances on a narrow, cobble-stoned street, accompanied by the sound recordings of their songs and music.

"And look at this gay caballero twanging his guitar to his fair Juliet. H'm, wouldn't plenty of our American sheiks be jealous," the announcer said while a mustached young Spanish peasant played his guitar in the shadow of the balcony.

"Romance lives in old Spain."

"I'd like to be there," Studs said.

"Me, too. Spanish broads are hot," Pat added.

WINNER IN NOVELTY ENDURANCE CONTEST

"And a new world's champion is crowned. Oscar Albert McGonigle wins peanut race for a five-hundred-dollar prize."

Six men, on their hands and knees, rolled peanuts along a cement road with their noses, followed by an amused crowd of spectators.

"The world's sure full of clowns," Studs said, as laughter broke over the theater.

"Hell, he got five hundred dollars for it. That's not so dumb," Pat muttered.

"And now, let us listen to Oscar Albert McGonigle tell how he won!"

The audience roared at the close-up of an adenoidal blond young man in his middle twenties with a raw scraped nose.

"I'm certainly glad to be the winner in this race," he said, nasal-voiced, "and it was sure a hard one. When I entered it, I said to myself Oscar you got to win, you got to win. My mother, she said to me, 'Oscar you haven't a long enough nose to win,' and I said, 'Maw, you wait and see.' Well, I won, and it was a hard race, and I'm sure the happiest man in the world today."

BUSINESS LEADER PREDICTS BETTER TIMES AFTER VISIT
TO WHITE HOUSE. OSCAR VAN GILBERT, BANKER, IN INTERVIEW

A stout, puffy, bald-headed man sat at a desk and mechanically read from a paper.

"A business depression is a reaction. For every action, there must be a reaction, and then a counter action, because that is the law of life and of economics. The business depression is a reaction to over-production. We are now through the worst of it, and have slowed down our processes of production in consonance with the law of supply and demand. We are again on a solid footing, and we shall see, in the next six months, another commercial upswing. In my recent visit to the White House, I found this same hope prevailing in official circles, and I concluded that what we all must do is to get behind our president and push forward, to the next period of prosperity. And when our next period does return, let us all be wiser then we were in the years of 1928 and 1929."

"I'm glad that's over," Studs said.

"Now we'll get the real stuff," Pat said.

III

GRANDIOSE FILMS CORPORATION

Presents

DOOMED VICTORY

Studs yawned without reading the credit list or cast of characters, and slumped in his seat ready to let the picture afford him an interesting good time.

Two shabby boys walked nonchalantly along a street in a poor district, the boy on the outside carrying a beer can with the handle resting over his right wrist. His companion, his cap back on his curly head, stuck his hands in his pockets and whistled. A beer wagon passed with a crunching of wheels and a rattling of barrels. They paused to stare at a drunk lying in the gutter, and the boy with the beer can looked up from the intoxicated man to an advertising sign across the street.

THE WORLD IS YOURS

"Holy Moses!" the curly-haired boy exclaimed.

The boy with the beer can gestured knowingly, handed him

the can, bent over, and forked two bills from the drunk's pocket.

"This is for you, Spike, and this for Joey Gallagher," he said, handing Spike one of the bills and taking back his beer can.

"Gee, Joey."

Whistling, they walked slowly along, past a row of wooden tenement houses.

"Joey Gallagher and Spike Malone, what are you rascals up to now?"

"Nothing, Mr. Kennedy. Just running an errand for the old man," Joey Gallagher replied, looking up into the face of the benign policeman.

"You little divvils keep out of mischief or I'll be running ye in."

"Kennedy's an old fool," Joey Gallagher said, and they walked around a corner building with the sign above it

O'BRIEN'S

Inside the saloon toughs and eccentrics lined the bar, some in caps and jerseys, others wearing plug hats, and sporty gray suits with narrow trouser cuffs. Full-rounded women with wide hats were scattered among the men at the tables. Waiters moved about with trays, and a thin-faced fellow tickled the piano keys.

The boys crept in by the side door, timidly walked to the edge of the bar, attracted the attention of the bartender with the florid mustaches, handed the can up to him. With the can filled, they turned to the door, and just before going out Joey Gallagher cast an admiring and wistfully boyish glance at the toughs lining the bar.

"So you're tough! You're tough!" a boy, huskier than Joey Gallagher, said, meeting them on the street, toying with Joey, like a cat playing with a mouse, by pushing him, pulling out his shirt, and jamming his cap half over his eyes.

Joey quickly shoved the can of beer to Spike and rushed into the bully, the two boys mauling back and forth. The bully plunked Joey's eye, and Studs, watching Joey rush in again with flailing arms, remembered how he at Joey's age had beaten up Weary Reilley, who was just like this bigger kid in the picture. He knew he was going to like this picture. It was going to be more like his own life than almost any picture he'd ever seen, he felt. He hoped, too, that Joey would have a sweetheart, who would be just like Lucy Scanlan.

"Yes, I'm tough, you big mutt," Joey said, his eye swollen,

standing over the bully who cowered at the edge of the dusty curb.

"And so am I," Spike added, dousing the bully with beer, and Studs laughed with others in the audience.

Handsome, with marcelled hair, Joey Gallagher sauntered into a poolroom, strolled by the talkers and pool players, and Studs wished that the old poolroom on Fifty-eighth Street had been like this one in the picture.

"What's wrong, Joey. Today a holiday?"

"Oh, no, Spike," Joey replied to a thin youth with greased-down hair.

"Canned again? I suppose it was another fight."

Joey shook his head negatively.

"Then what's the big idea?" Spike said, registering an expression of puzzlement, scratching his poll.

"Only saps like my brother work . . . Say, is the King back there," Joey said, gesturing toward a closed door in the rear.

While Spike followed in surprise, Joey Gallagher boldly pushed into the room, ignored the gorillas scattered about it and stepped up to a broad-shouldered, thick-lipped, bull-neck gangster.

"Hello, King," Joey said with familiarity, and the King drew his cigar stub from his mouth, winked at two of the gorillas.

"I got a little business I want to discuss with you."

"Oh, yeah?"

"Sure. I just quit my job and I want to hitch up with you. I'm a useful guy."

Studs laughed at the close-up of Spike's face.

"Look, boys, it wants to join up with me," the King said, and his mob erupted into stage laughter. "Kindergarten classes is on Sunday. Ho! Ho! Come on, keep it up, sonny, I haven't laughed so much since my aunt died," the King continued, again drawing the raw laughter of his mob.

"Which one of you muggs wants to be the chief attraction at his own funeral?" Joey hissed, glaring from face to face, his fists itchy for action.

"Listen, punk, scram!" a beefy gorilla snapped, towering over Joey.

"Keep those mitts of yours in women's pocketbooks where they belong and you won't get your puss marked up like a cross-word puzzle."

"What?"

"You heard me!"

"Wait a minute! Wait a minute! Maybe we can use the kid," the King said in a measured voice.

That was nerve! If he could have busted into something big that way, he'd be much better off today. But Studs Lonigan wasn't Joey Gallagher. The picture was too interesting for him to sit brooding, and it carried him along. His mind became like a double exposure, with two reels running through it. He saw Joey Gallagher as the hero, and he saw himself in Joey Gallagher's boots, and Studs Lonigan and Joey Gallagher together leaped up the career of gangdom's adventurous ladder to fame.

They hijacked. They spoke with crisp hard words, and with barking gats and tattooing machine guns, bumping off friends and foes, letting nothing get in their way. Ah, that was the kind of a guy Studs Lonigan wanted to be, really hard and tough, afraid of no goddamn thing in this man's world, giving cold lead as his answer to every rat who stepped in his way. Getting clothes, too, like Joey Gallagher, riding in the same doggy automobile, turning corners on two wheels, and the hell with traffic cops, giving the heat to another mugg who got soft with cold feet. This was a picture. Why hadn't Studs Lonigan lived like this? And the blond, tall, with those swaying hips. Joey was laying her, too, and he would be, if he was Joey, laying a tall blond in a satin dress with hips on fire, if he, if he was only Joey Gallagher. And again going out, with the gat on his hip, a man's business. Would he get it himself this time? How did a guy get the guts that a gangster like Joey in this picture had? But gangsters did have it. That was what was wrong with Studs Lonigan. No guts. But Joey had it. And now here in this show, Joey Gallagher and Studs Lonigan were together, the two of them were one, racing across the screen, and the dough was rolling in, and the blond she was sweet, and she was his, laying only for him, and oh, goddamn it, this was the real ticket.

Wearing a gray suit, a gray fedora tilted over the left side of his face, Joey Gallagher strode confidently down the same street where he had appeared as a boy. He stopped, looked across the street at a sign board.

THE WORLD IS YOURS

He smiled, tossed away the cigarette. His face took on an expression of recognition, and a policeman rheumatically stepped up to him.

"Getting along these days, aren't ye, lad?" Mr. Kennedy said.

"Oh, so-so."

"Better watch your step, me lad."

"Nobody's got nothin' on me."

"Son, now take it aisy. Aisy, lad! I see ye with the King and his boys. Now, take the advice of one that's in this game longer than yourself, and take it aisy, me lad. I'm tellin' ye for your own good."

The policeman wagged a sad head as Joey confidently passed along. The scene dissolved, and Joey entered the modest home where his mother sat knitting, and his shirt-sleeved brother read a newspaper.

"Mother, you old skate, I have a present for you," Joey said, bending down to kiss her and dropping a fat roll of bills in her lap.

"No, son, I can't," she said in the choking voice of a mother's sadness.

"Mother doesn't need tainted blood money," the brother curtly said, arising. "Look! Tell me you don't know anything about it!" the brother challenged, handing Joey the newspaper.

Joey read the newspaper disinterestedly.

TWO MORE SHOT IN GANG WAR

Bullet-ridden Bodies of Greasy Jones and Lefty Loomis Found in Alley.

"They probably didn't keep their noses clean," Joey aid.

"That's a good crack," Pat said to Studs, Studs shaking his head.

"Get out!" the brother said, in a quavering voice.

"Why, you dirty . . ."

A surprised punch from the brother somersaulted Joey into a chair. He leaped to his feet, but his mother faced him, in tears, pointing at the door. He picked up the roll of bills from the carpet, shrugged his shoulders, walked out.

"Swell acting," Pat muttered.

The blond lounged in pajamas on a cot in a large room filled with modernistic furniture.

"Joey, come here," she called in a cooing, asking voice, and Joey sat in a corner, his head sunken in his hands.

She walked toward him with her abdomen jutting out prominently, and he gazed up at her with disgust when she patted his head.

Studs hoped that it wouldn't turn into a scrap, because,

after all, with a dame like that wanting something, and he wished like hell he was Joey Gallagher folding her into his arms, kissing her in that long, close way, and knew that the next step was to pick her up, carry her to the couch and. . . .

Joey shoved her away from him angrily.

"Say, Joey, what's the matter?"

"I don't know. Just let me alone for a while," he said absently.

"What's eating you, Joey. Getting a swelled head?"

"Never mind taking any tailspins there, baby," Joey said in his curt, tough manner.

"Losing your nerve. Gettin' yellow," she sneered.

"Why, you dirty. . . ."

He hit her in the chin with the heel of his left hand.

"Keep your hands off me. Why, you, you're nothing but a small-time gorilla," she cried, stumbling against a table.

"Look!" he said, pointing behind her.

She turned.

"Just a present from a small-time gorilla," he said, planting his foot into her buttocks and propelling her into the table, smashing a lamp.

"Small-time, am I," he soliloquized, getting into his roadster. He cut around a corner at breakneck speed.

Studs wondered why Joey couldn't have let well enough alone with the blond. But still, that kick in the slats had been funny. The way to treat a high-hat broad like that.

"Come on, Spike, get your coat on," Joey said, entering a room where Spike sat in shirt sleeves with a baby-faced girl in negligée on his knee.

"Every time I get set, somebody tips the glass on me," Spike complained, knotting his necktie before a mirror.

"Say, what's the idea?" Spike said, perplexed, entering the roadster.

"Got to see the King. I got a hunch he'd like a more comfortable life."

"Say, what's this? We can't muscle the King out."

"Keep your shirt on and your head cool and you'll always land on your toes," Joey said, turning his wheels quickly to avoid a crash.

"Hi, boys!" Joey said, entering a room full of gorillas.

Studs was getting tense, wondering what was going to happen, thinking would he have the guts to pull the stunt

Joey was pulling. Studs Lonigan walking in on Al Capone. Maybe this was his funeral though.

"Well, King, you're living well, and look at that," Joey said ambiguously, pointing at the King's paunch. "I was just sort of reflecting, you know, and I sort of figured out that you might like a nice little house in the country with nothing to disturb your sleep but the cows and chickens."

Guts. Gallagher had guts, and Studs sat thinking how he wasn't so much, set up against a guy like Gallagher, and there they were, Gallagher and the King glaring at each other, and that meant trouble. He wanted to see Joey come through it all, and would he. A rap on the door, everybody turning, Detective Sloane sauntering in. He'd seen this fellow act a detective role in some other picture, and he tried to recall it. Would they all get caught with Sloane just dropping them the hint about the shooting of Greasy Jones and Lefty Loomis. Would the picture end with Joey going to the hot seat? He hoped not.

A gorilla rushing in after the dick's departure. Butch McKee and his north side mob were coming. Studs sat forward in his seat as if he was tied up in knots. Big touring cars careening through streets. The rat-tat-tat of machine guns, the clash of breaking glass, the King's mob falling on the floor with drawn gats. Silence. The King jumping up, telling his gorillas to come on. Joey Gallagher stepping in front of him, breathlessly urging him to wait. The King, unconvinced, rushing out to the street, the mob following. Another car, bullets flaming out of it, Joey wounded in the arm, shooting left-handed.

Studs asked himself could he face guns, and fight like a gangster, and he felt that Studs Lonigan was yellow, and couldn't be a Joey Gallagher. He sat breathless as the King's mob rushed in cars to follow up the north side mob. The picture was getting close to the end. He wanted to see how it would turn out. And still he didn't want it to end. He wanted it to go on for hours. Best picture he'd seen in a hell of a while. Butch McKee's headquarters in a gambling house. Butch bragging that he was the King now. The entrance of Gallagher, the King, and their gorillas, Joey speaking his piece, telling Butch to get out of town in twenty-four hours.

Studs wished Joey had bumped McKee off then and there. No use taking chances. Joey might be shot. But no, the hero in movies always pulled through. Still, this was a different picture. Joey would come through, he and the blond would get lined up, and it would end hotsy totsy. But no, he'd read about the picture in the papers, and if he remembered it right, Joey got shot. He didn't want Joey to get shot.

The reception, Joey at the head of the table, as gangland's acknowledged leader. Joey Studs Lonigan Gallagher laughing loudly as Spike jabbed his fork into a mug's elbow for taking up so much room. Charlie Chaplin had pulled that in *Shanghaied*. He'd seen it as a kid, but it was still funny. Joey leaving the reception with the blond, her apartment, staying for the night. Laying her. Such a woman! Daddy! Sloane again. Just a friendly call. Hadn't seen anyone who knew about the murder of Greasy Jones and Lefty Loomis. No, just a friendly call, and he'd be seeing Gallagher at the D. A.'s office one of these days. Why didn't Joey get out of the racket now that he had dough, a woman, and he could pull through. The mother reading of Joey as gangland's chief, crying, the brother soothing her. Life was tough on mothers, but then, they just didn't understand. The tightening net of evidence. The blond squealing, ought to have her puss slapped, couldn't trust that kind of a whoring bitch. Getting near the finish, and Jesus, he wanted Joey to come through it. Joey, unsuspecting, pointing to the advertising sign. . . .

THE WORLD IS YOURS

Joey Gallagher again fading, in the mind of Studs Lonigan, into Studs Lonigan. Studs Lonigan, the world is yours. Take it. Oh, Christ, why hadn't he had an exciting life like Joey Gallagher? It happened to some people. Look at Al Capone. Joey Gallagher escaping from dicks, over roofs, leaving town on a freight. Would he pick up somewhere, meet a decent girl, as in most movies, would he come back? Sinking lower and lower, living in a flop house, hanging around a poolroom. Hearing these cheap pikers talk about the man hunt for Joey Gallagher, and one of them reading Sloane's statement in the paper.

"Gallagher is yellow."

Gallagher meant business now. But it was dumb. Grabbing a freight back to show if he was yellow. Hell, he wouldn't have done that. Meant the hot seat. But that was guts, guts. Gallagher telephoning Sloane. Sloane tracing the call. Cars on wet streets. Studs wished now, hoped, told himself, Christ, Gallagher couldn't die. The cars. Gallagher rushing into the trap. Shot dead. He couldn't be dead, and they were taking him home to his broken-hearted mother. The brother and Mr. Kennedy comforting her, and the corpse of Joey Gallagher. Dead. Death. He would die, too, some day, maybe not a hero's death like Gallagher. But hell, it wasn't worth it. Doomed victory. But he would die. Why hadn't the picture ended differently, and he could think of how Joey Gallagher could go on in life, going up and up, meeting a dame hotter than the stool pigeon of a blond, go on and up like he wanted to himself. Dead. Like a part of himself dying.

THE END

Walking out of the show, he told himself that, hell, it had only been a picture. Still, why couldn't it have ended differently? They didn't have to kill off Joey Gallagher. He was gloomy.

CHAPTER FOUR

I

Dropping into his father's overstuffed chair in the parlor, Studs asked himself if he had been a sucker. He lit a cigarette. Determined hopes forced themselves into his mind, and he expressed them by slapping his thighs and clenching and unclenching his fists. He viewed himself as a gambler, a chance-taking fool, prepared to face the risk of losing all the money he had saved for years and to drop it with a game smile on his face. Ashes slipped from his burning cigarette. Disinclined to arise and get an ash tray, he carelessly rubbed them off his trousers. He hoped that the cigarette wouldn't burn too rapidly and cause more dropping ashes. He cast a drifting glance at the gray of the expiring day. And he heard the muffled shouts of boys at play.

He looked across the room at the crumpled copy of the morning paper. He hadn't understood clearly the meaning of the news account of yesterday's stock market, but it had fallen. His stock, though, had just slipped one point, and meant a loss so far of only eighty dollars. It could easily come back if today's market was better. He recalled how enthusiastically Ike Dugan had talked to him about the stocks. They were backed by all of the Imbray holdings and public utilities, and directed by the brain of a man like Solomon Imbray, and you couldn't go wrong on such stock. Jesus, he hoped the guy was right. But there was something snaky about that guy, and. . . .

The cigarette stub burned his lips, more ashes falling as he arose to squash it in an ash tray. Hell, you never got anywhere unless you took a chance, and that was Studs Lonigan all over, he counselled himself.

He looked at himself in the wall mirror. Guessed he was looking better. But his cheeks were still thin, not a lot of color in them. When he'd been beefier, he hadn't seemed to himself to be so small, but now, he looked pretty much like a weak little runt. He told himself to cancel this stuff. He imagined meeting Stan Simonsky or some other friend, and casually telling them how he had taken this flyer in Imbray stock, talking as if it were nothing more than risking a few shekels in a crap game.

And when his investment rose, he'd sell, bank his original capital, use the profits to play on other stocks. All these years he'd been so dumb he hadn't thought of making money this way. Other guys had cleaned up doing it, and he had been just 'too dumb to know it. Well, it still wasn't too late, and he'd be worth a hell of a lot more than Red Kelly ever would be, and it wouldn't be long, either. And what a nice little nest egg they'd have for their marriage.

He flung himself back into the chair, imagining himself and Catherine married, getting along as well as, better than, Phil Rolfe and Fritzie. Yessir, Studs Lonigan was going to be up in the bucks, way up.

He got up, nervous, and stood by the window, watching kids chase each other about the weedy vacant lot across the street, bang-banging and dueling with sticks of wood. Wouldn't they like to have what those Italian kids had that he'd seen in the movies about two weeks ago? Wooden guns, trenches, regular imitation war. And maybe Mussolini was smart, all right. It might be good for this country to give kids the same thing, training them, because when they grew up, if they were needed for war to repel a foreign invader like the Japs or the Russian Reds, they'd not go into it green.

"William, come and have a glass of milk," his mother called, and he turned from the window, grateful for the distraction.

He passed through the dark, narrow hallway and planked himself down at the enamel-topped kitchen table. He munched a graham cracker and slowly sipped milk.

"Your father will be coming home early," she said, a gray-haired woman with fatigue indelibly printed into her gaunt face.

"Dad seems to be in the dumps a lot these days," Studs said, grinding on a new cracker, glancing at her as she sat by the sink peeling potatoes.

"It's a downright shame that he should come to all

this trouble and worry in his old age, after being such a good man and a good provider for his family all these years," she muttered.

Tough, all right. But Studs Lonigan was not going to let himself get it in the neck the same way, he thought confidently.

"The Trents downstairs only paid half of their rent this month, and Mr. Trent's salary has been cut. They're complaining that the rent's too high. And how can your father reduce it, with his expenses, the upkeep on the building, his taxes, and the mortgage payments he has to make. The O'Connells, too, on the third floor, haven't paid a cent of rent in three months. Your father hates to ask Mr. O'Connell to leave, because Mr. O'Connell is a good steady man who always paid his rent right on the dot. But with his store failing, poor man, he's lost everything he had. And I was talking with Mrs. Schwartz down on the first floor this morning, and she was telling me how with their new car half paid for, they couldn't keep it up, and the car was taken away from them."

"Yes, it's tough all around," Studs mumbled, but if his stock only went right, it wouldn't be hitting him in the solar plexus. But had he, had he, after all, been a first-class chump?

"Times are harder than I can ever remember them. If they get any worse, I don't know what's going to happen to us. And I'd rather die than have to ask anything of my girls or their husbands. I don't know what I'd do but for my faith in God and in the power of The Little Rose of Christ. I pray to her every day for comfort, and for your father, and our family." Looking up, she arose, walked to the table, poured him a second glass of milk and said, "Here, William, drink another glass. It's good for you."

"I've had plenty," he said, rocking back on his chair.

"Drink it, William. It will build you up."

"I'm all right. I feel fine."

"No, William, you're so thin and pale I always worry about you. You must drink more milk and build yourself up. If anything ever happened to your father, you know, you'd be the head of the family."

"Dad's been hoping to get a contract to decorate an apartment hotel by the lake. If he does, I'll be able to go to work on it, and things will be much rosier for us all around," Studs said, taking a gulp of milk.

"I hope to the Lord he does. But William, I just dread to think of you going out to do all that hard work in your health."

"I'll be all right."

"But the Lord knows you'll have to work when you're married. This isn't the best time in the world for young folks to be getting engaged and married," she said, her voice growing faintly querulous.

Studs was tempted to tell her there would be no worry on that score if his investment came out right.

"Well, it's a comfort to know that you have money saved up in the bank and that you won't be going to her empty-handed."

He drank his milk more slowly.

"And I'm grateful to God that my girls married good providers, and have the comforts your father and I always wanted them to have when they got married." She sighed. "Of course, I wouldn't for the world of me say anything against a fine upstanding ambitious boy like Phillip, because he is very good to my daughter, but I do wish he could get into a better business. He's too smart a boy to be doing what he does."

"He's making a go of it," Studs said.

Some day Phil Rolfe was going to be a piker alongside of Studs Lonigan!

"He's a fine boy. He lives up to the faith, too, better than many of them that's been born in it. And I so often think what a shame it is that he's a gambler."

"He doesn't do the gambling. He's got the law of averages on his side."

"It would be so much nicer, and Loretta would have so much more . . . more standing with the right kind of people, if he was in something else, real estate, insurance, bonds."

"What could anybody do in real estate these days? Look at us with our building, and what Dad says about nearly all the big hotels and buildings being busted and in the hands of receivers. There's more money today in running a race-track book, like Phil does, than in such rackets."

"I know, but there must be something else besides gambling for a boy with as educated a girl as Loretta for his wife," she said wistfully.

"He's making good," Studs said, yawning, getting up. "I guess I'll go take a nap."

"Yes, do, son, it will be good for you," she said, peeling away at the potatoes.

II

"Well, Dad," Studs said, looking to his left at his father, who sat at the head of the supper table, "I'm getting to feel pretty good these days."

"That's fine, Bill," Lonigan said, the worried absorption seeming to lift from his ruddy face. "And I'm only sorry that I won't be able to be giving you as much steady work to do as I used to. The deal on that apartment hotel job flopped. The fellow who was going to supply the fresh capital got cold feet. So we don't get our contract, and it's going to put quite a crimp in our style. I had counted a lot on getting it."

"That's a shame, Patrick. But you mustn't worry. The Lord will provide for his own," Mrs. Lonigan said.

"I hope so," Lonigan said lifelessly, applying a knife and fork to his pork chop.

"Things will have to get better. That's just what Mrs. Schwartz and I were saying to each other in the hall this morning," she said.

"Maybe if we get a man in like Al Smith next year, and kick out Hoover, who's only a tool of the Jew international bankers, we'll turn the corner. This country is too great and too rich to be going to the dogs the way it seems to be these days. And you know, I was speaking to a fellow today who seems to know what he's talking about, and that's just what he was saying. But we got to get a strong man in the White House, a man like Al Smith or Mussolini, to kick out the bankers and grafting politicians and racketeers, and that'll make America a country for Americans only. If we don't do that, we give arguments right into the hands of the Reds who want anarchy here like they got in Russia," Lonigan said, and Studs nodded.

"Oh, Patrick, I meant to tell you, Frances telephoned today, and they're getting a new automobile."

"Fine! Fine! I'm glad to hear it," he listlessly said with a mouthful of food.

"What kind?" asked Martin, a tall, thin and gawky young man in his early twenties.

"She told me the make, but I forgot it now. You know, it's such a comfort to know that Carroll and Phillip are so good to my girls. Only it would be so much nicer if Phillip could get into a more refined business."

"Well, Mary, all business is much the same these days, dog eat dog, and when everything is said and done, the thing that counts is getting ahead. The boy's doing that."

"That's true, Dad," Studs said reflectively.

"And once you get the money, sock it, hang on to it! Don't invest in anything. I met another fellow today who's a good friend of Tom Gregory's, the chain-store man who made such a profit a year or two ago when he sold out his Peoples Stores.

I don't know Tom personally, myself, but he's an old-timer who knows the business of making money forward and backward and sidewise. He started with a little store over in back of the yards, and today, according to what this fellow says, he's an insurance man, Tom Gregory is worth a cool twenty million. He was saying he was out to see Tom the other night, and they were talking about stocks and investments, and Tom said to him, and as I was saying, Tom would know about the matter if anybody would, well, anyway, Tom told him that there's not a stock on the market today that's safe."

"William, don't eat so fast," Mrs. Lonigan said, noticing that Studs had lowered his head and was bolting down his food.

"Isn't a stock like, well, say, Imbray stock with public utilities all over the Middle West to back it up, and directed by a man with the brain of Solomon Imbray, isn't that stock safe?"

"Well, Bill, I was only saying what I had heard from this insurance man what Tom Gregory had told him. But I'm inclined, personally, to agree with Tom. The stock markets are manipulated by the Jew international bankers, and those are fellows I don't trust."

Should he sell his stock and take a small loss? Should he ask his old man's advice? God, if he lost his dough!

"I was talking to another fellow today, who knows things on the inside down at the City Hall, and he was saying to me, only don't let this go any further than ourselves, that the city is getting deeper and deeper into a financial pickle, and that soon the policemen, firemen, bailiffs and a lot of the politicians will be in the same boat as the school teachers, and will not be getting their pay envelopes. Now, you can't tell me that's natural and isn't just the result of graft somewhere. You bet, there's something rotten some place. Here men like myself pay out good hard-earned money for taxes, and where does it go? Where does it go that the city can't even pay the people working for it?" Lonigan said, his face flushing with anger.

"Did you say the bailiffs? Red Kelly won't be getting his pay then, and he won't like that at all," Studs said.

"He was kind of wild as a boy. I remember once seeing Sister Bernadette when the children were in school, and she told me that I should not have a fine boy like William running around with the likes of that Kelly boy. But he must have settled down since he's gotten married and turned out all right, much better than poor Mrs. Reilley's boy did."

"Red's all right, and he's got a drag with both Judge Dinny Gorman and the sheriff," Studs said.

"I don't care if Dinny is a judge. Judge or not, he's a damn old mollycoddle to me and always was, a high-hat mollycoddle if ever there was one. He's not human now, like Joe O'Reilley is. I sure hope, too, that Joe gets in for judge in the elections next month. If there ever was a fine and a smart man, it's Joe O'Reilley, and he would have been state's attorney years ago if the newspapers hadn't knifed him."

"I saw Red downtown a week or so ago, and all he talked about was his wife," Martin said.

"He loves his wife, all right," Studs said.

Mrs. Lonigan carted in coffee and angel-food cake, and served it.

"Well, if things only pick up some now, I'll be having plenty of work for you boys," Lonigan said smiling.

"I'm ready," Studs said.

"And, Mary, we'll make that trip to Ireland when times get better. We'll let the boys do their old man's work, and with two smart lads like Bill and Martin here, well, we need have no worries, and can enjoy our second honeymoon."

"Yes, Patrick. And I know that everything is going to come out ship-shape," she said, smiling at him in consolation.

"I guess we have to have faith and confidence, and not let ourselves believe we're licked," Lonigan said after a gulp of coffee.

III

Studs sank into a rocking chair opposite the radio, while his father, toying with the dials, produced grating static. The parlor suddenly filled with howling jazz, and Lonigan again tinkered with the dials, decreasing the ear-splitting volume. Out of the swift tempo the notes of a saxophone came like a clear stream of fluid sound that seemed to flow into Studs, shivering up his spine, spilling through his nerves, and pouring poignancy into every corner of his brain. He leaned back, a brooding expression settling on his face, and again the saxophone was lost in a rising cacophony that crashed into a wild conclusion. Lonigan looked at his bulky gold watch, its ornamented case flashing back a ray of electric light that had hit it.

"Amos and Andy will be on about ten o'clock. Gosh, they're funny, and when they get going they can touch anybody's funny bone," Lonigan said in an interlude between songs, while an announcer's eulogy of furniture went unheeded.

Studs nodded. Maybe in the morning he'd better dump

the stock, after all. But if he did, and the stock rose, wouldn't he want to shag his tail around the block six ways from Sunday for having pulled out with clammy feet? He looked at his father, wondering whether the old man were really listening to the radio music or not. He was getting along in years now, and it was showing, his gray hair thinning out, wrinkles coming into the blown red face, bags under the eyes, the look of all-around tiredness on it. Pretty tough, too, having worries in old age. He heard a faint wheeze with every breath his father took, and he continued to glance at the relaxed face. Tough!

And how would things be going in ten years—1941. Would his father and mother be alive? Would he? Martin, what would he be doing? Would he and Catherine have kids of their own? How many? Would they be well-heeled with dough? And Phil and Loretta? These questions disturbed him. He was kind of afraid of what might happen in the next ten years. He let himself slump into his chair to receive the song of a cloying-voiced radio crooner.

> *Just a gigolo*
> *Everywhere I go,*
> *People know the part I'm playing.*
> *Paid for every dance,*
> *Selling each romance,*
> *Every night some heart betraying.*
> *There will come a day,*
> *Youth will pass away,*
> *Then, what will they say about me?*
> *When the end comes, I know they'll say,*
> *"Just a gigolo,"*
> *As life goes on without me.*

He didn't like gigolos. They were like pansies, worse even. But he felt something sad in the music, and it seemed to make their home, the parlor, his father and mother, himself, seem sad, as the chorus of the song was crooned a second time. Wiping her bony, chapped hands in an apron, his mother entered the room and took a seat near a tall, ornate floor-lamp. He noticed his parents again, and he wondered when he and Catherine were old would they sit night after night the same way, listening to the radio, with hardly a word to say, and would they have children of their own to feel sorry for them in the same way that he was feeling sorry now for his mother and dad, and would he seem to his children to be ready for the ash heap as he dozed half-awake at nights?

He tried to shift to other thoughts, and words from the song stuck in his mind. *Youth will pass away, Life goes on without me*. His stocks could give him a start and prevent him from fearing lest he end up like the old man. Oh, Jesus Christ, why, why couldn't they just go up and double, triple, in value. If they went to a hundred bucks, that would be seventy-five bucks a share profit. And other people had made plenty this way. Why couldn't he?

And there they were, his father and mother, seeming to have other things on their minds. The old man's mouth hung open, his arms were dropped like lead over the side of his chair, and when he breathed, the loose roll of fat around his belly moved.

Poor old bastard! Studs silently exclaimed.

And there were so many wrinkles now in his mother's face, and the circles under her eyes, too, made her seem so old. She was the kind who must always be wearing herself out doing things for people, for the old man, for himself and Martin, for the girls, and Phil and Carroll. And she would go on doing things for her home and her family until the end. Suppose the old man did lose everything? How tough it would be on her! Jesus God, if his stock would only go up and he could save them from such troubles!

"And what could be more tempting, more refreshing, more delicious than. . . ."

"Those damn advertisements," Lonigan said, leaning forward to turn the dial, capturing successive snatches of song, more advertisements, speeches, static.

"The sun shines on yonder hill, friends in Radioland, through the courtesy of Bloop Blop and Doop, makers of solid whalebone non-skid rolling collar buttons," Martin said, entering the parlor.

"Martin, they have to have money for the radio, don't they, and I think you should appreciate what you get for nothing and not be making such mean remarks. I think it's nice of people and business men to spend good hard-earned money in these days so we can hear all the wonderful things we do hear over the radio, without you making fun and belittling," his mother nagged.

Martin cast a quick, pitying glance at his mother, shrugged his shoulders, picked up a morning paper from the piano bench, and slumped into a rocking chair.

"Martin, turn to the radio page and see if there's anything good due now," his father said.

"Father, there's going to be old-time songs on XAK at about this time. I remember seeing it in the papers," Martin said, and Lonigan dialed.

"And friends of Radioland, the Peoples Stores, situated all over the city for the housewives' convenience, will be gratified and amply repaid if you have enjoyed this concert which they have sponsored. This is station XAK, Norman Withers announcing. Stand by now for the time. It is now four seconds to eight, central standard time."

Melodious bell-like chimes rang out.

"And now, folks of Radioland, we have back with us the Midget Singers. Through the courtesy of the Soskimo Old Woolen Company, manufacturers of all lines of high-class woolen fabrics with their main manufacturing plant at Soskimo Falls, Massachusetts, we will hear the Midget Singers in an old-times song festival. Miss Marjorie Maginnis, Miss Florence Turtleback, and Miss Helen Ashencourt, the famous Midget Singers, will entertain us with those dear old songs of the days that are gone but not forgotten, when you and I were young, Maggie, and after the ball was over, you hitched old Dobbin to the sleigh and rode home on a bicycle built for two to pledge your troths in the shade of the old apple tree. Folks of Radioland, the Midget Singers."

Lonigan's face became alive. He smiled at his wife. Martin frowned, bored, and sank himself again in the newspaper.

> *Dear old girl, the robin sings above you,*
> *Dear old girl, it speaks of how I love you.*

Studs noticed the tender way his father looked at his mother. They loved each other, and he thought of how it would be terrible when one of them died. He figured, too, that they both must be thinking of the good times they had when they were young, remembering rich good things, and he asked himself would he and Catherine sometimes sit, still in love, looking back the same way, and also remembering rich good things?

> *After the ball is over,*
> *After they all have parted. . . .*

That beaming smile on the old man's face. He had once courted her, taken her out on dates, just as he took Catherine out, thought the same things of her that he thought of Catherine and had once thought of Lucy, kissed her in the same way as he kissed Catherine down by the lake the night they had become engaged. Once his mother, she had been young, like a flower to the old man, warm and hot and panting for breath in his arms, just like himself and Catherine.

He tried to visualize his parents when they were young, kissing, and the image would not stay fixed in his mind. To him, they were something different. He could not see them as sweethearts together. But it had once been. And now they were old, and he, himself, was nearly thirty, and he was going to be old, too, some day.

> *Daisy, Daisy, give me your answer true. . . .*

Martin yawned.

And in those days things had been a lot different, with bicycles all over the street, and almost no automobiles, and the women dressed so differently. He wished he could have known what those days had been like, what kind of a fellow the old man had really been. He watched him, too, nodding his head from side to side, looking at his mother still, his lips moving as he quietly sang the songs.

> *But you'll look sweet, upon the seat*
> *Of a bicycle built for two.*

Lonigan sighed deeply, wistfully.

> *By the lakes of Killarney, my home o'er the sea. . . .*

Studs guessed that this one must be making the old man think of Ireland that he had left as such a small kid. If the stock would go up enough, they could take that trip to Ireland, maybe with himself and Catherine going along, and that would be just jake. He wanted, now, very much, to be able to do something for the two of them. He was glad, too, to see them happy while these songs were sung, only he knew it was a sad kind of happiness, making them think of how they were once young and were now old.

> *It's a long way to Tipperary,*
> *It's a long way to go. . . .*

He remembered this one from his own days as a kid. If he had been able to go to war! He looked at his father, listening, remembering, at his mother, listening, remembering, and he was listening, and remembering, too, and he was remembering Lucy as a girl.

IV

"I'll walk down with you, Martin. I want to get the paper," Studs said as Martin stood in the parlor doorway with his coat and hat on.

"You won't be staying out late, boys?" his mother said, her expression one of concern.

"I'll be home early," Martin said, checking the disgust that almost broke into his voice, while Studs put on his hat and coat.

"Boys, don't be staying out late," she said.

"Try and get back by ten when Amos and Andy come on," the father said.

"I'd like to get barrelled tonight," Martin said as they stepped out of the building.

"I'm off of that stuff for a while," Studs said seriously.

"You ought to be."

"Well, I did drink my share of the world's bum gin in my day," Studs said proudly.

"You're beginning to talk and act like my grandfather. Back in them there days before Abe Lincoln was shot, we sure was hot stuff, huh, kid?"

"With my heart, I can't afford to be taking risks."

Martin extended a package of cigarettes, and both of them lit up.

"I remember that Christmas morning when you came home with a sprained ankle, smelling a few degrees worse than a sewer. Remember? Fran was so hot and bothered because you'd been sassy and threatened to poke her boy friend's teeth down his throat. Boy, the old homestead sure was no place for peace and meditation that day."

"Yeah," Studs smiled, "that was the night we kidnapped Vinc Curley to get his car, and told him we were taking him to church, and went out to Burnham. And the police raided the place when I had my pants down and I jumped out of a second-story window to get away. . . ."

"I know the story," Martin said, bored.

Getting too snotty for a kid brother, Studs thought, his face suddenly grim.

"You know, when I first found out about how you'd get shellacked, I thought it was pretty terrible. When I was a punk in grammar school, I thought that drinking and laying a cutey ticketed you straight for hell. But I learned a few things since."

"And so did I. I learned you can knock hell out of yourself with too much booze."

"Thus speaketh the veteran of a thousand gin brawls."

"No, kid, I'm serious. A guy's got to watch his step a little. I know I had my fun, but you can't play that kind of a game forever if you want to live to tell the story."

"You had your fun, didn't you? You're only young once,

and you got a right to have a good time. What else do you get out of life? Look at the gaffer! What's he got now? Goddamn near nothing. Well, I'm not going to sweat my can off working and saving just to end up like that. When the game's called on me, all right, boys, I was no sap. I had my fun, here's my hand, goodbye, and it's your turn to carry on. That's my idea."

Looking covertly at Martin, Studs suddenly felt slated for the ash-can. And he wanted to tell Martin a few things, how he ought to tone down a little. Cocky punk, too! Well, in his day Studs Lonigan had shown them plenty. The kid would have to do plenty of travelling if he even wanted to catch up to where he could see the dust Studs Lonigan had left behind him. But that was behind him, and it was ahead of Martin. Martin didn't realize what a break he had gotten by being born later, having so much more ahead of him.

"You bet, Studs, this idea of sweating your tail off with work and carefulness is the undiluted crap. With me, a bird in the hand and a cutey in a bed is worth dozens of them in a bush you can't reach," Martin said, while ahead of them, at Seventy-first and Jeffrey, they heard warning bells from the Illinois Central, and saw the train gates lower, red lanterns dangling from them. An electric train shot across the street and the gates were raised.

"I was pretty cockeyed last Saturday night," Martin boasted.

"Seems to me that's the same story nearly every Saturday night."

"Umm, now and then."

"Mostly now, instead of then, huh?" Studs said, and they laughed.

"By the time Saturday rolls around, a guy's seen all the shows he wants to see for a week, and he hangs around with the boys, feeling dumb, wanting something to happen, tired of everybody's bum jokes that he's heard before. So he figures, well, the way to make things happen is to get a bottle, and he does. So he gets snozzled and has some fun. And last Saturday, the cutey I had! Umm! I made her, too, only I was so cockeyed it wasn't no fun. But I'm figuring to fix that baby again . . ."

"Oh, hello, Austin," Studs said.

"Why, hello Studs. And how are you, Martin?" Austin McAuliffe, replied, his voice jolly.

"How things going?" Studs asked, noticing that Austin seemed much the same as ever, thin, narrow-faced, well-dressed. Austin looked like he was making the grade. But then, why should he feel ashamed, with his Imbray investment?

"I'm a lawyer now, Studs. Graduated from St. Vincent's. I went nights and passed my bar exams last summer. I'm lined up in a promising job with a good law firm, and even if I do say so, things look pretty rosy."

"Married, Austin?" Studs asked.

"Not yet. I guess I better knock on wood, huh, Studs?"

"Studs is beating you to the gun," Martin said.

"Studs, don't tell me you're married?"

"No, but he gave her the ring," Martin said.

"Well, well! Congratulations, Studs. Who's the lucky girl?" Austin said, enthusiastically pumping Studs' hand.

"I don't think you know her. Her name is Catherine Banahan."

"Well, that gives her the proper credentials. Nothing like an Irish girl."

"Yes, McAuliffe, the lad's in love," Martin smirked, making Studs show his embarrassment with nervousness.

"How's the folks?" Austin asked like a fellow trying to make conversation.

"Pretty good."

"Oh, say, by the way, did you hear that Father Gilhooley has been changed to a parish back of the yards, and Saint Patrick's has been turned over to some order of priests, but I can't remember which one it is."

"Is the school still running?" Studs asked.

"Yes, but the pupils are all jiggabooes, and the parish is very poor now, I guess," Austin lamented.

"Gilly was always a puzzle to us altar boys. When he said mass, he always drank so much more wine than the other priests did. We always expected him to go staggering off the altar," Martin laughed.

"You know, it was a shame the way that parish went down," Austin said, turning toward Studs after frowning at Martin. "Father Gilhooley must have taken it hard, because of the parish and the beautiful new church he built, for it was his life's work, and then it was no sooner up than his people moved away on him. My mother met him downtown not so long ago, and she said he had aged a great deal. And say, I saw Jim Clayburn the other day. He's put on a lot of weight, and he's taken over his father's law practice. Seems to be prospering."

"He was a nice fellow. Tell him I asked for him if you see him again. See anybody else? How's Art Hahn?"

"I haven't seen Art for about a year. He'd just lost his job then and was selling vacuum cleaners. And I saw Father McCarthy a few weeks ago. He's an assistant at some parish out West."

"His brother, Monk McCarthy, is getting along, too."

"Every time I see anybody from Fifty-eighth Street, Studs, I always say to myself how times change, how they change."

"Yeah, that's so, Austin," Studs said weightily.

"And Martin, the way you've sprung up, you look like Studs' big brother now. I suppose one of these days we'll be hearing the wedding bells ring out for you," Austin said, laughing.

"Not this lad."

"I don't doubt that Studs once said the same thing."

"One in the family at a time," said Martin.

They stood in an awkward silence, talked out.

"Well, boys, I'll be seeing you around again. Got to run along and turn in. It's been a hard day in court, and tomorrow I got to go out to Carmody, Indiana, and collect a bill."

"So long, Austin."

"Sappy, I'd say," Martin said.

"Oh, Austin's all right. He's a smart fellow. He always studied a lot, and got himself a good education, and now he's reaping the benefits of it."

"Education or not, he's a dope to me," Martin said.

Walking along with him, Studs began to see in his kid brother a lot of what he'd once been.

V

"I see we have the Lonigans in person with us tonight," Pat Carrigan said, smiling as Studs and Martin approached the group of fellows who idled and talked front of the chain drug store at the northeast corner of the busy, well-lit intersection of Seventy-first and Jeffrey.

"Hello, Pat. How's it going tonight?" Studs said, pleased to be in a group of fellows and in the midst of a little noise and light after the dullness of home. He thought, too, that he liked Pat, had liked him in the old days when Pat was one of the second generation of punks coming around the corner.

"Know all the boys, Studs?" Pat asked, a note of solicitude in his voice. "Boys, this is Studs Lonigan. Studs, Don Bryan, Al Schuber, Jack Allison, Steve O'Grady, and of course you know Kodak Kid O'Doul," Pat said.

Studs shook hands around, and coming to O'Doul, he said laconically:

"Still smashing the broads' hearts?"

"Studs, what's been on your mind since we went to that movie together a couple of weeks ago?"

"Nothing much to write home about," Studs said.

"What movie was that?" asked O'Doul.

"*Doomed Victory*. It's an interesting gangster movie, only in real life, a gangster would grease a dick a little instead of letting himself be run out of town," Pat said.

"Don't tell me about it. I want to see it," Bryan said.

"Did Ike sell you his stock?" Pat asked Studs.

"Well . . . not quite," Studs said, wondering if Ike would keep his promise not to mention to anyone that he'd bought the stock. Pat might think him a chump, and also tell Martin, and Martin might let it out of the bag at home without meaning to or something.

"It may be a good bargain. I don't know nothing about it, but I do know that Ike, while being a swell guy, is one first rate B.S. artist."

"Say, Lonigan, what's your racket?" Bryan asked.

"Painting with my old man," Studs said, glancing surprised at Bryan, not liking the fellow's thin, slightly-pocked, snotty face.

"Not much doing in it these days, huh?"

"Well, of course, everything could be better," Studs said seriously, seeing himself as older than these kids, a fellow with investments now, business interests, and talking to them as an experienced guy.

"There's nothing doing anywhere now, I guess, except for a few bootleggers. They're just about the only ones who cash in these days. I'm working with my gaffer in the plumbing business these days, and there ain't much for us, and we can hardly collect on the work we do do. The old man is bleeding his eyes out with sobs," Pat said.

"It's this guy Hoover with those Sunday-school collars he wears. First time I saw a picture of him with them collars, I said to myself, a guy who wears those collars must be a chump somewhere. Now if we had a Democrat in office," O'Grady said. Studs noticed that he was a short, stocky fellow, with a fedora slanted on the left side and a cigarette drooping between his lips.

"Yes. I suppose everybody would be better off if there was a different man in the saddle," Studs said profoundly.

"What the hell, that's all politics, that's all," Bryan said.

"What do you know about politics? Are you on an inside wire?" asked Schuber.

"I know this much. Politics is politics, and guys, even when they're big shots, don't go into it for fun. They all want to sink their claws into the grab bag. And so would I if I was in the political game," Don said.

"The way I look at it, boys, is this. A Democrat like Al Smith, or Tony Cermak, who's a cinch for mayor in the next elections, now if they were up to bat in Washington, they might not knock the ball out of the lot every time they stepped up to the plate, but they wouldn't just hit nothin' but foul balls, the way Hoover does," Pat said.

"Well, this boy right here wouldn't complain, and he wouldn't be giving a damn about anything else if he could just line himself up to another job that paid a little dough," Allison, a tall, raw-boned fellow said.

"It used to be that all the lads I knew was workin', and I was beginning to get so lonesome that I almost went to work myself. But when I would almost do that, I'd think of you boys, sweating your tails off in the offices and factories on hot days when I was lolling on the beach, with my head in the lap of a sweet pickup. But now, what the hell, I don't take any more pride in my idleness since so many of you boys have signed up as recruits in the Army of the Unemployed. If it keeps up like this with all you rookies crowding me out, Steve O'Grady will have to be shagging ass downtown one of these days and getting himself a job. Only if I did, the gaffer and the old woman might die from the shock," O'Grady said, and they laughed, Studs' laugh a trifle self-conscious.

"If you do that, Steve, do me a favor? Let me know where you get the job, and how you turned the trick. Because, brother, I sure pounded the pavements in the Loop looking for a job, until my fanny was drooping like a wilting lily of the fields and the soles of my feet just ached for a nice comfortable pair of carpet slippers and a soft rug. And all I got was the go-by. Me, now, I'm a guy who doesn't feel good if I ain't working. I'm no lazy bastard like O'Grady. . . ."

"That's why you've always been so dumb," O'Grady said, interrupting Allison.

"Dumb, hell! It's just that I got to have something to do, and dough in my pocket, and the feeling that I don't have to take nobody's crap. Then I can just go along and pay my own way, and I feel right. And Christ, this goddamn hanging around without a sou in your pocket, it just rips me up the back."

"Me, now, I might just as well be not working, with my salary cut to fifteen bucks a week, and my old man sobbing the blues every night about how broke he is. Holy Christ!" Bryan said.

"Sing 'em, brother, sing 'em!" Pat said, smiling. He turned to Studs as they seemed to split into two groups, and said, "Doing anything interesting these days, Studs?"

"Not a lot," Studs answered, as if his conduct were of interest to Pat, his feeling for Pat warmed more and more.

"I guess nobody's raising as much hell as they used to. Fellows like yourself are getting more settled, and anyway, there's not so much loose dough floating around for hell-raising like there used to be."

"Come to think of it, Pat, I did spend a hell of a lot of dough on booze and such things in the old days."

"Don't I remember! It used to be a sight to hang around the corner on a Saturday night until one or two when you boys of the Fifty-eighth Street Alky Squad came around pie-eyed," Pat said, he and Studs laughing, Studs having the feeling suddenly that it was still the old days.

Warning bells and the lowering train gates of the I.C. distracted his thoughts, and he watched a westbound electric suburban train clatter down the middle of the street, drawing into the Bryn Mawr station that reached westward from Jeffrey. He watched three young fellows racing up the station steps to catch the train, asking himself idly who they were, and what they were?

"Say, Lonigan, since your old man's a painting contractor, I was wondering about something. A lad I know, good friend of mine, was chump enough to get himself spliced when he was out of a job. He's damn nifty with the brushes, too, and now he needs work because his wife is having a kid. I'll vouch for him as a damn good worker, not at all like me, he just knows me. Would there be any chance of your old man giving him something to do?" O'Grady asked.

"Jesus, the kid brother here and I don't even work regularly," Studs said, Martin frowning at Studs.

"Well, no harm in asking," O'Grady said.

Studs regretted that he couldn't help out O'Grady's friend. He'd like to be a guy who could do favors that way, like a politician. If guys wanted something, they'd say, know Studs Lonigan, well, see him, he ought to be able to fix you up.

"Now that everybody has done his gassing, how about a bottle, boys?" Martin said.

"Studs, hear that?" said Pat, nodding his head at Martin.

"Yeah, Pat, these kids nowadays getting pretty reckless," Studs said, winking at Pat.

"Sure we are, Grandpa Lonigan. Tell about that time, though, during the Spanish American War, when you jumped out of the window of a can house with your pants down. I haven't heard that story for an hour. Now, come on, tell us," said Martin, his voice a cutting sneer.

"Yes, and I'll bet you just go rolling down the gutter every time you whiff a cork," Studs said, pleased when they laughed, because it showed that he was impressing them all as a guy with a real sense of humor.

"Listen, I'll eat mine if I can't drink you under the table," Martin countered.

"Pat, there's a lot of cocky young punks these days whose talk is louder than their actions," Studs said with strained casualness.

"And there's plenty of old boys, you know, in training to become bald-headed dryballs," Martin said.

"I'd call this nice brotherly friendship," Bryan said, Studs glad for the crack because he was stumped for a retort.

"Frankly, if you asked my opinion, I'd lay my dough on the line to say that your old man could spot both of you a good-sized pint and still watch you pass out," Pat said.

"The gaffer had his in his day," Martin said.

"And Steve O'Grady's old man whetted his gullet with plenty, too, in his time," O'Grady said.

"You know, it's funny. Now, you take my old man. I'm pretty sure he was wild and sowed his wild oats in his day. But he must have changed a lot since then. He acted toward Martin there and me as if he didn't want us to have what he had, and as if he didn't even understand why a guy could want to go out, tip the bottle, raise some hell. Funny, isn't it, the way people change," Studs said.

"Wait till you are married and you make me the uncle of some squawking little Studs Lonigans," Martin laughed.

"Going to march down the middle aisle with a flower in your buttonhole, huh, Studs? Well, congratulations," O'Doul said.

"That reminds me. Pete Webb just took a run-out powder on his wife. She's having a kid, and Pete, who never liked work anyway, didn't have a job, so he just took the run-out powder," Pat said.

"He was the skinny, dark-haired punk around the corner who was so chicken, wasn't he?" Studs said.

"That's Webb, Lonigan," Bryan said.

"What's his frau doing besides having a baby?" asked Schuber.

"Webb was crummy to pull a stunt like that," O'Grady said.

"Fellows, you can't always tell what a guy's reasons are when he does a thing like that. He might be wanting to explore new fields for nooky, and you know, a john has got no conscience. And then, the broad a guy marries might not be just what he's bargained for. There's plenty of dames walking the streets, keen babies, too, and a fellow looks at them, gets hot in the pants, takes them out and throws a little necking party, and he begins to think, now, well, here's the gal who's got just what it takes, and is the answer to all my prayers, and she's got everything plus. Well, what he wants really is a piece of tail, and she won't put it out without the ring on her finger, so he puts the ring on her finger for a piece of tail, and after he gets tired of that, he finds out that she's got everything minus, and a tongue and things like that. So he finds out that he hasn't gotten any bargain after all. You can't always tell a guy's reasons when he takes a run-out powder," Allison said.

"Still, it's pretty low to breeze on a girl after you've married and knocked her up," Studs said.

"You never could rely on Pete for anything," Pat said.

"That's the way I always doped him," Studs said.

"Say, that's the twelfth train I watched go by tonight. I counted 'em," O'Doul said, watching an eastbound train clatter out of the Bryn Mawr station.

"Jesus Christ!" O'Grady exclaimed in surprise. "That's my idea of nothing to do. Counting trains. Hey, O'Doul, how many automobiles has passed here going to South Shore in the last nineteen minutes?"

"Huh?"

"You're falling down on the job, boy," said O'Grady, and they laughed.

"Well, now that the barbering has gone so far, let's get a bottle," Bryan said.

Studs was tempted, and thought of how he could get 'em off on a rip-roaring drunk and show them what Studs Lonigan really was, and teach the kid brother a couple of tricks for good measure.

"Now, Bryan, you're showing me you got some stuff on the ball," Martin said.

"I'm game, Don. But since this is your bright idea, how about you shelling out for the bottle? Steve O'Grady will help you drink it," O'Grady said.

"Who was your chump last year?"

"You."

"Well, try hunting a new one this year," Bryan said while they laughed.

"Oh, by the way, Pat, you know that keen broad, Louise Mahler? She's getting to look more like hot stuff every day. Saw her at a dance at the Westgate last week," Schuber said, O'Doul turning to look at them.

"Has she been introduced into the mysteries of life and love yet?" asked Bryan.

"Don, your mind is lousy. She's a decent girl," Pat said.

"And sure, so was I a decent boy once," Bryan said.

"Say, Studs, how's Phil Rolfe making out these days?" Pat asked.

"That boy just rakes in the dough," Martin said.

"Phil Rolfe. Oh, that's right, he's your brother-in-law, isn't he, Lonigan? Sure, I would say he's cleaning up. I was over to his place a few weeks ago, played a buck on a nag, and she paid four to one, and was his joint crowded! Lots of women there old enough to be my mother, too, playing the ponies. With times kind of hard, everybody is trying to make a little extra, and a lot of 'em are playing the ponies and that's just up Phil's alley. I don't envy him his luck, though. He's a nice lad. I was talking to him a few minutes. Nice lad. I never associated it, Studs, that you and Husk were his brother-in-laws," Allison said.

Studs Lonigan, Phil Rolfe's brother-in-law. That it would ever come to the time that he was known this way, instead of Phil being known as Studs' brother-in-law. He suddenly felt out of everything. A new corner. A new bunch. Out of it. Others pushing along, to be where he used to be. He looked from face to face: Martin, cocky and surly; Pat, jolly; that snotty puss of Bryan. O'Doul, simpering, showing off, standing there all dressed up and no place to go, trying to act like hot stuff, just as he used to back at the corner of Fifty-eighth and Prairie. The world could change, but not Kodak Kid O'Doul, Studs thought, sneering. And Allison, bigger, younger, more powerful-looking than himself. Out of it. These lads, knowing him as Phil Rolfe's brother-in-law. His old contempt for Phil rose. Before he got through. Well, he had to take nobody's. He had his investment, didn't he. . . .

"Well, are we or ain't we?" asked Bryan impatiently.

"Count me out. I'm tired, and I'm going home to hit the hay early," Pat said.

"How about you, Lonigan?" Don asked.

"No, thanks. Not tonight," Studs answered.

"Don, can't you see that this gang is as full of vim, vigor, vitality, and ambition as a sleeping alligator?" O'Grady said.

"Well, I'm ready," Martin said.

"And try walking home on your own feet tonight to see how it feels," Studs said to Martin, smiling.

"Don't worry about me there, foxy grandpa," said Martin.

"Well, I'll see you again, fellows," Studs said.

"Take care of yourself, Studs, and don't take any rubber dimes," Pat said as Studs walked to the chain drug store entrance to go in for a malted milk.

VI

"You missed Amos and Andy tonight. Golly, they were funny," Lonigan said as Studs entered the parlor.

"I was talking to some fellows I know," Studs said, unfolding his copy of the morning's *Chicago Questioner* and letting his eyes run over the headlines.

ALBANIAN SLAIN IN WEST SIDE HOLDUP
Aged Newsdealer Shot
To Death Battling Robbers

REDS BATTLE COPS
Anarchistic Literature Seized
Patrolman O'Houlihan
Seriously Injured
Scores Arrested; Fifteen
In Hospital

MILK STRIKE RIOTS IN EAST
Scores Injured

BUS PASSENGER SHOT AS AUTOIST IN CRASH FIRES

BLAME AGITATORS FOR MINE STRIKE
Governor Invites Inquiry

JOBLESS FATHER SLAYS FAMILY OF SIX

BANKER PRAISES HOOVER
Predicts New Boom in Next Six Months

SHOTGUN BANDITS COW 19
Get $4,000

MOVIE STAR WINS FREEDOM
Names Society Woman Correspondent

SOLOMON IMBRAY PREDICTS GREATER CHICAGO
After Depression City Will Grow

CATHOLIC PRIEST ASSAILS SOVIET
Moscow Atheistic and Pagan

Father Dooligan Finds
Russia Unfit for Society
of Civilized Nations

"Anything in the papers, Bill?"

"Not much. A couple of holdups. And a Red riot on the west side. A cop was beaten up and taken to the hospital with a broken leg," said Studs casually.

"They ought to put a stop to those damn Reds, starting trouble when the country has its hands full as it is. The cops aren't even safe with them any more. I tell you, there ought to be a law against 'em, and they ought to be put at hard labor on an island like that Devil's Island the French got," Lonigan said with a rising self-righteousness that drew blood to his face.

"Yes, and it says here that some university professor named Lovett has protested to the mayor against police brutality."

"He must be an atheist. What does he want, the cops to stand there and let their legs get broken? They haven't got any respect for law, these atheistic university professors and Reds," Lonigan said.

Studs read the account of an interview with Solomon Imbray.

> *"The depression is only temporary, and the process of shrinkage and deflation of values has reached rock bottom. We can now expect and prepare for a period of expansion, during which we will know greater prosperity than we have ever known before. Of this, I am absolutely confident. And this new wave will carry Chicago forward to an unprecedented development. One day Chicago will be the queen of cities, the world over," said Solomon Imbray today, traction magnate and one of Chicago's leading civic spirits, in an interview granted upon his return from a visit to New York.*

Umm! Guessed that, after all, he'd better hang on to his stocks and wait a bit. Imbray ought to know what he was talking about.

"As I was going to say, though, Bill, I'm sorry you missed Amos and Andy. You would have laughed yourself sick at them." Lonigan's belly rolled as he laughed. "They're so much like darkies. Not the fresh northern niggers, but the genuine real southern darkies, the good niggers. They got them down to a T, lazy, happy-go-lucky, strutting themselves out in titles and with long names and honors, just like in real life." Studs wished that his father would finish, so he could read the paper without distraction. "Amos and Andy got their taxicab now." He laughed again. "But it won't run. Andy elected himself president, and calls their cab *The Fresh Air Taxicab Company of America*. And Amos, just like a nigger, he wants to be a president. Well, Andy, he's the wise one anyway, he tells Amos, so Amos will be able to tell Ruby Brown about his titles, you see, he says to Amos that he, that is, Amos, can call himself *Chief Mechanic's Mate, Fixer of Automobiles,* and *Chief Business Getter. Golly!*" Lonigan chuckled; Studs pretended to listen. "Well, Amos is satisfied because he has his titles, too, but he doesn't understand that his titles mean he must do all the work, while Andy sits on his you-know. So then, Andy tells Amos to fix the car, and Amos asks why, and Andy tells him that fixing the automobile is in his department, and it would be shameful if the president of *The Fresh Air Taxicab Company of America* had to fix the car like a mechanic." Lonigan laughed. "Golly, Bill, they sure are a card."

"I'm sorry I missed them," Studs muttered, flipping the pages of his newspaper to the stock-market quotations and reading that his stock was unchanged, 24.

"Martin still out?"

Studs nodded, and turned to the back page, his eye catching the picture in the upper left-hand corner, a scene from the day's Red riots, with a fallen man in the foreground, against an indistinct background of struggling figures. Over the fallen man on the left was a policeman with a raised club, and on his right a hefty detective in dark overcoat and gray suit who had, when the picture was snapped, just completed making a swinging punch at the fallen man. He glanced at the next photograph showing a young girl, seated, blond, with crossed legs and one knee in sight, who had just married a sixty-eight-year-old millionaire. Good legs. Nice. Poor old bastard of a husband, too old for such nice stuff.

"Bill, there's something I want to speak to you about," the father said in a heavy voice, and Studs looked up from the newspaper, noticing that his father was embarrassed by what he had to say. . . . "Bill . . . how much money have you got in the bank?"

"Why?" Studs asked, taken aback, immediately wishing that he had said something different, because his father flinched at his question.

"Bill, I never thought that I would have to ask any of my children for a cent, but lots of things happen that we never counted upon." Lonigan disconsolately wagged his head. "I'm afraid I'm going to need money goddamn bad. I haven't told your mother how bad things look to me, but they are bad. They're fierce. I've got to figure out how much I can rely on in a pinch. Well, I might as well tell you the whole story. I've got some stocks. I bought them on margin about two years ago, and I've had to keep feeding money into my broker so I wouldn't get sold out. I've pulled through this far, but I don't know what's ahead of me. And then about four months ago I got a hot tip on a stock, so I bought a little of it on margin, and that leaves me pretty worried now, because my stock hasn't gone up like I supposed it would. So you see, with it, and with the mortgage, and running expenses, and every damn thing that comes along, I'm in a pickle, and I want to figure out how much I can rely on in case I need it, and in case you're willing to loan money to your father."

"Why, of course, Dad. I got two thousand. When will you need it?" Studs said heedlessly, and instantly he regretted the lie and couldn't understand why he hadn't mentioned the stock.

"That's fine of you, Bill . . . and well, you know, it gives me a great feeling of pride to have a son like you."

"Things are bound to get better, dad," Studs said with suppressed emotion.

"It's those goddamn Jew international bankers. And Bill, it ain't fair. It ain't right that a man should have so much worry and trouble in his old age, after working as hard as I have all my life and providing so well for my family. Your mother and I have earned the right to peace and comfort in our old age," Lonigan protested.

Not knowing what to reply, Studs nodded agreement.

"I might just have to call on you, so I wanted to mention this matter in advance," Lonigan said, sinking down in his chair, his chin lowering against his chest. Studs wished there was something he could say to help make his old man buck up.

But suppose the old man asked for the money. Well, he could sell, pocket his loss, and let him have the rest. He asked himself why a guy's life had to be one damn thing to worry about after another, and why wasn't a guy never done with deciding things. Always, time after time, as soon as one thing was settled, and the worry erased, another thing popped up. A guy no sooner skirted out of one pickle than he had fallen into another one. It seemed as if almost every minute of a fellow's life a knife was swinging over his neck, ready to slash into him at any unsuspected moment. When he'd been a kid, it had been the same, trouble at home, worry about school, something, and he had wished for the time when he

grew up, because then he'd be free and not always having
worries and dangers on his mind like so many wet blankets.
Now he was a man. And he was damn tired, too.

"Bill, I only hope that when you're my age you have a boy
who's as great a comfort to you as you are to me."

"Yes, Dad," Studs said, embarrassed, touched by the gentle
note which had crept into his father's voice; and he liked his
old man a lot. It made him almost wince and feel like a traitor
to think that he'd lied to him about the stock, and that he
hadn't even bothered to ask his advice before buying it. And
if he mentioned it now, the old man would take it pretty
badly.

"Yes, Bill, I used to worry about you a lot. For a while you
were a pretty wild lad, but then, I guess all young lads who
are worth their salt have to sow their wild oats. I was the same
myself once. But now I have the feeling I can depend on
you, and I just wanted to say so," Lonigan said, mumbling his
words.

A lump gathered in Studs' throat. He was afraid because
of the strong feelings that seemed to break and well up within
him. And he felt like a louse, not worthy of his father's trust.
To regain his control, he lit a cigarette, inhaled, let the smoke
escape through his nose.

"And, Bill, you got to watch your health. You've got to
fight an uphill battle to win it back, just as I got to
fight an uphill battle to get back where I was before these hard
times set in." Lonigan sat up erectly. "A Lonigan can be
down, but he's never out!"

Studs nodded thoughtfully, his eyes wandering about the
parlor, at the baby grand piano, the legs scratched, the cabinet
radio, the mirror, the subdued gray wallpaper, the ornate
floor-lamp, the family pictures hung about the wall, and then
at his father, brooding and corpulent.

Lonigan arose stiffly and muttered as he walked out of
the parlor, "Goodnight, son."

"Goodnight, Dad."

Studs moved to the window and stood gazing down, hands
in pocket. Across on the other side of the street, a couple
emerged from shadows, arm in arm, walking slowly, passed
through an area brightened by the glow of a street lamp,
passed again into the shadows that fell from the large apartment
motel. The sight made him want a girl, to kiss, to love, to
talk to and hold at this minute, Catherine, Lucy, a girl. An
automobile passed. He glanced at the apartment hotel, its
lighted windows yellow squares against an indistinct, bulky
background. What were the people behind those windows

doing? What troubles, worries, problems did they have bothering them? He recalled how on the night he had graduated from grammar school, he had stood by the parlor window of their Wabash Avenue building, looking out after everyone had gone to bed. Then, he'd looked forward to a lot of things. Now, Phil Rolfe's brother-in-law, out of it, his old man almost on the spot. No, he still had things to look forward to, still was in the show. He turned from the window and picked up his newspaper to read in bed. Turning out the parlor lights, he thought, Jesus, Jesus Christ, if only his stocks would go way up!

CHAPTER FIVE

I

"Shall we go into the other room?" Loretta asked, arising.

"Nice supper, Marie," Phil said with false joviality to the plump colored maid, who, with a surly frown on her face, had commenced removing the supper dishes.

"Phil, I'll have to get rid of her. She's entirely too surly for a nigger maid," Loretta said in a low but exasperated voice as they led Studs through the French door into the parlor.

"All right, dear, as you wish, but can we get another as cheap?"

"Frances only pays hers seven dollars a week."

Studs jammed his hands into his trouser pockets, glancing about the clean, bright parlor, his eyes resting on the blue and gray walls. Easy to look at, and a nifty, neat job of paperhanging, he thought.

"Say, I never saw a chair like this one, except in the store windows or the movies," he said, pointing to his right at a low-lined, chromium-plated chair.

"That's one of our recent acquisitions," Phil said with pride.

"It's modernistic," Loretta said, seating herself on the divan whose maroon-red upholstering matched the wine-red cushioning of the chair.

"Sit in it, Studs," Phil said.

"Say, it is comfortable," Studs said after having sunk into it, and Phil beamed.

"Furniture like that is quite the vogue now. Frances telephoned me today, and she's getting a modernistic bridge set that must be simply darling from the way she described it," Loretta said.

"It's nice, all right," Studs said, feeling that he ought to say something.

Glancing to his left, he spotted the low, gray ash desk, and on it a terra cotta lamp with a silver parchment shade.

"Say, that's a nice desk," he said.

"Isn't it, though?" Loretta said, Studs wondering had she started to get high-hat. "Come here, Studs," she added, rising.

"Honey, Studs doesn't care about that," Phil said, a whine creeping into his voice.

Studs got up and moved toward the desk, a supercilious smile on his face. Taking in Loretta, he wondered if she had cut the figure when she'd told him at the supper table that she'd only gained twenty pounds since their marriage. She was pretty wide. But then, she was small, and being so small maybe made her look fatter than she was.

"Everybody who comes here has to look at those drawers," Phil said.

Loretta opened a desk drawer, withdrew some packs of playing cards and scratch pads, and pointed. Studs stared, puzzled at what he was supposed to notice.

"Isn't it nice, with the insides painted blue?" Loretta said, proud.

"Yes, yes, it is. Catherine and I will have to figure on getting things like that when we get married."

What would Catherine think of such furniture, and a place in a high-class apartment hotel like this one? And would they be able to afford it?

"In the daytime with the lake right below us, the view, too, is simply grand," Loretta said as she and Studs sat down.

"Here, Studs, cigarette?" Phil said, holding a box containing cork-tipped Melachrinos before him.

Studs glanced up at Phil, observing that Phil was taking on the poundage now, his baby face padded, the cheeks full and shiny, the neck thickening, and the stomach expanding. He took a cigarette.

"Thanks," he said as Phil offered him the flame from a nickel, initialed cigarette lighter.

"I'll take one, Phil, dear," Loretta said, and Phil walked toward her.

As Phil lit her cigarette, Studs caught them exchanging tender and knowing smiles.

His sister was changed, all right. She was a woman now, who got regular jazzing and knew what it was all about. Phil sank into a wicker chair with a blue cushion in the seat, and sighed in exuding comfort. Her man, Studs thought ironically. Far different from the virgin sister who used to squeak with embarrassment if he accidentally saw her in the hallway in her underthings. She'd been a stranger to him then, but now she seemed like even more of a stranger.

"It's too bad that Catherine couldn't come with you," she said, her arm languidly extended with the cigarette smoking between her fingers.

"She had her bridge club again tonight," Studs said.

"That reminds me, Phil. The Kavanaughs invited us to a bridge party next Sunday night."

Studs smoked self-consciously. He wondered had marriage done to Fritzie what it was supposed to do with most women, made her an easy lay for guys. But it couldn't. She'd always been too decent a girl. And she was keen on Phil. But she was sure different from what she'd been four or five years ago.

"Studs, you play bridge?" Phil asked, and Studs shook his head negatively.

"That's too bad. We could have such pleasant foursomes if you did," she exclaimed.

"I learned the game since our marriage and I like it. Once you get your teeth into the game, Studs, it's really keen. It's good for you, too, because it makes you think. You got to think harder when you're playing a good stiff game of bridge than you do reading a book," Phil said.

"It wouldn't be hard to teach him, Phil."

"Is it a go, Studs?"

Studs smiled, deciding that it wasn't much use arguing. Better let it pass, let them think he agreed, and just stall off any definite dates.

"Sometime it might be all right," he said.

"How about next Monday night?" Loretta asked.

"I'll have to wait and see Catherine."

"Well, don't just say you will and then forget about it."

He nodded his head, squashed his cigarette in a tray.

"Any pickup in business, Phil?" Studs asked.

"No complaints, Studs," Phil said, stretching his legs. "In a way, hard times are playing right into my hands. There's lots of people these days who've got to live on less than they used to. And, of course, the races give them a chance to pick up some extra change. For instance, every day I get a lot of women coming in to play the ponies. Married women, trying to win pin money or a few extra pennies for the household budget. And you should see how they take to the races. Just like a duck to water."

"That's a new angle," said Studs, smiling.

"Most of them make piker bets of fifty cents, but that all

adds up in the end. In fact, I'm thinking of lowering my limit to a quarter minimum bet on week days. If I do that, I won't only be helping myself, I'll be giving plenty of people who've been socked by the depression a chance to keep their heads a little above water by winning on the races."

"Studs, have you set a date for your marriage yet?" Loretta asked, looking at him. Studs, glanced away from her scrutinizing eyes, thinking that maybe both of them were thinking of when he and Catherine would be living together just as she and Phil were: the possibility of his kid sister thinking of such things in connection with him made him feel kind of queer.

"Oh, sometime early next year, I guess," he said.

"Catherine's a sweet kid. And, Studs, I consider this a real compliment when I say that I think you're getting as good a wife as I got."

"Go on with you," Loretta said, blushing, and then throwing a smile at Phil.

"She is so natural and spontaneous, too. I like her," Loretta said.

"Yes, I like her," Studs said in his clipped manner, but he wasn't sure if Loretta really meant what she said and wasn't just sugaring over a catty feeling about Catherine; he felt that maybe Fritzie thought her kind of common.

"Studs, let me give you some advice. Don't go up in an airplane on your honeymoon. I did. I got dizzy and sick as a dog," Phil said, a smile of reminiscence on his fat, contented face.

"I got so afraid. I screamed outlandishly when we went up, I saw the ground getting farther and farther away, and all the time I kept thinking suppose we fall," Loretta added.

"It might be fun," Studs said, succumbing to the temptation of acting devil-may-care.

"You can try. Never again for me, though. When we were landing, I said to myself, 'Phil, you're a lad who was born to strut your stuff with your feet solid on the ground, and not with the clouds mussing your hair.' "

"Gee, it was funny, thinking about it after we came down. It was like getting terribly scared on a roller coaster. I agree with Phil, though, never again for me. If I went up again, I know I'd be so petrified that I'd faint."

They smiled politely.

"So you're joining the Christys, huh, Studs?" Phil remarked after an interval of silence.

"Yes, I guess it's about time."

"I wish I'd known soon enough. I'd gone through with you.

I guess now I'll have to wait until the next initiation. I want to get into the same council as you do," Phil said.

"I think I'll be in condition to play in the baseball league a year from this summer," Studs said, noting the surprise that came into Phil's face.

"Studs, you really should take care of yourself," Loretta said.

"I am, I'm feeling better than I've been in a long time."

"I know. Mother told me you were turned down by an insurance company because of your heart and were going to join the Order of Christopher because of the insurance, and now you talk about playing baseball. Mother, you know, is more worried over you than she lets on."

"My heart's going to get better. That insurance company doctor was just too damn finicky," Studs protested, his pallid face flushing, a sense of humiliation driving a river of shame through his mind.

"William, stop being so foolish!" Loretta said to him as if he were a little boy who had angered her.

"I tell you, Fritzie, that this heart condition is probably not so bad as you think it."

"I was talking to Mother and she told me it's an enlarged heart and it is, too, dangerous."

"Have it your own way, but we'll see."

"Yes, if you live to tell the tale."

"By the way, Studs, how's Martin?" Phil quickly asked.

"Pretty good. He's gotten to be quite a cocky kid, though, full of wisecracks. You know how a kid his age gets," Studs answered.

"Martin's so cute. The last time I saw him he was telling me all about a dance he went to and the trouble he had with his girl. And he was so sweet. And he kept saying, 'She's a kicker.' I didn't know what he meant, so I asked him. He looked at me as if I were so hopeless, and said he meant she was a good dancer. I could have just kissed him."

"Why didn't you? As long as he's your brother, I won't protest. I'll even not object to first cousins," Phil said.

"He might have been embarrassed," Loretta said, smiling at Phil.

"Regular flapper, huh, Studs, she even has to flirt with her husband," Phil said with affectionate irony, nodding at her.

"Yes, and her brothers," Studs said.

"Oh, is that so?" she bantered.

"How about the kid, though, Studs, is he still hitting the bottle?" asked Phil.

"Well, sometimes, I guess, but maybe it won't hurt him."

"Studs, you should try and talk to him because you could do it better than Dad. Martin's always looked up to you, and you could impress him."

"He looks down on me now. I was trying to tell him a few things the other night and he just acted as if I was Foxy Grandpa and there wasn't any hope for me," Studs said, and after they had laughed, he continued with vanity creeping into his voice. "Of course, what I think is that a little drink now and then is a good thing as long as you don't overdo it the way I did."

"Studs, I'm awfully glad you've learned to be sensible about it."

Studs turned quickly toward her, nettled, but Phil was speaking.

"Well, dear, we were just kids in the old days and didn't see life the same as we do now."

A hot one, Studs thought sardonically.

"Ever see anybody from Fifty-eighth?" he asked.

"I see Red and his wife nearly every Sunday at Church."

"Phil ushers now at mass," Loretta said.

"He's talking nothing but politics these days."

"Who do you think'll win, Thompson or Cermak?"

"Cermak, of course. The Republicans have ruined the city."

"Oh, let's not talk about that. All I ever hear discussed nowadays is politics or hard times. Isn't there anything else to talk about?"

"Well, dear, you know men like to discuss the issues of the day," Phil said.

"I know it, only if people wouldn't bother their heads so much about it, and if they wouldn't be so pessimistic and always expecting the worst, maybe they'd be better off. If you think of the worst, you'll get it, and if you think of the best, you'll have more chance of getting it. I really believe that. It's called Telepathy, and Fran and I are going downtown to a lecture about it," Loretta said.

"There might be something to it," Phil said profoundly.

"Uhhuh!" Studs grunted weightily.

"You know, Studs, a lot of fellows I've known from Fifty-eighth Street and from the old days at Louise Nolan's dance hall are hard up. Many of them have come around to see me asking for jobs."

"I suppose so."

"And, hell, I can't do anything for 'em, much as I'd like to. You see, for the protection I get from the law I've got to take care of all the fellows who are sent to me from the Hall. I

hire all my men that way. Every time I've got to hire a new
man, I call up and they send me somebody. I got to keep out
of trouble myself, you know."

"So that's the way it's run, huh?"

"Yeah! But here, Studs, have another cigarette," Phil said,
approaching him.

"Thanks."

"Another thing, Studs. I've been thinking a lot about the
World's Fair we're going to have in '33. That's going to be
a great thing for business and the city, isn't it?"

"Yes," Studs answered after studious reflection.

"By then I hope we'll be sitting pretty."

"But, Phil, dear, if we want to have money saved up then,
or ever, we really ought to save. You know we've been spending
a dreadful amount of money."

"Yes, I guess you're right. You know, Studs, after you get
married, money goes faster than you think. That car we
bought, furniture, clothes, and the upkeep of a home and
bookies is damn high. Cops, politicians, high salaries, because
you know, as I just said, all the jobs I have to give out
are politicians' jobs."

"Yes, we'll have to economize. And Phil, dear, I'm going
to watch Marie. I've been letting her do the buying and I'm
sure she is stealing on me. You can never trust a nigger."

"I guess not."

"And she gets so much better treatment than most maids
do. Why, Fran is shocked that I pay her eight and a half
dollars a week these days when maids are so easy to get."

Studs yawned. His glance, drifting toward Loretta, caught
hers. She smiled, an understanding smile.

"But Studs doesn't care about such things, do you,
Studs?" Loretta said.

"Let's have some music," Phil said, dialing in upon
the crooning of *Just a Gigolo.* Studs leaned back in his chair,
bored during the announcement between songs. He wondered
whether when he married Catherine, would they spend many
evenings like this, getting fed up, talking just to make talk. And
his stock, down four points, eighty times four made three
twenty lost if he sold it. Suppose his father asked for the
two thousand bucks. Could Phil loan him the difference?

"Well, Phil, I suppose if things keep rolling your way,
you'll be coming out one of these days with a bank account
to choke an elephant."

"No danger, Studs. I got lots of expenses. But now that
we're settled, and got our car and furniture, I hope to save a
little."

"Fran and Carroll are much better off than we are," Loretta said.

It dawned on Studs. Preparing excuses in advance. He checked an angry impulse to sound off, and thought that yes, Phil was spending everything. He could just remember the Jewboy who used to be so tight in the old days and sold clothes to all his friends, he could just see him spending all his dough. He yawned.

"And now I present to you Mr. Horgath Kelson, the internationally renowned economist."

"Ladies and gentlemen, these days many people, from the man on the corner, to radicals, politicians who are amongst the outs rather than the ins, and even a few business leaders, are issuing gloomy statements. If we were to believe these, they would convince us all that we are whistling in a graveyard."

"Oh, get some music, Loretta."

"Yes, but let's just get what he's got to say. He's a famous man," Phil said.

"Who is he?"

"Oh, he runs some kind of service advising business men. I've heard of him."

"I never did before," Studs said.

"To the contrary, I would say that 1931 is going to be the year of opportunity. This is no pipe dream. Statistics show us that business reached its lowest point on the index in December, 1930, and since then there has been a gradual improvement. All indications show us that within six months we will be again at a peak. That's why I believe that many who were trapped in crashing stock markets can, by buying now before the upturn reaches its full swing, recoup their loses."

"Phil, darling, isn't that enough of it?"

"Yes, dear," Phil said, arising to get a new station.

> *Gee! it's great after bein' out late,*
> *Walkin' my baby back home.*

Um, Studs thought, better keep those stocks. In six months they'd make him rich.

"What he said sounds hopeful," Studs said.

"Yeah," Phil muttered.

"Maybe a fellow with some dough could clean up if he bought some stocks."

"Well, maybe, but I'd feel better with my dough safe in the bank, drawing its three per. I don't know much about stocks, but that's why you won't find me sinking my money in a racket I don't know much about. When it comes to such propositions, safety first is my middle name."

> *Arm in arm over meadow and farm,*
> *Walkin' my baby back home.*

Studs felt superior to Phil. Phil was a pinching piker, wouldn't take a chance. Even after hearing that economist, he wouldn't. Well, Studs would. He was clinging to that stock until it paid him back plenty.

"Coffee, Studs?"

"All right."

Loretta went to the kitchen to make coffee, Phil smiled affably. Studs returned the smile. Piker, wouldn't take a chance. No one would ever say that about Studs Lonigan.

II

"Well, old timer, I'm one boy who's going to be full of sweet contentment when the day's work is over," Studs said to old Mort over the restaurant table: his back ached and his arms were sore.

"Your dad wants us to finish up today and get cleaned up tomorrow with only a half a day's work. We got to step because that last bedroom is pretty big," Mort said, chewing on a hunk of pork chop, his face weakened, wrinkled, worn.

The thought of the afternoon's work made Studs gloomy. How in Christ's name would he get through it! He thought that he might lay off and go home. But no, that would be letting the old man down.

"Lad, I'm gettin' old, and it's gettin' pretty damn hard. There's not a lot left in me. And I was the fellow who used to think that when I reached my present age I'd take it easy, have a little saved up, and would have my kids to take care of me and my old woman. Well, a man doesn't get what he hopes for, not by a damn sight. Only one of my boys workin' and him doing part-time work."

"The old man's worrying his pants off these days," Studs said.

"Don't I know it, lad! Just now when business should be best, there's not a thing stirrin'."

Studs motioned to the waitress and, catching her eye, pointed to an empty coffee cup. Needed it to wake up for the afternoon grind.

"Well, things better get better!" Studs said, thinking how

yesterday his stock had dropped to nineteen. Goddamn it, they had to.

He looked at Mort, struck by the signs of age in the old man. His face like a map with wrinkles: hair, all gray: thinner, too, than he'd used to be. Studs wondered how there could be any strength left in him. Studs relaxed in his chair, still tired from the morning's work. And hell, five, six, eight years ago, he'd been able to go out on a drunk and work the next day without feeling the effects as much as he did now.

"Did you read about that bank on the west side failing? I know what that means. Poor people, workingmen like myself, lose everything they got, saved from years of work. It's goddamn tough when a poor man saves a little money and thinks that he's got something put aside for his old age, and then the bank goes bust. It's goddamn rotten. And I suppose the crooked bankers who stole all the money will go free."

"Tough tiddy, all right. Think many of them will fail?"

"Lad, I hope not. If they do, the people won't stand for it. There'll be a revolution or something."

"Mort, the whole shooting match puzzles me," Studs said, sipping coffee. "I don't understand it. I guess there was a depression right after the war, but I didn't pay much attention to it."

"It wasn't anywheres near as frightful as this one."

"I was younger and the old man was doing better. But I never saw anything like this," Studs said.

"I remember the panics of 1907, and 1893, and they were bad. But not as bad as now. I don't know how many millions of men there's on the streets."

"How did the depression in those years end?"

"Well, they got to end. There's action, and then reaction, and then action again. When a thing goes up, it has to come down, and then when it comes down, it has to go up again."

"Mort, what do you think of the stock market?"

As Mort shrugged his shoulders, Studs saw by the restaurant clock that it was a quarter to one. Fifteen minutes more, and work. Fifteen minutes was damn short . . . and then . . . Christ, if the day was only over and he was home, just sitting doing nothing or reading the newspaper, resting. If he was as tired when he got home as he was now, he'd have to call off his date with Catherine.

"I never had much money to fool around with stocks. And I'm no good at figuring, and stocks involve a lot of figuring."

"Maybe it isn't the thing to fool around with."

"If you got the money, it might be all right, and then again it might be crooked. Nearly everything in the country seems to be crooked these days, and banks aren't safe, a man's job isn't sure. So I guess if a man has anything it's best to thank the Lord for what he's got and not want more."

"Maybe you're right, Mort," Studs said reflectively, looking again at the clock: ten to one.

"It takes money to make money, of course, but I don't know. If I had anything, I'd rather hang on to it. But I'm a poor man. I tried to save, but it was no use, and my wife sick for so many years, and then the funeral expenses when she died, and the kids I had to raise and educate. And now one of my boys had to move in on me with his wife and two babies because he was evicted."

"I know how it is," Studs said.

As they rose, Studs laid a dime tip under his plate. He lit a cigarette and paid the check.

"Christ, I wish the day's work was done," he said.

"We'll get it done, all right. I never fell down on a job for Paddy Lonigan yet, and I'm too old a dog to be learning new tricks. I told him we'd finish today and by God, we will."

Studs noticed that Mort was a little stooped, and had about him the manner of a man weakening with age. Christ, would he become like that some day? Or like his father? Or wouldn't he even live long enough for that? The doctor turning him down for the insurance company. . . . Thinking of that, he hastily shot the butt of his half-smoked cigarette. His body was heavy, sluggish.

"Say, what's the crowd?" he said in sudden surprise, pointing at a crowd around the corner ahead, seeing a policeman whose car caught and reflected glints of sunlight.

"Must be the bank or else an accident."

"Let's step on it and see," Studs said, a sense of eagerness and curiosity tingling him into an energetic state.

"I don't see that it's worth hurrying about. We'll come to it."

"It's something funny, all right. Cops there, too," Studs said, walking a pace ahead of Mort.

Approaching, he saw that the crowd was milling about a bank, and that a line of people cut out from the bank entrance onto the sidewalk. He felt the same as if he were running to a fire. Excitement. He saw that there were a number of policemen and that people in the crowd were talking and gesticulating.

"Watch out," Mort called, pulling him back from the cartrack.

He heard the dinging gong of the street car and saw one

sweep past him. His heart beat rapidly. He held his breath in an after-fear.

"Got to watch yourself, lad."

He looked ahead and to his side for traffic.

"Close," he said, sighing, the terror of being run over clinging.

"Robbers," a thin and wizened man of about forty-five said loudly as they stepped onto the curb.

Studs edged through the crowd, squeezing close to the line of people, crushed together, waiting to go forward, held in order by police who swung and twirled their menacing nightsticks in the air. His eye ran up and down the faces, anxious men and women. He saw a Jewish woman, frantically biting her fingernails, and beside her a powerful man in his prime with a pale face, nervous eyes, almost trembling lips. Almost crapping in their pants, all right, he reflected. Maybe his dough was, after all, just as safe in stock as the banks? Hell, if it went on like this where would a guy's dough be safe? If he kept it home he might be robbed. If he socked it in a bank, the bank might go under. If he bought stock, the market might crash. Christ, what a goofy world it was becoming.

"Oh, God! And my mother home sick. Oh, God, what will I do if I don't get my money?" a middle-aged woman said, her eyes watery, her hair dishevelled under her black felt hat.

"I guess it's a bank going on the fritz, all right," Studs said to Mort, who had edged in beside him.

"There's no trouble. People just get excited. Irresponsible people, like the Reds, spread these rumors around, to cause trouble," a fellow near Studs said.

"You work all your life and put your money in the bank and dese robbers, dese robbers, take it. You woirk all your life, eh, and then you say no, maybe it's nothin' just excitement. Yah," a tall dour-faced, red-mustached foreigner in overalls exclaimed.

The fellow gave the foreigner a look of contempt and turned away.

"Nottin'! Nottin'! for a working man to lose his money. Yah, nottin'?"

Studs wondered was the foreigner in overalls a Red. He didn't like him because he looked too much like the type who became bald-headed crabby janitors.

"You got anything in it?" Studs asked.

"Working men don't have much money," the fellow said, growling, and Studs thought that he had a lot of crust shooting his bazoo off when it wasn't any skin off his teeth.

He noticed people squeezing out of the bank, and the line of people crushing forward. He and Mort edged toward the bank entrance, and they watched a gray-haired woman, with a creased, rough-skinned peasant face, a black shawl over her head, edge out with the blustering assistance of a policeman. Crisp money stuck from the edges of the bank book which she clutched fiercely in gnarled fingers.

"This way, Mother," a burly, ruddy-faced policeman said, taking her arm and leading her across the street.

"Lucky old bitch!" Studs heard someone in the waiting line grumble.

"Hot roasted peanuts. Get something for your money while you can. Hot roasted peanuts!" a greasy man, wearing a white soda-jerker's coat, shouted.

The crowd seemed constantly to be increasing, and the police shoved and pushed in their efforts to preserve order. Again and again Studs caught the glances of fright on people's faces, the nervousness they revealed by biting their lips, furtively looking about, grimacing. Something was wrong somewhere, all right, and he guessed these people would have a goddamn legitimate squawk if they lost their dough.

A well-dressed man, with a sleek face and a white carnation in his buttonhole, emerged from the bank, smiling.

"Nothing wrong. Only a scare. Why, even a priest got up on a table in the bank and spoke, telling everybody to be calm and leave their money in there where it's safe. He waved his bank book to show that he was leaving his parish funds in, and that's where I left all my dough," Studs heard the fellow say in a blustering, self-confident manner.

"You tink so?" a wiry little hook-nosed man asked.

"Sure thing, brother. Look," the fellow with the carnation in his buttonhole said, waving his bank book.

A cheer went up. Studs was caught in the middle of a wave of pushing people. He squeezed himself slowly to a curb edge and saw an armored car and four armed guards escorting two men carrying money through a lane to the entrance made by the police. Studs smiled. The bank maybe wouldn't fail, and these people wouldn't lose their dough. The fewer banks that failed, the better off everything would be all around.

Mort touched his sleeve and they walked away, another cheer arising behind them.

"Fierce! Fierce! Money makes people into dogs," Mort said.

"Hell on a lot of 'em if the bank fails. But maybe it won't.

They were bringing in more money, and I just heard a fellow saying that a priest in a parish around here was in the bank speaking to the people, telling them to leave their dough in."

"I hope so. I know what it means to people to be poor in their old age."

"Well, it's more than I can make out," Studs said, shaking his head.

"And it's a quarter after one. We got to hustle," Mort said.

Studs felt sluggish and tired again. Jesus, if the day was only over.

III

"Did you get finished, Bill?"

"Yes, Dad," Studs called from the hall, entering in his paint-splotched work clothes, tired.

"I'm glad of that. You know, by getting done today, you and Mort saved me some money, and these days I got to figure on every possible economy," Lonigan said as Studs walked into the parlor and slumped in an easy chair.

"There was a run on a bank on Seventy-fifth. I forget the name."

"Must be the Chemical Deposits. Did it fail?"

"No, because on my way home I asked a cop who was standing in front of it, and he said it hadn't. I asked him what had caused the run, and he said he thought the Reds had spread a false rumor. The bank officials gave every depositor who didn't take his dough out, a carnation to put in his buttonhole, the cop told me."

"What the hell good would that do the people?"

"I don't know. And the cop was a mick, and he was proud because a Catholic priest, pastor of one of the parishes near the bank, saved it by getting on a table and telling everybody to have confidence and go home. He left all his parish funds in," Studs said.

"Those damn Reds bellyaching and agitating in times like these when everybody ought to get right to it to help keep the ship afloat! And, Bill, I also heard the Reds were egging on the niggers in the black belt. That's sheer dynamite." Lonigan gritted his teeth. "Anyway, I'm glad I haven't any money tied up in that bank. But I've got a couple of bills due from fellows out there in that vicinity. I suppose, if the bank crashes, these guys will claim they lost all they own, whether they did or not, and squirm out of paying me. I lost three thousand bucks already from fellows who've pulled that gag on me. But even so, I collected some money today at last from a guy on the west side who's been welshing payment on a job I done for him six months ago. And he promised more next month." Lonigan seemed to drift into brooding. Suddenly, he .continued, "Collecting bills these days is sure one hell of a job."

Mrs. Lonigan appeared with a glass of milk, and Studs drank half of it in one gulp.

"William, you shouldn't drink so fast!"

"How were Phil and Loretta when you saw them last night?"

"Oh, pretty good."

"Phil say how business was going with him?"

"Pretty good."

"Well, that makes me glad. He's a smart Jew, I mean a smart boy. It's a relief on a man's mind to know that his two sons-in-law are getting along."

Studs was distressed with fear that his old man was going to get confidential. His old man would, when he got that way, lay parts of himself open, bare, and he would seem so weak that Studs didn't like it. And suddenly he was tempted to speak about his stock.

"What did you say, Bill?"

"Nothing, I was just going to say it's pretty damn swell Phil and Carroll are clicking so well."

"Yes, oh yes," Lonigan said.

"Well, I guess I'll clean up for supper," Studs said, leaving his father sitting immobile.

IV

"I'm still tempted to go along and watch you tomorrow," Lonigan said, arising from the supper table.

"Patrick, why don't you?"

"Maybe I will, Mary."

"I wonder if it is going to be like a fraternity initation?" Martin said, dropping a crumpled napkin beside his plate and pushing his chair back.

"Martin!" Lonigan said in an injured tone. "You know that the Order of Christopher is more serious than a bunch of high-school kids."

"William, I'm so glad you're joining," the mother said, while Martin smirked superciliously.

"I've seen a few initiations in my time and they were beauts," Lonigan chuckled.

"And won't I laugh if Studs comes home with his face full of lumps."

"Martin, get that out of your head. It's the wrong slant,"

Lonigan said ponderously. "The Order of Christopher isn't a gang of barbarians. Nearly every leading Catholic of importance in this country is a Christy."

"I was just kidding."

"But, Martin, the Order of Christopher is no more the kind of a thing that you should kid about than your religion is the kind of thing you would mock."

"Anyway, I hope that I'm not letting myself in for something," Studs said.

"Bill, that's not exactly the best way to express it. It's not something you just let yourself in for." A chuckle seemed to roll out of him, and he beamed. "But, golly, I've seen some initiations that were beauts, I've half a mind to see them put you through tomorrow."

"Father, do go. It'll take your mind off other worries," Mrs. Lonigan said.

"But if I did, I'd miss Father Moylan on the radio," Lonigan said, turning into the hallway and adding, without glancing back, "I'll think about it."

"Got a date with the sweetie tonight?" Martin asked, yawning.

"Yeh," Studs gutturally replied.

"William, do come home early, because you're going to communion in the morning and you must be up early."

"I know it. Catherine and I are going to confession, and then after we have a little bite of something I'll come home."

"That's fine, son. Do come home, because you need your eight hours' rest," she said, disappearing with an armful of dishes.

"William, you're a good boy," Martin mocked, turning his back on Studs to leave the room.

"Can that wise stuff before you get your puss slapped!" Studs barked before he realized what he was saying.

"Oh, you will, will you!" Martin retorted with a voice of challenging sarcasm.

"Yes!" Studs said, hoping it would go no further, and instantly so tense that he was short of breath. Martin was getting too wise for his own health anyway, and sooner or later, for his own good, some of that sass would have to be slapped out of him.

Martin lip-farted.

"Think you're tough and wise!" Studs said, moving around the table toward Martin, who stood by the hallway entry, sneering, nonchalant with his hands in his pockets.

"Tougher than you any day in the week."

"Listen, can that crap while you're all together!" Studs said, tempering his voice to give Martin an opening for dropping the quarrel.

"I'm all together and I'll stay that way," Martin loudly rasped.

"Boys! Boys!" Mrs. Lonigan called nervously from the kitchen.

"I'm telling you to cut it out."

"Cut what out? Make me!"

Studs shoved Martin slightly, and he was rocked backward by a hard clip on the jaw. Martin went into him with two swinging fists, and Studs, surprised off-balance, slammed against a chair, which catapulted to the floor. Groping and grabbing under a rain of blows, he worked himself into the protection of a clinch.

"Come on, you has-been," Martin sneered, freeing himself from Studs' arms.

"Patrick!" Mrs. Lonigan screamed, rushing in from the kitchen.

"Yes," he called from the parlor.

Another chair crashed. Martin freed himself from the clinch, and Studs drove up an uppercut. Martin grimaced and flailed into Studs. Breathing heavily, with no real heart for the fight, Studs took a stiff right on the jaw, a numbing sensation spread to his head, and he had a sickening headache.

"Pat, there's a lot of snotty young punks these days whose talk is louder than their actions," Martin said, curling his lips, pushing Studs back against the radiator, slamming him on the ear.

Mrs. Lonigan screamed shrilly, dropped to the floor like a sack.

His ear stung, hot with a buzzing sensation, and, impotently infuriated, Studs edged away from the radiator, knowing that he had used himself up. He tried to stall off by waving his left fist before him. Martin pounced down on him. A wild left punch grazed his jaw, and he clinched. Martin shoved him back, as if he were powerless. He knew that he was whipped, humiliatingly, and that he could not quit. Hatred flared in him, and again the nausea in his head, his pounding heart, jerking breath, tired arms and shoulders, stung ear, hurt jaw, his hatred and his will were vain. Martin was on him again. Studs strove to set himself in the in-fighting, grunted, maneuvered to work his shoulder up against Martin's chin, and almost crumbled from a sharp pain as Martin smashed down with kidney punch.

"Cut it out!" Lonigan bellowed.

He saw Mrs. Lonigan, pallid and unconscious on the floor, and pointed. The sons, surprised by his command, followed his finger, staring helpless, guilty. The three of them converged over the prostrate Mrs. Lonigan.

"A fine thing to do to your mother."

They sat Mrs. Lonigan on a chair and awkwardly revived her.

"Oh, God! Why do I deserve this? My own boys, my own flesh and blood, fighting under my sacred roof! Oh!"

Lonigan's lips compressed: shaking his mortified head slowly from side to side, depressed more than angry.

"I'm ashamed of you boys," he said, and neither of them dared look him in the eye.

"He was too wise," Studs mumbled unconvincingly.

"I'm not being pushed around. He can't even take a joke," Martin stuttered.

"Hell of a way to take a joke, if you ask me, knocking each other all over the dining room."

"He started it," Martin said.

"I did like hell," Studs flung back, his side stiff and hurt from the kidney punch, his breathing still too rapid.

"Come on, now, shake hands and call it quits!" Lonigan said as Studs turned aside and winced with the stabbing pain still remaining from that kidney punch.

The two sons looked at each other, their faces drawn.

"I haven't anything against him, but nobody's shoving me around," Martin said, he and Studs looking at each other, their faces drawn.

"No hard feelings," Studs said lifelessly, their limp hands clasping.

Lonigan glanced apologetically down at his wife, who sat with head lowered, hair dishevelled, quivering as she sobbed.

In the bathroom, Studs studied his face in the mirror, momentarily pleased that there were no marks on his face, except for the redness of his ear. But that sock in the ear had told. His ear burned yet. And he was sore from that kidney punch. His heart pounded on him and he was sick with a headache from jolting punches. He felt all in, just like a has-been.

Still observing himself in the mirror, he tried to convince himself that it was not important. His pride rose, mangled, torn, stepped on, hurting him even more than Martin's fists had. Treated as a has-been, completely dismissed by his kid brother, the same way Jack Sharkey would dismiss some broken-down palooka who didn't count.

He cursed Martin, and, unhappy, lit a cigarette. Again he

told himself that it wasn't important. No matter how tough you were, there was always somebody tougher. It wasn't important. And it hadn't been a fair fight because he wasn't in condition to battle. He'd like to have seen Martin get wise before he'd gotten that attack of pneumonia and his heart had gone flooey on him! It was no shame to be beaten when you were in bad health. And even so, he might still have slapped Martin down if he hadn't been taken by surprise.

But he knew he was kidding himself. He knew that he had had fear and humiliation punched into him by his kid brother, and he knew that Martin knew it.

You're the real stuff! he told his image in the mirror with self-pitying sarcasm.

He wanted to get out of the house. He didn't know how he was going to face his kid brother. Reluctant to leave the bathroom, he paced nervously to and fro in the narrow space between the window and the bathtub, rapidly puffing on a cigarette, feeling cramped, almost as if he were in jail. Standing with his ear to the door, he heard murmuring sounds from his parents in the dining room.

If it had only not happened. Grimacing, he violently flung his cigarette butt into the toilet and pulled the chain, listening to the flushing sound, dreamy and wistful, glad that he had something to distract him.

He tried to frown at himself in the mirror, and jerked away from it. Sitting on the edge of the bathtub, he remembered his fights with Weary Reilley and Red, telling himself that Studs Lonigan in his prime would have massacred a regiment of punks like Martin. He laughed at himself. What did it prove? It wasn't important. He should walk out of the bathroom, face Martin, treat it for what it was, a thing of no account. And he continued sitting on the edge of the bathtub, leaning forward, that sick throb in his head and the stiffness in his side persisting, hearing the beat of his heart. Rolling his tongue around the inside of his mouth, he felt a sting when his tongue touched a cut on the inside of his jaw.

Christ, but he hated Martin. He saw himself punching the holy living Jesus out of him, battering him without mercy into swollen and bloody unconsciousness. He knew he shouldn't have such feelings, and he should try and put himself into a right mood for confession. And no matter what had just happened, Studs Lonigan would go on living. But his kid brother had beaten him, and he imagined him revenging that licking, wading into Martin, punching with right, left, right, left. . . . He noticed by his watch that it was seven-thirty. He jumped to his feet, quickly washed.

Breathing rapidly with the tension within him, he opened the bathroom door. In the bedroom, Martin stood carelessly in front of the mirror, knotting a black-and-white striped necktie. Whistling a jazz tune, he turned. Meeting one another's eyes, they glanced aside, shame-faced.

"What time is it, Studs?"

"Seven-thirty."

"I'll have to be stepping on it, I guess."

"Me, too."

Martin put on his jacket coat and overcoat.

"So long," Studs said gutturally, buttoning a clean white shirt.

V

Abashed, Studs stepped into the parlor. Shutting off the radio, Lonigan cast a pained glance at his son.

"Bill, I'm very sorry."

"Well, Dad, I'm sorry, too."

"You got to be a father, I guess, to really understand what such things can do to a man."

"Well . . . I didn't want it to happen."

"Bill, a great many things happen in life that we don't want to."

"We made up."

"Fine. But, Bill, I'm sorry this happened between you and Martin. It's an evil sign when brothers fight and snarl at each other like dogs under their parents' own roof."

Goddamn, Christ, if he'd only let Martin's cracks pass off and had just acted sensibly. Why such false pride about whether or not he was afraid of his kid brother? He'd shown the world Studs Lonigan wasn't yellow and hadn't needed to be having a false pride at this late date.

"Bill, I know you and Martin won't let such an unfortunate thing happen again. Your mother and me, we're kind of getting along now, and these things hit us pretty hard."

Studs looked away. He knew that he ought to be hustling away, and he stood with his eyes fixed blankly on the wall. He wanted to say something more, and . . . what?

"Better go say goodbye to your mother and try to make her feel a little better."

"I will, Dad."

He walked slowly out to the kitchen, troubling over what he would say to his mother.

"Mom!" he muttered, seeing her bent over a pan full of dishes.

"Yes, son," she said, turning toward him, eyes still raw from crying.

"I'm sorry."

"Two sons of mine," she said, turning back to her dishes, "fighting like wild animals under a roof that God has blessed." She dreamily picked up a plate and set it down to her left. "My own flesh and blood, fighting like Cain and Abel. It's a sin punishable by God."

"It was an accident, Mom, and we didn't mean it. We made up, and both of us are sorry."

As she wiped away a tear with her soiled apron, she looked old to him. He guessed she must at least be around fifty-five. Christ! . . . He felt lousy doing this to her and the old man. He guessed, too, that they wouldn't have such an awfully long time more to live. How did a person feel when he knew that in five or ten years he would probably be dead?

"Son, I'd have given my right arm not to have let it happen."

"It won't any more, Mom," he said with hollow reassurance.

Anxious to get out, he quickly put his arm around her, gave her a pecking kiss, patted her back.

"Goodbye, Mom, and please don't worry or feel bad."

She turned a weak, unhappy smile on him and sniffled.

"Be good, son, and come home early."

"Yes, Mom."

He thought of how this thing would make them feel lousy all night.

"Goodbye," he called from the front door, and he closed it, feeling like a heel.

CHAPTER SIX

I

"I wonder what it's going to be like outside there?" a round-shouldered fellow said.

"I hope we're not going to be left shanghaied in here much longer," a wiry fellow on Studs' left remarked.

"It can't start too soon to satisfy me. My dogs have had enough wear already," Studs said, leaning against the back wall in the crowded little room that buzzed with talk.

"It doesn't particularly reflect to the credit of the Order of Christopher when the best waiting-room they can find for us is a sardine can like this stuffy hole. Hell, we haven't even got enough room to breathe in here," a well-dressed, beefy, middle-aged man sourly declared.

"Fellow, this is an initiation and an initiation is an initiation, isn't it?"

"Me, I no lika this," a swarthy Italian said.

"Me, neither, but an initiation is an initiation, and you can't expect it to be nothing else."

"I don't mind the waiting so much, but what I don't like is this waiting-room. How about you, stranger?" the well-dressed man asked, looking at Studs.

"The whole business is all Greek to me," Studs said.

He noticed slanting rays of sunlight cutting down through the dusty air from the small, rectangular and unwashed window above him. The sunbeams made him feel how it was a pleasant March Sunday outside, and here he was cooped up, and he didn't know what was going to happen at this initiation. Yawning, his eyelids seemed heavy. He wished that he'd had enough sense to have made an earlier break from Catherine last night and gotten a decent night's rest. His eyes fell absently on a group of fellows a few feet ahead of him, who seemed to be quite at home, talking and laughing, not so anxious as he and as most of these other candidates were. He wished he'd had a friend along with him. It would make it easier.

"I wonder what it's going to be like?"

"Well, the degree they put us through this mornin', it was nothin', I came expecting to take a lot, just like college boys do when they get initiated into one of their fraternities, but this mornin' degree, it was nothin'."

"That's why I feel so edgy. They probably saved this afternoon to give us the works."

"Hell, they can't do no more than kill you, and they won't do that."

"Whatever they're going to do, I wish they'd get started on it and not keep us here until the Fourth of July."

Them's my sentiments, Studs silently told himself, feeling a dryness in his throat. He thought of the morning's event. The mass with a church crowded tight with candidates and members of the Order of Christopher. What Father Gilhooley would have called an edifying sight. So many Catholic men from all walks of life, rich and poor, young and old, marching to the altar rail in a body, receiving Communion, like true Knights of the Church. Seeing that, being one of those in it, he had been proud of his Church, proud to be entering an order of men so closely connected with the Church. Remembering his catechism from grammar school, he told himself that the Church was One, Holy, Catholic, and Apostolic, built upon the rock of Peter, and that it would last until Judgment

Day. Yes, he was glad, damn glad, that he had been born on the right side of the fence.

"Me, I'm in the laundry business. Sure, I drive a laundry truck for the Vincent Laundry. I pick up much less laundry these days than I did a year ago, and my commissions have been going down," a red-faced lad near Studs said.

"I'm in the insurance business. I'm getting as many policies as I ever did, but the collections are not as steady, and it's like pulling teeth getting money out of policy holders. That reminds me, here's my card in case you ever want any insurance. Since we're both going to be Christys, we might as well help each other whenever we can."

"And any time you want any laundry done, well, give us a shot at it. . . ."

"Say, they don't seem any too keen on wanting us, from the time they're taking," a dark, frowning man said.

"Maybe they got to figure it all out. When I was in high school, we had a frat, and before each initiation we had to figure out what we'd do."

"This is different. The Christys aren't high-school kids, and joining the Christys is not like joining a bunch of high-school kids."

"Well, I didn't say it was. I was only saying maybe that's the explanation, and then again, maybe it isn't."

Yes, it had been a kind of a thrill this morning, Studs told himself. Walking to the altar he had felt how great the Church was, and he had seen that he was a part of it. And if the rest of the initiation was no worse than what they'd gotten at the degree they'd taken in the morning, it wouldn't be so bad. But when they'd been marched into the dark hall with the fellow in a red robe standing in candle light, he had gotten a creepy feeling that seemed to tickle and shiver up his spine. And that fellow in the red robe, whoever he was, he had sure talked like a hard-boiled baby. The minute he'd opened his trap, Studs had felt sure that the whole gang of them were in for some rough going. The snotty way he had called out names. And then when the candidates whose names had been called out would answer, the way the fellow in the red robe had asked a question from the catechism. He wondered, would the rest of the initiation be as clever?

"I played forward two years with the Mary Our Mother heavyweights in the Catholic High School League, and I'm going to try out for the Council team next season. Basketball is a great game, and in the Christopher League you'll see some of the fastest and snappiest basketball that's played anywhere in this city."

That fellow in the red robe, though, was smart, acted as if he might be a lawyer. If he wasn't one, he sure ought to be. Some of those who had been questioned had given the right answers from the catechism, and this fellow had tripped them up with questions until they changed their answers to the wrong ones. Studs smiled, remembering how the fellow had lit into those who had denied their right answers. What a wicked tongue he wielded.

"I wanted to go to high school myself, and play baseball, but my old man worked in a machine shop and lost his hand. They said it was his own fault, and he didn't get much dough out of the accident, and so I had to go to work when I graduated from Saint Catherine's grammar school. But the Order runs a commercial school, and I think I'll go to it nights and take up accounting, if it doesn't cost too much. I was good at percentage in grammar school, and I figure I ought to get on in accounting. I've got no hankering to spend the rest of my life running a machine in a button factory."

"There's not much doing in accounting. Better stick to what you got."

"Well, the way I figure is, that a little ambition won't hurt anybody."

He wished that his name had been called out this morning and he'd have been given a catechism question he could answer, like what are the attributes of the Church? And they would have all known that the fellow named William Lonigan couldn't be tripped up easily when he knew something. But it was sure damn clever. Getting them all in a dark, spooky room, questioning them on the catechism to show them that a member of the Order of Christopher should know something about the faith. Would the next degree in the initiation be as clever and as interesting?

"I'm getting fed up waiting," a young lad beside Studs said.

"I don't care what they do as long as they make it snappy," Studs said, his legs aching, that stiffness in his side from Martin's punch bothering him.

"It'll go on in time," a puffy-cheeked fellow, whose breathing caused a little whistling noise, said.

Studs thought that there was lots to the guy who breathed like an orchestra, lots of deadness, and he turned the other way so he wouldn't have to talk to the dope. Several feet away he saw a priest, surrounded by fellows, all butting in to get a word and show off. He sneered at such show-off bastards, thinking how he wasn't that kind of guy, blowing out crap by the pound to make himself look big. Still he'd like to talk to the priest. Most priests were human, and interesting to talk to, like Father Doneggan of Saint Patrick's had been. But gee, he never knew that Father Doneggan had hit the bottle, and it sure had been a surprise to him when he'd heard that Father Doneggan had left the priesthood.

"Hell, you don't call Art Shires a ball player, do you? He's just a jaw artist."

Perspiring, he felt his shirt stick and his arm pits a bit clammy. And the air was getting worse. How long, oh, tell me how long, must I wait. Can we get it now, or must we hesitate?

"You can't convince me, if you jabber till doomsday, that with the resources behind the Order of Christopher, it has any excuse for not supplying us with a better waiting-room than this crummy hole."

"Bah, it's the same as everything else, a racket. We pay our ten bucks, and then, what do they care," a blond fellow of about twenty-five said.

"Just a minute, young fellow, you're making serious charges against the Order," a gray-haired, sunken-jawed man countered.

"Well, why shouldn't I? Do you think I forked out my initiation fees to be plunked in here all afternoon without even room to wriggle my ears?"

Studs wanted to tell the fellow to wait and see, because if the Order put them in here, it must have a reason, and the men at the head of it had more brains than this fellow had, and if they had put them here it was with a reason, and the Order of Christopher couldn't be a racket. If it was a racket, Cardinals and Archbishops wouldn't tolerate it a minute.

"Give us room! Room! This man is blind," a husky voice shouted.

Amidst sudden crowding and shoving, a wave of constraint seemed to lay a band around everyone in the room. All thoughts, except curiosity and a fear lest some kind of trouble might start, were sucked out of Studs' mind. He slowly edged himself toward the fellow who had called out, and he saw a blind man cowering and trembling on the arm of a plump, dark-browed fellow in a gray suit.

"Say, I wonder what's the idea of all this?"

"That's what we're all wondering, lad."

"It's an initiation, isn't it?"

"Hell of a way to run one, letting a blind man into a crowded room like this where he could get stepped on!"

Studs slipped back to lean against the wall. Aches extended down his legs like troublesome wires, and the soles of his feet were getting sore. He mopped his face and felt sweaty.

"I hope we get out of here by Christmas," he said wearily.

II

"All right, you birds, line up!" a full-faced sergeant-at-arms in a red robe commanded before they had finished sighing with relief at his entrance.

There was a hasty and disorganized attempt to form several lines, and Studs hesitated between them.

"Get in there!" the sergeant-at-arms snapped, unceremoniously pushing a slowly responsive initiate; and Studs, catching his first good glimpse of the man, saw that he was a tough-looking customer with a hard expression and heavy brows.

"I will," came a sulky voice.

"Well, do it and shut your trap! I haven't got all day to fool around here!"

"All right!" the voice replied still with a trace of sulkiness.

"I don't like his looks," a fellow next to Studs mumbled.

"Looks hard-boiled to me!"

"Oh, so you're snotty, are you!" the sergeant-at-arms said with menacing irony.

"I can't figure why he should come here in that manner. He's acting as if he wanted to start a riot," Studs remarked to the fellow next to him who had just spoken.

"Well, if that's what he's out for, he might be accommodated," the fellow said, and Studs hoped that the initiation wouldn't be broken up by a free-for-all.

"This is a free country and you got no right to order me around like I was a coolie."

"Listen, wise boy! While you're here, do what I tell you! I don't need any instructions, so try and edify yourself with silence, because the Order is not particularly concerned with accepting loud-mouths."

"He wouldn't pull that crap on me!"

"Me, neither," Studs said in a low voice.

"All right, let's can the beefing and get going!" the fellow who had been passing remarks to Studs called out throatily, his head lowered.

"What's your name?" the sergeant-at-arms said, glaring at Studs, after having brushed through to him.

"Me?" Studs asked in surprise, unwittingly pointing his right index finger at his chest.

"Yes, you, shrimp!"

"Lonigan."

"A runt like you with an Irish name. The Holy Spirit must

certainly have deserted old Erin," he said with a contemptuous sneer, a mumble of low protest breaking out around the room.

"Why?" Studs asked, humiliated, wishing he was this baby's size, knowing he was the center of attention.

"Listen, Loogan, or whatever your name is, I don't need any help from you. If you want to hear the sound of your own voice, get up on a soap box after the ceremonies."

"I didn't say anything. It was somebody else," Studs said tensely, writhing under the insult, wondering why the loudmouth next to him, who was nearer this one's size, didn't admit that he'd made the crack.

"Get in line!" the sergeant-at-arms said, turning away, before Studs could reply.

"Don't let him put anything over on you, Shorty," an oily fellow said.

"Jesus, I was so surprised I didn't know what to say, because I hadn't batted my mouth open," Studs said, his face pallid.

And calling Studs Lonigan a *runt* and *Shorty*. God, he just wanted to break loose and start slugging right and left, jam that *runt* and *Shorty* down a lot of throats!

"Did you smell his breath? He's drunk as a soldier, if you ask me. Certainly isn't a good example to us who are new members."

"Something ought to be done about him," Studs said.

"Say, do you understand English, or are you another one of these Polacks who speak a foreign language?"

"You ain't got no right to get personal," a hurt voice replied, and another low grumble spread through the room.

"And what's your name?"

"I'm blind," a quavering voice replied.

"This man is blind, and you ought to be ashamed of yourself."

"Did I ask you for any advice?"

"But this man is blind."

"I heard you the first time! Snap in there with him—this isn't an all-day coming-out party!" the sergeant-at-arms exclaimed, turning from the blind man to edge toward the center of the room, where he frowned, placed his hands on his hips, and raised his voice. "We're going out of here to get started with the ceremonies of this degree when you fellows cooperate with me, and prove that you're at least half-intelligent and can understand the English language. I forgot my Polish dictionary, and I can't speak Italian or Hungarian, and I don't know Gaelic. So I'll have to give you instructions in English with my apologies. Now come on, line up!"

With the echo of grumbling and shuffling feet, Studs got into a line along the wall. He hoped that everyone would stop giving the monkey arguments so they could get going.

"Let's get started," someone called out.

"We ought to get that guy outside after it's all over," Studs said low to a muscular fellow before him.

"If he keeps on like this, we won't have to wait until then," the fellow replied.

"Is it necessary to continue like this? You know, we're not cattle," the priest said in a low voice of controlled anger, and Studs, silently applauding the clergyman, thought it ought to tone down that damn red-robed clown.

"I didn't ask for your two-cents' worth," the sergeant-at-arms quickly retorted in an insulting tone, while the room waited in awed and taut silence.

Studs shook his head uncomprehendingly. Insulting a priest! He'd never seen that done before. And an officer of the Christys doing it, too! That guy was just passing out hints that he wanted to be mobbed. And boy, wouldn't Studs just love to jam his fists between the rat's eyes!

"I'm a priest and I do not propose to be insulted by you!" the clergyman said stiffly.

"You tell him, Father, we're with you!"

"Don't let him pull anything on you, Father!"

"Let's get going!"

"BOOOOOOO!"

"And I'm conducting this initiation. . . ."

"Pipe down!" a bull voice called out, and many stamped their feet in unison.

Studs tried to crowd forward, but couldn't break through the solid wall of backs.

"Priest or no priest, the sooner you get into line the better off we'll all be!"

Studs, leaping quickly up on his toes, caught sight of the fellow's face. Hard, tough, didn't seem afraid. Certainly wasn't the kind of fellow to meet in a dark alley.

"We have the right to ask that you be civil to us," the priest said.

"Get in line. You're no better than anyone else in here."

"Help! Help!"

Heads turned. Studs saw beside him a quivering, thin, sickly-faced young man of about twenty-five, who looked as if he were going to throw a fit. The mere sight of him almost shocked Studs into a state of irresolution. He was afraid, looking at that distorted face. The sick man sagged. A stream of blood shot out of his mouth, splattering Studs' shirt collar and coat lapel. The sick man was caught under the arms and held before he hit the floor. There was a minor stampede about him, and Studs, wiping his bloody neck and soiled clothes, was jammed back.

"Man's fainted!"

"Get a doctor!"

"Gangway!"

"Pipe down!" the sergeant-at-arms bellowed. A pushing wave carried Studs forward, his neck sticky, a semi-coagulating stream trickling under his shirt. . . . The sick man emitted a shrill, pitiful moan.

"Open the door!"

"Man's died!"

"Give him air!"

"Get a doctor!"

Another wave dragged Studs forward.

"Get that guy!"

"Sock him!"

"Get a doctor!"

"Open the door!"

Studs, caught up in this excitement, lowered his head, crashed forward. Just as he got close to the sergeant-at-arms, an aisle seemed to open to the door, and the sergeant-at-arms shot through it, slamming the door behind him. They pounded on the door, milled, crashed into each other, shoved purposelessly, grumbling with rage, and the sick man again moaned pitifully.

"Open the door!"

"There's a man dying!"

"Open that goddamn door!"

"Break it down!"

The sick man moaned.

"Man dead!"

"Open that goddamn door!"

III

The door opened, and the head of the sergeant-at-arms appeared in the doorway.

"Get him!"

The cry rose, and the candidates like an irresistible flood surged forward. A jam at the narrow door impeded their exit, and as they drove through by brute pressure, breaking loudly and wildly into a large hall, the sergeant-at-arms gained distance on them.

"Get him! Catch him!" Studs bellowed like a maniac, breathlessly streaking down the center of the hall. The sergeant-at-arms dashed safely ahead, his robe flying behind him as he passed rows of empty camp chairs, and a stand upon which a sharp-nosed man in a ceremonial red robe stood awed. He escaped through a wedge in the solid wall of black-hooded figures formed behind the stand, and when the mob of initiates reached it, the black-hooded figures closed tightly, preventing any break. Their voices rising into a babble, the initiates turned and milled about the stand.

Exhausted, his chest paining, his heart racing, Studs gasped at the edge of the crowd. He started around the hall and saw, on all sides, a silent wall of hooded, black figures. This was too much for him, he thought, gasping again for breath.

"Please, please, gentlemen! What is the meaning of all this?" the sharp-nosed man on the stand called in a surprised and squeaky voice, rapping on the wooden railing with a gavel.

"We'll get that rat!"

"Drunk, and insulting a priest!"

"He's no better than a murderer!"

Studs, slowly regaining his breath, wondered what had happened to the blind man and the lad who'd gotten sick and puked blood all over him. Couldn't the fellow have just tried croaking all over somebody else? He spotted the blind man quivering nervously in a chair. Lucky he hadn't been stepped on, all right!

"Bring him out!"

"Massacre the rat!"

"String him up!"

"Gentlemen, what's all this? Goodness, I never witnessed such disorder before at an initiation."

"He socked a blind man and insulted a priest. Send him out!"

"Hand him over!"

Studs looked up at the squeaky-voiced master-of-ceremonies. Judge Gorman, he realized in surprise.

"Please, order, gentlemen, order, and let us know the cause of this outburst!"

"We're not interesting in jawing. Fish up that rat for us!"

"Who? What? Hit a blind man, what's this?" the Judge called out, a shocked expression on his thin face.

"We want that guy!" Studs bellowed to get back into the excitement, and he smiled when others took up his cry and megaphoned it through their hands in unison.

Studs wove through the crowd, closer to the stand.

"Will some one of you come up here and tell us just what has happened, please?"

Studs raised his hands, thinking that he would explain it to Gorman, make himself known to all the candidates here, and use his good offices in knowing the Judge to settle this trouble.

"Here's a gentleman now from your own number who will tell us. Come up here, please, sir!"

"Tell him the straight stuff, lad!" someone said as Studs mounted the stand.

"Mr. Gorman, don't you remember me, Lonigan, from Fifty-eighth Street?" Studs said, extending his hand.

"Why, yes, yes."

"Well, Mr. Gorman, you see, this sergeant-at-arms must have had a few shots too many and. . . ."

"Here, please, turn around and tell everybody."

Studs fidgeted at the sight of so many faces below him. He looked over their heads at vacant chairs, and opened his mouth without saying anything.

"Gentlemen, now we can get down to the facts in this situation."

Studs grinned weakly. He wanted to make a hit, and he'd never spoken to a crowd before, and he was no orator, and. . . .

"Well, first we in the room, ah, a room like sardines in a can and the fellow comes in and he shoves everybody around, insults the priest, and when one fellow gets sick, he locks us in. For all he cared, the fellow could have died," Studs said, beginning nervously, the last words of his argument dying as he uttered them.

"Unheard of! Unheard of!" Judge Gorman exclaimed, shocked.

"Well, it's so," Studs said doggedly, stimulating corroborative cries.

"Is there any more to this? Here, will you come up here and tell us what happened and back up this man's charge?" the Judge said, pointing to a thin fellow with a turned-up nose and over-sized ears.

"You bet your boots!" the fellow replied, confidently mounting the stand.

Studs, feeling that he had failed, unobtrusively slid down from the platform.

"That's the stuff, lad," someone said, lightening Studs' disappointment.

"Quiet, please, gentlemen, while we proceed with this investigation. We must get to the bottom of these facts, because

the Order of Christopher would be deeply humiliated if it
allowed these allegations against one of its officers to go
unpunished, if they be proven."

"All right, I'll tell you! We're candidates, see, and we come
here to be initiated. We plunk down our ten bucks, and we're
all anxious to be put through the degrees in our initiation.
That's the layout. We come here to be initiated and not to
be treated like a bunch of dogs!" the little fellow with the large
ears said in a resonant voice.

"Pardon me, but what has this got to do with the facts that
have been charged against our sergeant-at-arms?"

"I'm coming to that. All right, then, we didn't come here
to be treated like dogs, did we?"

"No!" the crowd boomed.

"All right! We come here to join the Order of Christopher
because we know that it stands for decent things, sports,
religion, good fellowships, the church, decent things."

"If it stands for men of God being insulted by the likes of
that drunken bully, give me my money back!" a voice cried
out with a trace of an Irish brogue in it, bringing cheers and
catcalls.

"All right, he comes into that room with a breath that would
make a Mack truck run backward, shoves us around, and
he says to one lad, 'Are you a Polack?' And then what does
he do? He insults a priest." Turning to Judge Gorman, the
speaker raised his voice. "Now, does the Order of Christopher
stand for insulting priests or doesn't it?"

"Of course not. If that be true, the proper punitive measures
will be taken."

"And we're going to take the same things!"

Studs added his voice to the riotous outburst, keen for excitement, watching the speaker and thinking how he might
have done what this fellow was doing instead of fizzling his
chance away.

"How was the priest insulted?"

"There's Father. He can tell you!" the speaker said,
pointing.

"It is true!" the priest called from the crowd.

"Thank you!" Judge Gorman said, his voice squelched in
applause, and when it died, he continued, "Thank you, Father!
We'll ask you for more evidence when this gentleman here
concludes giving us his testimony."

"Well, we're in the room just as I said, and we got a blind
man. He can't see, because he's blind. And this drunken
. . . I can't call what he is in public. . . ."

Funny guy, Studs thought, laughing with the others.

". . . He tells the blind man to get in line, just like he was a snotty cop, and the blind man, he can't see no line. And when Father protests, he tells Father to keep his face shut, I mean to shut up. . . ."

"All right. That's enough jawing. Let's get him!"

"Gentlemen! Order, please!" Judge Gorman squeaked amidst a disgruntled murmuring.

"All right, boys, just a minute," the speaker shouted, producing quiet by a confident wave of his hand, then turning a proud glance of assurance upon Judge Gorman.

"Thank you," the Judge said humbly to the speaker before facing the candidates. "Please, gentlemen, let us have patience for a little longer. This unprecedented and outrageous situation calls for more than mere vengeance. As soon as it is cleared up, we will proceed to the initiation. But first we must get to the roots of this situation, and prove to you the blamelessness of our Order in its occurrence. The Order feels keenly such insults upon its integrity. And because of this, I must get to the facts, because without all of the facts, this Order cannot act upon them. And it is in total agreement with your demand that justice be rendered, and that its honor be cleared as well as it insists that the wrongs which some of you have suffered, be righted. Again, gentlemen, I ask you not to be too hasty and impatient."

"Yes, fellows, we got to go about this the right way just as the master-of-ceremonies here says, because we're not out to get the Order, but only that drunken. . . ."

"This gentleman here is your spokesman. Mr. . . . ah . . . what, sir, is your name?"

"Eddie McCarthy."

"Now let us get Mr. McCarthy's complete story."

"Three cheers for Eddie McCarthy!" someone called, and a wave of cheering rolled over the hall.

"Now I got as far as to tell how this fellow was cockeyed and trying to insult us as well as injure the honor of the Order of Christopher. Now I said he insults a blind man and a priest. Am I right or wrong?" Their cries affirmed his statement. "All right. Well, there we was in there, insulted by a bum who seemed just itching to have his teeth slapped down his face!"

"Yeah, let any of you come outside and try it!" the sergeant-at-arms called sneeringly from the rear of the hall, causing the Judge to wince.

"Come on out, you palooka!" McCarthy called.

"Bring him out! Bring him out! Bring him out!" they cried, stirred.

Judge Gorman waved his skinny arm, pounded with his gavel, raised his squeaky voice, in vain. Candidates rushed behind the stands, but they were blocked by the unopening and unbending line of silent black hooded figures.

"Gentlemen, I am stunned! Stunned!"

"Come on out, you bum! Bring him out!"

"Gentlemen, I want to state that I believe every charge you have made, and that I am in full rapport with your righteous anger!"

"Three cheers for the master-of-ceremonies. For he's a jolly good fellow!" Eddie McCarthy shouted like a college cheer leader.

"Thank you, thank you, gentlemen," the Judge said with feeling after the cheers had subsided. "I do not know what I can do to apologize for myself and for the Order of Christopher. From the bottom of my heart, I offer you my own, and its, profound apologies. And I hereby expel forever from this Order, Kevin Joyce, sergeant-at-arms of this Council, for betrayal of trust, conduct unbecoming an officer, setting a bad example, and appearing in an intoxicated condition at an important function!"

"Hurray!"

"But, gentlemen, we will need a sergeant-at-arms to assist me in the initiation ceremonies which I hope to begin shortly. I ask you if you will give your unanimous vote to Mr. McCarthy here as your sergeant-at-arms?"

"We want McCarthy!"

During the fresh burst of cheers, Judge Gorman signalled to the rear of the hall, and a red robe was brought to him. While he placed it on the shoulders of the new sergeant-at-arms, deafening cheers resounded. McCarthy extended his hand for quiet, with superb assurance.

"Thanks, fellows, I'll do my best to fulfill my job as sergeant-at-arms which you and the master-of-ceremonies have been so . . . so . . . so decent to entrust me with, and I'll do my best, and if that ain't enough, boot me out of it!"

Judge Gorman shook his hand in congratulations. McCarthy walked off the stand and was quickly mounted onto sturdy shoulders and carried along past the rows of camp chairs. Studs marched in the cheering group, which swept around the hall. If he hadn't been such a damn tongue-tied flop with shaking knees, he'd have gotten the honor McCarthy had. He'd be an officer in his council of the Order of Christopher on his first day, known to the whole Council, an important figure. His noisy shouts were mixed with silent regrets. All his life he had waited for an opportunity like this

one. And he'd flopped. His throat became irritated, and he
cheered half-heartedly in a hoarse voice, marching behind
those who carried McCarthy in triumph. He passed the rows
of black hooded figures and arrived in the noisy group back
by the stand. But still, hadn't he been the first to speak
in defense of things that were right, even if McCarthy was
the hero? He had joined in defending a priest, a blind man,
a sick man. If, if he'd only been the first out of that room, so
that he could have torn along on the heels of that louse Joyce
and nailed him to the floor with a neat flying tackle. . . .

"Three cheers for Eddie McCarthy."

And these might have been for Studs Lonigan.

IV

"Mr. McCarthy," Judge Gorman began with an air of
helplessness, while McCarthy tried to act natural in his red
robe, "we depend on you to uphold and enforce the dignity
of our Order with courage. We expect that you will be of
great assistance to us by acting as a sort of liaison man
between us who are older members, and perhaps more set in
our ways, and all these new members whom we are welcoming
today, and whose initiation we will shortly begin, now that
this unfortunate trouble has been cleared up."

McCarthy gestured assuredly with a sliding motion of his
hands, and a nod, causing a twinkle to come into the Judge's
eyes.

"Now, gentlemen!" Judge Gorman began after the subsiding
of another roar, his squeaking voice rising like a slightly
rusty echo.

A revolver shot echoed like a loud explosion. The Judge
wheeled around and looked to the rear. Momentarily, he stood
like a statue. McCarthy followed the Judge with bewildered
eyes. A current of tenseness seemed to run through the
candidates. Studs closed his fists, leaned forward, hungry for
more excitement, hoping that something had happened that
would give him a chance to come forward more prominently
than McCarthy. A fear of unknown danger cancelled his
hopes.

"What was that? My God!" Judge Gorman exclaimed in
a throbbing voice.

A man in rolled shirt-sleeves burst through the black-
hooded ranks, rushed to the stand, spoke low and hurriedly
to the Judge, and McCarthy, listening, revealed by his
concerned brow that something serious had happened. The
Judge's hand rose automatically to his forehead. He stumbled
several feet backward as if he were on the verge of fainting.

The candidates impulsively drew more tightly together.

"How frightful! Lock all the doors! Lock all the doors!" Judge Gorman cried out in a fretful voice, wiping his face with a handkerchief as he spoke.

Studs tried to get closer to the stand, but could make no progress through the closely pressed backs. Jesus, what had happened?

"Gentlemen, I am distressed. The sergeant-at-arms, Mr. Kevin Joyce, who was the provocateur of the regrettable occurrences here this afternoon, contrite and disgraced by his actions and expulsion from the Order of Christopher . . . has just . . . shot himself."

The words were like jolts of electricity, and there was scarcely a sound or a movement from the candidates. They waited, creatures of the words and commands of Judge Gorman. Studs thought that it was as exciting as a mystery movie. He'd never been present before when so many exciting things had happened one on top of the other. He had to do something to get in the thick of it. And that man might be dead. Dead! *Jesus!*

"Gentlemen, please pardon me if I am a bit upset, and please be patient a moment until I can collect myself, and think of what we can do in this crisis. Such a tragedy has never before occurred in the glorious history of our Order."

Watching the Judge sympathetically, Studs thought of how tough a spot he was in, how glad he was that he wasn't in the Judge's shoes. And it was a scandal that couldn't be kept out of the paper.

RIOT AND SUICIDE AT O. OF C. INITIATION

The Order and the Church, too, would get a black eye from this. If it had only not happened!

He glanced around him at the drawn, anxious, worried faces. His anger was suddenly roused at a fellow who was smiling superciliously. How could a guy smile like that? Hell, this was serious.

"Are the doors locked?" Judge Gorman asked, receiving assurance from various parts of the hall. "Good! Don't admit anyone! Don't call the police! His eyes singled out the priest. "Father, will you go back immediately and administer to that poor unfortunate man!"

Studs watched the priest move solemnly forward and disappear behind the stands. He looked up at Gorman with growing respect at the way the Judge was handling this crisis.

"Has a doctor been called?"

"One's on the way here."

"Here, sir, I'm a doctor," a candidate called.

"Will you kindly go back there immediately?"

"This way, doctor."

"I want to ask you gentlemen to take a solemn and serious oath never to divulge one word of what has happened here this afternoon to any outsider. I ask this of you in fraternal spirit for the good of our Order, which is bigger than any of us individually."

"Yes, fellows, we got to show the master-of-ceremonies here that we're with him. Now, are we or aren't we? We are," McCarthy said.

"Raise your right hands with me, please, gentlemen, and silently pronounce a vow of secrecy. . . . Thank you, thank you, gentlemen. This mustn't get into the newspapers, besmirching the name of the Order of Christopher."

"Judge, Mr. Joyce has died," a voice called from the rear.

V

"In the light of what has happened here this afternoon, I believe that it will be necessary to postpone this initiation until a less tragic time. But before I dismiss you, I must ask a guaranty from you of your secrecy and of your sincerity in joining the Order of Christopher, and I believe that under the very unusual circumstances of this afternoon I am fully justified in asking this of you in the name of the Order. The most convincing testimony of your spirit and attitude toward the Order of which I can think is that you prove yourself willing to shed your blood for the Order. I am going to ask one of you to volunteer for this act which will be accepted symbolically as that of the entire group."

Studs fastened his eyes on Gorman's hawk-like nose. Since he had flopped once already, all he had done was cheer. And damn it, Studs Lonigan was one made to stand out and make others cheer for him and not always to do the cheering. A zeal of martyrdom, which he had not experienced so acutely since one Friday afternoon during his fourth-grade year at Saint Patrick's while Father Roney was talking on the early martyrs, swept through him. Watching the Judge, he knew that he had to volunteer. And he couldn't get out of his mind the thought that Joyce out there was dead, and that the police might come, and they would all be on the witness stand. They had to stand by the Order now, too.

"Gentlemen, let me repeat that this is very grave and serious, and I ask you to reflect before volunteering. I do not want this to be an impulsive act, no matter how noble or self-sacrificing. I want it to be an act that is the product of reflection. Think carefully! We are asking that one of you offer, as a sacrifice to the Order of Christopher, a pint of his blood in symbolic proof of your seriousness to accept all the responsibilities that will be incumbent upon you as members. This may result in serious, even fatal, consequences. I am fully conscious of the gravity of this request, and I am prompted to make it in the name of our Order only because of the tragic events of this afternoon."

Studs turned pallid; his head became light. He saw himself dying as a result of this sacrifice. He wondered why this sacrifice of a pint of blood should be necessary, but his emotions swept this question out of his mind. He saw himself dying for the Order of Christopher, and the idea of himself becoming the martyred hero of this surprising afternoon gave him a sad thrill. He wanted to raise his hand. But he couldn't very well, in his condition, afford to lose that much blood. He asked himself where was his guts? Guts would carry him through it alive. Here was a chance to show the real stuff in him, such as he had never gotten in his whole life.

"This act must be absolutely voluntary. We want to know whether or not you are prepared to pay for the privileges of membership with something dearer to you than mere money!" Judge Gorman said gravely, in a rising voice.

He could see that many around him were thinking it over, and the fellow who breathed with his mouth open like a flytrap, right near him, looked like he might bust a brain cell.

"Any volunteers?"

Wanting still to raise his hand, he felt that it might kill him. Nearby a hairy hand was raised, and Studs saw that it was a sandy-haired fellow with football shoulders, one who looked like he could well afford to lose a pint of blood. Yellow? Studs Lonigan yellow? Without will or thought, he shot up his right hand, and said, with a rush of breath:

"I will!"

They were all looking at him, just as he had wanted them to. Look at him! Envy him! But he was uneasy. He tried to act unconcerned. He had made his decision, too, and he was going through with it and face the music. But suppose he would be, like that poor bastard Joyce, carried out of here in a six-foot box! He seemed shrivelling up inside, losing his strength, and he kept telling himself that he must pull together.

"I congratulate you two gentlemen who have volunteered. You have proven to us that you are the type of young men we desire to have enrolled in our Order. But once again, permit me to offer a word of caution. Once the volunteer has been decided upon as the man who is going to shed a pint of his blood for the Order of Christopher, then the die will have been cast, the Rubicon will have been crossed. He will be expected to go through with his sacrifice, no matter what the cost and the dangers."

More eyes on him. That fat fellow in front of him, who looked like he had the mumps, his cheeks were so fat, smiling at him as if he were a goof. Studs knew his kind. The wise aleck, always interested only in himself, never showing any spirit. He prided himself that he was not like that. And he was ready, too!

"Heck, I can't dope this out at all. What good does it do to have somebody give up a pint of good blood? If it was to save that poor bastard's life, now, or for some reason, it would be all right," a middle-aged man beside Studs asked in whispers.

"What good did it do Christ and the martyrs to sacrifice their blood?" a blond lad answered.

"I look at it this way. It's a fine thing to belong to the Order, and we ought to be prepared to do something for it," Studs said hesitantly, understanding clearly to himself why it was right, but not being able to put his understanding lucidly into words. He tried to remember the words Gorman had used in explanation, but he was distracted when another hand went up. Which of them would be the one? He hoped it wouldn't be he. But that was reneging. He was ready, come what may. Only he wished it could be gotten over with. If he could walk out and get it over with this minute, it would be all right. This waiting. . . .

"All right, gentlemen, before we select the man, are there any more volunteers?"

"Bull," a fellow close to Studs muttered under his breath.

They began to murmur, and scrape their feet in restlessness.

"Will the volunteers please come forward?"

Studs edged slowly toward the stand, head lowered to avoid meeting anyone's eyes, wondering was he a chump, trying to keep calm, steeling himself for the ordeal. His face was colorless. His lips were clamped tight with determination. Suppose it did kill him? Just as he raised his eyes toward Gorman, the Judge pointed at the hairy-handed blond fellow with the face of a pugilist.

"Will you gentlemen agree on this young man as the volunteer. . . . Thank you. . . . And I want also to congratulate you others who have come here. Your willingness and courage moves me as an older member of our Order, I assure you we shall always be proud of members like you young men!"

Studs flushed, and sank back into the crowd, disappointed at this lost opportunity, and yet . . . suppose, now, it had killed him? The other lad, too, looked healthy enough to go through with it.

"That's the stuff, friend," someone said to him and he smiled.

"Will you sign a statement absolving the Order of Christopher from all responsibility in case your sacrifice should prove fatal?"

"Yes, sir, I will!"

"Ready," the Judge called in the back.

"Yes, send him out," a voice coldly answered.

The restlessness ceased. They waited.

Jesus, he hoped the guy came through it all right, Studs told himself.

VI

Eddie McCarthy leaped down from the stand. As he slowly walked across the vacant space between the stand and the camp chairs, which were now filled, a moan caused him to glance to his left. He saw the sick man from the waiting-room, his face twisted and distorted, his body convulsing. Emitting a howl, the sick man jumped toward him. McCarthy ran down the center aisle between the camp chairs, pursued by the sick man.

The afternoon's mounting tensions collapsed into howling laughter. The sick man stopped in the aisle, straightened up, laughed. McCarthy turned around, like a frightened boy, stared from face to face, hurt and ashamed. Seeing Judge Gorman chuckling, he scratched his poll quizzically.

The priest, the blind man, the blond fellow who had volunteered to shed his blood, and the sergeant-at-arms minus his red robe, appeared under the stand, smiling, like actors taking their encore bow.

"Say, wasn't this on the level?" McCarthy asked. Laughing, Studs shook his head, and thought that he had been taken in by it, all right. Funny. If he had only used his brains, he could have seen through it all. He laughed, watching McCarthy return the robe of office to the sergeant-at-arms.

"Now, I shall explain, because you must clearly perceive that these distressing events were really part of the ritual of this last degree in your initiation. But first, permit me to state that never in my experience as the master-of-ceremonies at initiations have I assisted in putting through a more spirited group of candidates. What is your opinion, Mr. Joyce?"

"Yes, Judge. And we had a lively time in the waiting room. I would have had it much livelier, too, if our plants hadn't proven such good shock-absorbers and helped me get out," Joyce grinned.

"The priest here is not a real member of the clergy, he has been serving as a plant in our initiations for a number of seasons now. And as you see, the blind man has been restored to sight, and the sick man to health. . . ."

"How did that guy shoot blood all over me?" Studs said to the fellow beside him, shaking his head, touching his shirt where it was stiffened with blood stains.

"Probably had a rubber ball in his mouth. Got you, huh?" the fellow replied, both of them grinning.

"Every new member of our Order, excepting priests, goes through this same initiation. Now, some of you may be thinking of it in its lighter aspects, and it may seem mere horseplay to you, contrived to afford pleasure and amusement to our membership. But I trust that this impression is not the predominant one which you will carry away. For if it is, our ritual will have failed to serve its purpose.

"This initiation has been carefully planned with the aim of implanting in you the moral lessons which should drive home to every candidate the principles and the aims of the Order of Christopher, and the obligations which it expects of its membership. To speak in the vernacular, we did not merely wish to pull your legs.

"You are probably wondering why Mr. Joyce deliberately set out to embroil you. It was to test your patience, your courage, your honor, your charity. What, then, are the lessons of this ritual? On the one hand, it is calculated to impress upon you the virtues of patience and fortitude, to suggest the dangers that lie behind action that is too impulsive and hasty. In other words, to suggest that it is not always best to fly off the handle before you know what is really happening, because things are not always as they seem. Thus, a priest was not really insulted at all, as you supposed, because it seemed to you that he was.

"Specific parts of the ritual, which seem like sheer buffoonery to a superficial observer, actually embody a moral lesson. Thus we plant a member among you in the disguise of a priest to instill in you the lesson of reverence and respect for the clergy, and to drive home to you the duty incumbent on every member of our Order, the duty of defending the Church and the clergy wherever and whenever that defense may be needed. In the same manner, a blind man is planted in your midst to impress on you the virtue of charity, which is a cardinal principle of our Order, and to tell you in concrete terms that every member is to be as charitable as circumstances may warrant to the sick, the lame, the halt, the blind, the unfortunate.

"The part of our ritual dealing with blood sacrifice also has its purpose. It should reinforce in your memories the lessons and glories of the Christian martyrs, and the grace and glory which shine resplendent upon him who earns the crown of martyrdom. It should inform you that when you come into this Order you come as a man prepared to defend his faith, his honor, and his country, to struggle to the utmost for these sacred causes as the needs require it. These are the principles on which this Order was founded, and on which it stands to date. And we believe that the best way of informing you of these principles, instead of merely telling them to you in a dry sermonizing talk, is by contriving a ritual of initiation which will inculcate them upon your minds in an unforgettable way.

"You have proven yourselves, and I am proud to welcome you in fraternal spirit into the Order of Christopher. Your conduct here this afternoon demonstrates to us that you have in you the best stuff of which Catholic American manhood is made. You have shown yourself ready to defend the faith, to sacrifice yourselves, to practice the virtue of charity. I am sure that our association in this Council of the Order of Christopher will be happy, enriching to our personal lives, fruitful in our mutual participation in the larger life of our Order, our Church, our city, and our great nation. I know that all of you, in joining us, will contribute your share to the manifold works which the Order of Christopher performs.

"As a final word, let me express the confident hope that you will appear regularly at our meetings, get acquainted with older members, and that you will immediately join the various phases of our activities for which you are individually the most suited.

"I will now administer the oath of admission. Raise your right hands, please!"

Studs raised his right hand, and in a mood of solemnity, repeated a simple oath pledging secrecy and the defense of his faith and his country.

VII

"I kind of suspected that it wasn't the real goods all along," a fellow in the lavatory line-up said amidst a rattle of conversation.

"It's clever. Only I didn't suspect it for a minute. I fell, hook, line and sinker."

"Me, now, did I play chump."

"You're McCarthy, aren't you? You were a very good candidate, though."

"And say, are my kidneys floating?"

"I didn't think it was all hoax until the guy shagged McCarthy down the middle aisle. Only I wish that when he pulled that fainting act he found another target," Studs said to the fellow behind him, revealing his blood-stained coat lapel and shirt.

"I didn't, either. The fellow who thought it up, whoever he was, was a smart man. I give him credit!" the fellow replied to Studs.

"They pulled it off so neat," Studs marvelled.

"The master-of-ceremonies is a brainy man. His talk at the end there, it was really inspiring, and made you understand just what the Order of Christopher means."

"I know him. He's Judge Gorman," Studs said with pride.

"He must be smart as a whip."

"I knew from the start it was all hooey."

"And say, was I ready to stand up and give three cheers when that long-nose ended his spiel?"

"I'm just waiting for the next initiation, when I can see some new chumps go through the mill like I did, and laugh behind a black robe, thinking how there are lads dumber than I was."

"Jesus, this place smells like a . . ."

"Yes, just like a crapper. Ain't that funny? And you know what flowers smell like? They smell like flowers."

"Dumb, hell! McCarthy, you're the stuff that the best of Catholic American manhood is made of. Didn't he say so?"

"That stuff must be hunger, because right now I'm made of just hunger."

"Anyway, fellow, the Order of Christopher is sure a fine thing. I'm glad I can call myself a Christy."

"Me, too."

Stepping outside, Studs breathed deeply. On the street car, he turned up his coat collar to hide the blood stains, and relaxed in his seat. He realized how tired he was. And he wanted to talk about the doings, regretting that he couldn't tell of it to anyone but a Christy. Well, he could tell the old man about it anyway. He drowsed. Waking up stiff, he rushed to the platform and got off the car. He thought that some day he'd be a big shot in the Christys, just like Judge Gorman. He proudly told himself that he was a Christy. And he had gotten a thousand dollars worth of insurance, too, in Catherine's name.

He let himself in quietly and hurried to his room to change his clothes so his mother wouldn't see the stains and go up in the air about them.

His father was drowsing by the radio, and smiled.

"Congratulations, Bill. And say, I'm sorry. You just missed Father Moylan's talk. Did he roast the bankers! Tell me, how was the doings?"

Studs smiled knowingly at his father.

CHAPTER SEVEN

I

His stocks were off eight points, and that meant that he was out over six hundred bucks. His brows knitted, and he determined that he would pray this morning as he had never prayed before.

"Honey, what's the trouble?" Catherine asked.

"Nothing. Why?" he asked, switching a forced smile on her.

"You look so worried and grumpy."

"There's nothing wrong. I was just thinking."

"About what?"

"Oh, nothing in particular. I was just thinking."

"No, you're worried."

"Not especially. Of course, in these times, you wonder about a lot of things that you never even thought of before."

"What things?"

"Well, business."

"Yes, darling, and I've been feeling the same way since I got that ten-dollar cut in my salary. But this is Sunday, and you're just going to give business and worry a nice kick around the block," she said with a dash of feminine decisiveness, as if she were energetically routing dust from a closet.

He smiled again, forced.

"Sometimes you are just like a boy."

"What do you mean?" he asked with a mixture of embarrassed pride and pleasure.

"You men," she exclaimed in mock contempt. "You try to be so big and important, and stick your chests out, and you're just like little boys playing games. That's why we find you so sweet and love you."

Feigning disinterest, he shook his head quizzically.

"Now, you forget all this serious business," she coaxed, sliding her arm through his.

Jesus, if he only could walk along with her on a sunny spring morning like this one and not have a worry in his head, no worry about his dough sunk in Imbray stock, about his health and weak heart, and the possibility of not living a long life, and not be wondering would he, by afternoon, feel pooped and shot. And then it was so gloomy at home that it could be cut with a knife, and it was bound to affect him, the old man's business going to pot, his dough lost and going fast, his expenses, unrented apartments, the mortgage. Just to have none of these things on his mind, and to be able to stroll along Easy Street with Catherine at his side, perfectly happy all day, and not having to feel that when he woke up tomorrow all these thoughts would pop back and keep going off like fire-crackers in his mind all day. And he had to decide about holding or selling his stock. Which?

Ahead of him along the sunny street he saw people moving, most of them also bound for church. To know that nearly everyone on this street was Catholic gave him a different kind of feeling than what he often had just walking along any street where the people on it were all going about to do any number of things. He felt that he had something in common here and he knew that much about them. They were all on the same side of the fence.

He glanced at Catherine, and she was pretty in her new black coat and her small black hat slanting on the left side of her head, and beneath her opened coat a black-and-white patterned dress with a wide black leather belt. Under-neath these clothes there was a white, untouched woman's body, and some day it was going to be his, and the thought of that unseen, untaken body of hers, hidden in clothes, made him kind of want their marriage to be soon. His woman.

There was something quiet and lazy about this street, with its three- and four-storied apartment buildings, its vacant lots, the earth beside the sidewalk loosening and muddy, the sun spread over it, the feeling of Sunday and early spring in the air. And around him other people going to church, walking slowly, and not seeming to have troubles on their minds. Did they? If things could be so quiet and peaceful and other people could walk along as if they had no bothers and worries, why couldn't he?

Across the street he watched a well-set-up fellow in a loud, snappy gray suit, with a girl whose slim, tall but meaty figure was wrapped in a stylish blue cloth coat, and when the fellow talked, Studs could hear her ringing laughter. Happy. . . . If they could be happy, so could he. Damn it if he couldn't!

"Look, Bill, two for-rent signs in this building. We ought to stop in on our way back. All along here there are for-rent signs, and it would be fun to look at them."

"We don't have to. We can have a big apartment in our building."

"But it's fun," she said.

But maybe these people weren't in danger of losing every penny they owned in the world, and they hadn't had a run of tough luck about their health.

"Bill, dear, when are you going to let me teach you bridge as you promised me you would?"

"I don't like the game," he answered in an annoyed masculine whine.

He had settled the question by telling her he didn't care about bridge, and here she was at it, showing no respect for his wishes.

"How can you say you don't like it, when you've never played, and don't know it, or how much fun it can be? You ought to be at least tolerant enough about it to wait and see how it is before you say, like a gruff old bear, that you don't like it."

"It's the game for tea-hounds and parlor athletes."

"Bill, you're just being silly. Nice fellows play bridge, and you're just trying to act like a great big tough guy. It's so silly."

"I couldn't learn it. I've never been good at cards, and bridge has too much to do with figures," he said, shifting his defense because he was stumped for a reply even if he did know he was right. And wouldn't he feel like a sap, sitting down at a bridge table?

"You'll like it a lot, I know you will, if you'll let yourself learn it."

"Well, maybe I will," he said to change the subject and postpone having to make a definite promise.

They turned a corner, and saw the low, sand-stoned, wide-façaded church with its broad steps and the large space of sidewalk before it. Pat Carrigan, in a group down from the church front, waved and Studs waved in response.

"But, Bill dear, will you start learning bridge with me this week?"

"Hello, Studs."

Studs was grateful, for the unexpected presence and solicitous greeting of Johnny O'Brien, and they shook hands. Studs noticed something familiar in the round, pleasing face of the expensively dressed blond girl on Johnny's arm, and he saw that Johnny was rather pale and thin in the cheeks.

"You ought to know my wife, Studs, Harriet Hayes from St. Patrick's."

"Sure, Roslyn Hayes' sister. And this is Catherine Banahan, Mr. and Mrs. O'Brien."

"How do you do."

"How do you do."

"How do you do."

"Yes, I remember you, and how is Loretta?" Harriet O'Brien asked.

"She's married now to Phil Rolfe, know him?" Studs said, and he wasn't sure whether or not the O'Briens had really frowned at the mention of Phil's name.

"He's a bookie, isn't he?" Johnny said snootily.

"Yes."

"Gee, Studs, I'm glad to see you, and how is everything going?" Johnny asked, his tone of voice changing.

"Fair, Johnny, fair. How's tricks by you?" Studs said, noticing that Catherine and Harriet had fallen into a conversation about the weather.

"I'm with Dad. We're in the coal business, and while as a whole the coal business is pretty shot, we've been more than holding up our end of the stick. In fact, considering conditions, we're doing well."

"I'm glad to hear it. Good."

"Well, you see, Studs, these mine strikes they've been having these last months have helped us. In fact, they have saved our neck. You see, we had our yards full of coal and couldn't do much with it. And these strikes creating some shortage, we're setting pretty, and the price of coal has gone up a little. That's helped us a lot, and I'm hoping the Reds who've been agitating the miners, according to some newspaper accounts, keep the strikes going a little more. It's certainly a godsend to O'Brien's Coal company. And then we do a big business with convents and churches and Catholic schools."

"Well, I'm glad to hear it, Johnny."

"Isn't it dreadful the way these high waist-lines in the new spring styles show off the figure? You've really got to be thin to wear them," Catherine said.

"I was thinking the same thing, and I'm going on that Hollywood eighteen-day diet with grapefruit, lamb chops and melba toast."

"Yes, I've noticed that nearly all the restaurants downtown are featuring it, and many of them have their windows stacked with grapefruits. What do you really think of it?"

"The movie magazine that I just read said it absolutely works and I'm starting on it tomorrow," Harriet said.

"What do you think of the election, Studs?"

"Good, Johnny, I've always been a Democrat."

"I voted regular, too. We're kind of hoping to get some contracts out of it, and it's certainly fine for the city to kick out the crooked Republican machine."

"Yes, I like to see the Democrats in. But I guess it doesn't mean much to most of us. It's like baseball. You like to see your favorite team win."

"No, I never went to Saint Paul's," Catherine said to Harriet.

"It was really a tragedy to see Rock die," Johnny said.

"Yes, he was a regular fellow."

"He was a great man. Why even Hoover sent a telegram to his wife," Johnny said.

"Notre Dame will miss him."

"I think the team will go on just the same. Rockne may be gone, but not his Viking spirit."

"There was one newspaper editorial on his death, did you see it, that was very good. It told of how he died, like he lived, in the saddle, and that he carried on the real spirit of the old Norse Vikings."

"What was it he was going to the coast for when he died?" Studs asked.

"He was connected with the sales department of an automobile plant and he was flying out there to open a sales campaign."

"I certainly hated to see Rock die."

"He was a great man and it's a great loss," Johnny said dolefully. "But, say, mass ought to be just about starting. And say, Studs, do drop over and see us. We're living at Sixty-ninth and Crandon. The number's in the book, and just give us a ring any time."

"I will."

Studs and Catherine followed the O'Briens into church.

II

"Today certainly has brought them out," Catherine said, crunching along a gravel walk in Jackson Park.

"Yeah, they're out sunning themselves, all right," Studs said, the sounds of automobiles purring steadily in his ears.

He heard the smack from a driven golf ball, and looked

past Catherine at the wide expanse of the golf course. It was nice to look at, with blotches of leafless trees and bushes along its edges, with shoots of fresh green bursting amidst dead wintry grass and catching shimmers of sunlight, and with golfers spread over it and moving about in differing directions. Taking her arm, he led her over soft and soggy ground to a tee-off where a bandy-legged man in khaki trousers and shirt stood with his feet widely stanced, measuring the ball perched on a small cone of damp sand. He cracked it, and the ball veered to the right on low line, landed, disappeared. The man shook his head disappointedly.

A man in khaki pants and shirt with a prominent Adam's apple drove quickly, an arching line which bounded neatly onto a patch of green before the hole. Studs watched them sling their golf bags over their left shoulders and tramp forward, and he wished he could drive golf balls like that last fellow, because it might be fun, and safe exercise with his heart. Those two seemed to enjoy it, and he might, too.

"Bill, let's learn to play golf this summer."

"That's just what I was thinking," he answered as they returned to the walk.

"It'll be lots of fun, I'll bet, but it would take me ages to learn how to hit the ball right."

"I imagine one could pick it up more easy than you suspect."

"Even if I couldn't learn to do it well, I think it would be nice as long as we did it together."

He studied the expression on the faces of passing strangers, wondering what went on in their heads, and were they worse or better off than he was. Three girls strolled by them.

"And Conroy, he was the biggest simpleton, and when he danced he just ruined my brand new shoes," one of the girls said.

"I had the grandest time, Katie, and Hal just said the funniest things," the girl in the middle, a frail blond, said.

"The only thing funny about my date was his face. He looked like . . . like some kind of a chimpanzee or something," the third one said.

Studs watched them wriggle on. Young, younger than girls he'd ever get, nice to look at.

"High-school kids talking about their dates," Catherine said sagely.

He turned his eyes toward her, and she blew him a kiss.

"We're going to have our dates, too, this summer."

"Sure."

"It won't be long now before we can go to the beach on

Sundays. And let's sometime get Phil and Loretta and Carroll and Fran and have a beach party. We can bring a picnic lunch and a guitar and roast marshmallows by a fire and sing. It'll be loads of fun."

"Sure, we'll plan on it sometime this summer, and we'll also ask Red Kelly and his wife."

It would be a good idea, but going to the beach that way would be a little different than it used to be when he'd go alone with some guys and be expecting to find some jane there, keen and lively, who would flirt and afterward put out and think of it as only fun and nothing serious. This was different, and those days and the expectation of that kind of a thing was gone. Still, he guessed that it was just natural for a guy to think of that kind of thing now and then.

"Bill, dear, I'm so happy thinking of all the things we'll be able to do this summer, beach parties, and picnics, lots of things we can do together, can't we? And when I get my vacation, if you can be free, too, we could go away together and find a nice summer resort where we can stay and have separate rooms, of course, and just be together in the same place, having two full weeks to do things together. Won't it be fun?"

He nodded. If they did, would she? He was getting tired of waiting for it from her, and he wondered would all this long wait make it any better?

Delayed at the drive by the procession of automobiles, she took his arm. They skirted across and walked along by the lake.

"The lake's simply grand today, Bill, look . . ."

They peered over the lake, its waters like a shiny cover being stirred from underneath, like a blue cloak being ruffled, and the sunlight on the lake seemed like a pattern sewn into the cloak.

"Darling, I'll never forget the night we became engaged and walked down by the lake."

"Yes."

"And will you ever forget it?" she asked.

"No."

"I know you will. You men, you think such things are sentimental or foolish, and you don't remember them. I know you don't."

"I do," he said with an effort to make himself sound convincing.

"Honest?"

He nodded.

"Cross your heart?"

He quickly crossed his heart.

"I love you."

He wanted to tell her the same thing, telling himself how he did, really did, think a hell of a lot of her. He grinned sheepishly.

"Love me?"

He nodded and she squeezed his hand. Then she clung tightly to his arm.

"We won't be able to come swimming here, though, this summer," he said, pointing to the low gray pavilion of rough-edged stone which housed the Jackson Park beach.

"It's become the hunkies' community center here now. I came here one day last summer, and I tell you I didn't think there was as many hunkies and polacks in the world as I saw here."

"Yes, isn't it too bad? And there was trouble here last summer with niggers trying to go swimming along here. Ugh. Think of it, going with niggers," she said, shuddering.

"Seventy-third-Street beach is much better, but every year you see more noisy Jews there. Pretty soon there won't be a beach in Chicago left for a white man."

Ahead, beyond the end of the park, they saw several close-packed, tall apartment hotels, lost in webs of sunlight which refracted from the windows and bathed the bricks with soft reflections of color. Looking persistently at them, Studs wondered if they, as well as Phil and Loretta, could afford to live in one of them. If they could, it would be better than living in the old man's building.

At the edge of the park she pulled him toward a bus, and before he realized what he was doing he was sitting toward the front of the upper deck of a downtown bus, idly watching the buildings and the people along Hyde Park Boulevard. They turned north at Drexel Boulevard.

"Lots of flats for rent around here," she said.

"I know, but this isn't a good neighborhood, like it used to be," he said as the bus bounced over the Forty-seventh Street car-tracks.

"And such nice places and homes, too," she sighed.

He slumped in his seat, liking the bus ride in the sun, Catherine close to him. He scented her perfume, saw people drifting along, looked at girls in new clothes, thinking whether or not they were nice. But he didn't want to trade her for the girls he saw. She was a damn good kid, best in the world for him. Wanting her to know it, he took her hand, smiled at her, received in return a squeeze of the hand and a grateful smile.

"Love me?"

"Uh huh! you're darn right I do," he said with false gruffness.

III

Already yesterday seemed like a blur to him. It was like some happy dream which was forgotten the moment he woke up, and all that was left of it was the memory of having felt good. On the bus with Catherine everything but her and his own feelings had seemed covered by a curtain, and he had felt in the future only good things and good luck could possibly come to him. He could see now that he had no right to feel that way.

He sucked malted milk through a straw, and watched the soda jerkers hustle orders amid the noise and clatter of the buzz of the electric malted-milk shakers. They worked their pants off and they didn't get a hell of a lot for it, either. He was glad he wasn't in their boots, and he guessed he was better off than most of them. It was a flunkey's job, and a guy must feel pretty lousy working at it day after day, with no future and only hard dumb work. It was something to know that there were others worse off than he was.

He licked his straw and set it back in the glass, swung off the chair by the soda counter, and walked by drug articles stacked on tables to the cashier's desk at the door.

"Hey, Dugan."

"Oh, hello, Studs. How are you? Gee, I'm glad to see you."

"See this? The stock market went all to hell today. Where's all the dough I was going to clean up on the Imbray stock of yours?" Studs asked, nettled, showing Ike the account of a stock-market break recorded in *The Chicago Questioner*.

"You know what that is, don't you?"

"What?" Studs asked anxiously.

"That's just fluctuation."

"That stock is thirteen, and I'm out nine hundred and sixty bucks. Is that what fluctuation means?"

"I'm out more if you pay any attention to this. I've been buying Imbray stock every week. But we don't pay any attention to this at the office. It's just fluctuation. You can't lose on Imbray stock with all the public utilities of the Middle West and the brain of Solomon Imbray behind it."

"That's what you said before, and the stock has lost twelve bucks a share."

"I know. And I stand to lose more than you do. I've been buying Imbray stock out of my pay for months now. And I'm not worried, I don't bother about whether it goes up or down a little on the market. It's thirteen now, isn't it? Well, when we signed the stock agreement, it was twenty-five, and we're still buying it at that price, and still I'm not kicking, because I got faith. I got faith because I know you can't go wrong on Imbray stock, and some day I know it's going to set me up sweet and pretty on Easy Street."

"Isn't it dumb, though, to buy it for twenty-five bucks when it's thirteen in the market?"

"Well, by our employee-stock agreement, we pay half and the company pays half for us. But I'm still buying it every week and I'm not kicking. . . . But just a minute, Studs, I've got to call a girl up."

"I got to be blowing."

"Well, call me up and we'll go to a show some night."

He watched Ike hustling to the phone booth toward the back of the drug store. Something sneaky about him. Still, what he said sounded like there was something to it. How could a man as big as Imbray or his companies go bust? And if he hung on, he'd be sure in the long run to get his dough back with plenty of interest.

Outside, he looked to see if Pat or any other fellows were on the corner, and he was disappointed because they weren't, so he started home. Down five points more. Big break in all stocks. He tried to force the belief that Ike was right and it was just fluctuation. Jesus, it better be! And if it wasn't would he sock Ike Dugan! And he'd take his medicine like a man and not bawl over spilled milk.

He knew that he was kidding himself, because he really was worried about the stocks. Still, how could a man so big as Imbray go bust? With deliberation, he lit a cigarette and calmly inhaled. People seeing him wouldn't know that he was worrying and nine hundred and sixty bucks out on his investments. He was just calmly puffing at a fag, and that, mister, was Studs Lonigan. But was it? And was it true that everything that went up came down, and when it hit the bottom it had to go up again?

A girl approached, and when she came closer, he saw that she was a hefty wench with sex appeal sticking out all over her.

"Going any place, sister?"

He heard her heels rapping over the pavement. Stuck-up bitch. But wouldn't it have been nice taking her to Jackson Park, forgetting every goddamn thing while he loved her up, for all he was worth. He just couldn't feel as confident as Ike Dugan had. Well, this experience should teach him a lesson, at least, he told himself bitterly. Already, the cost of his

honeymoon, of a hell of a lot of things, was lost. He tried to
make up his mind what he should do, and if he should sell
and take his loss. Then the nine hundred and sixty bucks would
simply be floating down the creek. Just like a drowning man
who's gone under for the third time. Nothing to say but too
bad.

Suppose he should walk up to this doggy-dressed old man
coming toward him and say, brother, I just lost nine hundred
and sixty bucks, hard-earned bucks, on the brain of Solomon
Imbray, and all the public utilities of the Middle West, what
do you think of that? Or suppose he should see Red Kelly and
pass it off as if he was just losing a nickel. Carry it off
and faze Red. But that would show nothing except that he
was a good loser, and where did it get him, being a good loser?

He lit another cigarette and thought how easy it seemed
for some people to make money. Jesus, why couldn't he have
that kind of luck? Others didn't deserve it any more than he
did. He wished he could meet someone to talk to, and make
himself forget it. Hell, just think how many guys there were
in the world who could lose that much dough just like it was
only cigar money.

He shrugged his shoulders and tried to squeeze consolation
out of the thought that that was the way the world went.
Only, hell, it seemed so simple to make money on stocks, so
easy for the market to go up rather than down, and after he
had cleaned up, for it then to go any damn way it pleased.
It had been pie for many guys, why not for him?

It was just like watching a baseball game. The pitcher on
the side you wanted to lose would seem to have nothing on
the ball, and would only appear to bob it up to the plate
with lanterns hung on it. Watching the batters on your
favorite team step into the batter's box, you would look over
the field. Suddenly it would seem as if there were so many
places where safe hits could be driven, and so many breaks
could happen to make your side win. And the batters would
swing hard enough to knock a house down, massacring the
air, popping up, poking out dinky, measly grounders. Or if
somebody would connect with a safe hit, he wouldn't be driven
home for a run. Inning after inning would pass, and it would
still seem so easy for your team to win, and maybe your team
would fill the bases with one out, and it would look sure like
they were going to put the game on ice. And then pop ups,
double plays, and you wonder why, Jesus Christ, why, it
seemed so easy for the game to be won, and still it was lost.
It was just the same with the market and his stock.

He tossed his cigarette away. He was very lonesome, and

he didn't want to be alone and thinking about such things. But it was always that way. You couldn't think of anything you wanted to, and when you were in the dumps you thought of all your gripes and troubles and felt yourself to be a miserable no-good, bad-news bastard, and that was just how he felt. He looked around at the quiet street, the night, half dark only because the moon was so full and shiny, and he looked at it, and at clouds covering it, and at the lamp-post-lights cutting areas out of the shadows, and he wanted things, wanted something, wanted his luck to change. He couldn't stand this, and he quickened his steps to get home and read the newspaper, listen to the radio, do anything to get those thoughts out of his head.

IV

"Hello, Dad," Studs said, still breathing rapidly as he entered the parlor.

"Hello, Bill. What's in the paper tonight?"

"A break in the stock market, and it looks like they got the goods on that Methodist minister who's mixed in that divorce suit out in California."

"The dirty Protestant A. P. A. Fooling around with a decent little girl who sings in his choir. Stringing him up would be too good for him. You wouldn't find a Catholic priest doing a thing like that," the father said with venom.

"How was Amos and Andy tonight?" Studs asked.

"Oh, they were all right," Lonigan said.

There was something on the old man's mind. Must be the stock-market break. He could see that the old man had something to say to him, too. He'd need that money now. For a moment, he felt as he used to when he was a kid, and his father was really a boss over him. He grew fearful of his father as he had done in those days when he'd done something the old man didn't want him to do. Then he realized that he wasn't a kid any more and he and his father acted differently toward each other.

"Let's see that paper, I want to look at the stock-market news."

Studs handed him the newspaper and watched his father's fretting face as he read.

"Looks damn rotten, all right, Bill," he said as if to himself.

"Think things are going to keep on this way?"

"I don't know what the hell it is, but something is wrong. It's the big fellows, the banks and Wall Street," Lonigan said laying aside the paper.

"I don't know," Studs said, because he hadn't listened closely and he hadn't anything else to say.

"Bill, I had my stocks sold out from under my feet today."

"Gee, Dad. That's rotten, I'm terribly sorry. How much?"

"Five thousand bucks more, Bill."

Studs lit a cigarette and rose to get an ash tray.

"Goddamn robbers," Lonigan cursed.

They sat in silence.

"Bill, I'm in a hole now. I can't collect on bills long overdue me, and I'm going to have to meet a big mortgage payment in the early fall. And with wages to pay out and the household expenses to meet, I'm in a tighter pinch than I ever was in my life. Can I borrow that money of yours for a little while?"

Studs' face dropped. He looked aside.

"Of course, Bill, I feel that I ain't got the right to ask you, and if you don't want to, why, I'll have to try elsewhere. I've already borrowed up to the hilt on my life insurance, and it's pretty damn hard raising any money these days."

"It isn't that, it's. . . ."

"What?" Lonigan said with questioning anxiety, as Studs, failing to continue, seemingly groped for words.

"Well, you see, Dad, after Catherine and I got engaged, I thought that I'd be needing all the money I could get, and that I ought to put my money in something that paid me a little more than just the bank interest, so I took a chance."

"You lost it?"

"I bought some Imbray stock at twenty-five a share, and it's down to thirteen. I'm nine hundred and sixty bucks out if I sell."

"Bill, you should have asked me. You should have asked me," Lonigan said regretfully, showing that he was deeply hurt.

"I meant to. And well, Dad, I just took a chance. I was just a damn sucker."

"God, Bill! Imbray stock is as shaky as a reed in the wind."

"I thought that since it is based on public utilities, and with a smart man like Solomon Imbray controlling it, it would be safe."

"I know. I had money in some Imbray securities, too, and that's why I'm holding the bag. That stock is paper and water. You better get out from under with what you got left in the morning, and take your loss. Something left is better than nothing."

"Think so, Dad?"

"Yes, Bill. Get out, and don't try that stunt again without asking me about it. I've learned now, myself. They just wait for suckers, sheep to fleece in the market. If you'd only asked me, I might have warned you. This is the wrong time to go fooling around in stocks. The reason I lost today is, I bought my stocks on margin, and they slid so I couldn't get out. The broker was carrying me along a little. But today it was the end.

"It's the wrong time, Bill."

Studs agreed with a meek nod. He could see that the old man had been hurt, all right. Lonigan turned on the radio.

> *Did you ever hear Pete go tweet*
> *tweet, tweet on his piccolo?*
> *No? Well you've missed a lot. . . .*

Lonigan did not listen, but sat down in his chair, brooding, and forgetting, with that same blank, sleepy look on his face, that Studs had noticed so frequently these last months.

A snappy jazz band broke out, stirring Studs, making him want a good time, fun, dancing, drinking, whoopee. The loud fast rhythm seemed to be in his nerves. He beat his foot on the carpet, swayed his shoulders.

"You better sell out tomorrow, Bill, and bank that money. I'll see if I can't borrow a little on my Order of Christopher insurance. And with the Democrats back in power, I'm hoping that I can line up some contracts. In fact, I think I'll go see Barney McCormack about it tomorrow," Lonigan said while an announcer eulogized a talcum powder. "You'll need what you got left out of it for your wedding. And these contracts or something will turn up."

"I'm going to sell, all right, Dad. But you're really welcome to the money. You better take it. Things will be much better by the time I'll need it, and you'll be able to pay me back then."

"Bill, I hope to be able to give you much more than that when you're married, if I only get some good breaks. But I won't take this yet. You bank it. I'll get out of this hole, all right, and there has to be a pickup. America is too great and too rich a country to go to the dogs. And we'll ride right back up on the waves."

Studs could see, though, that the old man was hit. He felt as if he'd stuck a knife in his dad's back. Judas Iscariot. He sank in his chair, dreamily listened to sugared sad music, feeling lousy.

CHAPTER EIGHT

I

Seeing the morning sunlight beyond the window, hearing the sounds of life in the alley, Studs was glad to be awake and to know that the distressing sadness he had been feeling was only a dream. He stretched himself out comfortably, and with his eyes on the ceiling tried to remember his dream. All he could remember was that he had been very sad and afraid in it. He sighed again because it had only been a dream, now it was morning, and he had a sunny day ahead of him with nothing to do but take it easy.

In the alley an automobile exhaust went off like a gun.

He guessed he might even wait a few days on his stock, and see if it didn't go up. Because if the market broke yesterday, it was only natural that there would be a little stabilization today. A man like Imbray with all his money would back up his stock, and if he waited a few days he would, anyway, not be out as much as he was.

He got up and stretched his arms. Looking down at the small, grassless, fenced-in square of a back-yard, watching an ice wagon pass, he thought of how good he felt this morning. And the sun slanting down the flat sides of the building across the alley! It was going to be a good day.

He took his time washing, and thought of how he would maybe go out in the park and sit in the sun. He dressed lazily and walked to the kitchen for breakfast.

"Your father looked very worried this morning," Mrs. Lonigan said.

"Well, there won't be much business now maybe until fall, and he's worried. By then business will be going again."

"I do hope that something does happen for your poor father's sake. He's like a changed and unhappy man these days."

"It will."

"You're not working today, are you?"

Studs stared at her, wondering. What was the idea of such a dumb question, because she knew he wasn't or he'd have been gone long before a quarter to nine.

"No."

"Rest, then, and take it easy."

"I am. I'm going to the park and get some sun."

"You better not sit in the grass. It will be damp at

597

this time of the year and you might catch cold. You must take care of yourself."

"I will."

After breakfast, he lounged in the parlor, reading the newspaper.

GRAPEFRUIT KING PREDICTS GOOD TIMES
Business Has Improved Forty Per Cent
Says Hiram Cole

That sounded good.

MUSSOLINI PLANS CORPORATIVE STATE

He guessed Mussolini was a smart man, but flipped the pages to the funnies.

Throwing the newspaper aside, he left, thinking of how Moon Mullins was a real character. Slug Mason had been a little like Moon, poor Slug.

He drifted toward Seventy-first Street, looking upon himself as a man with business interests who was puzzled by the problem of selling out or holding onto his investments. Maybe if he held, he'd lose more. Maybe not. Best to think it over so as not to make a mistake.

And he hoped something interesting or exciting would happen in the park. He crossed over Sixty-seventh Street, cut through a path in the bushes and emerged at the extremity of the large golf course. A feeling of being lost and empty, with nothing to do, came upon him, and he stood with his eyes fixed on the sprouting green before him. He'd been anxious to get here, and now that he was in the park, what?

He hoped that he would meet some girl and that they'd get on together. He set off strolling along the edge of the course, with the image of a girl in his head as if she were walking beside him, tall and dark, and sexy, and if he took her rowing she would sit facing him, showing off her thighs, and if they sat on a lonely bench she would wait to be kissed and felt. Jesus Christ, he exclaimed, his desire reaching a painful point.

He looked around, the trees in front of him having grown larger as he approached, the sounds of automobiles as they skimmed through the park like an overtone. He had the feeling that something was going to happen, and he was nervous for it to hurry up, whatever it was. He picked up a branch, swished it, flung it aside. He thought, Christ, he did want a girl, hot, and pretty, and willing, who knew tricks that would set him nearly nuts, the kind that would go shiveringly crazy for him the moment he laid his hand on her. And they would lie around together in the park, or else at her apartment, where they would be stripped, and even maybe taking a bath together.

He saw a patch of grass with surprise, and realized that he had lost his sense of where he was. He felt as if he had just come from a hot time with a girl, and then realized that it had only been wishes, and he wished it had been the real article in the flesh. Across the golf course, so small that they were like images in a picture, he watched a man and woman pursuing golf balls they had just driven. He wondered who they were, what they were, were they in love, and did they sleep together, and were they well off and not bothered by worries over money? Envy of them grew in him, because they had something to do, and he hadn't. He grew dreamy, forgot them, lost consciousness of the fact that he was even walking, and imagined himself a golfer like Chick Evans or Bobby Jones, only greater, smashing records in a tournament, with a large gallery following to cheer him as he made impossible drives and shots with ease, and even made a hole in one.

A frown suddenly settled on his face, and like a gloomy cloud the thought of his stocks came back to him. He walked in an aimless course, grabbed a handful of budding leaves off the bushes, scattered them, picked up a piece of broken branch, peeled the bark off with his finger nails, dropped it.

He lit a cigarette and looked around him, seeing with suddenness, and as if for the first time, the earth, grass in sunlight, with a few sparkles of dew, and in the distance, over trees, a light sky. A desire as if to catch these things he saw came on him, and then again the worry about money and stocks returned to fill his mind. He stopped to stare at an oak, its limbs rattling a trifle in the wind, hoping that by concentrating on it he would drive the worry away.

Christ, he was getting goofy as a loon! Studs Lonigan was a poet and didn't know it.

"Fore. Fore."

He turned to see golfers shouting and waving at him, and briskly returned to the bushes by the edge of the course. He saw a golf ball land, scud along the ground, stop. He saw grass and earth stretching away, people moving over the course, and, as he glanced upward, a bank of clouds smothering the sun and draping shadows over the park.

He had a sense he had often felt as a kid walking around in Washington Park, looking and wishing for something to do. But then he had had no real responsibilities, and he'd expected any damn thing to happen any minute. And now.

He saw in his mind, but not so clearly as he wanted to,

the old Studs in short pants, playing indoors, on the small
gravel diamond of the Washington Park playground, swinging, smacking the ball over the iron picket fence. And he
remembered a rainy day when he was alone in the playground,
and Miss Tyson, the playground director, had brought
him into her office which was between the boys' and girls'
cans in a rough-edged stone building. She had talked to him
about what he wanted to be in life, and he'd felt that she was
looking at him in a funny way. And when the rain had come
down harder, she had closed the door, and she had sat with
her legs crossed, letting him get a good eyeful, and she'd run
her hand through his hair. Why had he been so dumb and
innocent? He dropped into a bench along the walk that he
and Catherine had passed last Sunday, and meditatively puffed
at a cigarette. He felt as if he was the old Studs Lonigan, and
he would see Dan Donoghue or Helen Shires before the day
was out and. . . .

"Got a light, lad?"

Studs looked up and saw a sandy-haired fellow with
a seedy suit and blue shirt.

"What?"

"Got a match?"

"Sure. I was just sort of sitting here and forgot where I
was, and didn't hear you. Here."

"Thanks," the stranger said, accepting the book of matches
and lighting a cigarette.

"I suppose you're out of work like the rest of us."

"Well, in a way."

"I know I've been carrying the banner during these days
of Hoover prosperity."

"Yes, it seems pretty tough, but things ought to get better,
and Hoover probably won't be elected next year."

"Things won't get better for me, not under this system."

"How come? There's no use throwing up the sponge,"
Studs said, thinking that, hell, the guy looked on the level,
and like a white man and just down on his luck, and he might
just as well try to cheer the guy up a little.

"I'm not throwing up the sponge. I'm just learning things,
and I've learned, this last winter, that a guy like me isn't worth
any more than a rusty piece of machinery."

Studs lit a cigarette and tried to think of something to
say. The guy seemed sore at the world, the way he had just
made that last crack.

"If you're a workingman, buddy, none of those Democrats
or Republicans mean anything for you."

"Well, what's the matter with Al Smith?"

"The same thing that's the matter with all of them. They don't mean any good to me. I've carried the banner all winter. And by God, I'm not going to carry the banner forever, sleeping in that Hooverville under Wacker Drive."

"Things can't always go down."

"I know it. They can come up in war."

"Who do you think we'll go to war with, Japan or Russia?"

"By God, if the U. S. goes to war with Russia, I don't shoulder a gun."

Jesus, a Red!

"But you wouldn't be a traitor to your country?"

"My country, what do I own here?"

"Aren't you an American?"

"I was born here, but if I had the fare I'd go to Russia tomorrow."

"But aren't they Reds and anarchists there? Don't you read the papers?"

"Sure, I read the papers. Lies. Lad, they're filling us full of lies so they can rob us all. We got to wake up."

"But Bolshevism means revolution."

"How else are we going to win the means of production for ourselves?"

"But that's anarchy."

"What is it when guys like me all over the country carry the banner, sleep in Hoovervilles? What is it when they shoot down coal miners?"

"I'm not a Bolshevik. It's against the country and the church." Studs wished the fellow would go away. If he was his size and in better health, he might sock him. He got up.

"I got to be traveling. But you'll never get anywhere with those ideas, fellow."

"Yes, I'll never carry a musket."

"So long."

Studs laughed at the crazy bastard. A Bolshevik. He supposed the guy was a nigger lover, too. Well, let the Bolsheviks get tough. They'd be taken care of, just the same as the shines were during the race riots of '19.

He felt tired, and the hell with that nutty guy. He had been thinking about old times, too, when the fellow had interrupted him to give that phony Bolshevik spiel.

II

Studs stood on the grass edge of the large, rectangular skin-dirt athletic field, hearing the crack of a baseball bat while a group of fellows snapped through infield practice, and a lad in a khaki shirt fungoed flies to five others in the outfield. About five yards from him a group of four sat watching.

The third baseman, a lank lad in a faded blue shirt, fozzled a ground ball, and, seeking hurriedly to pick it up, kicked it around in the dirt.

"The bush leagues for you, Spunk."

"Get off your can and come out here and do better."

"The bushes, boy. You're getting old."

"All right, Cal, get the lead out of your tail," one of the fungo hitters called, lifting a long high fly which was easily caught by a swarthy left-handed fellow in a white shirt.

Studs watched the infield practice, the grounders slapped hard, cutting over the dirt, the ball snapped around from player to player. They were pretty good, and they worked fast. Even though he had never cared a hell of a lot for baseball, it was something to watch, neat, quick work. The shortstop ran low to his left, smeared a fast grounder with one hand, bobbed the ball, off balance, to the second baseman, who caught it, wheeled around in the same motion and whipped the ball to first base.

"Spunk, how do you like that?" one of those on the grass called while the ball was pegged around.

"This is the million-dollar infield."

"Yes, if it had a third baseman."

Studs edged a bit closer to the group on the grass. Looked like a nice bunch of lads, and they had enough for a game. He'd like to play.

"That boy Spunk is good."

"He ought to get a try-out in the big shows."

"He's good around here, but he wouldn't make the grade. Can't hit a sharp-breaking curve ball. A pitcher like Jack Casey, who was with me at the Braves training camp last year, could make him eat out of his hand. And Jack never made the grade."

"How about you, Artie?"

"Couldn't get myself lined up, so I'm playing semi-pro. Hell, this country is full of guys trying to get into the game, and plenty of them are good. With minor leagues folding up like tents, and with old-timers coming down from the big leagues and the Class A. A. outfits, and then with chain-store systems like the one the Cardinals run, it's damn hard getting lined up even in a dinky little X. Y. Z. league."

"Maybe you're right."

"Look at Jack. He thought he'd make a go of it in pro athletics, and he did have one good season in the Three I League but then he threw his arm out. He's up the creek, and he doesn't make any too much peddling insurance. If I could get a decent job, I'd throw the idea up, too, and stick to my job, maybe just picking up a few pennies on Sunday playing semi-pro and having some fun playing basketball in the Christopher League in winter."

A Christy. Studs looked at him, a light-haired, husky, square-faced fellow in his early twenties, the kind of a mugg and build a ball player would have.

"Let's get going with the game," Spunk called, walking in.

Studs watched them choosing up, hoping, because there were only seventeen.

"Hey, lad, want to play?"

"Sure, all right," he said, slowly taking off his coat.

"You're on my side," the fellow named Artie said.

"Say, I just heard you talking. You're a Christy, aren't you? I just went through Kempis Council. My name's Lonigan."

"Mine's Pfeiffer, Timothy Murphy Council. Say, a young kid named Lonigan went to Mary Our Mother when I was there."

"Yeah, that was my kid brother."

"What ever happened to him? I know he left M. O. M. to go to Tower Tech."

"He's working a little with my old man in the painting business."

Studs put his left hand in the fielder's glove offered him and walked nonchalantly out to right field. He stood with hands on hips, waiting. Easy pitching and he'd get by, even if he hadn't played in years. And it would keep him in the sun. He bent forward with his hands on his knees, while the pitcher lobbed the ball up to the right-handed batter, a short fellow in a gray shirt. A high fly soared toward right center and Studs, seeing the ball come somewhere near him, ran forward to his right, confused, afraid of muffing the catch. Seeing that he was misjudging it, he ran backward, still to his right, with his eye on the lowering ball.

"I got it," the center fielder called.

Studs stopped in his tracks, and watched the center fielder gracefully nab the ball on the run. Breathing quickly, but glad that his misjudgment hadn't been serious, he returned to his position. He waited, over-anxious. A line single was driven to left, the pitcher picked a pop out of the air, and a dumpy texas-leaguer over third base placed runners on first and second.

"You better go back and play in a grammar-school

league," Spunk said, stepping to bat after Pfeiffer had dropped an easy toss at first base.

Spunk waited, swinging left-handed, and Pfeiffer motioned Studs backward. Spunk connected, and the ball travelled high out to Studs, who wavered around in circles, the ball landing three feet away from him.

"Jesus Christ, what a Babe Hermann that was," the center-fielder exclaimed more loudly than he had intended, while Studs clumsily retrieved the ball. A pain cut paralyzingly into his shoulder when he threw wildly to the infield.

"Take it easy, Lonigan. It's only a scrub game," Pfeiffer said when Studs came in abashed at the end of the inning.

"Hell, I haven't played in years. I used to be pretty good but I'm out of the practice."

"Everybody muffs a few."

"Hey, Artie, bushel baskets are cheap these days," Spunk called from third base.

"I'm going to knock your hands off when I get up," Artie called.

Studs stood several feet away from the players on his side, who grouped themselves on the grass edge. When he came to bat he'd redeem himself.

Pfeiffer, a left-handed batter, stood at the plate after the first two batters had flied out and, swinging late, stung a line drive just beyond Spunk's gloved hand.

"What's that you say about bushel baskets?" he megaphoned through his hands, standing on second base.

"Save us a lick, Pete."

"I'm getting fed up with nothing to do but lay around this damn park."

"Write a letter to Hoover. Maybe he'll put you on some commission and you'll get a job to help keep other people out of jobs."

"No, Jack, I'm serious. I ask myself how long is this thing going to keep on."

"Well, do what I say. Write a letter to Hoover."

"The bathing beach is going to open soon and maybe we can all get on as life guards."

"I can't swim well enough."

"Hang around until 1933 and you can get a job at the World's Fair."

"Swell hit, Pete. Come on, Al, lean on it."

"All I can say is some damn thing has got to happen."

"Hire a hall, you ain't got no kick. Laying around in the sun, playing ball, looking at nursemaids, and hearing the birds sing."

"Swell catch, Spunk, you lucky bastard."

Studs waited anxiously in right field, but batter after batter came up without hitting to him. He walked in at the end of the inning more confident. He'd get a rap this time and sock one.

"Save us a bat, lad," a fellow in a dirty gray sweatshirt called while Studs stepped up with two out. The bat seemed too heavy and, facing the pitcher, he lost confidence.

"Hey, which side am I on?"

"Wait till the inning's up."

He decided that this fellow could take his place. He swung late, fizzling a grounder to the pitcher, and didn't even run.

"Hey, Pfeiffer, he can take my place."

"No, it's only a scrub game, Lonigan."

"Well, I'm kind of tired anyway."

"Come around again and tell the kid brother I was askin' about him."

He crossed the driveway and walked along the gravel path flanking the lagoon, which lay below in shimmering sunlight. He should have gone on playing. He would have gotten into his stride, hit some solid ones, and nabbed fly balls, too. It would have been nice passing the time, and they seemed like a decent bunch. He imagined himself driving a home-run over the center-fielder's head and then making one-handed and shoe-string catches in the outfield. He shrugged his shoulders, laughed at his sudden interest in baseball.

III

His watch pointed at eleven-thirty. What would he do? He could walk home to dinner and that would cut a hole in the long day ahead of him. He ambled on in a careless, unenergetic stride. Was the stock market going up, he asked himself, dropping down on a bench and lighting a cigarette.

His vague awareness of chirping birds and of automobiles rushing behind him was distracted by a strolling couple. Lucky lad with such a cute and neat trick, and maybe he was taking her to a secluded spot on the wooded island, and he would sink his head in her lap, and she would stroke his face and hair, and maybe she was nuts about him and wanted it from the guy so much that she'd even risk being caught in daylight. Wished he had a girl nuts about him like that. Of course, there was Catherine, but she was decent, and this was a different matter. It made a guy proud, let him sort of feel his oats, gave him something to brag about. After he and Catherine got married and she got used to it, would she feel that way about him? If she didn't, what would be the use of marriage? He watched the couple disappear around a bend in the park. Lucky bastard.

An elderly woman with a neat black suit and a haughty society-woman manner about her looked at him with disdain as if he were something like a piece of garbage. She thought he was a bum. He sat up erect, straightened his tie, dusted off his shoes with his handkerchief. He wasn't a bum. But what the hell, these people would probably never see him again, and what difference did it make? But still, he wasn't a bum.

Yawning, he examined his watch; a quarter to twelve. What to do? He wished someone he knew would happen along.

But even if it was dull, it was good having the sun on him. And if he did this regularly, he would get a good, healthy coat of tan. He removed his coat, carefully folded it and laid it over the bench beside him. He rolled up his sleeves and looked at his thin white arms. Good, too, getting them tanned. He sat realizing that it had suddenly become quiet with just a faint stirring of leaves and sounds of birds. Then, from Stony Island, came the rumbling of a street car. Automobiles passed, an engine dying, chugging, starting again, its hum dying away. Human voices echoing from a distance made him want people to talk to. Maybe he could take a walk to the old neighborhood later in the day, see the old streets, the old buildings.

It was just nice, though, to sit here, and through the bushes to see the water, the sunlight dancing on it, like it was alive. The same way the sunlight had danced on the lagoon in Washington Park when he and Lucy had sat in the tree. Oars splashed and a boat rode by. Might be a good idea to go rowing, but he changed his mind, because that was too strenuous a form of exercise.

He let a burning cigarette hang from his mouth until he coughed from a throatful of smoke. He leaned back and with shaded eyes looked up at a sky whose shimmering and pervasive brightness brought water to his eyes. He blinked at a squirrel moving swiftly across the walk and into the bushes. He was humble and soft, and felt that there was something behind all this that he saw, sun, and sky, and new grass, and trees, and birds, and the bushes, and the squirrel, and the lagoon, and people moving by him, and street cars and automobiles, and it was God. God made all this, moved it, made it live, himself, that Red he'd met who was against Him, the fellows playing ball. And God was the spirit behind it all and behind everything. Gee, if Catherine was only here now! He shook his head, as if to drive all these thoughts away because if he told them to anybody, it would just sound goofy. He wasn't a poet.

But Christ, this was the life!

From far off he heard twelve-o'clock whistles. They made him want to do something, and they made him feel the same as train whistles did.

A woman of about thirty, neat, good figure, hopped along holding to the leash of a straining Airedale. The dog forced her onto the grass, switched directions, tugged and pulled across to the grass on the other side of the walk. She did not return his glance. Maybe she, too, thought he was a park bum. He wished a neat trick, like his sister Fran, would come by, speak to him, he'd show her he wasn't a bum. He watched the dog drag her forward, and didn't give a damn what she thought of him, and silently exclaimed, Up your brown Lizzie.

He sat back, feeling that warm sun on his arms and face, contented again. Nice.

IV

The Greek restaurant at Sixty-third and Stony Island Avenue with the imitation marble counter and the modernistic gray and dull red furnishings was crowded with high-school kids, and as Studs entered he heard an uproar of talk, giggling girls at the booths and tables, a clatter of dishes, and, above it, a male chorus on a radio singing snappily:

My wife is on a diet,
And since she's on a diet,
Home isn't home any more.
No gravy and potatoes,
Just lettuce and tomatoes,
Where are the pies I adore?
Oh, oh, oh, oh. What a disgrace,
I'm ashamed to look a grapefruit straight in the face.

The stout Greek behind the counter, hearing the song, wobbled to the radio and twisted the dial, bringing forth a saccharine torch-singing love-song.

Studs, smiling at the incident and thinking that it was a good song for Catherine to hear, took a seat at the counter. On his left, he noticed a young khaki-shirted workingman, soaking up the gravy on his plate with a slice of bread, and on his other side, a tall marcelled blond lad, with a long face, who wore a blue sweater with a large white P on the front. Park High athlete, he thought. He watched a dumpy waitress pass and hoped his order would be taken soon because he didn't like it with all these crazy high-school kids around.

"Have you ever dated Irene Knisley, Jack?" the athlete asked the black-haired, baby-faced lad beside him.

"No, but she can be my big moment any time she wants."

"She's a big moment who will heat you plenty. I dropped up to the Park Community Center dance last Friday, and she was there. You ought to dance with her."

"Tompkins took her out and he says she's plenty strong on the lovin'. He's certain he can make her."

Studs thought that they were just drying the milk behind their ears. He toyed with his knife and fork, and thought about how hungry he was.

"Hey, Katie," the baby-faced high-school student called out at the clumpy waitress.

"What?"

"How'd you like to be my big moment?"

"Come around on Sunday. I have kindergarten then," she flung back.

Studs smiled. He followed her with his eye as she moved to the slot opening back to the kitchen and shoved a pile of used dishes into it. He gulped down the glass of water and saw, as she turned, that she was no chicken, and her breasts almost fell down to her belly. Not worth the making. How did broads like her feel, because they had so little to offer a guy? They must know they look like hell and that a guy would have to be pretty hard up before he tried to play around with them. In fact, they must, in dolling themselves up to be made, have a hell of a lot of nerve and think a lot of what they had. And from the looks of her tough face, crusted with powder, she didn't look decent, but the type that would go with anything in pants.

> *You've got me pickin' petals off o' daisies,*
> *Some say yes, some say no . . .*

Still, some guys went for dumb broads like her, and would be glad to get her. At times, he might himself, because a guy got that way.

"What'll you have?" she asked in a strident voice.

"Roast beef and mashed potatoes."

"My pater's sobbing the blues, too, about dough. He's cut down on my allowance, but the mater slips me something and doesn't snitch to him," the athlete said.

"My dad's swell, a real pal. He always says to me, 'Jack, I had my fun when I was your age and I don't want my kid to be an angel.' He doesn't want me to kill myself studying, either."

"My pater's a babbitt."

The plate of food, soaked with greasy gravy, was set before Studs. He dumped catsup beside the meat, and commenced eating rapidly. His mouth jammed, he thought that these kids didn't know how lucky they were, having a good time and a chance to get an education in high school, and they ought to make the best of their chance. An education didn't hurt you.

"I tried to date Daisy Dell for the Alpha dance, and she was oh, so sorry. So I said to her, 'Say, don't cry, baby, you're not Clara Bow.' She hung up on me," the baby-faced lad said, and the athlete laughed.

"Apple pie and coffee," Studs called at the dumpy waitress as she scuttled by him with an armful of orders.

> *I lift up my finger and I say*
> *"Tweet, tweet, shush, shush, now, now,*
> *Come, come."*

He wished he'd gone to high school and college and belonged to fraternities and had a good time. But then, wasn't he a Christy? Wait, too, until the next initiation in his council. It would be a knockout. And he ought to start going to meetings.

"Apple pie and coffee."

She didn't even notice him. He wanted to get out, too, away from all these high-school boys. Goddamn bitch! She ought to be glad she had a job these days instead of gassing like she was now with a punk down the counter during a rush period like this.

"Apple pie and coffee."

"I got it the first time, mister," she called back.

Nervy bitch, who did she think she was, getting so tough? But then, what else could you expect from such a dumb-looking waitress? She set a slab of pie and a cup of coffee, with the coffee slopping over onto the saucer, before him. Coffee dripped onto his trousers as he took his first sip of it.

> *I'm just daffy 'bout daffodils*
> *And especially you*

He slid off the stool, and walked by a table of giggling girls.

"And her new dress was simply stunning."

He took toothpicks at the counter, and stood outside, with a toothpick in the corner of his mouth, hearing the noise of the elevated trains, of street cars and automobiles, seeing high-school students drift by him. His stomach turned sour from the meal.

What next?

V

Maybe he might pick up a girl, a neat, sweet little Park High girl in the park, he thought hopefully, strolling along a shady gravel path which circled around the northern extremity of the lagoon. Other guys did, why not he? But did he really love Catherine when he wanted to do this? Love was one thing, and a good time with a stray pickup was another. He was only human and that was just natural, and when a guy went with a clean, decent girl like Catherine what else could he do?

Ahead of him was a burly girl hanging on the arm of a fellow who wore a checkered cap and needed a haircut. He walked close behind them, trying to hear what they were saying, wondering whether or not she was the fellow's lay. Looked like she knew her onions and liked them, too. Tough, hard kind of broad, he decided, hearing her loud and rather cracked voice.

"But, Charlie, I didn't. I didn't. Jesus Christ, I couldn't."

"Don't crap me, sister, because I'm not the kind of a guy who lets himself get crapped. See?"

He couldn't imagine a fellow talking that way to a girl if she was decent. They selected an unoccupied bench, and Studs, walking by, noted the concerned, pleading expression on the girl's cheaply decorated face, and the fellow's curt and unbelieving look.

"Charlie, you just got to believe me," she said in a throbbing voice.

He would like to have stayed near and heard more, but he couldn't just stand gaping while a guy scrapped with his girl. He guessed that the lad thought she was two-timing him. He wouldn't put it past that kind of a broad, either. He smiled, thinking that Catherine was different, and wouldn't ever pull such tricks behind his back.

He walked on, his feet dragging, in no hurry. Lots of people in the park, fellows with nothing else to do, he supposed. Like the one ahead of him on the bench, sitting like a mope, half asleep, looking ahead of him at nothing. Maybe he was a poor bastard more down in his luck than Studs Lonigan.

"I knew Dopey Ahern when he drove for the Continental Express Company. But he went in the beer-running racket, and they put him on the spot," a fellow said to two companions as they strolled by Studs.

He thought of how when you went out and listened to what people said, you heard all kinds of things, people washing their dirty linen in public, talking about friends and business and gash, and it made him think how the world must be, at every minute, so full of people fighting, and jazzing, and dying, and working, and losing jobs, and it was a funny world, all right, full of funny people, millions of them. And he was only one out of all these millions of people, and they were all trying to get along, and many of them had gotten farther than he. Hell, what right did he have to expect to get anywhere with all these millions and millions in the same game, with fellows starting out with dough and an education, and better health than he had? He felt small and a little goofy. He looked around, seeing old men on a bench, a woman with a baby buggy, three fellows who looked like college boys on the grass, a skinny park policeman. How many of all the people around him, how many of all the people in the park, were ahead of him so far?

His feet began to ache and he flopped again on a bench. One-o'clock factory whistles blew from somewhere. A long afternoon still ahead of him. Did many fellows sitting around the park feel the same as he did, wanting something exciting to happen? A fleshy, light-brown Negress came along the path, her dress splitting against her thighs, her breast nipples clear against her black-and-white dress. A tight feeling gripped him. Whee! And he whiffed strongly an odor of cheap scent. Plenty of guys would like what she had. Plenty of white broads would like to have as much as she had. It was a goddamn shame, too, that a broad with all that stuff should be black and not white, he told himself, wishing someone was around so he could have sprung such a witty crack on them. Should he follow her even if she was a nigger? He looked after her at her slender brown silken legs, and he was tempted to whistle, to get up and follow her. Hell, she might just be a whore because he guessed most black gals were hustlers anyway. And even if she wasn't, a dark-skinned baby ought to fall all over herself with joy if a white guy propositioned her. But kissing one of them. Ugh . . . He eagerly watched her disappear from sight, and he saw her naked in his mind. Jesus, he was pretty lousy getting so het up over a dark-skinned wench. And still, brother, white or black, she had it. But here he was engaged to a decent girl like Catherine, and wanting a nigger. Lousy . . . If the nice girls men married knew the dirty places they went playing around and . . . that was another witty one he wanted to spring sometime.

He yawned and watched a baby toddle bow-legged ahead of its mother. What would he do? An old man with an ear phone. He drowsed, fell asleep, awakened stiff and dirty. Two-thirty. He started strolling toward home. He felt like a wreck. The day was more than half over anyway. And maybe his stock had gone up too.

CHAPTER NINE

I

After the movies, Studs and Catherine went to a small restaurant on Seventy-first Street. Studs hung his coat on a hook beside the table and absent-mindedly sat down while she was removing her coat. He missed her frown, lit a cigarette, and settled comfortably in his chair. He thought of how his stock was now down to ten, and he had to make up his mind whether to hold it or sell. A drop from two thousand to eight hundred dollars, and Ike Dugan had said fluctuations. That bastard was going to have fluctuations the next time he met Studs Lonigan.

"You seem awfully interested in me," Catherine said, sitting down with a great fuss.

"What? What's the matter?" he asked absently.

"Nothing. Oh, nothing's the matter, I was just so pleased at the interest you show in me," she said with increased irony.

He looked at her, puzzled, hoping that she wasn't set on kicking up a row with him.

"You act like a perfect gentleman who is keeping within the proper bounds before a girl he doesn't even know, or something like that."

"Why, what's wrong, Catherine?" he asked, a vague whine in his voice.

"Nothing . . . Nothing," she snapped with mounting exasperation.

A bony waitress hovered over them, and Studs blushed, wondering if she had heard Catherine quarrelling.

"What'll you have, Catherine?" he asked solicitously, while she made faces at him.

"Coffee and lemon cream pie," she said haughtily at the waitress.

"One coffee and lemon cream pie, one milk and apple pie," he said, wondering what the devil was wrong.

He watched the waitress retreat to the counter, and to avoid Catherine's eye until she cooled off he glanced around the restaurant, at the neat pale green walls and the black-topped counter running almost the length of the opposite side. There were two fellows slouched at it over coffee, and two couples at tables near the window toward the front.

The proprietor emerged from the counter and dialed on the radio.

> *Singin' in the rain, just singin' in the rain,*
> *What a glorious feelin', I'm happy again.*

One of the fellows in the basket-backed chairs by the counter swung around, and Studs glanced back at Catherine, her expression revealing persisting displeasure.

"What did I do now?" he asked in a restrained voice, jittery because of her mood, thinking that if all girls were like Catherine, they all liked to fight with a fellow more than he liked to fight with them.

"Nothing," she said sharply, planting her elbows on the table, resting her fattish, dimpled chin in her palms, closing her lips poutishly, her eyes cutting intently upon him.

"Well, we're never going to get anywhere with you acting this way and expecting me to be a mind reader and read your mind when you're sore and I can't see the reason why," he said haltingly, hoping that she would snap out of it.

The waitress set the orders before them and went off.

> *I'll walk down the lane with a happy refrain,*
> *Singin', just singin' in the rain.*

"You men . . . You can't see farther than your noses. You've got as much delicacy and imagination as a . . . hound," she flung at him.

"Oh, come on. What the hell," he said with attempted persuasiveness, wanting at the same time not to lose his dignity or seem weak in her eyes.

"I cannot say that I distinctly approve of the language you use."

"Gee, don't you expect me to be a little natural, what's biting you?"

"Natural. I don't understand the same thing by natural that you do. And nothing is biting me. That's what I suppose you think, though, that just because we're engaged and I let you kiss me, that I am safely captured and won, and you can disregard me, even walk all over me, and I don't require any more consideration. You men, you're all alike, and think you only have to show consideration for a girl until you feel you are certain of her. Then you drop all politeness and reveal your real nature. You act *natural*. Well, if that's how smart you think you are, think again," she said, her anger feeding on itself as she spoke.

"Listen, I wish you'd snap out of it. I don't want fights, and don't like them," he said low, leaning over the table toward her, feeling like a clown with the two guys at the counter watching them and listening.

> *Singin' in the bathtub, happy once again,*
> *Watchin' all my troubles go swingin' down the drain,*
> *Singin' through the soapsuds, life is full of hope . . .*

"Yes, you don't like fights. You're a gentleman, too. Yes, a gentleman. You've hardly spoken a word to me all night, and you let me take off my coat, and sit down ahead of me. I know . . . You think you've won me, so I can be ignored. Well, I tell you this, I can play the same tune as you can, and just as long, too."

"Gee, is that all it is?" he smiled, but carefully so as not to give her grounds for thinking that he was laughing at her.

Catherine pouted, and stabbed at her pie with a fork. Studs concentrated on his pie and milk, and felt a tenseness hanging between them like a curtain dividing two sides of the table.

> *Reachin' for a towel, ready for a rub,*
> *Everybody's happy when singing in the tub.*

Studs looked up at her prepared to smile if she did, or if she gave a sign. She held her eyes on her pie, sipped coffee with the pout remaining on her plumply pretty face. He shrugged his shoulders and thought to himself, the goddamn women, how in hell could a guy please and satisfy them, and what the hell did they expect? Didn't he have enough serious stuff on his mind without this silliness?

"You're unbearable and insufferable," she said with excessive spite.

"What's eating you?" he countered, stunned by the unexpectedness of her remark.

"Eating me? What's eating me? I'll tell you what's eating me without any waste of words. You!"

"Oh, I am, am I? Well, isn't that just too bad!" he said, unwittingly raising his voice, attracting amused glances from the counter and other tables, flushing because they were putting on a show for strangers.

"You needn't tell the whole world, either. First, you insult me. Then you try to make a public disgrace of me," she said in a muffled but angry voice.

Hell, he guessed women just couldn't listen to reason. He finished eating in silence and waiting for her, smoking in assumed nonchalance.

> *Little brooklets breaking free,*
> *Work their way down to the sea.*

He smirked fatuously, and, catching him, she looked back in disgust, and he hadn't really meant it, either. With her last drink of coffee, she flounced up, grabbed her coat and stamped out of the restaurant. Feeling like a fool, he arose, laid a quarter under his cup. He could notice that the lads at the counter were laughing quietly. He laid another dime on the table, and put on his coat with determined nonchalance.

> *Birdies sing in cages, too,*
> *They know that's the thing to do. . . .*

He paid the bill.

"Goodnight," the proprietor said cheerfully.

"Goodnight," he said, hurrying out, seeming almost to feel eyes and laughter on his back.

Catherine was energetically walking along Seventy-first Street, her high heels rapping on the sidewalk. Hastening, he caught up with her and strode along at her left, breathing rapidly.

It was clear and pleasant out, and he glanced absently up at the skies, seeing star galaxies as if he were discovering them. It was nice. But he'd get a stiff neck and look like a sap walking along with his hands in his pockets and his eyes raised this way. Ahead, he saw the sidewalk, the red lanterns hanging from the railroad gates which pointed almost vertically from the street, buildings with darkened stores along the street. His mind wandered to his stocks. He forgot that she was beside him. A frail breeze tickled his neck pleasantly. He became aware of her clicking heels again. Christ, she was sore, all right, and that was just so much added to his grief.

"Listen," he exclaimed, trying to be forceful, this quarrel dragging too intolerably on his nerves.

"You needn't talk to me in that tone of voice. I don't have to stand for it."

"Well, come on, let's be sensible. There's no use in us going on like this."

"You're not talking to me, because anything you say goes in one ear and runs out the other."

"Oh, all right," he shrugged.

An electric train passed them with mechanical gruntings. Accompanied by the sound of warning bells, it rolled into the Stony Island Avenue station. Studs watched the lifting train gates. Automobiles and a surface car shot over Seventy-first and Stony Island Avenue. It struck him how queer it was that he should at this moment be walking along this street, past a block-long prairie, and of how, five or six years ago, he had never thought that his life would turn out this way, and he'd have laughed at anybody who'd have predicted that it would. Life was queer, funny, and most of the things that happened to you came without your ever expecting them.

"I suppose you consider yourself clever."

"I thought you weren't talking to me," he answered, his voice as ill-tempered and cruel as hers.

"I'm not. Only you're walking along here, so self-satisfied, acting as if you were so pleased, with a head like a big balloon full of false pride, acting as if you thought yourself so . . . indispensable. You men, you think a girl falls head over heels in love with you, and it makes you begin to think that you are the only and the best possible thing that comes walking along. You and your conceit."

Her remark hurt Studs, made him feel as if he had been socked in the jaw unexpectedly by his best friend, or as if he had suddenly discovered people talking about him behind his back.

"You're trying to act wise." His voice cracked, but he continued, "Listen, baby! Don't start getting top-heavy opinions about yourself, either."

A rush of blood seemed to charge to his face and he got more hot because he knew he wasn't carrying it off right. To appease his stricken pride, he silently exclaimed, Why, you goddamn bitch.

"Is that so?" she countered to his last spoken remark, uncontrolled tears running.

He wished they weren't quarrelling. He didn't want to hurt her and make her cry. But she made him goddamn sore, and what did she think she was, trying all this high-hat stuff on him, going off the handle the way she had, over nothing at all? And just at a time when he was worried over the money he had risked for their marriage? Just now when he felt he needed to depend on her, she pulled this trick. Goddamn nerve.

"I'll never forgive you for what you said," she sobbed as they came to Stony Island Avenue.

"You said nothing. You were just a sweet angel, the beautiful rose of no-man's-land, full of charity."

"I was in the right, and I've got a right to expect some consideration from you, and when you take me out you should show some interest in me, and some politeness."

"Well, I do," he whined defensively.

"Where? When do you give your demonstrations? I'd like to be present at one."

"Hell, you just don't understand," he said with melodramatic dejection.

"I guess I don't," she replied with dragging weariness. "I just don't understand why you act so mean and hateful. To understand that a person must have as much meanness and hate in them as you have in you. And I haven't, thank goodness, so I just can't understand. I know now. I learned something tonight. I learned your real value. And William Lonigan, I can never forgive you for the things you have said to me tonight."

Jesus Christ, when she sprang such goddamn silly chatter, he just ached to haul off and smack her down.

"I know you're a martyr, a poor stepped-on little girl, and I'm a big brute, a hairy ape of a low-brow. I know," he said sardonically.

"William Lonigan, I hate you," she sobbed, facing him with a compressed face.

"Well, if you do, and I'm everything you say I am, why do you go with me?"

"I shan't. I've learned my lesson. I learned my lesson," she said like a movie actress in a dramatic scene.

She looked at him, her facial muscles contracted, the lips firm and locked as if glued together, the eyes cloudy and wet with the tears which dribbled down her cheeks. Her look told him that she had said her last word, that her dislike and anger had become unspeakable. With a forced calmness and deliberation, while her tears choked her, she removed his engagement ring from her finger and handed it to him. Accepting it, he felt that he perceived a sign of weakening in her, and he thought that maybe she was hoping he would say something to break up the quarrel. But he wasn't sure, and he was afraid to seem weak to her. And Jesus Christ, he didn't want this.

"All right, baby," he said with a mask of exaggerated coldness for the tumbling feelings within him, taking the ring in his closed hand.

"I never want to see you or hear your voice again. Don't call me up. Don't ask me to forgive you, or to make up and forget this!" she said throbbingly.

"Jesus, ain't you acting a bit previous, as if I was going to come crawling around? Who do you think you're talking to?"

"A beast."

He left her in tears, thinking that at least he had carried out his bluff and not backed down. He walked slowly, evenly, his shoulders flung back theatrically. And he knew he wished it had never happened and he was glad she couldn't see his face, because he was moody, and it would give him away. He counted his steps. He was tempted to look back, turn, follow her home. He couldn't, and he heard her heels racketing as she walked. If she'd come back after him. If girls were different so that he could go to her and say come on, let's drop this, and still not be afraid of seeming weak in her eyes for doing it. Hearing footsteps behind him, he slowed down against his will. But they grew fainter. Going home alone. Crossing the street, he again heard feminine footsteps behind him. But it couldn't be her. A strange girl, tall and slender and neatly dressed, swiftly passed him. He looked after her. He thought of Catherine brooding, regretful.

He had won the quarrel by leaving her alone at night, sobbing in the street, and it was a victory which now impressed him as not having been worth the winning. He could tell anyone about it, and stand before them as one who hadn't backed down, or taken any crap. And he liked the idea of people seeing him as that kind of a guy. And yet, he had to pay the cost of it now, he had to think of her crying, walking home alone, never seeing her again. That was an idea he didn't like so well.

He lit a fresh cigarette from the butt of the one he'd been smoking. He felt a sudden sense of freedom, and realized now that after becoming engaged to Catherine, he had thought of her in almost everything he had done or planned to do. He'd had to consider not only himself but also Catherine in his ideas about the future, and that had been a change he hadn't even noticed in himself. And now he was free to think only of himself, and not of how she'd fit into the picture. And he didn't have to worry the same way about money. It was like being released from a kind of jail, he told himself, the same way he used to feel as a kid when the last day of school was over and the summer vacation had really started.

He remembered her sobbing voice. He had said things that had cut her deeply. A girl had her vanities, all girls, and a guy ought to know that. He'd hurt her. He smiled, enjoying one or two of his cracks, but he knew that it was a miserable enjoyment, and he wished the cracks were unsaid. Even so, she'd had no right to go making a mountain out of a mole-hill.

He shook his head, feeling like hell, not even knowing what to think, remembering her crying, her face when the angry tears had come against her will. Would she go home and cry all night in bed, not able to sleep? He was sure that she did care for him, no matter what she'd said. Poor kid, she must be feeling in the dumps this minute as she walked home. What the hell, if he had taken a little, just to straighten things out! He should have shown himself the stronger. But then, if he had taken crap, she might have lost her respect for him. He couldn't make up his mind, that was all there was to it.

II

Feeling almost chained under the bed covers, Studs tossed, wishing that he could sleep. He lifted his left foot outside the covers, the breeze from the opened window cool upon it. Lying almost semi-crosswise, he perceived Martin in the darkness on the small cot across the bedroom, and he emptily listened to his brother's even breathing. He saw the blue patch of sky against the dark background of the apartment hotel across the street, with streaks of moonlight splashed on lightless windows. People asleep in all those rooms.

Christ, why couldn't he sleep?

Twisting, he pulled his foot back under the covers. He determined that he would lie still, force himself to be quiet until he sank into sleep. He lay still for a few seconds, sensitive to his own breathing and the beating of his heart. He turned on his left side and closed his eyes, holding the lids shut for several seconds. Opening them, he looked at the sky and the apartment hotel.

Was Catherine awake at this minute? He imagined her quietly sobbing, her body quivering, her pillow soaking with tears, and he was proud to think of her in such a state over him, turning her bed into a river because she was afraid that she'd lost him. Wasn't he, though, a goddamn low sonofabitch to be taking joy out of such thoughts? If they pleased him this way, he must be pretty much of an out-and-out heel, and really, he didn't feel that way. He felt low and rotten.

He knew that he'd be better off if he forgot about it for the night. Already since coming to bed he had thought back over the quarrel detail by detail, and what was the use of continuing when it got him nowhere?

Wanting to distract himself by thinking of something else,

he drew up in his mind images from his memory of the night when he had last talked with Lucy over the telephone, and she had been no soap on a date. He had walked over to the park with the boys. Barney Keefe and Shrimp had razzed each other, and he had boxed with Morgan and had been shown up. He saw himself back on that night, getting a date with Lucy, lacing Morgan, and then boxing with Hink Weber, dancing around like a streak. He commenced to feel as if he were back on that night, lying in bed now after he had made a sucker out of Hink. And on Saturday night he'd take Lucy out, and coming home with her in a cab, feeling her nearness, smell her perfume. . . .

Was Catherine asleep now, and if she wasn't what was she thinking about?

A cloud, like a large, white island, was floating just over the apartment hotel, white, puffy, its edges like strand or even like the hockings of a man with the con.

The thought of consumption made him afraid, lest he have it. He rolled over to look at the shadowy wall, trying to shutter out of his mind the image of that cloud, which seemed to grow into an enormous lump of consumptive spittle. Martin breathing so easily in sleep. Christ, to sleep!

Perhaps it meant the finish of everything between himself and Catherine. How would he explain it to the family? And how would he feel about it, going back to the way things had been before he'd started going regularly with her? Wishing on so many nights that he would have his own girl to take out. And with the old gang broken up, and his health not permitting him to tear around, how would it be, fidgeting at night, too broke to spend a lot of money, nothing to do?

He realized that he was, no matter what he thought or tried to make himself think, pretty much nuts about Catherine. And now, whoops, goodbye and the end of it.

Was she awake, crying, sorry? He could see her going to a show with some other guy, in the hallway afterward, the fellow taking her in his arms, kissing her, she lifting her face to be kissed, her body close and another fellow touching her. He remembered how he would hold and kiss her, feel her hard and hot against him, and now another guy.

Well, if she was that way, it would only prove that she was a bitch.

But after they had gotten as far as they did, such a thing happening! He could see himself socking some guy who was trying to make her. And after he would have battered hell out of the guy, she would come to him humbly and say that it had all been a mistake, and then they would go on again just as they had before the quarrel this evening.

He remembered that night two weeks ago when they'd talked in her hallway and she'd suddenly flung her arms around him, kissed him hotly, opened her mouth, french-kissed him. And he'd lost control of himself, grabbed her, sat her down on the steps, bent over her, lay on top of her, run his hand along her warm thighs until she quivered. Never before had he been able to excite a woman that much. She'd wanted to, right then and there, and at the last minute she'd pushed him away, said no, stood up all ruffled, with her hair mussed, and rushed upstairs. She'd stood at the glass of the inside door, breathing heavily, that look still on her face, blown him a last kiss, gone up. The next time he'd seen her, she'd said they had to be careful with each other, because they would have to wait until they were married. And Jesus, after coming that close, not to get it, never to see or speak to her again! To have her in his arms this minute. He tried to remember and make himself feel just the way he had felt, holding and kissing her and stroking her thighs. Just thinking of it made him ga-ga. He could see, too, why guys liked to be married.

Brother, I want a woman, he told himself, thinking how he hadn't had a woman in one hell of a long time.

And he'd put his hands under Lucy's dress, too, once, and that had been all, and now the same with Catherine. That night by the lake when they'd become engaged, that seemed to be so far away. He closed his eyes, rolled onto his back, thought that she was only a broad, and the world was full of broads. In the old days, when Red Kelly got drunk, he'd call his girl up and tell her, up your back, Charlie.

Up your back, Catherine.

One thing after another was hitting him like bolts of lightning out of the sky. He pitied himself, with his health shot, a bum heart, most of his dough lost, the old man watching everything he had go straight up the creek, and now losing his girl. There was no fairness in him getting all these tough breaks when fellows like Red Kelly were starting to swim in gravy. He put his right leg over the covers and asked himself, why in the name of Jesus Christ he had to take so many jolts on the chin from every side? Hadn't that pneumonia been enough? He felt that all his bad luck dated from that New Year's Eve party because then the cards had been shuffled the wrong way on him, and now it wasn't easy to unshuffle the pack. He was just a goddamn mess, and he wanted to go to sleep, and felt rotten and all-in, and too nervous to sleep.

How often in a fellow's life just one thing goes wrong, and then that guy is through and doesn't come back! One wild, accidental punch below the belt or on the chin. Some little thing, getting too drunk and going to a party and then . . . If he'd met some girl that night, taken her to her room, slept with her, his life would have been different, and he'd have woke up with her instead of in a hospital. Just such things that gave a guy a deuce instead of an ace. And he'd been chump enough to let those little things happen, so here he was. Or was it that he was just the kind of a guy who couldn't take it? He fought the question out of his mind, told himself that the harder the breaks, the more he had to fight, and the sweeter it would be coming through.

He tossed until he lay on his back with his feet spread widely apart. Martin snored, and it made him ask why Martin was younger and healthier than himself, sleeping now when he couldn't sleep?

All along, always during the old days, he had felt that somehow, some day, he was going to pull a royal flush out of the deck of life. He tried to feel that way now, to convince himself that he was just stewing up unnecessary grief for himself. In the morning, maybe it would all pass away, the market would start going up, Catherine might telephone, and even if she didn't change her tune, well, he'd go right on living, and one loss might lead to a better gain later on. Maybe yes, things were just getting hard because they were going to lead to making it all easier later on. A hard-won victory might be in store for him. He and Catherine would patch it up, prosperity might now really be around the corner, it would all turn out hotsy-totsy, and Studs Lonigan would be singing in the bathtub, and singing in the rain, and singing.

Martin asleep there, breathing so easily, he didn't know how lucky he was. Studs rolled to the left side of the bed, looked vacantly out of the window, unaware of his thoughts still rolling around and around in his mind, seeing the sky, clouds, black buildings, as if in sleep. Suddenly he opened his eyes widely, sat up terrifyingly awake, afraid without knowing why. He lay back, laughed at himself, blankly held his eyes on the black ceiling. Jesus Christ, sleep, sleep, sleep. He bit his nails, scratched his head, asked himself was he going nuts. He turned on his right side, sank his eyes against his arm muscles, realized how dry, dull, tired, he was. In the morning if he only felt different. This was like having crabs on the brain. He heard an automobile pass outside, then Martin's regular breathing, then footsteps on the street.

Sleep, Jesus, anything so that he would just feel less alone.

CHAPTER TEN

I

Blinking his eyes, Studs stared up and down the sunny street as if there was something interesting to see. He felt dopey from his restless night. But anyway, it was a quarter to eleven, and most of the morning, at least, was killed. He wished that he'd caught Martin before the kid had gone out. They could have bummed around today. If he was with somebody it would be easier to keep his mind off Catherine. She hadn't telephoned, either, as he'd kind of hoped. Well . . .

An old man came toward him on shaky, twitching legs, leaning on a heavy cane with every step. Studs observed his dried and wrinkled face, his watery eyes, his drooling, quivering lips, his tight, death-like skin, the sack of flesh under the chin. Seeing the poor old duffer was like seeing death.

"Good morning, Mr. Dingby," Studs said.

"Eh?"

"I said good morning, Mr. Dingby," he repeated loudly.

Studs saw purplish gums as the old man laughed. With a blue-veined hand, he feebly poked Studs' ribs.

"Eh . . . they don't wear pants nowadays. He! He! He!"

Studs left old man Dingby leaning on his cane, his body jittering with palsied laughter. The sight of the old man was just too much. And how did such a fellow feel, knowing that there wasn't any life left in him, that he couldn't ever walk straight like a healthy man, eat a decent meal, ever again enjoy a fast and sweet jazz? All over but the shouting. And some day he, Studs Lonigan, might be like that. He shuddered.

Would Catherine telephone him while he was out? If so, it would leave him in a strong position and still give him a good excuse for calling her up. It might keep her worrying and he guessed that that was the best way to treat a girl. Then she wouldn't get the idea that she could ride all over a guy on her high horse.

He sauntered along to Seventy-first and Jeffrey, and bought a package of cigarettes and a telephone slug at the chain drug store. He walked out of the telephone booth, disappointed with his mother's message that no one had telephoned him. Catherine was showing just too damn much crust, and if she could act like that, it just showed that she didn't give two hoots in hell for him. Just as well to find it out now rather than after getting married.

623

But what should he do?

He walked by several store fronts, and halted at the entrance to a shoe store.

"Hello," said a beefy young policeman whom Studs had seen before, while Studs stood slumped, looking emptily at the people passing along the street.

"How are you?" he answered as if he knew the cop, anxious to talk with him.

"I've seen you around before. Live in the neighborhood?"

"Yes. Why?"

"Work around here?"

"No, I work anywhere," Studs smiled, and then, seeing the blankness and suspicion on the policeman's face, he grew uneasy with an old fear of cops from his kid days.

"What kind of a business is that?"

"I work with my old man in the painting and decorating business. But there's not much doing these days, and I've got more time on my hands than I know what to do with."

"What's your name?"

"Lonigan," Studs answered, controlling sudden anger, because anyway he'd done nothing, and there was no use in getting snotty.

"Around here much in the morning?" the cop asked, and Studs wondered did he think he was Hawkshaw, the great sleuth, or what?

"Oh, now and then."

"Listen, if you see any suspicious-looking characters around here any time, let me know. There's been too many histing jobs pulled off lately in this neighborhood, and the sergeant has been hopping on my tail about them. Some of these bastards, you know, are just getting too goddamn reckless, even holding up stores along the street here in the day-time."

"Sure I will," Studs said, wondering why the queer look on the cop's mug.

"Looks like it's going to be a hot day."

Studs took a cigarette and offered one to the policeman, who shook his head no. Lighting his, he tried to think of something to say to show the cop that he was somebody, and also a regular fellow. A stout, untidy woman wheeled a baby buggy by and a tall, thin young fellow with a smart-aleck smirk ambled along in her wake. A coarse-faced middle-aged woman dragged a dirty-faced inquisitive child eastward. Bells rang and a train swept by, and Studs watched people rush to catch it. His eye wandering, he casually noticed how the sun seemed to turn the steel tracks into glittering, dazzling thin bands.

"You say your old man's in the carpenter racket and you help him?" the cop said, his puzzling suspicion seeming to persist.

"Painting and decorating."

"Oh, yeah, painting and decorating. I see. Your old man's in the painting and decorating racket, and you ain't working today."

"I can prove it, too. I've got nothing to hide," Studs said, his face turning pale from a rush of anger.

"Take it easy! Take it easy! You know, we're used to handling guys who get tough."

"I ain't tough or trying to get snotty. Only you're acting as if I'd done something."

"How do I know you didn't?"

"I'm telling you, ain't I?"

"If I was to pick up Al Capone this minute on suspicion, he'd tell me he ain't done nothin' either. I just got my orders to watch for all suspicious characters along here. How do I know you ain't a suspicious character? Here, let's see if you got any heat on you?" the cop said, hastily and awkwardly tapping along Studs' pockets.

Studs was too sore to speak, and he noticed several people stop to look at the cop and himself.

"Now, what did you say your name was?"

"I told you."

"Oh, so that's it, huh?" the cop said ironically. "All right, you're arrested as a suspicious character and for resisting arrest. How you like that?"

"All right, my name is Lonigan. I've talked straight, and if you want me to prove it, I'll take you home with me. We own the building there. Or else you can go in the drug store and telephone my home. I'm no crook, and I can prove who I am. But I don't like to be manhandled around, and my old man wouldn't like it, either. He grew up with guys who got plenty of drag in this town, Barney McCormack, Judge Gorman, Judge Joe O'Reilley," Studs said, speaking rapidly and with growing pride.

"Just a minute, fellow. I didn't mean nothing personal. The sergeant's just on my tail because there's been so many histing jobs pulled off around here, and I got my orders to keep my eyes peeled for suspicious-looking characters. I seen you here, and the only way I could find out whether you was a suspicious character or not is by asking you questions and finding out, isn't it? It's nothing personal. And my name's McGoorty."

"Sure, I know," Studs said, toning down. "I was just walking around, and it sounded kind of funny because, hell, I ain't got nothing to hide, and I was just walking around because I didn't have anything else to do."

"A cop, you know, has to make certain about things, that's all."

"I know how it is," Studs said, thinking that Officer McGoorty had dumbness written pretty plainly all over his map.

"That's it. We don't take chances, because it's our business not to."

"Yes," Studs said.

"Well, so long, Lonigan. I'll be seeing you around. I got to amble along to the box at the corner."

Studs watched him move toward the corner. He turned eastward, thinking that it was pretty dumb, having nothing to do. What was Catherine doing, and was she, at this very moment, thinking of him? Had to keep his mind off her, though, or he'd go cuckoo. Couldn't have another night like last night. But had she, or would she telephone him? He could see her, begging forgiveness at their next meeting, while he was aloof, just to teach her a lesson. But he probably wouldn't act that way, because he wanted the scrap patched up.

> *Did you ever hear Pete*
> *Go tweet, tweet, tweet on his piccolo?*

Radios all over. And he hated that damn song. But women, now, they never did seem to know their own minds, or what they wanted, so how could a guy know it? Even so, and even if he was in the right, still, he needn't have been so goddamn mean to her. Yes, he was kind of sorry about it.

He haphazardly stared in a fish-store window at the unshaven man in a dirty apron behind the counter. He laughed, thinking that the fellow was a dead ringer for Abie Kabibble. He moved along, and stopped at the window of a book store and rental library, looking from a stack of greeting cards to books piled up and spread around the window, with their bright jackets, reading the titles, *Lumber, Jews Without Money, The Woman of Andros, The Crystal Icicle, Iron Man, The Mystery of Madame Q, Bottom Dogs, Arctic Quest*. Sometime he might rent one or two of the books they had and do a little reading, he reflected, turning away from the window. Nice, it was, walking along here at this time of day, sunny, people coming and going, young married women, some pushing baby buggies, neat, swell-looking girls with their figures developed just right, not at all bad on the eyes. Two of them ahead, dressed smartly in black suits. Funny, too, that girls like that would be walking along on the street so calm and haughty, and even high-hat. And yet they would, with their husbands or whoever was the right fellow for them, lose all their cold haughtiness. If it was the right time, and the right fellow was feeling and necking them, they would pant, burn up, their faces would change and they would become so passionate that they'd almost suffer until the guy fixed them up. Just like Catherine in the hallway when she'd run upstairs to prevent herself from going the limit. And wouldn't he like to be the guy to fix up one of these younger married girls around here? One like Weary Reilley's sister, Fran. Suppose he should meet her now, and that should happen. Just looking at her was enough to show how much passion she had in her. And now that she was married. To see her and get fixed up regular on mornings like this while her husband was down on La Salle Street. That's what would make life a little interesting.

He paused at South Shore Drive and looked across at the arched entrance-way to the club grounds, wondering again what should he do now. Carroll Dowson had just joined South Shore Country Club, he remembered, and was getting up in the world. Well, the day would come when Studs Lonigan could join a swell club like that if he wanted to. A train pulled out of the station, curved around onto Seventy-first Street, clattered along toward Jeffrey. He watched a passing succession of automobiles. He leaned against a mailbox and looked at the faces of people on the sidewalk, the women, the babies, a tall woman with a good figure whose face was crumbling. She must feel pretty rotten, he guessed, knowing that she was getting old. Tough luck, sister! And suppose she wasn't married. She had to go on living, knowing she would have to die probably without ever having known what it was really like. Well, he knew that much, anyway. But it was like candy. The more you eat, the more you want, and damn it, he wanted it now with a dame as neat as some of the ones he'd seen along Seventy-first Street this morning. It was only natural for a guy to want some tail when he didn't have anything to do, and he was natural. And it would relieve the tedium of the day. He watched a mongrel dog scamper along, avoiding people, smelling at mail-boxes and lamp-posts. He saw a train swing around into the South Shore station. Christ, what a life!

Walking back toward Jeffrey, he stepped into a corner drug store and got a slug. He perspired in the booth. No, he wouldn't call her. He inserted his slug.

"Return please, operator."

He laid the slug on the counter, picked up his nickel, stopped by the magazine rack near the door and thumbed through a copy of an art magazine, looking at the pictures of naked and veiled women. Hot babies, but why the hell didn't it show them in different positions to give the whole works. He set the magazine back and selected a copy of *True Confessions,* opening it at a photograph of a dishevelled girl. Her dress was torn down one shoulder as she gripped a door knob, her face trapped in fear, with a man looking beastly, lurching toward her, his shirt torn, his face scratched and bleeding. Studs quickly skipped through the story, written in the first person, coming upon the scene represented in the paragraph where the girl was attacked. He hoped the fellow would succeed, and it would be described. But she escaped, and his eagerness sapped away.

Now, I learned my lesson.

The clerk stared at him with cold suspicion. He replaced the magazine and left the drug store. Girls weren't always so lucky as the gal who'd written the story. Not that dame named Irene whom Weary Reilley had raped. And with a lot of girls, when a guy got that far they wanted it, too, and a rape became a nice jazz. He nodded at McGoorty, who doped by a squat mail-box, looking dumb. He crossed over Jeffrey and stood at the newsstand in front of the bank, idly and half-interestedly looking at the headlines.

WOMAN SLAIN IN CICERO FLAT
Jealous Husband Shoots Unfaithful Wife

SCHOOL TEACHERS DEMAND PAY
Mass Meeting Tonight

NOT TIME FOR DRASTIC EXPERIMENT: DAVIS
Cabinet Member Addresses Chamber of Commerce

He yawned, and started home for lunch. Another day, and it was only half over. Christ, what should he do? And had she telephoned? Would she?

II

Studs entered the cigar store thinking that maybe she would call him up after work. Well, if she didn't, phrigg you, Catherine!

A runty Jewish clerk with a peaked sensitive face sat leaning forward against the counter, as if in mysterious confab with a group of fellows who looked like poolroom hangers-on. Studs caught the clerk's eye.

"O. K.," he called lackadaisically.

A door opposite the entrance door opened, and Studs stepped into a familiar passageway.

"Let's have it," said a fellow of the slugger type in a soda-jerker's white coat, his unintelligent face built upon a solid muscular neck; and a door behind him closed, bolting.

Although he knew there was no cause for fear, still he felt queer facing this bouncer.

"I'm going to frisk you, lad," the bouncer said, tapping Studs from head to foot, under the armpits, the pockets, the chest, viewing Studs' hat and examining the inside, working with a speed and efficiency which caused Studs to remember how clumsy McGoorty had been doing the same thing in the morning.

"O. K."

"Let's have it," a voice from behind the inside door called, as if in the performance of some strange and mysterious rite.

Studs entered a large half-crowded room curtained with cigarette smoke, and the door was bolted behind him. A low counter ran along the opposite end of the room, behind which Phil, with a clean blue shirt, sat working, three fellows alongside of him bent forward over papers. Small groups were gathered around charts and scratch sheets along the wall, another group stood conversing near a ruled-off and lined blackboard, and men and women sat on camp chairs in the center of the room, talking, or working over papers, scratch sheets and pads, dope sheets, and various kinds of clippings. A hook-nosed fellow who needed a shave leaned against a wall reading a copy of *The Morning Telegraph*. There was movement back and forth, and in the left-hand corner of the room a crowd was bunched around a card table. He caught Phil's eye. Smiling obsequiously, Phil came from behind the counter.

"Gee, Studs, I'm glad to see you around. Why didn't you let me know you were coming so we could have had lunch together?"

"I didn't have anything exciting in prospect, so I thought I'd just drop around," Studs said, from the corner of his eye noting the glances cast at him and Phil, thinking maybe they would take him for somebody important; no, he was Phil Rolfe's brother-in-law, he reflected bitterly.

"I'm glad you came, Studs. Only today is just another

dull day with nothing special in the lineup."

"I just wanted to say hello, and maybe lay a buck or two on a race for the fun of it. How's business?"

"Fair, Studs, fair. In fact, it's really a little more than fair, only everything that is clear I'm putting aside, because in a few weeks we're going to start enlarging here. I'm going to have more space, more black-jack tables, a roulette wheel, a table for poker and craps, and some nice-looking furniture around. Make it a swell-looking place, and it will bring in twice as much revenue."

"Swell idea. And how's the kid?"

"Loretta, she's fine. And when are you coming down to see us again?"

"Oh, one of these nights."

"We're always glad to have you, and bring Catherine along, too."

"I will," Studs said dully, resisting his temptation to tell Phil about their scrap.

They faced each other as if talked out.

"Oh, yes, say, Studs, want me to tip you off for a bet or two?"

"No, thanks, Phil, that would take the fun away, and I'd just be taking your dough gratis."

"As you wish, Studs. But," Phil lowered his voice, "between ourselves, the odds are against you if you try to play the ponies day in and day out. That's why we are able to stick in business."

"I know," Studs sagely said.

"Say, listen, Studs, the first race at Jamaica starts soon, and I got to get back there. I'll be with you again a little later. And if there's anything you want, just ask me," Phil said solicitously.

"Thanks, Phil, I'll just hang around."

He heard the door behind closing, and noted that many newcomers had arrived since his entry. He moved over to a group studying a scratch sheet on the wall.

"Which one do you like for the first, mister? It's a race for maidens, and the dope doesn't hold so good for them. I've been betting according to the dope from Sykes in *The Questioner* and I've never won a cent on a maidens' race," a fat-faced woman of middle age said to him.

"Sorry, but I don't know much about it," he said apologetically.

She turned to a woman on Studs' left who held a pencil between her teeth, newspapers, scraps of paper, dope sheets under her arm, and a copy of *The American Racing Record* opened before her.

"Good Luck to place," the woman said, papers sliding from under her arm.

"How about you, Ma?" she asked, and Studs saw that the woman addressed as Ma was a squat and rotund Jewish lady of about fifty.

"I'm betting on Good Luck, Charcoal, Happy Hours, and Sweetheart, fifty cents on each to show," Ma said, ashes from her cigarette dropping onto the stack of papers she held.

"Taking big chances, huh, Ma?" a stout man said.

"Tim, this is not fun. It's a business. I'm here to make a little money each day, and I play my system," Ma said without removing the cigarette from her mouth.

"Last call for first at . . ."

Studs watched a flurried and excited rush to the counter for final bets, feeling out of it because he wasn't betting. But suddenly, he thought of them as chumps who just forked their dough over the counter on a proposition that couldn't win in the long run. There they all were, paying for Phil and Loretta's apartment and automobile. Trying to strike an attitude of indifference, he drew closer to the counter, hearing fragments of talk.

"All right, make it snappy!"

"Dollar on Hot Pepper to place."

"House odds or track odds, madame?"

"Dollar on Hot Pepper to place, house odds."

"Two, Hot Pepper, house odds."

"Three on Happy Hours to show, track."

"Fifty cents on Charcoal."

"If I only win something today! My brothers are both out of work, and I have to support them. I got to win."

Damn fools, throwing their dough down the gutter, Studs thought, priding himself. He felt so in the dumps that thinking he was superior to them helped him.

The books were closed and bettors scattered to the chairs and in small groups near the scratch sheets and elsewhere. Studs filtered back toward the door, watching newcomers enter and lose themselves in the crowd. Would they see him, take him for a regular around the place? He didn't know, though, if he wanted them to think that or not.

Sinking one hand in his pocket, holding a burning cigarette in the other, he struck a casual pose, glanced around. At the black-jack table the players went on unconcerned. Others all over were getting nervous, and he could see the strain and anxiety on many faces. He was glad he didn't feel that way and have their grief. But he had his own grief, didn't he, and it was bigger than a buck or two on a race.

More women in the place than he'd imagined. They were certainly taking to the ponies, he thought with persisting surprise. Were they battered-down old whores? Most of them seemed like housewives, maybe mothers. Perhaps a lot of them were getting on to the change of life, and the ponies saved them from going nuts. Ma, there, smoking another cigarette, with dope sheets sticking out of her coat pockets, looked tough and hard, and still she looked like she might not seem out of place in a kitchen cooking noodle soup and feeding matzoth to a family of little Abies. And there was one, neat, slender, wearing a blue suit, and she couldn't be over thirty. Plenty of lads would turn around on the street to get a load of her, because she was an eye-opener, and he knew that he would, too, if he passed her on the street.

Sister, I wouldn't kick you out of bed, he silently told himself, watching her sit cross-legged on a folding chair, studying a dope sheet.

And the ponies had sure put the bug into her. She was nervous and squirmed her shoulders around, leaned forward, sank back, put her dope sheet aside, sat waiting, biting her finger-nails.

Sister, I know what you need, and need plenty bad, he told himself.

He stepped forward a few paces to get a better sight of her legs, wishing he could see more than she showed. She stared vacantly at him. He glanced aside. Had she noticed him, or was she just getting hot and bothered over the dough she put up on the race? He walked down from her and noticed a tall, well-dressed man with graying hair about the temples, who leaned confidently on a cane.

A telephone rang. Conversations lapsed instantly, and those about him seemed to stiffen up. Ma, perched in back of the chairs, carelessly shoved her papers into her pocket, lit a fresh cigarette from the butt of the old one, and bent a trifle forward, her face sternly set. The woman in blue placed her hands on the chair in front of her occupied by a pimpled, ratty-looking guy, and Studs was jealous. The fellow with the cane, who looked like some kind of a big shot, looked suddenly older than he had, with his lips compressed, his face intent.

"At the quarter, Good Luck, two lengths, Charcoal one length, Sweetheart running third," Phil called out from the phone in stentorian tones.

"Hold 'em! Hold 'em! Hold 'em!" the man with the cane mumbled, snapping his fingers.

Studs fastened his eyes on the woman in blue, and, snapping her fingers rapidly, she seemed like a wound-up spring ready to snap.

Sister, I know what can relax you, he told himself with a self-confident smirk.

"Come on! Come on! Come on!" Ma bleated, cracking her fingers.

"At the half, Charcoal half a length, Good Luck two lengths, Sweetheart running third . . ."

Studs wished he had dough on Good Luck. The excitement that was choking them all up seemed to be getting him, and while many kept stamping and tapping the floor, and straining themselves, and snapping their fingers, and pounding their fists together, he looked keenly around, a little bit lost.

"Come on! Come on!"

"Hold 'em! Hold 'em!"

"Sweetheart, be sweet."

"Come on, Hot Pepper, get hot, get hot!"

"All right, Sweetheart Girl, keep comin', girl, keep comin', keep comin', girl!"

"Hurray!" a man half-yelled, leaping from his chair, to stride rapidly to and fro.

They were all tightened up, all right, like they'd bust, he thought.

The seconds of the race seemed eternally long, and there they stewed, racketed, made faces. Most of them looked like they were ready to cry, start a fight or even go nuts.

"The winners . . ."

He could see, too, how many of them took it hard, couldn't lose with a smile like Studs Lonigan could, bum gamblers. From the sour pans they put on, a person might have thought that they had just lost their best friends or dropped a thousand bucks or more on the stock market, the way he had. Some of them should just know that, and then realize how they were taking the loss of a measly half buck or a dollar so hard.

". . . Charcoal, Good Luck, Sweetheart third."

Several hysterical cheers rose, died abruptly. Murmuring conversation broke over the room, the many voices drumming out like men talking to calm themselves after meeting sudden dangers. Studs searched out the woman in blue, and saw her glancing wildly and distraught from face to face. The winners were verified, and the winning list chalked on the blackboard. She rushed to it eagerly, with an extravagant hope blooming on her face, read, turned aside, watched the winning bettors clutter up to the counter. She went to a chair, sat, crossed her legs, studied the papers, her lips firm and tight.

Studs sauntered to a group around a scratch sheet on the wall.

"Well, Ma, how did you do?"

"I never complain, that's my policy. I have my system, and I play it, and it works all right for me," Ma said, cigarette still drooping from her lips.

"I had a hunch to play Charcoal, but I've been balling myself all up with my system of handicapping, and like a chump I didn't have the nerve to play my hunch."

"I never play hunches. That's not scientific. I play my system," Ma said.

"Well, who you picking for the next at Bowie?"

"That's my business."

"The next is a steeplechase. You can never pick 'em because anything is liable to happen in a jump race. The best horse in the country is liable to miss a hurdle and lose its rider. Now, last summer in a jump race at Saratoga, well, I had it doped for Equal Sugar to win. Every expert in the country, nearly, picked Equal Sugar. Well, I don't usually play the favorites, but I laid my ten bucks down on Equal Sugar because I was in the dough then. And you know, at the first jump Equal Sugar breaks a leg. It all goes to show, jump races are never certain."

"Al's Pink Sheet picks Sir Canafe, and he's the consensus of the experts, too. And Al's Pink Sheet is pretty reliable. I've been following it now for a long time and it's given me some good pickings. Why, one day two months ago I bet on all Al's choices and I won twelve bucks. And the other night I didn't have nothing to do, so I checked back through a number of old copies of Al's Pink Sheet, and you know, he picked fifteen steeplechase winners over the period I checked through."

"I tried all the dope sheets, and I finally found that Sunshine Sam's is the most reliable. He picks more winners than any of 'em, and he's good on the jump races, too. He picks Fielder's Choice."

"I used to go by Sunshine Sam's dope, but it never did nothing but put my dough in a bookie's pocket."

"Al's Pink Sheet never won me anything but grief."

The door kept opening, admitting more and more newcomers. Studs moved around kind of wishing some lad he knew would happen in, keeping his eyes, all the time, peeled on the neat trick in blue, who, studying her dope sheet with her legs crossed, showed one leg a little above the knee.

"I wish I could have the luck I had four months ago. In

one week I cleaned up a hundred bucks. Since then, I've had lots of luck, but it's all been bad. You know, I made a pickup I met at the Bourbon Palace, and the bitch dosed me. And then, goddamn it, before I knew that, I made the grade with my girl. So now I got a doctor's bill on my hands, and my girl won't speak to me, either. She'll only send me the bill. Lots of luck, and all lousy."

"How about a job?"

"Well, I could work with my old man, only, hell, if I can have another lucky streak on the ponies, why I can clean up more here in a day than working a week for him. And I know a lad, Buddy Coen's brother, who gets tips on the races. I was supposed to see him today, but I missed him. Just my goddamn luck. But maybe I'll get the breaks again."

"Say, how does this horse Sugar Candy stack up in the next?" Studs asked a fellow in a talkative group.

"Whenever he travels in fast company, his name is Also-Ran," Ma, still smoking, dryly said.

"There's three-to-one on him, and the way I look at it, you might as well take the odds, because anyway, you never can be certain about a jump race."

"Don't play Sir Canafe."

"Why?"

"Don't, I'm telling you."

All those handicapping fools were a card. They knew everything wrong before a race, and everything right afterward. Detaching himself from the group, he strolled over to a scratch sheet and was attracted by the name of the fifth horse on the list, Hollow Tooth. Might as well lay a buck on the nag. It might win. He was low on dough, too, these days, because of his dates with Catherine and so little coming in, and a few bucks to swell the exchequer wouldn't hit him in the wrong spot. Might as well take the chance.

He laid a dollar on Hollow Tooth at the counter cage, and received a numbered card with the odds, two and half to win; scrawled in a corner. He stepped back from the counter, hoping the race would start. Suppose he had beginner's luck, pyramided his winnings, cleaned up twenty-five bucks, fifty, hundred, maybe, say two hundred. Wouldn't that be hard to take! And he might. He wanted the race to begin, with Hollow Tooth starting him off on a real streak of luck.

The woman in blue marched to the counter with an air of desperation. He saw she was short, but all put together in just about as neat a bundle as a guy could expect to pick up. He wondered how it would be like making her? She had all the makings of a nice steady piece on the side. And, hell, if she hung out at a joint like this, she oughtn't to be so innocent or dumb. Looked to him like the kind who said all right, daddy, if you just touched her and cracked out with a how about it, baby.

Still coming in. Easy a hundred and fifty people in the joint. All good news for Phil. He wished he was in on a good racket like this and had the money rolling down the alley to him every day as Phil had, a racket that gave him a kind of prestige, too. Lots of people were getting to know who Phil Rolfe was, envying him.

"All I say is you can never be certain on a jump race . . . ."

"Last call . . ."

He watched the final rush to bet. Then the phone rang. The same stiffening up. Hoped he would win. Tapping their feet, snapping their fingers, calling out, looking intensely with nothing else on their minds but the race and would they win. And Phil's voice, Hollow Tooth in the lead, come on, Hollow Tooth. He wanted to shout out, too, come on, Hollow Tooth, and he kind of knew now how they felt, come on, Hollow Tooth, come on, boy. Hollow Tooth still, the second lap, now step along, boy, step along. He was tapping his foot, too, it was like a contagion, Hollow Tooth, come on.

They were so tense in the room that an explosion seemed imminent, as if all the excitement and strain on their faces and in their heads would burst like bombs, shattering the walls and the building with a loud, crashing thunder. And he was the same way. He gripped a chair, his foot tapped, he held himself in as if afraid to breathe, and Hollow Tooth in the lead still . . .

"The winners . . . Hollow Tooth . . ."

He smiled with gratitude. His shoulders sagged. He stamped anxiously forward to the counter, smiles cracking on his face, and waited for the verification and pay-offs, hearing a happy babel of talk all around him.

"Any luck?" Ma asked him, again talking without removing the cigarette from her mouth.

"I got the winner."

"My system didn't work out that time. It just goes to show that no system is water-proof perfect. But there's more races, and my system is calculated for the long run, and while there's wins and losses, the wins are more than the losses."

"You had the winner?" the woman in blue asked, her voice surprisingly deep and husky, a tough broad's voice, all right, he decided.

"Yes. How about yourself?" he asked, thinking here was his opportunity to dent the ice.

"I never have any goddamn luck," she said disconsolately.

"Maybe the next one will bring home the bacon for you," he said, thinking, hoping, that she'd be easy.

"It better be."

"Who you picking for the next one?" he asked to keep the talk rolling.

"I got to sit down and figure that out now," she said, turning from him.

He collected and pocketed his pay-off, turned away from the crowded counter, saw her laboring over her papers, chewing a pencil as she worked. He decided that she was just what he needed to change his luck.

III

"How's it going, Studs?" Phil asked, nonchalantly lighting a cork-tipped cigarette, standing with Studs in a corner by the blackboard, while many moved and swirled about them in the let-down between races.

"Oh, it's all right."

"It's turning out to be a pretty good day for us. Some, you know, are better than others, and Saturday's the big day, but I can't complain about today. But after I get this all overhauled, I'm going to raise the intake plenty."

"Say, Phil, do many of these people come every day?"

"Plenty. Like one woman they call Ma. Did you notice her? She's a real character."

"Funny duck, isn't she?"

"Yes," Phil said, smiling and lowering his voice, "you see all different types in a place like this. It's a great place to study human nature. Some of them who come do it just for the fun of betting a dollar or two. And then others are just gambling fools. Many of the women, it seems, started coming here to pick up a little extra dough because of hard times, less dough coming in from the husband's pay envelope and things like that. But they take it up like a fever, and they become fiends at it. But then, it all goes to help business along."

"See that good-looking dame in the blue suit, on the chair, handicapping with all those papers and dope sheets? How about her?"

"She's here every day. It's like dope with her, all right, I hear she's married, and I guess it must be that her husband can't fix her up right. There must be something the matter with him. Because she certainly plays the ponies with a bang.

And you know, Studs, when women get that way and start hanging out at places like this, I always suspect that what's wrong with them is they need some guy to give them the right kind of jazzing."

"She's neat enough, so that there's plenty of guys who'd be ready to give her what it takes."

"She's not exactly a chicken, but still, she has her points and her curves. I wouldn't be surprised if a lot of the lads around here have tried to make the grade with her. In fact, I wouldn't be surprised if some of them succeeded."

"Hello, Mr. Rolfe."

"Hi, there, O'Donnell."

"Good day?"

"So-so."

Studs noted that they treated Phil with respect, all right. Phil was getting to be somebody. Smart boy, Phil. And yes, at present, to many he was just Phil Rolfe's brother-in-law.

"Say, Studs, I got to get back to business."

"See you later."

"How about coming home to supper with me tonight?"

"Can't tonight, thanks. Some other night, though."

"You know, Studs, you're always welcome."

He watched Phil walk back behind the counter with some of that same cake-eater's strut that he'd always had.

He smiled contentedly. All in all, it had been a profitable afternoon, and after this next race he'd be leaving, six bucks to the good. And it had been fun, betting and winning.

The phone rang again. The crowd quieted and listened in that tension that was like so much dynamite being put inside them. Just like dope, all right. And he was glad he hadn't bet on this one. He'd learned from his experience with the stock market to let well enough alone. Phil was barking out the progress of the race and they were like so many engines cranked up, snapping their fingers, shuffling, calling out and begging the horses, shaking their knees, almost praying. Jesus, it was something of a sight, all right. And the girl in blue, the way she shot her head forward with her jaw set, her lips closed as if they had been locked with a key, her eyes hard on the counter. Ought to approach her by talking about the races, and she'd be pie to make. With the announcement of the winners, he saw her sag limply, drop a card and some papers, sit back in the chair, while all around her others rose, talked, and the lucky ones began clustering at the counter. She switched sidewise in her chair, slowly crossed her legs, lifting one high as if trying to show off what she had. Maybe after the excitement she had to have some guy now to put her in the right shape. She had her head sunk in her hands, thinking. She was sore, now, and tearing up all her papers. She seemed to have caught him staring at her, and she was, or was she, giving him the eye? Getting up, coming toward him with a set look on her face. Was this too good to be true, or was she sore and going to tell him to quit looking at her? He turned as she came closer and swung around again, surprised, when he heard her voice, high-strung and ready to crack with nerves.

"You know happened to me?"

"Why, no. What?"

"I've lost all my house money, and if my husband finds out, he'll kick the devil out of me. I promised not to bet any more, but I had to. He doesn't understand. I have to have more house money than he can give me in these times, and he doesn't understand. And I haven't one cent for groceries for the rest of the week."

"Gee, I'm sorry."

"I simply must have money to preserve my happy home," she said, with a sudden and forced half-smile.

"I'm sorry but . . ."

"I'm not asking for a loan," she said sharply, interrupting him. She stepped back a pace. "Look at me!"

"I don't get you."

"Yes, you do. You've been giving me the eye all afternoon. Well, am I worth two and a half?"

"Well now. . . . Where at?" he said, flushed.

"At my home. Will you come?"

Studs shook his head.

"All right. Wait here a minute," she said, determined.

"Sister, you got it to give. You got a bunch of personality there and . . ."

"Skip it! Wait here a minute," she said, turning, studiously surveying various men as they milled around.

He watched her single out others, and he was confused by the unusualness of the offer, excited for her, and he decided that it had certainly turned out to be the nuts of an afternoon. Only, if he could get her alone, instead of with a gang. But maybe this might lead to it, and she might just be what he wanted to have on the string. She winked at him. He nodded knowingly, stepped toward the counter, but Phil was busy and he went outside. When she came out, three others joined her as Studs stepped toward her. She looked grimly at them.

"I don't know you fellows. You better step in the drug store on the way."

"You're not dumb, are you, sister?"

"Let's save that and get along. And you better stop in the drug store."

"O. K., little lady," a sandy-haired brute of a fellow said in a slow, almost stuttering manner.

She stepped ahead, and a thin Semitic lad took a quarter from each of them.

"We can toss for the extras."

"That's all right. You can keep 'em," a medium-sized fellow with a tough face and bushy brows said.

"It's just the rotten kind of luck I would have," she said, as if to herself, while they straggled around her and the thin fellow cut across the street to a corner drug store.

"Your bad luck is our good luck," the bushy-browed fellow said.

"What's your name, lad?" the sandy-haired slow-talking fellow asked.

"Lonigan."

"Mine's Al Coombs."

"Boys, mine is Burke," the bushy-browed fellow said.

"Well, that takes care of that," the thin fellow said, short of wind, as he caught up with them.

"What's your name, lad? Mine's Al Coombs."

"Cohen."

"Sister, don't take it so hard. This will never kill a girl. In fact, it's harder on a guy than a girl, and it's just a passing interlude that helps you out of a tough spot and is fun for all concerned," Coombs said slowly, and she smiled grimly.

"We're not the ape kind. It's just going to be a nice little party, with everybody cooperating to have the best time we can. You're married and know what it's all about, and know it's not going to hurt you. Just a little party to add to the glory of mankind," Cohen said, and they laughed.

"Skip it, fellow!" she said.

"Sure, if you say so. I only just wanted to let you know we all had the right attitude about it," Cohen said.

"Sure that hubby won't be around to catch us?" said Coombs.

"No danger," she answered decisively.

"It wouldn't kind of look so right if he did. And he wouldn't like it, would he? Ha! Ha!" Coombs said.

"He won't be home until at least seven."

"That's O. K. by me, sister. I like your looks, and I don't like to think of any irate husbands coming around to spoil our little round of fun," Cohen said.

Studs caught her wincing. He felt like walking out. Hell, they were all taking advantage of her, and she didn't like the idea of doing this. Her husband, too, he must be a tough, two-headed bastard or she wouldn't have propositioned them rather than tell him she'd lost the dough. Women were just too funny for his comprehension. Laying strangers, like a common whore, rather than tell her husband she'd lost the house dough on the ponies. Suppose the guy did come home? A mess then. But there were four of them, and this Coombs boy looked plenty big. And was she nice! Anticipating it made him feel just raring to go. He forgot everything else, and he tried to hold the image of her naked in his mind, her flesh soft and white.

"Play the races regular?" he asked, ranging himself on her left, wanting to make a better impression on her than the other lads might.

"Yes . . . but I never had such bad luck before as I had today. I lost on every single race."

"It runs that way," he philosophized sympathetically, thinking that he might tell her something about his own rotten luck with the stock.

"I know it. But this week has been my downfall," she smiled. "And I thought that I had worked out a good system to win. Oh, well, it's all in a lifetime."

"Yep, it's all to be charged up to the school of experience."

"If my husband knew it, he would darn near kill me. George has such a vile temper. And he just doesn't understand. When I win money, I buy extra little things for the house and the baby. And a woman has to have some excitement in life. I can't sit at home all day sweeping and cooking and washing diapers and twiddling my thumb, and then in the evening listening to him talk about business and politics. And when he turns on the radio, do you think he listens to music? Not on your life. Always to speeches."

"Wouldn't this make him sore?" asked Burke, and it led Studs to think, pleased, that he was going to tamper with another man's woman, put something over on the poor sap.

"What he doesn't know will be no skin off his ears. I got to have money, that's all there is to it. I've never done a thing like this before, and I wouldn't be doing it if I didn't need the money right away."

"You mean that all your experience has been with George?" asked Cohen.

She looked angrily at him.

"I know it's none of my business. But you know, it's just in such things that variety adds to the spice of life, and you look to me to be smart enough to have learned that."

"I keep my own secrets," she smiled.

"I can see that. You look smart to me, girlie," he said unctuously.

"I keep my own secrets. But even so, I've never had a secret like this one to keep before," she said, slipping her arm through Cohen's, and Studs, keeping pace with her, jealously thought that he was just a goofy-looking kike and she was making up to him; he quickly took her other arm.

"Me neither, sister. I ain't never done this before, either. But you know, I'm a charitable guy, and I couldn't resist helping you out. When I first got into the joint and saw you, I said to myself, there's a little sister I like and I don't mean maybe."

"The same goes for me."

"Thank you," she said sarcastically, freeing herself from their arms.

"But why all the temperament? A minute ago we were getting along swimming, and now you're ready to fly off the handle. This little business is natural, isn't it? If you didn't have the stuff, we wouldn't have bitten on this proposition, would we? I got a wife myself, and I like her. She's swell, and I don't want any other wife. But a pleasant little vacation, you know. You got your man, and know that all the time together it isn't so good. A little change and you can compare, see differences. It's like discovering new tricks and perfecting your own technique."

"I hope George doesn't try your tactics of vacationing," she laughed.

"With a little lady like you, maybe he shouldn't. I'll bet you keep him toeing the mark," Coombs said, stuttering as he butted into the conversation.

"I'll try and show you boys whether or not I'm able to make it worth while for my old man to be a one-woman man," she said, winking lasciviously.

"Well, I'm getting anxious. How much farther have we got to go?" said Cohen.

"Oh, tell me how long must I wait? Can I have it now or must I hesitate?" Studs sing-songed.

"I live on the second floor of the yellow brick apartment house right down here. Come up, one by one, and give me a few minutes start. I have a gabby old crowd for neighbors, and what they don't know won't hurt them."

"Looks like it's going to be a good little piece," Burke said while they watched her cross the street and trip on to her flat.

"What you say, Lonigan?" Coombs asked, grinning.

"She's built for a bed," Studs said, pleased that they smiled at his crack.

"I li-like her," Coombs said seriously.

"I've been watching her around the joint for a couple of weeks now. If you lads ask me, I'd say she doesn't get enough from George. Looks to me like she's built for endurance. So this is our chance, boys. There's smouldering passion in every inch of that dame's chassis, and why let it smoulder. Four good men and true, well, we ought to give her enough."

"Say, Cohen, I think you're right," Coombs said.

"I'm ready," said Studs.

"Them's my sentiments, I'm ready to face the test," said Burke.

"Well, somebody s-start off and go up," Coombs said.

"We're to go up and wait and when we all get there fix up our turns, huh?" asked Burke.

"Yeh," Cohen said.

"All right, Lonigan, you go and we'll fo-follow."

Nervous and anxious, he walked toward the building, kind of wishing he hadn't gotten into it, because it might be dangerous, and still glad, because he needed it, and she was as good a piece as a guy could expect to get on quick notice. And wouldn't this be some experience to talk about! He read the name on the second floor mailbox. George Jackson. Well, George, here goes.

When she admitted him, he saw her in pink bloomers with pink brassière, her milky skin patched with a few pink blushes, her hips wider than he had thought, her breasts saggy, her body strong and muscular.

"I was getting ready," she said, abashed.

"Yes," he said, ill-at-ease, wanting to look at her, not certain how she'd take it. "The others are coming."

One of her breasts flopped out from her brassière as she shut the door, and clumsy, forgetting everything, he clutched at it, kissed her, tried to force and press himself stiffly against her.

"I'm not sorry I came to see you," he said, roughly pawing at her, his voice hoarse.

"Wait, please," she said, struggling to untangle herself.

The bell rang. She pointed to the parlor.

"Well, this is certainly a surprise," Coombs said dully.

"Would you wait in the parlor, please?"

"I s-say, Lonigan, this is certainly a surprise, and this little woman is going to be a nice little treat," Coombs said, entering the small parlor which seemed overcrowded with cheap, gaudy furniture.

"She looks like she's got a high-powered engine of passion in her," Studs said, lighting a cigarette.

"I see you covered up, girlie," Coombs said when she entered the parlor, her body draped in a bright red kimono that kept slipping down one shoulder.

"Now, please don't talk too loudly. My baby's asleep in the next room," she said, striking a seductive pose with her abdomen flaunted outward.

"Oh, a baby," Coombs said.

She turned away to answer the bell.

"Well, sister, here we is, a-rarin' to go," Cohen said, rubbing his hands as he entered the parlor.

"And too much delay and anxiety now will weaken me," Burke smiled.

"I'll be right in," she said.

"Don't talk too loud. Her baby is asleep," Coombs said.

"Certainly low, isn't she? But still, she's the goods, and it ain't our look-out," Burke said quietly, shaking his head, his face showing disgust.

"I hope one or two of you boys go first and get the lady cranked up right for me," said Cohen.

Studs was reminded of the gang shag they had once had at Iris' on Prairie Avenue, when he had lost his cherry. Since then he had never had it and gotten as much out of it as he hoped for, except maybe once with that little bitch from Nolan's who had dosed him. He wished he was only as old as when they'd gang-shagged Iris, and going in to this woman.

"I never had tail under such queer circumstances," Burke said.

"Life, my boy, is stranger than fiction."

"It's much better than a can-house, and only half a buck more," Burke said.

"When I came, she answered the door in her drawers. Nice, isn't she, Lonigan?" Coombs said.

"Getting down to business, boys, take these to keep yourselves out of the rain," Cohen said, going around to each of them.

She entered carrying a pack of playing cards, and each drew. Studs was highest with a ten of diamonds.

"Lonigan, save us a little," Burke said.

"Listen, if you think you can say such things, you better leave. This is my house. I'm not going to stand for your lewdness," she said.

"I'm sorry. No harm meant," Burke said meekly.

"Watch your tongue then!" she said, softening her challenge. She collected two-fifty from each of them.

"My baby is taking its nap in the bedroom off here. Please be quiet. And you can come into the bedroom down the hall in a minute," she said, looking at Studs.

Studs nodded, trying to keep himself under control. As she left the room, Burke laughed, shook his head quizzically.

"Treat us like a pal. We'll be waiting anxiously out here," Burke said.

Grinning foolishly, Studs walked down the hall, opened the bedroom door.

"All right?" he asked.

"Come in," she said.

He entered the small, neat bedroom and saw her, naked, her black hair falling down her back, reclining on a high poster bed, with feminine clothes and a copy of *True Stories* magazine on a chair beside it.

"Well, I suppose we better get started," she said coldly.

IV

"Three cheers," said Cohen when Studs re-entered the parlor, interrupting them as they cut cards for nickels.

He was disappointed, because it had all happened so quickly.

"Boys, wish me luck," said Coombs, arising.

"How you like the lady?" asked Burke.

The baby began squawling as Studs grinned knowingly at Burke.

"Hey, Coombs, tell her the brat is bawling. Ask her what we should do?" Burke called. Turning to Cohen, he said, "That big mugg Coombs is dumb. Let's tell him to mind it."

Cohen grinned.

They saw her, naked, enter the bedroom, carrying the baby back. It still cried as she closed the door behind her.

Coombs was in the room with her, and the baby let out a long wail as Studs put on his hat and left. All over so quickly. He wanted more, but she'd said no encores without another two and a half. And he'd rather go back alone some morning than now with the others there.

He felt lazy, too, and he thought of how when he went back it would be better. She was nice, and he remembered her naked on the bed when he'd entered the room. But a married woman and mother who'd do such a thing, lower than a snake. What was the difference between her and a whore? None. And what a chump and sap of a husband she must have.

Women like her, and a girl like Catherine, now there was all the difference in the world between them. After being with her, and then thinking of a girl like Catherine, a guy wanted to go and fumigate himself. But what the hell? Just as Slug Mason had always said, tail was tail. Catherine didn't know about it, and what she didn't know wouldn't hurt her. If she wanted to be tough, as she had last night, let her, and then she could see what she was going to lose. Lighting a cigarette, he thought that this was a just revenge on her.

He stopped at a newspaper stand at Seventy-first Street, bought a paper, quickly opened to the day's stock-market quotations. Eight and a half. Hell, wouldn't it ever go up? Hardly any use now in selling it, losing so much dough.

The street was alive with people, women rushing through their last-minute marketing, people coming home from work. Suppose one of these men coming along was George Jackson. Nice surprise for Georgie.

Catherine. Was she home yet? What was she doing at this minute? And that broad, he wished he hadn't seen her, a broad who would do as lousy a thing as that made a guy feel contaminated. Still trying to kid himself. He'd wanted her, and he'd gotten just what he needed, and she was better than a whore. Catherine, though, was she home yet? Didn't she really give a damn about him? Had she meant the things she'd said to him last night? He couldn't make up his mind about it, or about her. Call her up? Forget her?

And now that the day was finished, he had to get through the night. Christ, things sometimes got dull for a guy.

But maybe she'd call up after supper, and he'd go over and see her. He thought she would. She really cared for him. Maybe when he got home there would already be a message for him from her.

CHAPTER ELEVEN

I

Was it going to turn out the same way as it had with Lucy? There had been a little scrap, and he'd waited for something to happen and for Lucy to take the first step, and days had dragged into months, and then it was about two years gone by and one day he discovered that she had moved. It was already three days since the quarrel with Catherine, and no word. He didn't want it to drag along and die out as it had with Lucy.

Since then, he would feel free and forget her, and then he wouldn't want to feel free, and the thought of her would pop right back in his mind. Then he would want to call her up, but he wouldn't because it might seem like he was crawling back, ready to eat dirt. So he had just had it on his mind, the fight, thinking of how they would act about making up, how they would get along better after they made up, and he would go off all over again into day dreams, and they would be busted wide open in disappointment with the question, What was he going to do about it?

He walked over to the parlor window, looked out at the street, wet and gloomy under the raw day, and he guessed he would just have to sit around home and not do much of anything. An automobile sloshed by. He stared at a space of blackened pavement, seeing the rain patter on it. He watched a man in a tan raincoat hasten by. A woman wearing a bright green raincoat came out of the apartment hotel building, buried her head under an umbrella, half ran in a clumsy, feminine way.

He turned away from the window, yawning, feeling imprisoned. And the damn gloomy weather made him feel twice as rotten. He looked wistfully at the crumpled copy of the morning paper, regretting that he had already read it. He picked up a copy of *The Argosy Magazine*, slumped in his father's chair, fitfully glanced through it until he came to a story of secret-service men who thwarted an effort of Chinese and shaggy-bearded Bolsheviki to blow up the Panama Canal. He read on, how the hero took a general's daughter into his arms, kissed her, and in the last paragraph they stood by a steamer rail, looking shoreward at the dimming outlines of land in the red sunset, kissed, talked of how happy they would be back in the good old U. S. A. where he would receive a higher salary serving Uncle Sam, kissed again. Drowsy, emitting a noisy yawn, he dropped the magazine, thinking that they would then have gone into their cabin and on to the next step after kissing. Interesting story, fast and full of action, with good descriptions, too. He saw himself as a secret-service agent, on the trail of Bolshevik agents and smugglers all over America. He didn't have the imagination to go on thinking how he would track them down, and he rested his eyes dreamily on the ceiling. Anyway, he wished that he had lived and was living an adventurous life, like a secret-service agent.

And instead of anything like that, here he was, nearly thirty, and just in a hell of a pickle, getting just about nothing but the sour grapes of living. He had lost nearly all of the money he owned, on the market. He had lost his girl. His health was on the fritz. The way things were going, pretty soon he probably wouldn't even have a pot to take a leak in. And just a couple of months ago when he and Catherine had become engaged, he had hoped for and planned on so many things. Already that night by the lake seemed long ago, and he was lonesome for it. He was still where he had always been. Just hoping. And where was his dough that was going to be backed by the public utilities of the Middle West and the brain of Solomon Imbray? The stock at seven. Wait till he saw snaky Ike Dugan again. . . . Now, too, didn't he realize how having a little dough of your own gave you confidence?

He leaned forward and turned on the radio, hearing an oily masculine voice.

One of the blotches on the name and civic reputation of Chicago is that during all these years of astounding growth in this great Athens of the Middle West no consistent and scientific method of solving the traffic problem has yet been devised.

Tough luck, Teddy, he thought, dialing on a new station.

Just a gigolo . . .

He returned to the window and forgot his worried thoughts by watching the rain hit the street, turn silver, almost bounce. The drops hung like crystals to the leaves of the small tree in front of the apartment hotel, slid off. An automobile passed with a clatter, and the rain splattered on its tarpaulin top. The sky, dull, heavy black clouds ranked above the tall apartment hotel. Bells, warning of a train at Seventy-first Street.

People seem to know . . .

A girl with tan raincoat and galoshes, a few inches of silk-stockinged leg showing. Neat. Who was she? Had she ever been made? How did being made change a girl? And before they were made were they as curious about what it was and how did it feel as he'd been as a punk kid? Good girls from good homes, once they got started, became the hottest. Or did they? She was out of sight. Neat little girl anyway.

Jesus Christ.

He had to do something, think about something, say something. And all he could do was curse and mope and look

out the window at the rain and at a passing girl. He realized
how so many times in his life he had just kept on living on
wishes, and the days had dragged along, and the wishes hadn't
come true. He returned to the chair.

> *Just a gigolo . . .*

He told himself that he was a clown clean through. Every
time a fly ball had been hit to him with men on the bases, he'd
muffed it. Hoping for one thing, then another, and when he
did get his chances—foul ball.

Girls, too. He'd never held one. Twice Lucy had given him
the cold shoulder. That girl he'd knelt next to at Christmas
mass in Saint Patrick's once—cold shoulder. Never got beyond
wishing about her. Now Catherine.

Football. He'd wanted to be a star high-school quarterback
and he'd not had the guts to stay in school. Fighting. His kid
brother had even cleaned him up. In the war when he'd tried
to enlist, a leather-necked sergeant had laughed at him.

He was just an all-around no-soap guy.

> *Happy days are here again,*
> *The skies above are clear again . . .*

And he didn't have anything ahead of him that looked so
keen. The old man was just about washed out and when he
died, he wouldn't hardly leave a nickel. And he had always
counted on that, too.

He jumped from his chair, determining that, goddamn it,
he had to break through somewhere. He looked at himself
in the mirror and frowned in an ugly, menacing manner. He
walked back and forth across the parlor, clenching and
unclenching his fists.

> *So let's tell the world about it now.*

He swung viciously through the air, as if he were ripping
into some bastard in a fight, slugging.

He paused, sat down, his tension relaxing, and he felt
ridiculous.

> *Let us sing a song of cheer again,*
> *Happy days are here again.*

Couldn't even make up his mind on any kind of a resolution.
On the stocks, he'd frittered around hoping, while they sank
to seven bucks on each of his eighty shares, and now it wasn't
even much use to dump them and get back only five hundred
and sixty out of his original two thousand.

He wanted to be with Catherine and to forget, and to talk to her, maybe tell her some of these things.

Hello, housewives of Radioland, this is Sally Saucer speaking.

He turned the radio off. Catherine would maybe still have confidence in him. It was just pride, false pride, that was keeping them apart, and it would cost them a lot to stick to it. Perhaps all she was waiting for was for him to telephone her. And that's just what he was going to do.

"Mom, I'm going down to the corner a minute."

"Son, not in all this rain."

"I got my slicker and it won't hurt me."

"But, son, if you want anything like cigarettes, you can telephone for it, can't you? It's raining cats and dogs."

"It won't hurt me."

"You'll get your feet wet, William."

"I won't be gone long or out in it enough for that."

"Well, at least wait and let me make you a cup of tea to warm you up before you go."

"All right," he said, walking into the kitchen and sitting down while she turned the gas on under a kettle.

"You haven't seen Catherine for the last two or three days?"

"I saw her three or four nights ago," he said, his voice so unconvincing that she turned to stare at him.

"Son, have you and Catherine quarrelled?"

"Why, no, of course not."

"Well, I know that something is on your mind, because you seem to be carrying on very strange. And you haven't gone to see her these last nights, or called her up, nor she you. Now, son, tell me the truth. Have you two been quarrelling?"

He showed his embarrassment. Hell, he wished he was a better actor.

"Well, it wasn't anything serious."

"Just a spat, or what?"

"Nothing much. We just had a disagreement and lost our temper," he said, wondering what made her so curious, regretting having given it away.

"Son, I didn't want to say this," the mother said, wagging her head regretfully, "but I have always believed that Catherine wasn't the girl for you. God forbid me from saying anything against the girl, because she's a decent Catholic girl who has good, hard-working parents. But I can't make myself believe she's good enough for a boy with the bringing-up and the family and the educated, refined sisters that you've got. God forbid that I would run her down, but it's the truth that she's a little bit *common*."

Studs looked bored and wanted to get out. And now she'd tell the old man and tonight at supper he'd have to do some explaining. The kettle steamed and Mrs. Lonigan put tea leaves and poured water into a crockery tea pot. She set a cup, milk, sugar, bread and butter before him on the table.

"Son, I'm talking to you because I'm your mother, and a boy can never do the wrong thing if he is guided by his mother. Now, tell me what was the trouble. Did she go out with another fellow?"

"It was nothing like that, I tell you."

"You know, William, it takes a long time to know a girl, and to learn what she has in her, and whether or not she is the right kind for you," the mother said, pouring him a steaming cup of tea.

"Catherine's all right," he said, controlling his gripe caused by her insinuations.

"Of course she is, son. God forbid that I say she isn't. I just said that it takes a long time to really take the measure of a girl, and to know if she'll make a good wife or not."

Hell, no use arguing with his mother. When she set her mind on something, there was nothing to be done and that was the end of it. He broke a slice of bread and buttered it.

"When did this trouble start?"

"There wasn't any real trouble."

"But you're not seeing her. Certainly there must have been trouble or you'd be seeing her. Before this quarrel you were seeing her almost every night, and the two of you were always hanging on the telephone."

"I might be seeing her tonight," Studs said to halt the talk. wishing that his words were true.

He arose from the table.

"I'll be back soon."

"Son, can't you wait until the rain lets up?" she asked, and he could see the disappointment on her face.

"It won't hurt me," he said, quickly leaving the kitchen before his mother could continue pumping him.

II

Studs dallied by the drug store entrance with soggy feet, blankly watching people pass the rain-swept corner of Seventy-first and Jeffrey. Quarter after eleven. He could wait a minute and get clear in his mind just what he would say to her. When she'd say hello, he'd say something like how are you, this is

Studs. Then he would go right on and say: Listen, there's no use of going on like this. We ought to talk it over. But suppose she slammed the receiver in his ear, or politely told him there wasn't anything to talk over. He couldn't stand to risk a thing like that.

He shouldn't have come out. As soon as he got home, he'd soak his feet in hot water and drink some more hot tea. Couldn't catch cold with his health and bum heart. He could call and pretend that someone had called when he was out, and ask had she called. And that would give her a chance to break the ice if she wanted to, and it would leave him a loophole to crawl out, and if she then said anything about his trying to make up, he'd have his excuse to show it wasn't so. He just couldn't take the risk of her cutting him cold. That was all.

He watched a man run stiff-legged around the corner onto Jeffrey. An Upton Oil Company truck rumbled over the railroad tracks. A stout flat-footed woman pushed toward the bank, her head hidden under an umbrella.

He guessed it would be better to wait until she was home. She wouldn't be able to talk much anyway from the office, because there were people listening in. He could catch the next downtown train and get down in front of the office building when she came out to lunch. That would be the best idea. It was easier to settle a thing seeing a person than over the telephone. He lit a cigarette and thought of how she seeing him, her face would pop with surprise. Then perhaps she'd smile and it would all be over. The bells rang, the gates lowered. People were running to catch the train. It rocketed into the station. Hell, no use to go down in all this rain. And if he did that and she passed him up he would be sunk. Couldn't bend too far with a girl, or she'd lose all respect for you.

If only he could meet her by accident somewhere, then his hands would be clean. He wouldn't then give her the impression that he was coming on bended knees, with his hat in his hand to get the thing patched up.

Maybe she would telephone him tonight, if she saw he was determined. If she could stand to let it go on, and he called up, he would just show all his cards. Then she'd think that he'd only been making a bum gesture when he'd walked away from her. Best thing to do was to go home, read a few nice stories, listen in on the radio, and sit tight. Let her come around. If she didn't think he was worth coming around to, well, maybe it was just as well to let it go smash.

McGoorty, with a shiny, black, caped raincoat, slopping along. How did they let such a dumb bastard on the force?

It would be dumb sitting home all afternoon, and the old lady would keep after him with questions about the scrap with Catherine. Mrs. George Jackson. That was the ticket. Nothing could be sweeter than a warm dame like her on a cold and rainy day. He pulled out his wallet. Ten bucks. Hell, why not afford the two and a half. It would put him in the right spirits, and he could lay around with her. Hell with Catherine. She didn't know what Mrs. George Jackson knew.

He bought a slug, looked up her number, and phoned. Temporarily disconnected. Couldn't afford to pay her bill, he guessed. Well, under the circumstances, he'd be a welcome and profitable visitor.

He hastened out of the store, bent his head, and trudged along in the pelting rain. This little hardship would make it all the nicer, and he could let his shoes and socks dry while he engaged in a real serious bout of love. Thinking of how she had looked stripped, he plunged his foot into a sidewalk puddle, cursed, proceeded at a more tiring pace.

Damp, his feet wet, he rang her door-bell and climbed the stairs. She stood in the doorway in a soiled apron.

"Hello, I thought I'd come around and see you again," he said familiarly, wiping his feet.

"Come in a minute, please," she said, startled, and he hopefully stepped in.

"On a bum and dreary day like this, a fellow needs someone like you to make him feel that he's a man," he said in a strained voice while she closed the door.

"But I never asked you to come back."

"I thought it would be a surprise, particularly if you've been feeling as dopey this morning as I have."

"You know, I'm not a chippy and my home is not a disorderly house. What do you mean by coming here like this?"

"I didn't mean it in that way. I just liked you, and wanted to see you under more favorable conditions than the other day, so I thought, what the hell, nobody would be the loser if I came," he said, trying to smile persuasively and break through her discomforting, unyielding glance.

"You'd better go see a chippy. I can't do that. I'm not that kind. If you had any feeling, you'd have realized the kind of fix that forced me to do that the other day, and you wouldn't have come back here like this, uninvited."

Nice little greeting after his trip in the rain.

"But you don't stand to lose anything, and it won't hurt your husband if he doesn't know about it. If you'll play ball with me, I'll give you five bucks. Come on," he said, pulling out his wallet and drawing out a five-dollar bill.

"Please go."

He felt like a clown and her voice seemed like a whip. He tried to win her by an intense and impassioned stare, and she returned it with a curling sneer.

"Come on, sister, you know the ropes and it's not going to hurt you. It'll mean five bucks extra for the ponies. I wouldn't have walked all the way here in the rain if I didn't think you were worth it."

"I'm sorry to inform you that I cannot return your compliment."

"I don't see why you should treat me this way," he said, knowing immediately that his words were a bull.

"Who are you that I should worry how I treat you? What do I owe you?"

"That's not what I mean. It's . . . aw, come on, sister, let's get to knowing each other," he said, reaching to grasp her hand.

"Don't!" she said, stepping back. "Whenever I'm as hard up as you seem to be, I can certainly find myself a better specimen than you."

"Listen," he said, sore.

"I wish that you would please get the hell out of my house."

"Say, what the hell's the idea? One day you hustle like a bitch, and the next you try to pull a high-hat gag like this."

"If you don't leave I'll call the police."

"And then we'll ride to jail together in the paddy wagon, and George'll come down to bail you out. There's a law against whores in this town."

"Who'd take your word for mine? My husband'll kill you, he'll break you in two. Get out before I scream. Get out! Get out, you dirty little rat!"

"All right, girlie. Keep your pants up. I ain't afraid of anybody getting tough, and you can send your husband around any old time."

"Are you going?"

"You can bet your boots I'm going. Sorry I made the mistake."

"If you ever come around again, I'll have you arrested. . . . Say, I remember how you acted yesterday, and I pity any woman who'd get the idea that you're a good time. Say, you don't even know how to jazz."

"All I can say is I feel sorry for George, having a cheating bitch like you for a wife."

"Get out before I scream!"

The door slammed behind him, and he hurried downstairs and out of the building.

The bitch . . . he repeated to himself, walking in the rain. That dirty, low-down, filthy. . . . He quickly turned the corner. She might set the cops on him. Well, she better not. That goddamn . . . and wasn't he glad he hadn't tossed his dough away for a pig like that! She was lower than a nigger whore or a pansy. Still, she was a neat trick. That dirty. . . . There wasn't any word filthy enough to describe her.

And what a chump he'd been coming all the way over in a rain like this for her. The rotten, goddamn. . . . She probably had some poor feeble-minded chump of a husband, too, who sweated his ears working to get dough she lost on the ponies. And hustling on him on the side. He hoped that dumb George would wake up and kick her all over the house. And the bitch, telling him he didn't know how to. . . . It made him appreciate how decent a girl Catherine was, and it all went to show how when a guy got a girl who was pure gold like Catherine, he should hold on to her. And he was going to. He'd just like to tell that goddamn bitch one thing. He had a girl who was clean and decent, a girl that she wasn't fit to walk on the same street with. The rotten, contaminated little . . .

He darted into a drug store.

"Slug."

"Bad weather today. Looks like it's going to keep up all day, too," the bald-headed druggist said.

Studs picked up his slug, and turned toward a booth. The druggist frowned after him.

Waiting to get her, he became afraid she'd turn him down flat, and he breathed in choking anxiety. Jesus, she couldn't. It was her voice.

"This is Studs," he mumbled with a prayerful hope.

"Yes," she replied, but in a friendly voice.

He coughed in the embarrassment of an extended thirty seconds of silence.

"It's a bum day and I guess I caught a cold."

"It is terrible out, and you should stay in today and drink tea and hot lemonade."

"I think I'll go home and do that," he gravely said.

He grunted during a second silence.

"How have you been?" he asked.

"All right, that is, in one way."

"Well, in what way?" he asked gently.

"Well," she said, and he liked her soft and caressingly friendly voice, and Jesus, he had to see her again.

"I thought I'd call you up because I didn't see any point in not calling and . . ."

"Yes," she said encouragingly while he struggled to find words.

"Anyway, when am I going to see you?"

"When do you want to?"

"When can I?"

"Come over to supper tonight. Mother and Dad are going out to a supper and bridge party, and I'll cook supper for you."

"What time?"

"Six-thirty."

"I'll be there."

"Goodbye, Bill."

"Goodbye, Kid."

"And, Bill, you go home now and put on dry socks and have your mother make you a hot lemonade."

"I will. So long, Kid."

He emerged from the telephone booth smiling.

"Bad day," he said to the druggist.

"Yes, looks like it'll rain all day."

"It's rained more than the flood already."

"Well, maybe it'll clear up tomorrow."

"Say, give me a coke."

"Yes, sir. Say, you know what I'll bet? I bet you've been fighting with your girl. When you came in, you had a face on you like a man ready to lick his weight in wild cats, and didn't even hear me talk to you. And you came out smiling like Easter Sunday. I said to myself, Wow, there's a lad, quarrelling with his girl friend or his missus. Well, here's your coke."

"Yeah, you guessed it. We had a dumb fight, and fixed it up. She's a damn fine kid."

"If she is, don't let a little spat draw you apart. These days there ain't many of them left that a man can have trust in. I know that with so many of them painting up and smoking cigarettes. They ain't out of public school before they're in here for cigarettes and making eyes at anything in pants."

"Well, my girl's the goods and I'm glad I got her."

"If she is, boy, hang on to her."

"I know that much."

"Well, it's still raining. Looks like an all-day rain."

"Uh huh! So long."

He could thank that Jackson bitch for one thing. She'd shown him what a decent girl Catherine was. Catherine was pure gold, and she was Studs Lonigan's girl.

III

Studs smiled apologetically at Catherine in the doorway.

"Come in," she said sheepishly.

"I'm not late, am I?" he asked, feeling the necessity of saying something.

"Why, no. I have things about ready, though, because I got off work a little early today to come home and cook."

"Well, that was certainly nice of you," he said hoarsely.

"Here, give me your hat and coat," she said, accepting them and hanging them in a hall closet off the front door.

They looked at each other. She broke into an effervescently spontaneous smile.

"Is this going to be all the greeting I get?"

"Well . . ." he said gravely.

"You're not even going to say you're glad to see me?" she said, showing disappointment.

Seeing the look of tragic discomfort on his face, she smiled lightly, drawing a grin from him.

"I'm glad, naturally."

"You men!" she exclaimed familiarly.

She flung her arms about him, kissed him, led him by the hand into the parlor.

"Aren't you going to tell me how glad you are to see me?" she said as they sat down on the small couch in the corner of the parlor.

"Yes, I am."

"And now, tell me, what have you been doing?"

"What do you mean?"

"These last few days."

"Oh, nothing much. There hasn't been anything to do. I haven't been doing any work because things are pretty quiet with my dad."

"Want to know what I've been doing?"

"Why, sure."

"I'll tell you. I've been wondering when you would have enough sense to telephone me. You're such a booby, taking things so seriously. You men, you're worse than babies when it comes to trying to understand a girl."

"Maybe it's because girls are babies."

"Oh, yeah," she smiled.

"Nice babies," he said heavily.

She mussed his hair playfully, kissed him, momentarily nestled her head against his shoulders. She jumped up.

"You wait here a minute until I call you," she said like a

mother instructing a child, shoving him back onto the couch as he arose.

He watched her vanish from the parlor, and leaned back comfortably in the couch. His eye travelled about the small, neat parlor, with the square piano against one wall, two flush easy chairs, a lamp with a flowery blue-bordered shade reposing on a doily in the center of a small table. Outside, the rain had stopped, and an after-glow endowed the street with a mellow coloring. A pleasant street, with homes and apartments, and it made him think of the 5700 block on Indiana Avenue in the old days.

He could hear her fussing in the rear of the apartment. She was doing things for him. He was gratified. Now he was sorry he had goofed around with that Jackson bitch. All she was good for was a jazz and he'd gotten that and finished. If they ever saw each other again they wouldn't speak. But wouldn't he love to sink his fist down her dirty goddamn throat! Still, it was a closed book, best forgotten.

"Bill?"

He walked self-consciously to the back, and he was struck by the pleasant sight of the dining room, the oval table set for two, the freshly baked chocolate cake flanked by two burning red candles. There were glasses of tomato juice cocktails before each plate, and the steak soaked with juicy gravy, the baked potatoes, and carrots and peas in a separate dish were already on the table.

"Now, dear, hurry up and let's drink our tomato juice so that the rest of the supper doesn't get cold."

Smiling, they sat down and drank the tomato juice.

"Well, what do you say?"

"Nice."

"Is that all?"

"Very nice."

"Hurry up, now, you serve the meat."

He cut two large slices of steak with an air of profound seriousness, and laid one on each plate. She served the carrots and peas. He reached for a baked potato, sank butter into it, buttered a slice of bread.

"How does it taste?"

"Swell," he answered with his mouth full.

"Is the steak seasoned enough?"

He nodded, still chewing, and during a brief silence he thought that anyway, he was grabbing himself off a girl who could cook.

"You're not saying a lot about the supper I cooked for you?"

"I was just thinking how good it is."

"You men, with your heavy compliments," she smiled.

He returned the smile, chewing.

"Aren't you glad now that you telephoned me and didn't go on being such a silly goose?"

"I wasn't silly . . ." he stopped short, determining not to let himself in for dumb baby talk, or even for a teasing argument, lest it lead to another serious row.

"Dear, you know, you did say nasty things to me the other night."

"You didn't seem to spare my feelings," he said, immediately fearing that it was the wrong thing to have said.

"Your feelings. . . . You acted like your feelings were hurt. You just went ahead like a bull in a china shop, insulting me right and left."

"I got sore, that's all. I got a bad temper, and I lose it sometimes."

"Don't I know your temper?" she smiled.

"Of course, maybe I was too quick on the draw in some of the things I said, and I guess I really didn't mean them. But gee, Kid, I couldn't see the reason for making so much importance out of an unimportant quarrel." He chewed into a slice of steak. "And listen, Kid, don't you ever let anyone try to tell you that you can't cook."

"I'm glad you're learning some things," she said, continuing to eat.

He helped himself to more steak. She blew him a kiss.

"How is your mother and everyone?"

"Oh, all right."

When they finished, she brought in the coffee percolator from the kitchen and set it on a pad. She poured coffee and pointed at the cake.

"I baked it."

"Looks swell."

"I hope it tastes as good as it looks. I'm worried about it. I'm afraid it'll be too heavy."

"It looks jake to me."

She cut large pieces, carefully placing them on plates. The inside was golden yellow color, and Studs, watching her, playfully licked his lips, made extravagant faces, smiled at her boyishly.

"You're a darling."

"Swell," he said with his first taste of the cake.

"No, I think it's too heavy," she said, her air almost professional.

"You're a dandy cook, Kid, and don't let anyone ever tell you anything previous."

"You're just trying to be nice to me and make up. Well, mister, I'm not going to let you off so easily. I'm going to put you through a long probation of good behavior."

"And suppose it isn't good," he said, his eyes almost twinkling mischievously.

"You men, you're so much like little children," she said with a gay laugh.

"And, girls, you're just old Father Experience herself," he said, and she returned his smile.

"And now you're going to play house with me and help wash the dishes," she said after they finished their coffee and dessert.

His face suddenly flushed. He arose and walked over to her.

"I thought I better bring this back to you."

"Put it on," she said, raising her hand.

He slipped their engagement ring back onto her finger. She kissed it, and looked at him tenderly. She pulled him down onto her lap, kissed him, toyed with his hair, pressed his head against her breasts.

"I don't want you ever to fight with me again," she said with assumed sternness, again kissing him.

He was proud to have his girl back, and to receive her attentions. But not wanting to show his feelings too much, he let himself act a little bored.

"We better get those dishes done," he said with transparent gruffness.

"I see you're beginning to get trained right."

He got up and commenced to pick dishes off the table.

"You're so inefficient," she said, smiling with a sense of superiority. "Here, scrape the leavings off the plates, and then stack them and save yourself extra trouble."

He helped carry out the dishes, thinking that there'd been a time when Studs Lonigan had never thought he'd be doing a thing like this—and liking it, too.

"Nice looking monkey-suit you got me into," he said with pretended discomfort after she had tied an apron on him.

She laughed and left the kitchen. Returning with her hands behind her back, she smiled impishly.

"Close your eyes."

He complied, and she placed a lace night cap on his head.

"You look so sweet and innocent and domestic now. . . . No, don't you dare do that. William Lonigan, you keep that cap on. Don't you dare! I won't let you take it off."

He looked at her, helpless and petulant. Laughing again, she threw her arms around him and kissed him.

"You're my dear, sweet, adorable boob."

"I guess I am," he sighed disconsolately.

She laughed.

"Nice compliments I'm getting."

"Beautiful compliments they are."

She let hot water into the dishpan and dropped in a handful of soap chips. Studs lit a cigarette, dropped the lace cap on the sideboard, and draped a dish towel over his arm, while she commenced to wash the dishes.

"Wait until it's rinsed," she said dictatorially when he started drying a soapy dish.

"All right."

"You men, you're such babies and incompetents in the kitchen. You talk so big and pretend so much for yourselves, and when it comes to doing simple, practical little things, you're all left-handed."

"Yeah," he countered with playful irony.

Drying the dishes, he admitted to himself that he liked this, and he liked her, and she sure was a rest and a consolation to him, and he was damn glad that they'd patched up their quarrel. But he couldn't say too much of such thoughts out loud because he'd look goofy and seem like a mollycoddle.

He wondered about the fellows like Red Kelly. Did he do things like this around his home and like it? Slowly and carefully, he dried the dishes and silverware. She put the dishes away, and he watched in a mellow, happy state while she perfunctorily swept the kitchen. It was going to be nice, too, when they got married, and she was going to make a real wife, and with her to help him he couldn't help but get along. And the difference between her and such a lying, low-down broad as that Jackson bitch!

"You get one hundred percent for this," she said when he meekly handed her the apron he had worn.

"Sure, I go to the head of the class."

"You're so funny," she said, kissing him, and they walked arm-in-arm from the kitchen.

IV

"Let's take in a show."

"Oh, let's not. We're going to be alone. Let's just sit and pretend that it's our own home," she said with an inviting smile.

He wasn't certain what it meant, and if it meant more than he usually hoped for from her. He looked at her nonplussed.

She seemed to grow a little vague and almost misty before his eyes, and he liked her, and the way she looked at him left him happy but uncertain, just as Lucy had done sometimes.

"It's nice here, isn't it, when it's just getting dark and it is so quiet," she said when they were seated on the parlor couch.

"Yes," he said dreamily, hearing an automobile pass outside, thinking how the quarrel had given him again a real appreciation of her.

"Bill," she exclaimed moodily.

"What?" he replied absently.

"Let's not ever fight again."

She placed her head against his shoulder, and toyed with his hand. She seemed soft, white, nice, and he was made tender by her nearness, and by the way she glanced up at him, coyly, wide-eyed. He kissed her. Her lips were feverish, and they excited him so that he roughly clutched her, clenched her firmly, and their bodies strained in an awkward embrace. Unable to check himself, he pushed her down on the couch and pressed against her. Their excitement lapsed and they lay peacefully, side by side. Suddenly she kissed him sensuously, and his hands eagerly strayed over her dress.

"Please."

He disregarded her words and she stifled her protest, opened her mouth when he bore against her, holding his kiss, while he ran his hand along her hot thighs, beneath her dress. She became like an instrument in his hands, quivering to his touch, panting from his heedlessly indelicate pressures and nervous hands.

"You're getting your dress all mussed," he said in uneven breaths.

"That's because of you, but I love you," she said, clenching her arms around him and straining herself until she lay on her back with him above her. Her body was strong, hard. He touched her, kissed her. He thought, as if through the voice of conscience, that she would hate him, turn from him in disgust for this. But he had gone too far to stop. And then she scratched his neck, pulling his face down to kiss him. She bit his lip. Acting, as if with an inspiration, he fumbled, trying to remove her dress.

"Just a minute," she gasped.

Studs sat beside her, humiliatingly impassioned, his hands almost trembling, and he felt that he must look like a fool to her. She sat up, smiling painfully. He sank back limply. He was thirsty, his hair was mussed, and he had lost all control of himself. Perspiration dripped under his armpits, making the hair in that spot stiff and sticky.

She arose and he felt it was goodbye. She pulled her dress over her head. He leaped to her and pulled it off. He quickly removed his coat, tie, shoes, socks, and shirt, and looked at her, partially nude in the semi-darkness. He choked with pride. She was doing this because of him, passion for him, because of his kisses, his touches, himself. She lay down wantonly, and like a grateful puppy he kissed her gently. She held him against her, and he could feel the warmth of her flesh. He tore wildly at the straps of her undergarment.

"No," she feebly protested.

"Come on," he muttered with hoarse impetuosity.

She sat up, and permitted him to strip her. She turned her head aside, shyly, and sat beside him, naked.

"I better save the press in my trousers," he said seriously.

She smiled. Suddenly he was beside her, feeling ridiculous in B.V.D.'s.

"No, we can't do that, please, please, darling," she begged, almost frantic.

He disregarded her. She sighed, moaned in pain. Clumsy, impatient, uncontrolled, he sensed that it was all a mess. She moaned again, and he winced. And then they lay together, their bodies warm and moist, and she trembled, sobbing quietly.

Darkness was covering the room like a cloak, and he felt as if they were off alone somewhere in space or the sky, away from all the rest of the world. A kind of lassitude filled him. He remembered what had happened, the way he had so messily hurt her, and shame, like the conviction of and contrition for, sin, grew in him as the weight of sins had often grown burdensome before he would go to confession. He kissed her gently.

"Catherine," he said huskily.

"Bill, I did this because I couldn't help myself, because I love you, and oh, you hurt me so much," she cried.

"Kid," he muttered, patting her arm, sitting up, gazing down at her in a state of helplessness.

She sobbed. Her naked body again trembled. He lay back, falling into a half-doze, with her warm beside him. As if in a nightmare, he began to see himself clumsily soiling her. He opened his eyes, and felt self-disgust. He became aware that she was breathing more calmly. He buried her face against his chest.

"I'm afraid."

She's my woman now, he told himself with pride. And again he remembered the act, visualizing himself like a goddamn bull. And all the mess it was, too. Ugh. He had hurt her, done something to her that could never be undone. It had not pleased him. It had been pain to her, a mess to him, and maybe in the morning she would hate him for it and only remember him on her like a goddamn, wheezing bull. Ugh. . . . Jesus Christ. . . . He was disgusted with himself as he had sometimes been when he had a hangover and remembered how the night before in his drunkenness he had been a chump and a clown.

He looked around the darkened room as if to fasten his attention on something that would make him forget what he couldn't just now forget. He heard footsteps outside, a telephone ringing in the flat upstairs, and he felt, again, removed from all the world with her burying her head against him, his skin wet from her tears. Would he ever be able to look her in the eye again? He had acted with her the same as with a whore or that Jackson bitch. And Catherine had been decent. This was the same way, the same way, too, it seemed with any girl, except that Catherine had been hurt, and she had been so stirred and excited by him that she had trembled and quivered. Never before had he done that to a decent girl. It made him proud, and again his pride left him.

"Kid," he said gruffly.

"Yes, darling."

"I'm sorry."

She lay against him, stroking his legs. They fell asleep for a while. She awakened, jumped up, ran to the dining room, returned.

"Bill, Bill. It's nine-thirty. Hurry up or the folks will find us like this."

She pressed the wall electric button, and they saw each other naked in the light. Mutually embarrassed, they dressed. Studs thought of love songs he was always hearing on the radio. *Secrets divine I am sharing with you. Like Love, you gayly come and go.* And this was the way it had turned out. He turned away from her in her slip, so that she would not see him buttoning his trousers.

Ugh. Jesus Christ.

V

"Goodbye, darling," she said, kissing him possessively.

He left, still in a state of uncertainty. She would get up in the morning knowing that she was no longer a virgin. And all because of him. No girl had ever cared that much for him before. She had proven she cared for him. Or had it been that she'd gotten too excited? Girls were only human beings, and Catherine was twenty-five, and by this time she should have been curious to know what it felt like.

It was clear out and he sensed a hanging darkness in the atmosphere. He saw himself as a man with experience, and he felt that the things he had just gone through these last few days had been dramatic, things that might have happened in a movie. Experiences that would make plenty of fellows envy him.

But his pride suddenly went out of him like a punctured balloon. He remembered the way Catherine had squirmed, strained in pain, moaned. He had ruined her, taken from her something very precious that was lost forever. Gee, he felt kind of rotten about it and then he didn't feel so rotten, because he was glad. A virgin. And now Catherine, who had never been made, was his woman.

But Jesus, what if she got sore and hated him? He shrugged his shoulders, thinking that he should worry. The cards were now stacked on his side. If she got tough now, or they had another fight and it got serious, he could always say, well, baby, I know everything you got. Getting sore wouldn't get her any place.

But that was not how he felt, either, and he didn't mean such thoughts. He could not get out of his mind the memory of her, naked and hurt, warm and moist, her little gestures, burying her head against his shoulders. He wanted her again, goddamn it. Once she got used to it, and it didn't hurt her any more, it would be swell. This time hadn't been so much as it should be, but it was going to be more. And it was different from going and getting a whore. Falling asleep, forgetting everything, awakening, dozing, hearing her breathing, her heart beating, feeling her beside him.

He crossed Stony Island Avenue, walked on past a gas station, a vacant lot, buildings. He wanted to tell someone about it, wanted people to know that Studs Lonigan had just copped a cherry, and that she was his girl, and his woman only. Somehow or other, things that you had to keep to yourself weren't enough, and you wanted others to know. But Catherine wouldn't want that. Still it was fun, thinking of telling guys about it.

He wished that he could have slept all night with her and had it again. But he would when they got married. He was going to get his just as regular as he damn well pleased. Still, when he got married, he would be getting damaged goods. But no, it had been only himself. He was sure of that.

But he had been a goddamn brute hurting her, and it was almost like pain to think back about it, her wincing, moaning, begging him to please stop. And she had been snow white, too, and warm in the darkness when she had moaned like that.

A stranger passed. Studs wished that the fellow could look into his head, see his thoughts. He wondered, though, wasn't he just thinking like a clown.

He saw Pat Carrigan and some other lads at the counter of that same restaurant where Catherine and he had fought. He entered, self-consciously returning the proprietor's smile.

"I say there, Studs."

"How's tricks, Pat?"

"Can't complain."

"The kid brother was around earlier tonight, but he dragged off to a show," Pat said.

"Coffee and apple pie. . . . I was down to see my girl tonight," Studs said, tempted to say more.

"Seeing your girl, huh, Studs?" Pat said.

"Yeah."

"Hello, boys, Hello, Lonigan, how they hanging?" said Bryan, seating himself at the counter.

"Oh, Studs, by the way, I saw Long-Nose Jerry Rooney the other night," Pat said.

"That's the Big-Nose himself," Allison called down the counter.

"If noses were gold, thousands of people would be shoving pans up that boy's nose and prospecting for gold in his snot," pimply Don Bryan said, and they looked at him in disgust.

"Oh, Jerry's singing the blues like everybody else because he ain't getting as much pay as he used to," Pat said.

Studs thought that some guys had a hell of a lot of guts singing them over a measly five bucks a week less when here he was out over a thousand bucks and not batting an eye. He felt like saying so, very casually.

"Well, boys, congratulate me," Allison said.

"How come?"

"I copped it. I copped that little dame's cherry. I'm putting her through an intensive course in the Allison Training School."

"Lucky rat," Bryan said.

"Lucky, hell! I worked two months before she came across."

"Is she nice?"

"Nice is the word for what she's going to be. Listen . . ."

A couple entered the restaurant and Bryan nudged Allison. They spoke low.

"How you feeling these days, Studs?"

"Pretty good," Studs said, but he was getting damn tired of being asked how he was feeling, as if he was a cripple.

He finished his pie and coffee and noticed Allison and Bryan still talking in whispers. Well, he had things he could talk about, too.

"Nothing much happening, huh, Studs?" Pat said.

"No, Pat."

"Same here, Studs."

He sat for a while.

"Guess I'll be going home and turning in," Studs yawned.

He arose, paid his bill, waved a final so-long, left the restaurant.

He walked home feeling pretty good.

CHAPTER TWELVE

I

Studs walked slowly to the center of the Bryn Mawr station platform, eyeing the scattering of people who waited for a downtown train. He hoped that some of these people would notice him and think that here was a fellow who didn't have to get up early to go to work but had time to himself. He stopped near the small waiting-room and dramatically stuck his hands in his trouser pockets.

"What else can I do? If our roles were reversed wouldn't he drive me into bankruptcy? He says it's not his fault. Well, is it my fault? So he's got until next Monday to pay up or my lawyer institutes bankruptcy proceedings," a stout, puffy-cheeked man said to a friend as they stood a few feet from Studs.

Tough tiddy for someone there, Studs thought. Anyway, over the telephone, Catherine's voice had sounded sweet and friendly. She wasn't sore. It was just that he had been the right guy and last night had been the right time. His eye caught a girl, neat, all right, walking past the restaurant on the north side of Seventy-first Street. He hoped she would be getting on the train, and he'd happen to sit next to her and they'd get to talking. He was kind of a bastard, and yet, she was damn neat. He lit a cigarette and let his glance trail wistfully after her. Last night had made him think of broads, and he'd had them on his mind all morning, naked broads, and he had kept thinking of making them, harems of them. And it was all damn dirty and unfair to Catherine. But a guy couldn't always help himself. Thoughts popped into his bean, and anyway he hadn't done anything but think about them. She was turning around the bank corner, gone. The world was sure full of broads. And this week, he'd had that Jackson bitch and Catherine. He must have some sex appeal to Catherine. He was going to marry her and he liked her, and other girls, they were just umm, nice orders of pork chops on the side, as poor Paulie Haggerty used to say. He saw himself when he was an old man, fondly remembering all the girls he had laid, from Iris down the line. And suppose he still had it in him when he was seventy? He still had years of it to go anyway and that was something sweet.

The warning bells distracted him. He looked eastward down the track at the approaching train and stepped back as it pulled alongside of the platform. Tossing aside his cigarette, he figured that he wouldn't smoke if he avoided the smoker, and he entered a car in the center of the train. The train rolled forward, and walking in the car aisle he looked to see if there were any girls he might sit next to, or anyone he knew. He took an unoccupied seat in the middle, by a window, and looked out as the train passed houses, vacant lots, people walking along Seventy-first Street.

When he saw Catherine, should he or shouldn't he mention last night?

"I saw her yesterday on Seventy-first Street, and do you know, she's wearing the same hat she wore last spring?" a a stout lady behind him said to a middle-aged woman.

The train shunted through a tunnel, and Studs developed an anxiety to be out of the tunnel.

"Of course, I don't wish ill of anyone. But she put on so many airs when she had it, that it serves her right."

The train broke into daylight again and rumbled into the Sixty-seventh Street station. He watched several men and women moving about the platform to enter the cars, and he thought of Catherine, of how he had met her. She had been a distant friend or something to the Dowsons, and anyway he had met her when his sister, Fran, had married Carroll. He remembered that Phil Dowson, Carroll's twin brother, who had married Gertrude O'Reilley, the niece of Judge Joe O'Reilley, had introduced her to him and she had said how do you do, or something like that, and he had just acknowledged the introduction in a formal way. She had looked a little fat, and not so hot that time. But there had been dancing, and since he happened to be standing next to her and there was no one else to dance with, he'd asked her to dance, out of politeness. She'd said something about his dancing nice, and he'd liked the compliment so he had asked her to dance again.

"Just as my husband, Arthur, says, he believes in the philosophy of compensation, and when you do something, there's always compensation for it. It's only a compensation to her now that her husband is not doing well because she was always flaunting herself and her clothes when she had it," one of the women behind him said.

Regular hen party there, he thought. But, anyway, at Fran's wedding, when Catherine was leaving, he had walked over to her and he'd said, because of some crazy impulse or other, that he might be seeing her again. And she had smiled and said that would certainly be something to look forward to, so they had made a date then and there. He'd been sorry he'd made the date after she'd left, but it had been done, so he'd taken her to a show, and he'd decided, the second time he'd seen her, that she was better-looking than he'd first thought she was.

"Annie Rothschild is really psychic. And over a year ago Annie said that that one is going to have bad luck."

And in the hallway after the first date she hadn't let him kiss her. She'd been very self-possessed and calm and had acted like she knew how to take care of herself. He'd taken her out again, until, suddenly, he had been going steadily with her. Funny how at first he hadn't even been able to kiss her and now, he'd copped her cherry.

He looked out the window and saw that the train was passing Fifty-seventh Street, and he noted the trees of Jackson Park below, and a block distant. And then the train was slowing beside the platform, and he saw people hastening to the car doors, and the trees and buildings of Fifty-sixth Street, and beyond it a patch of the lake, deep blue against the cloudy day. Two young fellows who looked like University students headed the procession of people entering the car, and they took the vacant seat in front of Studs. An asthmatic, graying man sat beside him and began making whistling sounds as he breathed.

"Then you really think that Annie Rothschild is psychic?"

"She's very good and she does it all with cards . . ."

The train was running, stopping again at Hyde Park Boulevard, and Catherine, what would he say to her when they met? He could see the tall apartment hotel buildings stacked beside the lake, and then the lake stretched, blue and gray and dotted with white-caps, on outward into a gray curtain of deep mist. He looked out at the lake, which was like a ruffling coat of gray and white, and he heard the two fellows in the seat ahead talking earnestly.

"Hal, we're old friends, and we were pals in high school together, and I'm talking to you for your own good when I tell you not to waste your time on such stuff.".

"Jack, I'm not wasting my time. I'm beginning to get my eyes opened for me."

"You know what Mr. Boardman said when we took Poly Sci 101 in our freshman year. He said that Communism was an asylum for neurotics. What do you want to hang around with a bunch of neurotics for?"

Reds or something. A guy who must have gone crazy reading too many books at the U. But hell, all that was nothing in his young life. He thought how, after last night, he had begun to have a feeling of really being able to say to himself that he had a woman who was his own, his only. He had never thought of love in that way, or how it gave a guy that kind of a feeling, made him feel proud, important, confident in himself when he walked down the street.

"Where did Annie get her psychic powers?"

"One is born with them."

He had felt so much different getting out of bed this morning from the way he had felt just two mornings ago. This morning he had not felt that he had a dull day ahead of him. He had been excited, and he had seemed to let his own excitement go out, and everything he looked at was not dull any more. He had awakened this morning with a whole new set of feelings.

"But, Hal, why don't you wait and study more? You're just young and what do you know about life? You're only a college junior, and you set yourself up to make such criticisms. There's a number of brainy men in the world who know more than you do."

"Can it. You can't convince me. I'm going down to this demonstration before the Japanese consulate, and that's all."

"But what'll it get you?"

Nuts, all right. He looked out the window at the lake, seeing first one part of the water roll and dip, then another part rolling, and then a whole succession of waves coming in. And far out he saw a boat as if pasted against the gray sheet of horizon, smoke issuing from its stack in a pencil-line of steam. Just like a boat in a picture.

"Roosevelt Road," a conductor bawled.

He watched people pass down the aisle. How many of the men getting off, or on the train, too, had been with a woman last night or this morning? And how many of the dames on the train had had guys? Every night there were thousands of guys with their women, and now he was going to be one of them and it was going to be damn different from the way it was with whores and bitches.

The train was at Van Buren, then moving again under a bridge through a dreary, smoky stretch of railroad yards and tracks.

"Hal, if you don't care about yourself or your family, think of our fraternity. What kind of a name will it give us if one of its members is arrested at a Communist demonstration and it gets in the papers? You know, at the present time when the treasury is so low and we need members that kind of thing can't happen to our fraternity."

What these college boys needed was a good piece of tail to educate them. The train stopped. Studs elbowed his way out of the car after the college boys. He was getting anxious. This was a new wrinkle for him, the first meeting with his girl, his woman, on the day after he had made her. He wondered what he'd say? How should he act?

II

"Oh, I didn't see you," he said, trying to make his voice sound very ordinary when she met him in the lobby of the building where she worked.

"Was it that you didn't want to?" she said in a chastened tone which made him feel sorry for her and for what he had done to her.

"I was just standing here waiting for you, and looking around, and I thought I had got here too early."

"Well, here I am."

"Where'll we go?" he asked, still over-serious in his effort to be casual.

"Wherever you say, dear," she said, her glance submissive.

"Let's go down to Randolph," he said.

They stepped out to the street and she took his arm.

"Glad to see me?"

"Yeah," he said, shaking his head.

"You don't sound very enthusiastic."

"I am, Kid. I was just thinking."

"Of what?"

"Something funny. Over in front of the public library, I saw a fellow in a cap and gown selling apples."

"What was it, a fraternity initiation?"

"No. He had a sign on him saying that he was a qualified engineer out of work."

"That's too bad."

"It would be a little different if he wasn't a college graduate and an engineer. If he was just an ordinary bum, it would be different."

"Maybe he was doing it for publicity, to get his name in the papers, the same way all these people are going in for marathons. Over on Clark Street there's a man in a music store window who's trying to establish an endurance record for saxophone playing. He's been playing the saxophone for three days now."

"It's goofy."

"Yes, it's so silly."

A round-faced man paced back and forth in front of a restaurant with cardboard signs tied around his chest and back.

JOHNSTOWN'S RESTAURANT
IS UNFAIR
TO ORGANIZED
LABOR

"These poor men have been walking back and forth here for three weeks. Yesterday in the pouring rain they didn't even stop."

"Who's in the right in the strike?"

"I don't know but I think the men were foolish to strike in times like these. And what the restaurant did was to hire girls."

"Yeh, I guess anyone who has a job these days better hang onto it," he said, and he felt a pressure on his elbow.

"You know what, Bill?"

"What?"

"I'm glad to see you."

"How do you feel?"

"I had pains," she said, looking quizzically at him.

He turned a frightened glance at her, wondering had he really injured her. The least he could have done was that he could have been more careful. Like any decent girl, she had a right to be disgusted with him. He was grateful for the smile she gave him, though. Still, it seemed like a suffering sort of smile.

"I had pains here," she said, pointing to her abdomen.

"Gee. . . . I don't think it can be serious. Maybe it's just natural. The first time, you know," he said haltingly, trying, as he spoke, to make her feel that he actually knew what he was talking about.

"I cried last night after you left," she said as they turned the corner of Dearborn onto Randolph Street.

A shifty-eyed man wearing a khaki shirt and dusty, unpressed, frayed suit forlornly held an apple out to him. Studs brushed by him.

"How is the Charlus Restaurant for lunch?" he asked, remembering the night he had proposed to her in that place.

"I think it would be nice. It's quiet, and I'd like to eat in a quiet place."

"Yes, it is quiet," he said with undue seriousness, realizing that she was different, a humbled Catherine, and he dreaded having to look into her eyes across a table, and yet he felt a pride of victory.

"Sure this will be all right?" he asked in front of the Charlus Restaurant.

She nodded affirmatively. They entered as a string trio played *The Evening Star,* and a tall, dark girl in a tailored black dress led them past tables where people talked in restrained voices to a small corner table. She almost made their seating a ceremony, smiled, pointed at the menus laid before them. Studs diligently searched his pockets for cigarettes.

"I always forget which pocket I put them in," he said self-consciously.

She smiled at him meekly. A fleshy, attractive blond waitress, neat in a white apron, laid water glasses before them.

"What'll you have, Catherine?" he asked, diligently reading the menu card.

"I wonder," she thoughtfully replied, her face also lost behind the menu card.

"I think I'll take roast beef," he said.

"Me, too."

They laid their menu cards aside simultaneously, and Studs watched the waitress hobbling away from their table.

"Nice place," he said, embarrassed by their lack of talk.

"Yes, and that's a beautiful piece they're playing."

"It is nice to have the music, too."

"Darling, darling. . . . What's the matter?" she said in a fright, seeing him become suddenly pale and throw his hand over his heart.

"I had a sudden pain. But it's nothing. It's passing now," he said while she leaned anxiously across the table.

"Bill, dear, I worry so about you with your heart. Are you sure you're taking the best care of yourself? And, honey, you're still smoking. I wish you wouldn't."

"I guess you're right," he said, squashing his butt.

The waitress set their order before them. He tried to shutter the sense of fear out of his mind, but it lingered after the lapsing of that sharp, sudden thrust of pain. His heart beat with labored and disturbing rapidity. He felt weak, and a sweat had broken upon his brow. He wiped his forehead perfunctorily with a fresh handkerchief.

"Bill, you must be careful. Promise me that you'll be very careful. If you die now . . . Gee, I don't know what I'd do. Honest, I don't," she said, and he could see how profoundly worried she was.

She loved him, she was crazy about him, he told himself. He was her man. He had a premonition of his own death, seeing himself stretched out in a casket, with her beside it, looking at his corpse, lonely, sobbing, red-eyed, hysterical with suffering from her loss of him. God, that couldn't happen. It wouldn't. He had to live for her, and for himself. This was even greater proof than last night that she loved him. He was beginning to see some of the things that love was. This was one.

"Bill, darling, you know, don't you, after last night, how much I love you?"

"Yes, Kid," he said, emotion cracking through his husky voice.

The heart pain had almost completely ebbed out, but he was still faint. He felt the same as he would have if he had just come through some danger, and the sense of danger hung in his mind like some after-image. He was more afraid than when he had been knifed with the brief and sudden pain.

"Yes, dear, you know, after you left last night, I felt funny and I cried," she said.

"You shouldn't do that," he said in a restrained tone, like a father talking to a child.

"I couldn't help it. I cried because I was afraid. And just now, I was afraid, too, that you wouldn't care for me any more. You'd think I was easy and without self-respect, and wasn't, well . . . good."

His expression became a combination of curiosity, lack of understanding, sympathy, tenderness. He realized, in a fresh perception, how much she cared for him, and could only express himself to her by quickly squeezing her hand. Her knees touched his under the table, remained firm against them. He wanted her again like last night, and he knew that he cared for her, a great deal. He wanted her. Last night had been only the first, and ahead of them there were many more times. And he wanted her.

"Because, dear, if you did feel that way toward me, I don't know what I'd do," she said.

He smiled reassuringly and tried to get at how he did exactly feel toward her, without showing that he was thinking seriously. He wondered, also, how many girls did let a guy go the limit before marriage, when they were really nuts about a guy? He began to doubt how much he thought of her, because after all she had let him. Did other decent girls, like his sisters, do that before marriage? Most who did, well, he didn't know? Was she an exception? He looked at her, felt her knees rubbing against his, and all he knew was that he wanted her. She'd gone the limit because she cared for him, couldn't resist him. But then Lucy hadn't. Still, maybe she had with other guys. Come to think of it, that night in the cab after the dance she had not acted just like an innocent broad. Broodingly, against his will, he looked at Catherine and wished she was Lucy. He smiled hurriedly and genially, so that she wouldn't worry or think he didn't like her. Because after hurting her that way last night, he couldn't let himself do anything to hurt her feelings.

"Bill, dear, now tell me frankly," she said, and he could see struggle and a determination to be brave mirrored in her face. "Tell me, after last night do you still want to marry me?"

"Yes, Kid, you know I do."

"When?"

"Whenever we can arrange it, just like you said. You said we shouldn't be in too much of a hurry."

"But that's changed. You know, dear, doing what we did last night, and our not being married, it's a sin. We can't do that ever again until we're married . . . and Bill, dear, I love you terribly."

The waitress cleared their dishes and Studs was glad for the interruption, because he was beginning to become afraid of himself, of the feeling of love and tenderness toward her that arose with her words, her nearness, the touch of her knees, the memory of last night like a spirit seeping through all these feelings to warm them and glue them together. He read the menu.

"Coffee and chocolate ice cream," she said.

The waitress stood nervously over Studs.

"Same," he said.

Catherine smiled at him, enigmatically, a smile that

was very brief, like a flash, and that he could not exactly get. In it she had seemed humble, and she seemed very understanding, and he could not quite figure it out.

He had never felt the same way with a girl, not even with Lucy. Sure of himself, and of Catherine, a feeling that he was the boss and not she, a feeling that he could do what he liked with her without being the loser, and still, also, a feeling toward her of kindness, a wanting to pet her and kiss her and stroke her hands, her face and her breasts and her body, and to make up to her with kindness for the way he had hurt her last night.

He could not understand himself, and how things had come to this development between them. And he could not understand how a girl could care so much for him. He smiled at her, weakly and hastily, and he still felt their knees touching.

"We're going to be awfully happy together, aren't we, Bill?" she said, and he nodded curtly, hoping as much as believing.

"And you still care for me and want to marry me?"

He smiled yes. He saw ahead how many nights they would have together after they were married; nights and years and years, and he would have that same feeling of being alone with her, half awake and half asleep, in a daze that was like a beautiful song.

"Well, we'll be married soon."

"Whatever you wish, Kid. There's no necessity of rushing it unless you want to, because we got to get more saved up and everything arranged right," he said, thinking of the money he had lost.

And how was he going to explain that to her?

"Bill, I could wait, oh, forever, if I knew you cared for me. But Bill . . ."

"I do, Kid."

"Tell me that again," she said with a sort of hunger in her eyes.

"I do," he said huskily, suddenly seeing himself like the actor in an important drama, as if maybe this was all a movie, showing before all the world.

And there was lots ahead of him now that wasn't just grief, and he would never get another girl who cared for him like Catherine. And still there was that holding back which made him feel like a traitor. And wasn't he just getting too goddamn mushy for words?

And she laughed free and gay.

"What's the joke?" he asked, surprised by her change of mood.

"I'm just happy and you're a darling," she said, her eyes seeming to flash. "You look and act so much like a boy, so gruff." She made a face. "So gruff when you don't mean it, and you have such nice beautiful eyes, just like a little boy's. I bet you must have been pretty when you were a boy."

"I suppose I ought to get a kiddy car," he said, but he liked it.

"Darling, I'd love to see you riding a kiddy car," she laughed.

"You get me with that chatter, Kid," he said, maintaining his air of gruffness.

"It's not chatter," she said in mock indignation.

"Say, it's one o'clock."

"Gosh, I got to get back."

They arose quickly and left the restaurant, and the string trio commenced *Love Me and the World Is Mine.*

CHAPTER THIRTEEN

I

"Let's take a walk in the park," he said, taking her arm possessively.

"I don't know," Catherine said, and catching her expression from the corner of his eye, he sensed that she had guessed what was on his mind.

Ahead of them at the Stony Island corner were passing people, automobiles and street cars with a brightly illuminated Nation Oil Company filling station in the background. Passing an open window, they heard a baby-voiced female radio songbird.

> *I've a pair of arms to hug and hold,*
> *But nobody's using them now . . .*

Once he had walked toward Sheridan Road with Lucy, and she had sung and. . . . But this was different now and, oh, hell with dragging up memories!

"Nice night out," he said.

"Uh huh," Catherine muttered thoughtfully.

"Too nice a night to waste," he said, lighting a cigarette and puffing on it vigorously. "That's why I thought we might take a walk over to the park. It might be nice there."

"You like nature," she said reprovingly.

"Well, it would be nice there because it is a nice night out."

"And isn't that all so awfully just too nice for words that it's nice," she mimicked.

"Well, don't you think . . . oh, can it," he said in growing confusion.

"I think you're perfectly right," she laughed.

"How do you feel?" he asked as they neared Stony Island.

"Oh, I feel all right."

They turned and walked aimlessly north along Stony Island Avenue, past stores and buildings and filling stations, with the sound of automobile tires swishing persistently.

"Well?"

"You men," she smiled.

"Why . . . what do you mean?"

"You want to go to Jackson Park and enjoy nature."

"Well, isn't it natural?" he said aggressively, and she blushed.

He shot his cigarette butt into the street and looked at a couple drifting along in front of him.

"Now, aren't you sorry you were so vulgar?"

"I wasn't vulgar," he said with embarrassment.

"Oh, no," she said, linking his arm. "Sometimes you're so like a boy."

"Well . . ." he stopped talking.

"Yes, well, it's a nice night, isn't it?"

"Well, it is."

"Beautiful night."

"And you're just trying to razz me."

"Did you just make that discovery, you sweet old . . . pumpkin."

"Anyway, Kid, what'll we do?"

"I know what we shan't do."

"What?"

"Go to the park and catch cold on the damp grass finding out that nature is grand. . . . Go on, you're making me blush."

"I never even mentioned that," Studs self-righteously protested.

"I know. But I'm not going to take any chances with you. I love you too much to be trusting you on a dark night in the park."

"You're putting thoughts into my head."

"Well, take them out, Mr. Tarzan," she said, shamming irritation.

"What did you put them in for?"

"You're so innocent."

"Yes . . . I mean no."

"William Lonigan, aren't you ashamed of yourself?"

"There's no reason for a guy to be ashamed of liking a girl like you."

"You're so sweet," she said, squeezing his elbow.

"Well, I know how you can make yourself even more sweet."

"But, darling, you know it's not right going on like this before we're married, and anyway I can't because . . . well, I'm sick."

"Yes," he said, striving to give the impression that he knew more than he actually did.

He looked at her, and tried to shutter the unwanted disgust out of his mind and to convince himself that after all it was only something that was natural. He wished he were alone.

"I know what I'd like to do."

"What?" he asked, masking that persistent disgust.

"Go to a dance marathon."

"Doesn't sound like my idea of a good time."

"Have you ever seen one?"

"Nope."

"Well, then, let's find out what they're like. A girl at our office goes to all of them, and she talks about nothing else, and it has made me want to find out what they're like."

"Let's take in a show instead."

"We can just try a dance marathon first to see what they're like, and if we don't like it, we can leave."

"Well, why not try one some other night?"

"Hurry, here comes our car."

Reluctantly he crossed to catch a surface car.

II

"Now what do we do?" Studs asked grumpily.

"Watch."

"Well, that's not my idea of spending a roistering evening, sitting here and watching a bunch of damn fools sleeping on their feet."

"Don't talk so loud," Catherine whispered as a broad and burly woman with Slavic features turned an angry face on them from the bench below.

They sat on the left-hand side of a large dance hall converted into an amphitheater. Below them, through a thick haze of cigarette smoke, was a large polished rectangle of dance floor bounded by the box-seat section which was decorated with bunting. An aisle separated the box seats from the benches of temporary bleachers which rose on all sides to the rafters.

The troupe of fifteen couples and two extra males trudged with wearying slowness around the edge of the dance floor. On a dais opposite Studs and Catherine a tuxedo-clad jazz orchestra idled. Below them, in a slide, Studs read from black cards: 366 HRS. A banner floated from the rafters in the center of the hall.

WORLD'S CHAMPIONSHIP
SUPER DANCE
MARATHON

A bell rang, the orchestra broke into a snappy song; and the contestants danced for three minutes. Again they trod slowly around the edge of the floor, solemn, silent, tired. The tall fellow of team number eight placed his head on his partner's shoulder, a small blond girl in ruffled, untidy pink beach pyjamas, whose face was so caked with powder that Studs could notice it even from his distance. The fellow's arms were ringed around her neck, and his face, stupid in sleep, was slung over her left shoulder. Walking backward, she dragged him around. Two other male contestants and one girl fell asleep and were also pulled and maneuvered around the floor. The music continued.

"Damn fools," Studs muttered under his breath.

"What do you mean?"

"Those two wasting their energy dancing that way," Studs said, motioning his head in the direction of team number sixteen, a sheiky fellow with sideburns and blue jersey and a tough-looking, thin, faded girl in scarlet beach pajamas who hot-stepped in a rapid, whirling dance.

Applause broke out from the half-filled bleachers, and coins were flung at them. Studs smiled knowingly. He glanced around at the crowd, fellows with regan haircuts, and the girls, hoods, fat Polack women, young broads who looked to be the kind that got crushes on movie stars, all kinds of people, a mixed audience no different from the kind that would be seen at a movie.

"When is something going to happen?" he asked, watching the contestants moving around and around.

"I don't know. It's funny, and I don't think there's anything interesting in it, either," she said.

"Damn fools, wasting their health. Look at the blond trying to keep number eight on his feet."

"I wouldn't like to be her."

"And I wouldn't want to trade places with that guy, either. He can have his dance marathon."

"Why do they do such foolish things?"

"I suppose because they can get people to come out and make damn fools of themselves, and then, too, there's the dough."

"Yes, the prize is something like a thousand dollars for the winners."

"Well, they earn it," Studs said, watching the blond girl of team number eight fight and strain to keep her partner from crashing to the floor.

"Look," Catherine said excitedly.

The blond girl had tripped, and her partner smashed to the floor on his face. A buzz of conversation rose from the stands. Other dancers crowded around him. The judge emerged from his small box beside the orchestra dais, and two male attendants in soiled white clothing rushed forward.

"Oh, I hope poor Albert isn't hurt," the woman with the Slavic features in front of them sighed.

"Gee, he got a shiner," Studs exclaimed, attentively watching the male attendants lift number eight.

Number eight shook his head in stupor and walked beside his partner. He received cheers, and coins were flung to him.

"What's that?" Studs asked a fellow next to him when male and female attendants assisted number eight and three other couples from the floor, following the resounding of a siren.

"Rest period. They all get ten minutes every hour, and they go off the floor in batches."

"What do they do, sleep?" Studs asked.

Three teams which had appeared unnoticed to Studs arose from benches along the side of the dance floor and joined the straggling procession, which wound around and around and around.

"How long will this go on?" Studs asked Catherine.

"They'll still be here in another month. They all got guts and they can take it," the fellow next to him said.

"It's beyond me," Studs said, puzzled.

"They do look like physical wrecks. And I can't understand why all the girls are so swollen out," he said.

"Uh huh," Studs muttered, watching the girl of team number three holding up the dead weight of her sleep-doped partner, and then he glanced from girl to girl, noticing how their buttocks were like pumped-up balloons.

"Let 'em hang, Jackie," someone called out as the male of number nineteen kept pulling up his falling knickers; the marathoner grinned sillily, marched with his knickers draping below his knees.

Studs watched a contestant in a brown sweater reading a newspaper as he walked. He thought, too, that the guys, poor bastards, must be pretty hard up. There they were, for twenty-four hours a day, so close to girls, touching against them, hanging onto them, holding them up, and not being able to get anything. And the girls didn't look so decent or hard, and probably wouldn't mind a little. That made it all the tougher.

"I wonder when something is going to happen?" he said to Catherine.

"I guess this is what happens," she said.

He watched number two, a little fellow with thinning light hair walk with a steadily more pronounced limp. Then he turned his attention to number seven, a solid, broad young lad of almost six feet who was without a partner. He walked, asleep, wagging his head, floundered. His head and shoulders lurched forward. He swerved sidewise. His head jerked back. He staggered like a man hopelessly drunk. He fell against the box seats below Studs. Two contestants turned him around, shoved him slightly. He reeled to the center of the floor, swayed precariously, stumbled to his right, and stood listing. He crumpled, his body hitting the floor with a thud.

"I suppose that guy is finished," Studs said to Catherine.

"He's been that way for four days since his partner was forced out with swollen feet," the fellow beside Studs said.

"The winners will earn their dough," Studs said.

Amid cheers number seven arose, shaking his head, grinning. He marched in the dragging procession. The orchestra played a snappy tune. The contestants dragged themselves around and around and around.

III

A medium-sized slick, light-haired announcer swayed his girlish hips before the microphone in the center of the floor, and the contestants clustered around him.

"Well, folks, we're now in our three hundred and thirty-seventh hour of the World's Championship Super-Marathon contest at the Silver Eagle Ballroom, and as I look around at the boys and girls, I can see that there are no signs of let-up. Game to the core, fighters all, these eighteen couples and two solos are still sticking. And when I say sticking, I mean just that, sticking it out, hour after hour, day after day, battling to win the world's marathon championship and the thousand-dollar prize which will go to the winning couple. The courage which we see here on the floor daily, even hourly, is something astounding, and it forces us to admire and pay tribute to all these game and courageous contestants out here on the dance floor of the Silver Eagle Ballroom where the World's Championship Super Dance Marathon is now in its three hundred and sixty-seventh hour.

"Some of the boys here are wide awake, folks, and getting spryer and spryer every minute like the well-known Squirmy Stevens of team number four."

He glanced at a squat fellow in a crimson jersey and tannish knickers, and the fellow's dark, heavy-browed, oversized Neanderthal face broke into a grin.

"How about it, Squirmy?"

"Squirmy says he feels like he could eat a couple of beefsteaks and then sleep until next year," the announcer said into the microphone, and Squirmy performed a brief, hopping dance, drawing applause and smiles when he clowned aside by sagging and bending his knees, creating the effect of deformed walking.

"Well, Squirmy, all you got to do is to strut your stuff longer than anyone else on the floor and you'll get your wish. And when you do go on that sleep, sweet dreams."

The contestant with the sore feet and thinning hair spoke to the announcer.

"Joe Hergel here says sleeping is natural to Squirmy and he should wish to wake up. Well, a little kidding adds to the gaiety of life, and let me say, ladies and gentlemen, that these marathon dancers we've got here on the dance floor of the Silver Eagle Ballroom in the World's Championship Super Marathon just have the time of their lives with all their jokes and good-natured fun. They all know how to give it, and, what's more important, to take it."

"Goodness!" Catherine exclaimed in shock while Squirmy drew a laugh by bending over, projecting out his broad buttocks and wriggling them.

"Now, folks, the contestants are going to strut their stuff, for you, and I'm going to bring as many of them as we'll have time to hear up to the mike for you. But, first, as a prelude, let me repeat for those radio fans who may have missed the opening of this broadcast. We are here now in the three hundred and sixty-seventh hour of the World's Championship Super Dance Marathon in the ballroom of the Silver Eagle, and we still have eighteen couples and two solos battling for the title and the one-thousand-dollar prize which will be awarded to the winning couple. Some of them had a bad night of it last night, and others have had trouble today, but now all of the contestants are cutting up here as spry as if they had just started. They will have interesting things to tell you, and the first contestant that I will call on is Louise Strang, of team number twenty-one, that game little blond girl from Carmody, Indiana. Louise is the smallest one on the floor here, but folks, is she game! Is she game! Night after night she's proven how game she is. And let me say this to you folks who haven't come out here on the south side of Chicago at the Silver Eagle Ballroom to see the World's Championship Super Dance Marathon Dance, let me tell you, it's worth the price of admission alone just to see little Louise Strang. Here she is now right beside me, as fresh and as pretty as a daisy, one of the favorites out here, and her partner Joe Joslyn agrees with me when I say that she's as game a girl as ever stepped out onto any dance marathon floor. Louise Strang."

"She looks horrible," Catherine said as a blond girl in a lacy black dress shyly stepped forward. She was brown and puffed, with her eyes sunken and circled with fatigue, and her face was hideously caked with powder. Loud cheering and a rat-tat-tat of hand-clapping greeted her.

"Hello, folks," she began, sleepy-voiced, "I'm awfully glad to be able to say hello to you tonight, and I wanna say hello to all my friends and admirers of Radioland. Now I'm going to sing my favorite song for you."

She smiled self-consciously into the microphone and cleared her throat. Her tired mouth opened into an O shape, and tunelessly and without energy she dragged out monotonous sing-songed syllables.

In Old Wyoming . . .

"She may be a marvel or something but she can't sing," Studs whispered to Catherine.

"She sings worse than you do," Catherine whispered back, squeezing his hand, smiling intimately.

"That's no compliment."

In Old Wyoming . . .

When Louise concluded, a shower of change spilled onto the floor and assisted by other contestants, she quickly picked up the money. A half dollar bounced, rolled into a corner. Squirmy made a nose dive for it and skidded on his stomach amid laughter. He cake-walked away from Louise Strang, who pursued him, ogling and giggling, with an outstretched hand. The spectators laughed.

"Now I'll call on another favorite, the inimitable Squirmy Stevens of team number four who scarcely needs an introduction. Squirmy."

Applause again broke, and Squirmy, handing Louise Strang the silver piece he had retrieved, cake-walked to the microphone.

"Hello, everybody, I want to say that I thank you one and all for your interest in me and in our World's Championship Super Dance Marathon out here at the Silver Eagle Ballroom and I'd like to say that I'd like to invite you, one and all, to come out here any time and see us do our stuff. And, folks, I wanna say this. A dance marathon is a fight, and the winner in a high-class field like the one we got here in our World's Championship battle has got to be a fighter, and stick to it, and that's what we're all out here trying to do. Well, everybody, I thank you one and all. So long, Squirmy Stevens signing off."

He cake-walked aside, a wide grin on his face. Money was thrown to him, and he made side-comedy grabbing it.

"You've just heard the inimitable Squirmy Stevens tell you what it takes to win a marathon dance like the World's Championship Super Dance Marathon which we are staging here in the ballroom of the Silver Eagle. Now, there's been a lot of letters asking for Georgia Ginger, the attractive and spirited little lady from the famous peach state, so I'm presenting to you, Miss Ginger, the Georgia Flash as she is known here among us. Come on, everybody, give this little girl a hand."

Loud clapping accompanied a bobbed, sandy-haired, plump girl in dirty, greenish beach pajamas, as she stepped forward, her coy, baby face a smothered picture of sleepiness.

"Hello, folks, I want to thank you all for wanting me to say hello to you all, and I want to say that we all here appreciate what you all think of us and the interest you all take in us, and, folks, I want to thank you all," she drawled, rubbing her eyes as she stepped aside.

"You've just had a word from that spunky little girl, Miss Ginger, the Georgia Peach, who expressed a feeling that all of us connected with this World Championship Super Dance Marathon at the Silver Eagle Ballroom have. We all feel the same way toward the public for its interest. You know, it means a lot to these people here to know you're interested in them and anxious to know how they're coming along.

Because they're out here twenty-four hours a day, battling for the coveted prize and honor. They're here every day, rain or shine, the weather doesn't mean much to them. Yes, sir, it means a lot to them when doggedly and persistently they fight sleep, it means a lot to them to know that you of the public are with them. Next, I'm going to present another favorite, Harold Morgan, one of our solos. Harold was coupled with Lilly Lewis, of team thirteen, and he thinks that his number is a jinx. Because a few days ago, after a game, game fight, his partner, Miss Lilly Lewis, was forced to retire. Well, Harold still has his heart set on the coveted honors, and his game solo fight here has been making dance marathon history. Harold Morgan."

"Hello, folks," Harold Morgan, tall, lanky and bucolic, began in a twangy voice, "I want to thank you all for the interest you have taken in my fight against odds in this here contest. Well, sirs, now my partner she put up a hard fight, a great fight, but, well, sirs, she got her feet blistered on the soles. She walked on those blistered soles of hers when nobody would have thought that she could have walked on such blistered feet. My partner, Lilly Lewis, she put up a ha-ard fight. So Lilly had to give up and here I am, and of course I don't wish bad luck to any of the boys here. They're one and all a fine fighting bunch of boys, and I don't wish them bad luck, but I am just wishing that somebody drops out and gives me a girl for a partner, because you can't win this here World's Championship Super Dance Marathon if you're a solo. And if any of the folks back home in Coonville, Missouri, are listening in, I want to say to them to tell everybody that Harold Morgan is agonna stick right in here until hades freezes over to bring home the bacon to Coonville, and also I want to say hello to Thad Shelden, and Ruth Allen, and to my ma and pa and tell them Harold is fine. Well, sirs, I thank you one and all for your kind interest and attention."

"Say, I'll bet he grows hay in his nose," Studs said to Catherine while there was laughter and applause.

"If any of the folks of Coonville, Missouri, are listening in, let me tell you Harold is one boy that Coonville can be mighty proud of. I've watched him sticking it out here solo, and I tell you, Harold is one boy who shows all the earmarks of making good here in the city. He's showing the real spirit of the hardy old pioneers who made America what it is today."

"That's putting it on thick," Studs whispered.

"Since the time for this broastcast is getting short, we'll

only have time to put one more of our contestants on the mike, and I'll now call on Katy Jones of team number two. Katy is another girl who has thrilled marathon fans out here at the World Championship Super Dance Marathon now in progress at the Silver Eagle Ballroom. You know, a week ago it looked like we were going to lose our Katy. She had already taken some bad tumbles, and then one night an abscessed tooth began to trouble her. If most of us had as painful a toothache as Katy's, we would have howled all night in bed. But not Katy. Holding ice packs to her swollen face, she stuck it out through the dog hours of the night, and took the pain philosophically. I remember how she said to me, 'The tooth makes it easier for me to stay awake.' And the next morning she refused to leave the floor, even to have it pulled, and then she marched gamely forward. Was that a thrill! Seeing this brave little girl join the marathon dancers here a few moments after that painful extraction of that abscessed tooth. Was it a thrill. . . . Now, here's Katy Jones, and she'll sing one of her favorite songs."

Katy Jones, built to barrel-like proportions, stepped forward in a short brown dress and sweater, her legs stockingless, her ripe-sized breasts bobbling. Her thick black bobbed hair was uncombed, and her face, white with powder, almost resembled a clown's mask. She sang *Rose of Picardy,* her voice whiny and monotonous in its even accenting.

"Now, folks, I am closing our regular evening broadcast for the World's Championship Super Dance Marathon at the Silver Eagle Ballroom which is now in its three hundred and sixty-seventh hour with eighteen couples and two solos still in the running. And let me say, in farewell, to all you radio ears, that the Silver Eagle Ballroom is one place these days that is always open, always interesting, always exciting, with thrills and humor and pathos galore. Make it a place to meet your friends and have your parties, the place to come when you want to see something new and exciting in the way of sport and entertainment. This dance marathon of ours and the contestants are the talk of the town, and if you haven't yet seen Squirmy Stevens, Takiss Filios, the Greek boy who sings *Yes, We Have No Bananas* in his native tongue, Harold Morgan, Katy Jones, Georgia Ginger, and all the other thirty-eight headliners competing in the World's Championship Super Dance Marathon at the Silver Eagle Ballroom, you've got something, and I mean *something,* in store for you. Thank you, and good evening."

IV

"Folks, we now have one final surprise for you by way of entertainment before I call it a night," the announcer addressed the spectators through the microphone. "Some of the boys have been practicing here on a little playlet called *The Midnight Ride of Paul Revere*, so please give them your kind attention. And oh, yes, the author of this skit is Squirmy Stevens."

Applauded, Squirmy Stevens bowed, grinned clownishly, and stepped to the microphone.

"I suppose you bozos didn't know that I wrote plays. Well, I does."

Studs looked on curiously while Squirmy stationed Katy Jones at a corner in the arena. Facing the same direction as Studs, he scratched and shook his head, studying the unselected girls on the floor. Katy Jones joined them and he drew a laugh returning her to the spot he had placed her.

"Oh," he loudly exclaimed, pointing to a tall brunette who wore a green sweater.

He led her by the arm toward a corner of the floor below and to the right of Studs. Her partner suddenly grabbed the girl's free wrist.

"Le' go," he called at Squirmy. Squirmy held to the other hand and both pulled, the girl's head and shoulders bobbing first in one way, then in the other.

"Seems like Ted Delancy of team twenty-two doesn't trust Doris Davis with Squirmy. I don't blame you, either, Ted," the announcer said through the microphone, the crowd licking it all in.

"Look, Squirmy," someone in the box-seat section called as Ted Delancy led Doris Davis away.

"I'll settle with you later," Squirmy shouted at the announcer. "Come on, baby," he coaxed, grabbing Doris Davis' left wrist.

"Get another girl," Ted Delancy said.

"Come on, baby. Doncha want to be an actress?"

"Yes, if I can be the leading man," Ted Delancy shouted.

"Looks like a case of where the eternal triangle bumps its isosceles angle against the artistic temperament," the announcer said into the microphone, and the amused crowd laughed.

"The announcer is witty, but that guy Squirmy is dumb," Studs said to Catherine.

"He's funny, though. Watch."

"Let go of her," Ted challenged.

"You . . ."

"I ain't afraid of you," Ted Delancy yelled, letting go of Doris Davis and sneering at Squirmy.

"I ain't afraid of your mother-in-law," Squirmy said.

"No?"

"No."

"No!"

"Say, you guys, what's the idea?" the announcer said like a vaudeville stooge, while the crowd roared.

"He's jealous because he's not in my play and Doris is. I didn't put him in because I couldn't think up a part dopey enough."

"I wouldn't act in his play. He wrote it so he could steal my partner."

"Well, I don't care about all that, but listen to me, you mugs, this isn't a prize ring, it's a dance marathon."

"All right, tell him to go dance in a corner with his head in a sack," Squirmy said.

"Well, are we or aren't we going to have this play?" the announcer asked.

"Yes, yes, yes, that's right, clear the floor," Squirmy shouted, excitedly running around in circles, drawing fresh laughs from the crowd.

"But he can't have my partner."

"But she won't be out of your sight," the announcer persuaded.

Ted Delancy sulked aside. Squirmy again stationed the girls about the floor. He stepped to the microphone.

"Ladies, gentlemen and others, this is going to be the performance of a play of which I am the one and only author, and also the hero. You didn't know that I could write a play, did you? Well, I fooled you that time." He waited while the crowd laughed. "This play by Squirmy Stevens is called *The Midnight Ride of Paul Revere*. I am Paul Revere, and these girls are in houses."

He walked to one of the benches along the side of the dance floor and fetched a cap and broom from under it. He put the cap on with the peak backward, and stood holding the broom between his legs in the fashion of a small boy playing that the broom was a horse.

"Giddyap. Clop! Clop! Clop! Giddyap!"

He stamped to Katy Jones.

"Rap, Rap, Rap. This is Paul Revere. The British are coming. Is your husband home?"

"Yes, he is."

"Well, tell him to shake his tomato out of bed and get out and fight the British."

The audience laughed.

"I saw this pulled in a vaudeville show once," Studs said to Catherine, while Squirmy repeated this scene. He lit a cigarette, and was beginning to feel stiff. "Shall we blow?"

"Yes, but wait until this is over."

"No, my husband isn't home," Doris Davis answered in response to Squirmy's question.

"Well, hurry up and open the door. I want to get in."

"Funny, even if I did hear it sprung before," Studs said, laughing.

"I don't think it's so funny," Catherine said.

The crowd laughed and applauded, and a shower of coins poured down onto the dance floor.

V

"This looks funny. He's asleep on his feet," Studs laughed.

"Play ball," Harold Morgan bawled from the center of the floor while the other contestants trudged slowly around and around.

Harold wound up to pitch, swaying as his arm circled over his head, half turned his left foot, rising, and performed the motions for an overhand pitch. Losing his balance, he fell on his face, and Studs roared.

"Don't laugh, he might be hurt."

"He ought to be."

"You're cruel."

"No. It's just funny."

Harold arose with a dazed expression on his face and a streak of dirt splotching his right cheek. He shook his head, opened his eyes like a man awakening, grinned sheepishly, joined the line which wound around and around and around the floor with a deadening slowness and a steady dragging of feet.

"Gee, it's late," Catherine said.

"Twelve-twenty," Studs said, yawning.

"The time certainly does pass here, doesn't it?"

He shook his head and looked sidewise at her. She leaned forward, watching, her dimpled chin resting in her left hand. She looked cute, pretty, and he wished he could keep her in that pose, just that way. And she looked no different either, from what she had before she'd been made. He guessed he liked her.

"They make me feel kind of sorry for them, some of them look so tired. And that poor partner of Squirmy Stevens, poor girl, having to hold him up when he's in such a dead sleep."

"Well, that's their racket and they get dough for it. Look at all the dough that was thrown into them. And then after that little play, they came through the stands here selling their pictures. It's tough, but they're getting something."

"You're heartless. I bet you would feel a lot different if you were going through what they are down there."

"I know that."

"But I wouldn't let you, Bill, not if it was for a ten-thousand-dollar prize. The things they go through! Look at that poor Greek boy falling all over that girl."

"It's a dumb stunt in one way, because they got to go so much, but they must be making a lot of dough. Still, your health is worth more to you than all the dough in the world."

"You bet it is."

"And say, they get a crowd. People are still coming in."

"Shall we leave, Bill?"

"All right."

"The air gets so bad and there's so much cigarette smoke. I bet this dance does no good for their lungs."

"Me, too."

The contestants silently circled the floor, marched around and around almost in slow motion.

"Shall we just wait until the next rest period and see if anything else happens?"

"All right," Studs said.

"Katy Jones is a brave girl. And that partner of hers, Honks Oliver, he's the deadest old thing. He's always asleep, falling all over her. And Katy, she's such a brave girl."

"Yes, look at her. She's having a time with him, isn't she?" Studs watched Katy Jones shift the strain her partner placed on her, his arms flung around her, his head lodged against her stomach, her large breasts wobbling. She shook his head and talked to him.

"If I was Katy, I'd give him a good kick in his ask-me-no-questions," the woman below them said.

"Say, the Romans were more humane. They fed their people to the lions and didn't leave them suffer," a fellow above them said.

"Yes, it makes me ill to look at them," a girl answered the fellow.

"They look worse than a chain gang walking around the floor," the fellow said.

Studs saw Katy hold her partner under the arms, again speaking. She locked his hands in back of her neck and dragged him, lightly slapping his face.

"That Jones dame is a tough gal. She's always fighting with Honks Oliver," a fellow to Studs' right said.

"He's an old no-good, always sleeping, and the poor girl has to carry him around," the woman below said, flashing an angry glance at the fellow.

"My, some of the people who come here take it awfully seriously," Catherine said very low, and Studs smiled, watching Katy Jones.

"Ouch," Honks Oliver yelled as Katy suddenly bit his ear.

"Good for you! Bite him again, Katy!" the woman below them shouted, standing up and waving her purse.

"Looks like a nice row. I'm glad we stayed," Studs said, while all over the hall people were shouting, laughing, talking with rising excitement.

"Well, I ain't a bed or a pillow," Katy said loudly while the referee and the contestants clustered around her and Honks Oliver.

"If I was Oliver, I'd sock that broad in her kisser. Hell, she sleeps on him, too," the fellow beside Studs said.

"Wake up, Katy," a woman cried shrilly from the stands.

The siren sounded. Katy and Oliver walked off the floor, followed by others, and a male attendant assisted Squirmy, whose face was besotted with sleep.

"We'll wait until their rest is over and see what happens."

"All right," Studs yawned.

VI

A cheer broke over the hall when Katy Jones and Honks Oliver smiled at each other and joined the dragging parade.

A half dollar landed at Honks' feet. He picked it up and handed it to Katy, who blew kisses toward the stands. Some dimes and nickels landed. The line wove around and around.

"Shall we go?" Catherine yawned.

"Yes, in a few minutes."

"Squirmy is still asleep after his rest period."

"He's a clown," Studs said.

"Yes, he's vulgar," Catherine said.

A bell sounded and the contestants danced to radio jazz. Ted Delancy and Doris Davis performed a tango in the center of the floor. At the end of three minutes, the marching line re-formed and Ted and Doris picked up the money thrown to them. A stout man arose in a box and waved to Doris. She walked over to him and he handed her a dollar. Katy Jones and Honks Oliver passed him, and he handed Katy a bill. Many cheered.

"Well, I guess we better blow," Studs said.

"Yes, we'll just wait a few more minutes and see if anything happens."

They yawned.

"That fellow who just passed that dough out to Katy Jones, he's been here for six days straight," somebody to Catherine's left said while Studs yawned.

"Ten after one," Studs said.

VII

"We must go now, Bill," Catherine said.

"Yeah, Kid. It's a quarter to three." They wormed to an aisle in the bleachers and walked downward. Studs watched Harold Morgan floundering.

"Poor Harold," Catherine said behind him.

Harold catapulted forward. He straightened up and shook his head. He walked zigzag, lurched, lost his balance, and pitched face forward on a bench.

"Oh," Catherine exclaimed, as the referee rushed to him.

Two male attendants appeared, Harold was lifted to his feet, his nose gushing blood. A woman fainted in the box. Nearly every spectator stood up, and there was a buzzing hum of conversation.

"Let's wait and see if he's seriously hurt. That was awful."

"Yes, he looks badly cut up."

Two ushers led past Studs the woman who had fainted. She was a stout greasy woman, and she was saying:

"That poor boy. Poor Harold. Poor Harold."

Studs shook his head to stay awake, and Catherine leaned against him. The contestants trooped around, and Squirmy Stevens' partner struggled to hold him up.

"Let's sit there," Catherine said, pointing at a vacant space near the bottom of the bleachers.

"Here he comes."

They saw Harold Morgan step back onto the floor, grinning sheepishly, his face clean, and a plaster patch pasted above his left eye. The cheers were deafening, and without realizing what he was doing, Studs found himself cheering. Catherine tugged at his elbow. The cheers continued as he and Catherine walked out, and he wished he was Harold, standing out there and bringing so many people to their feet with roars of admiration. But then, he'd rather be famous some other way.

"It is kind of interesting, though. It gets you interested without you realizing it, once you get to know who they are."

"Yeah. Exciting and funny things happen in it."

"I wonder who'll win."

"Hurry, Al, I want to get in. And I do hope that Harold Morgan has not dropped out," a girl said, passing them on the stairs.

"I didn't like that Katy Jones. She's awful," Catherine said sleepily.

"Uh huh," Studs yawned, leading her to the street car.

CHAPTER FOURTEEN

I

Studs drowsed in his B.V.D.'s while the drawn green window-shade waved a trifle from the hot and inconsequential August wind. Sunlight seeped around the edges of the curtain, and from somewhere outside kids could be heard whooping at play. He smiled wearily. Even if he was all pooped out, he could still look back on the last week and feel satisfied, and now that it was Saturday afternoon he could just take it easy and let himself feel good. But there was no use trying to kid himself. He just wasn't the man that he used to be. Yesterday he'd come home from work with his fanny dragging damn near to the ground. He'd seen Catherine every night in the week, and then in the park on Thursday night twice with her had not been calculated to make him any more peppy and energetic. And now the week was over, and here he was just lying almost half asleep, letting his mind drift.

Yet even with the heat wave he was glad that he'd worked. He'd salted fifteen bucks in the bank. Now, if he could just do that every week, he'd have a little extra money in double quick time.

He heard radio jazz from a nearby flat. Nice, hearing music when he was taking it easy like this. All week now, he had kept getting the feeling that it was old times. Mixing and grinding paints, slapping it on after having washed the walls, calcimining ceilings—it had all been something to do that he knew how to do right. If this job wasn't finished yet, or if only there was another one to do next week. Well, the old man had said he was going down to see Barney McCormack, the politician, and come to a showdown about getting some political contracts. Boy, if the old man got something, wouldn't that be just too sweet and rosy?

He shaded his eyes, spread his legs out wide, and tried to think of life with no worries on any side, nothing but working, himself and Mort, painting, seeing a dirty wall with the paint peeling, and turning it into a clean and nice and freshly painted wall that filled the room with its smell.

It seemed almost as if a rhythm pulsed in his head while he continued to see himself and Mort working. Just to have things like that, like they used to be, with no real griefs or worries.

But he'd been having heart pains all week, and Thursday night with Catherine he'd gotten one that was like a knife ripping through his chest. He had felt like a clown. And Jesus, think how awful to die from heart failure while you were jazzing your girl. He'd been afraid to look her in the eye after, because she might have thought he was weak and not much of a man. But she liked him. She had kissed him, and stroked his head, and talked that silly chatter to him that girls liked. He was beginning to understand more about girls, though. Once a girl was broken in, she wasn't to be stopped. And Catherine was learning fast. Thursday night, he'd almost gotten afraid of her, and she had even bit him. He'd never thought he or any guy could make a decent girl like Catherine get so excited. He smiled slightly, and felt that he could hardly wait until tonight when he'd be seeing her again.

She was nuts about him, he thought with gratifying assurance. But she wanted to get married. Somehow it was not right, either, to go on this way. But how could he get married now? Christ, what a chump he had been, hanging on to his stock. Letting Ike Dugan make a chump out of him, that snaky rat. He could just see himself meeting with him, swinging, pounding that skinny, ratty face of his into jelly. And then he'd just say, that puss of yours that I punched, it's only fluctuations, and you can go and get the brain of Solomon Imbray to fix it up for you and not let it hurt.

He had worked himself into a state of excitement, and he was breathing rapidly and could feel his heart knocking and going like a pump. He tried to relax and calm himself, and to smile about it and tell himself, what the hell, there was no use bawling over spilled milk. It was only that just when things looked like they could go so well for a guy, his luck just turned sour on him.

He listened to slow, sobbing radio music, and the indistinguishable cries of a peddler cut in upon the saccharine flow

of music. He lay still on his back and stared up at the white
ceiling, and a drowse seemed to lilt through his body, and suddenly he was hearing music again, feeling that period had just
been chunked out of his life. He had been lying looking at
the ceiling, and suddenly he heard the radio.

I love you, love, you, chérie . . .

The song made him think of French girls, of some ex-
citable young French dame, with a thin body full of live hot
wires who said oo-la-la, and ziss, and zat, and zose, and zese,
and himself with her. Fun to think of it, but with a real French
chérie he wouldn't maybe know what the hell to say or do.
And Catherine. Maybe he had let himself in for something
when he'd gotten engaged to her. But then, for years he was
going to be getting something regular that he liked, and that,
now, was something elegant, all right, and no matter what
else happened, that, sister, was something he would get. And
if he only had his money back so that he could marry her
right off. But Jesus, though, suppose she got knocked up!
But she couldn't. She couldn't, that was all, and he believed
it was true that a person's luck couldn't be all bad, or all
good, and his bad luck had all come. He couldn't get any more
tough breaks. Goddamn it, there was a law of averages.

He was distracted by a telephone ringing somewhere, and
he wondered what kind of people it was talking, and what
they would have to say to each other. But suppose now
that he still had his two thousand bucks. Suppose he had
even cleaned up on the market a little, two hundred, five
hundred, two thousand, five thousand, fifteen thousand. Getting
married to Catherine, and having fifteen, twenty thousand
bucks, and Red and everybody he knew saying, well, I never
thought that Studs would be so well-heeled. He could just
see himself with twenty-five thousand bucks to his name,
and that only a starter. Bank accounts, checking accounts,
buying anything he wanted to. Thinking of himself like this,
too, it gave him a pleasant, sleepy, lulling feeling. His eyes
grew heavy. A drowsing, dozeful sense of animal comfort
caressed his limbs, his nerves, his muscles, his brain. Studs
Lonigan, the big shot. He fell asleep.

II

Studs entered the parlor, wearing old trousers over his
B.V.D.'s. He rubbed his hand over his drawn and sleepy face,
yawned again, stood indecisive, with his arms, white and
thin, hanging at his sides.

"Hello, Bill. How are you feeling?"

"Pretty good, Dad. I took a nice nap."

"That's good. I always like a little snooze myself on a Saturday afternoon after the week's work. But today I just couldn't come home and take one. I was down to see Barney McCormack today."

"You saw Barney McCormack today, huh?"

"Yes, I saw him."

"What did he have to say?"

"Like everybody else these days, Barney's crying."

"That's funny. I should think Barney would be sitting in clover after the Democratic victory last spring. And that's nothing at all to the Democratic landslide we ought to have in the presidential elections next year if I know anything about it."

"The way Barney was crying, he would have felt almost as good if the Republicans got a few jobs."

"That's funny. How come?"

"Barney did nothing but cry all the time I saw him. He was crying about the Polacks and the Bohunks. He says that they just almost cleaned out the Irish. He kept saying to me, 'Paddy, if you want to get anything down at the Hall, you better put a *sky* on your name before you go down there.' And he made one funny crack. He said that these days, down at the Hall, they only speak English from one to two in the afternoon."

"That's funny."

"Well, Bill, tell you, you know for years all these foreigners have been let into America, and now they've just about damn near taken the country over. Why, from the looks of things, pretty soon a white man won't feel at home here. What with the Jew international bankers holding all the money here, and the Polacks and Bohunks squeezing the Irish out of politics, it's getting to be no place for a white man to live," Lonigan said, sighing as he spoke.

"You didn't line up any contracts then?" Studs asked, and Lonigan answered with slow and emphatic negative words.

"Barney said that these days, before a dead horse can be taken off the streets, you got to see one of the Polacks or Bohunks and get his O. K. They've just closed out the Irish. He told me it was just hopeless to count on any school contracts or anything like that. We're just out of luck. He says he doubts if anything could be done, even if I put a *sky* on my name."

"Gee, Dad, that's tough. I'm sorry to hear it."

"Bill, it's a fright. It's a fright."

"What are you going to do?"

"What can a man do? I can hardly collect a cent. And every guy who owes me money seems to owe it to everybody else and his brother. If I did press some of these bastards, they'd go in bankruptcy, and their creditors would be over them like leeches, and I'd be lucky if I collected a nickel or a dime on the dollar. It wouldn't be worth it. I suppose I might just as well plug along and hope for the best. But it's fierce, fierce."

"Gee, it's tough, all right."

"And I got to tell the Trents to go. I can't let them stay on any longer as long as they can't pay their rent. I just can't. I know it's a bad blow, a disgrace to an honest man to be thrown out of his home into the streets like a pauper, and I hate to do it. But I got to. And I tell you we're lucky we're not following them. That mortgage payment on the building has got to be paid next month, and they won't be stalled off on it. I just about got enough in the bank to cover it, too. I guess I better knock on wood. But if I didn't, well, we'd be on the street ourselves."

Studs nodded.

"The city is busted. Why, Barney was telling me today there's plenty of people working for the city, besides the school teachers, who aren't getting their pay. Bailiffs and clerks and people like that."

"Gee, Red Kelly won't like that."

"No, I suppose Red isn't getting his pay, either."

"I just know how he'll like it," Studs said.

"Well, that's what we get for letting the Jew international bankers get control of our country. You know what we need? We need a man like Mussolini here in America. A strong man to take things out of the hands of the Jew international bankers and the gangsters. If we had a man like Mussolini over here for two months, he'd straighten out a lot of people and put them where they belong, behind the bars or against a wall."

"Maybe there's a lot to what you say."

"No maybe about it. What does Father Moylan say? He tells what the bankers are doing. Loaning American money to Europe. If they had kept American money in America where it belongs, there wouldn't be any depression."

"Say, there's something in that."

"Then Hoover comes along and what does he do? This moratorium business. Telling Europe, no, they don't have to pay us. If Europe paid us and we kept undesirable aliens out of our country, so that there could be jobs and money for Americans, we wouldn't be having these hard times," Lonigan proclaimed with growing indignation, and Studs nodded agreement. "America was a fine country. And all these foreigners came here to take jobs away from Americans who have a right to them. And now we got too many men for the jobs we got. Well, I know what we ought to do. Put all the foreigners we got taking jobs away from Americans, pack them in boats, and say to them, 'Now, see here, America belongs to Americans. You go back where you belong.' And if we did that, we wouldn't have these Reds here agitating to overthrow the government. Say, you know what those dirty Reds are doing now? They're exciting the niggers down in the Black Belt, telling them they're as good as white men and they can have white women. I tell you, Bill, some day the American people have got to wake up and take things into their own hands."

"It's only right. America is America, and it should be for Americans," Studs said.

"You're damn right it should be. And you know who's going to wake Americans up? It's men like Father Moylan who speaks on the radio every Sunday. He tells 'em, and he talks straight. Men like him have got to wake the country up."

"And he's a Catholic, too," Studs said proudly.

"He's one of the finest and smartest men in America, and he tells the people what's what. He lays into the bankers, too, and by God, they've got it coming to them."

"I got to listen to him more often."

"Yes, Bill, you should. He's a brainy man and you learn what's going on from him," Lonigan said, and he chuckled. "Say, the way he gives hell to Hoover, it's a treat."

"If it wasn't for bigots, Al Smith would have been elected," Studs said regretfully. "I know. They played Al dirt," yawning and arising. "I guess I better be getting cleaned up and shaved."

Lonigan picked up his newspaper and resumed reading.

III

Catherine kissed him lackadaisically. There were no sounds around them, only the pleasing darkness, and they sat locked in each other's arms, their breathing tired, their clothing mussed and askew. Catherine looked away from him. He glanced upward at the overhanging tent of tall and leafy trees, idly watching stray rays of sudden moonlight that silvered the top layers of leaves. Away off somewhere, like a strange sound, he heard the noise of an automobile.

Freeing himself from her arms, he sat erect, and thought, Jesus, if somebody should come by now. Embarrassed and ashamed, he stood up with his back to her, buttoned himself, pressed down his hair, fingered his tie. Shyly, she turned, pulled down and smoothed her wrinkled dress, hooked up her stockings, pushed back her disarranged hair.

He slouched down beside her on the bench and looked at the black wall of bushes opposite, a narrow and uneven stream of moonlight unexpectedly flowing through them while a slight wind scratched the leaves. He shifted his glance, and partially closed his eyes to get a different sight of the bushes. He made an effort of lighting a cigarette.

Catherine sniffled.

"Bill," she sobbed.

Studs turned toward her, frightened, and took her hand.

"Bill, dear, I can't stand this. I can't go on sneaking the way we got to, as if this was something awful between us, afraid of being caught or seen by somebody, having to be ashamed of doing this when we love each other, and have to be sneaking about it in the park and in my hallway. And even that awful time in the taxicab. I can't stand even the idea of it, and if we were caught by someone, some stranger, I'm afraid I'd even kill myself."

"Kid . . ." he said, looking down at her while she sobbed with her head against his shoulder. He had no other words to utter. Puzzled, he shook his head slowly from side to side.

"Bill, we got to get married!"

"When?"

"Right away."

"But won't it seem a little queer to everybody? And it will take a little time for us to get ready, won't it? We'll have to have the banns published and fix things up."

"Tomorrow morning we can go to mass together, and right after mass we'll go to see Father Geoghan, and make arrangements then."

"Well . . . but . . ."

"Bill, darling, I can't stand this sneaking and skulking. And it's not right. It's a sin this way, and it can't be really wrong and sinful, because I love you. I love you so much!"

He was embarrassed and gratified by the way she flung her arms around him and kissed him, and still, he didn't know what to say.

"Kid," he said hoarsely.

"You love me?"

"Yes," he said, the reply coming as if it had been propelled out of his mouth by force.

"You mean it?"

He looked at her, nodded, leaned over, kissed her, held and patted her hand. He looked moodily away.

"Because I've been afraid to tell you, and now I've got to," she said.

He turned back to her, his face pallid in the darkness and moonlight, its expression trapped in worry and surprise. He glanced away again, then back at her, just as her round face was cross-cut by an exposure of moonlight.

"Something has happened to me," she said, looking aside.

"What?" he snapped out quickly in a choking voice, while at the same time, as if in a split part of himself, he was beginning to see his predicament as a drama filled with seriousness and importance.

"You know, Bill," she said, seeming to him like a soft, frightened, utterly helpless thing in his arms, "you know, I'm afraid that I'm going to have a baby."

Her head lowered, as in shame and modesty. She took and held the fingers in his right hand.

Jesus Christ! he thought to himself, even though he had guessed what she had to say from the way she'd led up to it.

"Can't we do something about it?" he asked.

"What?"

"See a doctor. Or maybe I can get some medicine to take care of it."

Looking up at him, she dabbed her eyes quickly, and he could see that she was fighting not to cry.

"Bill, darling, that's awful. We can't do that."

"But why?" he asked, his voice shaky, puzzled.

He tried to substitute a persuasive glance for the convincing words which he could not bring forth. He drew her gently against his shoulder, feeling the quivering of her warm and nervous body. Her fear made him feel strong and brave, and he began to feel a sense of power as if it were a pulse within him. He was the strong one, the one to be depended upon in a time of trouble, and it was up to him to be the captain steering a course out of it.

"Bill, it would be awful to do such a thing. I know! If you say that, you make me feel that you don't really care for me. You know you got what you wanted, everything I had to give you, and now you seem to be acting as if you only wanted to get out of trouble the easiest way."

"Kid, please," he said, still at a loss for words, wishing he could carry things off and lie better.

And he was just so goddamn mixed up and jumbled himself. He didn't want such a thing to happen. She'd be disgraced and ruined, and everybody would know that they had had to get married. And Christ, right off the reel they would have the kid. What would he do about a kid of his own? Studs

Lonigan, a father already! He didn't want to do that, and he
didn't know what to do about it. And how could they afford
it? There he would be in the future with cords about him, hand
and foot.

Join the Navy now, brother, he told himself sardonically.

He remembered how he used to hear fellows around the
poolroom kidding about it, and how he'd razzed fellows like
Wils Gillen when they were worried about girls they'd knocked
up. Goddamn it, it wasn't anything to laugh over, Jesus Christ,
it wasn't.

And there she was beside him, sniffling, and he had to
say or do something about it. He heard a distant automobile,
and it made him think of how, right now, there were people
driving around, free from having all the troubles and worries
he had. He just felt helpless, hopeless, with a sword swinging
right above his neck.

"Bill, tell me, do you love me?" she asked with a ring of
insistence and desperation in her voice, and he grew rigid
from the sudden thought that maybe in this mood she might
just go and jump in the lake or do something as bad.

"You know it, Kid," he said, still choked up.

"Well, you take a poor way of showing it. You don't even
hold me tight and kiss me when I tell you these things."

He kissed her, aware of warm tears trickling down her
cheeks, and they gripped each other in a mood of desperation.
Released, they sat side by side, surrounded by trees, alone
in a quiet where they could clearly hear each other's breathing.

"Bill, we got to do something. I'm afraid to go to a doctor
or take medicine," Catherine said after a period of silence.

"It won't hurt you."

"But I can't, I can't do such a thing."

"Well, it'll mean plenty of trouble for us."

"But if you love me."

"Yes, but, Kid, can't you see, right off the bat you'll be
tied down with a baby?"

"I don't care for myself. But maybe it's you. You're afraid
and you don't want to be tied down."

He knew that she craved some positive word from him,
and all he could do was pat her hand gently and hope that
his gesture would give her confidence and substitute for all
the words he could not speak.

"Both of us have money saved up," she said.

"I never told you, you know," he said awkwardly.

"What?" she said with fresh anxiety.

"Well, after we became engaged, I felt that we ought to
be able to start out with more money than it looked like we
were gonna have. So I bought some shares in a new issue of

Imbray Stock. I paid twenty-five a shot for it, and it's down to six dollars a share now, so my two thousand dollars is now worth, let's see . . . oh, about two hundred and forty dollars. It's hardly worth selling it, so the money's all tied up until we get better times and the stock market goes up."

Christ, now he was only beginning to fully realize what a chump he'd been. Oh, how sweet it would be to take Ike Dugan out and pound him full of lumps!

"But Bill!" she exclaimed, stunned with surprise.

"I thought it would turn out all right," he said dejectedly.

"But Bill, how could you do that and never say a word to me?" she said, breaking freely into tears.

He halted his impulse to say that it was his money, wasn't it, and he felt as helpless as she, sobbing beside him.

"And now we have no money," she said forlornly.

"I thought that things would get better and it would be a good investment. I took a chance," he said, shrugging his shoulders in an ineffectual gesture.

"But Bill, how could you?" she asked, and he saw that she was more frightened than angry.

"There's still a chance. Imbray, you know, is a smart man. And the stock is based on things that everybody needs, and they should be good investments in the long run. A man like Imbray can't fail when he's got stock backed by almost all the public utilities of the Middle West. I still think that I'm going to get more money out of my investments than I put into them."

"That doesn't matter, Bill darling. We're going to get along, all right. I know it. I can just feel it."

"Well, what do you want to do?" he asked nervously.

"Honey, you and me, we've just got to get married. And I'm not afraid of having a baby of yours, and I don't care what people say."

"Well, you know we'll be tied down."

"I don't care," she said, snapping her head, a note of defiance coming into her voice.

"It's going to be tough sledding. You know, I'm not working a lot with my dad, because there's nothing much doing."

"I don't care! I don't care! I don't care!" she said rapidly, clasping his hand tightly, digging her nails into his palm.

She slumped against him, sobbed, and in persisting confusion and helplessness he put his arm around her shoulders.

"Brace up, Kid!" he said, lacking conviction and looking vacantly at the bushes.

She ceased crying, and he seemed to drift into vague dreaming, forgetting everything, not wanting to move, liking the feel and pressure of her against him. Suddenly she sat up,

and to him her action was like being curtly awakened from
sleep.

"The dew is falling, and I don't like you sitting in the damp-
ness. You might catch cold, and summer colds are worse than
winter ones."

"I'm all right."

In the dark, she tried to arrange her hair. They walked
slowly, Studs hearing the crunch of their shoes on the gravel.
He remembered how he had so often seen fellows and girls
walking in Washington Park on nights like this, just as they
two were now. He didn't envy such guys now like he used to.
Walking just as he and Catherine were doing, as if they were
happy with each other, and had no worries in the world, nothing
to fear, happy in love with each other, as if there was nothing
else that counted. A sardonic smile came on his face, and over
and over again the line from a popular song hummed through
his mind.

Walkin' my baby back home . . .

Others, too, seeing him and Catherine, they'd think the same
thing. He shook his head ironically, and told himself, yes,
he was walking his baby back home. And it just showed, he
thought, that appearances were deceiving. Walking his baby
back home with everything seeming so tranquil, when things
were hemming him in, hemming both of them in more and
more.

But he didn't want to think anymore tonight of all these
goddamn griefs. And he didn't want there to be a tomorrow
when he would wake up and realize what he had to do. Tell
his family about it, and go to see the priest, face him when
the priest might get sore and bawl him out and all that stuff.
Start figuring out and preparing and arranging for the marriage.
And then, Christ, her being knocked up! If he'd only waited!
A few minutes each time, then feeling tired, feeling sometimes
disgusted and wanting no more of it, or else wanting it the
next time and hoping there would be more in it than there
was the time before, and now for that they were in all this
deep water. Or if he hadn't been such a chump and had taken
precautions every time. But it was always that way. Afterward,
when it was too late, you saw what you should have done.

And now all that he wanted was to be home and in bed
asleep, so that none of these things would be on his mind,
making him feel so tight and feel that any minute something
might happen. Even if he was going to sleep for only seven
or eight hours, and then wake up again to all these same worries, he wanted sleep. Eight hours of sound sleep seemed like
a century.

Catherine paused under a lamp-post and opened her purse. Studying her tear-streaked face in the purse mirror, she powdered, patted her hair, and turned a weary smile upon him.

"Do I look all right?"

Studs replied gutturally without even having heard her question. They emerged from Jackson Park at Sixty-third and Stony Island.

"Let's walk home," he said, too constrained within himself to stand waiting for a street car.

They crossed the street, and in front of the Greek restaurant with the modernistic decorations, a group of fellows stood, cluttering the sidewalk. Studs glanced to see if he knew any of them. Two drunks detached themselves and stood blocking the sidewalk. Studs' fists clenched automatically, and he watched them cautiously, hate suddenly overpowering him.

"But, George, if we call her up and she's not there, someone else answers the phone. So what? We lost a nickel."

"Suppose we telephone Marie instead. So what. We spend a nickel," the second drunken fellow seriously said, while Studs, tense and wary, led Catherine around them.

"They're having a good time," Catherine said with a thin smile.

"Yeah, a problem in high finance," Studs said, pleased because she laughed at his crack.

They used to be crowding around the street in the same way in the old days. And then, no cares and responsibilities like now. He guessed, too, that what he really needed was to go out and get himself uproariously drunk. And if he'd only watched his health more in the old days he could do that now. If!

"Honey, please don't let yourself get so worried," Catherine said.

"I'm not worried. I was just thinking."

"You were, too. I could see it on your face."

"No. I was just thinking about those two drunks and their problem in high finance," Studs answered, and Catherine's lips tightened as she looked away.

Studs stared ahead at the lights of Sixty-seventh and Stony Island. They passed a row of drab apartment houses, a line of darkened stores, a vacant lot, and then a brightly lit Upton Oil and Refining Company Greasing Palace, and Studs purposelessly watched an automobile back away from a greasing rack.

A group of young fellows approached, talking loudly, and Studs became nervous, in case they might start some trouble!

"Hell, he doesn't work! He's only the foreman and just walks around the joint. It don't take no brains to be a foreman.

You just got to be able to walk," a dusky fellow in the group shouted as the fellows passed, and Studs heard their loud voices while they moved on.

"Sometimes you hear people say funny things on the street," Catherine said.

"Yeh."

They entered a crowded chain drug store, and sat down at a vacant tile-topped table. Waiting for their chocolate malted milks, Studs looked around, gathering a general sense of noise and well-being, seeing the crowd lined along the soda fountain, the fountain men frantically working to fill orders, the white-aproned waitresses scurrying with trays among the tables where there were many couples and groups, and other customers around the drug counters on the opposite side of the store.

He began wishing that he was like some of the other fellows in the store who were at soda tables with girls, so carefree. Like the fellow in a palm beach suit several tables down who talked to a blond girl and then laughed so loudly. A couple laughing like that couldn't have a problem like he and Catherine had.

"It's crowded here, isn't it?" Catherine said after the malted milks had been set before them.

"Yes. These stores must be making money, depression or no depression," Studs said, thinking that it might have been a much sounder investment to get stock in a chain drug outfit like this one.

"Yes, they do a lot of business at a store like this one," she said, breaking open the small paper package of wafers that came with the malted milk.

"I'd be willing to bet they make money," Studs said, drawing the malted milk through two straws.

He finished it quickly, and while Catherine continued sipping he again stared around at random, and he began to think how all these fellows with their girls, they were guys just like himself. And maybe they had their problems, too. Fellows and girls when they went together always had that one problem. If they really felt about each other, they wanted to go the limit, and then there was the girl holding back because she was afraid, or thought that it was wrong, or if they did jazz, there was that worrying about getting knocked up, or else there was worrying over how they could get alone and not be seen and spoiling it by hurrying up so no one might catch them in the park or a hallway. Jesus Christ, life was one goddamn trial and tribulation, and love made it more of a trial and a tribulation. He wondered how many fellows there were in Chicago at this very minute who were in the same pickle as he was, with girls they'd knocked up. And yet, no matter if there were thousands of them, that didn't help him. Misery loves company, but what the hell good does company do?

"Bill, I want you to promise me now that you're not going to worry," she said, observing the set expression on his face.

"I'm not worrying."

"You are, too. You've furrowed up your face, and I can tell that you are."

He forced a smile as they arose. They proceeded southward along Stony Island, and Studs looked at the many strolling people, asking himself how many of them were better off than he was. He took a covert glance at Catherine. She seemed pretty enough. And she was showing him that she had guts. It was something to have guts.

But he wished, Jesus Christ, he wished for something, something!

IV

In the hallway, she was very troubled and worried, and she looked up at him with eyes of desire and anxiety.

"Darling, we're always going to be together," she said.

He nodded, kissed her.

"And we're not going to worry over this thing, either."

He nodded again, pleased with the sudden thought that this was a fight where he would have to overcome obstacles. But the idea of fighting and overcoming obstacles was one thing, and doing it was another, and tomorrow morning he had to start the doing. He'd realized all along that some day they would just stop being engaged, and marry, but now, with Catherine in his arms kissing him as if each kiss were their last one, he began to realize that he'd been kind of glad to have the marriage in the future. And it wasn't any longer. If it only could be put off a little, but it couldn't. He was in all the way up to his neck.

"We needn't worry, Bill, we're going to get along, aren't we?" Catherine said wistfully, relaxing in his arms and patting his cheek.

He shook his head, agreeing.

"I know that as long as I'm with you I won't have to worry because I can depend on you," she said.

He kissed her. Their eyes met in helplessness, and Studs knew that there was nothing more for either of them to say.

"What time will you be over in the morning?"

"What time do you want me to?"

"Let's go to eleven o'clock mass."

"I'd rather go to a low mass."

"But it would give you more sleep."

"I'd rather go to a low mass," he sulked.

"All right, little boy," she said with a smile. "You'll be over for ten o'clock mass? . . . No, I tell you, you come over and we'll have breakfast together. Come at nine o'clock."

"All right," he said, kissing her again.

He watched her disappear up the stairway within the inner hall doorway. He took the same path home that he always took after leaving her. Walking, he suddenly realized that they would have to start out on her money. He was going to her a pauper without a pot to. . . . Jesus Christ! Getting married on her money, after he had knocked her up, and having wasted his own like an out-and-out chump. And why, oh, Jesus, why did all these things have to come when he was losing his health and all jammed up? Now, as he had never realized it before, he could see just how important money was, and he told himself, yes, sir, your pocketbook is your best friend. Now it meant so many important things, and to think of all the dough he had pooped away since he had started working back in 1919.

He tried to see himself coming through and busting out on top, and it was like eating something that was sour and mouldy. With each step homeward he was shaken with a powerless anger, and it made him feel the imminence of some danger. He was getting afraid, almost, even to walk, because that danger might pop out at him from the next doorway and just put the clamps on Studs Lonigan with a pair of steel hand-cuffs.

He told himself to can it all, and trust to luck. Luck would have to be on his side. With luck, he'd win through. Trying to kid himself again. He yawned. He only wanted to sleep. To get home and fall into bed and forget it. But it wasn't like a jag, for that could be slept off. In the morning he was going to wake up, and know that it would be back again.

CHAPTER FIFTEEN

I

"Son, I don't see why you can't wait," Mrs. Lonigan said.

"Yes, Bill, isn't it kind of fast and sudden, you know, getting married on the spur of the moment? Of course, now, don't think that I don't like Catherine or don't want you to marry her. Because we aren't at all talking on that point. All we are trying to say is that maybe you better not rush into it and act on such a quick decision," the father said, and Studs commenced to grow nervous and very unsure of himself because he could see, sitting in the parlor and facing his parents, that they were both giving him fishy-eyed looks.

"Well, there's no particular reason why we shouldn't," he said weakly, sparring for time until he could think up better answers.

"Bill, now why don't you just think it over? Coming so sudden, it will look kind of . . . kind of . . . funny. And it gives us such little time to get ready," Lonigan said.

"We've talked it over and made up our minds," Stud said, bored, not wanting to argue it when all such talk anyway was just a waste of time.

"And how will Catherine's mother like this, with you taking her only daughter away from her on such short notice, and not giving her any time to make the right preparations for the wedding? It's not fair to Mrs. Banahan," Mrs. Lonigan said, still turning suspicious eyes on him.

He couldn't understand why they kept on hemming and hawing about it. But he was glad for one consolation anyway. There wouldn't be so damn much trouble about getting things ready for the wedding. Immediately he thought with regret that poor Catherine, she would miss all that fussing. She had, he was sure, like all girls dreamed of the time she would be married as some great special occasion. And now all these dreams of hers for a very romantic wedding were dampened plenty.

"Bill, I want you to promise me something," the father said in a man-to-man manner.

"Yes," Studs said, hoping to get this over because he wanted to meet Catherine and go swimming, and thinking also that when it came to anything important about himself, it was just about impossible to make them understand his side of the case, and it had been the same always, so far back as he could remember.

"Bill, I want you to promise me this. To think it over, and see if it isn't possible to wait at least a few months until the fall, when things will be better, and you'll then probably have more money and prospects to start on. Maybe by fall we'll turn the corner of this depression and have a real business pickup. And then I'll be able to have you working for me every day, and if money loosens up I'll be able to give you a tidy little sum as a wedding present. In days like these, a young fellow is foolish to get married when he's not sure of being able to work the next day."

"Two mouths always cost more to be fed than one," Mrs. Lonigan said.

"I've thought it over," Studs said, realizing there was nothing much to say to them about it, unless he told the truth, and he couldn't do that.

Both parents stared wistfully at him. The mother dabbed at her eyes, almost in open tears. She was his mother, and he could see why she should cry like this, and it made him feel kind of rotten. He thought, though, that she'd gotten married herself, hadn't she, and she and the old man had pitched in to try their luck without any bank to start on.

"I got to be going," he said, arising, wanting to get out of the house quickly.

"Now, Bill, think it over, you and Catherine, and if you do, I know you'll see where your old man is just telling you what's right and sensible."

Nodding affirmatively, Studs left the parlor. In his room, he quickly donned his swimming suit, and pulled an old shirt and pair of trousers on over it. He left the house, dashing so rapidly down the stairway that he emerged on the street breathless and tired, and he trudged slowly to Seventy-first and Jeffrey. He saw Catherine standing in front of the drug store, wearing an old blue skirt and brown pullover sweater, with a blue band around her head.

"How are you?" she asked, swinging a rubber swimming cap on her wrist and smiling wistfully, sadly, he felt.

"O. K. How about you, Kid?" he responded in an attempt at gruff cheerfulness.

"All right, darling," she said, taking his arm.

Catherine was silent as she walked beside him, her arm inserted in the crook of Studs' elbow. She seemed to him to have changed almost over night, and he realized that of late she didn't chatter on the way she used to. He wished she would.

"What did your folks say to you?" she asked.

"They want me to wait longer. They don't understand things, though. Of course, I didn't tell them the way things really stand. I only said we decided that since we were going to get married, we have figured it out that we might as well do it right away, because we want to."

"My parents are the same. They don't understand things, either. And what is the use of telling them or trying to make them understand? They would only get angry and fly off the handle, and it would make everything worse. But my mother is so suspicious. She didn't say a word to me, but I could tell that suspicion was just eating her up from the way she looked at me."

Studs checked himself before letting out the words that his mother was also suspicious. It would make Catherine nervous when she and the old lady got together.

"You know, Bill, if my father and mother were only as understanding as Father Geoghan was this morning. Wasn't he kind and tolerant?"

"Yes. He was very decent."

"I was so scared, too, having to go to him the way we did. And he was so nice. He didn't bawl us out or anything. He's the same way in confession. He's showed such an open-minded attitude I could have kissed him."

"Don't let me catch you!" Studs smiled.

"Why, Bill! Oh, go on with your teasing. But he was so understanding."

"What surprised me was that he kept saying not to marry if we didn't really want to."

"Yes, he's so understanding on things like that. You know this same thing must happen to lots of others, and they get married so there's no scandal, and they don't really love each other. I wouldn't want that. I would rather have our baby and face the world alone than marry if you didn't want to and didn't love me."

"Yes. You know that's where the Church is wise. It's in men like Father Geoghan who inherit all the Church's two thousand years of experience and wisdom."

"But Bill, we do love each other, don't we? And we want to marry?"

"Of course, Kid."

"I felt so much better after seeing Father Geoghan, too. He made me just feel different about it. That's what made him seem so much more understanding than Mother and Dad. They'd never understand, and all I could do was say we're going to get married, the same as you did."

"Well, my old man and old lady weren't any more hot on the idea than yours."

"I'll bet they don't like me."

"That's not it at all, Kid."

"I think it is maybe."

"Not at all. No! It was just like your folks felt, you know, surprised at the suddenness of it."

She seemed to him to lapse into a thoughtful mood. Without attracting her attention, he caught the reflective look on her face, blue. Her mood and his own both seemed to press down the more forcibly because of the sunny appearance of the Sunday street, the people dressed up, strolling along, the pretty girls, the couples laughing, going some place, people who didn't have the troubles on their minds that he had.

"Bill!" she exclaimed suddenly in a questioning tone of voice.

"What?" he asked in apparent apprehension.

"We don't care what anybody else thinks, do we?"

"Of course not, Kid," he said, trying to be casual.

"And today is a lovely day, and it's going to be ours, too, isn't it? No matter what we got ahead of us, we're not going to worry today, are we?"

He agreed with her by a cryptic nod of the head, and thought, if she would only forget to worry, and would go along, chattering away, it would make him feel lighter. It would be like a kind of sleep. It made him realize how, of late, she had seemed to slide away from all the things she used to do, from her girl friends, and bridge club, and everything like that. It made him feel a little lousy about it all, because look what she was getting for all this sacrifice!

"Maybe it would be a good idea for you to go to the next meeting of your bridge club."

"You're not trying to pawn me off, are you?" she asked, surprised.

"Why, no, no, Kid. I was only wondering if it might not be a nice change for you from a guy like me, and you know, help you to keep your mind off worrying."

"You silly boy! You men! You're not just a guy, and I'm not worrying, and I never will because I know you love me, darling."

"I don't want you to be worrying, you know."

"You're such a sweet boy. Why should I be worrying when you're going to be all mine, my husband in just three short weeks? What could I be getting to make me happier?"

"Well, now . . ." he halted because he didn't know what he really wanted to say.

"I hope the water isn't cold," she said.

"It won't be," he said, just to make the conversation go on.

"I won't be able to go swimming soon."

Her remark brought it all back to him clearly. Christ, if he could only get her to take some medicine that would bring her around. But after what Father Geoghan had said about such things: murder, killing an innocent, unborn soul, fat chance he had of convincing her. Maybe if she ran around the beach and got plenty of exercise, it might happen naturally.

"Come on, let's walk faster," he said.

II

Studs and Catherine descended over a small area of rocky, sandy beach to the shore line, and the lake, blue, with sunlight on it, stretched out and out, like some vast cloth.

"Gee, it's crowded all right today," Studs said.

"Naturally, since it's Sunday."

"But, no, it's crowded even for a Sunday," Studs said weightily, looking around him at the lively, noisy crowd, their bathing suits lending a variegation of color to the scene. His eye caught a slender girl, her body bronzed from sunlight and pinched into an abbreviated one-piece red swimming suit. She stood looking toward the water like a girl in an advertising picture, her head flung back. The glimpse of her caused Studs to see Catherine as small, and plain, and dumpy, and he felt sorry for her. He wanted to look again at the slender bronzed girl, but feared that Catherine might notice him. If she guessed his thoughts and wishes now when he saw other girls, she'd be hurt, and it would be damn lousy to hurt her, considering the circumstances. And yet he had these thoughts, these wishes that girls like the bronzed one were his instead of Catherine. And Catherine, too, she looked better dressed up than in a swimming suit. He glanced sidewise but closely at her. Nothing to notice yet, because she was a little round in the stomach anyway. Her skin was white, and it looked a little rough, and her thighs and legs seemed kind of chunky. Other guys got better-looking girls.

They paused at the pebbly shore line. Studs suddenly felt himself small and puny, and he stood, with the incoming waters curling over his feet, sticking his shoulders back and throwing out his chest. He ran through the waters, dove under in shallow water, and popped up wetted, with drops trickling from his mussed hair.

"Come on in, it won't hurt you," he called while Catherine waded in carefully.

"You let me come in my own way!" she shouted back, proceeding slowly, as if afraid to wet her swimming suit.

All about them the water was jammed with a shouting, splashing, joshing, kicking, swimming, diving, ducking, plopping crowd, and Studs' ears hummed from the noise they made. He turned his back on Catherine, who was up to her waist, dove under, bobbed his head up, swam out for about fifteen yards. He stood up in water that covered his chest, singled out Catherine by her white bathing cap, and watched her swimming breast stroke toward him. He cut back toward her, taking crawl strokes, and circled around her, blowing on the water, spouting it out of his mouth, diving under, coming up, a serious and studied performance which he wanted her to notice by thinking that he was just like a fish in the water. She swam beside him to the diving board, about two hundred

yards out and extending off the breakwater rocks that cut vertically through the water. Both of them puffed as they climbed
onto the jagged rocks.

"Come on and dive with me," he said.

"I'm afraid. I can't dive."

"I'll teach you."

"No, you go ahead, and I'll watch."

He crossed a few feet of jagged stones to the almost spring-
less diving board, and waited while a tall, solidly built, dark-
haired chap went off. He followed, hitting the water with
a big splash, and swam around randomly, liking it, taking
easy strokes. His arms began to seem leaden, and his back
started to ache. He labored toward the diving board, climbed
over the sodden piles and stones with lurching movements,
and, puffing as his hair dripped, stood over Catherine. A
brief spasm-like pain cut his heart, and passed too quickly
to cause him worry.

"You're a good diver," Catherine said as he sank beside
her.

"That one wasn't so good. I hit the water too heavy. I
used to be pretty good but I'm out of practice," he said, smiling modestly, breathing with effort.

His eyes roved the beach, colorful with bathing suits, alive
with a mass of people who stood, walked, sat, their shouts
and talks rising into a study, drumming roar. He watched two
fellows tossing a ball and he thought he'd like to join them,
and then he saw a girl falling off a fellow's back in a game
of leap frog. He felt a part of this scene, of many people all
having a good time. Close to shore, a group of fellows were
ducking a girl who screamed and giggled loudly. Nudging
Catherine, he pointed, smiling.

"They certainly have their nerve," she said.

"It's all in fun and she seems to like it."

"You men, you think that a girl likes anything you do
to her, just because it's you doing it. You're just babies when
it comes to understanding girls. And let me tell you further,
that being ducked is not my idea of fun."

"Look out or I might be ducking you."

"William Lonigan, don't you dare," she said in mock-
challenge.

"Is that a threat?" he asked, liking it as she tousled his
hair.

He watched a girl, her skin tanned almost the color of
chocolate, posing her athletic figure on the diving board.

"Mama, what a broad!" he heard a fellow nearby on the
rocks exclaim just after she had dived neatly.

Them's my sentiments, he told himself, trying to single

her out in the water. He feared, though, that Catherine might have caught him watching her.

"Nice here. I'm glad I came."

"So am I, darling," Catherine said.

He couldn't single her out in the water.

"I'll bet you can't make the grade with her, Joe," a fellow said.

"Well, if I do, won't I laugh at you. Here goes."

Studs watched the fellow, a curly-haired, hairy-bodied chap, dive quickly. He thought of how he couldn't do the same thing, and there was nothing that could drive home to him more forcibly the fact that Studs Lonigan was hooked.

"Let's go back and sit in the sand," he said, getting nervous.

He watched Catherine slip off the rocks into the water, and swim awkwardly toward the beach. Walking to the edge of the diving board, he saw the girl who had just gone off swim past Catherine like a fish. He gritted his teeth. He dove, went under water for several feet, and hit for shore with steady strokes. He snorted, speedily overtaking Catherine, and stood waiting for her in shallow water, all pooped out. She clutched his hand, and as they waded onto the sand he stared with quick anxiety about him. No faces that he knew.

A girl, chased by a fellow, scooted past him, tumbled, and the fellow purposely fell on top of her, both of them laughing.

Were these people, he wondered, trying to shutter troubles out of their minds, the same as he was? He caught a dark girl in a blue one-piece swimming suit and green rubber swimming cap standing alone like a young tree, fresh, virginal, untouched. If she was his girl! He remembered how Catherine had changed in these last months, a change that had seemed to come over her since she had given in, and that was so hard for him to put his finger on. To have such a girl, she couldn't be over seventeen, see her changing under a fellow's hand, growing to like what he gave, and all the rest of it. Already he was wishing to have over again those first weeks after Catherine had let him, and they were gone. But he couldn't give Catherine the idea he was looking around this way at girls. He looked at her, and saw, almost in pain, how plain she was without make-up, her chubby face framed by her white bathing cap. Suddenly, she seemed to him like a total stranger. He could not make himself believe that she was his girl, his woman who would be his wife in a few weeks, and who would, in about eight months, have a baby of his. Christ, for a lucky miracle! Have to make her exercise.

"Come on, I'll race you around the beach."

"I'm too tired, and I couldn't beat you anyway."

"Come on. I'll give you a head start."

"Please, no, Bill."

He became gloomy. He didn't want all these things to happen. He did not even seem to know her. . . . And did she really understand him?

"Where did we leave our things?"

"Around here some place. I know that much," he said, thinking that he was a bastard to be having thoughts so unfair to her.

He felt himself trapped like a rat in a cage. All this life around him, the sky, everything, were bars, and here he was, and here she was in this cage.

"Here we are," Studs said, finding the rolled-up bundle of their clothing.

He dug through it and found a package of cigarettes in his trouser pockets. Lighting one, he sat beside Catherine. He looked around the beach, as if looking through the bars of a cage, and he saw all these people in swimming suits, so many girls, so many fellows, and he wondered how many of them were trapped as he was, or would be trapped in the same way? He leaned back, supporting himself on his arms with his palms flat in the hot sand, and the sun was warm on his exposed neck and shoulders. Around him was the ebbing and rising of talk, and the constant eruptions of laughter. All this was not serious, and he wanted not to be serious, and he had something facing him that he had to be serious about. And right beside him was Catherine, who had to be serious about the same thing. She sat quiet, brooding unhappily, and his feeling for her was one of being very sorry. But he had to admire the guts she was showing. There was something! How many of these cuties on the beach here had as much guts as Catherine?

"Come on, let's take another plunge."

He looked wistfully over the lake at the horizon, where the merging of sky and water was like some mystery. He was struck with the desire to swim out to it and reach the center of where the sky fell into the water, and he knew there was no such place, and if he swam out, he would finally just sink, and this wish was like so many others that he had had all along. He was like a swimmer going out and out, and the farther he swam the more tired he got and the harder he had to swim.

"A penny for your thoughts, Bill."

"Oh, I was just looking at the lake. It's kind of nice to look out over the lake on a day like this."

They stared again at the horizon, but Catherine's eyes were more attracted by a child hobbling on unsure bow legs to the water to fill a small tin pail.

"Cute, isn't it?"

"What?" Studs asked.

"Darling, and our child is going to be more cute, isn't it, and it won't be bow-legged, either," she said, pointing as the child bent down with its pail.

He nodded mechanically. Her words brought back to him, with too much clarity, what was ahead of him, the problems and responsibilities he would have to face. He felt weak and powerless before them, and with his face clouding he began to pity himself, to feel almost as sorry for himself as he did for Catherine. Christ, what was he going to do? Himself, a father! How would he act, and what did he know about bringing up a kid? And the dough. Yes, goddamn it, he knew now what money meant. And while he began to understand such things, there were all those people here having a good time, all these fellows and girls flirting, some lads breaking the ice with girls they would lay and leave, and maybe others starting off with them on a road that would lead to the same place as Catherine's road and his own had led to. Why couldn't he have just made her, and then left? But how could he? Jesus, he couldn't take a run-out powder on her. And he didn't know if he wanted to, either. But he was out here at the beach to forget and have a good time.

"Yes, well, I'm nineteen," an almost flat chested, pertly attractive girl was saying nearby to a group of three fellows.

"And wouldn't I hate to hang until you reach seventeen."

"Well, hang then."

"Yes, Nellie, he's just a cynical old dope, isn't he?"

"If he tries hard and studies late at night, he might be a dope. He's not even that yet," the girl said, throwing sand at one of the fellows, jumping up to run screaming toward the water, pursued by them.

Hot little teaser, Studs thought, imagining how those fellows would grab and handle her in the water. His eyes met Catherine's, who also had been watching and listening. They smiled knowingly.

He laid his face downward in her lap, his right arm slung under his closed eyes. She toyed with his hair, and he liked the caressing touch of her fingers. So often he'd seen other fellows at the beach with their heads in girls' laps this way, and he had envied them. Well, some guys would be plenty dumb to envy him now.

"My darling little boy," Catherine whispered into his ear.

The world closed out of his mind, and the beach with its noises seemed far away. He was only half-awake, and he felt her fingers twining through his hair. Christ, if only life could be forever like this, no worries, no thinking of money, duties, responsibilities. If he had never to lift his head from her lap, and could just go on forever and forever feeling just like he did now.

He sat up blinking, squinting his eyes as he glanced around the beach. A girl, full and sexy, passed in front of him, kicking sand as she walked heavily, and he wondered how she would look naked. A bald-headed man sat in a family group about ten yards in front of him, and he watched the sun reflecting on the man's dome.

"Say, tell me now, no kiddin', you're a Polack, aren't you?" a fellow on Catherine's right was saying.

"Say, I don't catch your meaning."

"Meaning, baby, I know some meaning."

"I ain't that kind of a girl. Ha! Ha!"

A bitch. Still, he'd like to be lining her up. But what a lousy thought to have, so unfair to Catherine. Putting her in this jam and then wishing he was lining up some bitchy broad who sounded like the kind that favored only friends and had no enemies in pants. Wanting girls who wouldn't walk two steps for him, when he had Catherine who would go to hell for him. He must have the streak of a real bastard in his make-up.

He looked covertly at Catherine, and a horror like a cold sweat came over him. He saw her again as if she were a stranger. He didn't know her. Didn't know what went on in her head. He didn't feel that he would ever know her. He wondered how he could ever love her, and was this all that love really was?

"I wonder what time it is?" she asked moodily.

He shrugged his shoulders, and then noticed that she was looking thoughtfully ahead at those in the water and hadn't seen him shrug his shoulders. Was she having the same kind of thoughts that he was having?

"I don't know what time it is, but it must be about four o'clock."

"I was just wondering what time it was," she said abstractedly, and her voice, too, impressed him as the voice of a stranger.

"Come on, Hal, let's go in," a female voice behind him was saying.

"Darling, please," a man said.

"What's the matter, Connie, did Hal soak up too much moonshine last night?" another male voice asked.

"That wasn't all. We went to a party at Joe's and he and Joe's wife, Martha, hit it off swell. So he took her to his bed and board for the night, and Martha must be more wearing on a man than I am."

"Well, now, darling, it isn't that. It was just the liquor."

"Say, Connie, how about you and I trading off our mates for a night?"

"All right. But I'm taking a plunge now."

Studs and Catherine watched the one called Connie, a heftily constructed woman in a black bathing suit, run by them, followed by a bronzed-shouldered man in a two-piece blue-and-white suit.

"Terrible people, if you ask me," Catherine said, frowning disapproval.

"It's a funny way they talk," Studs said, puzzled by the conversation he had heard.

What the hell kind of a guy was it who'd let his wife play like that? Boy, he'd sock such a wife's teeth out and slam the crap out of the guy.

"That talk was just terrible. Why, I never even thought that there were people like that in the world. They ought to be arrested," Catherine said in a low but shocked voice.

"Yeh."

"The idea of it," she added with growing indignation.

He shook his head and asked himself how was it now, and how did it come about that he was marrying Catherine when she seemed to him suddenly like a stranger he could never know. And that a child of his was, at this very minute, growing inside of her. He scratched his puzzled head. He felt alone, so completely alone that it seemed as if there were no one near him. All these people, too, strangers. He closed his eyes and held in his mind the naked image of Catherine, and he imagined her with him in that act that was supposed to make a guy and a girl so close, and still she seemed a stranger, and he still felt all alone. His thoughts and feelings were padlocked, completely padlocked in his mind, and when he talked, most of the time, instead of expressing them he was using words to prevent himself from letting them out, fooling people by putting into their minds a picture of himself that was not at all Studs Lonigan.

He lay back, resting his head in cupped hands, looking at the sky, almost pale blue, while clouds floated so slowly, the sun glaring through it. He became light-headed, and thought of what a big place the world was after all, and he was sort of lost in it. He felt that he had always been like this. Ever since he had been a kid, he had wished and waited, and there had been no change except for the worst. He tried to laugh at this thought as if it were a wisecrack, but he couldn't, because it was too important to him. He had met lots of new people, become almost thirty years old, lost his health, and now he was getting married and going to have a kid of his

own. And what change would there be after he got married?
He'd already gotten it enough from her to know what it
was like, and maybe after the kid she might get fat and. . . .
He glanced sidewise at her. He liked it with her, though, and
wished it was dark now and they were together, and still
. . . oh, Christ Almighty! He was just a goddamn chump
trying to figure too much out.

"Let's go in," he said after jumping up sprightly.

She offered him her hand and laughed while he pulled
her to her feet. He dragged her swiftly to the water edge,
determining to make her get exercise, and he was thinking
that, all things considered, she was a damn good egg. They
stopped with their feet in the water, breathing quickly. Still
holding her hand, he suddenly asked himself who the hell
he was, wanting so damn much, and thinking she wasn't
enough for him. He was small and became ashamed of his
body and his size, and he wished he were a six-foot handsome
bastard, built like a full-back, attracting the attention of the
crowd of bathers. He splashed into the water.

III

With pain, he sensed a world that was black and twirling,
and with grooves which curved around and downward and
around and downward, and blackness shot through these
grooves. A great pain seemed to pulse and throb in this blackness, and at its ends, somewhere, there seemed to be a sense of
distant noise and excitement. He was somehow aware of spinning around and down and around and down these grooves, as
if on a roller coaster. The blackness seemed to contract,
and he felt himself growing smaller and smaller within himself,
and it narrowed, and he narrowed, and he was shooting straight
now toward a point in the center of the blackness, and a
greater pain coiled in his mind, and out of this pain there
grew the word death.

And he opened surprised eyes to find himself lying on the
beach, weak, his head, light and throbbing, resting on
Catherine's knee, while a man in a reddish swimming suit
with a close-cropped mustache worked over him, and a policeman drove back a gaping, circling, shoving crowd. He closed
his eyes, felt Catherine's hand on his forehead, moaned in
weakness and fright, and heard someone shout:

"Give him air!"

"Bill, darling, are you all right?" Catherine asked, her voice
almost frantic.

"Take it easy, Mr. Lonigan," the man with the close-cropped
mustache said.

"I'm all right. What happened?" he asked, opening his

eyes, still weak and dizzy, with a nausea arising from his stomach.

"Rest now a minute, Mr. Lonigan, and you'll be able to get up," the doctor said, touching Studs' forehead.

Shame mingled with surprise in him, and he felt like a circus with all the damn gapers crowding around to look at him. He remembered diving into the water, and nothing else. Jesus, he could have died! And the goddamn gapers. Jesus Christ, go way, go way, you bastards! He became more aware of his wet body lying on the sand, so tired, the wet suit clinging to him, the sand sticking uncomfortably to the suit, his arms and legs.

"You fainted in the water," Catherine said.

Catherine covered his face with a handkerchief, and he could feel the burning sun. He had just caved in, that was all, and his heart was pounding on him like a racing machine. He wanted just to lie where he was and fall asleep, forever. But he was ashamed of the weakness he had shown before so many people. Now they gaped at him as if Studs Lonigan was a monkey in a zoo. He tried to think of himself arising and walking off with a brave I-don't-give-a-good-goddamn air about him, while they gawked their pants off after him. But he was too weak, and he had a sick headache. He didn't want to move, but, ah, if he was only home lying between clean white bed-sheets, lying there for days with nothing to do, no worries. He heard voices, people still around him, what happened, who was it, is it serious, goddamn them. A flush came to his pale cheeks.

"Just rest a little longer, Bill, and we'll go home," Catherine said, petting him.

"I'm all right," he said, commencing to swoon.

Suddenly, he sat up, the handkerchief dropping to the sand. Still pallid, he looked at the greedy curiosity on so many of the faces in the crowd, many of them shoving to get a closer glimpse of him. A look of terror contorted his features, and the doctor gently eased him down.

"Darling!" Catherine exclaimed.

"I guess I fell asleep for a minute," he said grimly.

"How do you feel now?" she asked.

"I'm all right. Don't worry."

"Take it easy a minute now," the doctor said.

From his reclining position, he watched Catherine and the doctor step off a few feet and talk. He began to fear that he might die any minute, and he sat up to fight off this fear and prove to himself that he wasn't dying. His dizziness forced him to lie back, and in his persisting weakness he watched the doctor writing on a slip of paper the policeman had given him. They came to him, and the doctor timed his pulse with a borrowed watch, and listened to his heart.

"All right, go slowly now and you better take a taxicab home. With that heart, you got to be very careful and take it easy. You never should have gone swimming. Do you have a doctor? You ought to see one regularly."

"I do."

"You shouldn't exert yourself like this, not with your heart."

"I guess you're right, Doc," he said with a forced smile.

"Guess? Well, I know it."

He slowly sat up, then arose.

"How do you feel, Mr. Lonigan?"

"O. K., thanks."

"Want a ride home?" the policeman asked.

"I think we can manage, but thanks just the same."

"Well, you had a lucky escape and you better take it easy."

"I'll get along all right," Studs said, taking trial steps, uneasy because so many people were still watching him.

Catherine took his arm, and they turned back to the doctor.

"Thanks, Doc. Do I owe you anything on this?"

"Forget it, forget it. But do as I told you. Go easy, and see your doctor regularly. If you don't, the next time may be more serious."

"I'll see to it that he does, and thank you very, very much, Doctor," Catherine said.

"I better go and wash up a bit," Studs said to Catherine as they walked to their bundle of clothing.

"No! no, you can't. These are old clothes you have anyway," Catherine said, fiercely insistent.

He was just as pleased, because, anyway, he was afraid of even going back near the water. He caught the expression of worry knitted on her face, and he felt soft toward her, dependent. She was the one person on whom he could most surely rely. She was his woman, he told himself with mounting pride.

He lethargically pulled his clothes on over his swimming suit, and they trailed off the beach, glad to get away from people who kept staring and staring at them.

IV

"Bill, you must promise me that you're going to take better care of yourself," Catherine said, walking arm-and-arm with him toward South Shore Drive.

"I'm all right," he said gruffly.

"I know, Bill. I was talking to the doctor. He said you have to take care of yourself, very good care, too."

"I'm all right," he repeated, glancing away to keep her from getting a clear view of his face.

"You're not. You look very bad now, too. He told me. He told me you had a very weak heart, a cardiac condition, and you can't, under any circumstances, overstimulate it," she said, frowning at him when he pulled out a cigarette. "And the first thing you're going to do is to stop smoking," she snapped, snatching the cigarette from his mouth.

"I guess you're right," he said apologetically as they turned onto South Shore Drive.

"I know I'm right. And I am going to take care of you from this minute on."

"What else did the doctor say?" Studs asked with a foolish grin.

"He wrote out a prescription for some digitalis, and you're to take ten drops of it after every meal. And he said you must see a doctor."

"There's nothing really to worry about."

"You're not seeing your doctor now and you should."

"But I tell you forget it. It's not serious."

"Forget it! Forget it! How can I? You dove into that water and didn't come up, and I screamed and thought you were dead. And then the doctor tells me that you've got to be extremely careful. And you tell me to forget it."

"Doctors don't know everything."

"And Bill, you know, you don't, either."

"Well, I ought to know something about how I feel."

"Yes, you most certainly should," she said with kindly worry.

"It must have been caused by the sun or something I ate for dinner that didn't agree with me."

They crossed over to Seventy-first Street, Catherine clinging to his arm.

"How do you feel now, dear?" she asked after a period of silence.

"All right."

"Maybe we better take a taxi instead of walking."

"No. The walk will be good for me. We'll just take it easy, as we have been doing."

"But please, Bill, do what I ask you, because I'm only trying to think of what's good for you. So come on, take a taxicab the rest of the way."

"And what about you?"

"I'll ride with you and I'll walk the rest of the way home, and after supper I'll come over and see you."

"We'll go to a show tonight. I'll be all right."

"No, you'll rest and go to bed early."

"I'm better now, I tell you. It's all gone. It was just one of those heart attacks and it won't be serious if I watch myself."

"Oh, look, Bill, here come Fran and Carroll," she said, and Studs saw his older sister and brother-in-law strolling toward them. He was still pretty weak on his pins, but he didn't want them to know it.

"Hello, peoples," Fran said.

"Why, how are you, Studs? Gee, I'm glad to see you, and you know, old man, you haven't dropped around to see us in a long while. And hello there, Catherine, how are you?" Carroll said, and Studs guessed Carroll was friendly and all right, but he didn't like his talk and his gestures, too high-hat.

"And why don't you tell other people your secrets?" Fran said, smiling.

Studs could see that Fran was still a damn hot and pretty girl, and she looked nice with her white dress and her dark eyes and dark curly hair. And Carroll, with his classy light gray suit, looked like a hot shot, too. But he was sure picking up weight.

"I know. Mother telephoned me. Congratulations. We were just walking down to the beach to see if we could find you, because she told us you were there."

"And yes, Studs, my congratulations to both of you, and we both wish and know that you'll be happy," Carroll said.

"But isn't this sudden?" Fran asked.

"Well," Studs exclaimed while Catherine blushed.

"And as an old and experienced married man, Studs, let me give you one word of advice. Do what the lady tells you to the first time, and you'll save a lot of time," Carroll said dryly, winking as he ended his remark.

"Yes, darling, only why don't you practice what you preach?" Fran said, smiling at her husband.

"Oh, Studs will be all right. He can be trained," Catherine said, becoming more at ease.

"Gee, you kids must be busy as bees," Fran said.

"Well, I suppose we're going to be," Catherine said.

"Can I help you on anything, with your wedding dress, or something like that?" asked Fran.

"Why, no thanks, Fran dear. My mother will help me, and I think we'll get everything finished, all right."

"Well, you must come over. I want to have a shower for you, and when can I plan on it?"

"Fran, you shouldn't put yourself to so much trouble," Catherine said.

"Now, when?" Fran said authoritatively.

"If it must be, well, I suppose sometime next week," Catherine said.

"How are things going with you, Studs?"

"Oh, pretty good, Carroll, can't exactly complain. How about yourself?"

"All right, Studs. You know, I think that most of this depression talk is greatly exaggerated. I don't think that times are near so hard as people say they are, and all this gloomy talk just makes everything so much the worse. Why, with a little more confidence on the part of everybody or at least of all the people who count, and there wouldn't be any more depression. That's the way I feel about it. In our law office now, for instance, we've got more work than we can handle."

"Well, maybe there's something to what you say, Carroll, only some people have been hit pretty hard. I know I took a flyer in some Imbray stock, not a lot, just a little, and I got socked."

"Jesus, Studs, I wish you'd asked my advice before you did that. You know what's happening? People on the inside told me this. Imbray is in a bad spot. He's been fighting with a Cleveland financier, and this fellow from Cleveland has old Solomon with his back to the wall. It looks bad, because this Cleveland financier, his name is Goddard, he's got Imbray where he wants him. Imbray has to plug up his own stock and buy them on the market so that Goddard can't get them and get control of Imbray's companies. And to do that Imbray has to keep getting more money up issuing new stock. In consequence, he's built up a shaky pyramid, and now his stock is too watered. Imbray stocks are one kind not to buy. Get out of it quick, and buy some good government bonds, or radio stock. The future of this country is in radio and aviation, and when I buy stocks that's what I buy."

"Jesus, I think I will, and thanks for the tip. You say that Imbray is on the bust and his stocks won't go up?"

"They're so highly overvalued they can't go up much until the water is run out of them. There'll be a receivership. I think the story will break any one of these days. The old man is just going to be shoved out. I hope you didn't go in deep, Studs?"

"No. Just fifteen shares or so of a new issue."

"That's too bad. But take what you can get out of it, and get out right away. I got friends on the inside, and I'm not just talking rumors."

"I will, and thanks. It's not a great loss, but then a dollar is a dollar," Studs said, becoming suddenly uneasy, because he noticed how Fran was carefully scrutinizing him.

"Studs, are you running around very much?" Fran asked,

and Catherine flushed, her lips compressed in anger, and to mask it she forced a smile.

"Why, no. Why?" Studs asked.

"You're awfully pale. You ought to be taking better care of yourself."

"That's just what I told him. And after all my nagging I've only just now, at last, got him to stop smoking," Catherine said.

"Yes, he should," Fran said without looking at Catherine. "Studs, you look ghastly, and you ought to be taking better care of yourself. You should see Doctor O'Donnell regularly, drink a lot of milk to build yourself up, and you should do some other kind of work besides painting. That's too hard for anyone in your condition."

"I'm all right. I tired myself out a little swimming, but that's not serious," Studs said.

"It is too serious. You're getting married now, and you must take care of yourself. If you don't, I'm telling you it can be very serious. You look simply terrible. Catherine, you better watch him closely and make him take care of himself. He never would pay any attention to what my mother or Fritzie or I would tell him."

"Well, I tell you I'm all right," Studs said, smiling sheepishly.

"These men!" Catherine smiled.

"Yes, Carroll is much the same," Fran said.

"Studs, you and I better go crawl away and hide our heads somewhere," Carroll said dryly, filling an expensive pipe from a calfskin tobacco pouch, and Studs shrugged his shoulders non-committally.

"And Catherine, dear, I do want to see you alone sometime where we can talk. I'm going to be downtown Wednesday. Could you meet Loretta and I for lunch?"

"Why, Fran, darling, I'd love to."

"What time could you meet me in the Fern Room at Sheriff and Forest's?"

"Twelve o'clock."

"All right, dear, I'll expect you."

"And don't forget, Studs, we've got to see more of you," Carroll said, puffing on his pipe.

"Sure," Studs said.

"See any of the old boys much?"

"Not many."

"I see Kelly in court now and then. He's become a regular politician, with an alderman and all the other accoutrements. But I guess he's getting along. And I heard that Dan Donoghue's uncle failed in that string of movies he had up in Wisconsin."

"Gee, I'm sorry to hear that. Know what he's doing?"

"No."

"I'd like to see him. Good old Dan," Studs said.

"Dan's a fine fellow, and smart, too."

"Seen Phil's place since he fixed it up?"

"Have I!" Carroll smiled. "It looks like a movie set in a penthouse picture. But it was smart. It cost Phil plenty, but he'll get it back in time. Phil has a smart head on his shoulders."

"Well, people, I think we'd better be running along," Catherine said.

"And Catherine, darling, make him watch himself. See you on Wednesday," Fran said after the girls had kissed.

They parted. Studs felt very weak, and walked slowly, thinking of how healthy Carroll had looked.

"Carroll looks like he's up in the bucks, all right. But then his brother married the niece of Judge O'Reilley, and Carroll and Judge O'Reilley's nephew, Tommy O'Reilley, get all the business Joe O'Reilley used to have before he was elected. They ought to be getting along."

"Yes," Catherine said moodily.

"What's the matter, Kid?"

"Your sister, I'm afraid she thinks I'm responsible for your health. And then we have to meet them now when naturally you'd look pale."

"No, she doesn't. She knows me from old."

"Well, I think she does. And maybe that's how your whole family thinks."

"It's not. And anyway, you're marrying me, not my family."

"You don't understand," she said in a choked voice.

"Come on, Kid, snap out of it," he said gently, taking her arm. "We won't have to worry. The breaks are going to start coming our way now. You watch. A girl like you couldn't bring me anything but good luck."

"Bill, darling, I love you so."

Studs, because of his heart attack, had the feeling of being divorced from life and from the things that other people did. He was unsure of himself, and in his weakness asked himself would he be alive tomorrow, next week? He looked at people on the sidewalk, thinking that he didn't know how long he would still be a part of all this. He saw himself as if Studs Lonigan was already limping with one foot over the grave. But no, he knew that he wouldn't die. He knew that. He knew that he would pull through everything. Still, he could not shake away the feeling that he was cut off from life as if he was only half alive himself. He could not get it out of his head that soon he might die, and then all these strangers on Seventy-first Street would still be able to go out walking

on sunny Sunday afternoons. He stopped, concerned about
how he really felt. There was just a little weakness. These
thoughts were only like a bad dream. He took Catherine's
arm firmly, as if he were masterful and confident in himself.

"I'm all right now."

"Honest?"

"Uh huh!"

"We were having such a nice time at the beach, and I
was so happy. And I still am. I know you're going to take
care of yourself, and I believe in you."

A gray Stutz whirled toward them.

"Say, there's a beaut of a car. Some day maybe we'll be
able to get one like it," he said.

She smiled consolingly at him.

CHAPTER SIXTEEN

I

Where would he go to look for a job? And what would he
say? And on such a lousy day.

Studs glanced out the window of the moving Illinois Central
suburban train and saw the rain beating down on Seventy-first
Street. He turned over the pages of the newspaper, and his
eyes hit on the column of advice to the lovelorn. Should
the girl, who signed herself Terribly Puzzled, go out with
a young man to whom she had never been properly introduced? Jesus, she had a tough problem on her mind, he
thought ironically. If the gal asked him, he'd just tell her to
find out how much dough the lad had.

In just two weeks now, he would be married. And who
ever would have thought that Studs Lonigan would be up
the creek the way he was when he was getting married? He
had to get a job, too, because even if the old man could let
him work every day, there were the doctor's orders. With
his heart, he couldn't be climbing ladders, and he had to get
different work. And where would he get it? All the dough he
had was four hundred and sixty dollars out of the two thousand
he'd sunken. The brain of Solomon Imbray had guaranteed
the stock. Wait till he saw that rat, Ike Dugan. Wait! Lucky
he'd been able to get six bucks a share, and if he had waited
until Tuesday, instead of selling on Monday, he'd only have
gotten five a share. But now where was he going to get a
job?

With determination he looked to the classified advertisements.

> HAT SALESMAN—STEADY & SAT.
> XTRA. Expd. only. gd. refs. Abra-
> ham and Solomon.

Experienced. That let him out. Might, though, try bulling them. Experienced store workers. Nothing there. Commission salesmen. On that he and Catherine could eat air.

Executives and Managers

Could he find something here?

> SHOE BUYER and manager for
> women's, men's and children's shoes
> of quality. This position has great
> possibilities and we want the best
> man available. State age, nationality
> and full business history. For large
> west side department store. Address
> Box Xk 49.

Nothing doing again.

Professions And Trades

Engineer. No soap. Engineer Mechanic. No soap again. Fur designer.

> MAINTENANCE MAN—MUST BE
> EXPERIENCED on starch mogul
> machine. American. Protestant.
> South Side candy factory.

That guy must be an A. P. A. Protestant only. He'd like to run a business and fix 'em. Put in ads Catholic only. Dirty A. P. A.'s. Masseur. Nope. Physician. No.

> POLICE DUTY
> TEN MEN FOR NEARBY TOWN.
> ONLY THOSE WITH CITY POLICE
> EXPERIENCE OR LEGIONAIRES
> NEED APPLY. MUST FURNISH
> REFERENCE. MEMBERS OF UN-
> IONS NOT WANTED. APPLY RM.
> 216. . . .

He couldn't do police duty. Had to be tough for that. And he belonged to the painters' union, but that was just to avoid any trouble, and all he did was pay his dues. Sign Painter. Could do that if his heart was good. Window trimmer.

Clubs, Hotels And Restaurants

WAITER—ROADHSE., THURS. SAT. NTS. husky, sober.

Nothing there for him.

Salesmen And Solicitors

Might be something here. He knew, though, from the way he'd heard guys talk about looking for jobs, that most of the selling jobs advertised in the papers were sucker propositions. But maybe there might be a real steer in one of these. And he could sell without endangering his heart. Still, to sell, you had to have a line and he didn't have one. But what the hell, if other guys could develop a line, why couldn't he? Red Kelly had sold refrigerators for a while. And he had to do something. Anything he could. He would have to support a wife in two weeks, and a baby in seven or eight months.

LIFE INSURANCE MEN—FULL OR PART TIME. Comm.

He marked the ad with a pencil, figuring that even if he got another job, he might try selling a little insurance on the side. Phil Rolfe might take some, and Carroll, Red, lots of his friends. He'd see about it.

UNUSUAL SALES OPPORTUNITY FOR A-1 men calling on Funeral Directors. Metal vault with patented features, backed by live-wire merchandising plans. Good territory. Open and generous commissions that mean real money for man who can qualify. Write experience.

He would write a letter on this one when he got home. Might as well try everything. He imagined himself going around to undertaking parlors. Not the most pleasant sort of business.

CONFIDENCE INCORPORATED has openings for neat appearing, courteous young man to sell ice cream confections; commission basis. Apply.

• • •

He couldn't see himself standing outside the South Shore Country Club with a little wagon, selling ice cream cones.

TO SALESMEN—SELL SOBER-UP
CAPSULES taverns and roadhouses.

He smiled, thinking of how there were so many goddamn funny jobs in the world.

MAN—YOUNG (GENTILE) WHO
COULD SING AND PLAY UKE-
LELE EVENINGS. . . .

Employment agencies. He wondered if anything might be gotten that way, or would he just be handing his dough out. Jobs advertised by them for fifteen or twenty dollars a week, and only college graduates need apply. Things must be tough if that's all college graduates could get after four years of education. And trade schools.

LEARN SCIENTIFIC SWEDISH
MASSAGE

That would have been good work for Hink Weber.

THE IMPORTANT THING IN
LEARNING BARBERING IS
THE JOB AFTER YOU
COMPLETE IT
Hollywell not only creates the un-
usual jobs but the unusual graduates
by their distinctive individual short
course.

He could see himself going to a barber college. Studs Lonigan the barber.

Help Wanted Female

More jobs for women than men. Not too promising. Hell, he didn't even know where to go. Through the train window he saw the lake, gray, sullen, and he thought that, Christ, he did not see why he instead of someone else had to get a break like the one he had gotten. It hadn't happened to Red Kelly or Stan Simonsky. Stan at least had his health. But suppose his baby should be born crippled like Stan's? It couldn't. He couldn't have one additional jolt of tough luck. The world wasn't made that way. He turned back to the classified advertisements.

BE A TRAFFIC MANAGER. Learn
newest growing profession. Railroads,
industries, motor freight carriers need
men trained in modern methods. Big

pay and free emp. Help to qualify.
Class forming. Call 9 A. M. to 9 P. M.

• • • •

That was something it might be well to follow up. As
soon as he and Catherine got really settled down, he'd take
a course like this one, and see if he couldn't get himself lined
up with a job as a traffic manager. He saw himself a business
man wearing a classy suit, getting up from a glass-topped desk,
turning to a pretty stenographer and saying with an air of
authority, Lucy, I'll be back at two-thirty. And then, walking
out of an office with WILLIAM LONIGAN painted large
on the glass window. The train was crowded. Were all these
people going to jobs? Was the dopey fellow beside him going
to work or to look for it?

"Gee, kid, that association in our store is all a racket. I
know it. They take a quarter out of our pay every week, and
we don't ever get anything out of it," a girl in back of him
was saying.

"Well, if you die, they'll bury you."

He wondered what the girls looked like, but he did not
turn around to see. And damn it, he had to line up work right
now. Suddenly, almost over night, his whole life had changed,
and all this had come on him. So here he was with no future,
nothing ahead of him, unless he could go out and get it
for himself. The best thing, if it only could be done, would
be to get into politics. Red Kelly had, but he'd run in luck,
and was in now. How was he going to get in and get lined up?
Yes, how? Oh, Christ, wouldn't his luck ever change?

"But, kid, there must be some good in the association. Mr.
Goldensteiner says it's for us, and you know how much he
thinks of all us girls who work for him."

"Well, before I believe it's not a racket to get something
out of us, you got to show me."

He slouched in his seat, wondering what would come next,
feeling that his life was going to be short, and that he'd thrown
it away for nothing. He felt cramped, too, in the seat, damp.
And the day was so damn gloomy. He had no spirit. He
couldn't put his heart into trying to get a job today. And he
had to. Now there was no let-up. All day and always now he
would have to keep himself going, and all the boozing and
things he had done in his life, they had sure backfired on
him. And he had never really been happy. Always in the midst
of forgetting or getting over one trouble, he had always walked
into another. The image of Catherine seemed to flash into
his mind. It was for her now that he had to face things and

keep going on. Anyway, she would stick things out.

"But, Hazel, even if Mr. Browne is hard to work for, still, isn't he handsome?"

The girls in back of him sounded like dumb clucks. But hell, in the old days, he never would have pictured Studs Lonigan having to have someone like Catherine, or anyone, stick by him. And he remembered that night when he had a scrap with the old man, and he'd left home with a gat in his pocket to become Lonewolf Lonigan. Swell Lonewolf now, he was, hemmed in on every side. And how was he going to get out?

He saw that the train was pulling into Roosevelt Road. He jumped up and elbowed to the door. He didn't understand why this sudden idea hadn't occurred to him sooner. He could try getting a job in a gas station, and the Nation Oil Company offices were nearby on Michigan. Swell idea, he thought, stepping onto the wet platform.

II

His indecision grew as he stood sheltered in the entrance to the Nation Oil Building, watching the rain ink the boulevard, seeing people hurry by. Automobiles and motor busses passed, their tires swishing.

Across the street Grant Park was desolate, and over it was the heavy, downward sky.

He wanted to forget everything. If it was only a decent day, he knew he would feel better and maybe be able to look for a job with more confidence. He began to grow nervous, and wondered if the elevator starter was noticing him and would suddenly tell him that loitering in the building was not allowed. Now, what the hell would he say when he got upstairs? Maybe it would be useless to try here.

He compressed his lips, turned, approached the middle-aged uniformed elevator starter whose face was forbidding.

"Where is the employment department for the service stations?" he asked.

"Personnel Department, eighth floor. Take the last elevator," the starter said coldly, pointing as he spoke.

Entering the elevator he felt ashamed, because the starter knew his purpose. Three young fellows followed him and he wondered were they also looking for a job.

"Late today," the runty elevator man said as a pretty girl, wearing a blue raincoat, stepped into the car.

"Who wouldn't be in this weather?"

He closed the gates and the elevator shot upward. "It's

a bad day out, all right," the elevator man told the girl.

"Is it! Say, I could hang myself out on the line today, I'm so wet."

The girl left the car at the third floor. Studs became more and more anxious as one of the other fellows walked out at the fifth floor. The other two followed Studs out at the eighth floor. He walked along the narrow, tiled corridor, hearing the clicking of typewriters from behind glazed glass doors. Finding the door to the Personnel Department, he entered, followed by the other two fellows.

It was a wide office with dark rubber flooring. A freckle-faced office boy sat behind a closed gate, within which there were two large, unused desks. A line of applicants sat waiting on the two benches panelling the walls outside the gate, and seeing them, Studs' hopes again sank, and he wished that he had tried some other place. He walked hesitantly toward the office boy, permitting the two fellows who had entered with him to speak first, and then he immediately cursed himself for having let them get ahead of him.

"Is the Personnel Manager in?" he asked when his turn came.

"Want a job?" the office boy asked. Studs nodded his head.

"There isn't much chance. We're not hiring," the office boy said officially, handing Studs a card. "Fill that out and return it to me."

After waiting for the fellows ahead of him to fill in cards, Studs sat at a small desk in the corner by a water cooler and wrote in his name, age and address. The blank space for the reason he wanted to work with the Nation Oil Company stumped him. He noticed that another applicant was behind him, also waiting to fill out a card, and, feeling a mounting pressure within him, he wrote down in semi-legible handwriting that he needed a job with the prospect of a future in it. He returned the card.

"Take a seat," the office boy said, and Studs frowned, resenting this punk's snotty manner.

He noticed that the applicants on the benches were nervous and anxious. A gray-haired man with a kindly, friendly face sat in the center of the bench by the right wall, and beside him a thin-faced chap. From his looks, Studs decided he was a wise-guy bastard. Studs sat at the end of the opposite bench, and noticing the bull-necked applicant on the left of the wiry-looking skinny fellow, he guessed he must be in his thirties. He was dark-haired, with big ears and thick brows, a straight, long nose, and wide, thin, irregularly slanting lips. He sat as if holding himself together, giving off the effect of persistent sneering. Suddenly, his expression seemed to alter from a sneer to a pout. Studs decided he was a big sack of mush, and shifted his eyes to the floor, uneasy because he had stared so long at the fellow. Beside him, a weak-shouldered little man sat, nervously folding and opening his fingers, his wrists narrow and powerless, his face blown with yellowish unhealthy fat, a tb face. He wondered what about this fellow, and the bull-necked one, and the gray-haired man, and the others? They all must be hoping for a job, and maybe they needed one just as much as he did. If he got a job, it would mean some of them would be s. o. l. Well, the same would apply to him if they got jobs. It was just the breaks. A dark foreigner hurriedly emerged from an inner door on the right, crowded through the gate with eyes on the floor, probably to avoid meeting the questioning stares of the waiting applicants. He departed. No soap for that guy, Studs could see. The office boy barked out a name, and a little fellow in a loud shabby gray suit swung through the gate and disappeared inside the inner door on the right.

Studs felt let down because the fellow who had just come from his interview hadn't, it seemed, gotten anything. If these fellows ahead of him couldn't, how could he? Still, if he was to land something, most of these others would have to get the bums' rush, and each one who did meant one less rival. He tried to hope. And looking around, he could see the others must be thinking much the same as he was, because they all sat waiting, their faces hardening, their muscles tight, alert, scraping their feet, making all sorts of little motions and gestures because they were so nervous.

The freckle-faced office boy was checking over a stack of cards, and, watching him, Studs got the feeling that the punk was showing off, trying to tell them all that he had a job and they didn't. Just the kind of a face that Studs would like to have mashed in a little. He stared at the wall above the office boy. He wished the waiting could be shortened.

The small fellow in the loud shabby suit appeared through the gates, smiling artificially. Again Studs could feel how they became tense. The gray-haired man went in. Two tall fellows entered, spoke to the office boy, filled out cards, waited, standing to the left of Studs' bench and he enjoyed seeing how nervous and jumpy they were. He told himself that misery loved company. Well, if he failed here, he wouldn't be alone. If he made a fool out of himself, well, maybe others would, too.

The mush-faced, bull-necked fellow stretched out his legs and opened a copy of *The Chicago Questioner*. Studs pulled out his newspaper and looked at the front page. Police blamed Reds for recent eviction riots in the Black Belt. Reds must be nigger-lovers. Mayor says city finances in dangerous condition. That was bad, all right. Just what Barney McCormack had told his old man. Forced labor of women on Russian boats. Maybe every night the men lined up outside the women's cabins. How would the women like that? But there weren't enough details in the paper. He skipped the account of farmers rioting with guns and pitchforks, and avidly turned to one next to it. Sixteen-year-old girl found unconscious in forest preserve. Did a guy pulling such a stunt get anything worth the effort? He folded up his newspaper and noticed that the mushy-faced fellow had gone in, and that there were three more talking to the office boy. He looked at his watch. Ten o'clock already. Seemed he might waste the whole morning here and get out too late to look any place else until after lunch. Might as well get up and leave, because the way they kept coming out of that office, glum and hasty, there didn't seem to be much chance here. A nice smoke would go good, too, only for the doctor's orders. He'd stick it here, too, damn it if he wouldn't, and find out. Getting up and leaving now would just be showing that he had no guts. This might be just his chance. After all these guys getting the air, he might just walk in and get a job. But if he did, could he do the work well enough? He didn't want it long, just to carry him over and bring in regular dough until he could get started on that course in traffic managing and find a place in something that had a real future in it. Still, from the looks of it here, wasn't he wasting his time? But no, he ought to stick it out and see, since he'd waited this long. He slouched on the bench and noticed a roughly dressed Polack or Hunky whose face was deep with wrinkles, a coarse-skinned man of about forty-five or so with a dirty, tobacco-stained mustache. Reminded Studs of old Boushwah, the crabby old janitor he and the other guys had hated when he was a kid. And he'd be willing to bet that this Boushwah was as bad, and could hardly speak English. Such a guy had nerve looking for a job here. It perked up his own confidence. If such a guy thought he could get a job here, why shouldn't Studs Lonigan have more right to think the same thing? What could he say? Should he talk big? Walk in like he owned the office and this whole building and say, I'm the nuts, give me a job? He could just see himself getting a job that way. He imagined himself really getting a job, and he saw himself wearing overalls, working his ears off in a gas station on a hot Sunday. Anyway, he would just walk into the office inside and talk naturally to the Personnel Manager. Of course, though, he couldn't say that he only wanted a job for a short time. If business picked up for the old man, he could work with him, not painting, but just helping out. He knew enough about the business. But he was tired of it. What he really wanted to do was to be a high-class, well-paid traffic manager, and if he got this job, he would use it as a stepping stone to that.

But these other fellows? Were they as nervous and afraid as he was? And did they need a job as much as he did? Another exit. Another entrance. His turn very soon now. And what the hell would he say?

III

Behind a glass-topped desk, set diagonally on a dull, green carpet, Studs saw a thick-browed, full-faced, coldly efficient-looking man whose broad shoulders were covered by the jacket of a black business suit. He seemed to have the appearance of being fraternity and ex-collegiate, and Studs felt ready to give up.

"Mr. Lonigan, how do you do? I'm Mr. Parker," the man said, arising and extending a large, hairy-backed hand.

"How do you do," Studs mumbled, trying to act like an equal.

"Won't you have a seat?" Mr. Parker said, pointing to the chair at the near side of his desk.

They sat down, and from the corner of his eye Studs glimpsed the wet, dreary panorama of Grant Park, the blackened driveways, the gray lake, half-smothered in thick mist.

"Now, what can I do for you, Mr. Lonigan?"

"Well, I thought I would come down to see you about a job," Studs said, and the man's disconcerting smile made Studs wish that he was anywhere else but sitting opposite this fellow.

"I don't know if you are aware of it or not, but hundreds come here for that purpose every week."

Studs smiled weakly, feeling that he was giving himself away and showing by his smile that he had no guts, but still he was unable to check it. The man quietly studied him, his penetrating glance making Studs feel even more hopeless.

"How old are you, Mr. Lonigan?"

"I'll be thirty this coming fall," Studs answered, glad for the question because it would lead to talk and break that sitting in silence while that fellow looked through him.

"And how is it that you happen to come to Nation Oil Company? Did somebody send you, or do you know someone already employed here?"

"Well, I just thought that it would be a good company to work for," Studs said, hoping that his answer was satisfactory.

Studs felt as if he were a mouse in the hands of a cat while Mr. Parker looked down at his desk, toyed with his pencil. Then with a pointed glance he forced Studs to meet his gaze.

"When did you work last?"

"I've been working right along," Studs said, heeding a warning thought not to show his hand or reveal that he desperately needed a job.

"What sort of work have you been doing, Mr. Lonigan?"

"Painting," Studs answered, and the man seemed to raise his eyebrows.

"Artist, you mean?"

"No, house painting," Studs smiled, receiving a return smile which put him more at his ease.

"How does it happen that you want to come to work in a gasoline-filling station? Is it just a lull in your line, and a desire to tide over? Because, you should be informed, when we employ a man, we employ one whom we expect to stay with us and work his way up. Most of our salesmen and many of our executives here, you know, have worked their way up from the service stations. We consider our service stations as a training ground, and hence we cannot employ men just to tide over in dull seasons in their own occupation."

"Well, I'm giving up painting on account of my health, and I got to get a steady job right away. I have to get some other kind of work," Studs said, and, perceiving the frown his remark occasioned, he immediately realized that he had pulled a boner.

"What's the matter with your health, Mr. Lonigan?"

"Well, you know, painting, that is, house-painting, isn't the most healthy occupation in the world. You can get lead poisoning, and then, too, my lungs, I've got to watch them and get different work. I'm not in any serious danger, you see, but I just have to change and get some different work. And in changing, I've got to get a good job at outside work, and still something with a future in it."

"Of course, Mr. Lonigan, I trust that you don't consider the Nation Oil Company a health resort," Mr. Parker said after a moment of deep reflection.

"Naturally not," Studs said, not liking the crack, but holding his temper. "I've got to find a job and I'm willing to work hard, as long as there is a chance to get ahead."

He wondered would he have done better by putting all his cards on the table and shooting square. He didn't trust this fellow, but still, if he told more of his story, well, the fellow would have to sympathize with him and give him a break, if there was any break to be given.

"Married?"

"I'm getting married in two weeks."

"How long have you been a painter?"

"Since 1919. I've been working with my father."

"Business bad now?"

"Well, it isn't good. But that's not the reason. I'm leaving because I want to get into something new, and because I got to change my work. You see, on my getting married now, well, I lost two thousand bucks, dollars, that is, on Imbray stock, and then I'm broke, and then, as I said, I got to change my job on account of my health." Studs noticed the immobile, cold face before him, and it seemed useless to go on. "Of course, things are not so hot, good, I mean, with my father, and well, under the circumstances, I think I ought to go out and work at something for myself. I've been a painter long enough, and now, I'm looking about for a change."

"I see now. At first I wasn't able to understand why you should want to go to a new work that pays less," Mr. Parker said, but still there was that lifelessness in his features.

"And, of course, I'm only asking for a start in a station," Studs said, spurred on to win interest and sympathy. "And I'm sure I can work my way up. I'm not lazy. I've always worked, and I can work."

"What education have you had?"

"Grammar school and some high school."

"Some high school—how much?" Mr. Parker asked querulously.

"Two years."

"In Chicago here?"

"Yes, Loyola on the north side," Studs said, and he waited in uncertainty while the man made some jottings on a scratch pad. Maybe he would get it.

"Well, Mr. Lonigan, there isn't really an opening at present. Times are, you know, not the best, and we have only a limited capacity for hiring people. We would like to hire as many as we could, but that, of course, is out of the question. If you and your father have a contract to paint a house, and you hire more men than you need, there isn't any profit. And you say, you are how old?"

"I'll be thirty this fall."

"That, also, isn't so good. At thirty a man is still young. But we, you see, like to get our service-station men younger. Just out of college, especially, and train them in our own way. I can't hold out much hope for you, but I'll give you an application blank to fill out and mail in to me, and if there is an opening, I shall get in touch with you."

"Well, thank you. And, oh, yes, I wanted to say, also, that I can give you good references."

"Of that I don't doubt. I can see that you are an experienced man in your own line, and that you have undoubtedly made good at it."

"Well, I can give references like Judge Dennis Gorman,

and Mr. McCormack who's high up in the Democratic party."

"Of course, there is no connection between the Nation Oil Company and politics. But then, of course, such references are worthy ones, references of men in public offices, and they will count for you favorably when your application is considered. Now here is an application blank. It is self-explanatory. You fill it out tonight and mail it to me."

"Thanks, I'll do that," Studs said, accepting the blank.

"I'm very glad to have met you, Mr. Lonigan," Mr. Parker said, arising and offering a limp hand.

Studs hurried out past the waiting lineup on the benches. In the corridor, he looked at his watch, eleven-thirty, and pressed the button for an elevator.

IV

From the entrance-way to the Nation Oil building he watched the rain sweep Michigan Boulevard like a broom. The damp atmosphere seemed to penetrate to his bones and he felt lousy enough as it was, without having to take any disappointments.

What now? He tried to make himself believe that he hadn't been dumb in the way he had talked upstairs, but he knew differently. Goddamn it, why did he have to go through this? Giving him the same kind of a go-by they would hand to a chump. It would just be a waste of time filling out the application and mailing it in. He wasn't a dummy, either, and if they'd only give him the chance, he'd show them. He saw himself getting the chance, working himself up, becoming a big shot in the Nation Oil Company. But things had gone too far for him to be kidding himself with such dreams.

That Parker was one cold and clammy bastard. A fake high-brow, lording it over every poor guy who came along looking for a job. What education? What the hell was college anyway? But still, he did wish he hadn't been such a mutton-head as to pass up the chance to get an education when he had had it. Just now, when he needed help most, an education would put him a long way ahead of many others.

Studs noticed a fellow who had been after him in the lineup waiting upstairs. He wanted the fellow to speak, but he passed out. He guessed the guy had gotten the same kind of crap that they'd given him.

A bum shambled by the building. A taxicab skidded on the wet street. Still, what next? He looked at the Help Wanted column of his newspaper, again figuring that he had time for one more attempt before lunch. Opportunity for a salesman. And the building was just over on Wabash Avenue. It didn't look any too hot, but a chance was a chance, and he couldn't afford to ignore anything if it looked at all likely. A green-slickered girl passed the doorway, and Studs thought how nice it would be to follow her, spend the day forgetting everything by fooling around with her. He wished to all holy hell that he didn't have to go through with all this, and he stood watching the splattering rain. He felt sorry for himself.

And maybe the ad for a salesman wasn't even worth trying. He stepped out onto the sidewalk and ran, hugging the building. He soaked his left foot and trouser cuff in a puddle, cursing as he hastened on. Turning a corner, breathless, he was forced to pause because of a stitch in his side and an aching heaviness in his back and arms. He jammed his hands into his raincoat pockets, gasped for breath, and began to worry over his wet feet. Rain beat off his hat and back, and a drop oozed inside his collar, slid coldly down his back.

On Wabash Avenue he found his number, a dirty, brownstone building, and he entered the gloomy cavern of the tile-floored entrance-way. Reading the bulletin board, he was depressed by the general seediness of the building, and decided to follow up the ad only because it would keep him out of the rain. The iron-grilled elevator jerked and rattled upward, and Studs reflected that such a rickety elevator ought to fall, anyway, and smash itself at the base of the elevator shaft. Stepping out at the fifth floor, he shook his wet hat, and heard the elevator doors clanking shut and the creaking and straining of the car. He pulled a comb out of his pocket and quickly ran it through his dampened hair. Again he heard the slamming elevator doors as he searched for the right room number along a dim corridor with soiled, yellow calcimined walls.

He entered a small, dim office and found six others waiting on a bench to the left of the door. Same thing all over again with a line ahead of him, he thought spiritlessly. What time did one have to get out to be first in following a lead for a job? Was it necessary to bring a tent along and camp outside the building all night? There was certainly something wrong between seeing the lineups for jobs and listening to Carroll Dowson tell how times weren't so bad, the way he'd done last Sunday.

Studs timidly approached the flapper with thickly rouged lips, who sat before a typewriter at a desk in a corner. Shame came upon him, and his cheeks were hot. Coming here and going to this dame and admitting to her that he wanted a job, putting himself at a disadvantage because it was acknowledging a kind of failure.

"I saw your ad in this morning's paper," he began with attempted casualness.

"What's your name?" she interrupted.

"Lonigan," he answered, feeling as if the hostile eyes of those on the bench were boring into his back.

"Well, Mr. Lonergan, will you sit down and wait? Mr. Peters will see you just as soon as he gets through seeing those ahead of you."

"Thanks," he said, not bothering to correct her mispronunciation of his name.

He sat down at the edge of the stiff bench. He was wet and chilled. His trouser legs were soggy, and the rain had soaked through his shoes. He watched the girl at the desk chew gum as she typed rapidly. Hard and tough-looking baby, all right, the kind who knew what it was all about, he guessed.

"Nasty day," the fellow beside him said.

"Damn rotten, and I'm soaked," Studs replied, surprised.

He watched the stranger squeeze slimy bubbles of ooze from his shoes by pressing continually on the balls of his feet. Noticing the rip on the instep of the right shoe, he guessed that here was a guy who was plenty hard up, and he seemed at least forty, his face thin, wrinkles under the eyes, the cheeks sunken.

"Hell to be looking for something to do on a day like this," the fellow said, revealing discolored teeth when the spoke.

"Damn right," Studs said, telling himself that the fellow's teeth gave him the willies, they looked so ugly.

"But then, these are hard times. I've been through other depressions, but none of them can match this one."

"Yeah, times are tough," Studs said, holding back the impulse to talk about his own troubles.

"Me, maybe I don't look it, but I once was up in the class. I'm a college graduate. Michigan, and I've been up in the class. Maybe I don't look it, but I was a ten-thousand-dollar-a-year man, and I had my money tucked neatly in the bank. And the bank failed. So here I am, holding the sack. But I'll come back."

Studs nodded agreement. The other went on, "Stranger, these are tough times. And don't I know it! It's quite a comedown from being a ten-thousand-dollar-a-year man to this, but I'll come back."

Studs saw clearly that this fellow was full of bull, but the guy had a good line anyway, ought to make a good salesman.

"You know it's these rich louses who ruined the country. They want to take everything for themselves and leave nothing for anybody else. So all of us, even those like myself, who've been in the class, we're just underdogs to them. But they can't keep a man like myself down. I'm a college graduate, Missouri University, and I'll get back in the class."

"Well, I was getting along. I studied to be a traffic manager, but things are bad and I had a set-back. I've got to get something for a little while to get back on my feet."

"You and I, well, just to take a look at us, anybody could tell we're not the underdog or working-stiff type. And when we got to go out looking for something to do, and the breaks have gone against us, well, it only goes to show how hard times are."

Studs nodded. He saw that the heavy fellow next to this guy was giving the two of them a fishy eye, and he wished this fellow would stop shovelling out so much crap.

"I'll tell you, stranger, it's a dirty shame when you and I and our type have to take it on the chin. Take myself now, I get pretty damn sore when I think of what I had. A swell apartment out on Wilson Avenue, gals, all the wine, women, and song my little heart desired, and a nice wad socked away. Nothing in the world to disturb my peace of mind, or my night's rest. And then, the firm goes bust, the bank closes its doors, so here I am. But I ain't through, not by a damn sight. I was in the class once, and that's where I'll be again."

Studs turned away, not wanting to see any more of the fellow's teeth, hoping the others on the bench or the girl typing wouldn't take him to be the same type of crap artist.

The girl walked out of the office, wriggling with each step. The way they all gave her the once-over reminded Studs how the boys used to line up in front of the Fifty-eighth Street poolroom and undress every girl who passed. And this dame, he could see that she was a teasing bitch who liked to be looked at. Well, let her flaunt herself. He wasn't exactly hard up.

"Jesus Christ!" he heard a little fellow at the opposite end of the bench exclaim in an enthusiastic half-whisper.

"She's something that could make a man forget whether or not he had a job on a day like this," the crap artist beside him said insinuatingly, slyly poking Studs as he spoke.

A wiry, nervous, bald-headed man came from an adjoining office, followed by a barrel-like fellow who walked out of the office, carrying a folded newspaper under his arm.

"Who's next?"

A tall lad arose and walked into the adjoining office after the bald-headed man.

The girl returned.

"Sticks what she's got right up into your face," the crap artist whispered.

Sitting down, the girl flashed an annoyed glance at them, and Studs flushed. But how could a guy help getting het up when a dame did everything she could to tantalize him? She was crossing her legs, showing one leg above the knee. Ought to be a law forbidding broads to tease that way. She pulled the gum from her mouth, stretched it several feet, pulled it back into her mouth, resumed chewing it, and began typing as if the lineup on the bench were non-existent.

He looked toward the unwashed windows at the opposite end of the office and, staring at the heavy pall of gray sky, he became aware of traffic noises from the street below. He was damp, wet, and what would he do if there was nothing decent here? And how long would he have to wait? He looked at his watch: a quarter to twelve.

Two shabby men entered and walked to the girl. The tall lad came out of the inner office. Didn't look like he'd gotten anything. Maybe, then, it might be a good job. And if he got it, his troubles might be ended. If not, a whole morning wasted.

V

Studs saw the wiry, bald-headed man sitting at the littered desk of the cramped adjoining office, and beside him there were stacks of paper cups.

"How do you do, ah, Mr. . . ."

"Lonigan," Studs volunteered, taking the chair opposite the man.

"Glad to meet you, I'm Mr. Peters. Now tell me, Mr. Lonigan, are you, or are you not, a live-wire?" the man said, giving Studs a penetrating look.

Too stunned to answer, Studs stared back, puzzled.

"I have here a proposition that is for live-wires, and for live-wires only. Slackers, slow-pokes, easy-going, unambitious fellows, I neither want nor can tolerate. I am not even interested in the kind of salesman who thinks that because he has made a few sales in the morning, his day's work is done and he can knock off. The reason I'm saying these things at the beginning of this interview is because if you are that type, we are both wasting our time in even discussing the proposition I have to offer you."

"Well, I'd like to hear what your proposition is," Studs said, not liking this oozy bastard, but trying to act up to him.

"I've got here the kind of proposition a genuine live-wire recognizes immediately for what it's worth when it is presented to him. He sees that it is a sure-fire proposition that he can make plenty of money out of. I can prove it, too, that I've got a real money-maker here by showing you the reports of some of our salesmen." Mr. Peters dug through the papers on his desk and found a blocked-off, criss-crossed sheet.

"Here's a report from one of our salesmen who earned sixty dollars commission last week."

Studs' eyes opened widely, and his suspicions momentarily quieted. Sixty bucks in one week. If sixty, why not seventy or seventy-five? Leaning his elbows on the desk, his head bent forward.

"Here's another whose net was fifty-four dollars. And fifty-four dollars a week in these days is real money. It's big money for salesmen new at the game, who are selling a new product which is just being put successfully on the market. I can vouch for that. Our product is new, and anyone starting in with us at this stage of the game has boundless opportunities ahead. There's no telling where the limits are, and he can make, from his very first week, more money than thousands and thousands of men are earning today after years of work in one line. The opportunities are boundless."

Perspiring, Studs wished this goofy bald-headed bastard would come down to earth. But, gee, if this only was the genuine article and he could make sixty a week!

"We don't want coming to us the type of man who cries he's licked before he has even started, and who blames his failure on the business depression. A business depression is a smart man's opportunity. Too many people, today, are crying they're licked and not putting forth their best efforts. Well, that only means so much more opportunity for the live-wire. It's the time for him to plug, while others whine. It gives him less real competition in selling and if he throws his heart and soul into his efforts and his sales talks, he wins out, just because of the simple fact that so many of his rivals are beating themselves by whining. It is worth repeating that today is the smart man's opportunity. Today is the time for the real, high-class salesman to show his real mettle. And any man can sell if he has the courage and ambition to make a live-wire of himself. The stuff is there in every man. The question is, if you'll pardon my language, whether he's got the guts to bring it out."

Studs squirmed in his chair. Guts. Well, he had the guts. Studs Lonigan had guts, even if he had nothing else.

"Why, today so many people are whining, and whimpering, and prostrating themselves to Old Man Gloom, that the good salesman has an ocean of clear sailing ahead of him. Because this country is not licked and it won't be. And the service the good salesman can perform for this country today is to show it that it isn't licked. What we lack today is confidence. It is contagious. It peps up the sales prospect. Because people, even though they whine and whimper, sigh and decry and put faces on a yard long, cry out that times are bad and they're licked, people still don't want to believe it. They want to have faith. They want confidence. And remember this, they are going to pay the man who gives them confidence and faith. This is the one cardinal principle of salesmanship, the principle of the irradiation of confidence," Mr. Peters emphasized with a snapping gesture of his right fist.

"Yes, I think you're right. . . . But now, what is the proposition?" Studs asked, trying to make his tone of voice circumspect.

"I'm coming to that," the man said, knitting his brows.

Studs was sure it was all bull. But Jesus, if it only wasn't, if he only could knock off sixty a week. Then he wouldn't have to be marrying Catherine like a damned gigolo.

"Now, to continue, I have here the kind of proposition that only a real salesman wants. If you're not a real salesman, you don't want this proposition, and there is no need of prolonging our interview. Now, do you have faith enough in yourself to believe that you can bring out that something in you that is the makings, the basis of real salesmanship?"

Trying to conceal his surprise under the man's direct stare and pointing finger, Studs shook his head in affirmation.

"Well, speak up!" Mr. Peters said frettingly. "Speak up! You know a real salesman has to be able to talk. Nodding your head, you know, that's not a positive answer. You got to speak out straight from the shoulder, crisp, straight, hard language. Even when you only say yes and no, you should say them with a punch."

"Well, I think so. I haven't ever sold, but I'd like to know what this business is, and then we could see."

"That's the idea. Now, if you want to handle our product, you got to be a real salesman. But if you are, there's big money waiting for you. . . . Are you married?"

"I'm getting married."

"And you want a job. Well, you've come to the right place. If you're the right person, you'll have no further worries. With the money you'll earn on our product, you'll be able to furnish that little love nest for yourself and the little girl. And you know what you need for smooth sailing on the stormy seas of matrimony? Money. As I have said, if you're the right kind, if you can speak up, always dance on your toes, grasp your opportunities, be a character psychologist on sight, read a man's mind, see the weak spots, the Achilles heel in his armor and drive a telling wedge through it to carry the sales off, and above all, always remember that cardinal principle of the irradiation of confidence, well, then, you and I can talk business."

Studs glanced aside to prevent himself from smiling. He

was sure that it was a sucker proposition, but then, there was one born every minute, and if there were enough chumps in the world, well, maybe, fifty, sixty dollars a week.

"Our proposition is this. We have a new sanitary paper cup. Now there are in Chicago hundreds and thousands of industrial establishments, stores, offices and the like that are backward and unsanitary, because they use the medieval method of letting employees drink from one drinking glass, or even a tin cup. These are old-fashioned, backward, stone-age methods, unmodern, unscientific, and they help to spread disease. Nobody likes to use another person's, a stranger's, drinking glass, and particularly not some rusty old tin cup that scores drink out of. Throughout this city there are people who spread diseases through drinking cups and glasses. That's one of your principal selling points. It constitutes an irrefutable argument, and if you are clever it will gain you a high percentage of sales. The man who refuses to listen to it, who refuses to substitute our sanitary paper drinking cup for the old-fashioned, antiquated, disease-ridden drinking glass or tin cup, that man is backward, and he is risking the health of countless people." The man pointed his index finger at Studs and glared until Studs felt like reminding him that he wasn't making anyone drink out of a rusty tin cup. "A sanitary drinking cup, such as ours, is first of all scientific, and this is the age of science, the era of hygiene. Also, it is an aid to efficiency in a store, office, or factory. Why? Because it ministers to the better health of all concerned, and this makes for that increased efficiency. How does it achieve the purpose? Ha, proving that argument is like knocking over a straw man! If people are well, if they have less fear of disease, they work more efficiently because their psychology, their psychological attitude, is the right one. If there is a diseased employee in an office using an unsanitary medieval drinking glass or cup, the baneful, the dangerous, the mortal, results can be incalculable. That person can infect a valued member of the office force, and require him or her to remain out of work. A new person must be temporarily employed. The new person does not know the work, and must be broken in. There is resultant inefficiency. Inefficiency means demoralization and there is a contagious spread of inefficiency. The employer himself is not immune to disease, and probably, in some instances, uses the same backward drinking glass or cup that his employees use. He can become infected with a contagious disease, and can carry it home to his wife and children. They can become sick, even die. You see the point? In selling you stress it, only make it more concrete than I have done. Pick out someone working in an office, the secretary, concrete, you know, and speak of some specific disease like consumption." Studs nodded courteously, thinking that this guy was a new one to him. And he could see himself stringing out a line like this guy's. "Now as to our cups, we have an unusual offer of five hundred paper cups for a dollar, and with any order of twenty-five hundred or more cups, we will give as a premium an attractive glass container that is not only useful but also decorative in an office, store or factory. Now, isn't it worth a dollar to insure efficiency in your office and home? That's our argument to the buyer. Here is our proposition to the salesman. You buy the cups for fifty cents, and a cardboard carrier box goes with it, free. You sell them for a dollar and make your own delivery. We assign you a territory which is large enough, and has sufficient potential sales in it, to insure you a good living income, fifty, sixty, even a hundred dollars a week."

Studs tried to think of something to say that would permit him an easy exit.

"What do you think? How does it sound to you?"

"All right," Studs said to prevent the fellow from unwinding into another long breath-taking spiel.

"Well, would you like to try it?"

"I might."

"That's no way to be a salesman," Mr. Peters said, his expression pained as he emphatically shook his head from side to side. Rising half way from his chair, he surprised Studs by pounding his fist on the desk and gimleting Studs with a searching eye-to-eye gaze. "You got to be positive, direct, forthright. You'll never be able to sell with that wishy-washy kind of an attitude and manner."

"I think I might try it, but I can't today because I haven't any money with me to buy the cups," Studs said apologetically, but determined not to be roped in.

"You know every day lost is so much money lost. So much time squandered. And time is the most valuable and precious possession of mankind."

"I didn't think to take money with me."

"Usually an initial order of our new salesman is five packages of cups for two-fifty, but you might start with a lower order, one or two packages. One package is only fifty cents. You could sell in the territory I assign you here in the Loop and earn the price of your lunch and carfare. Then you could come down early tomorrow prepared to dig right in, or even, you could buy one package, sell it, and come back for two more with your dollar from the same."

"I couldn't even do that. I've only got my I. C. ticket and the price of my lunch."

"That's too bad, and it may be your tough luck. By tomorrow many good territories will have already been given out. First come, first served. That has to be our motto. Each day you lose means you are sacrificing the prospects of so much good money. After we get our product on the market, we will change our methods, and employ regular salesmen. Then the opportunities will be less than they are now. If a man starts in with our organization now at the beginning, he is in line for advancement. Inside of a year, we'll need sales managers, and they will have positions that any man would envy. They'll go into the real money, over a hundred dollars a week, and they will have the guarantee of a future of useful and profitable work. If a man goes in with us now, and he shows he has the genuine goods, his worries, for the future, are over, depression or no depression."

"Well, I could come back tomorrow."

"Think it over, Mr. . . . ah . . ."

"Lonigan."

"Mr. Lonigan, yes. I interview so many people daily that I can't remember new names always. Now, Mr. Lonigan, if you are interested, I'll be glad to discuss this proposition of ours with you further in the morning, and start you off on the right foot. But don't forget, every day, every minute that you lose means that valuable territories and Loop buildings are going to others."

Studs arose.

"Think it over, Mr. Lonigan," the man said, lifelessly shaking Studs' hand.

"I will."

Studs walked from the office, tired, almost dizzy, from the man's talk. There was a lineup on the bench, but the girl was gone. He examined his watch: twelve twenty-five, and left. But, gee, if it had only been a real and genuine proposition that would have netted him his sixty bucks a week.

VI

He walked in the rain, north along Wabash Avenue, worn out, with his feet soaked, fighting the discouraging idea of giving up for the day, wondering where to go and what to do next. He dashed into a Thompson restaurant to get out of the rain. He noticed the clock to the right of the cashier's desk. Seven minutes to one. I probably wouldn't do much good to try any other place until at least one-thirty. He could sit here over a cup of coffee until then. Should have taken longer with his lunch. He carried his cup of coffee from the counter, put sugar into it at a service stand, and found a one-arm chair. He slouched, and stared around at the many people scattered over the place, noticing a shabby, graying man wolfing a sandwich. Two chairs away from this man, a bum snoozed half asleep over a cup of coffee. At a table, two young lads talked rapidly over plate dinners. Near them two bell-hops or doormen in braided uniforms drank coffee. Down to his right, an old man with shaking hands slobbered as he drank. All these people, some happy, some not, how many were worse off than he?

He drank coffee, and determined to force his mind on the problem of what to do this afternoon, and what to say when he went out looking again. He lifted the cup and noticed the manager, a sour-faced fellow in a clean white coat, move officiously around, seeming to give orders to the hustling bus-boys. The man took a position near the door and stood with folded arms as if he owned the joint. Studs thought of how he would hate to work for a nasty-looking bastard like that manager. In a far corner two girls talked at a table. What about them?

There was no urge in him now to do anything. He was too damned tired. His feet were wet, and they felt dirty. His suit seemed not to fit, hanging loosely and unpressed on his body, the trousers about the cuffs heavy from rain. He told himself that he was whipped. He told himself that no, damn it, no, he wasn't whipped. He would just sit here awhile, rest himself, get his bearings, figure out a clear line to use in getting a job, and then go and look until he did get something.

He walked to the cashier's counter and bought a package of cigarettes. He knew he shouldn't smoke, but now, in his present state, wouldn't hurt. Returning to his chair, he saw that his cup had been removed. He walked to the counter and came back with another cup. He lit a cigarette and inhaled deeply. He shook his head, thinking that Christ, the times sure must be hard, all right. At both places where he'd been this morning, fellows had kept streaming in. And there would be some chumps, so dumb, or so hard up, that they would fall for that bald-headed guy's paper-cup racket. Have a scientific drink of water in a scientific paper cup, he smiled to himself, drinking coffee. But Studs Lonigan had not been one of that boy's suckers. No, sir.

"Well, Joe, I got a job." -

Studs turned to his left, and saw two young lads in blue suits a few chairs down from him.

"Anything good?"

"You can't tell. It's commission selling."

"That ain't a job, that's a question of reducing weight."

He had to get a job, because if he didn't he would be

living on Catherine's dough, and on what she could earn until she would have to quit because of the kid she was having. Jesus, it was just dumb, tying themselves down with a kid in the first inning, refusing to take anything or have something done about it. His eye, wandering over the restaurant, caught a coal black and perspiring Negro, in an almost filthy white apron, who slung a mop rhythmically back and forth along the dirty tile floor.

"It's this way, Joe. Now, what gave us good times? The automobile industry. Why? Because it was something new to develop. Now, what do we need now to bring back better times? Something else that's new, to develop. Well, that's the idea, see. This outfit I'm with has got something new. An electric shaver. All right. If it can sell an electric shaver to every man in the country who is working, well, think of what that means."

"Don't let anybody from the barber's union hear you say that."

"I'm serious."

If he could think of something new, or get in on something new that was really a good thing and not just a racket like that paper-cup dodge. If he could go back to painting.

From somewhere outside he heard fire-engine sirens, and he sat on the edge of his chair and saw that all over the restaurant people got excited. A man arose, hurried out of the restaurant. He felt like dashing out to see the fire. But he couldn't. Not in the rain. And anyway this afternoon he had ahead of him the serious business of getting a job. The Negro passed him, humming quietly as he mopped. Looked like a happy shine. Wished he was as naturally happy as all the shines were. Suppose he had been born a jigg. Christ! That, at least, was one thing to be thankful for.

"Joe, it's a chance. But it's worth taking. There's a whole new virgin field here, just as Mr. Cathaway, he's the man I just got the job from, just as he said."

"Sure, you wear out your shoes, feed yourself, and take the change. If you sell anything, he collects, and then you do."

"You're just cynical, Joe."

"Sure I am. I've worked at enough jobs and seen enough rackets to be cynical."

"Well, I'm not."

Studs was too nervous to keep sitting. He got up and paid his check. He walked along Wabash Avenue, rain pelting him, worried over getting wet and catching cold, not knowing what to do, a feeling of confusion spreading like a fog over his thoughts. He scarcely knew where he was. He heard an automobile horn and stepped back two feet on the sidewalk, standing in momentary paralysis. He had to laugh at himself. In the middle of the block, jumping back, afraid of being run over because he heard an automobile horn in the street! He had to, damn it, just pull himself together.

Oh, my Jesus Christ, if only something would happen! Again that confusion, like a fog, numbed his senses, and he became unaware even of the rain battering against his raincoat. Suppose he should just clear out on a freight, and go to-hell-and-gone, letting everything just go to pot. What then? Consumption, like Davey Cohen had gotten on the bum. Or maybe lose a leg or get killed under a train, or freeze to death riding the rods in winter, or just poop out with heart failure. He imagined himself a politician, with a fat cigar in his mouth, a bigger shot in the racket than Red Kelly, a boss sitting over a table with Barney McCormack, deciding on what to do with jobs and rake-offs.

"Buddy, can you spare a man the price of a cup of coffee?"

Studs turned to see an unshaven man in a soaked, torn coat. He walked on, turning east on Randolph Street. Women's dresses in a window. The same window that Catherine had looked at the night they became engaged. Maybe he should take in a show this afternoon and get started bright and early in the morning. He passed the public library, seeing hoboes cluttered around the entrance way, looking out at the rainy street. He turned north on Michigan Avenue. Well, he at least wasn't a bum. He asked himself where he was going. Well, maybe he might just stumble into a job some-wheres along here. He entered a building near the bridge and read the bulletin board, his eyes stopping at the name, Royal Insurance Company.

On a hunch that it might be his ticket, he rode on the elevator to the tenth floor. He stood outside the entrance door to the insurance company offices, trying to pump courage into himself. What the hell, wouldn't be anything doing there. He walked back to the elevator, and riding down he told himself that he didn't want to go around begging his friends to buy insurance off him. And anyway, it might be a little too early to go looking for a job in the afternoon. Best maybe to wait until about two-thirty.

Walking back toward Randolph Street, Michigan Boulevard lost itself in the mist, and the Art Institute down at Monroe Street was like some very distant building. People were hurry-ing by, and the crawling, honking traffic beat a confusion into him. He collided with a stout woman, hurried on without an apology. Maybe he ought to go home. He was too wet and mussed to look for a job. At Randolph, he dashed across the street and up the steps of the public library building, winded by the short run. He looked at the small crowd of people who stood sheltered from the rain. The boes made him laugh. So many of them looked like mopes. He watched a stream of people pour up from the Illinois Central subway exit. Train had just pulled in. Lots of women. Some neat girls, too. If it was only a hot sunny day, they wouldn't be wearing raincoats and slickers, and he could get a better look at their figures. He watched one girl in a yellow slicker, with blond hair curling out from a black hat, as she minced to a taxicab. Neat little parcel of femininity, young and budding just like Lucy had once been. Lucy again. If he could only see her, talk to her, even if she was fat and used up and another man's woman. Lucy, like she used to be. Even to see her would give him a feeling of those other days, when he had never dreamed that he would be in the kind of a hole he was now in. Or to see good old Helen Shires, a girl he could talk to, tell her of his feelings and troubles, and she would understand. Another cute dame, her dainty steps, the shocked look on her face as she avoided a puddle. He laughed. An old Jew with black whiskers getting wet, maybe a rabbi smelling of gefillte fish. Boy, what wind tormentors that old Abie had! They fell halfway down his chest. He watched the automobiles curving onto and off Randolph Street. Two students entering the *Cresar* Library Building across the street caught his eye. Lucky boys getting an education. And the cartoon coming up the library steps with books under his arm. A nose that hooked and stuck out all over his face, blue corduroy pants, leather jacket, no hat. Must be one of those Bohemians or a pansy. Lots of goofs in the world.

"Got a cigarette, Mister?"

Studs turned to face a jerking little gray-haired man with ill-fitting old clothes that hung over his body like a wet sack.

"Thanks," the man muttered, taking a cigarette from Studs' extended pack.

Studs nodded as if he had done the man a great favor.

"Got a match?"

Studs handed him a book of matches, looking on as the fellow unconfidently and excitedly wasted four matches before getting a light.

"Terrible weather," the man said.

Studs grunted agreement. The bum stood beside Studs as if expecting something. Studs watched a green-bellied surface car swerve onto Randolph Street and clang to Wabash Avenue surrounded by automobiles.

"Say, Mister, you couldn't spare a dime for a bite to eat?

I've been carrying the banner all night, and I'm goddamn hungry." Studs did not hear, and his thoughts dragged up Lucy again. The bum walked off, muttering curses. Studs stood watching people pass in the rain, thinking of Lucy, and wondering, now what would he do?

VII

Studs stepped out of another building. Four straight turn-downs, one right after the other. It was about a quarter to three, and disappointment was deep and like a worm inside of him. Walking again in the rain, he was afraid, afraid that he was no good, useless, that he would never be able to get anywhere. If the old man lost everything, he would just be a pauper without a pot to take a leak in. He walked rapidly, half running until he was forced to slow down. He knew he shouldn't exert himself in this manner, tiring his heart, getting more and more soaked, his clothes hanging wet on him, his trouser legs and cuffs heavy and soggy, his shoes sopping out wetness with every step, his hat dripping. Again he hurled himself forth, with head lowered, street sounds beating in his ears while he kept telling himself, goddamn it, he had to have a stretch of luck. There was nothing he could do but paint, and that was out, and at anything else he'd be lucky to make a measly fifteen bucks a week.

He entered a building on North Wabash Avenue, read the bulletin board. Emmett Jewelry Company. He took the elevator, hoping again. A girl by a telephone board in an outer office looked at him impersonally.

"I want to see the man in charge."

"For what purpose?"

"I'd like to interview him about a position."

"I'm sorry, but we have no openings."

"Well, couldn't I just see him?"

"He isn't in."

"Is his assistant or secretary in?"

"She's busy."

He turned away, slammed the door behind him. Another defeat. He told himself that he didn't give a good goddamn. Let himself get sick. Let anything happen. He'd already had so much tough luck that what the hell difference did it make. He stepped carelessly into the rain, faintly aware of streets and people.

He had a picture in his mind of Studs Lonigan courageously telling life and the world to shove itself up its old tomato and let it stick there. He saw himself walking in the rain, wet and tired, with things crashing down on his head, being screwed at every turn, forced to do something. He saw himself walking south along State Street in the sloshing rain, past department stores, past attractive windows full of suits and ties and shirts and dresses and furniture and baseball bats and football suits and feminine lingerie and refrigerators. Walking past tall buildings full of people at work who didn't have the troubles Studs Lonigan had. He looked at people on the streets, their faces indistinct, and an unquenchable hate rose up in him, and he wanted to punch and maim and claw them. He caught a close-up view of a fat male face, a sleeping contentment in the features. There went another sonofabitch, another sonofabitch who had a job and did not have to marry a girl he'd knocked up when he was sick and didn't have any dough, a sonofabitch who wasn't afraid of dying of heart failure. And there was a high-hat black-haired broad who probably thought that hers was gold, a broad who ought to be raped until she was exhausted and couldn't take another goddamn thing.

The sneer from the old days, the old Studs Lonigan sneer of confidence and a superior feeling came on his face, and he threw back his aching shoulders. He wanted to be noticed by these passing strangers, wanted them to see his surly expression telling them, he hoped, that here was a guy who did not give a good whooping goddamn and just walked along, taking his time and did not run to get out of the rain and hide from it in doorways, worried and afraid. A guy who had a perfect right to worry about plenty of things, plenty, and still did not worry. He stopped in a building entrance-way and drew out his package of cigarettes. Shouldn't smoke. Phrigg you Doctor O'Donnell! Phrigg you Catherine! Phrigg everybody! He made the act of lighting a cigarette into a gesture of defiance. He stood watching a street car crawl northward, its roof blackened by rain. Automobiles swished past it. Its gong clanged. A second surface car crawled behind it.

"Look at the rain, just like a silver stream from the heavens, Martha," a sallow fellow with a ruined panama hat said to a girl.

Studs glanced at them, sneered. But she was nice.

"It just looks wet to me," she said.

"But you don't see it with the poet's lyric eye."

Poet. He better watch himself before somebody slapped his wrist and kidnapped him.

"Now, as a poet, what does it mean, this silver rain, these puny crawling little packages of wet mortality?"

"Oh, Alvin, please."

Studs sneered at the nut, walked out of the entrance-way laughing to himself. Anyway, he wasn't like that pansy. He tried to forget the discomforts of wet feet, soaked clothing, the feeling of dirtiness he had. That pansy poet. Silver rain. B.S. A cold rain-drop spattered on his cheek. Some day, some day, goddamn it, if he wouldn't make the f——n world take back everything it was doing to him. Some day he would make the world, and plenty of damn bastards in it, too, eat what he was eating, and in bigger doses. Some day, he, Studs Lonigan, was going to bust loose like hell on wheels, and when he did, look out, you goddamn world!

He lit a fresh cigarette from his soggy butt. He sneezed. He had to laugh, and couldn't get over what that lily of a poet had been springing on the dame. Tell it to Martin tonight. He sneezed again, and the sneeze made him fear he was getting sick. He felt himself growing weak, and under the armpits he was sticky and clammy. He was afraid of poverty, and the fight he would have to make. He was afraid that he would get sick, die, from being exposed in this rain. He wished, with a weak will, that many things that had been done could be undone. If he had never met Catherine. If they'd never had that scrap and made up just the way they had. If he had never gone to that New Year's Eve party in 1929. If he hadn't drunk as much as he had in the old days. If he had only let himself get an education. If he hadn't lost his dough in Imbray stock. He stepped into the crowded entrance-way of a music store near Van Buren Street and stood listening to radio music. He noticed the faces on the men about him, blank and dull and dreamy, hopeless-looking. They seemed half asleep on their feet. Mopes. Studs muttered to himself. Look out, boys, or you'll wake up.

He slouched near a window, moped himself, and a sugary male voice sang.

> Just a gigolo,
> Everywhere I go,
> People know the part I'm playing . . .

The song filled him with a soft kind of sadness, and he listened, forgetting things, feeling as if the music was a sad thing running through him.

> When the end comes,
> I know they'll say,
> Just a gigolo.

And he looked like he would be something of that, marrying Catherine without a job when she'd have more dough than he had. Hot, ragging, snappy jazz music broke

loose, and Studs sneered at the sight of a kid of seventeen
or eighteen, with down on his upper lip, snapping his
fingers, shaking his shoulders, gyrating his legs to the music.
Disconcerting and shrill static cut into the music, and then
it beat again in quick rhythms. Studs tapped with his foot,
dreamily thinking of himself as just going along the same
as he had in the old days, strong and tough and with nothing
serious to cramp his style and his fun. Studs Lonigan, hard
as nails, chased by broads who just begged to lay down for
him.

His lips twisted in a sneer at himself, and he thought that
he was just a goddamn washed-up has-been. Sneezing again.
He was catching cold, and he ought to go home and get
in bed. The music softened into a slow and sighing sentimental tune, and it struck at Studs, made him brood with
pity for himself, worry, regret. Lucy, Catherine, the days
when he was a punk kid. A crooner sobbed with the music.
Felt low, walking in the moonlight of a summer night,
because she had left him. He now, well, he had gotten
something else again. He smiled ironically. If Catherine had
left him, he might have felt the song, but he wouldn't feel
like he did this minute. Vacant-eyed, he looked over objects
in the window, music rolls, violins, saxophones, sheet music,
Victrola records, piccolos, horns, tuning forks, mouth organs.
He turned from the window. He clenched his fists and
compressed his lips in explosive tenseness.

Goddamn it! he silently spit at himself.

What he needed was something to make him forget such
things. A burlesque show. The hottest ones were south of
Van Buren. He crossed under the elevated structure, and
on toward the cheap shows on South State Street.

VIII

The urinal smell of the ten-cent burlesque show made
Studs feel as if he would become diseased or contaminated
just by sitting in it. Four beefy women in narrow strips of
colored cloth slowly rolled and twisted their abdomens to
the tune of catching, tinny music. The music beat more
swiftly, and the belly movements of the dancers quickened.
Studs clenched his hands, leaned forward in his seat located
at about the center of the small theatre. He watched
closely while the women stood, legs spread, orgiastically shaking their wobbly bellies. Washed-out, painted whores. But
they sure could shake that thing. His whole body seemed
to narrow into one canal of desire.

"Take 'em off," a man cried.

With a final beat of the music, and a last lascivious twist, the girls trotted off the stage, their large breasts bouncing with each step.

A page-boy placed a sign at the right-hand corner of the stage.

SHIMMY CONTEST

A peroxide blonde, with purple tights and breast cloth, heavily skipped to the center of the stage. She began slowly, worked herself into rapid, shimmying twists, flung her head back in abandon, stood with her feet planted widely apart, her belly thrust forward. Sick with desire, wanting to see, and imagining the sight of the woman's hidden flesh, Studs watched the rippling of muscles beneath the purple tights. The woman let go completely, and with a final crescendo of jazz drew wild applause from the male audience.

"Take 'em off. Take 'em off," a man cried, and Studs joined others who took up the cry, stamped their feet, clapped.

The woman removed her breast cloth deftly, shielding her breasts almost with the same movement, robbing her audience of the desired sight. She coyly winked, turned about, projected her fat buttocks to her applauders, wriggled them, trotted off the stage.

Just enough to make a fellow want more. This one was stringy with legs like poles, black-haired, lousy-looking. And she shimmied in an annoying, jerky way. But there was hard bone and muscles behind those scarlet thighs, flesh and muscles and bones, meat to be laid against a guy. Come on, sister, shake it, shake it. Her breasts bounced. He wanted to see the rest.

Faster, sister, faster, baby, oh, sister, shake yourself.

"Take 'em off. Take 'em off."

Tough luck. Too quick in covering to let them see her boobs. Another blonde, shaking the same way, oh, Jesus Christ, he wanted a woman. One of these would be the trick if he could put a towel over their faces. Come on, sister, let it go, come on, sister. Jesus Christ, this was too much, that flesh wriggling beneath pink tights, faster, head flung back just as if she was taking it standing up, and oh, sister, stop it, stop it, this was too much.

"Take 'em off. Take 'em off."

Studs relaxed in his seat. His hands unclenched. He sighed, wished he hadn't come in. Glancing to his right, he saw, two seats away, a man's hand running up the thigh of a young kid of eighteen or nineteen. Ugh!

He arose, crushed out to the aisle, walked to the

exit. Dazed, sleepy, he walked back toward Van Buren Street, past barber shops, employment agencies, cheap and greasy restaurants, shows, shooting galleries, flop houses, without seeing them. Stray bums scurried past him. He was so disgusted with himself that he could almost vomit. He felt as if he could puke himself right up. Watching such lowdown broads, letting them send him off as if he was a sixteen-year-old punk who still had his cherry. How different Catherine was from them. She was decent. And look what she had and was giving up for him. And then his going to a dime girl show, and liking it, getting so hot. Ugh, but he had acted like a slimy bastard. Pride in his woman Catherine mounted in a rush of dizzy hot-blooded thoughts. Catherine so clean, where they were dirty. He was just a louse, unworthy of her.

He sneezed, coughed, full of fear. He was sick. He wanted to go home, get his clothes off and fall into bed. He was tired. His arms pained, and an ache wormed straight down his backbone. His feet were so leaden that walking was an effort. His underwear was sticky, his clothes heavy. To get home and in a bed of clean, white sheets, resting, sleeping endlessly, forgetting everything that was on his mind. He tried to walk fast, but slowed down. Too much for him. His heart was leaping. His feet were getting more soaked with every step.

He had just made a mess of every damn thing. The thought of Catherine, her love and devotion alone, gave him confidence, and he wasn't worthy of her, he had been false to her. He was through. Studs Lonigan, hang up your glove. Studs Lonigan, you're through. He was beaten and whipped and he did not know what to do. He could only crawl to Catherine, ask her to forgive and take care of a louse named Studs Lonigan.

He sneezed again, and his head pounded. He realized that he had a headache. A nauseous taste arose from his stomach. He had to get home. He walked through the tunnel leading underneath Michigan Boulevard to the Van Buren Illinois Central Station. Waiting for the train, he bought a newspaper and read a headline.

RIOT AS BANK FAILS

But he was too tired, too tired to read.

"South Chicago," an announcer barked.

Studs staggered through the doors to the long, narrow platform, slouched into a seat by a window. He sneezed and coughed, and damp, dirty, tired, he wished the train ride would end quickly. He touched his cheeks. Warm. Thirsty.

Must have a fever. He was sick. Maybe he was going to die. Oh, God, please don't let him die. Please only let him get home to sleep, sleep, sleep. He let his chin sink on his chest. He felt as if he were going to vomit. He wanted to moan, and fought back his impulse.

"I was walking down Sixty-seventh Street, and he smiled at me. And he had such a nice smile. He! He! I didn't mean to smile, but I couldn't help myself. But then I walked right on like a good little girl, and he came along, and when I was looking into the window of a hat store, he stood there, and I smiled again. And he had such a nice smile," a girl in the seat in back of him was saying, and he heard her dimly.

Broads and people in the train, and, oh, he was sick. He was sick, he silently repeated to himself. His eyes closed. His head and body sagged. Opening his eyes, he saw the broad, wet expanse of Stony Island from the moving train window. Almost home. The broads in back talking. Soon now, a bed, clean white sheets. He got up, tried to walk straight to the end of the car. Leaning against the side of the car platform, he saw a flashing picture of Seventy-first Street. Oh, Christ, what was going to become of him?

"Bryn Mawr."

He stepped off the train, forced himself to walk west to the street, and he ran down Jeffrey for about a hundred yards. He halted from exhaustion, stood gasping with his heart pounding like a dynamo. His cheeks were hot. His tongue felt coated. His underwear was wet with sweat. He could just drop right down on the sidewalk, and sleep, sleep. He walked feverishly on, his shoes sopping oozy bubbles with every step, his side cut with a pain, his over-stimulated heart a bombardment with his diaphragm. A feeling of congestion and pressure grew in his lungs. He sniffed. His nose drooled. He coughed up slimy green mucus.

He stopped and like a drunken man watched an automobile splash by. Suddenly, a cold chill iced his body, and the rain slapped against his cheeks, dripped from his hat. Dizzy, he staggered off the sidewalk and supported himself against a building, looking dazed at an apartment hotel building, seeing, as if in a nightmare, two men come out of it and walk rapidly toward Seventy-first Street. The building began to waver and dance before his eyes. Funny. The building was doing the shimmy. He shook his head, as if that gesture would clear his mind and permit him to see clearly. He lurched to the sidewalk, zigzagged, telling himself, Christ, God, Jesus Christ, God Almighty, he had to get home. Against his will, he closed his eyes, walked with lowered head. His shoulder slipped against a lamp-post, and, feeling himself falling, he opened his eyes like one awakening from sleep, circled the post with his arms, hung to it. He straightened up and walked on, his face burning, his body wracked with a succession of hot spells and chills. He could feel his shirt wringing wet against his back, and there was an unpleasant tightness in his crotch. With the sleeve of his raincoat, he wiped his dripping nose, streaking his upper lip. The rain beat on him, and he lurched up the steps of his father's building, set his shoulders against the door, strained, pushed, fell into the hallway, bruising the shin of his right leg. He crawled up the stairway on hands and knees, and lifted himself to his feet against the railing outside his door.

"William!" his mother exclaimed in shock as he stood before her at the door.

"Mom, I'm sick. Put me to bed," he said feebly, throwing himself weakly into the house.

As she closed the door, he crumbled up and his mother screamed.

SECTION TWO

CHAPTER SEVENTEEN

I

The thin-faced, prim nurse read the thermometer and wrote on the chart.

2:00 P. M.——103.

Shaking her head prophetically, she studied the patient, observing that the forced and shallow respirations continued. The face was flushed and emaciated. Glazed eyes. Nostrils drawn out from the effort to breathe, each emission of breath accompanied by a forced, expiratory grunt. Lips that seemed blue with raised, grayish-red fever blisters, pinhead size, on the angle of the upper lip. An anxious expression on the suffering features.

A sudden cough wracked his body, and out of his mouth there came a feeble drooling of sounds. Bending closely and listening, she distinguished the words, Please God. He became more restless. Looking vacantly up, he saw a figure of whiteness, as if through a mist. He was on fire, his legs, and his arms, and his chest, and his face. There was a nauseous taste in his dry mouth, and he could feel the coating on his tongue. That pain in his side was like a constriction or a boil, and there were aches all over his body, persisting like toothaches, or earaches, subsiding, returning in waves that shot up and down within him. Again there came that cough, coming up from his chest like a razor-bladed knife, dragging up rusty, infectious sputum. The nurse bent over him to wipe his drooling lips. She mopped his face with a cold cloth. Again he coughed, and when the cough ceased, he moaned in restlessness, dribbled out a confusion of sounds, which grew into articulated words.

"I'm dying."

He looked up, a beseeching expression tearing his face, and he sensed himself alone and helpless, removed from the commotion of a world that beat and hummed in his ears. He sighed. Still again that cough.

"Priest," he muttered.

The nurse shook her head. She knew the meaning of this. Again she wiped his drooling lips, and momentarily left the room while Studs lay with the feeling that he was sunk in a low bed on a rough mattress, surrounded by walls that towered up on the high ceiling.

Outside the afternoon sun beat like a torch on backyards and rear porches and the dusty cement of the alley. The exhaust pipe of an antiquated automobile backfired like a gun going off. A peddler, half a block away, was heard calling his wares in an Italian accent. A mother shrieked for her boy. A love song was crooned, and two boys walked through the alley singing *Just A Gigolo* out of tune.

And again that cough, sputum oozing from his heated mouth, a sense of his heart fluttering in pain, an ache which seemed to eat into the marrow at the base of his spine, pains in his shoulders and in the muscles of his arms and legs, a nauseous taste in his mouth, a pounding between his half-opened eyes, that expiratory grunt with the struggles that produced shallow breathings, and the world outside a buzz and a din and a humming in his ears.

II

"Mrs. Lonigan, you had better call Dr. O'Donnell. And also, he is moaning for the priest," the nurse said to Mrs. Lonigan, who was haggard and worn, her face pinched, shadows indented like circles beneath his eyes.

"Oh, God! Is he dying? Is my boy dying? Oh, Blessed Mother of God!"

"Please, Mrs. Lonigan," the nurse said patiently and with gentleness.

"Is he dying?"

"He is in a restless coma, and his condition is critical. His temperature has gone up to one hundred and three, and we had better have the doctor. After Dr. O'Donnell comes it will be best to have the priest, because he may come out of this coma and be able to confess. We'll just hope for the best."

"Oh, my son! My first-born son!" Mrs. Lonigan exclaimed, blessing herself.

"We must give him all the chance we can and let the will of God and Nature take its course. Come now, dear. I know how you feel, and I want you to bear up like the brave mother that you are."

"God have mercy on me, a poor mother carrying this cross at the end of my old days. Oh, Blessed Mary, Mother of God, be with me in my hour of tribulation."

Following the nurse into the sick room, Mrs. Lonigan dipped her hands into the holy water fount hanging by the door, blessed herself, sprayed the room, formed the sign of the cross over Studs with wetted fingers while the nurse wiped his lips. She looked down at the emaciated and tortured parcel of flesh that was her son. She blessed herself, muttered words of prayer, walked out of the room, and the nurse heard her at the telephone.

The window curtain stirred. A troop of shouting children passed in the alley, and Studs tossed with the echoing of their cries. He quivered, coughed deep from his chest. He looked up beseechingly with glassy, half-opened eyes as the nurse wiped his lips. Why must he be tortured with a rough mattress?

III

His eyes closed. He knew that he had been left alone to burn up, to be bruised and hurt by a rough mattress. His ears buzzed. Turmoil seethed in his head. He had to get out. To sleep, to die, even death, anything but this fire and weakness in him, and this stiff, hard mattress. With relief, he felt a cold cloth on his face. His head sagged. He was aware of an enveloping blackness, and colors, colors that seemed sick and mysterious, orange streaks, green and scarlet bands, purple lines, wheels and rainbows of colors shot like firecrackers and skyrockets, scarred all this blackness. He knew now what it was. He was dying, and he felt fear, like a great puke, sweep through him. And somewhere in this world of colors and blackness God awaited him. And the voice of God rumbled out of this blackness like some tremendous command.

Verily, verily, I say unto you if you want a soft bed, honor thy father and thy mother.

And the thin distorted figure of his mother rose against a purple background, and the flapping lips of her witch's face opened in a moan.

You'll never have another mother.

I'm damn glad of that, he said, knowing that his words would only sink his soul more deeply in Hell.

Bloated to about a half ton, and wearing the uniform of a clown, his father dropped off a moving band of color that was like golden sunlight, stood beside his mother, and cried out.

The son who put one gray hair on the head of a mother or a father will rue the day, rue the day, rue the day.

What you say, Charlie? Studs asked.

A fat priest in a black robe with a red hat stepped from behind a wide band of wine red, like an actor making an entrance on the stage, and spoke in a solemn pulpit voice.

Remember, O Lonigan, that thou art dirty dust, and like a dirty dog thou shalt return to dirtier dust.

Hey, don't talk so much, Studs said.

Sister Bertha, with the twisted face of a maniac in a motion picture close-up, danced a drunken jig around him, flung her nun's black robe high, exposing the legs of a skeleton, and wailed in a toothless idiocy.

Now you die like a thief because you shot spit-balls in the class.

And his mother knocked Sister Bertha over, to get in front of her, and said:

No one loves you like your mother.

And George Washington appeared in moth-eaten rags with a purple cloak flung around his chest and a bartender's towel wrapped around his gray wig, and he shouted, striking a Napoleonic attitude:

Your country right or wrong, but your country, my boy, jazz her.

And the Pope of Rome, with a thin face, was carried by six dark-skinned altar boys and dropped unceremoniously on his buttocks. In a stern authoritarian voice, he asked:

Do you receive the Sacraments regularly?

And like drunken Indians they did a war dance, whooping and bending, while bands of gold and yellow and orange and green and red like a fiery rainbow shot and whirled behind them. And out of the dancers, his sister Loretta, with a pregnant belly, called:

Cleaniness is next to Godliness.

And Sister Bertha halted and shrieked like a drunken hag.

Don't throw erasers in my classroom.

And President Wilson tripped before him like a fairy, with rings on his fingers, green earrings, and said, pursing his lips:

Join the colors now.

And his mother stepped in front of President Wilson and said, in tears:

The home is the most sacred thing on earth.

And Father Gilhooley in gold vestments thumbed his nose at Studs and said:

Contribute to the support of your pastor.

And Red Kelly and his father, Sergeant Kelly, staggered drunkenly before him with gin bottles held aloft like torches and shouted:

Obey the law.

And his father stepped up, took off a clown's mask, and said:

Drink is the curse of mankind.

And Dr. O'Donnell, carrying a syringe and a hypodermic needle, came to him, and said:

If you jazz, you'll get the clap.

And Mrs. George Jackson wriggled her tattooed belly, and sneered:

You can't jazz.

And the wife of Mr. Dennis P. Gorman in the red robes of the master of ceremonies of the Order of Christopher came forward and said:

Join the boy scouts.

And Father Shannon, on the arm of Lucy Scanlan who was naked and bleeding from her young breasts, stopped before him and said:

Be a man.

And his father reappeared and said:

Come home early tonight.

And his sister Frances in a transparent nightgown said:

Wash your face. . . .

And again they danced around and around him like drunken Indians in a war dance, and colors fell like sparks raining upon them, and Studs knew they were dancing the dance of his own death, and he wanted them to go away, and he arose and ran shouting.

Save me. Save me. Save me.

And they chased him and he ran, still screaming, and they shouted:

Stop thief.

Save me! Save me! Save me!

"He's dying," Mrs. Lonigan screamed, and the nurse rushed

into the sick room. Mrs. Lonigan soaked her fingers in the holy water fount, and stood over the bed, sprinkling her tossing, squirming, delirious son with holy water in the sign of the cross. She dropped to her knees and prayed, her body shaken with sobs.

IV

"Well, Mary, how is Bill now?" Dr. O'Donnell asked, stepping into the house.

He was a short, thick-faced man with a clipped gray mustache, gray hair, ruddy complexion and a large head.

"Oh, Doctor, he's very bad. I'm so worried."

"Well, we'll take a look at him. Maybe you're more worried than you should be. You know, sometimes in these pneumonia cases the patient will look to be much worse than he is," Dr. O'Donnell said, hanging his hat on the hall tree and setting down his bag.

"Doctor, I do hope so," she said.

"Mary, don't you worry. What you want to do is to take care of yourself, and let us watch Bill. How are the girls?"

"Fine, Doctor. Both Frances and Loretta are happy. They both married such fine, decent boys."

"Ha, I remember them when they were tots. And Paddy, how is he?"

"He's not so well, Doctor. You know these worries he has on his mind."

"Mary, check the worries now, and you'll be better off."

"Doctor, it's just what I hope Paddy will do."

"You'll tell him I prescribed it. And now I better take a look at Bill."

"Yes, Doctor."

He walked to the sick room, followed by Mrs. Lonigan.

"Mary, I think you had just better let me look at him, and I'll come out and tell you."

"Yes, Doctor. And Doctor, would you like a cup of tea?"

"No thanks, Mary. I have another call right after this one."

"Well, how is he?" Dr. O'Donnell asked the nurse.

"He's been in a restless coma, and here is his fever chart, Doctor. He doesn't look very good, so I advised Mrs. Lonigan to call you."

"Yes. It was lucky she caught me," the doctor said, wrinkling his brows as he read the fever chart. He opened his bag and, with the nurse's assistance, turned Studs over on his back. Sitting on a chair beside the bed, he felt Studs' pulse and found it feeble, one hundred and ten a minute. He noticed the flushed and fevered face, and, opening the mouth, perceived a thick and ugly coating on the tongue.

"It doesn't look so good, does it?" he said meditatively.

He found that the respirations were shallow, forty a minute, and that the patient, in his coma, was very weak.

"He's not as restless as he was when I telephoned you, Doctor."

"In a case like this, there is not much to do. We must let Nature take its course and hope for the best."

He again looked at the patient and saw the blueness around the mouth, heard the grunting breathing, and Studs mumbled inarticulately.

"You gave him digitalis?" the doctor asked.

The nurse shook her head.

"He has rales, and a great deal of congestion. What we must watch for is cardiac failure. I'm afraid the heart is going to give us trouble, and I'll leave a prescription for strychnine. It had better be administered at once."

"Yes, Doctor."

"If he survives, I'll be greatly surprised."

"He seems to have been losing steadily all day."

"Well, we might as well do what we can and make him more comfortable," the doctor said.

He and the nurse bathed the patient's limp, thin body by giving him an alcohol rub. The patient was set face downward again. He drew irregular breaths with a small clicking noise, and uttered feeble moans, and then a wailing, sad cry. The doctor looked meditatively at Studs, closed his case, left the room, meeting the shaken mother in the parlor.

"Doctor, how is he?"

"In such cases, Mary, it's difficult to say. Nature must take its course. All we can do is hope for the best and trust to the will of God. We'll do all we can and the rest is not in our hands."

"Oh, Doctor, I know it. I know it. He's going to die. I was told it last night in a vision."

"Now, Mary," Dr. O'Donnell said gently, patting Mrs. Lonigan's shoulders, "you must wait and be prepared. There is no use jumping to conclusions."

"Doctor, I'm his mother. Tell me the truth."

"There's a great deal of congestion, and naturally the pneumonia infection has sapped his strength. The pulse is bad, and the heart action is unsatisfactory. The greatest danger in a case like this is heart failure with complications, so I'm leaving a prescription to be filled."

"I knew it, Doctor. Oh, my son, my son," Mrs. Lonigan

said, looking confused while Dr. O'Donnell wrote out and handed her a prescription blank.

"Now, Mary, you must bear up. It's not lost yet," Dr. O'Donnell said, patting her shoulders.

"Doctor, isn't there anything else we can do?"

"Well, I could put him in an oxygen tent which would make his breathing easier and help clear up the blueness of his lips and face. But that would be very expensive. If you can afford it, it would be good."

"I'll talk to Patrick, and he will telephone you. Patrick has just taken a bad blow, you know, Doctor, the day my son came home to me sick, and cried like a little boy, 'Mom, put me to bed,' that very day Patrick's bank closed and he's lost a lot of money, the money he had for the next mortgage payment on our building. Oh, Doctor, it's hard times indeed. That such misfortunes should be visited upon us in our last years!"

"It's sometimes for the best, Mary, so you must buck up! Tell Paddy to telephone me at six o'clock and we'll talk about that oxygen tent."

"Doctor, I have called the priest."

"That was wise, Mary. In cases like these, it is best not to wait too long, particularly since you know the patient's heart is weak and his illness is putting a severe strain upon it. Yes, that was wise, and it might be helpful. The hand of God in a case like this is likely to be of more help than us doctors."

"Yes, Doctor," she said, sighing, then facing him speechless.

"The nurse will keep me informed by telephone of Bill's condition, and you'll have Paddy telephone me at six so I can talk to him about an oxygen tent. Now, Mary, you're a brave mother, and I can vouch for it because I tended you when you brought your children into the world. I know you are going to keep up your spirits. You look tired yourself, and I'd advise you to take a rest."

"Oh, Doctor, I can't. I can't!"

"Mary, don't say you can't. You just go lie down and take a rest."

The doctor returned to the sick room, spoke to the nurse, and took his hat from the hall tree.

"Now, Mary, don't forget. No worrying from you," he said.

Puffing, he walked downstairs.

V

"Is Bill any better?" Catherine anxiously asked as Mrs. Lonigan admitted her.

"I called the priest. He's in a bad way. A bad way, I fear," Mrs. Lonigan said mournfully, looking at the girl as if to drive and wedge into her a sense of guilt because of Studs' illness.

"Can I see him?" Catherine asked with deference, removing her hat.

"I don't know. The doctor said there must be complete quiet in the sick room, and he must have absolute rest, and only his mother should see him besides the nurse."

Catherine was so hurt that she could have cried. She had a flashing impulse of anger. But seeing, as if on second sight, this haggard and tired mother with eyes raw from tears, a natural womanly sympathy stirred her.

They moved to the parlor, and sat down, silent. The girl was suddenly struck with envy, because she thought that now she would never be able to bear the same name as this woman, Mrs. Lonigan. She felt, too, that even though she had hardly begun to swell, Mrs. Lonigan would sense her condition, because women who have been mothers seemed always to notice so much more readily than others.

"You say William is not better, Mrs. Lonigan?"

"He's a very sick boy, and I don't think he'll be able to pull through," Mrs. Lonigan said challengingly.

"Won't I be able to see him?" Catherine asked, a beseeching expression on her face.

"Well, the doctor's orders is for absolute rest and no visitors," Mrs. Lonigan said, acting like a martyr.

"Hasn't he asked for me?"

"No. . . . William has not been conscious."

Catherine's mouth opened in shock. She sat rigid, trying to face and accept the fact that he would die, that she might never again hear his voice, his dear voice. She broke into tears and the mother watched her with curious and envious eyes, eyes that blamed the girl. She wished, also, that Catherine would stand up so that she could get a good look at her. She was suspicious.

"I must see him," Catherine sobbed, lowering her head and struggling to check the flow of her tears.

Mrs. Lonigan wiped her eyes, and stared hard and calculatingly at the girl, as if she enjoyed seeing Catherine suffer. She believed that the girl would now, perhaps, understand her own feelings, her mother's feelings. She turned on Catherine all the suffering, worry, apprehensiveness that had wracked her these last few days. Catherine was the cause of all this tragedy and unhappiness that was being brought upon her home, her poor home. Chippy! Whore! Street walker! She had done it to hold him and to force him into marriage. Well, now, if it was so, she could pay the penalty of guilt before all the world. Mrs. Lonigan resolved that she would fight and forbid a death-bed marriage to save the girl's name.

Mrs. Lonigan thought, too, in envy, that this girl was young, and she had known her own flesh, her own son in a way that she herself never could have known him. She remembered when she was young, a girl like Catherine, the things that had happened in those days between herself and Patrick. She was sure that there had been the same thing between Catherine and her boy, William. Her jealousy persisted like a cancer.

Catherine, catching Mrs. Lonigan's fixed stare, flinched. She had never expected such treatment. She was afraid of this woman. She didn't know what to say. Should she tell? Her own mother was suspicious. Or was she just imagining these suspicions?

"Catherine, dear, why did you and William decide to get married on such short notice?" Mrs. Lonigan asked, sweetening her voice with false cordiality.

"Bill wanted to," Catherine mumbled unconvincingly.

She could not bring herself to tell Mrs. Lonigan, bring into public such intimate feelings and the condition she was in as a result of them. It was something so beautiful to her and to Bill, but others, even his mother, might not understand it.

"My son might not have been where he is today, only for that. He took sick after he had gone in the rain, against my wishes, to look for a job." Pride came into the mother's eyes, and she continued, "He came home a sick, exhausted boy and he said 'Mom, put me to bed.' He went out looking for work in the rain, against my wishes, because he needed money to get married on."

"Please, please, Mrs. Lonigan, don't say things like that. I love Bill," the girl beseeched.

"At times like this, we have got to look at the truth, no matter how hard it might be," Mrs. Lonigan said, each of her words like the thrust of a sword.

Catherine did not reply, and the silence between them was interrupted only by the sighs of their breathing. Catherine began to feel that they had sat, so quietly facing each other, for a long time. And the poor woman. Even though she was treating her this way, Catherine could sense the woman's sorrow. She was sitting, stiffly erect, her face changing from that hard, cruel look to one of brooding and worry. Then that sad expression would leave her face, and she would narrow her eyes. Her face would seem to grow more thin and to come to an intense point, as she leaned a trifle forward, again directing a calculating and suspicious look at the girl.

Catherine began to feel that the mother was staring clean through her. Upset, she could not return Mrs. Lonigan's glance. She was looking at her in such a way, so mean, so heartless. It was a double struggle for Catherine not to cry, because in crying she could give herself up to being sad, exhaust herself, and then all that she had on her mind would be forgotten. But she would not, she was determined, cry and expose herself in Mrs. Lonigan's presence.

Mrs. Lonigan suddenly assumed a possessive attitude, as if to indicate that she was nearer to Studs than Catherine was, an attitude which wordlessly, but like the slash of a sword, told the girl that she was Studs' mother, and Studs was hers now. Catherine held herself drawn tight, when she could have just screamed to the housetops that Studs was hers, that his child was in her womb, growing and living this very minute. She could have jumped to her feet and let the world know this, and she sat there, her control like a sealed lock over her tongue, lest she do that. And there was Mrs. Lonigan facing her, suddenly turned into a spectacle of heartbreak and sorrow. And again, her hard crafty look. The woman was hurting Catherine so deeply that she knew, until her dying day, she would never forgive Mrs. Lonigan. She knew why. The woman sensed it, sensed that she was pregnant.

What could she say? What could she do? Tell her? She wanted to. She had to tell someone, and she feared that her own mother would not understand any more than Mrs. Lonigan would. And she did need someone to talk to now. Someone on whose shoulder she could lay her head and sob, cry her heart out, exhaust herself utterly in tears, until her eyes were so raw that she would enjoy their very chafing. But Mrs. Lonigan was not the one to whom she could talk. Oh, God, she told herself, what could she do?

And still only silence and suspicion between them, blame on the side of the older woman, a wound that was raw and festering into hate on the side of the girl, and between them a continuing silence that was oppressive. Every little sound, the irregular and strident breathing of Mrs. Lonigan, slight movements of the nurse in the sick room, the sounds of life and movement, of men walking and talking outside and of automobiles and playing children were all magnified, and each sound and echo was like a bullet driving terror into this room and this home. Both of them sat, contained, lest they scream and shout. And still that persisting relentless look of Mrs. Lonigan. God, Jesus, Mary and Joseph, please help, Catherine prayed. She was afraid now even to stand up for fear that Mrs. Lonigan should catch the very slight swellings of her stomach and breasts.

Could she talk with the father? She was afraid to, and he was a man. The idea of telling them made her shudder, and the very thought of it made her feel muddy. Tell them of such a beautiful, intimate thing, so that they could scorn her, call her names, blame her, make it all dirty when it was so clean. She couldn't do it. But could she sit here forever? If only the telephone would ring, if only someone would come, if only Mrs. Lonigan would be called away. The woman looked at Catherine more and more like a witch.

"The priest is coming. I had better prepare things for him," Mrs. Lonigan said, suddenly arising.

"May I help?" Catherine said.

"I can do it myself, thank you," Mrs. Lonigan said, curtly shaking her head.

VI

Weakness and lassitude flowed through Studs. He fixed his half-opened eyes on a burning candle which seemed to be high above him on a dresser. A tall, dark priest entered the room, and Studs saw him with wavering sight, heard him speak in a strange muttering which he could not understand.

"Pax huic domui."

When he wanted to sleep, why didn't they let him? Only to sleep, to close his eyes and sleep and sleep, and forget everything until he was rested and strong again, forget the parched dryness of his mouth, the feeling that there was something coated and dirty on his tongue, the aches that seemed to worm themselves through his bones, all this. His eyes closed, and he wanted to sleep, and thought what a joke it was on them all. They thought that he was going to die, and were having the priest for him when he wasn't going to die at all. They thought that he was unconscious, and dying, and did not know all this. And here he was able to see and hear it all, the priest saying something to his mother. What a joke it was! He would tell them when he woke up. And now he was going to sleep and lose all sense of pain and these aches, and all his hotness that was like fire in his body. His eyes opened, and he could see them all, his mother, the priest, the nurse, Catherine, and Lucy Scanlan kneeling in a corner. They did not know it. Sleep. That was all. He was going to sleep this minute. What a joke on them, when he was only going to sleep and would wake up and say I fooled you that time. His lips opened in the effort to tell them he wanted to sleep.

"Yes, son," his mother said anxiously, bending over him, hearing only a weak, grunting sound.

They wanted to torture him. They put him on a bed on

the floor, with a hard mattress and heavy quilts over him and they wanted to torture him because they thought he was dying. Again he tried to tell them. It was a big joke. Thought he was dying, did they?

The priest laid a small vessel of holy oil on the table near the bed, where there were two holy candles burning in holders, a cut-glass bowl of water, a small saucer of bread crumbs, a saucer of small cotton balls and an empty saucer, and two clean linen napkins. Doffing his coat, the priest vested himself in his surplice and purple stole. Bending down, he placed a small crucifix on Studs' lips, and Studs made the gesture of kissing it. Straightening up, the priest dipped his right hand in holy water, and gesturing with it in the sign of the cross, sprayed Studs, the bystanders, the room, sing-songing simultaneously:

"Asperges me, Domine, hyssopo, et mundabor: lavabis me, et super nivem dealbabor.

"Miserere mei, Deus, secundum magnam misericordiam tuam.

"Gloria Patri, et Filio, et Spiritui Sancto, Sicut erat in principio, et nunc, et semper, et in sæcula sæculorum. Amen."

Studs looked up glassy-eyed when the priest asked if he could talk to confess. It was a joke, and he wasn't dying, and why was he on the floor? Sleep. A joke. The priest heard only an inaudible sound.

The bystanders knelt after the priest, Mrs. Lonigan and Catherine looking into the white-covered prayer book which Studs had carried the day he had, long ago, made his first Holy Communion.

"Adjutorium nostrum in nomine Domini."

"Qui fecit cœlum et terram," Mrs. Lonigan and Catherine read from the prayer book in response, mispronouncing the Latin.

"Dominus vobiscum."

"Et cum spiritu tuo."

"Oremus. Introeat, Domine Jesu Christe, domum hanc sub nostrae humilitatis ingressu, aeterna felicitas, divina prosperitas, serene laetitia, caritas fructuosa, sanitas sempiterna: effugiat ex hoc loco accessus daemonum: adsint Angeli pacis, domumque hanc deserat omnis maligna discordia. Magnifica, Domine, super nos nomen sanctum tuum; et bene—" the priest gestured in the sign of the cross with his right hand,— *"dic nostrae conversationi: sanctifica nostrae humilitatis ingressum, qui sanctus et qui pius es, et permanes cum Patre et Spiritu Sancto in sæcula sæculorum."*

"Amen."

"Oremus, et deprecemur Dominum nostrum Jesum Chris-

tum, ut benedicendo bene,"—the priest again made the sign of the cross with his right hand,—*"Dicat hoc tabernaculum, et omnes habitantes in eo, et det eis Angelum bonum custodem, et faciat eos sibi servire, ad considerandum mirabilia de lege sua: avertat ab eis omnes contrarias potestates: eripiat eos ab omni formidine, et ab omni perturbatione, ac sanos in hoc tabernaculo custodire dignetur: Qui cum Patre et Spiritu Sancto vivit et regnat Deus in sœcula sœculorum."*

"Amen."

Catherine's attention strayed from the prayer book to the priest kneeling at the bedside, her gaze concentrating on his dark curly hair, and she thought that he was a handsome young priest, and he was strong and healthy and he was bringing strength and the grace of God to her poor, sick Bill, his dying body stirring on the bed. Her glance turned to the flame of the holy candles on the table at the priest's right, then back to his purple stole. She heard the continuous half-sung words of the Latin prayer, a prayer which lifted and flew on wings to heaven, a prayer to restore his health, or to prepare him for the joys of heaven. But if he died, oh, she couldn't bear the thought! Bill, her Bill, she would come to him in Heaven. And now the priest had risen, turned toward her and Mrs. Lonigan, and she could see his face, thin and drawn, the cheeks pinched inward, a saintly-looking face. He was talking, pray for him and recite the Penitential psalms. Mrs. Lonigan beside her flipped the pages of the prayer book, and Catherine looked, her knees stiff from kneeling, silently mumbling a Hail Mary.

Studs looked up, and saw high above him the extended right hand of the priest, and he wanted them to know it was a joke, but they didn't even listen to him when he told them.

"In nomine Pa—" the priest made the sign of the cross, *"—tris et Fi—"* again he made the sign of the cross, *"—lii et Spiritus—"* and again his fingers traced the cross in the air, *"—Sancti, extinguatur . . ."*

The three kneeling women looked into the prayer book, reading in slow and frightened words that mingled with the priest's solemn Latin.

"Remember not, O Lord! our offences, nor those of our parents! and take not revenge for our sins.

"O Lord! rebuke me not in Thy indignation, nor chastise me in Thy wrath.

"Have mercy on me, O Lord! for I am weak; heal me, O Lord! for all my bones are troubled.

"And my soul is troubled exceedingly! but Thou, O Lord! how long?

"Turn to me, O Lord! and deliver my soul; oh, save me for Thy mercy's sake!

"For there is no one in death, that is mindful of Thee; and who shall confess to Thee in hell?"

And the priest with his right hand over the suffering head of Studs Lonigan, an intense pride in his ascetic features, slowly intoned.

"Patriarcharum, Prophetarum, Apostolorum, Martyrum, Confessorum, Virginum, atque omnium simul Sanctorum. Amen."

And the priest dipped his thumb into the holy oil, while the window curtain moved slightly and the three bystanders bent their heads toward the prayer book in Mrs. Lonigan's hand. The nurse recited the Psalms without conviction in her voice, thinking that he would die soon, wondering, drowsy and tired, would she get all her pay. Mrs. Lonigan and Catherine recited with fervor, fear and piety in their faces, struck with awe and wonder by the un-understood Latin and the mystery of the sacrament which would save their beloved from the fires of Hell.

"Blessed are they whose iniquities are forgiven, and whose sins are covered."

"Blessed . . ."

"Per istam sanctam Unctio"—the priest administered the Unction on the closed eyelids of Studs Lonigan in the form of a cross,—*"nem, et suam piissimam misericordiam, indulgeat tibi Dominus quidquid per visum deliquisti. Amen."*

"I have acknowledged my sin to Thee; and my injustice I have not concealed," the three bystanders intoned.

The priest wiped his thumb with a fresh ball of cotton, and dropped the cotton onto an empty saucer. Mrs. Lonigan watched as he again dipped his thumb into the oil, and she thought that her son might once have been such a man, a priest, bringing solace and strength to the dying, and she saw him not on the death bed, but as the priest, reciting the Latin words, bending over one whose soul was flying.

"Per istam sanctam . . ."

And Studs Lonigan lay half in coma, mumbling to himself only of sleep and escape from the aching tiredness that was like a river flowing in his body, while the priest anointed his ears in the form of a cross.

"For Thy arrows are fastened to me, and Thy hand hath been strong upon me."

"There is no health in my flesh, because of Thy wrath."

"Quidquid per auditum deliquisti. Amen."

The Latin words, the recited Psalms, were disturbing noises in Studs' ears, and he lay restlessly, his breathing coming with clicking noises, thinking over and over again how it was a joke for them to think of him dying, and would they only hurry up, go away, let him sleep. And next week he would be back in Sister Bertha's class at St. Patrick's telling kids in the class about how he had fooled them all by not dying at all, and he could hear Lucy Scanlan praying for him, and he would tell her, too, about this joke, and he wanted to sleep, he was so very, very tired.

"And I became as a man that heareth not, and that hath no reproofs in his mouth."

The voices of the mother and sweetheart throbbed, broke. Tears streamed down their faces. Breathless, tired, their backs straining, their knees hurting, they recited, smearing their faces by hastily wiping their tears with the backs of their hands. As if through tear-dimmed eyes, Mrs. Lonigan saw her boy in the cradle, saw him receiving his first Holy Communion in a Buster Brown collar and a blue suit, and Catherine saw herself and Bill again walking in Jackson Park on a Sunday, and the nurse, beginning to tire, wished this Catholic mumble-jumble would end.

"But my enemies live and are stronger than I; and they that hate me wrongfully are multiplied."

And the priest signed the cross on the blistered lips of Studs Lonigan.

" . . . —nem, et suam piissimam misericordiam. . . ."

"Forsake me not, O Lord! my God! do not Thou depart from me."

And mechanically the priest's voice intoned while a fierce pride of justification swept like a torrent within him, repaying him in this moment of the exercise of his powers to succor the dying, for all his struggles with the world, the flesh, the devil, the temptations arising out of his own nature.

" . . . per gustum et locutionem deliquisti. Amen."

Envisioning Heaven in an unclear sense of perfect happiness flying about like an unseen bird, Heaven and God Whose ministrations he was performing on this dying man, the priest wiped his thumb with an additional clean ball of cotton, dropped it into the saucer containing the previously used balls of cotton. Contrite for the false pride that had stirred him with this exercising of his mysterious powers, he thought of God, an Unseen Spirit, looking down upon this little scene, preparing Himself to receive another soul redeemed at death from the clutches of Satan. Again he dipped his finger in the Holy Oil.

"Per istam sanctam Unctio— . . ."

He pressed the sign of the cross on the backs of the wasted

hands of Studs Lonigan, observing the bony protuberances of wrists, knowing that it must be the Will of God taking this suffering sinner's life.

"For behold! I was conceived in iniquities; and in sins did my mother conceive me."

Her face distorted with tears, Mrs. Lonigan brokenly read the Psalms, thinking that in sin did she conceive him, her own flesh and blood dying while she was powerless to die for him, protect him, help him; and Catherine sobbed, and told herself that in sin had she conceived Bill's fatherless baby. Oh, God, no, please, please God, no!

The curtain waved, the burning candle flickered, and the radio crooning from outside drifted into the room, causing an expression of annoyance to cut the priest's face.

> *Just a gigolo,*
> *Everywhere I go . . .*

". . . per tactum deliquisti. Amen."

"Turn not away Thy face from me; in the day when I am in trouble, incline Thine ear to me."

The telephone rang. Catherine and Mrs. Lonigan looked at the closed door. The nurse, glad to get out of the room, signalled to Mrs. Lonigan, arose and tiptoed out of the room.

With the sheets drawn down from him, Studs felt a cooling draft on his legs and body, and he wanted to sleep, and to end this joke of them thinking he was dying when he wasn't. A joke was a joke, but he wanted to sleep, and his limbs were so tired and there was such a dragging ache in his back, and he wasn't dying, only sleepy and weak. He felt the touch of something oily on his feet, heard voices as an indistinct blur of sound, told them he wanted no more of this joke, but they wanted to torture him and wouldn't listen. A sudden smile twisted on his emaciated fevered face. Or was he playing the joke on them?

"For the stones thereof have pleased Thy servants, and they shall have pity on the earth thereof."

". . . per gressum deliquisti."

And after this final anointment the priest wiped his thumb with bread crumbs, washed his hands in the cut-glass bowl, dried them with a linen napkin, the women looking hopefully at his tall back, thinking, as if in unison, that he, he would save their beloved.

He knelt by the bedside.

"Kyrie, eleison."

"Christe, eleison."

"Kyrie, eleison."

While the priest's lips moved in a silent Pater Noster, a peddler passed down the alley, calling out in a deep and singing voice . . .

"Ba—nan—oes! Ba—nan—no—oes!"

Mrs. Lonigan quickly arose, tiptoed to the bed, drew the sheet over Studs, returned to kneel by Catherine, who sobbed with restraint, her head lowered.

"Et ne nos inducas in tentationem."

The priest paused momentarily, as if awaiting a response, and the women looked questioningly at one another. Mrs. Lonigan turned the pages of the prayer book. While the priest continued, she looked with sad hopefulness at the framed picture of the boy, Christ, above the bed, a clean, clear, sensitive young face with large eyes and longish hair. Christ, the son of Mary, had died. Oh, Mary, Oh, Blessed Virgin Mary whose mother's heart was wounded by the death of a son! Catherine lowered her head, limply tired. She could neither think nor pray. A haze curtained her head, and she waited for the end of the prayers, waited for this sacrament to work a miracle and give her back her Bill. She knew it would.

"Let us pray. Lord God who hast spoken by Thine Apostle James, saying: Is any man sick among you? Let him call in the priests of the church, and let them pray over him, anointing him with oil in the name of the Lord: and the prayer of faith shall save the sick man: and the Lord will raise him up; and if he be in sins, they shall be forgiven him: cure, we beseech Thee, O Our Redeemer, by the grace of the Holy Ghost, the ailments of this sick man; heal his wounds, and forgive his sins; drive out from him all pains of body and mind, and mercifully restore to him full health, both inwardly and outwardly; that, having recovered by the help of Thy mercy, he may once more have strength to take up his former duties, Who, with the Father and the same Holy Ghost, livest and reignest God, world without end."

"Amen," the two bystanders chorused.

"Let us pray. Look down, O Lord, we beseech Thee, upon thy servant, William Lonigan, failing from bodily weakness, and refresh the soul which Thou hast created, that being bettered by Thy chastisements, he may feel himself saved by Thy healing. Through Christ our Lord."

"Amen."

"Let us pray. O Holy Lord, Father Almighty, Eternal God, who, by shedding the grace of Thy blessing upon our failing bodies, dost preserve, by Thy manifold goodness, the work of Thy hands: graciously draw near at the invocation

of Thy name, that having freed Thy servant from sickness, and bestowed health upon him, Thou mayest raise him up by Thy right hand, strengthen him by Thy might, defend him by Thy power, and restore him to Thy holy church, with all desired prosperity. Through Christ, our Lord."

"Amen."

VII

The priest gathered up the cotton balls to carry them to the church, burn them, and throw their ashes into the sacrarium.

"Oh, thank you so much, Father," Mrs. Lonigan said.

"The sacrament may help him, Mrs. Lonigan. I have attended sick beds with the sick person closer to the end than your son is, and they have recovered. So you must have faith and give yourself into the hands of God."

"Yes, Father. Father, I'm ready. If it is the will of God that he must go, I will face it. Father, he's been so sick. He came home here and he couldn't walk in the door. He fell into my arms."

The priest seemed shy.

"Father, did your family live in Brighton Park?"

"Why, no, Mrs. Lonigan, I was born in Buffalo."

"I used to know some McCaffreys in Brighton Park."

"No, no relatives of mine. I have only one cousin in Chicago, and they live on the north side. Their name is O'Halloran."

"I once knew some O'Hallorans who lived in Saint Ignatius parish."

The priest edged toward the hall door.

"Father, take this as an offering, and say a high mass for the Souls in Purgatory," Mrs. Lonigan said, handing the priest a five-dollar bill.

"You're a good woman, Mrs. Lonigan, and I'm sure that Our Lord will bestow His graces upon you and your family. And I'll pray for you and for your boy. We must, on occasions like these, put our trust in the hands of the Lord and pray."

"Yes, Father. You've been so good, and you've given me so much hope."

"Goodbye, Father, and thank you," Catherine said, coming forward as the priest placed his hand on the doorknob.

Mrs. Lonigan stood facing Catherine while the front door closed, and Catherine was again afraid of her.

"He's like a living saint," Mrs. Lonigan said.

"Yes, Mrs. Lonigan. And it ought to help Bill, too."

Suddenly Mrs. Lonigan hugged Catherine, drew her tight, and held her firmly against her own body.

"Oh, Mrs. Lonigan, I feel so much better, and I know now Bill will pull through. God won't let anything happen to him."

"Yes, child. I know, I know how you feel."

"Maybe we ought to say a little prayer," Catherine said.

The mother and girl sobbed in each other's arms.

VIII

Catherine fixed a sightless glance on a man alighting from an automobile and disappearing in the apartment hotel across from the Lonigan parlor. She was empty and dull after the administration of the last sacrament to Studs, and her eyes were dry. She turned from the window and walked to the easy chair by the radio where Mr. Lonigan always sat. He would be home soon, and if he seemed kindly and understanding, she might tell him. Or should she? Now she might wait, because Bill was resting more easily, and she had faith. God was now going to spare him.

Unnoticed by Catherine, Mrs. Lonigan entered the parlor and stood over the girl. A deep sigh caused Catherine to look up, surprised, at Studs' mother. Mrs. Lonigan stroked her hair gently, and Catherine thought that Mrs. Lonigan had just been upset before the priest had come. Now there was sympathy between them, and they would be able to understand each other's feeling. Catherine smiled gratefully, unsuspicious, and a glow of emotion from the administration of the Sacrament of Extreme Unction seemed to lull through her. She dismissed a sudden and passing thought of warning to be careful.

"Catherine, if my son lives, you are going to be my daughter-in-law, like my daughter, because I have begun to feel toward you the same as if you were my own daughter. Now, my girl, you must not hold back anything from me. You must remember that I am William's mother, and that to both of us William means a great deal. He would want you to tell everything to me."

Gazing up hopefully at Mrs. Lonigan, and seeing the woman's face, kind, sad, understanding, she again dismissed a cautioning thought. She could not keep it silent any longer. It had to be known sometime. She had to talk, or else, she felt, this secret would drive her crazy. She lowered her head, sobbed. Mrs. Lonigan gently patted her hair. She looked up, her face torn with distress. It simply had to come out now.

"I'm having a baby," she cried, lowering her head onto her arms.

Mrs. Lonigan's face pinched, tightened, and she coldly watched the girl's unrestrained sobbing.

"You know we shan't be able to do anything to help you. Mr. Lonigan's bank has just failed, and he is, poor man, near bankrupt. And if William dies, with his Order of Christopher insurance made out to you, he will have on his shoulders the extra burden of a funeral. So I am afraid we shan't be able to do anything to help you," Mrs. Lonigan said with a calculation made doubly vicious by her even voice.

Catherine knew she had made a mistake. She feared looking up, meeting Mrs. Lonigan's eyes. She wanted sympathy now. After kneeling and praying with his mother, she didn't want to, she couldn't, fight or quarrel. She continued sobbing, trying to pretend that she had not heard these last words of his mother. But this insult. She couldn't pretend. It was like a shame growing in her. She looked, forcing an angry expression on to her face.

"I didn't ask you to," she said curtly, but she could not contain herself, and with another sigh she flung her head against her arm on the side of the chair, permitting an uncontrolled flood of tears.

"You shouldn't have done such a thing," Mrs. Lonigan persisted, clucking her tongue, shaking her regretful head from side to side. "You should have had more decency and self-control about you."

What could she say to this woman? Already she felt as if she had taken off her clothes in a room full of strange men. And she didn't care if it was Studs' mother, she was an old witch, and Catherine couldn't tell any more to the old witch. Mrs. Lonigan had been young once, and she should know how people feel when they're in love, and how when a girl loves the way she loved Bill, she couldn't help herself, and had to let herself go and do whatever he wanted her to do. She remembered intimacies with Bill, her cheeks hot with shame because she feared that Mrs. Lonigan was thinking of what the two of them had done, forming pictures in her old witch's mind of herself and Bill naked in each other's arms.

"What are we going to do?" Mrs. Lonigan asked with insistence, standing over the girl, a gleam of apparent enjoyment in her eyes as Catherine cried. "You'll have to do something. It is hardly possible that you can save your name, even if my poor sick son is not called above. And if he does pass away, you will not be able to save your name by a marriage at the last minute, because he is too weak, and he might never even regain his senses."

"Please. . . . Please, Mrs. Lonigan!" the girl beseeched.

"And you won't be able to hide it from people very long. You're already beginning to show it. If my son dies, I'll be ashamed at the funeral, and it will scandalize everybody. What are you going to do?"

"Oh, God, please! What can I do?"

"You can't just stand and be a disgrace to my family and to yourself and your poor mother. You can't do that. And your poor mother, does she know? What has she to say of your goings on?"

"I'll scream! I'll go crazy. I don't care . . . I don't care! I can't stand this! Please. . . . Please!"

Catherine was light-headed, dizzy, and this woman was still standing over her, like a devil, using words so that they cracked and lashed her more than if Mrs. Lonigan were beating her with a whip. Her cruel words, her face, oh, God, she hated that thin, hard, wrinkling face, calculating, intense, insane, yes, insane, and saying these things to her now.

"I won't say that you killed my son. I won't. I won't say that, but when a girl sins, it is not the boy's fault as much as it is the girl's, because the girl is different. And she should have more pride and self-respect and a sense of decency than to act like a mongrel dog or an alley cat. I won't say that you killed my son. But I will say that by making a chippy of yourself, you have helped to ruin his chances. If you hadn't thrown yourself on him like a streetwalker, he might not be on his death bed this very minute."

Catherine crumbled forward to the floor. She had fainted.

CHAPTER EIGHTEEN

I

"Mort, old man, I'm sorry to see things come to a pass like this," Lonigan said, standing by a scratched desk piled with papers and samples of wall paper, and glancing away from Mort at a smoke-dulled scene of railroad tracks and sooty buildings.

"I know. I know, Paddy. I was saying to my oldest kid only the other night, I said to Joe, it must hurt Mr. Lonigan more than it does me, because I've been working for him all these years, and it isn't just like he was my boss, because we're friends. I know, Paddy, that times is hard, harder than I've ever known them before. Business is business, and we're all in a rough spot."

"That bank failing, Mort, has just put the kibosh on me. I had my money for the next mortgage payment on my building that's coming due next month. And the bank won't give me any time."

"Yes, it's a shame, Paddy. An honest man like you, the squarest man I ever met," Mort lamented.

"I don't understand why it's got to be me, Mort. I've worked like an honest man all my life, and I pulled myself up by my own bootstraps. I earned every penny I ever made. It isn't right, Mort, and it isn't fair. It ain't fair. Why do I have to be a goat? Why?"

"Yes, Paddy, it's a dirty shame."

"I'll tell you what it is, Mort, it's the Jew international bankers. They did it. They are squeezing every penny out of America and Americans. And it ain't fair."

"Paddy, you took the very words out of my mouth. Here are you and me, two men who worked hard all our lives, honest men who were good providers, and the worst we have ever done is tip the bottle once in a while. And now, at the end of our lives, they take everything we got."

"Mort, it's all, everything, has been turned into a skin game, and the Jew international bankers are running it," Lonigan said, Mort nodding agreement.

"And, Paddy, I wanted to ask you, how is Bill?" Mort asked, worry clouding Lonigan's sagging, ruddy face.

"Bad. Bad, Mort," Lonigan said, shaking his head, emphasizing his words by lowering his voice.

"Bill's such a fine fellow, too. Many's the times he and I have worked on jobs, and I never worked with a better man."

"A man could not want a finer son than my Bill. But the game's up for him, Mort, I fear. He's sick, very sick."

"Paddy, you sure have your troubles."

"Troubles, Mort, always come in bunches."

"Isn't it so, Paddy?"

"I'm afraid, Mort, that only a miracle can save Bill."

"Well, Paddy, maybe the best will happen yet."

"Goddamn it, Mort, some good luck has to come to me."

"Paddy, you sure deserve it. You're the squarest shooter I ever met."

The two men stood facing each other, gloomy and silent.

"Anyway, Mort, if I line up any jobs, I'll call you first. But all I've got to say is that things look pretty fierce. A

long time ago I said that things would happen just like they
have, because Hoover was elected. He's just a tool, if
you ask me my opinion. If there hadn't been such a dirty
A. P. A. anti-Catholic prejudice against Al Smith, he would
have been elected, and this country would not be where it
is today. Because Al Smith would have been a president
just like old Abe Lincoln was, a man of the people, governing
for the people," Lonigan said, and Mort agreed with
strenuous affirmative nods.

"And Paddy, another man who would not have let
the country come to the pass we're now in is Cal Coolidge.
Coolidge, now, he was too smart for them. He saw what was
coming, and he cleared out so they couldn't pin the blame
on him. And say, Paddy, do you read what he writes in
the paper? He writes wonderful things. A smart man,
Coolidge."

"Yes, sometimes. He's a brainy man, even if he is
a Republican. He got out just because he was too smart to
let them give him the rap for these hard times."

"I cut out one of his articles and saved it. I wanted to
show it to you. He says in it just what's what!" Mort said,
drawing out a worn leather bill-fold and extracting a frayed
clipping from it.

Lonigan took the clipping. A sudden hope arose in him.
It would tell him what to do. He wanted it to tell him why,
why he was being broken and ruined, why, why?

Faith without work is vain. But he had always worked,
damn hard. *Although many millions of people are enjoying
record wages, there are others, who are unemployed, some
of whom can live on their savings, while the rest will have
to be supported directly or indirectly by those who work.*
If things went on as they did, it looked like he would have
to be dependent on public charity.

*People are out of work because the things they could
produce are not being bought.* True. True. The things
he could do, people didn't want. Too many buildings already,
and owners couldn't afford painting and decorating them.
With all our wealth, why didn't Coolidge tell the truth about
our wealth, tell who was getting control of it? If he,
Paddy Lonigan, knew, Coolidge must know, *it is difficult
to suppose that our consuming power has greatly diminished.
It is not being exercised. It will help somewhat to increase
public and private construction.* Bully. Smart man. An
increase in construction might give men like himself more
business. Men like himself were the ones who needed
a boost these days, the ones who deserved it. They were the
real backbone of this country. And if he did get contracts,

he would be spending money, buying supplies, hiring men. Smart man, Coolidge, even if he was a Republican. *But the principal consuming power is in the people who have work. Unless they buy of the other fellow he cannot buy of them.* He'd buy plenty if the bankers weren't robbing him.

If those who are working and have the means would pay all their retail merchandise bills and in addition purchase what they need and can afford, if those owing him money, Morris at that Jew apartment hotel, Olson, that damn Westside Swede, if they would, *a healthy commerce would quickly be created. Our nation has plenty of resources to support all its people comfortably through a mutual exchange of products if everyone will do his part.* Goddamn it, he only wanted to do his part, and he had always done it. He would still be doing it only for those dirty, crooked bankers. And yes, he had always paid his bills. *Those who have employment now run the risk of losing it by refraining from buying and paying within their means. No one who has the money can afford to defer settling his account.* Golly, he'd like to show this piece to Morris and Olson.

Lonigan smiled.

"True, isn't it?" Mort eagerly asked.

"Yes, and, Mort, I'd like my own debtors to see it."

"Can't you sue, Paddy?"

"I got to, but I'll be lucky to get a nickel on the dollar. I got a letter today from the bank holding the mortgage on my building, telling me I got to pay up on the date. How am I going to? The bank with my own money in failed. How am I going to?"

"Paddy, my only wish is that I had the money to loan you," Mort said.

"It ain't right. It ain't fair, Mort."

Mort wagged his head sadly from side to side.

"Mort, I'm sorry I can't help you out any more than this dollar," Lonigan said, handing Mort a dollar bill, and then putting his panama hat on.

"I understand. Thank you, Paddy. I understand. And I always say that Paddy Lonigan's a square-shooting man with a heart of gold when he has it."

"Thank you, Mort. I've always tried to be fair. And I suppose that all we can do is to keep a stiff upper lip, grin and bear it, and try to hang on by the skin of our teeth until business gets better."

"Yes, Paddy, that about hits the nail square."

"We've gone through the mill, Mort, and both of us have known hard times before. But this depression looks like the worst we've ever had. And Mort, neither of us were born with silver spoons in our mouths. We know what tough breaks mean. But I tell you, Mort, things have never been as tough as they are now." Mort nodded in eager agreement. "Why, I've hardly got a penny left."

"Paddy, I always think that I've got this one consolation. Maybe it was the wisdom of God taking my woman away from me before she had to go through times like these."

"Yes, Mort, often mere mortal men like ourselves cannot see the ways of the Almighty and what looks to us like misfortune often turns out different and only proves the wisdom of God," Lonigan orated.

"True, Paddy, true."

"Well, goodbye, Mort, old man, and whenever I have any work for you, I'll get in touch with you. Goodbye and good luck, old man," Lonigan said.

"So long, Paddy. I know how it is. I know," Mort said as the two men spiritlessly shook hands.

Mort trudged out of the office. Lonigan stood as if transfixed, thinking that Mort was too old and too slow to do much work for him. He had to use younger men, who could do the work quickly.

He picked up the telephone, put it down. He was afraid to call home and get bad news. Bill might be dead. Was in bad shape when he left this morning, and Mary had spoken of having the priest.

He locked his office door and left.

II

Lonigan sat at the wheel of his battered, dusty Ford coupé. There was really no place to go, and it didn't matter where he went or why. If there was ever a man plagued by the seven devils, he knew that man was himself.

He stepped on the starter. The engine turned, and the car lurched forward. Driving mechanically, Lonigan decided that he might pay a visit to St. Patrick's. He parked his car before the broad and pillared façade of the church. Inside, he looked around in awe and wonder, rediscovering the stained-glass windows, the hollowed dome of colored glass, the marble altar, the statuesque stations of the Cross along the wall. He knelt in the last pew on the right of the center aisle, his eyes fastened on the candle burning with flickering steadiness inside a red glass hung above the altar.

A sense of mystery filled him, an awe of God, his God. He blessed himself a second time, palmed his hands together, looked from the altar light to the golden tabernacle door which housed the Lord in Whose honor the candle burned perpetually. He beseeched comfort and solace. Divine help, that his God would intervene, if it be His Will, and spare his son. His *Our Father* was interrupted by the remembrance of how Dr. O'Donnell had shaken his head and said that Nature would have to take its course in Bill's case. His eyes shifted from the tabernacle door to rest on the hanging imprint of the bleeding and crucified Jesus set high in the hollowed half dome which curved above the altar. He begged it for hope, feeling that he was a weak and tired man, deserted, at the mercy of a world beyond his powers.

His knees tired, he sat back in the pew. Bewildered, he tried to force himself to understand what was happening to him, what was happening in the world, why so many things should be crushing down on the shoulders of Paddy Lonigan who had once been so confident, so well equipped to deal with his difficulties.

Vaguely, he remembered an afternoon in October, 1929, when he had come home around a quarter to five as usual. In the newspaper, delivered at his door, he had read the account of a break in the stock market. Now he saw that that was the beginning of this depression, this depression that was robbing him of everything he had acquired through the long years of work. And more clearly he remembered that New Year's morning of 1929, when he had been awakened by a call from the Washington Park Hospital at Sixty-first and Vernon and told to come down and see about his son, who had been picked up on the street, in the gutter, drunk and unconscious. That day was one he could never forget. And both of these days had brought upon him troubles that now linked up in one whole series that was breaking him. And he was getting old himself. This all meant the ending of Paddy Lonigan.

It was neither right nor fair. He could not see why these troubles must all come to him. What had he done? He wanted to know. Here he was, a man who had always done his duties. Hadn't he earned his place in the world by hard work? Hadn't he always provided for his family to the best of his abilities, tried to be a good husband and a good father, a true Catholic, and a real American? Hadn't he always made his Easter duty, contributed to the support of his pastor? And hadn't he done all in his power to bring his children up the right way? He had wanted them to be a comfort to himself and Mary in their old age. And now, Bill, his favorite, was dying. And he and Mary, after all their work and struggle, must come to such misery in their old age, be reduced almost to the state of paupers. It wasn't right. It wasn't fair. He had done nothing to merit this punishment. Why, why was it?

Anger flared in him. He silently heaped a curse on the Jew international bankers. They were the causes, he assured himself. They did not want America to collect its just debts from Europe. If America did, they wouldn't make enough greedy profit. That was why there was a depression. The bankers. And hadn't that radio priest, Father Moylan from the Shrine of The Little Rose of Jesus Christ, told the bankers where to get off at?

But why was he, and not others, being ruined? Old man O'Brien who ran the coal yards was still above water. So were his two son-in-laws, and Judge Joe O'Reilley, and Dinny Gorman. And Paddy Lonigan wasn't. With his back against the wall, he had to make the grimmest fight of his life, and he didn't have the heart to fight any more. Those dirty Jew international bankers.

It was the Jew all over again, he told himself with grumbling, morbid pleasure. The Jews queered everything they put their hands on. This neighborhood, for instance, had been a good neighborhood, with decent, good people in it. The Jews had come in, and then that meant that the Irish and the other white people had had to clear out. Because the Jews hadn't been satisfied by themselves, but they had sold their property to the niggers. Trickery, Jew trickery, had ruined this neighborhood. And the trickery of the Jew bankers was causing the depression and ruining him.

He knelt again, and commenced to mutter an *Our Father,* but his mind slid into a daze and he was like a man half asleep. He found himself remembering that Sunday morning, now it seemed like many, many years ago, when with dirty shovelled snow along the edges of the sidewalk, and a winter sun melting it, he had come to the first mass to be celebrated in this very church. All the old parishioners had come and knelt in these deserted pews, and in that marble pulpit to the left of the altar the Cardinal Archbishop of Chicago had preached. On that day he had been filled with the confidence that things were going to go on getting better and better. He and Mary had both felt that they would coast on Easy Street into a long and happy old age, and die in this parish, respected, leaving something behind for their children. And now Bill was home, sick, thin, suffering, dying. God, Christ Almighty, if on that winter Sunday he had only seen ahead to what would happen to him and his family. Again he listlessly mumbled *Our Father,* his mind a fatigued blank. Unaware of what he was doing, he again sat in the pew, and began to feel convinced that it was only the day after that Sunday morning when the new St. Patrick's church had been opened. He saw himself going home to the building on Michigan Avenue, thinking of how he would take Bill into the parlor and talk to him in such a way that Bill would see eye to eye with him and would take care of his health. And then he would sit down and calculate his money and his investments and see that the money was put into sound investments. But his money had been soundly invested in real estate and a building. What could have seemed safer? The trouble had been that too much money had gone into construction and real estate. The Jews again. If less Jews had rushed in to make easy money, then real estate values would not have been ruined.

Again he knelt, prayed in an exalting fervor, abjectly asking his God to spare his son from death, to give him back just Bill. If only Bill lived, he would take the loss of everything else with Job's patience. He imagined Bill recovering quickly, their moving into a small flat, economizing, he and Bill fighting back to where they had once been. He saw himself coming around to a large building where he had a big contract, seeing Bill in paint-stained overalls, up on a ladder like it used to be. He saw a future of Bill and the other children with their kids, himself and Mary as happy grandparents, a family reunion, with him and Bill laughing as they talked about the hard times of 1930 and 1931, and how they had pulled through those days of hard times.

His mind cleared. He thought of his home, and wondered how Bill was. He knelt, rigid with the paralyzing conviction that Bill was dead. Again he beseeched his God for Bill's life.

He arose, and with fear creating tremors in him he slowly walked to the altar, knelt before the statue of the Blessed Virgin, dropped all his small change in the slot for money, and lit eight candles to burn in honor of the Blessed Virgin as prayer and offering that Bill might be spared. He arose, turned, walked to the rear of the church, a corpulent old man, his body slack, his shoulders drooping, his abdomen sagging, his eyes heavy and baggy, suggesting sleeplessness, his loose face drawn in a fretting expression.

III

He stood on the church steps looking at the drab row of three-story brick apartment houses across the street. Looked old, not worth much. Probably run down inside, too. Nigger buildings now. He watched a stout shabby Negro woman across the street walking to the corner with a waddling gait, disappearing around the corner store.

The feeling of having nothing to do, no stone to turn, no

help in his present difficulties, weighed upon him like
something heavy. He stood indecisive and watched a street
car cut across Michigan Avenue, followed by a succession
of three automobiles. He smiled at a neatly dressed Negro
boy of about twelve who passed him singing, and he thought
that, golly, the eight-balls sure could be happy. He stared
while a slender, pretty mulatto girl wheeled a baby buggy
along the sidewalk below him. Nigger babies were cute little
ducks. But they grew up into black dangerous buck niggers
who flashed razors. He nodded, bewildered by his observation.

He descended the steps, got into his Ford, and without
thinking of what he was doing drove north along Michigan
Avenue, past the Carter School playground where black
children romped and played in the same place and in
the same way as his own kids had romped and played. He
halted the car in front of the building he had once owned,
approached it. With his hand on the knob of the outer
entrance door, he realized with the pain of loss that it was
no longer his building and that all the life, hopes,
expectations lived in this building, these were all gone,
and that he was now an old man on the verge of ruin,
and when he went home tonight, he might find his oldest
son . . . dead.

Jesus Christ, he agonizingly exclaimed to himself.

Nervousness accumulated in him, and feeling the need
of doing something, he lit a cigar. He stepped back to his
automobile, and drove northward. At Fifty-sixth Street he
came to the sudden realization that he was driving heedlessly, and swerved, scratching a fender against the curb
to avoid colliding into a Nation Oil tank truck. Shocked,
he watched his driving, puffed on his cigar, turned west
onto Garfield Boulevard. Turning north again, he saw by
a sign in one of its windows that the bank of Abraham
Clarkson was closed. Served Clarkson right because Clarkson
was the shine who, in the old days, had refused to
move from the neighborhood when no one had wanted a
nigger in it, depressing real estate values and living among
white people where he didn't belong. He wouldn't get out,
even though his house kept getting bombed. Lonigan
suddenly remembered reading in the papers that Clarkson
had been indicted. Served him right. A banker and a
nigger.

At Fifty-first Street he wheeled westward, driving along
a dreary, dusty street, with shabby stores, wooden houses,
sooty, low, brick buildings. A train roared overhead as he
went under the viaduct, and he drove on, turning onto

Wentworth Avenue, seeing again a dusty street filled with people, for-rent signs in store windows, and on his right a drab, low fence, in need of paint, with post-no-bills announcements spaced regularly along it. Several firemen lounged back on chairs in front of the fire engine house at Forty-seventh Street, and he thought that they weren't getting paid because the city was broke. A crowd of men were cluttering a corner, two blocks down, and he guessed they were out of work. That was bad, because with nothing to do they got into trouble, especially the younger ones. He honked vigorously when a dirty-faced boy dashed before the car, dodged in front of a truck on his right, and leaped onto the sidewalk. Crazy kid. He'd get killed doing that some day. A street car donged behind him, and he curved off the cartracks. Another closed bank. Golly. More men on the corners. Women in shawls. Kids. More idle men.

He turned on Thirty-fifth Street and followed a surface car along the west-bound tracks, annoyed by the slow progress, the repeated stops of the car, the people who cut in front of him at the street crossings. Nervous, he passed the car, and jammed his machine to a quick halt to avoid running over an old woman in a blue coat. He cursed, and followed again in the wake of the car, cursing, telling himself that he would have to watch his driving. Dingy, smoky street. Wooden houses, buildings stained from smoke, drab stores, for-rent signs in dirty windows. Another closed bank. It made him suddenly realize something of what this depression was beginning to mean in people's lives. When a bank in a neighborhood like this one closed, there must have been many men like himself, many poor working people who lost all their life savings. It meant that they were made paupers. Dirty crooks of bankers, he hissed to himself.

Halted by the traffic lights at Halsted Street, he understood why he had come to this neighborhood, and where he was going. His mood softened into one of deep nostalgia, and he told himself that he was going back to an old neighborhood, to look at places where he had lived and played as a shaver. He remembered his Irish father and mother, his sister who had become a whore, Joe, getting old and tired, working still on the street cars, plugging along, Joe's oldest son Tommy in the pen for sticking up a store. Ought to see Joe. Joe, poor fellow, had had a hard life. And he and Joe were the only ones left, he guessed, unless Catherine was still alive. And Joe's wife Ann, she was sick, not much life left in her. Once she had been like Mary also, a blooming, innocent young girl. He felt kindly toward Joe, toward Ann, even toward the memory of Catherine. He wanted to see them again, talk to them. And all he could do was to shake his head sadly and sigh.

"Ah."

Horns tooted behind him. Blocking traffic by falling asleep at the wheel. He drove forward, and he parked his car by a vacant lot that was thick with weeds and littered with rocks, refuse, papers, tin cans. Stepping out of the car he caught a whiff of stale garbage from the prairie. He turned back and locked the door of his Ford. He glanced down a block-paved street, with tumbling and sinking wooden houses stacked between old brick buildings of two and three stories, most of the houses appearing uninhabitable in a pall of gray smoke. The neighborhood still looked something like it had in the old days, only worse. He slowly moved down a narrow cracked sidewalk, unable to recognize most of the houses. He halted before a boarded, untenanted structure that was weather-worn and lop-sided, as if threatening to fall into a heap of junk at any minute. He noticed that the windows were broken, black with dirt and soot, and the grassless plot of dirt in front of the house was messed with papers, small broken pieces of board and rusty tin cans, and the steps dropping into the cellar entrance were barricaded with refuse. Chewing on his cigar, he tried to remember what family had lived there. O'Learys? Doyles? Schaeffers? He scratched his head. Golly, he couldn't remember. And all those who had lived along this block then, where were they, and what had happened to them? He flung the cigar-butt away. Some of them, like all the older folks, dead. The last O'Leary boy had been killed by an automobile. Dan Doyle dead, his oldest son killed in the war. The Schaeffers disappeared. He sighed.

Across the street from the abandoned house some boys were playing ball in a narrow lot, shouting like hell. Golly, he had played ball like that and so had his brothers, Jack and Mike and Joe, and so had Bill and Martin around Fifty-eighth Street. And now here were these boys.

"Go on, you sonofabitch, I'm safe."

He laughed. Tough kids, all right. A whole new generation, going through the same mill that he had. Going through the same kind of a mill that Bill and Martin had. No. Bill and Martin had been given advantages that he'd never had, and these kids weren't getting them, either.

"If I'm a sonofabitch, you're a . . ."

Swearing like teamsters. Well, when he was a shaver he'd done the same thing. What would become of these lads? They'd scatter like the kids he'd known. Some go to jail. Some just get nowhere. Some pull themselves up by heir own bootstraps just as he had done. He remembered Packey Dooley. Packey had died young, of consumption. His mother had wanted him to learn the violin. Maybe if Packey had lived he might have been a great violinist. Ah, life was a funny thing, and Boots Brennan, the toughest kid in the whole block, who had always sworn like a trooper, Boots was now Father Brennan. But most of the kids hadn't turned out so well, and they had come to no good end. He had escaped all that, but for what? Only now to be ruined and bankrupt. And was he coming to a good end? And how many generations of kids had come and gone since his time, and how many more would follow after those kids cursing and playing ball in the lot across the street? Oh, life was a funny thing.

He hadn't remembered his childhood in years as he was remembering it today. Poverty, the cold house in winter with the wind breaking through the cracks. Days without food. His father, a big strong man, worrying, coming home drunk. He remembered his father once staggering in with not a cent of pay left. His mother had cried and cursed him. The old man had punched his mother and she had fallen, and Catherine, like a little tigress, had ripped into the old man until she'd gotten a whaling. And then for two weeks his parents hadn't spoken. He could remember his mother, day after day, working and slaving, washing, scrubbing, cooking in their crowded little home. Ah, life was a funny thing.

Thrilling with pride, he told himself that he had taken his family away from such a life. Even now, if he was a ruined man, he had lifted them up, and they would have something better. His girls would. Martin? He was worried about Martin, and Bill. Oh, if only. . . . But where was he? He tried to convince himself that he was worrying too much, and he stood watching a black-shirted blond boy hit the ball over third base and run the bases while the others shouted. Oh, to be a shaver again, playing like these kids, stealing coal from the railroad yards. And then the days when he was a young buck, sowing his wild oats, the nights at dances and in saloons, and Mary. Mary such a sweet young girl, winning all the races at picnics. Mary whose dark eyes went only for him, Mary who had really made a man out of Paddy Lonigan.

> *When I first met Mary . . .*
> *When I first met Mary . . .*

He turned, staring ahead of him, slowly pacing this familiar, and yet not familiar, street. An old woman came toward him. Her skin was rough and wrinkled, her gray hair stuck out from a black shawl pulled tight around her shrewd, peasant face. Bent, walking slowly, she made him sadly remember his old mother in her last years. She had ended up like this poor old woman was, before any of the children had been in a position to help her. She must, though, be getting her reward in Heaven. A wave of sympathy, such as he had not experienced in years, overpowered him, almost dragged tears out of his eyes. He wanted to say something kind to this old woman, who was thrusting a suspicious glance at him, something jolly, he wanted to smile at her and call her mother, drop a little word of cheer into her life. She passed on, and he watched her, scurrying on toward Thirty-fifth Street.

He lit a fresh cigar and tried to fancy himself as the prosperous Paddy Lonigan he had been just a couple of short years ago, walking back through these changed scenes of his boyhood, trying to keep his mind on the distance he had travelled since those days. He suddenly caught the odor of decay and stink from the nearby stockyards that were just south of this section. He smiled. Just like old times. That was something he hadn't thought of in years, golly, the stockyards smell. In those days he had always lived in that smell and gotten not to mind it. He tried again to keep his mind on the distance he had travelled since those days. But what did it mean now? He cursed. They were robbing him. Goddamn it, they couldn't take his building. They couldn't. He'd get a shot-gun and defy them.

A crowd was gathered at the end of the block, and he walked more rapidly toward it, noticing, as he approached, that there were policemen. Trouble. Coming up to the crowd, he saw a bailiff and two workingmen removing an assortment of ancient and scratched furniture from a three-story brick tenement while three broad-shouldered policemen stood about with surly, challenging expressions. A lean woman in a ragged black dress sat in a stuffed chair with a baby in her arms. Beside her, a leathery man stood, talking down at her. Two unwashed girls of ten or twelve, and a small boy with holes in his stockings stood beside the man, crying.

"Get back," a policeman said to a ragged kid who ran toward the furniture.

"This can't go on forever," a small, nervous man in overalls and a blue shirt said, too loudly, and a ruddy-faced policeman walked quickly toward him.

"What did you say?"

"Come on, break it up. Break it up," a second cop called, quickly joining the first.

Lonigan stepped off the curb and aside.

"I didn't say anything."

"Break it up."

"Move on. Don't block the sidewalk."

Their faces surly, the crowd was edged down the sidewalk. Lonigan walked around the sidewalk, toward the corner. Might be trouble, and he didn't want to be mixed up in any riots or trouble. There had been riots, started by the Reds, in the Black Belt when niggers had been evicted. But that poor family. Losing their home, four children, too. Poor fellow, must be out of work. He remembered the remark of the small, nervous man. Could these hard times go on forever? His own building, they were taking it away from him, the building into which he had put all the money earned by the sweat of his own brow. Yes, it was earned by the sweat of his own brow. They couldn't take it away from him. They couldn't.

He passed a box-like, red-brick factory, sooty, with smokeless cylindrical chimneys. The windows were dirty, many of them broken. He guessed kids had done that. Closed factory. That meant men out of work, machinery rusting, people with money invested in it getting no return. Ah, hard times were hard, and we needed a new man of the people in the White House, to end all these hard times and unemployment.

Two short blocks ahead he saw a crowd gathered on a corner. He hastened forward on tired feet, breathing asthmatically, to see what was up.

IV

Strange music filling the street, the shouts and cries of an approaching throng headed by an overalled white man and a Negro carrying an American and a red flag, policemen stretched along the curbs in both directions, shabby people behind the line of bluecoats, a crowd constantly augmenting in front of the corner speakeasy saloon, children scampering and dodging through the group; all this befogged and confused Lonigan, and he puzzled with himself trying to figure out what it was. He heard a snickering voice beside him, and his face livened with the discovery that it was a Red parade. Goddamn Reds. They shouldn't be permitted to march in the street. Wouldn't if he had any say about it.

The noise and music swelled in volume, and he told himself, as if in an argument with someone else, that with things as bad, why couldn't the Reds let well enough alone, put their shoulders to the wheel, try to help things along back to prosperity instead of making conditions worse by parading to foment all this trouble and agitation. Kicking was all right, he continued with himself, and the Lord knew that he had as much reason to kick as any man. But that was no cause to want to tear down everything and have anarchy like in Russia. Why did these Jews and foreigners and Reds want to go on disrupting the way they did?

An explosion of shouts burst against his eardrums, and he stiffened with fear and surprise. He saw the head of the parade, half a block down, moving toward him like a howling mob. He remembered *Scaramouche,* a movie about the French Revolution that he and Mary had seen a long time ago in the old neighborhood. Were these Reds going to burn, and kill, and destroy the way the mob had in that picture? He looked at the broad back of a bull-necked policeman a few feet in front of him, and he guessed that the cops would be able to take care of any trouble if it started.

The shouts of the paraders broke upon him, the flag-bearers passed, several feet in advance of the parade, and he saw a swarm of faces, poster signs, banners, for blocks and blocks back. A tall, solid blond man in an unpressed blue suit, with frank features, followed the flag bearers, and Lonigan guessed that he was a Swede or an American. Behind him came Jew, a Negro, and another tall, solidly built fellow who looked to Lonigan like a white man. A band followed, playing that strange tune, and Lonigan saw a sunken-chested little fellow in a gray shirt step beside him and raise his right fist and forearm. He couldn't understand it. A white and a black marcher carried the poles supporting a large banner.

TRADE UNION UNITY
LEAGUE

They passed in a steady and confusing flow, men and women, white and black, blond and swarthy, carrying crude signs, slogans written on cardboard and attached to sticks and poles, singing and shouting, a succession of slogans breaking forth clearly, causing Lonigan to knit his brows and shake his head in wonderment.

> *Down with Imperialist War*
> *Hands Off Nicaragua*
> *We Demand Unemployment Insurance*
> *Down with the Cossack Police Terror*

"Comrades, join our ranks," a plump girl called, passing Lonigan.

File after file strode forward. Poor people. Shabby people.

Hunched and underfed men and women. Tall and powerful young men. Hefty, buxom Slavic girls. Lonigan looked idly from face to face, and singled out a tall buck Negro, his face black and surly, his pleated wide-bottomed brown trousers frayed, flopping and dragging at the cuff. Not a nice-looking customer, Lonigan decided. At the outside of the next rank a fat Negress with a red bandana about her head waked flat-footedly, constantly jerking her head about, smiling in a broad, white-toothed grin. She saw two flimsily-dressed, red-lipped, Slavic-faced girls on the curb ogling two corner hoodlums who had stepped out of the corner speakeasy.

"You ain't too pretty to starve," the Negress called out loudly in a deep, rich voice, causing laughter to rake the marching ranks.

"Go on back to your washing," one of the girls flung back, applauded by the loafers.

"Come on, folks," the Negress shouted with a wave of a beefy arm and flashing a broad smile as she flat-footed by Lonigan.

"Comrades, join our ranks."

Lonigan's mouth popped open in surprise. He watched a column of children in light blue uniforms with red armbands swinging behind a large banner.

YOUNG PIONEERS

A silent anger flushed his cheeks. Children shouldn't be let parade with all this riff-raff, taught socialism and anarchy and atheism and ideas against God and America and the home in their tender years. The children chanted in unison.

> *We want Hoover,*
> *We want Hoover,*
> *We want Hoover,*
> *With a rope around his neck.*

Not right or decent. These youngsters should be taken away from their parents by law and placed in institutions so that they would not be contaminated with all their vile Bolshevism.

NATIONAL STUDENTS
LEAGUE UNIVERSITY
OF CHICAGO

From the University, too, he thought, slowly shaking his bewildered and shocked head, seeing students pass. And many of them were Jews, too. Father Shannon in his missions at St. Patrick's had told what the A. P. A. professors at the University did.

We Want Scholarships Not Battleships

And this was what the A. P. A. professors did. They ought to be jailed, run out of town on a rail, tarred and feathered. A corpulent policeman with stern features and fattening cheeks smiled cordially at Lonigan. The face seemed very familiar to Lonigan, who returned the cop's glance, smiling, searching his memory to place who it was. He had an impression of a swarm crowding past him, and from the corner of his eye noticed a group that looked like workingmen, singing with their clenched right fists raised.

> *Arise, ye prisoners of starvation,*
> *Arise, ye wretched of the earth,*
> *For justice thunders condemnation,*
> *A better world's in birth.*

"Hello, Mr. Lonigan," the policeman said. Lonigan still struggled to remember who it was. "I'm Jim Doyle."

"Oh, how are you? I'm glad to see you. And I see that you're on the force now."

"Yes, I'm on the force," Jim said. "This is a surprise to see you here, Mr. Lonigan," he added as a file of marchers caused Lonigan to flinch by booing him and Jim Doyle.

"I had some business to transact near here, and I stumbled into this. And years ago, when I was a kid, I used to live around here. The neighborhood's sure changed a lot, though, since I was a shaver."

"The Reds are making a lot of noise today. They call this an anti-war demonstration."

> *Long-haired preachers come out every night,*
> *Try to tell you what's wrong and what's right . . .*

"This is a disgrace and it shouldn't be permitted. The city shouldn't allow these dirty Reds to be out here agitating and disrupting the way they are," Lonigan said with a rising, self-righteous anger, aware of the scuffle of passing feet as he spoke.

"Most of them are just poor people. That's the reason a lot of them are in the parade. It's being out of work and having no money that makes Communists out of many of them," Jim said.

"But look, Doyle," Lonigan said with a perplexed stare, "they're inciting the poor people around here to revolution.

I saw a poor family down a few blocks being put out on the street, and if these people get to a poor man like that, they might make him desperate. Why, there was nearly a riot as I passed. And look up there," Lonigan pointed at the second story of a grimy brick building across the street. Jim and Lonigan watched a stout woman, with a dirty rag about her head, energetically wave a red blanket and receive cheers and salutes from the marchers.

"Comrades, join our ranks."

"I know. And I'm not a Red, and never will be one, because they're against the church and the home."

For we'll hang Herby Hoover to a sour apple tree . . .

"But I know most of these people are out here because they're poor and want something to eat and a job. Times are hard, and people are beginning to feel it. A lot of other cops, I know, club and beat hell out of them whenever they can. We've got one big mick down at the station named Gavin who always brags about how he can call the spot where he'll land on a Red's head. But some guys are like that. I don't like to hit anybody with a club unless I've got to."

"They ought to be clubbed until they get some sense knocked into their heads. This is America, not Russia, and the sooner we teach them so, the better."

"Comrades, join our ranks."

Lonigan thought that he had a bigger squawk than these people, because he was losing more. And still he wasn't a Red, was he? The marching feet shuffled and scraped, and he watched uneven columns pass, noticing the shifting faces, the different types and sizes, the clothing of the demonstrators. A pimply young man along the side of the parade thrust a handbill into his hand. Embarrassed, he looked at the boldfaced type.

FORWARD FOR A WORKERS' WORLD

Only a Workers' America can give peace and justice

He crumpled the paper, threw it down.

"How is Studs? I haven't seen him for a year or so?" Jim asked, noticing a wistful look come into Lonigan's face.

"Bill's got pneumonia."

"Why, I didn't know that. I'm awfully sorry to hear it. He always was a fine fellow, and so healthy. I'm sure he'll pull through."

"He's pretty sick, and naturally we're worried. But we're hoping that he'll pull through."

"Gee, Mr. Lonigan, that's too bad. I'm very sorry to hear that."

No Work No Rent

"In cases like Bill's, we got to let Nature take its course. It's all in the hands of God, and we're hoping for the best."

Jim shook his head sadly, and both of them turned back toward the parade, with nothing more to say to one another.

Remember Sacco and Vanzetti

Lonigan watched like a man in a trance. His few words with Jim Doyle had brought his mind back to his son. He shook his head in impotent sadness, compressed his lips. All these troubles coming down on his head at this late date in his life.

And still they were passing. Suddenly, like a man making an intellectual discovery, Lonigan realized that these people were happy. He could see them laugh. He could see how, between their yells and cries, they grinned, and their faces seemed alive. That stiff-legged fellow with the gray mustache, hobbling. He seemed happy. That frail little woman in blue. They were happy. And they didn't look like dangerous agitators, that is, except the eight-balls. All black boys were dangerous, and they couldn't be trusted farther than their noses. But the white ones, they looked like men and women, with faces the same as other men and women. He could see that most of them were poor, and many of them, like that fellow in gray dragging his feet, were tired. He wondered how they could be Reds and anarchists, so dangerous and so perverted that they even made innocent little children into atheists. He shook his head in bewilderment, and repeated to himself that these people were happy.

FREE TOM MOONEY

"Say, is that the Mooney they got on the coast in jail they're yelling about?" Lonigan asked Doyle.

"I guess it must be."

"Well, if these Jews and jiggs are yelling about him, he must be guilty, and he belongs in the pen," Lonigan said.

"I'll be damned. There's two of the O'Neill kids," Jim said.

"Who?"

"Remember Danny O'Neill from the old neighborhood? He used to live on South Park Avenue?"

DEFEND THE SOVIET
UNION

"Oh, yes, I think I've heard Bill and the girls speak of him."

"Well, his kid brother and sister just passed."

"Where?" Lonigan asked, searching the ranks.

"They're gone now."

"What a shame! What a crime! And they were taught by the sisters at St. Patrick's. Once, you know, they must have been decent kids like my own. And they came to this," Lonigan said, sighing as he spoke.

> *The workers' flag is deepest red,*
> *It shrouded oft our martyred dead,*
> *And ere their limbs grew stiff and cold,*
> *Their life-blood dyed its every fold.*

"Their brother went to the A. P. A. University, and he's probably responsible for it," Jim said.

"Somebody ought to put a stop to them A. P. A. professors, all right."

"I'd like to see them stand up to a smart priest like Father Shannon."

"Yes, he was a smart priest. And an even smarter priest is Father Moylan, who speaks over the radio. He gives hell to the Reds, the same as he does to the bankers."

We Want Bread Not Bullets

Lonigan looked down the street, and it seemed as if there were blocks and blocks of marchers still to come. He placed his weight on his right hip and leg, tired. He wondered if he hadn't better be going?

DOWN WITH THE
HOOVER WALL STREET
GOVERNMENT

Good. But why couldn't they be sensible about it? Be against Hoover and the bankers, but not want violence and anarchy. But Bill? How was he? And God, how was he himself going to end up, with all his worries, needing money as he did? He laughed, forgetting his thoughts completely while a stout Negress jigged before a policeman. He watched her pass on.

Again he thought of Bill. His boy couldn't die. It was impossible. It wasn't so. Bill couldn't die. He heard boos behind him and saw two young Irish fellows with slanting caps. He turned to the parade and saw a banner carried at the head of the column.

IRISH WORKERS
CLUB

"Say, they must be left-handed turkeys and Orangemen to be with this outfit. You'd never find a good Irishman who was true to the church and the memory of his good old Irish mother in this outfit," Lonigan said.

"Maybe they're all Jews," Jim said.

"They're micks, all right. That big, red-faced smiling fellow. But they must be insane to be Reds." He smiled superciliously. Still, they seemed happy. And himself? But there was a funny little Abie. He watched the stunted, unshaven man who megaphoned through his hands with a pronounced Yiddish accent.

"Hens off China."

The demonstrators choked the street from curb to curb. Lonigan watched, spotting a fellow in blue denim overalls. The guy looked like a bum. Beside him, a Jew in a spotted blue suit. A tall, handsome brown Negro, limping. Powerful shine. A large woman wearing a blue gingham apron over a reddish purple dress, brushed by him.

"We'll starve no more," she shouted loudly, in an Irish brogue.

Must be a drunken biddy, Lonigan decided, seeing her step beside a thin Negress. The marchers cheered her, and repeated her slogan in a multi-voiced cry.

We'll Starve No More

The menacing roar gripped Lonigan with fear. These people were the mob, coming to wreck, and they would take all that he had and live in his building without paying rent, and maybe send him and his family to live in a hole in this neighborhood. His shoulders dropped in relaxation. Before they would come to take his building, the banks would have it.

> *No more tradition's chains shall bind us.*
> *Arise, ye slaves, no more in thrall . . .*

He just couldn't make anything out any more. Too many

things had been happening to him. He couldn't piece them together, and he felt that the world had passed him by, and he was no longer able to deal with it.

> *Oh, why don't you work like other men do?*
> *Oh, how can I work when there's no work to do?*

Just an unhappy old man, and even these people, anarchistic Reds, communists, niggers, hunkies, foreigners, left-handed turkeys, even they seemed happier than he.

WE WANT BREAD NOT BULLETS

"*Daily Worker? Daily Worker?* Comrades, buy your paper," a stolid girl called out, holding up one copy from the bundle of papers under her arm, and Lonigan turned his head aside until she passed.

Hands off Haiti

He turned to speak to Jim Doyle, but Jim had moved away. He saw a singing detachment of young fellows and girls stride forward, keeping step.

> *You'll have pie in the sky when you die (It's a lie).*

Decent-looking youngsters. These Reds must be vampires putting evil-eyed spells on young lads, Lonigan decided. He heard a loud noise behind him, and glanced around to see a pimply, thin, unpleasant young fellow in a flashy gray suit.

"Why don't them damn I-Won't-Work bastards shut up and get a job, or else go back to Russia?" the pimply fellow said, revealing yellowed teeth.

"Mister, they have no jobs. There are no jobs to be gotten, and there are millions of workers on the streets."

"They wouldn't work if they could."

Down with Imperialist War

"Why don't you work?"

"Now don't get personal," the pimply fellow said, speaking out of the side of his mouth.

"Well, they want work, and the bosses throw them out on the street. The bosses don't throw their machinery out on the street and say to the Starvation Army, 'Here, you take care of these.' No, the bosses throw the workers out on the street and say to the Starvation Army, 'Here, they're only workers, give them mouldy doughnuts and black coffee, and when I need some more slaves, send them back.'

But the day will 'come. The day will come and the workingman will own the world."

"Aw, nuts."

"The day will come."

"Bull . . ."

Defend the Soviet Union

"Dirty-neck Reds," the pimply fellow hissed, ranging himself alongside of Lonigan.

"What I don't understand is why they are allowed to make trouble and incite to anarchy like this. With times so bad, and people so poor, this stuff is dynamite, especially with them getting the niggers in it. If the police allow these people to carry on like this, there might even be a revolution," Lonigan said, his voice intense with protest.

"If I was the cops I'd haul 'em in," the pimply fellow smirked, raising his left hand in a gesture of assurance. "Then, bam. Banana stalks."

NO WORK NO RENT

"I don't suppose most of them would work if they had the chance, and the instigators of it probably get their palms greased by Moscow gold," Lonigan said as if he knew a lot.

"Say, got a cigarette?"

"Sorry, but I don't smoke 'em," Lonigan said, uneasy in the pimply fellow's presence.

Lonigan was attracted by a marcher in a light gray expensive suit. The lad looked refined, like he came from a good home. He looked as refined as his own son-in-law, Carroll Dowson. What was such a boy doing here?

"All right, get back! Get back!" barked a husky cop with a beefsteak face.

Lonigan was slow in obeying the command.

"You're wise, huh?" the policeman said, shoving out his jaw at Lonigan. "Maybe you'd like to take a little ride and have a talk with the judge, huh?"

"You'd just better figure out who you're fooling with," Lonigan said, while people crowded close to gape at them.

HANDS OFF HAITI

"You're resisting arrest and inciting to riot. I've a good mind to run you in."

"Go ahead. I'll be right out, and you might find out you

made a mistake," Lonigan said, determined to show this cop.

"Who are you? What's your name?"

"Lonigan."

The cop eyed Lonigan with an apparent and growing indecision.

"Well, I got to keep people back, you know, Mr. Lonigan. No hard feelings. Only try and keep on the curb. These bastards around here are tough to handle, and it's no soft job for us. This is all extra duty. We got orders to prevent trouble today and I'm only following my orders. But if I had my way," the cop raised his club slowly, winked, "It isn't no picnic for us."

"Have a cigar.'

"Thanks, I will. My name's Roonan," the policeman said, inserting the cigar in an inside pocket.

Down with Hoover

"I suppose that makes Hoover afraid," a young fellow with Semitic features said, and Lonigan turned, noticing that he was well dressed and carried a briefcase.

"Hoover is a tool of the capitalists just like the Czar was," a well-built, middle-aged Jewish man in a brown suit said with a slight Yiddish accent.

"Yes, but I suppose that makes his knees quake."

Down with Cermak

"Young fellow," the older Jewish man said, "in Russia they say I will never see the revolution. So I will never live to see it, hanh? So we couldn't make the Czar afraid, hanh? Vell, I heard all that before."

Down with the Bosses Government

"Back in the old country they told me I will never live to see the Czar overthrown and the Ochrana kicked out. And the Cossacks and peasants, they told me, they will murder you, not follow you. That was in 1905. My sainted mother, she cried, 'They will find you, kill you, send you to Siberia, my darling.' And they did. They chase us, they beat us because we are Socialist, they hunt us like wild animals."

We Demand Unemployment Insurance

"Twelve years later, I see it all. I see it. We kick the Czar out on his *tuchas*, the Ochrana, and the Generals, too. Now Cossack and Jew are friends, work together to build Socialism. Tomorrow? Hoover is not afraid?" The older man spit contemptuously and the younger one smirked. "Tomorrow, here we will see. Tomorrow we will throw out broker and banker, and Pershing and Hoover on their *tuchases,* and white and black, Jew and Gentile, we will build Socialism in America."

"Well, why don't you go back home to Russia if it's like that?" the younger fellow sneered, looking at the older man as if the latter were insane.

"I'll stay here and we'll make America like Russia," the man in the brown suit said. Cheers greeted him as he joined the demonstration.

FREE TOM MOONEY

"Nuts, all right, thinking they can overthrow the government. Wait till Hoover hears of this. It'll give him apoplexy," the young fellow with the briefcase remarked to Lonigan.

"I don't see why the police permit this," Lonigan said, shaking his head sagely.

"It's just as well. They got to get off steam some way, and if they do it in the open, they won't be conspiring."

"Maybe you're right," Lonigan said.

The last column passed, filling the street, singing with raised right fists.

> *'Tis the final conflict,*
> *Let each stand in his place,*
> *The International Soviet*
> *Shall be the human race.*

He watched the moving backs, turned, walked back slowly to his automobile. Home now, the home the bankers would be getting soon. And Bill? Was he dead? Oh, but Paddy Lonigan was an unhappy man, and those people in the parade, they were happy, happier than he was.

V

Lonigan stepped out of the police station, still cursing. Those goddamn kids. Stealing his spare tire. There wasn't any chance, hardly, of getting it back, either. The sergeant had said that the neighborhood was full of thieving kids. What was going to become of them when they grew up?

He drove off. Thieving little bastards, stealing a man's spare tire right off the car! When they grew up, a man's life and property wouldn't be safe. What was Chicago coming to, what with the kids like the ones who'd snatched his tire, the Reds and the niggers? He shook his head sadly, thinking of how the shines had already ruined so much of the south side. Had it been so good to free the slaves? Of course, all men should be free, but a nigger was a nigger. You couldn't trust them and they didn't know their place as it was. And now the Reds were agitating them. Dangerous stuff. Maybe if old Abe Lincoln had lived, he might have settled the black problem by giving them a place of their own to stay in, the same as the Indians had been put on reservations.

All those south-bound automobiles on Michigan. People in them going home. Were the men and women in all these automobiles happy? What did they have on their minds? For-rent signs in these fine buildings on Michigan. Property ruined by the niggers. And a closed bank at Thirty-ninth Street. God, how long could it all go on? And Bill? He had a feeling that Bill was dead. He didn't want to go home to the house where his son had died. Unthinkingly, he drove his car more slowly.

Near White City he stopped in front of a speakeasy, deciding that one good, stiff shot would jack him up. Several men were lined up at the bar of the small saloon when he entered.

"Shot of whisky," he told the ruddy-faced bartender.

Lonigan gulped it down, convincing himself that a man in his shoes had to brace himself up with something, and this one would make him feel better about going home.

"And, Pat, I suppose you think I'm only a toothless old drunkard, headed for an alcoholic grave?" a stunted old man said, hanging over the bar.

Catching Lonigan's eye, the bartender winked. Lonigan smiling in response, drank half of the whisky before him and gulped down a chaser of water.

"Pat, don't tell me I'm no good. Because I swear to God on it, and to the memory of my saintly old mother in Heaven, that there's no Irishman alive who hasn't some good in him. Pat, we belong to a race blessed by God. But we have been oppressed for centuries by John Bull, the curse of the human race. And by God, I'm proud to proclaim that my name is McGuire."

The drunkard laughed repulsively, staggered from the bar, jigged clumsily, fell forward, toward Lonigan, and looked at him sternly, slouching against the bar.

"Sir, doesn't God love the Irish?"

"You're right, Dad," Lonigan said with a smile, finishing off his drink.

"Dad, bejesus no. I want the likes of all you to know that Timothy McGuire is a granddaddy," he said shaking with laughter that sounded ribald.

Two lads in their early twenties, one wearing a nicely pressed blue suit, the other in splotched working clothes, entered and strolled up to the bar smiling. They reminded Lonigan of his son, and he saw Bill in other days, stopping off after work for a drink, stepping up to a bar the same as these lads, talking, kidding with a drunk as these two were with McGuire, maybe thinking the same kind of thoughts as they were. Martin, too, was like these lads. And once he himself had been. He wanted almost to cry, and he sipped his third glass of whisky.

"Boys, I'm just a no-good Irishman," McGuire said, staggering up to the newcomers.

"You're no good, and we're no good. That's what we got to brag about. Ha, ha," the lad in the blue suit said.

"By Jesus, I'll shake on that profundity. No good. Was there ever an Irishman that was good for anything but the bottle and a song and the ankle of a pretty lass? Ha, ha," McGuire drooled, shaking hands with both of them.

"Come on, Pop, have one on us," the lad in the blue business suit said.

"By gosh, you're gentlemen, even if I do say so," McGuire said, supporting himself against the bar.

"Join us, stranger," the lad in working clothes said, and Lonigan raised his fourth drink in response, feeling warm with a sense of companionship.

"Well, spittin' in your eye," McGuire said, gulping a thimble-glass of moonshine.

McGuire staggered to a thin man who sat slumped at a table over a cocktail.

"Why so pale and dour, fond friend?" he said, unsteady before the man.

The stranger frowned. McGuire made a face and returned to fall over the bar.

Lonigan looked into his fifth drink with melancholy, feeling like he wanted to hear songs, to sing sad old songs himself, like *The River Shannon,* and *Dear Old Girl,* and *When I First Met Mary,* and *Silver Threads Among the Gold,* and *After the Ball Is Over.* With a gesture of despair, he downed his whisky. His head began to feel light, and he did not think that he could control himself any longer. And he ought to go home, but he didn't want to. Those two young lads, talking of girls and whorehouses, forced Bill's image back into his mind. What should he do, just sit down here and cry? He frowned. Goddamn it, he cursed, thinking how he had done nothing to merit these sorrows. He didn't care now. He was beyond caring, and he was going to drown his sorrows in drink.

"Another."

"Friend, you look glum. Why look glum? Why look glum and sour? Why so glum and dour? Sing, friend, sing. I always sing, and sing again, and sing. Listen!" McGuire babbled.

> *Since Maggie Dooley*
> *Danced the Hooly-Hooly,*
> *Ireland's been fading away.*
> *The Sweeneys and Dalys*
> *Have sold their shillelaighs,*
> *The fat Miss Kelly*
> *Wiggles just like jelly*
> *To that taunting sway.*
> *And all the colleens on the street*
> *Are all dressed up like shredded wheat*
> *Since Maggie Dooley*
> *Learned the Hooly.*

McGuire, exposing his gums in a grin, acknowledged the applause he received.

"Have one on me," Lonigan called to McGuire.

"Oh, 'tis a pleasure to drink with a gentleman. Sir, what is your name? You are speaking with Timothy McGuire."

"Lonigan."

"Irish, too. Well, friend, drink to the dear old sod," McGuire said, Lonigan smiling, proud to be Irish, trying to drag through his foggy brain remembrances of old days in saloons, when Paddy Lonigan was young, and free, and light-hearted.

"I'm a Kilkenney Irishman," McGuire said, touching glasses with Lonigan.

"Let's sit down," Lonigan said, beginning to tire.

He walked unevenly to a vacant chair, and McGuire crashed into a chair opposite him. His eyes grew misty, and he looked at the figures at the bar in a semi-daze. The insides of his head spun like a top. He told himself that he was drunk and he didn't give a good goddamn.

"My friend, these are hard times, and the world, oh, the world exists in a dreadful state of confusion. So smile, my friend, smile, smile," McGuire slobbered, and Lonigan grinned foolishly. "Me now, I lost everything, I lost every red copper in this vale of tears. So what do I do? I drink, and I smile, and I sing, and I say," his head tumbled forward, "I say, my friend, whisky is an Irishman's best friend."

"I've lost plenty, plenty," Lonigan said, his chin sagging. He silently warned himself to hold his tongue. "I lost everything. Money. My building. And now my oldest son lies home, dead."

"Condolences, friend, condolences," McGuire muttered, extending a wrinkled and dirty hand.

"I don't mind the money," Lonigan said, weakly sighing. "But my boy. My oldest son, the best damn son a man ever had. He died today of pneumonia."

"Friends," McGuire called, arising, supporting himself against the table. "Friends, Romans, lend me your ears. My friend here, an Irish gentleman, they took all his money, and now his son is dead. Friends, Romans, lend him your sympathies."

McGuire fell back into his chair. Lonigan slumped, his face puffed, his expression saddening, the fat bulging around his jowls. He arose and floundered blear-eyed toward the two young lads at the bar.

"Pardon me if I bother you, boys. You make me think of my own son lying home, dead. I've been a good father, and he's been a good son to me and my old lady, and he's dead. Dead! A good son, know him, Bill Lonigan? Everybody calls him Studs. Did you know my boy?"

"Where's he from?"

"I raised him near here, down at Fifty-eighth Street."

"No, sir, I don't. How about you, Jack?" the lad in the blue suit said.

"Friend," McGuire said, pawing at Lonigan's coat sleeve.

"Boys, you'll excuse me for troubling you, but you don't know what it means to a father in his old age to lose his son."

"Friend, here, take my sympathy," McGuire said in tears.

"What was the trouble with your boy?" the bartender asked.

"Double pneumonia."

"Tough. Here, friend, better have a drink on the house. It'll brace you up," the bartender said, pushing a whisky toward Lonigan. "My brother, he had an attack of the same ailment, and while he pulled through, he's never been a well man since. I tell you, sometimes the death of our dear ones is the mercy of the Lord, and we must abide by His will."

"God called him, and there is no gainsaying the will of the Almighty," Lonigan said, shaking his woozy head. "But

I'm an old man. Why couldn't it be me? I'm old, and I'd give my life if my boy could have been saved."

"Many are called but few are chosen," McGuire said, toppling, saved from striking his face on the bar by a stranger. "Chosen," he muttered while the stranger leaned him against the bar.

"God's will is God's will," Lonigan muttered.

Drinking, Lonigan spilled half his whisky on his coat and tie. His head turned like a merry-go-round, and he had a vision of his home, all of them waiting for him, the father. Mary, her mother's heart suffering a mother's agony. They would put Bill under the sod, and the crooked bankers would take his building. He was drunk and he did not want to go home and face it, and he felt like a traitor for not going home.

"Brace up, friend," McGuire said, his feet sliding from under him as he pitched face foremost on the floor. "Brace up," he repeated, groveling on the floor.

Lonigan puffed, lacking the strength to lift McGuire. The two young lads dragged him to his feet and dumped him in a chair.

"It's a tough old world," the bartender said, meeting Lonigan's eyes in a glance of mutual sympathy. "Now I well remember the day my poor old mother passed away. She was ninety-two, and you know, after she died, they couldn't get her mouth closed. My sister, she was crying, and cutting up for a fright, because she was sad to see my poor old mother lying there so cold, and nobody able to close my mother's mouth. And my aunt who was ninety-four, when my sister told her how they couldn't get the mouth of my mother closed, she, that's my aunt, she said to my sister, 'Well, you children never let her open it when she was alive. Let her open it in death as an act of charity.' And since that day I have never spoken to my aunt, and she's alive to this day. She's a hundred and two years old."

"My mother is dead, years dead," Lonigan muttered.

"That's one thing that's sure in this life. Everybody dies," the young lad in the blue suit said.

"And 'tis soon we'll all be out of this sad vale of tears," McGuire bemoaned.

"Maybe you should brace up now and go home, friend," the bartender said.

"Yes. You know, I'm not a drinking man. I drink, yes, but not like this. Only today. . . . I'm a ruined man. I can't go on facing troubles without a few drinks to buck me up. I'm a painting contractor and a goddamn good one, but there are no contracts or jobs now, and I can't collect what's owed to me. And they're taking my building away from me. They're taking the sweat of years of hard working. And now my son. . . . He's dead. Sir, I've been on the square all my life. There's nobody can say Paddy Lonigan isn't on the level. They ain't got no right to do this to me. An honest man all my life, and now, look at me." His head swam. Through disordered images he saw his son's bed, and white sheets drawn over the stiff corpse. "My son, Bill, he was like a pal to me. I was going to leave him my money. He was going to carry on my business," Lonigan commenced crying. "And he was marrying the finest girl, s' finest girl in God's world. In two weeks. And now he's dead. Gentlemen, do you know what that means?"

"I do, sir. Indeed I do. Only you must brace yourself up, and not flout the will of God. What happens is His will and works for the best," the bartender said.

Lonigan leaned flabbily over the bar, crying, his facial muscles relaxed, suggesting an ugly approach to old age. McGuire, his head on a table, snored loudly. Several strangers entered, and a slick fellow, with a cropped mustache, laughed at Lonigan.

"Poor old bastard," the lad in the blue suit said, and Lonigan caught the words through his drunken fog.

Nothing but a poor old bastard. Brace up. Buck up, Paddy boy! Holding onto the bar, he staggered to the two young fellows. He had to talk, and they knew, they felt sorry for him.

"Lads, I'm older than you. I'm older than you, and I've been through the mill. I'm a father with four kids, and they're the world to me and my old woman. Boys, I'm talking to you like a father. Take care of your health, lads. Guard it. My boy Bill didn't, and he's paid the penalty. Dead. . . . The dark angel hovered over my unhappy home like a thief in the night, and snatched him up. That's why I'm drunk. That's why I'm just a poor old bastard. I had to get drunk. I'm not a drinking man. I had to. When everything a man has falls from under him, he's got to do something."

"Ought to put him out of his misery," the fellow with the close-cropped mustache said low and superciliously to a companion.

"It's tough," the lad in the blue suit said sympathetically.

"Dad, you better grab a cab and go home," the lad in working clothes said.

"Boys, I can get home," Lonigan said, looking at them with shrewd suspicion. "I can take care of myself. Paddy Lonigan has always taken care of himself. He's pulled himself up by his own bootstraps, and he'd still be on top but for fate. Fate and the international Jew bankers. Lads, my son died today. He's dead. He was a regular fellow, like you boys are, chip off the old block, a man's man, a fighter. All Lonigans are fighters, fighting hard, even when it's a losing battle," he drooled.

"Come on, Dad," the fellow in working clothes said, taking his right arm, while Lonigan wiped tears away with his dirty left hand.

"You two boys make me think of my Bill," he said as they supported him out of the saloon.

They put him in his Ford.

"Now where to?" the lad in working clothes asked, getting in the driver's seat.

Lonigan mumbled an address, sank back in his seat.

CHAPTER NINETEEN

I

"I can't help it. I'll never forgive her. I can't help it," Mrs. Lonigan said.

"But Mother!" Fran exclaimed.

"Mother, you know she loves Studs, and if he lives, she'll make him a very good wife," Loretta persuaded.

"That day he went downtown in the rain. I asked him not to, but he went to find work, because of her and her condition. And now he lies at death's door."

"But Mother, it could have happened to anybody. She and William loved each other. You know you were young once," Fran said.

"Why, my own daughter saying such a thing," Mrs. Lonigan exclaimed, looking at Fran outraged. "My own daughter. Well, I'll have you know that I went to your father's marriage bed a decent woman."

"Oh, Mother, times have changed a little, and Studs and Catherine were . . . well, they were going to be married," Fran said.

"Sin is always sin," the mother said with a wrenched pride, and the two sisters exchanged helpless glances. "Oh, God, that I should have a grandchild born in sin. Well, I never want to see it. I won't see it. I won't. It will never darken my door."

"Mother, it will be William's child, and William is ours. Catherine is a decent girl. The only reason she did such a thing was because she loved him. You know, William is not blameless in this affair," Fran said.

"You would say that about your poor brother while he lays at death's door?" the mother said, frowning at her oldest daughter.

"Oh, Mother, now come. Please be sensible. We must be sensible, and we have to be fair to poor Catherine. When she left here, she was ready to break down, poor girl, and she's facing a hard future. She loves Bill, and he was going to be her husband. We owe it to him to be fair to her," Loretta said.

"And well she might feel sorry. Well she might. Disgracing herself and her hard-working mother and father, and my poor unhappy family. Disgracing us when we must bear this cross of sorrow. Well might she regret."

"Mother, you simply must be sensible," Fran said with controlled exasperation.

"Well she might, with the curse of God on her. I will not raise my little finger to hurt her. She's in the hands of the Almighty and He has put His curse on her. The first time I met her, I could see that she was possessed by the devil. She never brought him good luck. He killed himself for her. There's no good luck in such a one and I could have told him so the minute I first set eyes on her."

Fran left the parlor with a gesture of hopelessness. Loretta walked over to her mother, patted her head.

"Mother, now come and get yourself some rest."

"Rest when my son is dying?" Mrs. Lonigan broke into tears. "And the day he went out in the rain, he looked so pale and tired. I could see that morning that the strength was no longer in him."

"Mother, we must be brave," Loretta said, gritting her teeth, and the mother sighed, as if unhearing.

"That as fine a boy as William should be dying for the likes of her. With his education and all we did for him, that he should go traipsing after her. She's not good enough for him. She's common. The chippy. Oh, I tell you the curse of God will be put on her, and she will never know a happy day."

Mrs. Lonigan drew out a pair of black rosary beads and commenced mumbling the rosary. Returning to the parlor entrance, Fran signalled Loretta, who walked to the hall, unnoticed by her mother.

"Mother is awfully upset," Loretta said.

"We must be kind to Catherine. Poor thing. She never would have let herself get into such a condition if she didn't love William."

"I know it. Poor thing. Won't she do something to prevent it?"

"I tried to talk to her. She said that an abortion is murder," Fran said.

"God couldn't want her to have the baby now."

"I'll try again, but she is very set. Poor foolish thing," Fran said, and Loretta nodded her head, dismayed.

"If she needs the money, Phil and Carroll could provide it. It will disgrace her and us. That people should know about William having a son after he is dead. It will be terrible. What will they say?" Loretta said.

"Of course, she is a little common," Fran said, nervously tapping her foot on the floor. "William should have selected a girl more suited to the station in life where he belonged. But after all, she is his girl, and for his sake, at least, we've got to help her."

"What can we do about Mother? She is terribly upset, and dead set against Catherine. I can understand how Mother feels, but still, it isn't fair. Oh, gee, Fran, why must this happen to our family?"

"Don't cry, darling. We'll both of us just have to see Catherine and try to talk some sense into her. It's still time enough for her to have something done. She could stay with you while she was resting, if necessary, or we could send her to a hospital."

"Hospital will be best. Phil has put every cent into improving his place, but we could still manage to scrape together half of what it would cost."

"Carroll has just lost a lot of money in stocks, but we could manage something also. And I'll see her tomorrow. We'll just have to drum some sense into her head."

"Yes, dear."

"And I'm going to tell Dad to talk to Mother. Oh, if he only hadn't come home drunk this way. But poor Dad, he never would have done it, if he wasn't just heart-broken. Poor Dad." Loretta wiped her eyes. "And we, everything is thrown on our shoulders. Everything. Oh, why must this happen to us?"

Loretta laid her head against her oldest sister's shoulder, and cried.

II

Mrs. Lonigan remembered the day that her oldest son was born. She recalled him as a youngster in a sailor suit. And the day she had enrolled him in the first grade at St. Patrick's school. The pride she had felt. He had been such a sweet

boy, too, in that blue sailor suit, and he had held her hand
so tightly, and when she had started to leave after talking
to the sister, his eyes had grown big with tears, and he had
run after her. She had swept him up in her arms and kissed
him, her son. And then the night he had graduated
from St. Patrick's, looking so like a little man in his
first suit of long trousers. The dream and the hope she had
had that night of her boy going into the priesthood. If he
had, he would not now be suffering on his death bed, and
this awful tragedy would not be visiting her poor home.
God showered grace and blessing on any home that gave a
son anointed to His service.

And if he was a priest now, Father William Lonigan,
what joy she would have known. She could die in peace,
happy if her boy was a priest. This was a penalty from God,
because William had ignored his vocation. God had called
her son. She knew it. Because had she not so many times
in her sleep seen God, and had not God spoken to her in
dreams, told her that He had called William. And William
had turned a deaf ear on Him. Whoever did that would never
have luck on this earth, and that ill luck passed to his family.

If Patrick, poor man, had only taken her side, helped her
make a priest out of William, he, neither, would be a broken
man tonight. But he, too, had flouted God's wishes,
encouraged William to set himself against his God, and now
where were they? It was a punishment from the Throne of
the Almighty that was being visited upon her and hers this
very evening.

Her fingers moved from bead to bead, as she silently mumbled
prayers. If God would only give her the strength to go
on. She, too, she wanted to go home to Him. Wasn't she old
and tired? Hadn't she worked her fingers to the bone all
these years? And she was being smitten with God's punishment
because her own had flouted Him. Oh, she wanted to go
home to Him and rest forever in happiness. Oh, if God would
take her and spare her son.

She thought of Jesus in Gethsemane, sweating blood for
the sins of man, and of Jesus on the cross, wearing a crown
of thorns, drinking vinegar and gall, his side pierced with
a lance, Jesus, crucified, muttering to God, not my will, but
Thy will be done. She lay her trust in Him. She would bear
the burdens He sent her. If William must die, it
was His will, and she would bear it.

Again she saw a vision of her William in a black cassock.
She saw herself kneeling in St. Patrick's while William
celebrated his first mass. She saw herself giving a reception
to friends and relatives, after his first night. Father William

Lonigan smiling, meeting everyone, bestowing his blessings, she at his side, his mother. What a pride! What a blessing to her and her family!

Again she prayed.

Hail Mary, full of grace, the Lord is with Thee, and blessed art thou among women, and blessed is the fruit of thy womb, Jesus . . .

And the fruit of her womb. Was there a mother in this world, suffering tonight as she was, she asked herself?

III

His face revealing an alcoholic stupor, Lonigan hiccupped. He laid his face on the kitchen table and cried. Paddy, buck up and be a man! He moved unsteadily to the stove and lit the gas under the coffee pot. He drew a cup and saucer from the cupboard and set them on the table.

Paddy, buck up and be a man!

He wheezed and wiped his perspiring face. He lowered his head on his left forearm, thinking that he might just rest a minute until the coffee boiled. He raised his head and stared at the calcimined ceiling. He looked at the clock on the window sill, above the table. A quarter to two.

The coffee slowly bubbled and commenced to boil.

He was acutely aware of the clock ticking in the quiet house. He wished that it would stop, that time would come to a dead halt. He had a nauseating headache, but he was beginning to sober up and the coffee would fix him just right.

Buck up, Paddy, and be a man! he told himself.

Tired, he laid his head again on the table, waiting for the coffee to boil.

"Goodness, Patrick, what's this? Is the house on fire?" Mrs. Lonigan excitedly said as she rushed into the kitchen sniffing, seeing her husband asleep. She shook him.

"What, Mary? Oh, hello," he said, looking at her dazed, his words seeming to float listlessly in the air as if there were nobody behind the utterance.

She rushed to the stove, and burned her hand removing the burning pot and dropping it in the sink. He gazed at her with the guilty expression of a boy while she sucked on her fingers. She went to him, and he stood up, clenching her in his arms.

"Father," she moaned.

"Now, Mary, we got to be brave and strong, and face whatever the Lord visits upon us. I know it's hard, Mary, but you and me, we've come through a lot, and we've still got one another, and our other children. And I have a feeling that Bill will pull through."

He patted her head, gently kissed her eyes, her cheeks, her lips, the top of her gray head.

"Oh, Patrick!" she sobbed.

IV

Martin Lonigan paused at the first landing and warned himself to be quiet because his brother was pretty sick. He steadied himself against the banister, and staggered up the stairs. He withdrew his door key from a trouser pocket and thudded against the door. He rebounded. He tried to fit the key into the lock, jabbed it against the metal, and heard subdued voices from within. As he again strove to insert the key, the door opened and he fell into the house. His father gripped him. Mrs. Lonigan appeared behind her husband, and at the sight of Martin, she blessed herself.

"Jesus, Mary, and Joseph. First the sweetheart tells me she's having a baby. Then the father and son come in drunk."

She fainted.

"Mother. Mother," Lonigan exclaimed, staggering with her into the parlor, while Loretta rushed to the kitchen for water.

Martin hung his coat and hat on the rack, his mother's fainting having had a partially sobering effect.

"Hello, Fran," he said, floundering into the parlor.

"You should be ashamed of yourself," Fran snapped, looking daggers at him.

"Now Fran, you know I like Studs. Always did. Studs was a great guy. It ain't right for him to be sick like this, and he's my brother, you know. I hate to see him kick the bucket . . . die. I want to see him alive. He's my brother, and I respect him. Don't want to see him sick. We all like Studs, don't we?" Martin said, lighting a cigarette.

"Aren't you ashamed of yourself?" Fran said, vigorously shaking his shoulders.

"None of us wants Studs sick, do we?"

She led him off to bed, and the father and Loretta revived the mother.

V

He seemed to be choking.

"Mother, it's getting dark," he called feebly.

He gasped. There was a rattle in his throat. He turned

livid, his eyes dilated widely, became blank, and he went limp. And in the mind of Studs Lonigan, through an all-increasing blackness, streaks of white light filtered weakly and recessively like an electric light slowly going out. And there was nothing in the mind of Studs Lonigan but this feeble streaking of light in an all-encompassing blackness, and then, nothing.

And by his bedside was a kneeling mother, sobbing and praying, two sisters crying, a brother with his head lowered hiding a solemn and penitent face, a father sick and hurt, and an impatient nurse.

Lonigan went to the kitchen. He poured himself the remains of a bottle of whisky and gulped it. He sat by the table, his face blank, his mouth hanging open. He heard his wife scream.

The two daughters led the hysterical mother out of the room, and the nurse covered the face of Studs Lonigan with a white sheet.

1929-1934

A Wide-Canvas American Epic!

THE
SMASHING
COAST-TO-COAST
BESTSELLER

VOYAGE

A NOVEL OF 1896
STERLING HAYDEN

"A ROUSING EPIC . . . BIG, MUSCULAR,
PROFANE, CYNICAL, ROMANTIC."
Chicago Daily News

"A FAST-MOVING, HEART-POUNDING SAGA
. . . PURE PLEASURE TO READ."
San Francisco Examiner

MAIN SELECTION OF THE
BOOK-OF-THE-MONTH CLUB

 Avon 37200 $2.50

The National Bestseller by
GARY JENNINGS

"A blockbuster historical novel.... From the start of this epic, the reader is caught up in the sweep and grandeur, the richness and humanity of this fictive unfolding of life in Mexico before the Spanish conquest.... Anyone who lusts for adventure, or that book you can't put down, will glory in AZTEC!"

The Los Angeles Times

"A dazzling and hypnotic historical novel.... AZTEC has everything that makes a story appealing ... both ecstasy and appalling tragedy ... sex ... violence ... and the story is filled with revenge.... Mr. Jennings is an absolutely marvelous yarnspinner.... A book to get lost in!"

The New York Times

"Sumptuously detailed.... AZTEC falls into the same genre of historical novel as SHOGUN."

Chicago Tribune

"Unforgettable images.... Jennings is a master at graphic description.... The book is so vivid that this reviewer had the novel experience of dreaming of the Aztec world, in technicolor, for several nights in a row ... so real that the tragedy of the Spanish conquest is truly felt."

Chicago Sun Times

AVƆN Paperback   55889 ... $3.95

Available wherever paperbacks are sold, or directly from the publisher. Include 50¢ per copy for postage and handling: allow 6-8 weeks for delivery. Avon Books, Mail Order Dept., 224 West 57th St., N.Y., N.Y. 10019.

Aztec 1-82

"A masterpiece. . . . One of the best novels of our time . . ."

The New York Times Book Review (front page)

THE BOOK OF

EBENEZER LE PAGE

BY G.B. EDWARDS

Introduction by John Fowles

This novel of a crusty Guernsey Island inhabitant has been acclaimed by reviewers on both sides of the Atlantic as one of the literary finds of the century.

"Breathtaking . . . gripping. . . . The bold assault on our feelings is irresistible."

Newsweek

"It amuses, it entertains, it moves us; it can shift from pain to bawdy humor and back again, effortlessly, as convincing in its tones and shifts as the voice of a worldly, cunning and soulful blues singer. . . . He becomes a universal figure and his story becomes the story of our century."

Washington Post Book World

"A brilliant reminiscence: one man's homage to the simple life . . . (and) the qualities of honesty, integrity, humor and endurance."

Chicago Sun-Times

"The characters, as well as the many remarkable incidents, will long linger in the memory. . . . Ebenezer himself, by turns wise, perceptive, foolish and irascible, is one of the most human characters you will encounter in many a day . . ."

Dallas Morning News

CONGO

The National Bestseller by

MICHAEL CRICHTON

Author of THE ANDROMEDA STRAIN

"Darkest Africa. Strangling vines. Rain forest. Pygmies. Clouds of mosquitoes. Rampaging hippos. Roaring gorillas. Killer natives. Gorges. Rapids. Erupting volcanoes. An abandoned city full of diamonds, lost in the jungle. Maybe a new animal species, a weird cross between man and ape, but unheard of in 20th-century anthropology. Zaire. Congo. Michael Crichton's newest thriller. And of course: technology, which is what it's all about today, isn't it? Zoom!"

The Boston Globe

"A gem of a thriller!"

Playboy

"Oh, is this ever a good one!"

Detroit News

"The master of very tall tales plunges into the heart of darkness. . . . A dazzling example of how to combine science and adventure writing."

People

"What entertainment! . . . Crichton has created in Amy a 'talking gorilla' of enough charm to enshrine her in pop culture as firmly as R2D2."

Saturday Review

Available wherever paperbacks are sold, or directly from the publisher. Include 50¢ per copy for postage and handling; allow 6-8 weeks for delivery. Avon Books, Mail Order Dept., 224 West 57th St., N.Y., N.Y. 10019.

AVON Paperback

56176 • $2.95
Congo 10-81